THE VERY THOUGHT OF *You*

DUET

THE VERY THOUGHT OF *You*
DUET

ÉTOILE SERIES
BOOK 1 + 2

SUFEN ADAMS

THE VERY THOUGHT OF YOU DUET

Copyright © 2022 Sufen Adams

All rights reserved.

The reproduction or use of this work in any part is forbidden without the prior written permission of the author, except in the case of brief quotations embodied in reviews.

This is a work of fiction. Names, characters, places, incidents, and events are the product of the author's imagination. Any resemblance to actual persons, living or dead, or actual events is purely coincidental.
The author acknowledges the trademarked status and trademark owners of various products referenced in this work of fiction, which have been used without permission.

Character from:
Perfume: The Story of a Murderer by Patrick Süskind

Lyrics from:
Itsy Bitsy Spider by Unknown
You are the reason by Calum Scott
Je t'aime by Kelly Sweet

Cover: Sufen Adams

To my husband,
who is always patient and supportive

BOOK 1 1

BOOK 2 353

BOOK 1
The Very Thought of You

PROLOGUE

> Life is not what you expect:
> It is made up of the most unexpected
> twists and turns.
> ~Ilaiyaraaja

FIVE women and I were forced to entertain those so-called VIP clients in the mirrored-wall drawing room. Perhaps I was the only reluctant one because all of them seemed to do this willingly and blithely.

And they called me *the newbie*.

Vera, the madam, led me to a maroon velvet settee occupied by a large middle-aged man. He was in an expensive black suit, and his salt and pepper hair was combed back and plastered with greasy hair pomade.

So... This is the man I am paired with, or should I say assigned to, tonight. I thought, my stomach clenching and my hands sweating.

Vera introduced me to the man in a foreign language, sounding like Italian, and then said to me, "Mr. Cantu especially requested you. Be a darling and make sure he enjoys himself." She tilted her head, gesturing for me to sit next to him, who was eyeing me in a lecherous manner.

When I did not move, she reached for my wrist and firmly locked it with her long fingers as a warning. Remaining her sugary smile at Mr. Cantu, she whispered menacingly in my ear, "Do not try my patience. You know better."

Her words sent a chill up my spine as I recalled what the consequences would be if I disobeyed her. I plucked my wrist from her grip and sat down on the sofa far away from the man. It was a loveseat, so he easily snagged my arm and pulled me close to him.

While the beefy hand dragged me across the seat, I quickly crossed my legs and pulled down the hem of the short dress, which was so short that it barely covered my hips.

Expressing a satisfied smile, Vera wished Mr. Cantu a good time and left us.

My heart pounded and I flinched when the man put his arm around me. Pulling the dress in place with one hand, I tried to keep him from getting too close with the other.

"You are so beautiful. I love American girls." He flattered me to give in to his loathsome behavior and kept putting his big fat hands on my bare thighs, knees, and arms, no matter how many times I pushed them away. The odor of his unpleasant cologne was suffocating me, and his alcohol breath was nauseating me.

Feeling frightened, angry, helpless, and disgusted, I was absolutely sickened by the whole environment and was on the verge of getting physically sick.

Out of the corner of my eye, I saw Vera sauntering in my direction. She must have perceived my hostile attitude towards her precious guest and my appalled expression.

I dared to look into her eyes, hoping she would get me out of here. But whom was I fooling? She was the reason I was here, and I was her money-making tool. Feeling a lump in my throat, I tried to fight back tears.

She caught my glance and flashed me a disapproving glare. Her hips swiveled from side-to-side in a seductive sway, and the emerald sequin gown flattered her with a plunging v-neckline and a thigh high slit sheath skirt. She threw coquettish smiles at other patrons when she walked past them.

"Stop it!" I huffed and slapped Mr. Cantu's demeaning hand away from my breast, feeling violated and disgusted.

But my action only infuriated this condescending man. He started yelling loudly in his language and turned towards Vera, who put on an ersatz smile when she approached him.

She placated him in his language and sat down between us, facing the irritated man and puffing out her barely covered chest.

Quickly, I shifted to sit on the arm of the sofa to be as far as possible from them.

The man looked annoyed but seemed mollified. He nodded at whatever Vera was saying and gave me an irksome glare.

Staring down at my trembling hands, I tried to hold my tears in.

Vera startled me when she reached for my hand. Gracefully, she stood up and pulled me up, giving me a frigid stare in the process.

She must be enraged at me. I could not see it, but I could feel it. She had never shown her displeasure in front of her clients. As a matter of fact, she had never shown her anger in front of us either. Her icy glare and indifferent remarks were more mortifying and petrifying.

Obediently, I followed her and left the room through the side door. She took the narrow staircase, heading upstairs.

Vera stopped in front of the foreman of the security, Max, who was leaning against the landing newel, blocking the stairway, and had no intention to move.

Vera stepped close to him and gently pulled on his black tie to bring him closer. He leaned in, gazing at her seductive eyes.

"*Sie ist wieder krank,*" Vera said to Max in German, telling him I was sick again.

They did not know I understood German—not fluently but at least the basics—and I intended to keep it that way. I pretended to look lost and confused.

Frowning, Max scrutinized me with his piercing blue eyes.

Turning my head away, I avoided his penetrating glare, in case he found out that I understood them.

"I will send Monique back down after I take her back to her room." Vera switched to English for my benefit, and her voice was lazy and luscious just for Max. She walked past him, brushing against his toned body.

Leaning against the wall across from Max, I tried to keep a good distance from him while passing him.

Suddenly, he stepped closer.

I halted and squeezed my eyes shut. His face must be less than an inch away from mine as I could feel his warm breath and smell his fresh scent.

"Maybe I should teach her how to stay healthy," he said to Vera in his deep voice.

Astounded by his comment, my eyes flew wide open and met his midnight blue eyes, which were perfectly outlined by long black eyelashes.

Giving me a mocking smile, he stepped aside.

Promptly, I ran upstairs, my heart racing.

Hate these heels! I stopped, took off the sky-high stilettos, and ran as fast as possible towards my room. Hot tears were welling up and running down my cheeks. I quickly wiped them away because I would not give them the satisfaction of seeing or hearing my weakness.

I sprinted into the room and slammed the door shut, not caring whether Vera was behind me or not. Throwing the shoes across the room, I slid down against the door and fell onto the floor. I could not contain my anger and sorrow anymore. Hugging my knees, I wept in silence.

It was supposed to be a fun night out in Paris, but my life was turned upside down. The last thing I remembered was sitting on the chaise lounge in the ladies' room of Étoile, an upscale nightclub by the Seine. I was feeling short of breath and extremely tired, so I decided to lie down and rest for a couple of minutes. When I opened my eyes again, I was nowhere near Paris....

That night had been playing in my head countless times...

I should've stayed close to my friends.
I shouldn't have drunk anything at the club.
I should've just stayed at the hotel.
I wish I didn't go to Paris.
I wish this was a nightmare.
I wish...

CHAPTER 1

*A good friend is like a four-leaf clover;
hard to find and lucky to have.
~Irish Proverb*

THREE Months ago...

My dear friend and business partner Jasmine, aka Jojo, was turning thirty, and she wished for Paris. So Antonio, the business genius of our interior design firm and also my childhood buddy, suggested that we surprise her with a trip to Paris. And I went all in for her: Flying first class and staying at the opulent Shangri-La Paris. Wanting to give her a royal treatment with the former home of Prince Roland Bonaparte, I booked her a terrace suite with amazing views of the Eiffel Tower.

Jojo was thrilled when we took her to dinner at Restaurant Le Meurice Alain Ducasse. She immediately fell in love with their Versailles inspired interior decoration and could not praise the elegant and high-grade cuisine enough. She oohed and aahed at everything in front of her eyes.

After dinner, we took a short taxi ride to Arc de Triomphe and strolled along the Avenue des Champs-Élysées. We decided to save the shopping for another day and went back to the hotel to have a private celebration in Jojo's luxury suite before heading out again to party in the city of light.

Antonio and I were reclining on the outdoor lounge chairs and sipping wine while Jojo was leaning against the railing, mesmerized by the magnificent Eiffel Tower light show.

"You guys, I don't know what to say... This...this is..." She turned around, tears in her big brown eyes.

"Honey…" Antonio got up and walked to her. He held her in his arms, gently rubbing her back.

I wanted to join them for a group hug, but I might burst into tears if I did.

Jojo was from a small town in Kentucky. She moved across the country to California to pursue her dream after graduating from high school. She fell in love with the sunny weather and beaches and decided to make the golden-state her new home. She was four years my senior and a project designer at my first paid job after college. She took me under her wing, even though I was not assigned to work with her.

She was free spirited, optimistic, and down to earth. We quickly became very close friends, and both of us being named after flowers was like a sweetener for our friendship. A few years later we started our own design firm with Antonio, who was the reason for the speedy takeoff of our business.

Even though our burgeoning success had already freed her from student loans and provided her the financial security to purchase a small condo, she still lived a frugal and simple life and would never spend money on herself like this.

"Consider this trip your birthday and quarter bonus," Antonio teased her. Kissing the top of her head, he held her tightly and said, "You deserve all of this, so enjoy yourself."

"Here." I got out of the chair and handed her the wine glass. "The night is still young. We are going to dance through the night and give you an unforgettable birthday."

"You, come here." Antonio pulled me in for a group hug. "Two gorgeous women in my arms. I am the luckiest man in Paris."

"LOOK at the line…" I sighed when we got out of the taxi.

This was our third club tonight. The first one was mediocre, and the second one was so dull that we stayed there for less than an hour and decided to come to the famous Étoile.

Ignoring the people waiting in line to get into the club, Jojo marched right up to the two sinewy bouncers.

One had a beautiful shaved head, and his muscles were fighting to rip through the black turtleneck and slacks. He had dark skin, a square jawline, and ebony eyes, oozing charm and hostility at the same time—sort of reminding me of a Venus flytrap.

And the other one—fanning myself—was a manifestation of a sexy Viking rocking an all black suit and fitted black shirt. He had a flowing mane of light brown hair draping over his wide shoulders, medium length full beard, and a pair of light green eyes glittering with wickedness. I imagined him minus the facial hair and was surprised to find that his face was actually very delicate and pretty. He must have grown the beard to make himself look tough and masculine.

Both bouncers were now staring down at Jojo.

"Hello." She adjusted the pink, satin birthday-girl-sash and sparkling tiara, which she insisted on wearing, and smiled from ear to ear. Batting her eyelashes, she looked up at Mr. Viking.

So, I had this nicknaming-people quirk, which my brother called it an adorable eccentricity—I might have added the *adorable* part myself—while my friends thought of it as an oddity. Some acquaintances might find it offensive if they were the receiving parties who did not attract my affection. I had my very reason for developing this idée fixe though. Ever since I was a little child, I had had great difficulty in remembering people's names because I truly believed a person should *look and act* like his or her name. However, I could not really blame the parents for giving their children the *wrong* names, could I? They would not have known their baby *John* would grow up to look and act like *Jerry*, right? Therefore, I came up with this *method* to help me remember people. And later on nicknaming-people became a peculiar habit for my own amusement.

Now, where were we? Right, Jojo and Mr. Viking…

Jojo stood right in front of Mr. Viking and asked in her fake British accent, "Love, can you grant me my birthday wish?"

Irksome murmurs in French were coming from the people in line, but since I did not understand a single word, they did not sound unpleasant at all.

"What is your name, beautiful?" Mr. Viking asked, slowly scanning her face, her birthday attire, and all the way down to the nude killer pointed stilettos with his dreamy eyes.

"Jasmine. Princess Jasmine." She tossed her wavy long blonde hair back and touched her tiara, emphasizing her status.

I tried to hold back my laughter, but Antonio let out a loud laugh. He immediately got punched in his arm by Princess Jasmine.

Mr. Viking gazed at her in silence, looking amused.

In my opinion, his gaze was a bit intimidating and lasting a little too long.

Jojo stood tall, pushing her chest forward and returning his gaze with an enticing smile.

Keeping his eyes on Jojo, Mr. Viking raised his right hand to his right ear.

A sparkling ring on his index finger caught my eyes, but I only glimpsed a white diamond star framed by black gemstones because it was immediately covered by his long hair when he pressed the earpiece in his ear.

"I have Princess Jasmine and her two friends coming in. Please have my table ready for them." He spoke into the tiny microphone connected to the earpiece in English with a sexy French accent.

Wow... Antonio mouthed the word to me.

I know... I mouthed my response.

I believed it had nothing to do with her birthday or the *Princess* title. Her coquetry and sexy as hell pink silk mini dress could not go unnoticed.

"Welcome to Étoile, Princess Jasmine." Mr. Viking winked at Jojo, lifting the purple velvet rope to let us in. "Andy at the main bar will take care of you."

"*Merci beaucoup!*" She expressed her gratitude, blowing Mr. Viking an air kiss.

We walked through a short entrance hall illuminated by color changing lights from the ceiling, which was covered with dangling teardrop crystal pendants. It felt like we were walking underneath sparkling rainbow rain. Heart pumping music became louder and louder as we approached where the action was.

This club was screaming *posh*.

The focus point of the main room was the DJ station with a TV wall background, which was live streaming the dance floor filled with writhing beauteous people.

It's Fall Paris Fashion Week. I guess all the gorgeous people are here in Paris, I thought.

"Main bar!" Jojo exclaimed, pointing to the right, where stood a huge bar with a long purple glowing counter and striking color changing floating liquor shelves.

We shoved our way up to the bar and were immediately greeted by a very attractive red-haired lady.

"Welcome to Étoile. I am Andy," she greeted from her spot behind the bar, smiling warmly at us. "Princess Jasmine?" she asked, fixing her eyes on Jojo.

That tiara must have given out the clue. I chuckled.

"*C'est moi.*" Jojo pointed at herself with a grinning smile, and then waved her hand in front of us. "These two are my entourage."

Antonio crossed his arms over his chest and rolled his eyes.

"We adore her, don't we?" I entwined my arm with his, resting my head on his shoulder.

A waitress swathed with a white, latex body-contouring-dress showed us to our table, or should I say Mr. Viking's table, in the roped section, which was furnished with booth seatings. A bottle of complimentary champagne was delivered to our table soon after we were seated.

"Cheers!" Antonio filled our flutes and raised his own to us.

"Cheers!" We clinked our glasses, and I took a small sip of my drink. I already had two glasses of Moscato d'Asti earlier in the hotel. Being a light drinker, the third one would probably push me over the limit.

"This is so yummy. Drink up, Iris. It's my birthday." Jojo stared at my still full flute after tossing off hers.

Not wanting to spoil the fun, I took a big gulp just for her.

"Yay, let's dance!" She grabbed my hand and wrapped her arm around Antonio, dragging us to the dance floor.

Strobe lights were meshing with deafening music. I could feel the powerful baseline reverberating in my chest. Jojo was bouncing in front of me, hands aloft. Antonio was in his element with all the women moving in on him.

Many would have mistaken him as one of the fashion models here because of his over six-feet-four fit physique and charming features of thick eyebrows, golden hazel eyes, and kissable full lips...

Kissable full lips? Ewww... What was I thinking? He was Antonio, my childhood buddy who had no problem sharing all his bedroom conquests with me, had no boundaries in our friendship, and wore this rakish attitude I depreciated—but honestly, he sported it well.

A brunette Barbie doll with legs for days was rubbing her back against his chest. He had his hands on her tiny waist, seemingly enjoying his new dance partner very much.

I gave him the thumbs up, knowing he would not be going back to his hotel room alone tonight. He returned me a wink, moving his hips closer to the brunette beauty.

Just then, the song flowed into a slower one. Bodies in motion around me started to move titillatingly. Jojo had her eyes closed, losing herself to the music.

A smile spread across my face. I was glad she was enjoying this special trip.

As I was scanning the exhilarating surroundings, a tall man standing by our table caught my eyes. Hands in his pockets, he was looking in our direction intently.

"Jojo," I yelled over the music, but she did not hear me. I nudged her to get her attention. "Jojo," I yelled again.

She opened her big brown eyes, leaned closer to me, and shouted in my ear, "Yes?"

I winced at her thunderous voice and pointed at the man.

Giving me a bewildered look, she turned in the pointed direction and exclaimed, "My Bouncer!" Grabbing my arms, she jumped up and down. "Let's go say *merci* to him."

Without waiting for my response, she started to push through the sea of bodies and head towards *her* bouncer.

Looking around, I wanted to tell Antonio where we were going, but he was nowhere near us.

Where did he go? I frowned, following Jojo back to our table.

"Hello." Jojo walked right up to Mr. Viking, looking up at him just like their first encounter plus exchanging flirty glances with each other.

"Hello, beautiful." He gave her a gentle smile and nodded at me when I gave him a small wave before sitting down in the booth.

Even though we were away from the dance floor, the music was still overpowering and vibrant. I could not hear Jojo and Mr.s Viking over the music, although I could see they seemed to hit it off.

I was just glad she met this hot guy who was now making her laugh at whatever he was saying. She had not laughed so unreservedly for ages. I knew she had been carrying a heavy financial burden of supporting her family back home. She did not share much and I did not pry.

We had been working so hard since day one, and there was really no time for romance. I had a boyfriend from college. He was supportive of my decision to start my own company, and I was really grateful for his understanding of my busy schedule. But when my heavy workload became his excuse for putting his penis in other women's vaginas, I dropped him. *Hard.* Cheating was verboten, forbidden, and prohibited. Big *no no*!

Burying myself in work was the antidote to my broken heart, and my family and friends were the panacea for all the stress and difficulties I had. Our hard work was paying off, and the blooming business was rewarding. Here I was, happily single and partying in Paris with two of my best friends.

Jojo and Mr. Viking's heated flirtation started to make me feel like a third wheel, so I decided to go to the ladies' room and explore the club after.

I walked up to them and put my hand on Jojo's arm gently to get her attention. "I am going to the ladies' room," I said to her.

"Wait." She put her hand on mine and said to Mr. Viking, "Give me a minute."

He nodded politely and stepped aside. He waved a waitress over and slid into the booth.

"I am sorry, Iris," she said, squeezing my hand.

"What for? You are having a great time." I winked at her.

"His name is Marcus." She sounded either infatuated or drunk.

Marcus? It suits him.

"He is so hot, isn't he? Like a cup of hot white chocolate latte," she said. She peeked at him and caught him gazing at her. I could feel her blushing in the dark.

"I hope he tastes as good as the white chocolate latte," I joked. "Don't waste your time chatting with me then."

"Are you coming right back?"

"I think I am going to track down Antonio."

"He's probably getting lucky in one of the dark corners now," she said dryly.

"You are doing pretty good yourself, too." I tipped my head towards Marcus who was now speaking to the waitress, probably ordering drinks or discussing club security.

"I am *not* a slut like Antonio," she protested in a lowered voice.

She was not wrong. She was never a one-night-stand girl when Antonio was... How should I put it? I really did not want to call my friend a manwhore.

Jojo glanced at Marcus and said clandestinely, "I might let him get to second base." She took another peek at him and met his alluring eyes. All giddy and dippy, she pulled me closer and added, "If he keeps looking at me like that, he might get to the third."

I laughed as I gave her a hug. "What are you waiting for? Have fun. I really have to go pee." Without waiting for her response, I walked towards the main bar where I saw a *La Toilette* sign earlier.

The ear-splitting beats of drum and electrical bass were blasting behind me when I followed the sign, rounded the bar, and walked down a narrow hallway.

Someone pushed the restroom door out just as I was reaching for the handle.

Wow... I stopped abruptly before slamming into the door.

A woman—supermodel looking—bumped into me accidentally

when she walked out. Profusely, she apologized to me in English with an exotic accent and gently touched my arm to make sure I was okay, her expression sincere and apologetic.

She smells so sweet. I thought to myself when I caught a whiff of fruity perfume. I gave her an assuring smile and walked around her to open the door.

A luxurious sitting area furnished in Baroque style appeared when I turned the corner of a small foyer behind the door.

Walking into the room, I saw dark purple velvet upholstered sofas and fanciful marble-top tables. I sat on the three-seater sofa, running my hand on the exquisite fabric. One of my occupational habits was hands-on approach to feel different materials, no matter when I was.

Just as I was feeling the sumptuous material, I suddenly felt a sensation of whirling. I only had three drinks all night. Maybe they were more than I should have. And when I tried to stand up, I felt lightheaded and boneless.

I should get help, I started feeling panicky. *I need to get back to Jojo.*

Looking around, I just realized there was no one in here, and I did not hear any sound coming from the toilet area.

This is too strange...

Then I started to feel short of breath and extremely tired.

Maybe lying down and resting for a couple of minutes will help, I mollified myself while I rested my head on the arm of the sofa.

Don't fall asleep, Iris. Don't fall asleep...

CHAPTER 2

> The oldest and strongest emotion of mankind
> is fear, and the oldest and strongest kind of fear
> is fear of the unknown.
> ~H. P. Lovecraft

SLOWLY wakening... My eyes were so dry that I had great difficulty opening them. I blinked many times, slowly gaining consciousness and slowly growing accustomed to the bright surroundings. I took a deep breath and stretched my body...

"Ow..." I groaned in agony, squeezing my eyes shut, as every part of my body was aching. And I was surprised by my raspy voice. I could feel my throat and mouth were extremely dry.

How long have I been sleeping?

Giving a small cough to clear my throat, I raised my hands to touch my neck. A sharp pain in the back of my left hand startled me, and my eyes flew open. I was stunned to see an IV injection in my hand and find myself wearing a white patient gown.

Am I in the hospital?

Feeling so confused and disoriented, I tried to sit up but was held back by my sore muscles.

A grating sound like a metal chair scraping on tiles drew my attention to my left. I turned my head and saw a young girl, probably fifteen or sixteen years old, standing by the bedside.

I tried to speak but could not make a sound. After giving a harder cough to clear my throat, I tried again. "Am I... Am I in a hospital?"

She did not answer me. Instead, she turned around, opened the door, and left the room. Before she closed the door behind her, I caught a glimpse of a big man in black standing outside by the door like a guard.

Perhaps she's getting a doctor for me. Why is there a guard outside the room? I shut my eyes, trying to remember what had happened: We were in a nightclub; we danced; I did not see Antonio; Jojo was with Mr. Viking; I went to the ladies' room; I felt nauseous and rested on the sofa and... Nothing.

I must have fallen asleep because I could not remember anything after lying down on the sofa. Nothing at all.

Wait... A sweet scent. I remembered I consistently smelled something very sweet like that woman's perfume. I almost forgot that a supermodel-looking woman bumped into me outside the restroom.

But... Can people smell things in their sleep?

I opened my eyes and scanned the room. It did not look like a hospital room but a well-furnished bedroom.

Where am I?

Slowly, I tried to sit up, wincing at the pain. As I was cracking my neck and rolling both shoulders, the bedroom door was opened, and a woman in her mid-forties walked in, followed by the same girl.

The woman walked closer to me, making a loud click-clack sound with her high heels.

"How do you feel?" she asked, her English in a hard accent, her voice apathetic, and her expression impassive. She reminded me of the military scientist played by Cate Blanchett in Indiana Jones, especially her short raven bob hairstyle.

"Where am I?" I asked.

"Please don't worry," she said, checking the IV. "This solution will help you feel better soon."

"I need to call my friends," I said.

She ignored me and asked the girl to prepare clean clothes for me in German.

Wait... German?

Several courses of German in college really came in handy now. I put on a confused face, hiding the fact that I understood the language.

Where am I? I am supposed to be in Paris. Why are they speaking German? Suddenly, a horrible thought struck me. I stared at my left hand injected with the IV, overcome with panic.

"Are you drugging me?" I yelled and pulled the tubing, trying to rip off the IV catheter which was secured firmly in place with a transparent film.

Ahh… It hurts. Note to self: *never manipulate anything that was stuck in your vein.*

Still shocked by the twinge, I was suddenly pinned down on the bed by both of them.

"Are you drugging me?" I eyed between them, my voice trembling.

"This is saving you," the woman rebuked, seemingly irritated. "Don't make me use a restraint belt."

Restraint belt? My body was shaking with terror and rage.

Iris, be calm and be smart if you want to get out of here, my pragmatic voice whispered to me.

I tried to control my rapid breathing and stopped struggling. "I… I am so…sorry…" I breathed out the words.

Skeptically, they watched me.

Happy thoughts, Iris. Think happy thoughts. Closing my eyes, I tried to focus on my breathing and happy thoughts. However, all possible dreadful apprehensions but happy thoughts were going through my head. My heart was racing.

Mommy, Daddy, DD, Janie, Jako, Johnny, Jenny, A-Ma, Ojīchan, Nana, Papa… Silently, I started to call all the people I loved, tears stinging my eyes.

Their grips become loose, and finally, they let go of me.

The woman commanded the girl to guard by the door, her voice grating, and then she clicked-clacked out of the room.

I opened my eyes when the door was closed and saw the girl pulling the metal chair closer to the door. She sat down, avoiding eye contact with me.

Wiping the tears with my hands, I tried to sit up again. More tears were gushing out, but I was afraid to wail, afraid to upset those people, whoever they were.

I scanned the room more closely this time. Plains walls, no window, a door on the far corner…

Bathroom? Maybe there was a window in there. I can tell her I need to use the toilet and climb out of the window… I started to plot my escape plan to save myself. Then… I looked down at the thin patient gown I was wearing. There was nothing underneath the gown. And I had no shoes, no passport, no phone… I had nothing. Desperation and pain pervaded me as I was not sure if I was brave and strong enough. I wrapped my arms around my knees and buried my face between them, weeping this eerie happening, the unknown, and my helpless state.

This is unreal… This is just a dream… Wake up, Iris! Wake up!

I must have drifted off and was awakened with a start by talking noises. My eyes were blurred by the dry tears, not able to see what was happening, but my ears heard them talking about food, about a house…

The young girl put a tray on the bedside table. "Eat, please," she said in English, her voice soft.

I glanced at a bowl of oatmeal of some kind on the tray and turned away.

Sighing, she moved closer to me and reached for my hand.

I smacked her hands away, staring at her angrily.

"It is done." She pointed at the empty IV bag.

Unwillingly, I gave her my left hand.

Gently, she removed everything. She did it so carefully as if she was afraid to hurt or bruise me.

I tucked both of my arms underneath the blanket as soon as she was done.

She wrapped everything in a cloth and said to me again, "Eat, please." Then she turned around and left the room.

I thought about running out of the room since the IV injection was removed now, but that big man outside the door could easily catch me.

Suddenly, a really horrific thought popped into my head. I quickly checked all over my body, especially my inner thighs and private spot between my legs.

Thank God. There are no bruises and soreness. I let out a sigh of relief, knowing I was not violated when I was unconscious.

Footsteps and voices were approaching. I could hear a group of people gathering right outside the door. I quickly covered myself with the blanket, poking only my head out.

The door was opened, and the ruthless woman walked in. The young girl was behind her again, holding a set of clothing and shoes.

"I need to examine you now," the woman said to me with authority.

I guessed she was waiting for me to uncover myself. Afraid of her using the restraint belt she threatened to use earlier or other torture instruments she might have, I lowered the blanket to my waist.

She frowned as she started a physical as if we were in a doctor's office. When she untied the patient gown I was wearing, I flinched and gripped the thin fabric. Then her cold stare made me cringe, and I cowered in fear and let her remove the gown.

Gently, she held me still with her warm hands and started to examine my skin thoroughly.

Her behavior was bewildering as she seemed to care or worry about my health very much, but at the same time she treated me with no compassion at all. The whole situation felt more like a kidnap now. Perhaps they needed to make sure that I was unharmed so they could get the ransom. The very thought of me possibly being kidnaped made my blood run cold.

Don't be afraid, Iris. Nothing bad will happen to you…

Pep talk was absolutely not working in a situation like this. My body started to quiver, and my mind was running hundreds miles an hour, surmising how they would abuse me mentally and physically. I wished I were never a big fan of Law & Order Special Victims Unit and Criminal Minds because those shows hardly had happy endings.

What is going to happen to me? My family must have known I am missing by now. They will do everything to save me…

"Are you cold?" the woman asked.

"No…" My voice was trembling.

"Good. Now, please raise your arms and hold them up," she said.

I did what she asked. And she held me still before I could shrink away and started touching my breasts. I looked up and stared at the ceiling to avoid the awkwardness.

"Perfect. Now, please get out of the bed and stand by it," she commanded.

Grabbing on to the gown to cover myself, I slowly moved to the edge of the bed. My legs felt weak and shaky when I tried to stand on them. Sitting back down on the bed, I was perplexed by my physical condition.

"Try again," she said, giving me a hand. Literally.

Letting out a frustrating sigh I held her hand and tried to stand on my feet again. This time I managed to balance myself on my wobbly feet and was able to stand up straight, holding my head high.

She removed my gown, leaving me completely naked. And she walked around me, touching, and examining my skin thoroughly. Whatever she was doing was absolutely creepy and disturbing.

My body would not stop trembling. Shutting my eyes and clenching my fists, I felt so disrespected and violated.

"Put on the clothes and shoes." She gave me another order.

I opened my eyes and saw her beckoning the young girl.

Love to. I grabbed the pile of clothing and shoes, fled into the adjoined room, which I assumed was a bathroom, and shut the door. I was so disappointed when I found it was just a half bath with no window. And of course, the door had no lock. So much for my escape plan: Getting changed and climbing out of the window.

After I put on the undergarments, black sweatsuit, and sneakers they gave me, I sat on the toilet seat, procrastinating about going back out to face my unfortunate fate.

Loud knocks on the door startled and distressed me, and then the door was opened. The young girl was standing by the door.

"Time to go," the woman said in a harsh voice. She opened the bedroom door and walked out.

Where are they taking me? I followed her, the young girl right behind me.

I froze when I saw two big men flanking the door outside. Both were heavyset Caucasians. They clapped their hands in the front and stared straight ahead, standing tall and carrying no expression. One was clean cut and had shaved-side short-top sandy blond hair, and the other had a dark brown buzz cut and patchy beard. Both of them looked heavily muscled, even though they were fully covered by their black suits.

"*Sie ist bereit.*" The woman was telling someone that I was ready in German.

Ready for what? It immediately grabbed my attention, and I turned in her direction.

She was walking towards a man who was leaning against the wall across the corridor. He was in all black as well, looking severe and assertive, probably someone in charge.

Did she just stroke her hair coquettishly? My eyes followed her.

"*Herr Martin, noch ist sie—*" She addressed him Mr. Martin and told him I might be weak but was well enough to travel. Her voice was soft and congenial, completely contrasting with her attitude towards me earlier.

The man looked past her and gazed at me with his cold piercing eyes. That set of sapphire eyes was so dark and overawing. I quickly turned away, my heart palpitating with fear.

The two men by the door moved to stand right behind me but did not touch me like I had assumed they were going to drag or push me.

Maybe they are not allowed to touch me, I wondered.

But their presence intimidated me so much that it forced me to move forward to keep my distance from them.

The blue-eyed man, or should I call him Mr. Martin, turned around and strode down the corridor. The two guards started to move in the same direction, forcing me to follow Mr. Martin, who I assumed was their boss, the one giving orders here.

I walked past the woman, who was still ogling the man I was following, gave her a glare, and quickened my steps to catch up with Mr. Bossman.

Following the man in charge here, I studied him...

He was at least over six feet tall. The muscles of his back flexing underneath the slim fit black suit told me that he was muscular and ripped.

Dang it!

Even though he was not as buff as the guards behind me, this man could easily overpower me. There was no way I could fight all three of them and run for my life.

Just stay calm and wait for a good opportunity, I thought to myself.

This long passage had no windows, just like the room I was in earlier. I could not tell whether it was night or day.

Arriving at a large metal door, Mr. Bossman pushed the door open, and I was disappointed to see it was dark outside.

Since I had no idea who these people were, what day it was today, where I was, and where they were taking me, I believed the best and smartest thing to do now was go with the flow and stay calm. It was not easy, but I just had to try.

The porch light revealed a black Mercedes-Benz cargo van parked at the bottom of the stairs, waiting for me, waiting to take me to my next destination.

All emotions exploded in my chest, my heart jumping wildly and my lungs gasping for air. I was fearful of what was going to happen to me once I stepped into the van. My legs suddenly lost their strength, and I fell forward. One of the guards behind me seized my arm, saving me from collapsing.

"Don't touch me!" I yanked my arm back, scolding the guard, but immediately lost my balance and fell backward because of the force of my own sudden movement.

But I did not fall onto the concrete steps, which could have cracked my head open. Instead, I fell into someone's arms.

I was in shock, frightened, and befuddled. Looking up, I saw those blue eyes again. They were so dark that they were almost black under the dull porch light

"Are you all right? Can you walk?" Mr. Bossman asked me in English with a smooth baritone accent, nothing like the woman's harsh German intonation.

"Of course I can walk," I snapped at him, pushing myself away from him. I stood up straight, put on a brave face, walked around him, and stepped into the van.

There were no windows—what a big shocker—and the driver sliding door partition was closed. I could not see if we were driving in the city or the woods, nor could I recognize any landmark for that matter. I frowned and slumped into a random seat, arms folded across my chest.

Three men got in the van after me. Mr. Bossman and The Beard took the seats behind me, and I shrank away when The Blondie sat down next to me. I stared down at the sneakers I was wearing, hiding my weakness. My eyes were flooded with tears of agitation and fear.

The van started as soon as the door was shut. I shut my eyes, preparing myself for the unexpected.

When we came to a stop and the engine was turned off, my heart palpitated suddenly. It was a short drive, or perhaps it was a long one. I was not sure because my attention was focusing on every sound and every turn, hoping for a clue as to my whereabouts.

Mr. Bossman opened the door, and a cold burst of wind gushed in. He closed the door straight away, leaving The Blondie and The Beard in the van with me.

There were muffled voices outside the van. They sounded far and low, too hard for me to hear the content of their conversation.

Then the door was opened from outside. The Beard got out first. He stood by the door and extended his hand, signaling me to follow.

Slowly, I moved towards him, shivering with cold and fear. He extended his hand to help me, but I did not take it. Taking a deep breath, I moved closer to the door and poked my head out to see what was out there.

There were more guards in all black attire, a brightly illuminated driveway, and a big structure.

A house? I stopped by the doorway, hesitating.

The Beard motioned me to get out.

Sighing, I held onto the door frame and carefully stepped down the steps, followed by The Blondie.

"This way," The Beard said to me, marching in the direction of the house.

Knowing I had no choice but to follow him, I graded my feet. Huddling, keeping my head down, and staring at the rear of The Beard's shoes, I traveled behind him and really did not care where he was leading me.

"Welcome, Iris." A sweet-sounding female voice surprised me.

She knows my name. I raised my head and saw a striking beautiful woman standing in the doorway and smiling at me. She had silky black hair, tanned skin, flawless features, and a perfect lithe figure.

"I am Vera," she said, slowly walking down the steps.

When she reached for my hands, I nearly sobbed in consolation. She gently pulled me closer to her and whispered in my ear in a soft voice, "We will take good care of you."

Before I could ask her why she knew my name and why I was here, a red-haired woman appeared from nowhere. I was probably too distracted by Vera's beauty and tenderness to notice this woman earlier. She gently put her hands on my shoulders and steered me into the house. Her touch on my shoulders was comforting. She looked probably only a few years my senior, affable, and kind.

Two beastly looking guards followed us into the house. They made The Blondie and The Beard look kind and lovely.

When I turned back to find Vera, she was already gone.

"Wh…where am I?" I asked the red-haired woman.

She did not answer my question, nor did she look at me or even acknowledge me. So I slowed down to get her attention, feeling annoyed. She sighed, tilting her head to the guards. Either she was trying to warn me of the impending threat from them or to signal for them to handle my indiscipline, it worked. I reluctantly moved along, her touch no longer comforting.

My instinct was telling me not to be fooled by her amiability and friendly façade. I would pretend to be placid—totally opposite from my true nature—and stay out of trouble before figuring out how to escape.

Up two flights of stairs, they brought me to a fully furnished bedroom. A young woman was sitting on one of the full size beds, watching me as she was expecting me.

The Gingy—she would have been given a less controversial moniker if she had answered my question earlier—closed the door and left me to get acquainted with the young woman.

"I am Mia. Have a good rest," she said to me, her voice sleepy and uninterested. She turned off the lamp by her bedside and went to sleep.

I felt confused by her casualness.

Oh, Iris, enough of being astounded or stunned. You should expect all of the unexpected by now, my pragmatic voice said loudly in my head. I had to admit its opinion was true.

Dragging my feet, I walked towards the empty bed by the window, assuming that was *my* bed. I crawled into bed and under the blanket, not bothering to take off the shoes. I felt exhausted, and tears welled in my eyes.

This is a dream. It will all go away when I wake up in the morning...

CHAPTER 3

> Reality is crushing.
> The world is a wrong-sized shoe.
> How can anyone stand it?
> ~Jandy Nelson

THE changing of the guard must have taken place before sunrise. When I left the room the next morning, The Beasties were replaced with two much gentle-looking guards. Mia led me to a small dining room to have breakfast. I only had a cup of coffee, just to stay alert. After breakfast, I followed Mia to a large living room where I saw Vera, The Gingy, and many women dispersing around the room. Some were lounging on the sofas while the others were chatting away.

"There she is." Vera spotted me and announced my arrival. "Ladies, meet our beautiful Iris."

Vera apparently was the one running the show here. I was introduced to fifteen women, including Mia and The Gingy, aka Adeline. I believed I was the only newcomer because all of them seemed to have already come to terms with this frightful situation: Human trafficking, captivity, or confinement, whichever could define it.

After the introduction, The Gingy took me to a stockroom in the basement. A middle-aged woman took my measurements and gave me a few changes of clothes and toiletries. And I was, of course, escorted back to the bedroom by the same guards and given very little time to wash up and change clothes before I was summoned to Vera's office.

She was sitting behind a spectacular white executive desk with gold wood appliqués and trims all over—seemingly excessive in my opinion. She stood up when I walked in, giving me an ear to ear smile.

"Walk with me, darling," she said, approaching me. That sounded more like a command to me.

What a... I had not granted her a *pet name* yet. *The Bitch? The Madam? The Vixen?*

She linked her arm with mine and steered me out of her ridiculously fancy office. She seemed kind and pleasant, nothing like what I thought a procuress would be.

We walked around the mansion, and she would not stop emphasizing how luxurious this dwelling house was. It was an opulent mansion, if not estates, with endless green lawn, hedge gardens, several luxury pavilions, and a grand swimming pool integrated with landscape—brilliantly designed in my opinion. Nevertheless, security guards were all over the place, not to mention those who were following me everywhere. I really did not see a magnificent place but only a restricted living space.

Vera continued to show me the amenities of this place: Countless bedrooms, lounges, rooms for dining and entertainment, spas, and a small library, where I lingered a bit longer. There were no live TVs and radios, not to mention the Internet. We were completely isolated here.

She played up how comfortable and enjoyable my new life would be, although what I heard was what she did not say: *Only if you play by my rules.*

She told me I would soon be working for her highly organized, top-end, and exclusive escort agency, and all her clients were either wealthy or powerful, or both. She said I was specially chosen, but the fact was I was abducted and trafficked.

I was silent, simply moving alongside her, and listening to her justification for my abduction. My stomach was churning. She nauseated me.

I must be dreaming. This kind of thing only happened in TV shows. It did not happen in real life, right?

It's happening to you now, Iris. My pragmatic voice spoke again. I started to dislike this voice. It was pessimistic, and it depressed me.

I will survive this. I must survive this!

Everything was still so raw. I had to figure out a way to save myself, but before then, I would have to play alone and feign obedience. I knew Vera was using her charm and fake affability to lower my guard, and I also knew she was smart enough to know I did not fall for it.

"Enjoy your new home, darling," Vera said to me, the word home chilling my blood.

Thankfully, she was done with me and turned in the guards' direction; otherwise, she would perceive my misty red eyes and nose.

"Walk Miss Iris back to her room now," she said to them.

That was actually my cue. Flanked by two big menaces, I walked towards the hallway we passed through earlier, and then I stopped at a landing, feeling so disoriented.

Upstairs, downstairs, or down the hallway?

"This way, Miss Iris." One of the guards extended his hand, showing me the way going up.

"Of course, thank you," I muttered and walked upstairs.

I supposed it could have been worse, right? They could have tortured me and left me for dead, but instead, they had fed and clothed me well, and this place was not a dump. I might be held here and forced to do things against my will, but I must look at the bright side: I was still alive.

DAY went by in a blur.

Vera had not sent me to entertain any guests yet because, as she pointed out, she had to groom me first. To enhance my appearance, I must wear exaggerated makeup, sky-high stilettos and next-to-nothing dresses. To ameliorate my entertaining skills, I had to learn to flirt, to flatter, and heaven knew what else. And the most important preparation was to condition me to accept these circumstances.

I assumed most of the women were abducted from different countries because many of them spoke languages that I had never heard before. And I believed they were all *specially chosen* just like what Vera said about me. All of them were young, gorgeous, sexy, and attractive.

But why me? I was twenty-five already—still very young in my opinion. I was older than all of them, and I did not see myself as gorgeous, sexy, or attractive.

Vera told me I was *unique* and *exotic*.

Being multiracial, I surely heard those words a lot. My father's Scandinavia and Italian descent and my mother's Chinese mixed with Japanese/Irish heritage made my brother and me look absolutely unique and exotic. Our DNA was all over the map. I used to feel special when being praised with words like those, but I loathed them so much now.

Vera also said, "Some of our clients have very specific tastes. Your popularity will be in great demand. I promise you that you are going to be a star."

S*pecific tastes?* How disgusting, twisted, and wicked it was.

A star? How ironic? I was abducted from a club named Étoile.

Mia delineated that Vera only had parties in this mansion for drinking, dancing, gambling, etc. except sexual activities. Clients had to pay much higher prices for additional services. The sex act would be held at other locations agreed and arranged by both parties because those wealthy and powerful clients demanded their privacy.

Mia surely did not have any problem flaunting her fancy wardrobe and her splendid rewards, which were given to her by the patrons for her *special* services. She told me her life before Vera was penurious, and she was grateful to her.

I thought she and some other women had traded their dignity and self-respect for luxury gifts and lavish lifestyles, but… Should I feel sorry for them or pity them? Perhaps my definition of morality was different from theirs; if so, who was I to judge?

Mia also warned me that whoever did not fit in here or became useless to Vera were taken away.

Taken? What a horrifying word... Perhaps that was why they all seemed to be enjoying the life here because they were suited here.

At the beginning Mia did gain closeness with me and had my sympathy. I was thrilled when she told me she was also from the States—her English made me homesick. And my maternal instinct kicked in when I knew she was only twenty years old. She was too content with her life here that I wanted to shake some sense into her. However, after a few private conversations, I was certain that she was more than my roommate and was assigned to influence and brainwash me. How did I know? Because she only had good things to say about Vera, her life here, and all the patrons she had ever entertained.

"What about your freedom, Mia?" I once asked her. Ever since I was brought here, I had never been able to go anywhere without at least one guard following me.

"You will earn your freedom. Once you are ready, you can go places like me," she said with excitement. Except that her *going places* was being transported to different locations to meet with men paying extra for special services. She was proud to be a courtesan.

I will never be ready... I kept this thought to myself because I certainly had learned my lesson about sharing too much with Mia, The Snitch. She reported everything back to Vera. And being chastised by The Vixen—I happily granted Vera her pet-name, and it was perfect for a female fox—was not a pleasant experience, which I had had too many of since I arrived here.

Here I was, summoned to The Vixen's private chamber again. I started to sense that I might have pushed my luck a little too far now.

The Vixen was lounging on a Rococo tufted-seat-back chaise by the window, luxuriating in the warm sunshine. She sat up when she saw me.

"Sit," she commanded, smoothing her skirt without sparing me a look.

I sat down in the same style single seater across from her, waiting for my lecture. I had learned to tune her out, stay quiet, and look remorseful.

But somehow, this meeting felt different... She did not use any endearment, such as *my loveliest*, which she used quite often on me.

And she just stared at me, not speaking a word. Her silence was daunting.

Maybe she's waiting for me to confess or to apologize?

Just as I was considering what was the best thing to say, The Gingy knocked on the open door and walked in, a tray in her hand.

"Ma'am." She placed the tray on the coffee table by the chaise, picked up an espresso cup and its saucer, and put them down closer to The Vixen.

Ah, she's waiting for her caffeine shot. I felt instantly relieved.

The Gingy gave me a sympathetic glance before walking out of the room. I gave her a nonchalant shrug, bending my head and dusting off the invisible lints on my skirt.

In my peripheral Vision, Vera picked up her espresso and took a sip elegantly. Holding the cup in her hand, she said, "Iris, I—"

So it began...

I put on a repentant face, my hands folded in my lap. And I tuned out her voice.

Punishments? Wait what? I turned to look at her, listening carefully to what she was saying.

She did just state explicitly that I would be punished if I did not drop my resistance immediately and accept the reality.

Do I care? I sneered at her in silence. I was not in the least concerned about whatever disciplinary actions she had in store for me. Starvation? Isolation? Or scaring me with whipping or caning? Ahem, tolerating pain was probably not my forte...

However... If I was weak or injured, I would be excused from the parties. That was actually a good plan.

She gave me a withering glance and continued, "I have plenty of procurers wanting to buy my rebellious girls. And also, sex slaves are in high demand." And then she turned her body to face the window and closed her eyes. She moaned, soaking up the sun.

Sex slaves...

Her words made my blood curdle.

"You are excused," she said in her usual low and indifferent voice.

I stood up, hands gripping the hem of my cardigan, and could not get out of the room fast enough.

CHAPTER 4

> Man can live about forty days without food,
> about three days without water,
> about eight minutes without air,
> but only for one second without hope.
> ~Charles Darwin

TWO months ago, I made my debut in a high-profile client's birthday celebration held in the biggest ballroom. Vera demanded me to stay close to her during the party, not because she cared about me, but because she wanted me to watch, to absorb, and to learn from the best.

She chatted, flirted, and mingled with her client and his guests while I shadowed her ungainly in a super-short, crimson Christian Dior dress and a pair of super-high, red and black, snakeskin Christian Louboutin sandals—Vera dressed all her women here excellently and expensively.

"Red is your color, my loveliest," she said to me once, and she filled my closets with all different shades of bloody red.

I still remembered how dirty I felt after that party. I soaked in hot water and scrubbed myself for hours. My skin was wrinkled and scratched, but I still could not get rid of the reeking smell of cologne and cigar mixture.

Here I was, working at another big celebration in the ballroom today. I could not even remember how many times I was forced to work at big parties like this. However, attending big parties was always better than entertaining small groups of lecherous men or dealing with one prurient man who specifically requested for my company.

The eighth? Or probably the twelfth? Do I really care?

Sighing, I scanned the room and met a pair of admiral blue eyes.

Do those eyes change colors all the time? I stared back at them. It was probably the mood and atmosphere lighting in this room that gave those eyes hints of velvety purple and black.

Why do I care? I scowled at the man who possessed those blue eyes.

The security foreman Max, aka The Bossman and Herr Martin, was always on duty when there was a big party like this. He and his minions kept their eyes on the clients because there were two strict rules here. Number one: The guests were not allowed to touch us improperly; number two: Rough and rude behaviors were not allowed. I had seen The Beasties removing a couple of men off the premises before, and they were absolutely menacing when they escorted them out.

The guards' presence was appreciated if I was at a party, big or small. But other than that, I wished they could give me a break. Who would like to be monitored every waking minute? They were everywhere! And Max was always around. Every corner I turned, he was there. Even when he was off duty, I would run into him, too.

The Bossman had enchanted all the women here, even Vera, with his dream-come-true looks, gentlemanly manner, and bad-boy coldness, but he could never fool me. I knew his type. His charisma was just his scheme to control women, and that would not work on me. He was a bad person to his bones because he was making his living on someone else's misery. All of them were all evil and immoral as far as I was concerned.

I averted my eyes from his gaze and suddenly was choked with emotion.

Today is... I turn twenty-six today...

Not wanting to be caught crying, I sneaked into a powder room. The sudden absence of the revelry was almost comforting.

Dragging my hurting feet, I walked towards a bench by the window and plunked myself down. I kicked off the towering six-inch stilettos, and my feet got an instant relief from the pain.

I looked out the window, staring off into the distance and letting my silent tears run free.

On my birthday, I would call my mother to thank her for enduring almost forty hours of labor to bring me to this world. After my parents moved from Laguna Beach to Monterey, which was almost four-hundred miles away, they would order my favorite cake, Black Forest gâteau, and have it delivered to me.

Oh my, Antonio's bizarre birthday presents... I smiled at the thought of them.

He would give me the most unusual, strange, or funny things he could ever find on this planet. One year, he gave me a screaming Rubber Chicken and said it reminded him of me—seriously, why did I call him my best friend? However, he could be thoughtful at times. He gifted me an ostrich pillow one year so I could take good naps; and a bright pink pee funnel last year so I... His exact words were 'When you gotta go, you gotta go.'

I chuckled in tears, wondering what he would get for me this year if...if...

Dejection enveloped me, my stomach churning at the thought of my misfortune.

Living like this was intolerable, but I was afraid to be taken or sold. Everything I did now was to survive.

The cooks, maids, and security guards here spoke German, French, Italian, and a little English, so I assumed I was still somewhere in Europe. If they spoke German, then I was able to pick up some key words and guess what they were talking about. They were actually very careless when they discussed their business, especially Mr. Bossman. I often overheard him instructing his guards on the security plans regarding the upcoming parties. Since no one knew I understood the language, I used it to my advantage. Once I got the details, I would plot to refrain from attending to as many patrons as possible.

I used to resent my poor alcohol tolerance because I would either have an instant hangover or flushes or blotches all over my face and body after I consumed alcoholic beverages. Now, I thought it was a blessing. I would drink more than I could handle, usually only two glasses of wine, and become all groggy and red—The Vixen did say red was my color, didn't she?

Unfortunately, she soon perceived my intention and would make sure that no one offered me more than a half glass of wine.

I feigned sickness. And when my acting no longer convinced Vera, I would make myself become ill for real by taking cold showers, being on a complete fast, or not sleeping at all—I was feeling like hell.

I tried to find allies to cover for me. And when they stopped helping me, I would deliberately start fights with women who disliked me—It hurt like hell when the fights became physical.

I forced myself to fit in, but every single cell in me refused to comply—I felt like living in hell.

I was surviving...barely. The longer I stayed here the more despairing I became. I was afraid I was going to lose hope and go completely insane before I ever saw my family again...

A sob escaped. I hastily covered my mouth and nose with my hands to stifle it. The emotion was so overwhelming that my body was shaking violently. Not able to suppress my anguished cry anymore, I grabbed a hand towel from the rack and covered my mouth to muffle my wail and allowed myself to give vent to my anger, grief, and sorrow.

When I finally recovered from my meltdown, I felt a little better... Emotionally. Letting out a deep sigh, I got up and stood in front of the mirror to clean my face, which was a disaster.

How long have I been here? I wondered. And I was surprised The Vixen had not sent a search team to look for me already.

Looking at my face in the mirror, I gave myself a bitter smile. There was only so much I could do to conceal my cried-out eyes, and I really did not care.

Sitting on the bench again, I tried to put the heels back on.

Oh no... I squeezed my feet into the shoes in agony. Note to self for future reference: *never take the high heels off if I planned to put them back on again.*

I balanced on the stilettos and took a couple of steps to make sure I could still manage them for the rest of the night. I walked to the door, ready to get back to reality.

Facing the door, I combed my hair with my fingers and smoothed my skirt.

Here we go... I opened the door and saw a guard standing right outside the door. He faced away from the powder room and blocked the doorway.

"What the…" I muttered. *Seriously? Do they seriously think I will pose a serious threat to them or to myself?*

The guard turned around when he heard me.

Those blue eyes again…

Frowning Max stared down at me, arms across over his chest. He didn't look angry or irritated. His expression was very hard to read.

I was completely in shock and unnerved by his somber demeanor.

His gaze darted back and forth between my eyes for a minute or two and then stepped aside.

Blinking away my fear, I drew in a deep breath and headed back to the party.

CHAPTER 5

> The best way to find out if you can
> trust somebody is to trust them.
> ~Ernest Hemingway

"GET your dirty hand off me!" I was screaming and kicking when this lascivious man I was entertaining tonight slid his hand under my skirt.

I must have kicked him really hard because he was yelling and cursing in his mother tongue—whatever it was.

I stood up, trying to get away from him, but he immediately grabbed my thighs and dragged me down, so hard that I fell on the sofa. I was in shock, and my mind just went completely blank.

He got on top of me, one hand holding my arms over my head and the other pulling my skirt over my hips.

He's going to rape me... A wave of panic swept through me.

"Get off me! Hel...help!" I screamed at the top of my lungs.

Just when he was going to put his hand over my mouth to stop me from screaming, someone grabbed his wrist and yanked him off me.

"No," Max said to the man, his voice low and authoritative and his eyes full of rage. Without waiting for the patron's reaction, Max scooped me up effortlessly.

"Don't touch me!" My initial reaction was to fight him. I shouted furiously, struggling to get free from him.

"Settle down," he whispered in my ear tenderly. "Let's get you out of here first." Carrying me in his arms, he strode towards the door.

All my anger and rage suddenly turned into fear and grief when the heavy door slammed shut behind us, tears scalding my eyes.

I heard Vera's severe voice approaching, along with her entourage's footsteps. My heart was pounding out of my chest. I quickly shut my eyes and buried my face in Max's chest. I felt him turning his body, turning me away from them.

She sounded mad, so mad at me now, because I just upset her most important client.

"She has to go!"

"Get rid of her!"

"Nothing but trouble!"

She's going to get rid of me... Horrible thoughts of what they could do to get rid of me were going through my mind. My body started shaking uncontrollably.

Max held me tighter. "Don't worry," he whispered.

Why is he so nice to me all of a sudden? I wondered, although his comfort was all I had now. I burst into tears, sobbing in his arms. *I might die today...*

Max carried me back to my room. He set me down on my bed and stepped out of the room right away, closing the door behind him.

I was plunged into despair.

Surviving these past few months was unbearable, but facing death was behind everything I could imagine. I broke down and wailed.

"Iris..." Mia's voice startled me.

I loathed her! She told me as long as I behaved and entertained the patrons in the mansion, I would be safe. But what just happened in the lounge was...was...

"Iris..." She sat down beside me and touched my shoulder, wanting to comfort me.

I flinched, turning away from her. I could hear her loud sigh, which sounded especially irritating to my ears now.

"What did you do this time?" she asked.

What did I do? How dare she ask that! I blocked her voice out, curling up in a fetal position and shedding tears.

I had been encouraging myself to stay positive and convincing myself that there must be a way out of here and I could survive this, and I constantly reminded myself that my family would never stop looking for me.

But at this very moment, I just wanted to give up...

I was so tired of constantly feeling frightened, disgusted, and hopeless. I would rather die than being a prisoner here and a toy of those wicked people for one more second.

"What's going on?" Mia mumbled as she stood up.

There were loud arguments going on outside. Many people were talking at the same time, so I could not understand a word.

I opened my eyes and saw Mia walking towards the door. She opened the door, but a security guard shut it close right away. The loud bang startled both of us.

"You really pissed them off this time." Mia turned towards me, frowning. "Why can't you—"

"Shut up, Mia. Just shut up," I cut her off, giving her a wrathful stare.

She shrugged and walked back to her bed.

Suddenly, the door was flung open. Max marched in, looking terrifying as if he was going to break someone—maybe he was...

"Mia, go outside," he demanded.

"Mia..." I looked at Mia, begging her not to leave me, and what I saw was a timid coward.

Of course she would not defend me because no one defied Max. All the women here wanted his attention. The tender-and-loving kind and not the getting-on-the-wrong-side-of-Max kind.

Mia gave me a look full of pity.

"Mia, please—" I pleaded, hoping she could have some sympathy for me and decide to stay.

"Now," Max cut me off, growling.

She lowered her head and quickly walked out of the room.

Max slammed the door behind her. It was so loud that I felt it echoing in my chest, and my heart might have skipped several beats.

What...what is he doing? I saw him locking the door.

Taking a deep breath, I stared at his back. I was going to look into his eyes when he turned around to hurt me or killed me.

I saw him breathing heavily, his shoulders going up and down. He did not turn around. And I waited, on alert and ready for his attack.

When he finally moved, he scanned the room, frowning and surveying. The anger on his face was replaced with concern and contemplation.

And when he finally looked at me, his blue eyes looked pained and made me forget my own sorrow.

However, all the fears resurfaced when he moved towards me.

"Max, please…" I begged. "That man tried to rape me. I was just… I was just… You were there. You saw it." My voice was hoarse, tears gushing down. "Gi…give me… Give me another chance. Plea…please. I pro…promise I…I'll be…be… good." I lied because I knew I would fight even harder next time, but I had to lie to survive now.

Max knocked the lamp off the bedside table when he walked closer. I screamed in panic.

"Please, don't… I am begging you…" My body trembled violently when he grabbed my wrists and pinned me on the headboard. *Somebody, help me. Anybody…*

"Listen, Iris," he whispered in my ear. "I need you to keep yelling and screaming. But, listen to me very carefully." His voice was calm and comforting, not what I had expected. "Please," he added.

Keep yelling and screaming? And did he just say the word please? I was so confused. *What kind of sick game is he playing?*

"Scream now," he whispered in an authoritative tone.

Although it was a whisper, it sounded absolutely imperative.

I did what he asked: Screaming at the top of my lungs.

And strangely, he turned his face towards the door and shouted, "Be quiet!" He deliberately wanted people outside to hear him.

"What?" I was so puzzled. "But you…"

Looking apologetic, he whispered to me, "Trust me. Please."

Trust you? You are acting like a mad man. I did not say it out loud because I also did not want to get on the wrong side of Max.

He looked into my eyes, pleading, and his gaze was both earnest and unfeigned.

For some reason I felt calm and trusting, so I nodded.

"I am going to let go of you now." He kept his voice down. "Don't fight me, Iris. Please. I need you to trust me," he said, asking for reassurance.

His voice held genuine sincerity, so I nodded again.

He slowly moved his hands off my wrists.

I backed away from him as soon as I was free.

"Tonight I will relocate you—"

"Relocate me?" I cut him off in a horrified voice.

"Lower your voice," he hushed me, frowning. "Or scream if you want." He looked around and spotted a water glass on the bedside table. He grabbed it and threw it at the door. It smashed to smithereens, and the water splashed on the door and carpet.

I screamed, shocked by his sudden and violent move. My frightened eyes met his.

He leaned closer, wanting to say something, but I immediately shrank away from him. He sighed and said above a whisper, "Iris, no matter what you hear later, I need you to stay calm and don't worry. Okay?"

I hesitated, unsure how to respond. He was obviously crazy and making no sense.

"Okay?" he asked again, his voice becoming impatient.

Strenuously, I moved my head up and down, up and down, and up and down, not wanting to upset him.

"Good. We are going to put on a show now," he moved even closer to me. His fresh earthy scent enveloped me, and his proximity made my heart race. "Can you do that?" he asked, his voice tender again.

"What… How?" I asked in a whisper.

"Vi…" He averted his eyes and said in hesitation, "Violating you."

"Vi…" I almost raised my voice but quickly lowered it. "Violate me? To work with *you* to violate *me*? Are you insane?" I huffed, staring at him. *Oh my… Did I just call Max insane?*

"No. No. I will never assault you." His brilliant blue gaze was back on me, blinking his nervousness.

Max was nervous… Really? I gave him a quizzical look.

"Please, Iris. I need you to trust me and work with me," he pleaded. His earnest entreaties and heartfelt eyes were weakening my willpower.

"O…okay…" Although I still had my doubts, I agreed because he was my only hope now.

He gave me an appreciative smile before moving closer, and I did not flinch this time.

"Iris…" he whispered my name, and it sounded like an endearment, enchanting me. "I am going to rip your dress now."

"What?" I was shocked and shrank away from him. Again. "You… What?" My voice was shaking with fear.

He sighed, looking regretful. "Just putting on a show, Iris. To make them believe that you are being punished—" He paused and added, "By me."

My eyes could not get any wider and angrier, and my mind was trying to make sense of his words…

Isn't he going to get rid of me tonight? The thought sent chills down my spine.

But why putting on a show? If getting rid of me was his plan, then why did he want to make others believe he was in here to punish me?

I felt so exhausted. My dismal befuddled brain was going to shut down soon.

Just a show, right? Fine…

"Now?" I asked, my voice trembling.

"When you are ready. But…yes, now please, if we want to fool them," he said impatiently.

I quickly assessed my other options and found nothing. *None. Zero. Keine.*

"Okay…" I breathed out the word and shut my eyes, waiting for his big move. I felt his warm hands touching my arms gently. It was so comforting that I failed to anticipate his action.

Suddenly, a sound of ripping fabric startled me, and then a gush of cold air brushed over my chest.

Max covered me with a blanket straight away and breathed apologies in my ear.

Even though he had prepared me for this and I knew we were just putting on a show, it still devastated me. I felt powerless and violated. Hot tears rolled down my cheeks where the old tears had not yet dried.

"I am so sorry..." He gently held me in his arms.

I could no longer hold back my fear and sorrow. I lost control of my emotions and cried uncontrollably.

Max just held me.

Pull yourself together, I thought to myself. Taking a deep breath and choking with sobs, I pushed myself away from him and said, "I...I...I am...I am o...kay."

"Are you sure?" His voice was full of regret and concern.

I nodded, avoiding eye contact with him.

Out of the corner of my eye, I saw him standing up and looking at his watch. He became silent and pensive for several minutes. And then he looked at me and gave me that apologetic look. Again.

"I am going to turn around and..." He paused, gazing at me in hesitation. "I know you are absolutely terrified right now, but I must ask you to do one more thing. Please, trust me and work with me."

I nodded without hesitation. He had not harmed me or intentionally frightened me so far. Although I did not know what his plan was, I knew for sure he would not hurt me.

"Thank you. I... I need you to remove your undies and toss it on the floor. Please..."

This is too much. Just too much. I shook my head vigorously.

"Please, we need to make them believe this," he explained. "I will send Mia back in here, and she will see the evidence."

Evidence? Oh... I just realized what he meant. Frowning, I nodded very slowly and reluctantly.

Max gave me an appreciating smile and turned around. He folded his arms across his chest, waiting.

I kept my eyes on him, making sure he did not peek or move before I was ready. Although I did not know this man at all, I trusted him. Well, at this point, I had to trust him. I covered myself with a blanket from neck to toes first and then removed my thong.

"I... It's done," I whispered after tossing the panties on the carpet.

"Thank you," he whispered but did not turn around or come close to me again.

I fixed my eyes on him, watching him walking towards the door and standing by it for a couple of minutes. Then he unlocked it and threw it open.

"Do not let her out of the room!" he commanded the guards standing outside, sounding like the cold and heartless Max again.

Can I really trust him? All my emotions and fears were coming back. I gripped the blanket that covered my half-naked body tightly.

Mia was at the door almost immediately after Max stepped out of the room. She stopped in the doorway and scanned the room, astounded by the mess. Moving her eyes to me, she gave me the same pitying look she threw at me earlier and walked towards me.

And my thong caught her eyes. "Oh god..." she thought out loud. "I would never... Max?"

We have to put on a show. Max's voice was echoing in my head.

"Did Max..." Not able to finish her question, Mia sat down on the edge of my bed, staring at me with her bulging eyes.

I looked at her with my watery eyes and nodded, trying to be as convincing as possible.

"Oh, Iris... I am so sorry..." Gently, she touched my shoulder.

I pushed her away and got out of the bed. I scampered into the bathroom and shut the door.

The reflection in the full length mirror standing against the wall startled me. I turned to stare at the person in the mirror...

I am such a mess... I could not recognize myself at all. Messy hair, smudged mascara, black tear lines, my arms and legs covered with red marks caused by the man in the lounge tonight, and...and the torn dress.

Totally swallowed up by the despair, I fell onto the floor and bawled like a wounded child.

"Iris, are you all right?" Mia knocked on the bathroom door. She must be troubled by my anguished cry.

Am I all right? Would I be all right if I were really raped?

"Leave me alone!" I shouted, wiping the tears away.

Sadness turning into anger, I got up and went around the bathroom to turn on all the faucets, hoping the sound of running water would be able to soothe my uncontrollable rage.

CHAPTER 6

> Just as despair can come to one only from
> other human beings, hope, too, can be given
> to one only by other human beings.
> ~Elie Wiesel

A hot bath had calmed me down, and then the reality hit me so hard when I stepped out of the bathroom and saw the lamp and broken glasses on the floor. Tears were threatening to emerge again.

There was no sight of Mia. I glanced at the clock on the wall and found it was after nine already. She was probably entertaining her loyal patrons now. I walked into the closet and put on leggings and a sweatshirt.

Tonight I will relocate you. Max's words were playing again and again in my head.

Tonight? When? How? Should I pack? I didn't even know what to pack because nothing here belonged to me.

It was so quiet outside the door. Usually, some women would be lounging in the sitting room, chatting, or playing cards and board games when they did not have clients to attend to. Therefore, it was very unusually quiet tonight.

I took courage and opened the door and was surprised to see The Beard standing outside, completely blocking the doorway.

"Max ordered—" he answered my unspoken question.

"I know. I know," I cut him off. And before closing the door, I peeked behind him and saw an empty living room.

I guess I just have to wait.

I had been staring at the clock for hours, wondering when the relocation was going to happen, if Max was going to be with me, and what was going to happen to me now...

It was a nerve-racking ordeal.

Finally, I heard chatting outside the door around midnight. I jumped from the bed and stood against the wall far away from the door. My body was trembling with fear and apprehension.

The door was opened, and The Beard beckoned me.

Where is Max? My feet refused to move.

"Now!" He commanded, his voice impatient.

I was startled by his loud, hoarse voice, which only made me move farther away from him.

"Is there a problem?" Max's voice had never sounded so heavenly.

I scurried out of the room, past The Beard and towards Max's voice. Then I stopped abruptly when I saw a scowling and irritated Max standing by the living room exit.

Disdainfully, he shot me a sidelong glance of annoyance and turned away, making me feel snubbed and worthless.

He exchanged some words with The Beastie standing next to him. And then he turned around and headed in the stairway direction.

Wait! Don't leave... Although feeling confused and hurt, I wanted to call him. Before I could react, The Beard grabbed my arm and hustled me to follow Max.

"Don't touch me!" I shouted, wanting to shake his hand off me. And my reaction only made him grip my arm even tighter. "You are hurting me!" I huffed.

They obviously were permitted to be rough with me now because I was no longer precious to Vera. I looked at Max's back, expecting a little sympathy, but he kept walking and did not respond to my shouting and yelling. Feeling disappointed and irate, I resented myself for trusting him. My eyes were again welled with disheartened tears.

Once we were out of the backdoor, I saw a black sedan parked near the entrance. Max got into the car and sat behind the wheel while The Beard opened the backseat door, tossed me inside the car, and shut the door. Max stepped on the gas before I could sit up.

I tried several times to move myself up to a sitting position in the speedy car but failed miserably. Finally, I gave up and just lay face upward, staring at the car ceiling.

Why is he driving so fast? Cannot wait to get rid of me? Tears ran down from the corners of my eyes. I was surprised there were still tears left in me.

The car finally slowed down. I hastily sat up, wanting to see where I was, and maybe, just maybe, I could jump out of the car.

"Please, put on the seatbelt," Max said. His voice was gentle and soft again.

I'm not falling for that again. I readily pulled the door handle. *Come what may. If I die, I die.*

But, the door stayed closed, shut, sealed. The child-safety-lock was on. Of course.

I saw Max's frowning face in the rearview mirror and shot him an angry glance.

"Seatbelt. Please." His voice was kind, not upset by my reckless action.

Since I was stranded in the car anyway, I might as well ride safely. I fastened the seatbelt and leaned back in the seat, my arms folded across my chest.

We must be far away from the mansion now because I looked out the windows and did not see the glow of its bright security spotlights. It was very dark outside. Through the windshield, I saw a narrow winding road ahead illuminated by the headlights. The darkness and uncertainty frightened me. I could not believe I was going to jump out of the car earlier.

"Are you all right?" he asked with that kind voice again.

I did not answer him, not wanting to give him the satisfaction. Then I met his concerned eyes in the rearview mirror. They melted my heart.

No. Not going to fall for that again. He's taking advantage of my vulnerability. Bastard!

I quickly averted my eyes and leaned back in the seat, trying to shelter my weakening mind and emotions.

Max did not say or ask anything again and left me alone.

We were on the road for a while. I glanced at him several times in the rearview mirror and saw him checking on me through the mirror as well. When our eyes met, I never missed a chance to give him a spiteful look.

Where is he taking me? Looking at the road in front of us, I could see we were heading towards a bridge.

Lights! I saw a sea of lights on the other end of the bridge. I could not conceal my exhilaration. I leaned forward, fixing my eyes on the lights of my possible freedom.

Just as I was feeling hopeful and believing I could finally get help, Max slowed down.

"Wait. What are you doing? Why are you slowing down?" I asked anxiously.

He did not answer me but made a right turn at the intersection right before the bridge.

No... Turn back... I felt devastated. My eyes followed those lights, to my left and then behind me. Those bright dots became smaller and smaller.

Suddenly, he stopped the car.

I whipped around and found we were behind another black car.

Switching cars? Handing me over to another abductor? Selling me as a slave? Oh my god, I am going to be a sex slave. My mind was running a thousand miles an hour, wondering what was happening now. My body was trembling, and my heart was pounding in fear.

"Iris..." Max turned around and called me softly.

I looked at him, blinking back tears.

His brow furrowed and let out a sigh of guilt or probably dejection. Perhaps it was a sigh of relief, feeling relieved that he could finally get rid of me.

"Wait in the car. I will be right back." He turned off the engine but left the headlights on.

"Max, please..." I begged, hoping he would pity me.

"Trust me." He gave me a reassuring look before he got out of the car and closed the door behind him.

I was able to see him because of the moonlight and the headlights. My eyes followed him as he walked towards the other car.

My survival instinct kicked in, and I pulled the door handle anyway, even though I knew the child-safety-lock was on. I would push it, kick it, or break it open if I had to.

And the door opened with a thud on my first try. It was unlocked...

He must have unlocked it by accident. It's my chance now. My adrenaline was going through the roof.

Calm down, Iris. Be smart, I thought to myself. I had to sneak out quietly because I knew he carried a handgun and could easily shoot me.

I took a peek at Max to make sure he was not looking in my direction, and I saw a person stepping out of the other car.

A woman? A procurer? Or worse, a sex slave buyer...

And then they totally had my attention because it looked like she was scolding Max. He folded his arms across the chest, his eyes cast down to the ground.

Against my better judgment, I moved closer to the front seat to get a better look—my curiosity was going to kill me.

Now, Iris. It's perfect timing to sneak out now. My pragmatic voice shouted at me.

Time to go. I decided to listen to the loud voice in my head and carefully pushed the door open. But I halted when I heard the crunchy sound of them walking on gravel. Towards me.

I just lost my chance of getting out of the car.

Too late for regrets, I quickly sat back down, trying to act casual.

"Iris," Max gently swung the door fully open, not surprised at the already-opened door at all. He extended one hand out for me and said, "You are safe now."

Safe? I gave him a skeptical glance.

He returned it with a reassuring smile.

I hesitated, unsure of what to do.

"Let me introduce you my friend." He bent lower and extended his hand closer to me.

I shrank back, staring at him with fear.

"She's a very good friend of mine." He saw the concern in my eyes, his voice becoming even softer. "Trust me, please."

I really did not have much of a choice, so I took a deep breath and moved to the edge of the seat. Without taking his helping hand, I stepped out of the car. Then I immediately hid behind Max, peeking at the woman.

She was dressed all in black like Max, had short blonde hair, and looked masculine and feminine at the same time. What was the word? Androgynous!

"Iris, this is Julia," he said to me, introducing the woman.

"Hi Iris," she greeted me and gave me a benevolent and compassionate smile.

But instead of responding to her, I shrank and huddled, looking down at the ground and hiding myself completely behind Max.

Max turned around slowly.

I could sense him gazing down at me. Feeling intimidated by him, I stepped a couple of steps backward to keep a safe distance. Out of the corner of my eye, I saw him raising his hands up—probably wanting to hold me still—and then putting them back down—probably changing his mind. He clenched his hands into fists—seemingly struggling with something in his mind—and then put them in his pockets.

"Iris," he called me softly. And since I did not respond, he continued, "Julia is going to take you to the U.S. Embassy now."

I raised my head in shock, my eyes widened.

The corners of his lips slowly turned up, his gaze serious and sincere.

"U.S. Embassy? Really?" I asked, my voice shaking and tears blurring my vision.

Julia stepped closer and put her hand on my shoulder.

I flinched, not wanting to be touched. And when I saw the concerned expression on her face, I felt terribly sorry for my rudeness.

"I am sorry..." I offered her an awkward apology.

"Don't be," she said with a gentle smile, keeping her hands behind her, and said, "They are expecting us. Shall we?"

"They are?" I looked at her intensely and then turned towards Max for reassurance.

Max nodded and gestured for me to follow Julia, who was walking back to her car.

I hesitated, looking in Julia's direction and feeling uncertain.

This must be real... They did not need to lie about where they were taking me. If I could trust Max, I should be able to trust this woman, right?

I turned towards Max again and asked, "Will I see you again?"

Wait... What? Why did I want to see him again? He worked for Vera. I regretted my impulsivity as soon as the words left my mouth.

He looked surprised, and then he turned away, staring off into the distance.

I drew in a deep breath, knowing he had turned cold and disinterested again. Feeling rejected, I scampered towards Julia, who was standing by the passenger side and holding the door open for me. I dived into the car and buckled myself up immediately.

Before Julia got in, I heard Max's car door shut and the engine started behind us. I turned around and looked through the rear glass window, wishing to catch another glimpse of him, but the headlights' glare blinded me. I heard the car turning around, and then he drove off.

I forgot to thank him... I stared at the taillights.

"Iris..." Julia pulled me out of my thoughts.

I shrank back in the seat and whispered, "I am ready."

Julia made an u-turn, like Max just did, and then turned right towards the bridge.

I should feel relieved, but for some reason I felt lost in Max's absence.

He saved you, Iris. That is the reason. My pragmatic voice pointed it out for me.

"He saved me..." I murmured, turning to look at Julia for confirmation.

"He did, indeed," she said, her voice full of emotions.

I turned my head to my right and looked out the window, staring off into the darkness. Hot tears were flowing down. They were grateful and hopeful tears, but my heart was aching.

Julia left me alone, leaving me to process what had just happened at my own pace.

I saw some signs at the side of the roads but could not recognize any of them.

"Excuse me, Ju…Julia."

"Yes, Iris?" she responded eagerly, keeping her eyes on the road.

"Would you… Would you tell me where we are going?"

Frowning, she glanced at me and said, "Bern."

"Bern?" I felt so confused. "I am in Switzerland…" I murmured.

"You don't know where you are?"

I shook my head, not able to answer. I did not know how to explain to her that I should be in Paris.

"Don't worry, Iris," she said in a comforting voice. "You shall be able to go home soon."

Home…

I had been dreaming of waking up in my own bed, but the disappointment had welcomed me every morning.

Am I really going home soon? I would not dare to dream of that, not yet…

CHAPTER 7

> And one has to understand that braveness is not
> the absence of fear but rather the strength
> to keep on going forward despite the fear.
> ~Paulo Coelho

WE had been on the road for a long time. I was exhausted, tired, and sleepy. I had been awake since early yesterday morning, and so many things had happened. When I woke up yesterday, I would not have thought, or dreamt of, I would be on my way to the U.S. Embassy in Bern now. I kept pinching myself to make sure this was really happening and to keep myself awake as well.

Julia suggested I take a nap or at least rest my eyes, but I did not want to, afraid to, actually. I was afraid I would wake up in Vera's mansion if I fell asleep. And I also wanted to know where I was. I read every road sign, trying to memorize every road she took and every turn she made... I felt my brain was overloaded and fuzzy. I pinched my thigh so hard that I uttered a yelp.

"Are you all right?" Julia asked.

From the corner of my eye, I saw her glancing at me and quickly focusing on the road again.

I nodded, too tired to make a sound, except the yelp earlier.

I might have dozed off because one minute we were on the highway and the next we were in the city. I hastily sat up straight and looked out the window. Although it was dark, I was excited to see all the lights, cars, and people on the streets, even just a few of them at this hour.

I felt anxious every time Julia made a turn, hoping the building at the corner would be our destination, and then I was disappointed when she kept driving. My emotions were on a seemingly never-ending roller coaster ride.

I am going crazy. I'd better stop this. I sank back into the seat, trying not to be too eager. However, when Julia made another turn, my face was pressing against the window again.

When she made a left turn at a three-way junction, I soon saw a line of silver bollards along the sidewalk by some concrete walls and tall fences on our right hand side.

My heart palpated when I saw the illuminated letters CONSULAR SERVICES mounted on a small concrete wall, and then my eyes were glued to the sign, EMBASSY OF THE UNITED STATES OF AMERICA, and the Great Seal of the United States on a wilder wall.

We are here... The sight took my breath away.

Julia kept going, and I saw a light grey office building behind the tall metal fences. She continued to drive along the fence and around the guardhouse on the corner. She stopped in front of the metal gate right next to the guardhouse, and it started to slide open. A man in uniform walked out and motioned her to move forward. She followed the instructions and stopped before the closed second gate, and the officer walked around the car to the driver's side.

I glanced at the time on the GPS screen. It was almost three in the morning.

"Ma'am," he greeted Julia, and then he looked me in the eyes and nodded. "Ma'am," he greeted.

I shied away from his courtesy, staring my hands folded on my lap.

"Mr. Hoffmann is expecting us," Julia said to the officer.

"Yes, ma'am. I was informed. Mr. Huffman is waiting for you at the front entrance," he said to her in *perfect* American English.

I stared at him, feeling overwhelmed.

Then the second gate slid open slowly.

I held my breath when Julia slowly drove past the gate.

I...I am really safe now...

A young man was standing at the end of the driveway. I assumed he was *the* Mr. Hoffmann they talked about. He walked closer after Julia stopped the car and opened the car door for me.

"Ms. De Waal," he greeted me.

He knows my name... I could not speak nor move. I just stared at him with hesitation.

"James, I got this," Julia said to him. She got out, walked around to my side, and crouched down to my eye level. "Iris, I will stay by your side. I promise," she said, her voice soft and comforting.

I nodded, blinking back my tears.

James stepped up, offering to give me a hand, but Julia stopped him. He got the message and stepped aside to give me more personal space.

I gave Julia an appreciative smile and slowly stepped out of the car.

"This way. Let's settle you in first," James said, motioning us to the front entrance.

I was not sure if I was too overwhelmed with excitement or with fear. I could barely walk. Dragging my feet, I followed James into the building. And Julia was just one step behind me.

We rode the elevator to the fifth floor. When I stepped out, all I saw was a long corridor with many doors on both sides.

"This way." James continued to lead the way. Halfway down the hall, he stopped in front of a door and proceeded to open it. "This will be your room for now." He walked in and held the door open for us.

I followed him into the room, not sure what to expect.

It looked like a dorm room, nowhere near as nice as the bedroom in Vera's mansion, but it made me feel content and safe. I saw several clothing items on the bed and a pair of flats on the floor.

"Ms. De Waal, you must be exhausted. Have a good rest first, and we will talk tomorrow," James said in a very comforting voice.

I looked at him and Julia, tears flooding my eyes. "Th...thank you," I said in a trembling vice.

"M..." James choked up. He cleared his throat and suppressed his emotions before he gave me a warm smile and said, "My pleasure."

"Are you going to be all right? I can stay." Julia's eyes were red as well.

Awkwardly, I reached for her hand. "Yes, I am. You have done so…so much for me already." I gently squeezed her hand. "You need rest, too."

She nodded, holding my hands with hers. "I will be back…" She glanced at her wrist watch and continued, "It's almost four now. Have a good rest and don't worry about anything. I will be back around noon, and we will go from there."

I nodded, letting go of her hands and wiping my tears with my sweatshirt sleeves.

"If you need anything, James is here for you."

"Anything you need," James echoed her and pointed at an intercom phone on the wall by the door. "My extension is 335. The security is 0. Right here," he said, pointing at a sticky note above the phone. "You can reach me or the security anytime."

"Th…thank you…so much."

Julia took a deep breath and walked out of the room, followed by James, who closed the door behind him.

I walked to the door and locked it right away. I knew nobody would come in, but I needed reassurance.

I kicked off my shoes and climbed under the thick duvet.

Is this real? I burst into tears, drowning in unbearable emotions.

CHAPTER 8

> Hope is the thing with feathers—
> That perches in the soul—
> And sings the tune without words—
> And never stops—at all—
> ~Emily Dickinson

AWAKING with a racing heart, I was covered in sweat. Looking around, I could not recognize the room. Suddenly, I panicked and hastily checked my hands and arms. When I did not see any IV injection, I let out a heavy breath of relief.

Light broke in through the gaps of the window curtains. I jumped out of the bed, scurried to the window, and opened the curtains. And a peaceful and beautiful scenery greeted me. Looking down, I saw a big green lawn and lots of trees, and then I looked around to see if I could recognize anything.

Wow... To my left through some tall trees and off in the distance, I saw a beautiful garden and...and... I pressed my hands and forehead against the window as if I could get any closer to the object I just saw. It was an American flag dancing in the air.

I am in the U.S. Embassy Bern! I did not want to move my eyes away from the flag. My mind was in total chaos. I remembered... I remembered Max, Julia, a kind officer, and James. *Mommy! I have to call her. I need my mom.*

I whipped around and scanned the room again.

The phone! Wait, that's an intercom. Then I remembered what James said to me: Anything you need.

Wait, Julia said she would be here around noon. Everything seemed to be coming back to me now but going reversely, counterclockwise, backward...

Max... Suddenly feeling out of sorts, I sat down on the edge of the bed. I pressed my hand on my chest, feeling unsettled and unresolved. I didn't even know who he really was, but I...I missed that enigmatic man, who had saved my life, and I wished to see those saturated blue eyes one more time.

I quickly shoved off the thoughts, drawing in a deep and heavy breath.

"ANYWAY..." I spoke out loud to myself. It was all in the past now. No need to dwell on the past. I glanced at the bedside digital clock. It read 12:43 pm.

Julia! She's probably here already, I thought and quickly walked to the intercom.

The exhaustion must have knocked me out. I had not slept for so long since...

I shook my head, pulling my thought back to the present, and picked up the intercom phone to call James.

After speaking with James, I took a quick shower and changed into the new clothes. They were just big and plain sweatsuits, but they felt better than everything I had in the last few months.

When I was ready to leave the room to meet James and Julia at the elevator lobby, I froze. My hand was on the handle ready to unlock the door, but it started to tremble. I took a couple of deep breaths and told myself repeatedly that I was in the U.S. Embassy before I was able to unlock the door. I opened it just an inch wide to hear if anyone was outside. And when I did not hear anything, I opened the door a little wider so I could peek out the door to see if anyone was in the hallway.

The coast is clear. I thought to myself and stepped out of the room.

James and Julia were standing by an elevator, and the door was open already. I gave them a small smile, not as nervous as when I first arrived here.

James gestured for me to go into the elevator first but I insisted on following them. When I walked into the elevator, I immediately leaned against the wall, my eyes focusing on the elevator panel.

On our way down, James told me they would answer all my questions and explain everything I needed to know.

I nodded my appreciation, still feeling tense and anxious.

The elevator door opened to an open reception area. James gestured for me to step out first, but again, I insisted on following them.

Other than a young lady sitting at the reception desk buried in paperwork, there was no one in here.

I quietly let out a sigh of relief…

"*Guten Tag*, Elley," James gently tapped on the reception desk and greeted the young lady 'good day.'

"*Guten Tag*, James." The young lady looked surprised to see us.

"We will be in one conference room. Please do not disturb us," James said and proceeded to head to a pair of black double doors. Julia and I followed him.

"Yes, James," Elley replied, and her voice was muffled by the closing door.

We walked into an open office space. I assumed the office should be busy at this hour, but it was empty. I would save this question for later.

"I have prepared this room for us." James walked into a room and stood by the door.

I walked in, followed by Julia, but whipped around when James closed the door.

"Would you like me to leave it open?" James asked, opening the door again.

Both of them looked concerned.

"It's…it's fine," I said, twisting my fingers nervously.

"Let's leave it open," James said, giving me an understanding smile. "It's Sunday. Hardly anyone will come in here anyway. We have plenty of privacy."

Sunday? That explains the empty office. I mentally crossed the question out.

"Have a seat, please," James said, taking the seat closest to the door.

I looked around and took the one across from him. Julia sat down next to me. I noticed there were several folders on the table and a telephone. I suppressed the urge to pick up the phone to call my mother right at this minute.

"You all right?" Julia asked. She must have perceived my anxious expression.

I nodded, folding my arms across my chest. The new shirt felt very soft and comforting. I embraced myself a little tighter.

"You must be hungry. I have coffee, hot chocolate, and many pastries prepared." James stood up again.

"No, I…" I was going to decline the offer and hoped we could get to business right away, but my stomach answered otherwise. I frowned in embarrassment.

"How about I will get them for you, and James can start answering your questions," Julia said, looking at me. "Coffee? Or hot chocolate?"

"Coffee, please." I gave her a much appreciative smile.

"The breakroom, right?" Julia asked James, standing up and walking towards the door.

"Yes, and thank you so much." James sat back down.

"I will be right back." Julia gave me a tender smile and left the room.

Taking a deep breath, I turned towards James with anticipation.

"You must be very eager to call your parents," James said, pushing the phone closer to me. "I have already contacted them—"

"You have? They know… They…" I interrupted him, my voice choking with emotions.

"Yes." He nodded with a reassuring smile. "They are expecting your call. So, why don't you do that first, and we can talk later."

My body was shaking, and my eyes were flooded. I reached for the phone but realized I didn't remember their numbers by heart. I did not even remember my own number. All my contacts were stored in my phone, which was long gone. *Who remembers phone numbers by heart nowadays anyway…*

Just as I was feeling discouraged, James placed a folder in front of me. It was opened to a page listing all my family members and close friends' contact information.

Staring at the page, I blinked back tears.

"I don't know anyone who remembers phone numbers by heart." He shrugged and walked out of the room, giving me privacy.

I like him, really like him.

I scanned the list, grabbed the phone, and called my mother.

MY parents sobbed with joy during our whole conversation, and so did I. They told me my brother David, the world's most protective big brother, was waiting for my call as well.

"Hello?" My brother picked up the phone on the first ring, his voice urgent, expecting, and nervous.

"DD…" I burst into tears when I heard his voice.

When I was littleI, I could not pronounce the word David, so I called him DD. And it also happened to be his initials, a perfect nickname for my big brother.

"Don't cry, honey. Everything is all right…" He tried to comfort me, but he was choked with emotion as well.

"Honey…" My sister-in-law Janie's voice was like a warm blanket. It was comforting and soothing. She could not hold back her sobbing either.

There was so much we wanted to tell each other, but all we did was sobbing. I almost emptied out the tissue box James put on the table for me earlier.

"I already booked the flight leaving Monday." DD was on the phone again.

"Da…Daddy said—" Hiccuping and sniveling, I kept breaking off.

"Yes, hon. They are flying out from San Francisco. I will travel from LAX to meet them in Bern. We are bringing you home."

"I…I will see…see you when you…you come home," Janies said.

Home...

I wanted to tell them I missed them and their kids so much, but I could not stop bawling and hiccuping.

DD put on his big brother mask and finally calmed me down. Then we said goodbye reluctantly.

I hung up the phone, wiping my eyes and nose, and then I noticed that James and Julia were standing in the doorway with watery eyes. I quickly looked away, hiding my crying face.

They both walked in. Julia put my coffee and a plate of pastries in front of me.

"Th...thank...you." My nose was stuffy, so I breathed out the words.

"Do you need a minute?" James asked, sitting down.

"I am fine," I said with a stuffy nose, reaching my hands to grab the coffee.

The temperature was perfect. I guzzled it, needing fuel and caffeine.

"Iris, I need to go over some things with you, but I can wait until you are ready," James said, holding a folder.

"I am ready," I said right away because I wanted to get it over with, and I wanted to go home as soon as possible.

"Wonderful," he said, fixing his eyes on me.

I averted my eyes because his blatant stare was making me uncomfortable. I knew he meant no harm; however, I had received an awful lot of unwelcoming stares in the past many months. I really could not stand it any more.

"I am so sorry," he apologized sincerely after perceiving my reaction. "It... I..." He hesitated for a couple of minutes and then continued, "I have been following your case for months. I...I cannot believe you are sitting right in front of me now."

"My case?" I faced him again.

"Your family and friends were all over Europe looking for you. All over the world, I should say."

"They were?" I looked between him and Julia, who nodded, agreeing with James.

"Your family has a quite impressive diplomatic influence," he added.

I looked down at my coffee cup, smiling at the thought of my maternal grandparents. I had no doubt that they would take the measure of their diplomatic connections to extreme when their beloved granddaughter was abducted.

That was how Grandpa and Grandpa met. He worked for the Minister of Foreign Affairs of Japan when she was dispatched to the Taipei Economic and Cultural Representative Office in Japan. They met in Tokyo and fell in love, and the rest was history.

"When we were informed by fedpol yest—" James went on.

"Fedpol?" I interrupted him.

"Would you like to shine the light?" He looked at Julia, and I followed suit.

"It's the Federal Office of Police of Switzerland," she said.

"You are a police officer?" I should not be surprised, but I was. She did act like a police officer and was not afraid of Max.

But a friend of Max? Does she know what kind of horrific crimes Max is committing? Now I had more questions to ask her.

Julia paused a minute, considering her answer, and said, "Yes, I am a police officer." She then faced James, not wanting to say more. "Go on, James. I think Iris is eager to know what you can do for her."

"Yes, of course." James smiled at me and said, "When we got a phone call about you last night, we were asked not to contact anyone until they were able to safely bring you to us. It was very urgent."

I was not sure how to react as I was still processing everything myself. *It was urgent, and it was also anguished, bewildering, and frightening...*

Perceiving my unsettling expression, James' voice changed to a much more comforting tone. "Iris, I am here to help you with everything you need. First of all, I am going to take care of your travel documents so you can go home as soon as possible."

I nodded my appreciation.

"Second, I would like to arrange counseling for you if that is all right with you."

I nodded anyway, frowning and not really sure what he meant.

"Wonderful." He looked relieved. "Julia and other officers are going to con—"

"Other officers?" I interrupted James again and looked at Julia, frowning.

"Yes. They are from different agencies." She gazed at me, studying my expression. "Will you be more comfortable just talking to me?"

Frowning, I wanted to say *yes* but was not sure if it was all right with her. I really did not want to make her job more difficult.

"Iris, we can arrange that." She seemed to read my mind.

I nodded, feeling relieved. "Are you going to conduct the interview today?" I asked.

"Not necessary." She sat back in her chair. "I will work with James and figure out the schedule. Before you leave, of course."

"I'd like to do it as soon as possible." I looked between Julia and James. "My parents and my brother will be here very soon. In a day or two, I am sure. I'd like… I'd like to go back to the States as soon as possible."

The truth was I really did not want to talk about what I had been through. I did not know if I was able to talk about it. I just needed to get it over with so I could go home and forget all about it.

"James?" Julia asked.

"Of course, Iris. Of course. We will, and I personally will, accommodate you with that." James leaned forward and gave me the most earnest look I had ever seen for a long time. "If you would like to start right now, I will make a pot of fresh coffee." He stood up, ready to head to the breakroom.

"Thank you." I looked between them.

James gave me a smile before leaving the room.

"You haven't touched any of the pastries yet. Are you not hungry?" Julia asked, her voice concerned.

I really did not have any appetite, but I grabbed a Danish just to ease her concerns. "How… How would you like to start?" I asked.

Julia gave me a much worried look while she reached for a folder in front of her. "I don't want to lay too much stress on you." She paused for a minute and asked, "How about you tell me anything you would like to share with me first?" She opened the folder and took out a pen from her pocket.

I stared at the Danish in my hand, not sure where to start. However, there were questions I really wanted to ask her.

"I will also try my best to answer your questions," she said, reading my mind again.

I nodded and said, "Can I ask you some questions first?"

"Of course, you can," she said earnestly, putting the pen down on the table.

"You are a police officer…" I said in hesitation. "So, do you… I mean…"

How can I put it so I don't place Max in jeopardy?

"Iris, are you worried about something?" she asked, leaning closer. "How about all your questions now are off the record? Feel free to ask me anything, and I will give you my most honest answers."

It was like she could really read my mind. Or I was too easy to read…

"Max told me that you are his friend…" I observed her expression, making sure I asked the right questions.

"Correct. We have known each other for years."

"So, do you…" I was going to ask if she was aware of Max's involvement with those criminals, but I saw her dark brown eyes glinting with curiosity—not that I was a facial expression expert and understood what it meant—and decided to change my question. "Did Max ask you to help me?"

Julia took a deep breath, considering her answer.

"You don't… You don't need to…" I felt bad for asking such a relevant question, especially regarding her personal relationship with Max.

"Yes," she gave me an honest answer—the shortest one also.

I waited for her to offer me more information, but she did not say anything else. I had a feeling that was all I was going to get, but I pressed on. "Does he do this a lot? I mean, asking you to drive someone away."

"No," she gave me another one-word answer, but at least she did not need to consider this one at all.

I nodded, pretending to be satisfied with her answers, and Max was still a mystery. I took a bite of the Danish mindlessly, staring at my empty coffee cup. After I swallowed the bite, I put the rest of it down. It tasted really good, but I did not think I could keep food down once I started to tell her my story.

"What is the date today?" I asked.

"March twenty-seven."

I did a mental calculation. "Almost five months..." I murmured.

"Pardon me?"

"I was in Paris with my friends last October..." I started telling her my misfortune.

CHAPTER 9

> Call it a clan, call it a network,
> call it a tribe, call it a family.
> Whatever you call it, whoever you are,
> you need one.
> ~Jane Howard

AFTER I recounted my dreadful experience, I excused myself and went back to the bedroom for the remainder of the day. James brought me dinner and a change of clothes. He even let me borrow an iPad and have internet access to get in touch with my family and friends and also to learn what had happened in the world when I was held captive. I hesitated when he told me his supervisor would like to meet with me Monday morning. And that would be tomorrow morning. I agreed because James and the embassy had done so much for me. That was the least I could do.

But everything went downhill the next morning when I was awakened by the chatter outside the bedroom…

I jumped out of the bed and hid in the bathroom until James called. He rushed to me, comforted me, and kept me company for a couple of hours before he really had to go back to work. And he promised me no one would bother me. I stayed in the room for the remainder of the day *and* the following days.

I was not sure how much the embassy would and could do to assist their citizens, but James absolutely did his utmost to look after me, even though he kept telling me it was his job.

He obtained medical care for me; but I declined because I did not want to meet with any stranger until my family arrived. He told me a psychiatrist was available for me if I needed to talk to someone; but I did not take him up on the counseling offer because I just wanted to bury all the memories—burn them if I could—and move on with my life.

My brother gave me his and my parents' flight information so I could track their flights. They arrived today. Three days after our phone calls.

James picked me up from the bedroom and brought me to the same conference room. I did not know how he did it, but we did not run into any person on our way there, not even the receptionist.

I had been sitting in the conference room since my mother called me from the airport a couple of hours ago. My hands were sweaty, and my heart was palpitating with anxiety.

Then... I was in my family's arms the minute they walked in. The emotion was more than I could bear. We did not want to let go of each other. I was afraid I would be alone again if I did.

I was told Antonio and Jojo were devastated when they could not find me and reach me after the club was closed. The club owner offered his security team to look for me in the nearby area and encouraged Antonio and Jojo to wait in the hotel, in case I was simply out somewhere in the city and would eventually go back to the hotel. They waited the entire day before going to the police to report my disappearance. Then they went to the U.S. Embassy for help and contacted my family.

My family and friends reached out to many international organizations, such as DoeNetwork and ICMP, International Commission on Missing Persons. They also posted and reposted my information on social media.

"You've done so much..." I said, overwhelmed by knowing my family and friends had never given up on looking for me.

"It's nothing compared to what you've gone through..." My mother sobbed even more sorrowfully, holding me in her arms.

A knock on the door made us all turn our heads.

"Please, come in," DD said.

I was surprised to see Julia standing behind James. I thought I had answered all her questions.

"I am so sorry for interrupting you," James said, walking in with Julia. "Officer Zoss would like to have a word with you." James then introduced Julia to my parents and brother.

My mother gave her a hearty hug and thanked her again and again for saving me.

Julia looked surprised and obviously did not know how to respond to my mother's wholehearted appreciation. "It's a group effort," she said politely, gently patting my mother's back and smiling at all of us.

"I have good news to share with you," she said after we all sat down. "We are ready to crack down this specific group of criminals." She gave me an encouraging smile.

Vera and her gang... I detested even the mention of them. I took several deep breaths to keep myself calm.

"However..." She paused, looking at me in hesitation.

I had a feeling I would not like what she was going to say.

"Iris, we still need your help because—"

"No, it's out of question," my father cut Julia off, sounding upset. "She has been through enough." His voice was determined and harsh.

"We are taking her home now," DD added, his voice calmer than my father's but definitely firm.

I felt so protected and content at the moment because I had my family here to shield me and take care of me. I decided to let my father and brother do the talking for me and leaned my head against my mother's shoulder. She protectively held me in her arms, resting her head against mine.

"I absolutely understand," Julia said sincerely. "Her well-being is our first priority as well. She can absolutely go home now. What we are hoping for is that...Iris can be our witness." She continued to offer more explanations, emphasizing their operation could save so many more people if they could put everyone behind bars.

But my father and brother insisted on keeping me safe and away from fedpol's operation.

This is exhausting... I looked between Julia and my father and brother. *Maybe I should listen to what Julia needs from me first.*

I had not had the chance and courage to tell my family what I had gone through as it would devastate them. They also did not know how bad a mess I was now.

"Julia, what do you need from me?" I asked, trying to sound calm.

"Honey?" My mother looked at me, sounding worried. "You don't need to do anything you don't want to."

"Mommy, I know." I gave her an assuring smile and looked at my father and brother. "I will explain it to you all later. I promise."

Julia gave me an appreciating nod, glancing at my family in regret. "First of all, we hope you can identify some—"

"Identify? I don't want to face any one of them," I interrupted her, my voice calmer than I had expected.

"Iris, I would never put you through that," Julia said, her voice kind and sincere.

"Okay…Please go on."

"The operation could take up to weeks, and then the trials will take up to months…"

Weeks? Months? I felt dizzy already. My brow furrowed, and I shut my eyes in pain.

Julia seemed to read my expression. She paused and somehow changed her tune. "When the trials start, we hope you can be here to assist us. However, if you don't think you can do it then, just let me know. You are under no obligation to do anything."

My eyes flung open. I gazed at her, wondering what had made her change her mind not to persuade me.

Everyone was silent, waiting for my reaction. I could feel my mother's trembling hands on my shoulders.

"Can I get back to you later, Julia?" I asked politely.

"Of course," she replied straight away. "You do not need to decide it right now. Just get better, Iris. Please, call me if you have any concerns or questions."

She and James excused themselves and let us get back to our family time.

"Honey, is everything all right?" my mother asked me softly, caressing my cheek with her warm hand.

My eyes were saturated with tears, and I started to explain my concerns and what I had experienced the past three days.

Just as we were ready to leave, I froze when DD opened the door. Strangers were walking by, and all kinds of noises suddenly became deafening. I backed into the corner of the room, shaking my head frantically and gasping for air. Suddenly, everything became blurry; all noise muffled.

"Go get James," someone said aloud.

I had my first severe panic attack.

Paramedics and an ambulance were called. And I became more panic-stricken when surrounded by more strangers. I did not calm down until I was back in the bedroom and cradled in my mother's arms.

So, for my safety and well-being, my family and I decided I should stay in Bern and received treatments first before heading home.

Two days after the episode, Dr. Eva Thompson, a highly recommended psychiatrist specializing in counseling victims of human trafficking, came to see me. I was diagnosed with PTSD, and the anxiety, panic attacks, insomnia, and mistrust were severer than we thought. I was not able to step out of the embassy to go to a hotel or a hospital, a completely unfamiliar environment where I would be surrounded by strangers.

Under this special circumstance, the consular services allowed me to continue using the bedroom in the embassy. My parents extended their stay, but my brother had to go home to his family and business, even though he wished to stay longer. I wanted him to go home so he could hug Janie and my beautiful nephews and niece for me.

My parents got me a new phone, and when I tried to sign in to my account, it showed that the account did not exist. I assumed it was hacked by whoever abducted me and they wanted to erase me. Although I was upset, I told myself that they had failed because I still existed and was free from their control now.

My parents also wanted to buy me a whole new wardrobe and many things I did not even think I needed. They told me they wanted me to be as comfortable as possible while staying in Bern, and they would feel better if they knew I had everything I needed.

Who would turn down new clothes and shoes? However, I ended up only asking for a few things. I guessed once one experienced having nothing, one would be satisfied and happy with the minimum.

I could not be more grateful for Dr. Thompson's training and experience. She suggested that psychotherapy would be the most effective therapy for me, and she came to the embassy once a week for two hours to talk to me and teach me different methods to help me manage the symptoms. She did prescribe medications for my insomnia and anxiety but encouraged me not to rely on them.

It took me more than a month to finally ask my parents to go home. I assured them I would be safe in the embassy, and they promised me they would come back and visit me every month until I was ready to get on the plane and go home with them.

Julia was not able to tell me much about the operation, but she kept me updated. And what I appreciated the most was she did her best not to involve me in the investigations.

Time flew in the blink of an eye, and three months had gone by. I had less unwanted memories and nightmares; my insomnia was improving; I did not waken frightened and disoriented as frequently as before; and I was able to manage my anxiety level when meeting with strangers. I was still unable to deal with crowds, but I was working very hard with Dr. Thompson, hoping I could soon deal with daily activities normally and go home soon. Slowly but surely, I was getting better.

James had become my bestie here in the embassy. He introduced me to his boyfriend Tim, who was just as delightful as he was. They understood I was not comfortable with the idea of leaving the embassy, so they spent lots of time here with me—I had officially become their third wheel.

Tim was from California like me—no wonder we hit it off right away—and was working on his doctoral dissertation in social cultural anthropology at the University of Bern. He and James met when he visited the embassy to inquire about traveling documents.

"It was not just a spark. It was a firework…" James described the moment they saw each other.

Finally, Dr. Thompson believed I was ready to fly home during our last session, and I called my parents before the session even ended. I had been on cloud nine since then, and James and Tim celebrated with me in the embassy garden, joined by the few friends I had here.

"YOU have a visitor, Ms. De Waal." Eddie, a marine security guard and also one of my very few friends here, called on the intercom.

"Thank you, Eddie. And it's Iris." I said, "I will be right there."

My parents and DD are not here yet. Who would visit me? I wondered as I was heading downstairs.

Dr. Thompson? She would not be here without scheduling an appointment first.

Julia? Maybe she was here to say good-bye after I texted her the good news.

Who else? James filtered everything and vetted everyone before scheduling any meeting for me, and I did not recall there was any meeting today.

Then, who is here to visit me?

I started feeling anxious when I stepped out of the elevator and headed towards the front desk.

I am in the embassy. It's safe. I can do this. I was giving myself a pep talk because it was still very hard for me to meet and talk to strangers. James had always been a great support and accompanied me in every single meeting, even the first several sessions with Dr. Thompson. Now that I was ready to go home, I could not and should not rely on him anymore.

"*Guten Morgen,* Sunshine!" James surprised me. He was

standing by Eddie's security desk, greeting me good morning.

"*Guten Morgen...* Are you my visitor?" I asked, grinning.

"I wish I had the pleasure," he said, walking towards me.

We gave each other cheek-kisses.

"Why are you here?" I asked, feeling quite relieved to see him here.

"Ed rang me and told me you have a visitor," he said and looked at Eddie. "He's the best."

"Thank you." I gave Eddie an appreciative smile.

Eddie gave us the thumbs up and went back to stare at the monitors. He reminded me of Antonio, a younger and more serious version—not that I meant Antonio was older and frivolous…ahem.

Speaking of the devil, Antonio had been calling me everyday since he got my number from my brother, and Jojo had as well. They wanted to fly here, but I asked them not to because I wanted to embrace them in my arms when I felt safe and stress-free at home.

"I am glad you are here." I linked my arm with James' and scanned the lobby. "You don't know who is here?" I asked suspiciously.

"No, that is why I rushed down here as fast as I could."

"*Danke schön.*" I gave him a gentle nudge, thanking him.

"*Bitte zehr,*" he responded to my gratitude, holding my arm tighter, and said, "Let's go see this mysterious visitor of yours." He steered me towards the visitor area and continued, "The visitor is in the small conference room. Ed said—" He paused and looked at the note in his hand. "His name—"

His? A man? I faltered, and James' voice just became muffled. I probably should just turn down the visit since I did not know any man in Bern other than those in the embassy and Tim.

Did one of Vera's people or patrons track me down here? My heart started to pound heavily in my chest, and I felt nauseated all of a sudden.

"Iris, are you all right?" James' voice brought me back from my little panic attack.

I nodded, taking several deep breaths.

"How about you let me speak with him first?" he asked, looking worried. "You don't have to meet or talk to anyone."

I nodded vigorously, losing my ability to speak. I unlinked my arm and walked behind James. And I stopped about five feet away from the conference room while James made his way to meet my visitor.

"Good morning. I am consular officer James Hoffmann. You are?" James' voice was somber.

"Thomas Torian. I am here for Iris. I mean… Ms. De Waal," the visitor replied.

Wait… I recognize this voice. That tranquil tone, the staccato accent, and the endearing way my name rolled off his tongue.

I scurried into the room…

CHAPTER 10

> I believe in being strong
> when everything seems to be going wrong.
> I believe that
> happy girls are the prettiest girls.
> I believe that
> tomorrow is another day and
> I believe in miracles.
> ~Audrey Hepburn

MY visitor's eyes lit up, and a tenderhearted smile spread across his face when he saw me.

"Max?" My head was tilted to one side, my eyes widened in complete bewilderment.

This man looked dapper in a fitted dark gray suit, compared to the rugged Max who was always in black. This man had shorter, wavy hair, compared to Max's medium-length, messy mane. He looked nothing like Max except those brilliant blue eyes. They were gleaming with the same gravity that I saw in Max's eyes when he asked me to trust him.

"Max?" James sounded confused as well, looking at me with concern. "Are you all right, Iris?"

"Yes. Yes, I am," I answered James, my eyes fixed on Max. Or Thomas…if I heard it correctly.

"How are you, Iris?" His familiar confident voice aligned with his vibrant blue eyes assured me who he was.

"I am…I am very well. Thank you," I replied, trying not to sound eager, edgy, and elated, but my heart was going to jump out of my chest. Blinking away my widened eyes, I turned to face James. "James, this is Max." And my eyes were back on Max.

"THE Max?" James asked and, of course, had to accentuate the determiner when I was trying to conceal the fact that I had mentioned *The* Max to anyone and *The* Max was very significant to me.

James stared at him and asked, "But you just told me you are Thomas Tarion…"

"Torian," Max corrected him.

Thomas Torian… It suits him so well. I thought, not able to move my eyes away from him.

I had so many questions to ask him. For months, not a single day I did not think about him. A man whom I loathed so much saved me and then walked away without a word. I racked my brain for all the possible explanations: He was an obliging villain, and he simply performed a good deed since he had done so many wrongs. Or… He could be a double agent or undercover police officer.

In the mansion, I tried to stay away from him because I felt absolute repugnance towards him for what he did and who he was. If I had paid more attention to him, I would have detected something *not*-villainous about him.

"Iris?" They both tried to get my attention.

"Yes?" I looked between them vacuously, but my mind was plotting what to do to get all my questions answered. And I would not accept just *yes* and *no* like Julia' answers.

"James," I said in a very collected voice, turning away from Max so he could not see my face. "I am fine here. Weren't you in a meeting before you came down here?" I winked at him, hoping he could get the hint because I really needed to speak with Max…wait, I meant Thomas, in private. Desperately.

"I was?" James asked, looking confused.

"Yes. With Mr. Meiner." I was dragging Eddie into this, but I was sure he would understand.

"Mr. Meiner?" James crossed his arms over his chest, one hand scratching his chin. Then he smiled at me with mischief and said, "Very well. But I can stay. I am sure Mr. Meiner will understand."

He winked at me.

"I. Am. Really. Fine. Here. I don't want to trouble you." I shot daggers at him.

He ignored me and stared at Max. Ahhh... I meant Thomas.

Please... I mouthed the word.

"Are you sure? I can stay..." James was giving Thomas a full scan with his eyes, from his dark chocolate quiff to the black wingtip Oxford shoes.

"Absolutely," I replied, gripping his arm.

"All right then." He gave Thomas one last look and said to him in a serious tone, "She is under the protection of the United States Department of State."

One arm over my chest and one hand massaging my temples, I shook my head, feeling absolutely embarrassed while James added, "You. Be nice to her."

"Of course," Thomas replied, sounding amused.

"Call me if you need me," James said to me before walking out of the room.

My eyes followed James, and then I just stood there, afraid to turn around to face this man whom I thought I would never see again.

"Iris, I..." His voice was so tender and... apologetic?

I took a deep breath, forced a smile, and turned around. Then my facade was overpowered by my emotions when I saw his concerned smile. My eyes were burning, tears threatening to emerge. I quickly suppressed my overloaded emotions and said, "I... I've never had a chance to thank you."

"Don't mention it. It's my job," he said with a little shyness in his expression.

Wait... What? Saving me is his job? I frowned. *Julia is a fedpol officer. They have been friends for years. Saving me is his job. Does that mean...* A smile surfaced on my face.

He smiled back in contentment and said, "I thought you would figure it out."

"Officer..." I was waiting for him to fill in the blank.

"Thomas Torian." His answer was gratifying.

He was a hero not a villain...

I sat down, gesturing for him to sit down as well.

He took the chair across from me, and then an awkward silence was making both of us very uncomfortable. He was staring at me, and I was glancing around the room.

"I am going home next week," I said, trying to break the ice.

"That is fantastic," he responded in a broad smile, his voice now relaxing. It was absolutely pleasing to my ears.

"I cannot wait..." I mumbled.

Thomas seemed to notice my sudden despondency, so he changed the subject. "I have been wanting to visit you, but—"

"Don't worry about it," I interrupted him. It was not important anyway, for him or for me.

The awkward silence fell on us again.

"Have you gotten a chance to visit Bern?" He spoke first this time.

I shook my head and shifted uncomfortably on the chair, crossing my legs and uncrossing them again.

"Are you not doing well?" he asked with concern.

"I..." I took a deep breath, not sure how to start. I was not sure he could understand, but I felt so comfortable with him that I did not mind telling him my condition. "I am having great difficulty being around people, especially strangers."

He frowned but did not give me the pity look that most people did when they saw me or talked to me.

"So... I...I have been in this building since I arrived," I said, eyeing my surroundings and suddenly feeling a little sad and embarrassed.

"Can I take you out?" he hastily asked.

"It's... Don't... Haha..." I waved my hand in front of me, dismissing his absurd idea and giving him a fake laugh.

But he gazed at me, both sincerely and eagerly.

"I don't think it's a good idea..." I said, knowing that once I stepped out of that metal double-gate I was going to freak out, and that would freak him out.

"I did not mean today," he said with a sincere smile. "I actually have to go back to the office soon. Can I visit you again?"

I nodded instantly with a big smile. How could I decline his visit?

"Fantastic." His smile was big and radiant.

I had never thought *Max* had the ability to smile like that. His smile was contagious, and I broke into one as well, grinning like a schoolgirl.

He took a business card and a pen out of his jacket's inside pocket and wrote some numbers on the back of the card. "This is my personal mobile number." He handed me the card. "And I will ring you tomorrow."

I looked at the card, finding that it was a police business card printed with just an official logo, his name, and a number. I turned the card over, smiling at his neat hand-writing.

"Can I borrow your pen and have another card if you have one?" I asked.

"Of course," he took another card out of the pocket.

I wrote my number on the card and gave the card and his pen back to him. "You can call me directly instead of the embassy."

He glanced at the card with a pleased smile. "Thank you." Putting it in his pocket, he stood up and said, "I will let you get back to your day now."

I stood up as well. "Thank…thank you for visiting me," I said. How much I wished he could stay a bit longer. It had been a long time since I felt so at ease.

"It's my pleasure. I will give you a ring tonight if that is all right with you," he said in hesitation.

I nodded, feeling my heart beating a bit faster—in a very good way.

"Does eight o'clock work for you?"

"Ye…yes. Eight is perfect." My heart was racing now.

"Brilliant…" he said, still standing in front of me and gazing at me.

We both did not know how to say good-bye…

Extending my hand to shake his did not feel quite right. It was too business-like, wasn't it? Leaning in to kiss his cheeks was just plain awkward.

Deciding to keep it casual, I said, "Thank you for your visit." I stepped out of the conference room first. "I will walk you ou—"

I scowled. *Walk him out? What am I talking about? I haven't left this building for months.*

"I mean I will walk you to the front door." I gave him a forced smile.

He followed me out of the room, still fixing his eyes on me, then he walked up next to me, keeping a nice comfortable distance. We were both quiet for the rest of the short walk.

"Thank you," I said again when we reached the front door.

"My pleasure." He leaned in and gave me cheek-kisses, his hands gently touching my arms. "*Tschüss.*"

"*Tschüss.*" I said goodbye, lightly touching my cheek with his.

He gave me another warm smile before walking out of the building.

I didn't freak out! I was freaking out now because I did not freak out when he leaned in to give me cheek-kisses.

I wanted to do a happy dance right in the lobby! I stifled my excitement, fixing my eyes on him as he walked across the parking lot and into the entrance structure.

He probably walked here or parked on the street. I thought and could not stop smiling.

CHAPTER 11

> I never wanted a Guardian Angel.
> I didn't ask for one. One was assigned to me.
> ~Mercedes McCambridge

"**YOU** what?" James exclaimed, his eyes bulging.

He reminded me of Matt Bomer with dark brown, caring, and sincere eyes. I called him Bomer sometimes, but he just ignored me because he said he was better looking than the actor. However, this bulging-eye James was nowhere near the good-looking category.

"He promised only to drive me around the city, and I would be in the car the entire time. So, I thought I could give myself a chance to finally leave the embassy," I said, batting my eyelashes, not to flirt with him, but to be persuasive and cute. "And… And I trust him," I added.

Last night at eight o'clock sharp, Thomas called as he had promised. We had a relaxing, pleasant, and very long conversation. It seemed much easier for me to breathe if his almost-perfect blue eyes were not gazing at me. I let him decide when and where he would like to take me out for a ride, but I did not expect him to suggest the next day.

"But you just met him *yesterday*." James did not even try to hide his irritation.

I winced at the rebuke in his voice. I wanted to argue that I actually met Thomas over ten months ago, but I did not want to have an argument or debate with James. If he asked me to cancel this outing with Thomas, I would do it, even though I really, really, really, did not want to.

"Fine…" I pouted. "I will call him back and cancel—"

He shushed me with a hand over my mouth and took out his phone and tapped on it, giving me a furrowed-brow glance.

He has Thomas' number? I was surprised and panicky because I really did not want to cancel it yet. I thought I might be able to convince him. "I…I can call him myself."

James ignored me and held the phone to his ear, waiting for the call to be answered.

I felt sort of upset now. I was an adult. I really did not need his permission. "Jam—"

"Hi Officer Zoss, this is James Hoffmann…"

He called Julia? I became speechless, just staring at him.

"Everything is great. Thank you for asking. The reason I am calling is I have something that I need to verify with you," James said, staring right back at me.

Stop! I mouthed the word to him, but he just waved me away.

"Wonderful. Thank you. It's regarding Officer Torian." He continued his conversation with Julia, completely ignoring me.

Is he seriously doing this? I grabbed his arm and whispered, "I don't want to get Thomas in trouble."

He put his index finger to his lips to shush me, continuing his conversation with Julia, "Yes… Hmm…" Nodding his head, he looked at me, raising one eyebrow.

Nodding head is good, right? I tightened my grip on his arm.

"*Wunderbar…*" he said, the corner of his mouth tugging upward.

Saying 'wonderful' is good, right? I started shaking his arm.

"That is all I need to know. Thank you so much. Yes, I will. *Auf Wiedersehen.*" He tapped his phone to end the call and said to me, "Julia said hi."

"So?" My eyes went wide.

"Not until you let go of my arm. It's cutting off my circulation." He glanced at my hands which were still gripping his arm.

I quickly let go of his arm and folded my hands behind me. "I can't believe you did that."

"You should thank me, young lady," he said, rubbing his arm like it was really hurt.

"So?" I asked again.

"So. Julia actually knew Thomas visited you yesterday, and she said lots of good things about him."

"And?" I grinned.

"And... You are an adult. You can do whatever you want." He gave me a straight face and said, "Give me your phone." He put his hand out, waiting.

"Ooookaaaay..." I put my phone on his waiting hand and said, "You know I need it when I go out, right?"

He did not say a word but held my phone up facing me to unlock the phone. Then he started to tap away on it.

"What are you doing?" I stared at the screen.

"I am sharing your location with me..." he explained, still tapping on the phone and looking quite serious.

"Okay..."

"Done." He turned off my phone and handed it back to me. "I must know your whereabouts."

I nodded and suddenly felt a little emotional. "I am sorry..." I whispered.

"What for?" he asked, his voice so concerned.

"I...I should've been more considerate. I make you worry..."

"Oh, honey. Worrying about you is my job. Stop the sentimental *Scheiße*." He wrapped his arms around me.

I laughed, leaning closer to him.

He did not use curses often. Although when he did, they were usually German, and they always made me laugh.

"That is what I want to hear. Laughter not whimper." He gave me a warm smile and asked, "When will he be here to pick you up? Four or five? I blocked your voice out the moment you told me you were going out, and therefore I did not catch the rest."

"Five thirty..." I rested my head on his shoulder. I knew he heard everything I told him and was just giving me a hard time.

"I will be downstairs with you. I need to give him some verbal warnings. And also..." He looked at me, looking serious. "I won't go home until you come back in one piece."

He's going to make me cry now... I gazed at him with my

almost-watery eyes.

"Stop the—"

"*Scheiße.*" I finished his sentence.

"Just be careful." He chuckled.

"I will. Thank you, Bomer."

"Stop calling me that."

"James Bomer... It actually sounds really good. Don't you want to consider it as your stage name?"

He rolled his eyes and walked away.

JAMES was called to a meeting and could not wait here with me. Therefore, here I was, waiting anxiously in the lobby sitting area alone and ready to leave my comfort zone for the very first time.

Many cars had entered the gates and parked in the parking area, but there was no sign of Thomas. It was not because he was late, but rather because I was too early. I was early because I needed time to prepare myself.

I tried to see it as a practice since next week I would be going to the airport and board the plane with hundreds of people. Although my parents and DD would be by my side, just thinking about it was still frightening. However, I was determined to go home this time, even if I had to beg Dr. Thompson to prescribe me the strongest anti-anxiety and sleeping pills—crossing my fingers and hoping it would not be necessary.

Staring out the windows, I was so nervous about leaving this building and also seeing Thomas.

Nice ride... A cold white Bentley continental convertible with black soft-top just entered the gate. I recognized this specific car because my father had a dragon red one. We all thought he must have a late midlife crisis when he drove home one last year. And then my mother was the one driving that car all the time.

How very interesting that a car could distract me from feeling nervous and make me think about my parents instead. *I cannot wait to see them next week.*

Five more minutes… I glanced at the time on my phone.

I looked out the window again, and a man stepped out of that Bentley, all dashing and tall. My heart sped up when he turned around.

I stood up from the chair, fixing my eyes on Thomas, who was in a black polo shirt and blue jeans. He walked towards the building and through the front door and stopped at the front desk.

The security guard pointed in my direction. We both smiled at each other at the same time.

He walked towards me casually.

"Very punctual, Mr. Torian," I said.

"You look very lovely today, Ms. De Waal," he said and leaned in to touch my cheeks with his.

He smells good… I could feel my cheeks becoming warm by his proximity.

"Nervous?" he asked.

"Nope!" I avoided his engaging gaze and started walking. "I am excited."

In the mansion, I always felt intimidated by Max when he was around. Now I was just crazily nervous.

I gave Eddie, who was actually off duty today but standing by the front desk now, a small wave.

He returned with a soft smile, giving me a thumbs up, and then his friendly gaze immediately shifted to a cold stare, aiming at Thomas. He pointed two fingers at his own eyes first and then turned them towards Thomas in a I-have-my-eyes-on-you gesture.

James must have put him up to this. I shook my head.

Thomas returned with a quick salute, two men exchanging acknowledgements of each other in silence.

Out of the door, Thomas led the way to the Bentley and opened the passenger door for me.

I admired the beautifully crafted machine when I got into the car. "Either your job pays very well or…" I trailed off.

"Or…" He gave me a wink with mischief before closing the door.

The thudding sound of the closing door somehow unnerved me.

A surge of anxiety stormed up in me. Holding both my hands tightly on my lap and drawing in deep breaths repeatedly, I tried to ease the unwelcome feeling.

Thomas gazed at me when he got into the car, his brow furrowing. "Trust me..." He put his hand on my trembling hands.

I looked into his eyes, feeling an instant serenity.

"I do," I whispered with a grateful smile.

We drove through the inner city and crossed the Aare at least three times. I was completely drawn to the splendid scenery and architecture, anxiety gone, verschwunden!

Either Thomas knew Bern very well, or he did some homework before picking me up. He was an amazing guide. I learned so much about the city and also where all the good restaurants were.

Yes, restaurants. He said he would have become a food critic if he did not join law enforcement first.

"You can do both," I told him. "Fighting bad guys by day and tasting gourmet food by night." I teased him.

Stroking his chin, he was seriously considering the idea.

I laughed heartily, and it felt so good.

When he parked the car near Rosengarten Park, I glanced at the time on the touch screen of the car and was surprised to see that it was already past eight-thirty. Sun was about to set in an hour or so.

"Are you hungry?" he asked.

I was, but I was not ready to go back yet. Gazing at Thomas, I suddenly felt sad and even a little bit lonely, already missing his delightful company and our carefree conversations. But dining in a restaurant? I knew I would get all hysterical when someone simply walked by me, and Thomas was going to think I was a total nutcase.

I was in a dilemma, not able to produce a simple answer to his question, not even just a yes or a no.

"I am," he said, answering for me, and got out of the car.

My eyes followed him to the back of the car. He opened the trunk, and my view was blocked.

What is he doing? Getting food from the trunk?

After he closed the trunk, he laid a blanket over the trunk lid and put a bottle of wine and a big paper bag on top of it. Then he walked towards my side and opened the door.

"Please, join me," he said, offering me his hand.

This man really surprised me in many ways. I took his hand and stepped out of the car. He held my hand and steered me towards the back of the car.

He gently patted the blanket, motioning me to sit on it. "May I?" he asked, holding both his hands near my hips, wanting to help me get on top of the car.

"Ye…yes." I put my hands on his shoulders and pushed myself off the ground while he gave me a little lift and placed me down on the blanket.

I believed I was blushing because Thomas did not even try to hide his amused smile.

He reached over me—intentionally—for the paper bag.

Holding my breath, I kept my eyes on his face which was less than an inch away from mine. I still remembered how frightened I was when Max came near me, but now I was desirous of his proximity.

"I picked up some sandwiches and bresaola rolls." He opened the paper bag, took out a couple of containers, and put them on the blanket.

My stomach was cheering for the food.

"As you can hear, I am hungry. Haha…" I let out a fake laugh, trying to hide my embarrassment.

"In this case," he said and opened the containers. "You will definitely enjoy these delicacies."

"Wow…" I was impressed by the presentation. They did not look like they were from a regular deli but a Michelin three-star restaurant.

"I promise they taste better than they look."

"They look gorgeous," I said. "May I?"

"Of course." He handed me a napkin.

I picked up a well-crafted bite size grilled cheese sandwich and took a small bite. The crispy buttery baguette crumbled and blended with the warm, rich, and nutty flavor cheese, arousing all my taste buds. I closed my eyes, savoring the divine dainty. Who would have thought a grilled cheese sandwich could taste this good.

"I assume you enjoy it."

"This is amazing...." I exclaimed in delight, opening my eyes and meeting his pleased gaze. "Brie?" I asked, tilting my head.

"Yes, your favorite," he said casually as if he was supposed to know that.

I frowned in surprise. "How do—"

"Oh, I forgot the wine. It pairs beautifully with the sandwiches," he suddenly changed the subject—purposely—and opened the paper bag again.

How does he know Brie is my favorite cheese? Those Vera's cooks must have told on me. I got into trouble with them because I would steal Brie and crackers from the kitchen all the time.

He lifted his chin, indicating the wine next to me, and took out two small wine glasses and a bottle opener from the paper bag.

I handed him the wine.

"*Danke.*" He winked at me with a flirty smile.

"*Bitte,*" I replied, bending my head to hide my blushing cheeks.

I was enjoying everything too much, in particular his company, and that scared me. He would be the perfect man to fall for, but he had such a dangerous job. The thought of him working among despicable people gave me chills.

Five days... I drew in a breath, realizing how fast the days were approaching. *I am leaving in five days.*

He uncorked the bottle and poured just half a glass of the red wine for me.

He remembers... I stared at the ruby liquid, surprised that he remembered my alcohol intolerance. And Brie. *How? I mean... unless he paid attention to—*

Of course not, Iris, my pragmatic voice cut me off, bursting my bubble. *He was there to save all the women. And don't forget that you are flying six thousand miles home in five days.*

You are such a killjoy! I huffed inwardly.

"Iris?" Thomas' calling pulled me back from my private conversation with Miss Killjoy. He was holding a glass in his hand.

"*Prost!*" Saying *cheers* aloud, I clinked my glass on his and gulped down the wine like beer, concealing the fact that I thought he might have been paying attention to me and…he might like me.

He gazed at me in amusement, sniffing the wine and slowly taking a sip.

I stared back at my empty glass, avoiding eye contact.

From the corner of my eye, I watched him slowly savoring the wine and then swallowing it, his Adam's apple dancing slowly—I might just start calling him Mr. Adam now.

"—rolls?" Thomas asked, pulling me back my reverie

My eyes flew up to his eyes. "Pardon?" I asked, feeling embarrassed and wondering if he had caught me ogling his Adam's apple.

"Would you like to try some bresaola rolls?" he asked, holding the container.

"Yes, please." I reached for a tastefully crafted little thing, praying he did not notice my fascination with what I saw earlier.

As we were enjoying the delicious food, fine wine, and delightful conversations, the sky was slowly turning gold. The sun was setting down behind Bern Minster, and the view from where we were was magnificent. I looked into the far distance in awe.

Thomas placed his hand on mine gently.

I turned and met his violetish eyes looking at me thoughtfully.

The sunset had contributed the reddish shade in his blue eyes and made them look like two round-brilliant-cut purple sapphires. They were so profound as if they were trying to tell me that he was watching and protecting me from a distance since day one.

Was he?

I had repeated my story again and again to so many people who had interviewed, counseled, and comforted me. Some were good listeners, and some felt sympathetic towards me while some pitied me. However, no one could truly comprehend what I had been through.

Thomas was there. He saw how lost and terrified I was when I first awoke in the recovery house. He grasped how much I despised all the enticements that were used to lure me. He knew how hard I had fought to survive. And he witnessed how close I was to giving up hope.

There was no word that needed to be spoken and no story that needed to be told. He understood…

I suddenly felt so overcome with the realization. Tears already flooded my eyes and were rolling down my cheeks. Through my blurred eyes I saw his doting smile becoming a worried frown.

"I…" I wanted him to know that I had been so sacred. And I still was.

"I know," he whispered softly, wiping my tears off my cheeks with his thumbs, his gaze tender and understanding. He leaned closer and wrapped his arms around me like a guardian angel enfolding me with his invisible wings.

My breathing was becoming slower.

My muscles were relaxing.

My heart started to match the rhythm of his gentle heartbeat.

The tranquility had found me…

I felt safe, protected, and indescribably content. I thought I would never have those feelings again.

"Better?" he whispered, still holding me.

I nodded, gently pulling myself away from him. I didn't mean to show him this weak and vulnerable side of me. "You know… I am… I am not an emotional wreck."

"I don't think you are," he said, looking at me with his affectionate eyes.

His gaze… I had to avert my eyes, or I would forget to breathe. Trying to lighten up the mood, I laughed lightly and said, "I just turned the perfect kissing moment into an emotional mess, didn't I?"

Thomas did not respond. He gently lifted my chin, making me meet his gaze again. And he leaned in and placed his lips on mine.

It was so sudden and unexpected. I could feel his tender lips craving my response.

Leaning closer, I answered his desire.

Times seemed to stop.

CHAPTER 12

> When everything is lost, and all seems darkness,
> then comes the new life and all that is needed.
> ~Joseph Campbell

MY parents and DD arrived two days before my departure. I wished so much to introduce Thomas to them, but he had not returned my phone calls or replied to my text messages for three days.

Since our outing, picnic, and that unexpected kiss, he had been calling and texting me everyday, therefore I really did not understand why he was ignoring me now.

Not wanting to meet my family? I thought, feeling upset. When I told him about their arrival, he told me he would love to meet them. He could have been honest about it, rather than faking eagerness.

Another assignment? The thought made me worry. Although he could have sent me a quick text and let me know he was not available.

What do you expect, Iris? It was just a spontaneous kiss. Miss Killjoy voiced her opinion.

My opinion was: One should not just ghost people. I was a big girl, and I could handle it.

Can you? Miss Killjoy asked.

Of course, I can. I have too much on my plate now and have no time and energy for a love affair. I decided to drop the unnecessary pondering and get ready for my journey home.

Today, I was going to move from the embassy to Hotel Bellevue Palace, where my parents and brother were staying. And it was only a two-minute drive away.

James arranged a town car for us and followed us to the hotel in his own car.

I was sitting between my parents in the back seat, and DD was in the passenger seat. I held my parents' hands so tight, and this two-minute ride felt so long.

I was so certain and truly believed that I was able to do it until the car pulled up in front of the hotel entrance.

All the unfamiliar faces going in and out the entrance were staring at me.

Why are they all staring at me? My heart started pounding heavily.

My father and brother got out of the car first. My father held the door open for me while my brother helped with my luggage.

"Honey?" My mother must have felt my sudden tight grip on her hand. "Are you all right?"

"Why are they staring at me?" I asked, keeping my head down to hide from those eyes.

"Who?" My mother's voice sounded confused and horrified.

"Who? What's the matter?" my father asked, bending down to look at us.

"Everything all right?" James asked, standing right next to my father.

"Iris? Honey?" DD's voice was so worried.

"She said people were staring at her," my mother said to them.

"Who?"

Their voices sounded all blended together.

The air became thinner.

I was gasping for air.

"Iris? Iris? Can you hear me?" James' voice became recognizable now.

I nodded, blinking my eyes, turning towards his voice.

"Good. Now take a deep breath. Slowly... Just like how Dr. Thomson taught you." James' voice was soothing.

I did what he said, taking a deep breath. Now I could see James.

He was sitting to my right, holding my hands.

"Wonderful... You are doing great. Now take another one. Focus on your breathing..."

I did what he said, taking another deep breath slowly.

"Honey..." My mother's voice sounded so soft and...sad.

I turned to my left and saw her in tears. "Mommy..."

She gently held me in her arms and leaned her head against my temple. "It's all right... It's all right..." she whispered.

James let go of my hands, and I hastily wrapped my arms around my mother. He got out of the car and gently closed the door.

Out the window, I saw my father, DD, and James having an intense discussion.

That doesn't look good. I thought and turned back to my mother. "I'm sorry..."

"Oh, honey. It's not your fault. It's never your fault," she said, stroking my hair.

I was so disappointed and discouraged by myself now. I would not be able to go anywhere and do anything if I could not overcome this.

I taped on the window to get their attention and lowered the window.

"Honey, you all right?" my father asked, his voice sounded both concerned and troubled.

"I...I am... I would like to try again," I said bravely, but my voice was trembling.

They all looked at each other, frowning.

Instead of waiting for them to open the door, I pulled the door handle, and the door clicked open. And that made them all look at me in panic.

I closed my eyes and took a deep breath, telling myself that it was all in my head. Nobody was staring at me, and no one was going to abduct me.

Then I opened my eyes and focused on my hand holding the door handle. I slowly moved my eyes higher and looked at these three men who cared for me so much.

I can do this. Keeping my eyes on them, I pushed the door open.

A loud honk startled me, making me turn towards its source. I lost my focus…

Suddenly, all the noises around me became thunderous, and my head was pounding so hard that my chest hurt. And I saw several burly figures approaching me.

"No!" I yelled, withdrawing back.

My mother wrapped me in her arms, sheltering and cradling me.

"Don't…don't let them take me." I hid in my mother's embrace. "I can't… I am sorry…" Starting to feel lacking air again, I started to beg, "I need to go back to my room. Please…"

Then, everything was a blur to me until we drove through the embassy double gates. I felt calm again when I saw the grey building.

DD held me in his arms when I got out of the car.

I burst into tears, not able to suppress my disappointment and anger anymore.

"Don't worry, honey. We will take you home." He kissed my hair and squeezed me tight.

———

AFTER lunch we just stayed in my room.

My mother and I were lying in bed, each using an AirPod to listen to music together. My father was on the phone with Dr. Thompson. DD went back to the hotel to pick up my mother's suitcase because I asked if she could stay with me tonight.

A knock on the door made us all stop what we were doing.

"Come in," I said, removing the AirPod and getting out of bed.

James opened the door and gave us a big smile. "I have wonderful news for you." Walking into the room, he greeted my parents first and said to me, " You might want to sit down for this."

"My apologies, Doctor. I will have to call you back," my father said and hung up the phone.

"Are you ready?" James asked.

"Just tell me. What wonderful news?" I could not imagine anything could be wonderful now.

James cleared his throat and announced, "A private jet will be arranged for you tomorrow. It's going to take you all the way back to Los Angeles."

"No…" I was glad James had asked me to sit down first.

"Yes…" James nodded his head.

"A private jet? Does the embassy have this kind of budget?" my father asked.

I had no idea how much it cost to charter a private jet, but it did sound expensive, especially flying internationally. My father did fly private quite often for work, so he knew the cost. Maybe that was why he was questioning such a nice gesture.

"Who cares, right? As long as it can take you home." James brushed off my father's question.

That's an odd answer, but he's right. Who cares, right? As long as I can go home. My smile was so big that my face hurt.

"But…" My father sounded hesitant about accepting the arrangement. "I will reimburse the embassy for the jet after we arrive home."

"No, no, no. Don't worry about it. All will be taken care of," he said to my father and immediately turned towards me, giving me a sweet and caring smile—but more like not wanting my father to ask him more questions.

Hmmm, interesting. But who cares? I am going home! I jumped up and gave him a hearty hug. "Thank you so much."

He hugged me back and said over my shoulder to my parents, "I need all of your passports, travel details, and contact information to get the thing rolling. You know, getting the clearance for departure and setting up with the U.S. customs for arrival."

"I am on it!" I exclaimed, letting go of James.

Collecting our passports and writing down all the information James needed, I kept looking at James, frowning in disbelief.

"David will be right back. I will ask him to bring you his passport," my mother said.

"Wonderful," he responded.

"Here you go." I handed him the documents and wrapped my arms around his neck with joy again. "Thank you so much, James."

"My darling, it has been my pleasure," he whispered in my ear, squeezing me tightly.

ALTHOUGH my parents promised me that the whole process of chartering a private jet would be easy and private, I still fretted about how I might react once we arrived at the airport or the private suite in the hangar when I saw all the strangers. I took my medications, which Dr. Thompson made adjustments to yesterday, so I should be able to handle one or two fly attendants. However, it was still nerve-racking after what happened yesterday.

Instead of a hangar, we drove up to a huge airplane. I was impressed when I saw the size of the plane. I was expecting a much smaller jet like those in other hangars we drove by earlier. I guessed they needed a bigger one to fly internationally.

There was a lady in a soft velvet uniform standing by the cabin door, smiling at us. I assumed we were boarding right away as we were told all our luggage was transported here and loaded into the airplane already.

James got out of the car and walked up the steps to talk to the lady in velvet while we were standing by the car.

"Everything is ready," James said, walking towards us with a big satisfied smile.

My father extended his hand for a handshake first and then pulled James in for a man hug.

I felt a burning sensation in my eyes. I quickly blinked away my emotions, or James was going to tell me to drop the sentimental *Scheiße*.

My mother and brother exchanged their appreciation and farewell with James and boarded the plane after my father.

Now it was my turn…

I let my emotions take over me. I wrapped my arms around his waist—because he was so tall, and I was in flats—and wept.

"There, there, don't cry. You are going home." He stroked my hair.

"I will miss you terribly, and Tim."

"I know you will, but forget about Tim," he joked, but his voice was choked with emotion.

I chuckled, holding him even tighter.

He turned around and steered me towards the plane.

"This is Emma," James introduced the lady in uniform. "She will take good care of you." He was doing this to make me feel comfortable with a total stranger.

"Ms. De Waal," she greeted.

I gave her a small smile, not able to engage in eye contact. Yet. I would try harder later.

James kissed my hair and rested his chin on my head. He enfolded me and said, "Take care, honey. Call me anytime."

I lost my voice. All I could do was hold him tightly.

"Now you are cutting off my circulation," he joked, gently pulling away from me. "I promise I will visit you if you offer free lodging and complimentary three meals."

I laughed and stood on tiptoe to kiss his cheek.

CHAPTER 13

*In the sweetness of friendship
let there be laughter, and sharing of pleasures.
For in the dew of little things
the heart finds its morning and is refreshed.
~Khalil Gibran*

SOAKING up the salty ocean air and basking in the California sunshine, I was standing on the living room balcony of my oceanfront house in Laguna Beach and doing my daily breathing exercise. Slowly, I inhaled through my nose and then exhaled through my lips, my eyes closed, my mind peaceful.

When I awoke in my own bed every morning, the first thing I did was look out the glass balcony door to see the magnificent ocean view. Although it had been more than nine months since I came home, I still needed that to assure myself this was not a dream and I was really home.

Dr. Thompson referred me to a wonderful psychiatrist, Dr. Warren. She made house calls so I could continue to have my psychotherapy sessions. My recovery was as smooth as it could be.

My parents went back to their Monterey Peninsula home after staying with me for six months. After they left, DD, Janie, and my friends took turns staying with me for a couple of more months before I was comfortable to be by myself in this big house *with* the security system on.

We were all beach people. When my parents decided to move to a less crowded city in Monterey Peninsula, I took over this beautiful three-story house with breathtaking views of the Pacific Ocean. It was situated on a hill. The front entrance, garage, and living spaces were on the top floor; all the bedrooms were on the floor below; and the ground floor had a large entertaining room with beach access.

My brother was an animal lover—from birth, according to my mother—and was now a veterinarian. He loved beach life and horses, so he bought a piece of land in Laguna Canyon and built a ranch, living his dream with his wife Janie and three little monsters whom I adored so dearly.

Antonio also grew up in Laguna Beach and lived not too far from me. He and Jojo came to see me right after I arrived home, and both of them would not stop sobbing. When Jojo refused to let go of her arms that wrapped around me so tightly, I finally understood what James meant when he complained about me cutting his circulation.

Speaking of Mr. Bomer... He called me every week, keeping me posted with all the gossip in the embassy. I warned him the CIA might be listening as he might leak national security information by accident.

I could not be happier when I started to work again, even though I had to work remotely from home.

I had ambition and dreams before...

Before? It sounded pretty sad as if I no longer had them. I always wanted to open another studio in New York, travel the world, and speak French. Now all of those would have to be put on hold. For now, I hoped.

Here I was, back to where I grew up and trying to be better one day at a time. Other than hiding in the house, life had been good because all my friends and family were more than thoughtful since I came home.

A warm gentle breeze blew my medium length hair around, tickling my nose. I missed my long hair...

I had my waist long hair cut into a blunt pixie bob right after I came home. I did not hesitate when I asked Janie to cut it for me and did not even wince at the snipping sound. I found it very therapeutic, like having a new start.

Antonio gently tapped on the glass balcony door to get my

attention. He had been here since seven o'clock in the morning to make me breakfast and enjoy it with me before our meeting with Jojo today.

Did I mention he was our business genius? He had secured two remodeling projects in Pasadena, and we were going to discuss the budget and design concepts today.

"Jojo just texted us. She's almost here," he said when I walked into the living room.

"She is late. She is *never* late." I glanced at the oven clock when I walked into the open kitchen adjoining the living room.

"Well..." He averted his eyes, suspiciously evasive.

That's rare. I looked at him, one eyebrow arching all on its own. Something was not right because he would never miss a chance to make flippant remarks about Jojo.

One might wonder why I did not have a nickname for my best friend. I did, and those monikers—not just one—started with letters A as in ass, D as in dick, and J as in jerk. I called him by those endearments all the time until my mother banned me from using them. So, he was only *Antonio* to me since nothing else suited him.

"Antonio?" I gulped down water, side-eyeing him.

"She might be busy," he said, shrugging his shoulders.

"Busy doing what?" I pressed on. "Her life has nothing but work."

He ignored me and walked to the big conference table, aka my elegant white marble dining table, and started going through his papers.

"Unless..." I started to consider all possibilities. "Wait. Is she seeing someone?"

He did not pay any attention to me. At all.

"She will tell me if she's seeing someone, right?" I asked him.

No reaction from him. At all.

"Oh my god! She *is* seeing someone!" I exclaimed. I grabbed my phone and headed to the security panel. I turned on the camera's live view screen so I could see her when she arrived. I could feel Antonio rolling his eyes at me, but I did not care.

Soon enough, her white Toyota Prius appeared and parked in

front of the front gate. And she was getting out of the *passenger* side.

I quickly tapped on my phone and called her, my eyes on the monitor.

"Hi Iris, I just got here." Her phone was in her hand, so she answered my call right away.

"I know. Who is driving you?" My tone was harsh.

She looked around, and then her eyes landed on the security camera.

"Jojo, who is driving you?" I sang my question, opening the door and walking towards the front gate.

"Uh… A friend…" she answered with hesitation.

"Which friend? I know all your friends." I was bluffing. Of course I did not know all her friends.

"Not this one…" Her voice was just above a whisper.

"Then I must meet…her? Him?" My hand was on the gate lock.

"Iris…" Her voice sounded strangely stressed.

I did not ask more questions but opened the gate.

She looked shocked, still holding the phone against her ear.

"Aren't you going to introduce me to your friend?" I asked, standing inside the gate, which protected me from the outside world.

She bit her bottom lip.

"Your friend is my friend. I promise I won't freak out. You know I have been making great progress," I said, giving her those puppy eyes.

Jojo sighed, looking defeated.

Why doesn't she want me to meet her friend? I was now really intrigued by this mysterious friend of hers.

Just as I was bending sideways, trying to look past Jojo and through the car window to take a peek, the driver side door was opened.

I stood straight again, watching a burly man stepping out.

He looked at me with a shy smile. Tall, clean cut, long hair…

Have I seen this man before? I stared at him, tilting my head and furrowing.

"Iris…" Jojo's voice sounded nervous as if I was supposed to become panicky.

I beckoned Jojo to come closer, and she did. "Do I know him from somewhere?" I whispered to her.

"Y…yes…" She was really nervous. She turned around and introduced us, "This is Marcus. Marcus. You remember Iris…"

"Marcus?" I frowned, trying to match the face with the name—which I was very bad at.

"Hi Iris." His smile was more confident now.

"Do…do you remember him," she asked cautiously.

"Iris." Antonio was standing behind me now. He gently put his hands on my shoulders. "Hi Marcus, how was the flight?" he asked Jojo's mysterious friend.

Antonio knows him, too. I tilted my head up, looking at Antonio.

"Very well, thank you," Marcus said to Antonio.

My eyes flung back to Marcus.

"Iris," Jojo held my hands and asked, "Do you remember the bouncer from the club Étoile in Paris…?" Her voice was becoming smaller.

I knew she was afraid she might trigger some bad memories, and I truly appreciated her thoughtfulness. I had been working on my PTSD for more than a year now. Mentioning Paris or the club where I was abducted would no longer cause me to be emotional or panicky. Not anymore. However, everyone around me was still overly cautious about mentioning anything related to the trip two years ago.

I gave her a mischievous smile and said, "Of course I do, Princess Jasmine."

I had learned to make jokes or be frivolous so people would not feel like they were walking on eggshells around me.

Looking past her, I scrutinized Marcus carefully. "Mr. Viking?"

"What?" Antonio and Jojo responded in unison, and Marcus widened his eyes.

"What did you do to your beard?" I asked, my brow furrowed.

"Oh…" Marcus touched his chin, a bright smile spreading across his face.

"You remember!" Jojo covered her mouth with one hand, her big eyes wide like saucers.

I nodded. Giving Mr. Viking another curious look, I turned to Jojo and said, "Why don't you park the car in front of the garage and invite him in." And without waiting for her to respond, I stared at Antonio and said, "And you. Come with me. Now."

JUST as I had suspected, they thought talking about the club was not a good idea, not to mention meeting a person we met there.

"You could still mention something!" I scolded Antonio.

He shrugged and added, "He's her boyfriend. It's her call not to tell you."

Boyfriend? I turned my head toward Marcus, who was now walking into my living room, hand in hand with Jojo.

She asked him to take a seat on the sofa and then went to the kitchen. Probably getting him a drink…

I took a seat across from him.

"So, tell me. Marcus," I said, grabbing a pillow and putting it on my lap. "Are you on vacation?"

"Yes, I am." He gave me a babyface smile.

I was completely accurate about him wearing the beard to cover his delicate and pretty face. I wondered what Jojo did to persuade this pretty man to shave his long beard. *Hmm…* I would have to grill her about that later.

"Tell her what you do for a living," Antonio said and took a sip of his cappuccino, his voice teasing.

"What's wrong with you?" Jojo smacked Antonio's shoulder when she walked past him. She handed Marcus a cup of coffee and sat down next to him.

"Are you dealing drugs besides being a bouncer?" I joked.

"No drugs, I promise." Marcus chuckled. Then he looked at Jojo and asked, "Would you like to explain to her?"

"Tell me, tell me, tell me!" I acted as if I was really eager.

"Marcus is one of the owners of the club. They actually own several clubs in Europe and here," Jojo said.

"Can't you afford more security guards so you don't have to be a bouncer yourself?" I gave Marcus a mocking glance.

Antonio burst out laughing. Holding his coffee in one hand, he looked at the couple and said, "I knew what happened, so I am going to work on the projects. Good luck." He got up and walked away.

"Don't mind him," I continued. "I was just joking. I am sure you were just filling in the bouncer post when we got there."

"He also owns the security company that does the security for all their clubs," Jojo said, but her voice was not proud or excited anymore. It was sort of downhearted.

"Man with many talents," I said to Marcus, but my eyes were on Jojo. "What's going on? You look…troubled."

She glanced at Marcus and continued, "When we couldn't find you, Marcus asked his crew to search the club and the surrounding area thoroughly."

I gave him a grateful smile when I heard that, and he acknowledged my appreciation with a gentle nod.

"He also personally watched all the security footage," Jojo added.

Did the camera catch who and how they abducted me? My heart started palpitating with anxiety, my palms sweating.

"He didn't see anything at first," Jojo continued.

"What do you mean *at first*?" I looked between Jojo and Marcus.

"I noticed they had been edited," Marcus said.

Someone edited the security footage? I let out a long deep breath, sinking into the sofa.

"Iris, are you all right?" Jojo asked, sounding concerned.

Antonio was back and sat down next to me. He wrapped one arm round my shoulders, one hand holding my hands.

"Marcus, please continue," I said, nestling against Antonio.

"I was able to analyze the edited footage and figured out which time period had been edited out," he continued. "We believed that was when they took you. I am truly sorry that it happened in my club. On my watch."

I just looked at him, not sure what to say. I did not really catch his apology because my mind was dwelling on what he said about the security footage. *Does that mean it was an inside job?*

"I fired the security team and all the staff at the club because I couldn't find out who did it," Marcus interrupted my thought. He suspected the same thing: Someone working in the club that night was involved.

"All of them?" I asked mindlessly.

"Everyone. Even the cleaning crew," Jojo answered.

"My partners and I couldn't risk having unlawful employees. And I gave all their information and everything I had found out to the police. Unfortunately, they did not help. I am truly sorry, Iris."

I just shook my head, wanting to tell him it was not his fault, but I could not voice it.

"Are you all right, hon?" Antonio whispered.

I nodded, giving him a forced smile. I was so shocked by how well planned my abduction was.

"Iris, that's...that's the reason why Marcus hesitated to meet you," Jojo said.

"It was never your fault." I looked at Marcus and was surprised by my own words. Dr. Thompson and Dr. Warren would repeatedly say those words to me when I blamed myself for what had happened.

"I really appreciate your understanding," he said politely.

"I...I will be right back..." Suddenly feeling suffocated, I stood up and went out to the balcony, closing the door behind me.

CHAPTER 14

> If we do not expect the unexpected,
> we will never find it.
> ~Heraclitus

TODAY I slept in because of…no reason. And also because it was Wednesday and I had no plans to do anything.

It was already one in the afternoon when I finally got out of bed. I made myself a bowl of cocoa puffs and milk and lounged on the sofa. I resumed the movie I did not finish last night. Or was it this morning when I finally fell asleep?

My cell phone vibrated, making a big noise on the coffee table glass top. Well, vibrating meant an unknown caller. I tapped the decline button without even looking at the caller ID or number.

And it vibrated again.

Who is calling me? I picked up the phone and looked at the locked screen notifications: Two missed calls from +41 031 xxx xx xx.

+41 031 is for Bern, Switzerland. Did James use a different phone? Without a second thought, I called back the number.

"Torian." The call was answered after two rings. It was not James' cheerful voice but a deep, mellow one.

I regretted calling back, but I guessed I could at least be polite and say something in English. "Hi, you called me twice. I believe you had the wrong number."

"Iris?"

Wait… Did this person answer with 'Torian'? How did I miss that? I had not heard his voice for…for almost a year. I deleted his number after I came home and never thought I would hear from him again. *No… It's impossible.* I suddenly felt upset and annoyed, but my heart sped up, totally betraying me.

"Iris?" He called again, his calling bringing me back from the shock.

"This is she," I said casually, pretending I did not recognize his voice.

"This is Thomas," he said. His soothing and soft voice was making me…making me so mad!

"Thomas…" I lowered my voice, trying to sound uncertain. I did not want him to know he still mattered to me. I hastily glanced around, trying to come up with a last name, and the cover of a Dwell magazine on the table caught my eyes. Clearing my throat, I asked, "Mr. Thomas Dwell?"

Then, silence… I thought I heard sighing.

No, no, no! I did not want him to hang up, so I gave in and spoke in my normal voice, "Hi Thomas…"

Another moment of silence passed, and I was sure I heard him sighing.

"Hi Iris, how are you?" His tender greeting was so comforting.

"I…I am good… You?" I sounded absolutely nervous. I did not understand why he still had such an impact on me after so many months.

"That is fantastic. I am quite good as well," he replied. "Did I… did I catch you at a bad time?"

He sounds nervous, too. Good, I'm not the only one, I thought and said, "No, you didn't. What a surprise? So, what have you been up to?" I sank into the sofa, my hand on my chest. *This man…this beautiful man…*

"Traveling," he said. "As a matter of fact, I am in California now."

I suddenly became silent, gripping my chest. *I think I am having a heart attack now.*

"Iris?"

"Really? Where…where in California?"

He cleared his throat and said, "Laguna Beach."

"Thomas, this is not funny…" My voice sounded harsh. My mood dropped as a mixture of feelings swarmed over me.

"I am serious, Iris," he said in a very genuine tone. "I am…I am right outside your house now…"

What? I jumped up from the sofa and ran to the front door. I looked through the glass…

Dummy! What am I doing? He would be outside the gate not outside the front door.

"I apologize. I do not mean to intrude. I am calling to see if you are home…" He paused, sounding like he was taking a deep breath, and then added, "Are you home? Now, I mean."

I looked down at my baggy t-shirt and shorts—my middle of week and no visitor outfit.

"It's absolutely fine if it's not a good time," he said after I did not say anything.

"I am home," I said quickly. "Can…can you give me a couple of minutes?"

"Of course. Please take your time."

"I will open the front gate for you. You can wait in the front yard," I said, walking towards the security panel on the wall by the front door.

"Thank you, Iris."

"I…I am going to hang up now. I'll see you in a few minutes."

"See you in a few minutes, Iris."

We both hung up at the same time.

I turned on the security camera's live view screen, and there he was…

Oh, right. The gate. I quickly disarmed the security, buzzed the front gate open, and quickly ran downstairs to my bedroom.

I changed into another t-shirt that fitted better and put on jeans.

Does he always surprise people like this? First at the embassy and now here… I took another look at myself in the mirror before heading back to the front door.

Very wonderful surprises though. I grinned.

I could see him through the glass panel. He looked slimmer and a bit darker, and his eyes were covered by sunglasses. I really missed those blue eyes.

But, he ghosted on me. I hesitated, not sure if I wanted to let him in now. *So he ghosted on me. Big deal. There was never anything serious between us anyway.*

I groaned, reaching for the door to open it before getting sentimental about something that never happened.

"Hi!" I greeted him in a cheerful voice.

Thomas removed the sunglasses right away when I opened the door and gave me a smile, a little nervous and a little awkward one.

"Please come in." I stepped aside, holding the door open.

"Thank you." He walked in with an easy gait and leaned in for cheek-kisses, but I backed up instinctively.

I completely forgot about the Swiss cheek kissing etiquette. Here in the States we did hugs which I was not going to give him any.

Respectfully, he stepped back, giving me my personal space.

I closed the door, feeling his gaze on me.

"This way, please." I led him towards the spacious room with spectacular ocean views.

"You have a very beautiful house," he said.

"Thank you. Please have a seat." I gestured for him to sit in the living room. "Can I offer you something to drink?" I asked and stood by the kitchen island.

"Water, please," he said and sat on one of the kitchen island stools instead.

"Bottle or tap water? I also have sparkling water. Or flavored water? I have lemon, peach, and lime. With ice? Or no ice? Or you just want hot water?" I was rambling

Hot water? Seriously, Iris? He just stood outside at midday in June. Miss Pragmatic, aka Miss Killjoy, decided to show up.

"So many choices," he said and laughed softly. "I will have whatever you have."

Oh, I hate him. Why does he have to be so charming? I walked to the refrigerator and grabbed two bottles of Saratoga sparkling water. I put one bottle on the counter in front of him and then moved a couple of steps away from him.

He frowned as he watched me step away. "Thank you," he said, reaching for the bottle. He unscrewed the cap and took a big gulp of water.

Awww, I made him frown... I stared at his frowning face. *Look away, Iris. Look away! I am not as vulnerable as I was a year ago.*

"You look great," he said, his voice nervous.

"Than…thank you." I noticed his eyes landed on my hair. Unconsciously, I touched my shoulder-length hair and twirled the end around with my fingers, remembering he only saw me with waist-long hair.

"I…I must apologize for showing up like this," he said, sitting up straight.

"Don't…don't worry about it." I averted my eyes to hide my diffidence.

"I have been wanting to—"

"How did you know my phone number and address?" I interrupted him, not wanting to hear any excuse from him. I looked at him with a puzzled expression, doubting he would abuse his police connection to find my personal information.

"James was really helpful."

"James…" I murmured, not sure if I should scold him or thank him.

"Please don't be upset with him. I…I put a lot of pressure on him," he quickly explained, his brow furrowed.

And then there were moments of silence.

"California, huh?" I changed the subject, not wanting to make him feel more uncomfortable. "It's a vacation paradise. I am glad you chose it as your holiday destination. How long have you been here?" I was rambling again and really needed to stop. Now! "Have you done some sightseeing yet?"

"I…I arrived last night."

"Last night?" I exclaimed—not really the reaction I should have.

"Yes. It was too late to give you a ring, so I waited till today."

"You came to see me right away…" I murmured.

He gazed at me with his vivid blue eyes, looking both uncertain and anticipating.

"That…that is very nice of you." I had to turn away from his heavenly beautiful eyes that I missed terribly.

"Iris…" His voice suddenly became very serious. "I owe you an apology."

"No, you don't." I darted a frowning look at him because I knew exactly what he was talking about. "You don't need to explain anything."

"I do…" He leaned closer. Regardless of my response, he continued. "A special assignment was allotted to me, and it required me to report for duty immediately. I did not have access to my personal phone when I was away. I…I regretted very much when I saw all the missed calls and messages."

I had nothing to say because I had already put it behind me, and his reasons or excuses were not going to make any difference anyway. It was almost a year ago. There might have been some attraction between us then, but it was long gone now.

Is it? I took a deep breath, knowing the attraction was still there. Just his voice on the phone earlier had stirred up something in me. *Maybe he doesn't feel the same way. He could have contacted me if…if he really cared.*

"Don't worry about it," I said, walking towards the balcony.

He reached his hand out, wanting to stop me.

Usually, I would flinch if anyone touched or wanted to touch me without my knowledge, but I just stopped when his fingertips touched my arm.

"I wanted to contact you right away, but…" He stopped talking, his fingers lingering on my bare arm.

But? What a heavy and extenuating word… I looked at him and met his wholehearted gaze.

Should I hear him out? We enjoyed each other's company, shared an amazing kiss, and had some nice phone conversations and text messages. But that was all…

You can never repay his bravery for saving your life. Doesn't he deserve five minutes of your time? What do you have to lose? Miss Pragmatic was trying to talk some sense into me.

"I should not find any excuse. I am sorry," he said, and his voice could not be more apologetic. "I am truly sorry."

"There…there is really nothing to be sorry about." I blinked my eyes to break his spellbinding gaze and quickly turned away and walked towards the balcony, or I would drown in those alluring eyes, which were bluer than the ocean and the sky.

I looked out the window, missing his touch already. I sensed he walked closer and then stood right next to me.

"The view is amazing," he said, changing the subject. And I was glad he did.

"Do you want to go outside?" I asked.

"To the beach?"

"Oh no…" I chuckled at the idea. He would not have known I was still having great difficulty in being around strangers.

"The balcony." I opened the door and stepped out. He followed suit.

"The view is magnificent," he said, walking to the edge of the balcony.

"We are on the top floor of the house. The bedrooms are on the floor below us, and the ground floor is the fun room."

"Fun room?"

"Pool table, exercise machines, games, and the access to the beach." I leaned on the glass railing, looking down. "The Pacific Ocean is my backyard."

"Do you spend lots of time on the beach?" he asked, turning his face towards me.

"Used to…" I stared at the beach, not sure how to explain to him.

Even though this section of the beach was much more secluded, there were still people playing in the sand and the water, and there were still people walking and jogging on the pathway. I walked to the beach with DD once and had a panic attack when a little kid ran past me. It was so embarrassing.

"Would you give me a tour?" he asked, seeming to read my hesitation.

"Yes, of course." I led the way back into the house.

WE walked around the property, and Thomas was very impressed with the design.

"It's my daddy's vision and my imagination," I said to him when we were standing on the wooden deck outside the fun room facing the ocean. "We used to live on the other side of PCH…" I noticed a little furrow appearing in his brow when I mentioned PCH. "I mean the Pacific Coast Highway. Did you drive here or take a taxi or Uber?"

"I drove here. And I took the Pacific Coast Highway."

I gave him a smile and continued, "My father and I took walks on the beach all the time when I was a child. He was a fine architect and would explain the structures to me. We would point at different houses, admiring, or criticizing them." I smiled at the thought of the sweet memories. "Once I said to him, 'Let's build a house here, Daddy.' I didn't realize he took my words to heart."

Thomas listened to my story so intensively. He did not interrupt or probably did not even blink.

"Then, he brought this property and rebuilt it," I said with pride.

"Your father must have a great influence on you."

"He does," I said, turning around and heading back to the house, gesturing for him to follow me. We ascended the stairs, heading back to the living area.

"He is an architecture critic and a guest speaker at many universities now. If you google Lucas De Waal, you will find many of his articles. He's the reason I am doing what I love the most."

"That is fantastic. I always think being able to work in the profession you love is the most fortunate and fulfilling," he said.

"I agree." I turned around and saw his smile, which made me blush. I quickly turned back to where we were heading. "How long will you be here? I mean California, LA…" I asked, trying to hide my sudden nervousness.

"A couple of weeks or maybe longer. It depends on how things go."

"What things?" I didn't mean to pry as the question just came out.

We now came back to the living room. I sat down in the middle of the three-seater and motioned him to the other sofas, just to avoid any future awkwardness in case he decided to sit next to me.

He sat down on the single seater, ignoring my question. Looking curious and amused, he picked up a magazine on the coffee table. "Dwell?" he smiled at me.

I smiled back awkwardly and changed the subject. "Where are you staying?"

"DeMont Beverly Hills," he answered casually, putting the magazine down.

"How luxurious!" I exclaimed. "It was one of my favorite hotels in Beverly Hills." Then I realized it did not sound quite right, so I added, "Not to stay, of course. I used to go there for lunch and dinner with my friends."

"Why is it one of your favorites?" he asked, probably asking for some advice to take advantage of his staying.

"Exceptional service, divine cuisine, beautiful decor... Absolute top of Relais & Châteaux standard," I replied and asked, "What do you think about it?"

"I think it has great potential for improvement."

That's an odd comment, I thought. And then, I noticed him looking at his watch, again. He had done that a couple of times when we were downstairs.

Does he have to leave but didn't want to hurt my feelings because I wouldn't stop talking? I suddenly felt a bit self-conscious and disenchanted. *I shouldn't enjoy his company...*

"Do you have somewhere else to be?" I asked, my voice small.

"How rude I am!" He covered the watch with one hand, sounding regretful. "My apologies."

Get a grip, Iris! I took a deep breath and decided to retain respect for myself. "It's quite all right if you have to go. As a matter of fact, I do need to catch up on my work."

"I...I do have an engagement to attend, and I am already late."

"Oh." I quickly stood up, not sure what to say. I let my silence make us both feel quite uneasy.

"Can I... Can I visit you again tomorrow?" He stood up as well, asking with hesitation

Visit me again? I widened my eyes, not sure I had heard it right.

"If you are busy tomorrow, I can—" He said when I did not respond.

"You want to visit me again tomorrow? Why?" I interrupted before he could finish, frowning.

He looked completely nonplussed by my question.

"I mean... I mean you are busy now and you might be even busier tomorrow. I am a boring person... Über boring..." I started babbling nonsense.

"You are not boring, Iris." He smiled.

"I am not?" I frowned. *Then why do you keep looking at your watch?*

He gently shook his head, banishing my unnecessary presumption. "I really had a business meeting at three," he added.

I glanced at the oven clock: 3:47PM. "I am so sorry..." I mumbled.

"Don't worry about it. So..." He walked closer. "Can I visit you tomorrow?"

"Yes..." I nodded. "I'd like that...very much."

CHAPTER 15

> Fear not the unknown.
> It is a sea of possibilities.
> ~Tom Althouse

THOMAS called about an hour ago and should be here any minute. And I was standing in front of the closet, wearing nothing but my bra and panties.

My hair was down and curled, and I already put on a little eye makeup and lip gloss. All I needed now was an outfit, but I had changed countless times, and nothing felt right. I was anxious and nervous, just like eleven months ago when I was waiting for him at the embassy. Actually, I felt worse. What happened to my progress?

Floral sundress? I removed it off the hanger, put it on, and turned towards the full length mirror.

Negative. It looked like I was trying too hard. Quickly, I took it off and hung it back.

Casual. Must be casual. What are more casual than a t-shirt and jeans? Feeling confident, I picked a pink fitting v-neck t-shirt and skinny jeans. I shimmied and wiggled to put on the jeans and waddled to the mirror.

Nice booty. I admired the image in the mirror. It was not easy to squeeze into the jeans, but it was worth the effort. Then I remembered he saw me in a t-shirt and jeans yesterday. I immediately peeled them off.

Glancing at my dress collection again, I grabbed the champagne color maxi dress and walked to the mirror. Holding the dress in front of me, I studied my reflection in the mirror.

Okay, sophisticated and cute. Ding, ding, ding. We have a winner!
 I hastily took off my bra as the dress already had a shelf bra and slipped into the dress. Grabbing a pair of white sandals, I rushed upstairs.
 I rearranged the pillows on the sofas at least three times and then scampered to the security panel to turn on the camera's live view screen. Then I walked back to the sofas and rearranged all the pillows again.
 I checked the live view screen every five minutes, and nothing had changed.
 Traffic shouldn't be too bad at two o'clock in the afternoon on Thursday—
 My cell phone chimed and sounded notably loud, interrupting my thought.
 Thomas: My apologies. I could not find a closer place to park my car, and the nearby streets are very packed as well. I shall be there a bit later.
 Me: You can park in front of my garage door.
 Thomas: Fantastic. I am right here.
 He's here! I walked to the front door with anticipation and saw a black car on the security camera's screen.
 I buzzed the front gate open with my trembling finger, more nervous than yesterday. I then opened the front door and stood in the doorway, waiting for him.
 Thomas pushed the gate open and walked in, looking as dapper as always in a white polo shirt and rustic blue jeans, and he looked so much more relaxed than yesterday.
 How can a person stay relaxed after driving around looking for a parking space? I wondered.
 He was carrying a bouquet of irises and a paper bag which reminded me of our sunset picnic.
 He brings me irises... My heart was melting. I stepped aside, inviting him in.
 He stepped into the house and leaned in to touch my cheeks with his—the Swiss etiquette I had now grown to be very fond of.

The tension and awkwardness from yesterday were long gone. This time I did not take a reflexive step backward but returned the same cheek-kisses, discreetly breathing him in. He smelled deliciously masculine. This refreshing, subtle spicy, and woodsy aftershave or cologne suited him so well.

"You look very beautiful today," he said softly and handed me the bouquet. "This is for you."

"Thank you," I replied with a bashful smile, receiving the flowers, and my puckish mind insisted on saying something about it. "You know, I was not named after the flower." I held the bouquet against my chest, inhaling its elegant and powdery fragrance.

His confused and repentant expression was priceless.

"I was named after Van Gogh's still life painting, Vase with Irises. The one with the yellow background," I said solemnly, suppressing my laughter.

He blinked his eyes and tilted his head, still processing what I just said.

I looked into his eyes, which were almost the same color as the flowers in my hands, and gave him a mischievous smile.

"Very witty, Iris," he said after coming to the realization.

I winked at him and walked towards the kitchen to put the flowers in a vase.

Thomas closed the door and followed me.

"It's a true story," I said, filling the glass vase with water. "My parents decided to name me Iris after they visited the Van Gogh Museum in Amsterdam."

"I think it's a wonderful story," he said, putting the paper bag on the counter, and added. "This is also for you."

"More presents?" I glanced at the bag with curiosity as I untied the blue ribbon of the bouquet and put the flowers in the vase. "Perfect…" I mumbled, admiring the arrangement.

"I did not bring them with me yesterday because I was not sure if you would be home or not."

"I am intrigued." I reached for the bag. Pleasantly surprised, I took out a bottle of ice wine and a box of dark chocolate.

"There is one more item." Thomas pointed at the bag.

I looked inside and found a small cello bag with white silvery sea salt in it.

He remembered...

When we were chatting about food and wine in his car, I told him ice wine and bittersweet dark chocolate with a bit of sea salt drizzled on top equaled pure happiness.

"Thank you. These... They are wonderful."

He looked satisfied with my reaction—the same look he had when I took a bite of the grilled cheese sandwich.

I did not realize how much I had missed that day, every detail and every conversation we had.

"I am all yours now. No engagement at all," he said cheerfully.

I like that...a lot.

WE spent a couple of hours in the fun room playing pool and throwing darts. I declared that all games ended in a tie regardless of the actual scores. This man showed me no mercy when it came to playing games.

After that, we came back to the living room. We had coffee, and I told him about my progress here with my psychiatrist and how much I appreciated James for all his help and support.

"Enough about me. Your turn now." I wanted to know more about him.

"I am a very boring person," he chuckled.

How can he be boring with the job he has? I thought. "But I knew so little about you."

"Ask me anything you fancy knowing," Thomas said, leaning back on the sofa.

Challenge accepted. I gave him a smirking smile and asked, "Did you always want to be a police officer?"

"No," he answered straight away without hesitation.

"I need more, not a one-word answer," I protested.

He frowned, seeming to consider his answer.

"I am sorry... Don't worry about it." His solemn expression

made me regret my fuss.

"I am just thinking about what to say. I want to give you an honest answer," he said and looked so sincere and…doleful.

Why the mournful look? Did I cross the line? I really regretted my words now. "It's really o—"

"My sister was abducted sixteen years ago," he interrupted me as if he had to say it now or he would change his mind.

I was speechless, my eyes fixed on him. This was not what I expected to hear.

"I just started my first year at the university in Oxford," he continued.

I did a mental calculation of his age… He would be thirty four or five now if he was a freshman sixteen years ago. I would have guessed he was in his late thirties, about my brother's age. His dangerous and stressful job must have aged him.

"I rushed home, and we did everything we could to find her."

Just like my family…

"She was found in Italy after almost three years."

Three years? I felt a sudden dizziness.

"Are you all right?" he asked, his voice worried.

He's worried about me when he has so much pain in his eyes. I gazed at his mournful eyes.

"You don't have to…" I said to him, knowing how painful the memory must be for him.

"Iris, I…I want to tell you this."

I nodded softly, drawing in a deep breath.

"When she was found, she was very ill, physically and emotionally. We brought her home immediately, and she was hospitalized for months," he said and took a deep breath. "She ended her own life soon after she came home from the hospital."

I could feel her pain… Tears welled up in my eyes. I looked away, trying to take slow and deep breaths to calm my emotions that were awakened.

"I am sorry," he said. "I did not mean to upset you."

"Please continue," I said, blinking back tears. I grabbed a pillow and hugged it tightly.

He gazed at me dubiously.

"I am okay. I promise." I gave him a reassuring smile.

He nodded and continued, "My sister and my mother were very close, just like sisters." A slight smile appeared on his face when he said that. "After my sister passed away, my mother gave up her cancer treatment."

I wanted to walk over to him and hold him in my arms. It must be so devastating for him and his family...

"That was when I decided to be a police officer." He looked down at his hands, trying to ease his emotions.

"Thank you for sharing this with me," I said in a very soft and low voice, truly appreciating his honesty.

He looked up, his expression hesitant, and said, "Iris, there is something else I need to tell you."

"Okay..." I wondered what it would be.

"I... I was there when you were abducted...in Paris." His voice was low and regretful.

My mind just went completely blank. I could not think, could not process his words, and could not suppress my emotions anymore.

I need a minute. Alone. Standing up from the sofa, I walked out to the balcony. I could sense his eyes on me, watching my every move.

I paced back and forth, trying to ease my anxiety.

He saved me, he saved me, he saved me... I repeated the words in my head, refusing to have the horrible thought of him being one of the people who abducted me and stole my life.

There must be much more to it. I finally stopped the pacing and looked at him, who was sitting still on the sofa gazing at me.

"Tell me more, please," I said when I stepped back into the room. I walked to the kitchen instead of back to where I sat earlier.

Thomas stood up from where he sat, wanting to come closer to me, but I gestured for him to remain where he was.

He respected my wish and continued, "They had their eyes on you soon after you arrived at Charles de Gaulle Airport."

"What?" I was shocked. It sent chills down my spine.

Thomas nodded. "I know it's very upsetting."

It's more than upsetting. It's sick and...and... I found myself gripping the edge of the counter top so hard that my knuckles were becoming white. *Do I really want to hear this?*

"Iris, just remember most of them are in prison now."

I looked at him, frowning. I wanted to know why he did not save me then if he was there. "You...you said you were there. Tell me more. Please."

He closed his eyes, taking a deep breath, his expression pained. "I was..." He took another deep breath and opened his eyes. Then he said, "I was always Vera's bodyguard when she traveled. You were already in the van when I saw you." He paused, waiting for my reaction.

Everything he was telling me right now felt like a stab of agony. Now I knew I was drugged and loaded in a van like freight.

"I could not interfere or do anything..." he continued as I did not say anything, sitting back down on the sofa. "So I tried to stay close because..." He paused and let out a deep breath. "I had wished someone would have done that to watch over my sister..."

Oh God, he looks so miserable... My heart ached for him, but I still needed to process what he just told me.

We were both silent. He was staring at his folded hands while I was gazing at him.

How does he do it? I could not imagine what he had endured when taking on a job like that.

I was so blind... That was why he was always around, in the hallways, staircases, parties... To watch over me.

Wait... Did he? He stood guard over me outside the powder room when I had a meltdown on my birthday.

Oh, Thomas...

"What is your sister's name?" I asked, my voice quivering.

"Laila," he said with a gentle smile, still staring at his hands as he was remembering his sister.

"That's a very beautiful name."

"Thank you." He looked up. "I know she was brave and must have done whatever she could to survive. Just like you."

But she ended her own life after she was free... Would that happen to me if...if Thomas didn't save me? I felt hot tears rolling down my cheeks.

He stood up, seemingly wanting to come closer, but he did not move. He just gazed at me with his dejected eyes.

"Why...why did you risk giving away your cover to save me?" I asked.

Ever since I knew he was an undercover officer, I had been wanting to ask Julia or him about this. I knew he took the risk because those who were no longer useful for Vera were picked up, but I was driven away by the security foreman.

"I had to..." His eyes became tender and caring. "I...I could not bear to see you getting hurt."

Slowly, I walked towards him, biting my lips to repress the overwhelming emotion. I wrapped my arms around his waist and buried my face in his chest. "Thank you..." I whispered.

He hesitated for a moment and then gently held me in his arms, letting out a sigh of relief.

My guardian angel... I was once again enfolded in his invisible wings, feeling protected and content.

"The itsy bitsy spider climbed up the waterspout..." Suddenly, the room was filled with my nephews and niece's voices singing Itsy Bitsy Spider.

We looked at each other and busted out laughing.

"It's my brother. I must get it."

"Of course," he said, freeing me from his warmhearted embrace.

I picked up my phone on the coffee table and answered, "Hi DD."

"Someone parked the car right in front of the garage door and didn't leave a number. Can you come out and get the grocery first?" DD said, sounding annoyed.

"I'll be right there!" I completely forgot DD was supposed to be here today. Hanging up the phone, I said to Thomas, "My brother is here. Would you mind moving your car?"

"Of course not," he said and followed me to the front gate.

"I will open the garage door for you. Just park the car in the garage."

He nodded and stood right behind me when I opened the gate.

DD's eyes could not be any wider when he saw Thomas. And I thought his jaw just dropped to the ground.

"David, Thomas. Thomas, David…" I quickly introduced them.

"Pleasure," Thomas greeted, extending his hand.

DD was still speechless. He stared at Thomas when he shook his hand and kept holding it.

"Let's take care of the parking first," I said, separating their hands.

"Do you still want me to park in the garage? I can drive around and look for a place to park," Thomas said, walking towards a beautiful black four-door Bentley parked right by the garage door.

"Yes, please," I said and pressed the garage door remote. "It's a two-car garage." My red Land Rover Evoque occupied less than half of the garage.

"Let me move my car first," DD said to Thomas. He jumped into his gigantic Chevy Tahoe and drove it a little farther to give Thomas more room to turn the car around. And then he came right back and stood right by me. We were both watching Thomas parking the car.

"Thomas?" he asked, putting one arm over my shoulders. He and my parents had heard about Thomas when they went to Bern to pick me up but never had a chance to meet him.

"Yes, THE Thomas." I wrapped one arm around his waist.

"Are you all right?" he asked.

"Better than all right, DD." I looked up at my brother and met his concerned eyes.

My brother checked on me every chance he had, and every Thursday he would come here with groceries and have dinner with me. I could not ask for a better big brother.

"I am glad…" DD kissed the top of my head. "Okay, my turn now."

Thomas' car was inside the garage now so DD could park his car in front of the garage door. I shut the door after Thomas walked out.

"Did you empty the store?" I asked because the second row and the cargo space were full of bags and boxes.

"Just things you need and might need," DD said, unloading the groceries.

We had to make a couple of trips to bring all the bags and boxes into the house. I noticed my brother was observing Thomas very carefully.

"Stop it," I whispered to DD.

"Stop what?" DD walked towards Thomas, who was carrying two big grocery bags into the kitchen. DD put the box he was carrying on the counter and then sat on an island stool.

I scampered after my brother and walked into the kitchen casually. Giving him a warning glance, I opened the refrigerator and started putting away groceries.

"Thomas, I apologize for my rudeness earlier. I was just really surprised. I'm so glad to finally meet you!" DD said.

"No apology necessary," Thomas replied. "I am glad to finally meet you as well." He walked closer to me and handed me fruits and vegetables.

"So… Are you here for work or pleasure?" DD asked, resting his folded arms on the island counter.

"Both." Thomas politely gave DD a respectful glance while gently putting a carton of eggs on my hands.

"Never mind him," I said out loud to Thomas so that DD could hear it.

"Do mind me, please," DD said, giving me a smug smile. Then he looked at Thomas sincerely and added, "My family cannot thank you enough."

"I was just doing my job," Thomas replied. "Iris was incredible and brave. She still is…" He looked at me, gazing at me with his caring eyes, which made me blush and hide behind the refrigerator door.

"She sure is," My brother said. "I wish Iris had told us about your visit. My parents would love to meet you, too."

"Oh, she…she did not know…" Thomas explained, sounding a bit unease.

"Thomas didn't want to make a big deal," I said to my brother. "Imagine what Mom would do if she knew he was coming. She probably would arrange a red carpet welcome with a marching band for his arrival."

Really? Thomas widened his eyes, mouthing the word to me.

"That's very likely," DD said to Thomas. "Iris is not just my mom's baby. She is her companion for reading, traveling, chatting, shopping, et cetera. They are best friends."

I glanced at Thomas and saw him looking at me intently in thought. I had a feeling we were thinking about the same thing: His sister was his mother's best friend and I my mother's.

"So, you can imagine how my mother was when Iris was missing," DD continued.

"I sure can…" Thomas kept his gaze on me.

I blushed again, turning my whole body to the refrigerator and rearranging groceries on the shelves aimlessly.

"Are you staying for dinner?" DD asked, changing the subject, and added. "You must. Iris is a very good cook."

"Then, I must," Thomas replied, sounding a bit too enthusiastic.

"Great!" DD said and stood up from the stool. "I am going home now before the traffic gets too crazy."

"What? You always stay for dinner!" I exclaimed.

"You have a perfect company," DD said, pointing his thumb at Thomas, who was nodding in agreement.

These two are acting like they are buddies already.

"See, he agrees." DD turned his pointing thumb into a thumb-up. He walked up to me and kissed my forehead. "I will call you in the morning."

He turned towards Thomas and extended his hand for another handshake. "It's really a great pleasure meeting you."

"The pleasure is all mine," Thomas responded, holding DD's hand in his.

"I know my way out," DD said and headed out.

Then, he was gone. Just like that. My brother was here less than twenty minutes, and that was a record. He always stayed at least a couple of hours and fretted about everything. He made sure I ate well and slept well, and he would double and triple check the security system before he left.

Thomas and I were silent, and the atmosphere became a bit

awkward when we heard my brother closing the door.

"So, what is on the menu?" He broke the ice. "I heard you are a good cook."

This is a man who wants to be a food critic. Do I dare to cook for him? I gave him a nervous glance and said, "He exaggerated."

I scanned the refrigerator to see what I could make. Taking out a package of ground turkey, I ask, "Does spaghetti sound good?"

"Perfect." He gave me a broad smile.

CHAPTER 16

The best is yet to be.
~Robert Browning

AFTER dinner we sat on the balcony, enjoying the ocean breeze. The sun was yet to set for at least a couple of hours. I was sipping on water while Thomas was enjoying the Pinot Noir we had for dinner.

"Let's take a walk on the beach," he said spontaneously.

I looked at the beach spread out below, not really sure if it was a good idea because there were still people dotting the whole area.

"Maybe later?" I asked in hesitation. I didn't even know why I asked him that because I would not be ready later, or even later than later.

"Do you know there is a dark cloud hanging over your head now?" His brow furrowed, but he sounded amused.

I exhaled deeply and stood up. I walked closer to the edge of the balcony and leaned against the glass railing, staring down aimlessly.

He followed suit, stood right next to me, and put his hand on the small of my back. "I will be right by your side," he said to me in a tender voice.

I turned my head to look at his loving eyes and beautiful face. His five o'clock shadow reminded me of Max, whom I used to think of as an evildoer and loathed so much. Who would have known that he was now the person I trusted the most?

I nodded without realizing what I was doing. *I must be mad...* I thought to myself.

"Fantastic." He interlaced his fingers with mine and led the way downstairs.

I decided not to worry too much and live a little. Today. With him.

It had been a long time since I felt so…so carefree and happy. Today was going to be a day to remember for a long, long time after he left, just like that day in Bern. I had never stopped thinking about his eagerness to take me out, his quick and inventive humor that made me laugh so much, and his love for food and wine. Especially when I felt…*forlorn*.

Was there another word I could use to describe this void emptiness that made me lose all my perspective? To express this heart-wrenching grief that trapped me in the labyrinth of sorrow and loneliness? And to explain this immeasurable regret that I could not see any light in my future?

The grief and regret often struck without warning… For instance, I would suddenly feel so lonely and hopeless while I was having dinner with DD; and the next thing I knew I was bawling in his arms.

I had learned to coexist with those emotions, but sometimes they were just too overwhelming… And when I could not handle them anymore, I would close my eyes, thinking back to that special day, remembering Thomas's embrace that soothed me and our unexpected first kiss that melted my heart. And then, I would find the serenity again, feeling centered again.

Thomas did not let go of my hand until we arrived at the backyard gate to the beach. He took off his loafers while I felt more comfortable if I had my sandals on.

I froze, casting my eyes down, when he opened the gate.

He stepped in front of me, facing me, blocking the view of the beach full of strangers.

"Look at me, Iris," he said, gently placing his hands on my shoulders.

I gazed up at his both concerned and sincere eyes.

"I promise I won't let go of your hand." His left hand softly brushed down my arm and took my hand, intertwining our fingers again.

I drew in a deep breath and gave him a confident smile.

He turned around and led me through the gate.

We zigzagged towards the water, keeping a good distance from the beachgoers. When we were at the edge of the ocean, I held my long skirt higher with my free hand, kicked off my sandals, and let my bare feet sink into the sand. When the cold waves flew over my feet, I laughed. Brightly and wholeheartedly.

Thomas laughed along with me and never let go of my hand.

I turned towards him and smiled my appreciation, my eyes misty.

He slowly stepped closer and leaned towards me, his eyes fixed on me. I closed my eyes, thinking he was going to kiss me... Then he gently held me in his arms.

No kisses? Only a hug? I was both surprised and disappointed. However, his warm embrace was very much welcome, and his woodsy and a bit citric scent was intoxicating.

"Excuse us!" Suddenly, several young voices spoke in unison. They were coming from behind me, thundering to my ears.

I instinctively huddled against Thomas, shutting my eyes, my body trembling slightly.

And just like my instinctive reaction, Thomas hastily enfolded me tight in his arms, sheltering me.

My heart did not speed up, and my breathing remained calm.

I have found my safe haven...

"Are you all right, love?" he asked softly when we were again surrounded only by the sound of the ocean waves crashing against the shore.

I didn't get panicky! I was screaming in my head.

A sudden realization dawned on me: He must had seen that group of young people coming behind me. He held me in his arms to distract me and shield me from them.

He released me and cradled my face in his warm palms. "Are you all right?" he asked again.

Looking up, I was hypnotized by his doting gaze...

The Sun was sinking below the horizon behind me. His sky-blue eyes reflected the golden sunlight, so beautiful and celestial. I could not answer him as I did not want to disturb this aura of tranquility around us.

Slowly, he leaned in, eyes closed, and placed his lips on mine, so softly, as if he was afraid to break me. I rose up onto my toes, wrapping my arms around his neck, and kissed him back passionately. His kiss became intense as well, tasting my lips both tenderly and eagerly. Everything was so familiar but so much more enticing than our last sunset kiss.

When our lips parted and our eyes opened, the sky was already dark. The silver moonlight was shining on the surface of the ocean, and the hills were ornamented with colorful illuminated houses and streetlights.

"Shall we?" he asked, wrapping his arm around my shoulders.

I nodded, wrapping my arms around his waist.

We strolled on the empty beach back to the house.

I heard music when I came out of the bathroom, not something I recognized.

Thomas was sitting on the three-seater sofa, playing the music from his phone. He gently patted the seat beside him, inviting me to sit next to him.

I smiled at him first and then flashed him a little flirting eyebrows—I probably should practice how to flirt again. I walked towards the kitchen instead of him to get two glasses of cold water for us. I could sense his gaze on me.

Putting the water on the coffee table, I sat down next to him, my feet tucked under my legs.

He wrapped his arm around me and cradled me in, making me feel both anxious and content. He was a little too quiet, just staring at the water glass, lost in thought.

I noticed his pensive frown and suddenly felt discouraged. Just as this night was going so well, he looked hesitant and uncertain now.

"What a beautiful voice…" Out of nervousness, I chatted, "Who is the singer?"

"Jon Batiste. You have never heard of him?" He faced me, turning the volume down.

"Don't..." I stopped him from lowering the volume.

Although I was only trying to break the silence, the voice of this singer was enchanting. "His voice is so...so calm and rich. Luscious like sweet wine..."

Thomas smiled in surprise. "That is a very unique way to describe his voice."

"The pianist is wonderful, too." I closed my eyes, enjoying the soothing piano.

"He is also the pianist for this song."

Opening my eyes, I looked at him. "He is so good. And the voice..." I put a hand over my heart and sighed with amazement.

He nodded his agreement, a smile spread across his face.

I leaned against him again, resting my head on his shoulder, trying to enjoy the music and his company.

"Iris," he finally spoke after moments of silence.

Is he going to tell me he has a significant other back home? Or... No, nothing is worse than that. My heart started palpitating.

Iris, do not forget the BYLAW! Never get involved with someone married or in a relationship. Miss Pragmatic appeared from nowhere.

I know! I scolded Miss Pragmatic in my head. After dumping my cheating ex-boyfriend, my circle of friends established the Bylaw of Constancy and Dependability Alliance, and I was the president.

I took a deep breath and responded, "Yes?" My voice sounded a bit shaky, and I was ready to catch my already-sinking mood, and probably a broken heart soon.

"I am no longer with fedpol," he said.

My little brain, which was busy planning a one-person-pity-party, paused to process what he just said. Those words were not what I expected to hear. I was ready for something more dramatic and for something that was going to hurt my feelings. But this...this was actually...worse!

Was he fired because of me?

I sat up straighter, turning fully towards him and asked, "Did I...

did I jeopardize the operation? They fired...they fired you because —"

"No. It was nothing like that," he quickly clarified, gently caressing my arm, reassuring me.

"No?" I was not convinced, my forehead scrunching.

He shook his head, giving me a tender smile, and continued, "After my last assignment, I reassessed everything in my life and decided it was the right thing to do."

Okay... That's good. Right? No more dangerous assignments. I gazed at him.

"You are so quiet..." He asked, his hand stroking my hair, tucking a lock of hair behind my ear.

Blinking my eyes, I gave him a half-smile but stayed quiet, not sure what to say...

Asking if he was between jobs sounded so rude. I was certain he was doing great financially since he could afford staying at DeMont Beverly Hills and renting a Bentley; plus, it was really not my business. And congratulating and wishing him good luck was not quite right, either. I thought I would just ask him to talk more since he was a man of few words.

I snuggled closer to him. "Anything else?"

"Such as?" he asked, his fingers playing with my shoulder-length curls.

"Girlfriend or wife... Somewhere?" I asked nervously.

The question was silly and a little desperate, but it was better than finding that out later. Right? Let me quote Article I of the Bylaw here: Fidelity is the basic principle of courtship.

A shy and broad smile spread across his face. "None of those. I did have a girlfriend before," he answered in a sincere tone.

That's it? Less than ten words? I tilted my head.

The police academy must have trained them to use as few words as possible. That was fine. There was nothing else I needed to know anyway.

"Okay, that's good enough," I said in a very low voice, resting my head on his shoulder.

"Good enough?"

I nodded and said, "Either you made a special trip to visit me or just dropped by to see me, I am happy, very happy that you are here."

He turned fully towards me, so I glanced up at him, expecting more confessions from him. He did not say a word but gently lifted my chin up to face him, his intense blue eyes making me breathless.

This time I took the initiative. I leaned in and kissed him, just a gentle, soft touching of lips.

He definitely answered this kiss well, one hand cupping my face and the other pressing the nape of my neck. He pulled me closer to him and deepened the kiss. His lips were soft and warm. And eager.

A moan escaped me, and that only enticed him to want more.

Gently, he put his hand on my knee through the long dress and pulled me closer. He lifted my leg and sat me down astride his lap. One hand rested on my thigh and the other pressed my back, holding me closer. Slowly, he moved his full lips to my earlobe, and my body tensed up. A small amused smirk flashed over his face. He looked seemingly pleased he had found my sweet spot. He gave it a tender suck, a wave of arousal rushing through me, goosebumps proliferating all over my body.

Jon Batiste's *The very thought of you* was coming out from the speaker, his euphonious and tantalizing voice mirroring our amorous fervor.

I cradled his face, the stubble rough to the touch but titillating me, his heavy-lidded, blue gaze glinting with lust. I knew we both craved each other badly, and I especially recognized how much he had affected me yesterday…

No, it was way before that. I had never forgotten his embrace and our first kiss in Bern.

Or… Was it after he saved my life and drove me out of the mansion? I had never stopped thinking about him since.

No, wait… I had always sensed his steadfast sapphire gazes watching over me…

Our lips met again, and this time his velvet tongue joined in, eagerly finding its way to seduce me. I opened my mouth for him but only touched the tip of his tongue, returning his seduction with tenderness, needing him to slow down.

He breathed out my name, knowing he needed to take it slow to find the perfect rhythm within us. Slowly, he ran his fingers over my arms, shoulders, and then trailed them over my back, his featherlight touch stirring all my senses.

My reserved lustful desire was so close to being released. I wrapped my arms around his neck and brought myself closer to him, unintentionally grinding against his excitement beneath his jeans. I was not sure it aroused me more or him because our breathing had picked up and our kisses had deepened. His palm cupped my head, and the other pressed my bottom to bring me even closer. His hip gently pushed up, and his hardness unquestionably was pronounced.

Oh, my goodness… The room is becoming very hot.

"Stop… Stop…" Suddenly, he whispered against my lips, holding me still. His chest was rising up and down heavily.

I leaned back, my eyes blinking rapidly and my breathing matching his.

"You are killing me, Iris." He gazed at me, running both his hands through his short dark hair.

Am I too forward? Feeling discomfited, I slowly moved backward.

"No…" He tugged me back and said, "You are amazing, so wonderful…" Pressing his forehead against mine, he continued in a deep, rich voice, "I…I might not be able to control myself any longer."

Then don't… I wanted to say that to him, but the words did not come out. My eyes casted down, unsure what to say.

"And…" He brushed the hairs on my cheeks, tucked them behind my ears, and lifted my head to look at him. "I don't have condoms with me," he whispered.

My face must have turned bright red because I could feel the heat and he looked amused. I casted my eyes down. Not only did I not have condoms, I had not had sex since I broke up with my ex. That was centuries ago.

So what now? A cold shower?

He drew in a deep breath and kissed my forehead. He took my

hands, kissed my fingers, and then held them against his taut chest. "I can go to—"

Wait... I remember...

"Come..." I interrupted him, trying to stand up from his lap.

He looked at me, raising a curious brow when I grabbed his hand and pulled him up from the sofa.

I led us downstairs to one of the guest rooms, which my brother and his family would use when they were here.

Thomas looked so puzzled when I let go of his hand and walked into the bathroom, but he followed me anyway.

"I remember I saw it...somewhere..." I mumbled, glancing around the room. And I started going through the drawers of the double-sink vanity. Moments later, a black Trojan box came into sight when I opened one of the bottom drawers.

"Yeah! Look what I found!" I exclaimed—probably too enthusiastically. I picked up the box and whirled around, showing it to Thomas as if I just won the grand prize.

I uttered a surprised yelp and burst out laughing when he unexpectedly wrapped his arms around my thighs and lifted me onto his one shoulder. The black box flew out of my hand and landed on the vanity top.

"Grab the box," he said, tilting me closer to the target.

I hastily snatched it as if it was going to make a run for it. And we both laughed aloud.

He carried me in a fireman's lift style to my bedroom in just several long strides and gently put me down on my feet at the end of the bed.

I combed my hair back with my fingers, giving him a radiant smile.

He stepped into my personal space, cupped my face in his big warm palms, and whispered, "You sure?"

I answered with a bashful nod. I did not know what to expect, but I was very certain that we wanted one another. Badly. I would miss him terribly after he left, but I would lick my wound then. So yes, I was sure.

He leaned down and pressed his lips on mine, giving me a soft, luring, prolonged kiss, which made me breathless and my knees weak.

"Where did you come from?" I whispered, gasping for air when he pulled away.

He fixed his eyes on mine, taking the box from me and tossing it on the bed near the headboard. Wrapping his arms around my waist, he slowly walked forward, bringing me with him until my calves touched the edge of the bed. Slowly, he leaned in, guiding me to sit on the edge of the bed, and gave me another lustful and heated kiss.

When we broke apart for air, his hand gently caressed my thigh through the dress, his blue eyes glinting with wants, eagerness and… hesitation.

I slowly pulled my skirt up and over my knees, just up to my upper legs, my eyes watching him, wanting his touch.

His alluring eyes followed my movement and then shifted back to meet my gaze while his warm palms skimmed over my bare skin and rested on my knees. He gently pushed my legs apart and moved closer between them. I leaned in, meeting him halfway. He tilted his head and kissed my neck. His warm lips inched along my neck higher and higher until they touched my ear, and he teasingly nibbled my earlobe, enkindling my libido. My breathing picked up, arousal damping my thong.

He ran his fingers along the neckline elastic strip of my dress and slowly pulled it over my shoulder, dipping soft kisses on the exposed skin. He cupped my breast through the dress, kneading it tenderly. The thin bra pads could not conceal the peaks of my arousal, and his gentle caress only made them more sensitive to touch.

"Mmm…" I could not hold back my moan, titillated with desire. I was so ready for him, and he was surely taking it slow…

"Sit back a little," he whispered in my ear.

I did as he asked. When I pushed myself up a little, he wrapped one arm around my waist, lifted me up, and laid me down gently on my back. He propped himself up on one elbow, one hand stroking my cheek. "Iris…" he whispered my name, gazing down at me intently. "I…"

"Yes?"

"I have never stopped thinking about you...."

Me too... I did not know why I could not say aloud to him. Sheltering my heart, maybe?

I did not think I was capable of being loved or letting anyone into my heart anymore despite Dr. Warren's persistent encouragement: Iris, you will be trusting enough to love and be loved again.

I trust Thomas with my whole heart... My heart sped up. *But he is not here to stay.*

My eyes flicked between his adoring eyes, my throat tightening, tears threatening to emerge. Concealing my sudden doleful emotion, I reached my hands up and pulled his face down to give him a kiss, and another one, and another one...

He returned my longing kisses, his hand roaming along my arm and down to my hip. When he put his hand between my thighs, both our breathing became harder.

He gave a low moan of surprise, or maybe delight, when his fingers brushed along the edge of my seamless thong, gently touching my freshly sugared, smooth skin.

I put my hand over his hand, not sure if I wanted him to stop or more of his tender caress. I guessed it was the latter because I spread my thighs slightly wider and guided his hand to the center of my desire.

"You are so wet..." he whispered, tracing my folds slowly through the satin fabric with his fingers.

I gasped in pleasure when he moved his fingers underneath the barrier, his fingertips slowly tracing up and down my labia. He kissed and nibbled my bottom lip, his fingers tucking the thong aside and sliding into my inner folds eagerly.

I grasped his arms when he entered a finger inside me slowly, his thumb running circles around my immensely sensitive happy button. I opened myself wider for him, my back arching, my heart speeding up.

He started rubbing me with perfect pressure when he added a second finger.

Panting, I opened my heavy eyelids and saw his blue lustful eyes watching me blatantly. My cheeks heated. I reached my hands to bring his gorgeous face closer, needing his lips on mine.

He glided his fingers in and out, the thumb doing its magic. They were building me higher and higher. My hips moved to his rhythm all on their own, all the muscles tensing up. I wrapped my arms around his neck, catching up my breathing. And before I knew it, I tilted my head back, letting out a guttural moan when an orgasm burst. My muscles were spasming around his fingers that did not stop thrusting.

"You look so beautiful when you come...," he whispered in my ear when I was coming down from the peak. He slowly pulled his fingers out, dipping a kiss on my shoulder.

I tittered, covering my blushing face with both hands and closing my thighs.

"Don't hide your beautiful face," he said, his voice deep and tender.

I peeped at him through my fingers and whispered, "I... It's just... I have never come so fast..." Not to mention I was still fully dressed and already had an orgasm.

"My pleasure," he said, moving my hands away from my face.

A giggle escaped from me when I saw his smirk smile. He was definitely pleased with his *handy* work.

He moved atop me, pressed his body against mine, and brought my hands above my head. He threaded his fingers through mine, flatting our hands on the mattress. Leaning down, he caught my mouth with his, turning my giggle into a moan.

Letting go of my hands, his fingers skimmed down my arms. He broke the kiss and propped himself up on his left elbow, right hand brushing over my collarbone and down between my breasts, his fingers drawing little circles there and then slowly pushing my dress neckline to the side, his lips trailing his fingers.

"Hmm..." I mewled aloud when he sucked my nipple in his mouth, the tip of his tongue licking it softly. "Thomas..." I breathed out his name, my hands running through his hair, tugging slightly.

His knees nudged my thighs apart, and he settled his hips against me. He ground his hardness on my still sensitive lady-part when he pulled the other strip of the dress over my shoulder and tugged it lower to reveal my other breast. He abandoned the nipple in his mouth and licked the newly uncovered one with his warm tongue.

I moaned... The sensations were spreading throughout my body, overwhelming me. I pulled on his shirt, needing to touch his bare skin.

He hastily got on his knees, reached the bottom of his shirt, and pulled it over his shoulders and head.

I propped my upper body up, covering my breast with one arm—remaining modest no matter how horny I was—and ogling the shirtless Thomas.

"Like what you see?" He tossed the shirt onto the floor, his biceps and chest muscle flexing in the process.

I nodded eagerly, biting my lower lip, waiting for him to lean in for another fervid kiss.

But he got out of the bed...

I furrowed my brow, watching him walking towards the headboard, grabbing the black box. He removed the contents and set them on the bedside table.

My mouth formed an O, eyes blinking rapidly.

Fixing his gaze on me, he started unfastening his belt and unbuttoning his jeans. My eyes darted to where his hands were.

Feeling a bit embarrassed and awkward, I averted my eyes while he removed his jeans. I heard him tossing the jeans on the floor—hoping more than jeans—and then felt the mattress depressed down.

His fingers touched my chin, lifting my face to meet his enticing gaze. He kneeled towards me, still in a black boxer brief, his tanned skin, taut bare chest, and toned muscles on display. My breathing picked up just by looking at him.

He took my hand covering my breast and put it on his chest. His skin was so warm, his soft chest hair tingling my palm.

He leaned in, laying me down on my back again. His hand gently and slowly roamed along my thighs and upward underneath my dress. I gasped when his hands touched my thin satin thong again, my face turning red with embarrassment as my thong was soaked with my arousal. He dipped a kiss on my heated cheek while his hands slipped my panties off.

"Take off my brief," he whispered in my ear, and my hands moved at his command, reaching and tugging his brief down. He helped with the process and reached for a foil wrap.

I took a quick peek at his erect manhood.

Impressive!

He kneed between my legs and pulled my dress down slowly. My body slightly trembled with nervousness and anticipation. He moved atop me right away, embracing me, calming me. He kissed my temple, his body pressing against me. My thighs parted when he wedged between them.

"Are you mine tonight?" he whispered in my ear, one hand traveling down behind my knee and lifting my leg over his hip.

"Yes…" I breathed out my reply, feeling hotter and wetter for him.

His hand guided his erection to my entrance and slowly slid in.

I resisted a little, inching my hips back when he stretched me.

"Am I hurting you?" He paused and asked, his voice tender and his eyes concerned.

"Just…" I palmed his face with my hands, taking deep breaths to relax my body. "No. It's just…" I closed my eyes, the slight pain and discomfort already easing. "You are too big," I whispered, boosting his ego. "But I like it…"

"Is that so?" He leaned in and whispered in my ear, slowly gliding in further. He nibbled my ear and sucked on my earlobe, knowing how to tease my sweet spot.

I lifted my hips, already used to his thickness and needing more of him. He covered my mouth with his and slid in fully with one thrust. I drew in a sharp breath, my body tensing up.

"Are you all right?" he asked softly, one hand caressing my thigh.

I nodded, stroking his cheek when he began to move within me. His rhythm was slow, and his motion was gentle. My gaze flicked between his blue eyes, which were glazed with desire and wants. His thrust intensified, so did the hunger and needs in his eyes.

My body was eager to reach the climate again, craving for physical gratification, and then an intense emotion suddenly flamed in me, a sudden longing for emotional connection with him.

No, I can't. This is just us seeking relief... My thought did not help a bit; instead, it turned my longing into dejection.

Suddenly, his hand went underneath my knee and lifted my leg high, pulling me out of my wandering mind. My body responded to his deepening thrust before my mind did, aloud moans breaking free from me, followed by his arousing groan.

My fingers dug into his shoulder blades, my body writhing underneath him when he picked up the rhythm. My head tilted back, my eyes shut, and my lips half opened, panting for more.

A mix of emotions in me ruptured, sending into ecstasies and then tossing me in sadness and loneliness. Tears were seeping out of the corners of my eyes.

My heart ached when his warm lips touched my eyes, kissing away my tears. I palmed his backside, urging him not to hold back. He pulled almost all the way out then back in forcibly, again and again.

"I am so close..." I whispered, my breathing erratic, but the peak was elusive and unreachable...until...until his hand reached down between us and found my needing spot.

I gasped at the first touch as if his fingers had powered up all my senses and lit an enrapturing fuse inside my body. My hips writhed when he began to massage the most erogenous part of my body, building me up.

I cried out when the orgasm sent me over the top, my body trembling.

He buried his face in the crook of my neck, his movements escalating. He followed me soon after, his groan raw. I could feel him throbbing and pulsating inside me. I enclasped him as if I could bring our bodies any closer, relishing his weight on me. Both of us were panting and out of breath...

Slowly, our breathing became regular, and our heartbeat returned to normal. I felt absolutely languorous. He lifted himself up on his elbows so he could look at me, his gaze doting and satisfied. He smiled at me and then leaned down to kiss me passionately. I could feel him twitching inside me.

None of my formal boyfriends ever kissed me like this after they finished. This man made me feel cherished and adored...

"Don't move. I will be right back," he whispered, slowly pulling out.

Blinking my eyes, I watched him rolling out of the bed, walking into the bathroom, leaving the door half-open. The view was magnificent. I could not contain a silly smile spreading across my face.

Although he told me not to move, I still hastily got under the duvet. Lying naked on the bed waiting for him was sexy and all that, but I just could not do it.

He is really...amazing. Having someone putting my pleasure first is amazing. I gripped the duvet firmly over my chest, processing what just happened, and then I heard him turning on the water.

Is he leaving soon or...? I wondered, wishing he could stay here tonight, or just a little bit longer.

Ask him to say! Miss Pragmatic chipped in—perhaps I should call her Miss Reveler instead.

Can I? Maybe he likes his fancy hotel room better. I could not believe I was trying to talk myself out of the idea. I really wanted him to stay, but it would be so awkward and humiliating if he said *no* —even politely.

My thought was interrupted when the water was shut off. There he was, walking out the bathroom with a towel wrapped around his hips. He flashed me a smile as he walked closer.

"Here," he said, sitting down near my legs and lifting the duvet up to uncover me.

I bent my knees without thinking, widening my eyes and wondering what he was doing.

He showed me a wet washcloth in his hand and asked softly, "May I?"

How did I miss that? I blinked at the washcloth. Right. I was busy ogling his almost-naked body. I reached for the cloth, but he withdrew his hand.

"Allow me," he said tenderly.

I was hypnotized by his charm and tenderness. I parted my thighs, opening myself to him again. He gently cleaned my private area and inner thighs with the warm cloth, his expression concentrated. My heart was pounding in my chest as if I was having another orgasm. This was purely physical and just a casual thing with Thomas, but it was the most intimate experience I had ever had.

"All done now," he said, looking up at me. "I will be right back." He leaned in and kissed my forehead.

"Stay." The word escaped—I mentally high-fived Miss Reveler.

"Pardon?"

"Stay here tonight," I said, trying to sound confident, but a complete nervous wreck underneath the smile I pasted on.

He was silent, seemingly surprised. And his silence felt a little bit too long for me and made me feel absolutely mortified.

Just as I was going to hide underneath the duvet for the rest of my life, a broad smile spread across his face.

"I would love to," he said, reaching out and caressing my cheek.

I tilted my head, leaning into his warm palm, biting my lower lip to hold back a silly—probably a little naughty—smile.

"I will be right back," he said again, gripping the wet cloth, and walked back to the bathroom.

He had a big smile on his face when he came back. It warmed my heart, knowing that he was willing and happy to stay.

I patted on the spot beside me.

He removed the towel and placed it on the bedside table, giving me a full-frontal glimpse of his brawny body before getting under the duvet. He embraced me in his arms immediately. I snuggled up to him, letting out a satisfied and content sigh.

CHAPTER 17

> The moments of happiness we enjoy
> take us by surprise.
> It is not that we seize them,
> but that they seize us.
> ~Ashley Montagu

SLOWLY awakening, I blinked my eyes to adjust to the brightness of the room.

I had not slept with the curtains closed since I came home, even though *closed curtains* were supposed to have a strong effect on the quality of sleep. And according to many studies, sleep and mental health were closely connected. Maybe that was why I was such a mess.

But being awakened by the sound of the ocean waves and California sunshine gave me reassurances that I was home, and I needed that to keep myself sane.

Hence, I had never closed any curtains of this house since I came back.

I stretched my body and took a deep breath, feeling absolutely well rested. I had not felt this relaxed and peaceful for a long, long time.

Opening my eyes, I found myself alone in bed. Although I was not completely awake yet, I knew last night was not a dream because my body was sore…in a very good way.

I sat up and habitually looked out the glass balcony doors to confirm my whereabouts. And instead of the usual ocean view, I saw something even more spectacular…

There he was, standing straight and tall on the balcony. He was fully dressed already, holding a coffee mug in one hand and looking out over the ocean.

I smiled, feeling content.

I was reluctant to get out of bed because it felt so toasty and smelled like him, but I really needed to do my business. I looked around for a blanket and saw it on the sofa all the way by the balcony doors. So I pulled the bedsheet up and wrapped myself with it. While I got out of the bed, I noticed my clothes he tossed on the floor last night were gone.

I padded into the bathroom and closed the door behind me.

Standing in front of the vanity, I could hardly recognize myself in the mirror, hardly recognizing that radiant smile.

When was the last time I felt so happy? I thought, my smile growing broader.

My body was aroused again by the thought of last night's intimate kisses, touches, and his enchanting scent which was still lingering about me. I cupped my heated cheeks with both hands, letting the bedsheet fall down to the marble floor and pool around my feet.

I let out a satisfied sigh and grinned at myself in the mirror. Glancing down, I saw a toothbrush and an opened travel size toothpaste in a paper cup. He must have found them in the guest bathroom.

When did he wake up? Already brushed his teeth, dressed, picked up the mess on the floor, and got himself a cup of coffee or tea...

"Well, I'd better hurry," I said to myself, opening the top drawer to get my toothbrush.

I paused when I saw my prescriptions kept in the drawer. Staring at the sleeping pill bottle, I just realized that I did not take one last night and... I slept like a baby and felt so relaxed.

The sleeping pills just simply shut off my brain and put me to sleep while my whole body was still wide awake, and I would wake up with a headache or dizziness and feel exhausted.

Perhaps it's the sex... or Thomas... or both. Wouldn't it be nice if I had Thomas instead of sleeping pills? I sighed.

Shaking off what was in my mind, I turned on the water and started my morning ritual: Brushing teeth, washing face, taking a shower, and doing my morning skincare routine.

I walked into the closet adjoining the bathroom to get dressed. It was much easier to decide what to wear since I was not a nervous wreck this morning. After putting on a short lilac sundress, I double-checked everything in the mirror before I opened the bathroom door.

Thomas, the one who pampered and pleasured me last night, was leaning against the wall by the door, wearing an enchanting smile.

"Morning..." I said, heart beating a bit faster.

He leaned down to give me a soft kiss on my lips and handed me the mug. "Coffee?"

"Thank you." I received the mug and took a sip.

Ahh... Perfect sweetness and creaminess. I closed my eyes for a moment, appreciating the perfectness—not only the coffee but also the man serving it to me.

"Can I make breakfast for us?" he asked, caressing my cheek with his fingers.

"Of course..."

So good in bed and also knowing how to cook. Can things get even better than this? I thought, giving him a grin.

"Shall we?" He offered me his arm.

"Yes, we shall." I looped my hand through his elbow crease, casting down my head to hide the silly grin spreading over my face.

―――

THOMAS gestured for me to sit on a barstool and made me a cup of coffee before he started taking out ingredients from the refrigerator and pantry.

What a treat... Sitting back luxuriously in the plush upholstered barstool, I sipped my coffee and watched this beautiful man cooking in my kitchen.

"What are you making?" I asked when he was whisking together eggs, milk, cream, and seasonings.

"*Pain perdu.*" The words rolled off his tongue, sounding

something French and fancy, and he added, "With a twist."

I got the *pain,* bread in French, but still had no idea what it was. Arching my brows curiously, I took a mouthful of coffee, wondering if I should pretend I knew what he just said.

"French toast's cousin," he said, giving me a wink.

I hastily covered my mouth so the coffee would not spurt out of it while I laughed.

"I promise that you won't laugh after you taste it," he said with a cocky smile.

"Challenge accepted," I responded, grabbing a napkin to dab my mouth.

He put ham and Swiss cheese between two thick slices of French baguette and soaked them in the egg-mixture goody. While the sandwiches were absorbing the custard, he melted a generous amount of butter in the frying pan. Then he gently placed the custard-saturated sandwiches in the pan. They instantly sizzled in the bubbling butter.

I had never had savory French toast before. The smell was absolutely mouthwatering. I know I had already lost the challenge. I slid off the stool and walked into the kitchen to get silverware and placemats, just wanting to be of some help.

He leaned in to give me a kiss while I opened the drawer next to the stove.

Oh my god, this is so domestic… My heart palpitated.

With two set of silverware and a couple of placemats, I walked back to the other side of the island and set down the place settings. Getting back on the stool, I sipped my coffee, hiding my silly grin.

When the sandwiches were cooked to a perfect golden brown, he turned off the stove, dished one out, and put it on a plate.

I waited with anticipation, but he did not put the plate in front of me. He cut a small bite with a fork, stuck his fork into that little bite, and brought it towards my mouth.

I leaned in and took the bite. "Mmm…" I moaned, giving him the thumbs up.

He still did not put the plate in front of me. He took a bite himself and put the rest back in the pan; then he put the pan in the oven, assumingly, to keep them warm.

"Patient," he said and started whisking egg yolks and lemon juice in a saucepan.

Is he? No, he is not... Yes, he is! He is making hollandaise sauce from scratch! Just as I thought everything was perfect, he just made everything better than perfect.

"Is that what I think it is?" I asked in astonishment. "It's my favorite…"

"I saw so many packages of hollandaise sauce mix in the pantry," he replied, suppressing a smile, or probably a laugh.

"One will never know when she needs hollandaise sauce." I justified myself.

"Totally agree," he winked at me, finishing cooking the sauce.

He took the pan out from the oven, distributed the beautiful pain perdu on two plates, and cut them diagonally. And here came the best part: Pouring the creamy yellow sauce over the golden brown delicacy.

He placed the plates on the placemats and then sat down next to me.

"It looks and smells divine. Thank you, Thomas," I said, admiring his culinary art.

"I like how you call my name," he said, his voice suggestive.

I blushed, thinking about how many times I called his names last night. "*Gu…Guten Appetit,*" I quickly wished us a good appetite in German to conceal my bashfulness.

"Gutten Appetit, Iris."

As we were enjoying the food and each other's company, my phone started to sing *Itsy Bitsy Spider.*

DD! I just remembered he said he would call in the morning.

"It's your brother. Go ahead," Thomas said, recognizing DD's ringtone. He picked up his plate and coffee and walked to the dining table to give me some privacy. Taking the seat facing the ocean, he continued enjoying the breakfast.

"Thank you," I said, walking to the kitchen counter where I left my phone last night. I took a deep breath before picking up the singing phone and sliding the button to answer the call.

"Hi David," I answered in a flat voice, trying to sound as casual as possible—probably too casual because I sounded like a robot.

Seriously, Iris? His given name? When was the last time you called him David? It felt as if Miss Pragmatic just gave me a smack upside the head.

And I believed I just silenced my brother with his name.

I heard him clearing his throat before he said, "Morning, honey." His voice was always comforting.

"Morning."

"How are you?"

"Fine."

"Did Thomas stay for dinner after I left?"

Right to the point, Big brother. I thought and replied, "Yes."

"How was the dinner?" He pressed on.

"Good."

"Only Good?"

"Yes…," I answered, not really sure what he had expected.

"What abu—" He was interrupted by Janie because I heard her talking to him but was not able to make out what she was saying.

"Did he talk about the case at all?" He was back again.

"No."

"Did he explain why he came to visit you?"

"No."

I knew he was worried about me, but I was not ready to share anything with anyone yet. Everything was still too raw for me. I glanced at Thomas, who was seemingly enjoying the breakfast and the ocean view very much.

"No? And you didn't ask?"

What's up with all these questions? I rolled my eyes and answered, "No."

"There must be a reason for his visit. Don't you think so?"

"Sure." My voice might have come out a little annoyed.

I heard Janie's voice again, sounding as if they were whispering to each other.

"He's still there, isn't he?" DD asked just when I thought he was done with the interrogation.

I suddenly was not able to talk. I glanced at Thomas again and really believed I saw a smirk on his face.

"What's the matter, Iris? Cat got your tongue?" DD asked, his voice derisive.

"No... I mean, yes..." I had no idea what I was talking about.

"Honey, we would like to invite Thomas over for dinner. You two can come over earlier and spend some time at the ranch," he said.

"I...I'll ask him."

DD was quiet, meaning he wanted the answer right away.

"Fine. Wait a second..." I said, rolling my eyes, and walked over to Thomas.

Thomas turned towards me and said, "Yes."

"Yes? For what?"

"Whatever you are going to ask me. My answer is yes." He looked amused by my puzzled expression.

Oh, that's easy... I thought and held up the phone, ready to give DD Thomas' answer.

"Great, see you guys later," DD said and ended the call before I even made a sound.

"Have you two been chatting?" I mumbled, staring at the silent phone.

"So, what is the plan?" Thomas asked enthusiastically.

"You are invited to dinner at their ranch. What if my brother invited you to swim with sharks?" My brow furrowed.

"That would be amazing, but I would need a wetsuit," he said and took a sip of his coffee...all casually and sexily. "There is an issue though."

"What issue?" I crossed my arms across my chest.

"I have been wearing the same clothes since yesterday morning."

"Hmmm, there are some items in the guest room closet, but I am not sure if—" I was thinking aloud.

"That is quite all right," he interrupted my thought. "I will call the hotel later and ask them to bring me something," he said and finished the last bite of his sandwich.

Does DeMont Beverly Hills really offer such kind of VIP

concierge services? I tilted my head, looking at him. Not wanting to sound inexperienced with hotel services, I replied casually, "That's great. Issue solved." I hastily turned around and headed back to my breakfast so he would not see my goofy grin. I was excited that he was going to be around today.

Thomas took his empty plate and mug to the sink. "I shall bring something," he said, turning towards me. "Wine? Maybe flowers for your sister-in-law? What do their children like? Chocolate?"

It made me happy, so happy that he had accepted the invitation and thought about making a good impression.

Four hours later, someone was at the door delivering a carry-on suitcase, a bottle of wine, a big bouquet with flowers I suggested, and a fancy box of milk chocolate. I did not know how he did it, but I was very impressed.

He took a shower and was in black jeans, dark brown Chelsea boots, and a white button-up linen shirt when he came upstairs, looking classy but casual. He offered to drive us, and I could not feel more at ease to have him with me on this ride to the ranch.

CHAPTER 18

> Gravity is love and
> every turn is a leap of faith.
> ~Warren Miller

DD and Janie's two-and-a-half-acre ranch was off Laguna Canyon Road, very private and serene. And the best part was it was only a ten-minute drive from my house.

About a couple of months ago, I started driving to their ranch every Friday *by myself*. Stopping at a red light made me nervous, but I was able to manage it as long as I knew the car doors were locked and did not engage eye contact with anyone. It was a huge step for me. I could finally be out of my house without relying on others.

I loved spending time at the ranch, playing with the kids and animals—they practically were under the same category—and hanging out with my favorite and only sister-in-law. I used to pick up the kids from their schools and take them to the downtown ice cream shop all the time, and now I would have to go with either DD or Janie and wait in the car. The kiddos did not quite understand the changes, and it was too hard to explain to them what had happened to me. They were still too young to comprehend why someone had wanted to hurt their Auntie Iris.

We were warmly welcomed when we arrived. Janie was thrilled with the bouquet, and Thomas gave me the credit for choosing the flowers. I was looking forward to seeing my baby Liam, a miniature pug I adopted five years ago, but he was nowhere to be found. Janie said it was probably running around with their puppies somewhere at the ranch, and that made me feel good about leaving him here with them. I could no longer take care of him because I could not take him out for a walk and play with him at the beach anymore. And since the kids had been taking care of him while I was gone, I truly believed he was happier here.

After exchanging pleasantries, DD and Janie gave Thomas a tour of their huge house. In contrast to my modern and compacted oceanfront home, their house was rustic and spacious. After the tour, my brother suggested a walk around the ranch. They had a male horse named after the superhero Flash, two adorable pygmy goats, and many dogs.

"He is a beauty," Thomas said when DD brought Flash out of the stable. He approached Flash from the side, whispering something to him and rubbing on the side of his body and neck.

"You know horses?" DD asked.

"My family has an equine property as well. I grew up with horses," he replied.

Growing up with horses? Now, DD is going to love him.

And I was right as my brother just asked Thomas if he would like to ride Flash.

"I would love to." Thomas sounded thrilled and asked, "David, is Flash willing to carry double?"

"Yes, Jane and I ride double all the time. He's a smooth gaited beauty," DD said, gently rubbing Flash.

"Fantastic. I would like to take Iris for a ride. But, of course, only if it's all right with her," he said, turning towards me.

Widening my eyes, I looked at Thomas while all three of them were looking at me.

"Do you fancy a ride with me?" Thomas asked.

"How sweet," Janie said, gripping my arm.

"Y...yes," I answered.

"Bareback or saddle?" DD asked Thomas.

"Bareback?" Thomas asked me instead of answering my brother.

I just nodded my head, having no idea which one was better or easier.

"Bareback, please," he said to DD.

"Wonderful, I will get the bareback pad," DD replied and tilted his head towards me. "She will need to use the mounting block to get on Flash," he said and headed to the stable.

"Are you nervous?" Janie whispered in my ear, linking her arm with mine.

"Yes!" I whispered back, turning away from Thomas, who was now having an intimate moment with Flash, and dragging Janie with me.

"Just enjoy the ride and have fun," she said, smiling broadly.

"Shh…" I squeezed her arm, needing her to lower her voice.

"Sorry… Do yo—" Janie said but was interrupted by DD when he placed the mounting block by Flash. "We'll talk later, okay? Love you, hon." She kissed my temple and scampered towards her husband.

"Ready?" Thomas asked, giving me his hand.

"Yup!" I took his hand and walked towards Flash.

Then three pairs of eyes were on me again when I stood at the mounting block, waiting for Thomas to get on Flash first.

"What?" I shrugged.

"You are riding in the front," Thomas said, waiting to help me get on the block.

"I am?" My brow furrowed. I thought I was supposed to ride in the back and hang on to him for my dear life.

Thomas nodded, extending his hand to help me.

Well… I let out a breath and stepped on the mounting block while DD held Flash still.

I held the reins and got on Flash quite easily with the help from both Thomas and DD. Thomas moved the block away and got on Flash right behind me with one easy spring, his broad chest pressing against my back.

I held my breath as he held the reins by my hands, enveloping me from behind and breathing right by my ear. Although we had already been intimate with each other last night, he still made me blush and made my heart race.

"Are you ready?" Thomas whispered in my ear.

"Yes," I replied, sitting up straight, my body stiff.

"Relax," he whispered, squeezing Flash with his calves, and we were slowly heading towards the trail around the ranch.

"John, I think she's in good hands," Janie said to DD.

"John?" Thomas asked.

I smiled, turning my head around a bit so Thomas could hear me. "She is his Jane, and he is her Tarzan John Clayton." I could not see his face, but I could feel his smile behind my neck.

"I see…" he whispered as if he was remembering something.

"I will take the credit because I was the one calling them John and Jane when they started dating," I said, grinning.

He laughed, and his laughter was music to my ears…

We did not talk much on the horseback. He was in control of Flash, rocking with its movement, and I was just enjoying the ride and focusing too much on his proximity.

"Try to move with me," he said and explained that we should move in the same motion and rhythm so we would not give different and confusing signals to Flash.

I wondered if he grew up on a farm or in the countryside since he said he grew up with horses.

"Iris," he whispered in my ear.

"Yes?" I leaned back so I could hear him better.

"There is a black-tie charity gala I must attend at the hotel tomorrow night," he said, slowing Flash down.

Tomorrow night? Does that mean he's leaving later today or at least tomorrow? My mood shifted, not sure what to expect.

"Would…would you like to join me?" he asked.

"Whoa… Hold on…" I was not sure I was talking to myself or him.

"Are you all right? Do you want me to stop Flash?"

"No… I mean, yes, I am all right…" I could feel my heart pounding. He just asked me to go to a gala with him. Wasn't that what I wanted? To spend more time with him… I should be on cloud nine now, but I was not because *gala* equaled lots and lots of strangers… I did not want to decline his invitation, but I could not accept it either.

He must have noticed my hesitation because he enfolded me and whispered in my ear, "Would you consider it?"

I nodded.

"Thank you," he whispered and placed a soft kiss on the crook of my neck, sending heat straight down between my thighs.

Not wanting to tire Flash, we headed back to the stable after going around the trail once. Thomas took care of Flash and walked him back to the stable.

"So hot, let's go back inside the house," I said when he walked out.

He pressed a kiss on my hair and put his arm around my waist, so casually and naturally. We strolled back to the house in silence.

MY brother and I were so different. He was born a country boy, and I was a city girl. When he met his country girl, Jane, he fell head over heels in love with her.

He was an animal science major freshman in UC Davis and she was a high-school junior when they first met. She followed him to UC Davis and majored in plant sciences while DD continued his training at UC Davis School of Veterinary Medicine. John and Jane, they were meant to be together.

I always envied their relationship and wished I would meet my special someone when I was in high school just like Janie. But, of course, it never happened.

"Something to drink?" Janie asked when we walked into their huge family room with a stone fireplace and floor-to-ceiling windows overlooking Janie's garden. "Beer?" She looked at Thomas.

"Yes, please."

"Lemonade for you, of course." She gave me a sweet smile.

"Are you hungry?" I asked Thomas in a whisper. "I am going to make a sandwich. Would you like one?"

He nodded his appreciation.

"Janie, can I make a sandwich? We had a late breakfast, so we haven't had lunch yet."

"Of course, hon," Janie replied with her cheerful voice, linking my arm with hers. We headed to the kitchen together and left the boys to get to know each other better.

Once we got to the kitchen, Janie gave me a grinning smile and walked to the refrigerator for the beers and lemonade.

"Pour yourself a cup and take whatever you need for the sandwiches. And I will be right back." She handed me the pitcher and headed back to the family room with the beers.

I walked into the pantry to get bread first and then started to browse what they had in the refrigerator.

"So, tell me everything!" Janie startled me with her excited voice when she was back.

"About?" I pretended not knowing what she was talking about and started grabbing ham, lettuce, mayonnaise, etc., whatever I thought I might need, out of the refrigerator.

"Honey, your knight in shining armor," Janie said, her hazel-green eyes glinting with excitement.

This was why I loved Janie so dearly. She was always so lively and warm. DD was so lucky to have her as he was such a nerd.

"Janie..." I stared at the baguette I was about to cut, but my mind was completely blank, or should I say it was fully occupied by the thought of my knight in shining armor.

"Let me." She took the knife and baguette away from me. "Let's start with what you did last night."

"Janie!" My voice became a little bit high.

"Fine, you can skip that part," she teased me and started making the sandwiches for me. "Honey..." She gazed at me with her very caring eyes. "You look so happy."

"I am..." I took a deep breath, thinking about these past two days. "Janie, he makes me very happy."

"That's good," she said, patting my hands.

Only good? Janie was a big fan of exaggerating words. I was expecting words like super, amazing, marvelous, or at least wonderful. *Does she not like him?*

"I think he's wonderful," she added as if she just read my mind.

Am I really that easy to read? I frowned.

Janie finished cutting the sandwiches and placed them on the plate. She handed me one bite piece and said, "It's time to pick up the twins. Let's talk in the car." She then handed me the plate. "Go feed your knight first."

"Yes, ma'am." I took the plate and headed back to the family room. "Where are they?" I was surprised to see the room was empty.

"Oh, probably in the study." Janie was right behind me and turned towards the study. "Let's go tell the boys we are leaving now."

I put the plate on the coffee table and followed her. I heard their voices when we walked down the glass corridor leading to the study and the bedrooms.

My father helped DD and Janie design this house, and this corridor was one of my favorite spaces. It had glasses on both sides and connected the common activity rooms and the private rooms.

When we arrived at the door, my brother was telling Thomas something about horses, gesticulating passionately, and Thomas looked quite interested, arms crossed, beer in one hand.

"There you are." Janie walked right up to DD and gave him a kiss on the cheek. "We are going to pick up the twins now."

DD wrapped her in his arms, kissing her hair. "Drive safely."

I loved their relationship so much. Fifteen years and counting and still on their honeymoon…

"Hey…" Thomas walked up to me and wrapped one arm around my waist.

My heart might have just skipped a beat when his warm hand rested on my hip. I wanted to show him the same affection, but it just felt…not there yet. And I also had to remind myself again that he was not here to stay…

"I am going with Janie. Sandwiches are in the family room," I said to him, gazing at his bright blue eyes.

"Thank you," he whispered and kissed my temple.

"Let's go." Janie hooked her hand on my elbow and dragged me with her. I threw Thomas a quick wave.

I did not think we were late for picking up the kids, but Janie seemed in a hurry.

She grabbed her purse and the car key and headed out of the door.

I followed her and scurried to the big SUV, matching her speed.

"Honey, he seems like a very nice gentleman." She could not wait for another minute before she continued our conversation. "I love his accent, by the way, so charming. I was so surprised when John told me he was at your house yesterday. I was dying to call you, but he told me not to bother you two." She buzzed the front gate open with the remote and continued, "I am thrilled to see you so happy. But…"

The word but is never good… I sighed, casting my eyes down, waiting for what she was going to say. Then she was quiet…

I looked up and saw her focusing on steering the giant SUV onto Laguna Canyon Road. Watching her small frame controlling a big car was quite amusing sometimes.

"Tell me about him," she said after we were on the road.

"*But* what, Janie? You said *but* earlier."

"I want to know how you feel first."

"Well…" I stared out of the windshield. "He's very attentive and protective. He was like that back in Switzerland, too."

"How do YOU feel?" Janie asked, the stress falling heavily on the word 'you.'

How do I feel? I suddenly found no word to describe how I felt. *Happy?* "Janie… It's like…my heart would skip a beat when I see his smile. He makes me feel so…so safe and protected. We went to the beach—"

"You what?" Janie cut me off, almost shouting. "You went to the beach?"

"We took a walk."

"And…?" She took another quick glance at me, and then her eyes were back on the road.

"I didn't panic." I knew that was what she wanted to know.

"Oh, honey…" She reached her right hand over my shoulder, giving me a hug.

I leaned towards her and met her half way. "I surprised myself, too."

"That's wonderful. It's a huge step, don't you think?" She sounded so enthusiastic and excited.

Janie was with me during my early therapy sessions with Dr. Warren, just like James did when I was not able to be in the room with the just-met Dr. Thompson. I saw Janie wiping tears furtively during the sessions, but she always gave me the brightest smile when she was around me. I knew she wanted to settle me in their house and never let me leave her sight, but she also wanted me to heal, to recover, and to be the optimistic and sociable Iris again.

"I guess…" I murmured.

"Did you call Dr. Warren?"

"No… Not yet. It just happened. I don't even know what to say to her." I sighed. "I don't know, Janie. Maybe I should call her… But I really want to just enjoy some normal time with him without analyzing every minute of my feelings and anxiety level."

"I understand, honey." She took her eyes off the road for a second, gazing at me and touching my cheek with her right hand.

Janie pulled up to the curb of the pick-up zone and shut down the engine since we were early.

"I…I think he likes me," I said in a very low voice.

"Oh honey, the way he looks at you… I think it's more than that. How about you?"

"I do like him a lot, but…" I had a feeling that Janie's *but* meant the same concern I had.

Janie put her hand on mine, encouraging me to talk.

"It's so confusing, Janie." I looked at her concerned eyes, suddenly feeling emotional.

"Remember what Dr. Warren said. One thought at a time, one feeling at a time, and—"

"One day at a time," I finished her sentence.

She pulled me in, embraced me in her arms, and whispered to me, "You are the bravest…"

"It's been almost a year. And I… I've never stopped thinking about him," I finally said what was in my mind.

"Iris…" She frowned. "You've never told me that."

"I know… It's just… I hated Max so much, and then he saved me. That's a lot to take in already. I talked to Dr. Thompson about him and learned to cope with that. And then this caring police officer,

Thomas, visited me, took me out, and texted and called me everyday. And then... Poof! He vanished. I've never talked about him with anyone because I felt so confused and pathetic."

"Pathetic? Why do you think that?"

"Because I didn't think I would see him again. It just felt unrequited..."

"Does it feel requited now?"

"It doesn't matter, Janie. He lives six thousand miles away, on a completely different continent." I pulled away from her and leaned back in the seat, taking in a deep breath. "Maybe his visit can finally give me closure."

"Did he explain why he decided to visit you? I mean, after so many months?"

"He thought he owed me an apology..."

"Flying all the way here to apologize to you? Don't they have a phone in Switzerland?"

I gave her a sidelong glance.

"Coming all the way here to see you means something. It could mean—"

"Janie," I interrupted her. "I don't think... I mean, I don't want to get my hopes up. I don't even know why he's always on my mind. It can be because he saved my life and I am in his debt. And he's doing this because...because he feels sorry for what I've been going through..."

Or he saved me only because he wished he could save his sister... My mood just sank deeply.

"I am sure his job doesn't require him to fly all over the world to check on all the people he's saved."

"Well... He told me he left fedpol."

"Really? That's... Wow... Why?" Janie's forehead scrunched with disbelief.

"He's helping his family now. I didn't want to pry, so I didn't ask more questions."

"Of course..." she responded, looking pensive.

"Janie, don't worry about me," I said to her, knowing she would alway worry about my well-being, no matter what I told her. "He's going home sooner or later, so I won't…I won't get too involved with him." I looked down at my hands.

"Oh, Iris…" She held my hands. "You know what I think?"

I looked up at her bright smile, already feeling comforted.

"You should enjoy every minute with him if he makes you happy," she said. "I'm not Dr. Warren, so I probably shouldn't give you any advice. BUT…" She did the emphasizing tone again. "I remember Dr. Warren once said that facing what had happened might be able to help you deal with the triggers for the anxiety attacks. I don't remember exactly what she said word by word, but it's something like that. Maybe Thomas represents the what-had-happened because he was there." She frowned and asked, "Does that make sense?"

"It does…" I felt a burning sensation in my eyes, remembering our conversation yesterday. "Especially now that I know he was always around and watching over me…"

"He was?" Janie looked at me in astonishment.

"Yes, he was." A smile spread over my face, and tears flooded my eyes. "Maybe that's why I feel so safe and protected around him."

"Honey…" Janie stroked my hair, tears in her eyes as well. "So, I am right. He is your knight in shining armor."

"Janie," Wiping away the tears, I said to her, my voice solemn. "I really need your advice."

"Anything," she said in an emphatic tone.

"He asked me to go to a charity gala with him tomorrow night."

"A gala? What did you say?" She acted as if I was asked to the prom.

"I…I told him I would think about it because I didn't know how to say no to him. I cannot accept the invitation…" My voice suddenly became distraught. "I am like a walking bomb. What if I have a panic attack when…when he introduces me to his friends or some important people at the event? I will embarrass not only myself but also him."

She took a deep breath and looked into my eyes, her lips curving in a caring smile. And then she said to me in a calm and sincere voice, "I think you should take a leap of faith. Thomas knows your condition very well, I assume, and still wants you to be by his side in a public event. If you do have a panic attack, so what? Just leave. Call me, and I will be right there to pick you up."

Take a leap of faith... Her words were sinking in.

"Thank you," I wrapped my arms around her.

Suddenly, we were startled by a loud pounding sound on the car window, along with muffled voices outside the car.

I spun my head around and saw two little faces pressing against the car window.

"Auntie Iris!" Both kids exclaimed in unison.

Janie unlocked the car, and Johnny and Jenny quickly dived into the back seats. They were fighting to give me kisses and hugs, so I embraced them both in my arms.

"I am the luckiest auntie," I said to them.

CHAPTER 19

> The best way to pay for
> a lovely moment is to enjoy it.
> ~Richard Bach

WE did not come home until almost midnight. I was happy—over the moon kind—when he asked if he could spend another night here.

I was exhausted from horseback riding, the sun, and entertaining three kids, and I was sure Thomas was tired, too.

He reached for my hand when we walked into the house, pulling me closer.

I looked into his eyes, which were asking for a kiss.

Without a second thought, I wrapped my arms around his neck and kissed him passionately. I had been wanting to do this all afternoon and all evening when I caught him gazing at me from the other side of the room, when he gently touched my thighs underneath the dining table, and when he enfolded me in his arms while we sat in the family room chatting with DD and Janie.

"I want to give you my answer to the gala," I said when our lips parted.

"I am listening." His voice was full of anticipation.

"I am happy to accept your invitation," I said. "But… There is an issue though." I furrowed my brow, trying to imitate his tone from this morning.

"What issue?" He grinned, knowing what I was doing.

"I don't have any proper gown or dress for a black-tie event." I even shook my head and furrowed my brow to emphasize the issue.

"It's not a problem. You can pick one at the hotel tomorrow," he replied right away, a huge smile spreading across his face.

"At DeMont?"

"Yes. There are many stores there."

Those luxury boutiques at DeMont? I was a little taken back at his reply, "I... It's..."

Does he know those boutiques don't even put price tags on their merchandise? I blinked my eyes, not sure how to tell him I was not going to spend a fortune on a dress, which I probably would only wear once. *Maybe this is a bad idea...*

He leaned in and whispered in my ear. "I am glad you are going." His breath tickled me, and my mind became fuzzy when he nibbled my ear.

Maybe I can afford the cheapest dress there...

"I think there are still condoms left in the box," he whispered.

"You think, huh?" I reluctantly pulled myself away. "About the dress..." I had to be realistic. There was no way I could afford anything in Hotel DeMonet. "I will ask Janie to rent a gown for me before the event. When should I be there?"

He looked at me, frowning, as if he could not understand what I was talking about.

"I need time to rent a gown and get ready," I explained.

He smiled and cupped my face with his warm hands. "Don't worry about it. I will take care of the gown."

"No—" I was protesting because I would not let him buy me anything, but he silenced me with a fervid kiss. I sighed with gratification. This man really knew how to kiss.

My eyes were still closed when he parted his soft lips from mine.

"Come with me tomorrow morning," he said.

In a daze, I opened my eyes.

"I have to attend a meeting tomorrow morning. Bring whatever you need to get ready for the gala and come with me." He looked intense. "And an overnight bag. Spend a night with me."

I just nodded. *Is it me or was it getting hot in the house?*

"Fantastic..." He gave me a panties-soaking smile.

"Whoa..." I fanned myself. "I am really hot. Let me turn on the AC." I needed an excuse to keep a safe distance from him. His charm, temptation, kisses... All of those were making my brain foggy.

I walked to the AC control panel, which was next to the security panel in the foyer. It was in the auto mode to keep the house at a comfortable temperature.

So it was me!

"I'm going to get some water..." I said to him and headed to the kitchen. I needed cold..., no, ice water to cool myself down.

He did not follow me, but I could feel his eyes on me when I was walking away.

"I am going to take a shower first," he said.

"Sure." I turned my head to give him a smile.

"You are welcome to join me," he added. He had his hands in his pockets, smiling, and looked absolutely enchanting.

That made me speechless. I just gave him another smile and quickly walked into the kitchen, blushing.

"I am going now..." he said.

"Enjoy your shower..." I replied, and then I heard his footsteps walking downstairs.

I could not believe I was still so nervous after...after last night. Opening the refrigerator, I buried myself in it, along with my silly grin.

I did not join him in the shower even though I wanted to so badly. I needed a clear head to process what I just agreed to and gave myself a pep talk.

Just attending the gala and spending a night at the hotel... No big deal. Right? I was taking a shower in the guest bathroom since Thomas was in my bathroom. The hot water was washing away the tiredness and sleepiness but not the apprehension.

Can I really do it? I haven't gone anywhere else besides the ranch since I came home. Absently, I was washing my body with a sponge underneath the shower. The lather had already been rinsed off, but I was still scrubbing. *But Thomas will be with me...*

I smiled at the thought of him, but suddenly a growing despondency threatened to overpower my short lived happiness.

No, no, not now. Please… Let me enjoy just one…, no, two more days with him. I felt my eyes burning. I knew he had to go back to Switzerland, maybe soon after the gala, and I would… I would…

I dropped the sponge and buried my face in my hands. Maybe the sadness would go away after a good cry. It always did…

No! I tried to push the overwhelming emotions away. I would not let Thomas see my puffy eyes and my vulnerability. I knew I would miss him terribly, but I would be okay.

I shut the water off and took several deep breaths before stepping out of the shower to dry myself off.

I can do this. Standing in front of the vanity, I smiled at myself in the mirror. *And first of all, I will tell him I cannot accept the gown. I will pay for it myself.*

Wrapping myself in a bathrobe, I went back to my bedroom.

Thomas was not lying in bed but sitting on the sofa by the balcony window, looking contemplative. Then his face lit up when he saw me.

"Is everything all right?" I asked.

"It will be if you sit by me," he said, reaching for my hand.

I held his hand and sat down next to him, thinking about last night, about how everything started after I sat down next to him.

Leaning against him, I perceived furrows in his brow. Instinctively, I put my hand on his forehead, wanting to erase whatever was worrying him.

He took my hand down and kissed it tenderly. He then gazed at me, both adoringly and seriously. "There is something I need to explain to you before we go to the hotel tomorrow."

"Okay…" I was not as nervous as last night and welcomed anything he wanted to share with me.

"Remember I told you I am helping my family now?"

I nodded.

"I am here to…" He paused, looking hesitant about what he was going to tell me. "Well, let me put it this way…" And then he paused again.

Now my brow furrowed in perplexity. He made me laugh by putting his hand on my brow this time, smoothing out my scrunched forehead.

"Just tell me. Rip the bandage off," I said, giving him a reassuring smile.

He held my hands and said, "DeMont Hotels is one of my family's businesses." He then paused, presumedly expecting some kind of reaction from me.

Did I hear it correctly? His family owns DeMont Hotels? I just looked at him, processing and waiting. I knew he had more to tell me.

He cleared his throat and continued, "I am visiting all locations now, conducting assessments of the management and the properties."

No wonder he said the hotel had great potential for improvement. I scrutinized him for a bit longer.

"That's why you could have your clothes and the gifts delivered here." I exclaimed as if I had solved the biggest mystery in the world. "I was so impressed by the superb service. Now it makes sense."

Thomas grinned and kissed my forehead.

"Well… I am surprised for sure. I would've never thought… Anyway, thank you for telling me…" I was more distracted by how long he would be here since he was going to move on to the next hotel soon…

"I thought I should explain to you now because I have some business to attend to after we arrive at the hotel tomorrow. I don't want you to feel confused or surprised." He held me in his arms. "I am sorry that I did not say anything to you when I first got here."

"There is no need to apologize," I said and held his hand in mine, intertwining our fingers together. "Is that why you are invited to the gala? What kind of event is it?"

"That is another thing I am going to tell you." He gently squeezed my hand. "The hotel is hosting an annual charity gala. It…" He paused as if not sure what to tell me. "I will have to show you the information when we are there tomorrow."

"Of course." I gave him an understanding smile.

"Anything else you like to know?"

I wanted to know when he would leave but did not want to

sound too eager. How should I ask about it? Maybe talking about his job would lead to that subject?

"You said you are visiting all locations. Where have you been so far?" I wondered if he had been on the road all these months.

"This is my very first business global trip. I started from Asia two months ago," he said. "I flew home a couple of times during those two months. It would be too stressful just going from one city to another, and another."

"I would think so too…" I thought aloud.

He smiled and added, "Especially since I am working, not on holidays."

"Where did you go in Asia?" I became excited. "My maternal grandparents are in Osaka… Wait, maybe in Taipei now."

Thomas gave me a confused look.

"Oh, I should explain this. My grandpa is from Japan, and my grandma is from Taiwan. They live in Osaka and often visit my grandma's family in Taipei. And I visit them quite often…" I suddenly trailed off, thinking when I could visit them again.

Thomas gave my hand a comforting squeeze, interrupting my wandering thought.

"I… I miss them." I gave him a smile and continued, "I traveled there every year until I started college. Those were the best worry-free and being-spoiled-by-grandparents vacations." I grinned.

"Do you speak their languages?"

"Very rusty. I wish I had spent more time with them and learned their languages better." My voice sounded a bit down as I remembered the phone calls we had and their visit after I came home.

Thomas perceived my sudden quietness and gently touched my cheek with his warm fingers. "Are you all right?"

"Which cities did you visit?" I asked, trying to lighten my mood.

"DeMont has hotels in Hong Kong and Tokyo."

I was a bit disappointed that he did not visit my grandparents' cities.

Then he added, "And I was in Taipei and Singapore to evaluate the potential of opening hotels there."

"You were in Taipei!" I exclaimed.

"I was, but I did not have a chance to visit the city," he said. "Maybe you can be my guide next time."

I looked at him, forcing a smile on my face. *Be his guide next time? He's just being polite.* "Where are you going next? And when?" My voice was so little that I could hardly hear it myself.

"New York," he replied and kissed my hand. "I don't know when yet."

"And after New York?" My voice was now just a whisper.

"I will go home first before I travel to different cities in Europe," he answered, his voice soft.

I looked at him, wondering how to ask him my next question… *Will I see you again?*

No, no, no. I'm not going to do this to myself. I decided not to ask the question, so instead I said to him, "New York. Nice. I studied Urban Design and Architecture Studies at NYU for two years."

"Only two years?" He did not question why I changed the subject.

"I went there thinking I wanted to be like my dad and then realized it was not my passion. So I transferred to the Art Center College of Design and came back to California." I gave him a plain and straightforward answer as my mind was not really focusing on our conversation… It was probably still processing his surprising news regarding his family and his new job, wondering when I would see him again after he left, or worn out by the tiredness. Or missing this short period of dalliance already…

You should enjoy every minute with him if he makes you happy. Janie's voice was replaying in my head.

I should… But why am I making myself all miserable now? I let out a deep sigh.

"Are you all right?" he asked, noticing I had become quiet.

I nodded and got out of the sofa. "Do you fancy a nightcap, Sir?" I asked in his accent.

"Sure, what do you have?" he asked, looking amused.

"I have Grand Marnier, Godiva dark chocolate liqueur, Hennessy cognac…" Suddenly, I burst out laughing. "I sound like a heavy drinker, don't I? These drinks are my dad's collection. I am sure he won't mind sharing."

"What are you going to have?" he asked, smiling as he knew how little I could drink.

"Warm milk," I said, and that made his smile broader, and his smile just made my heart skip a beat.

"Then I will have the same." He stood up and followed me heading upstairs to the kitchen.

Does this have to end? Can I have this content and safe feeling for a little longer? I turned away from him so he would not see my disheartened expression.

We cuddled on the sofa, sipping the warm milk. I tried to keep our conversation light and fun, not wanting to spoil the moments if the time we had was limited.

"I know exactly how that feels!" I exclaimed when Thomas told me how often Louis, his older brother who was five years his senior, had treated him like an annoying little child. "My brother is only seven years older and still thinks I am a little baby."

It must have been very late because I kept yawning and was trying to keep my eyes open. And…

I must have fallen asleep because when I opened my eyes again, I was alone on the sofa and covered with a throw. And then I heard a very soft and familiar voice coming from the staircase. I smiled because I was not alone.

I followed the voice, descending the stairs. Thomas was sitting halfway down the stairs, softly speaking on the phone. I tiptoed towards him, trying not to make any noise.

"I am sorry, love. Did I wake you?" Covering the phone with one hand, he asked me.

"No…" I sat down next to him. "I will be quiet," I whispered to him.

He pressed a kiss on my forehead and went back to his conversation. In French!

His voice was low and soft. I stared at him in admiration, listening to his conversation as if I understood the language.

Something, something, something, Merci, and something Iris, and then something, something…

"I heard my name," I said after he hung up the phone.

"I told Louis I had to put you to bed now." He winked at me.

"No, you did not!" My cheeks burned with embarrassment.

"Mon amour, let's go to sleep." He held my hand and helped me stand up.

Mon amour… I like it.

We were like an old couple, dragging our feet back to the bedroom. I glanced at the clock on the bedside table. It was past two already. No wonder we were so tired…

I went into the bathroom to brush my teeth first. When I came out, he was already undressed and underneath the duvet.

He lifted the duvet up, inviting me.

CHAPTER 20

> The past is gone,
> the future is not here,
> now I am free of both.
> Right now, I choose joy.
> ~Deepak Chopra

WE left my house around eight in the morning because Thomas had a meeting at ten. Although the rush hour traffic was heavy, I really enjoyed the drive because I had a wonderful company and I felt normal. Then I started feeling anxious when we were approaching a fascinating Second Empire style building—the DeMont Beverly Hills. I was worrying about how I might react when we entered the hotel entrance. It had been almost a year since my last episode in Bern.

I can do this... I was too fragile then, but I was better now, much better. Plus, Thomas was by my side now. He would not let anything bad happen to me.

Just as I was boosting my courage, Thomas made a turn and drove us straight down to the basement parking lot.

I mentally let out a sigh of relief.

He soon pulled up at a plain glass double-door entrance. A young liveried porter was standing by the doors, smiling at us. He walked up to my side when Thomas turned off the engine. I instinctively lowered my head and turned my back towards the young porter, and I regretted my reaction right away...

Am I really able to handle the whole gala thing?

However, the car door remained closed. From the corner of my eye, I saw the young man still standing by the door, smiling radiantly. I sat up straight, eyes cast down, feeling awkward and self-conscious.

Thomas reached for my hands, which were held tightly together. I looked up and met his worried gaze.

"I am sorry…" I whispered.

"You never have to apologize for this." He gently squeezed my hands. With his eyes he gestured in the direction of the porter and said, "That is Chase. A brilliant young college student. I rang him this morning and asked him to wait for us here. When I am not around, he will be the only person you need to talk to if you ever need anything. Okay?"

I nodded, surprised and moved by how he had thought about all these details to make my visit easier.

He then beckoned the young man over to the driver side and got out of the car.

"Chase, our suitcases are in the boot," he said and gave him the key fob.

Thomas walked over to my side and opened the door for me. "This is the employee entrance, less crowded," he said, extending a hand for me.

"Thank you…" I took his hand and stepped out of the car.

He held my hand tightly and led us through the double-door. "We are going to take the employee lift to our floor."

There were just a few people in uniform around. They all looked so friendly, smiling at us and greeting Thomas.

Thomas never let go of my hand, not even after we stepped into the elevator. He swiped his index finger over a small black square on the side of the button panel and pushed a plain button on the very top, above the PH button. I did not ask questions as I was too curious and anxious about everything around me.

"Are you doing all right?" he whispered, caressing my cheek with his free hand.

I nodded, watching the floor display changing numbers as we ascended. It showed HM after PH.

HM?

And the door opened to a big sitting area, much like a cozy living room. Then I saw a stunning woman on a sofa looking anxiously in our direction.

She stood up, her long, shiny, blonde hair falling on her slender shoulders, her huge, light blue eyes glittering. I caught her eyes twitching when she saw me. Seemingly, she was not expecting me like Chase. And Thomas' grip on my hand tightened. I assumed he was not expecting to see her here.

Interesting...

She was wearing a white fitted suit and pin heeled sandals. The gold bangle bracelets on her wrists were jingling with one another when she walked towards us.

"Tom," she called, her voice as womanly as she looked.

I suddenly felt so...so unimpressive, unappealing, and crappy about myself. Before we left the house, I just threw on a sundress and put on my most comfortable wedges, and the only thing I wore on my face was my go-to red lipstick.

"Vic." Thomas stepped in front of me like a personal bodyguard.

She walked closer, looking at me curiously with her crystalline, pale blue eyes, seemingly waiting for Thomas to introduce me.

I was unnerved by her confident and intimidating demeanor, and her proximity was definitely making me anxious.

Thomas must have felt my trembling hand. He tugged me closer to him and led us out of the elevator.

"Iris, this is my assistant, Victoria. Vic, this is my friend, Iris," he introduced us.

"How do you do?" Victoria greeted, reaching out her hand.

"How do you do?" I drew in a deep breath and forced myself to do the same, my hand shaking.

Victoria looked a bit uneasy when she touched my shaking hand. I hastily withdrew it, and out of the corner of my eye, I saw Thomas frowning.

"I will see you at the meeting later," Thomas said to her and was eager to end this unexpected encounter. Without waiting for her response, he wrapped his arm around my shoulders and steered me towards the corridor.

"Of course, Tom," Victoria responded softly.

That's so awkward... I thought when we were walking away.

Then my attention was drawn to the elegant design of the corridor. The sitting room was furnished with flair as well, but I did not have a chance to admire it earlier.

"Here we are," he said when we arrived at a set of double doors without any number.

I looked around, realizing none of the doors had numbers like hotel rooms. "Is this floor not for the guests?" I asked.

"Correct." Reaching into his jeans pocket, he took out a metal key instead of a common hotel key-card to unlock the doors.

"Welcome to my home," he said as he opened the door.

Home? I followed him through a small foyer and then into a spacious living room.

He walked up to the curtains and pulled the heavy fabric open. California sunlight rushed in through the French terrace doors and windows.

"May I" I asked, standing by the doors, hands on the handles.

"Of course."

I unlocked the doors and pushed them out. The terrace was bigger than my living room balcony and furnished with sectional outdoor sofa and tables. I leaned against the black wrought iron railing, taking in the incredible panoramic view of the Beverly Hills area.

"My family used to travel together frequently. And we stayed at our hotels, of course. So my grandparents converted the best part of the hotels into our far-away-from-home living and working spaces." He stood behind me and embraced me. "It does not have the cool ocean breeze like your house," he whispered into my ear. "It's too hot. Let's go inside." He steered me back into the living room. I did not fight him because it was really hot.

Home? Far-away-from-home? I was contemplating what he said. "HM..." I said it out loud.

"Excuse me?"

"HM means Home!" I exclaimed. "Am I right?"

"The lift display?" He thought for a second and said, "Yes, you are right." He grinned.

Then I caught him glancing at his watch.

"Do you have to leave now?" I asked.

"Soon, but I will wait until Chase brings the suitcases here," he said, holding my hand. "Let me give you a tour."

First room we walked in was the kitchen with high-end appliances.

"Does your family really cook in the kitchens in the hotels?" I had to ask as many of my wealthy clients only wanted the top brands but never really used them.

"I do. Sometimes. My family has not traveled together for a long time, so I don't know if they do or not. My grandmother and my mother cooked quite often when we traveled… And I miss that." He opened the refrigerator and gave me a bottle of Saratoga sparkling water.

I looked at the bottle in astonishment.

"I asked the housekeeper to stock the kitchen with things you like. I want you to feel at home when you are here." Leaning in, he gave me a soft kiss.

I need to call Janie now… Everything is too perfect.

After the kitchen, we came to an elegant study with floor-to-ceiling bookcases.

"I spend lots of time here," he said. "I told you I am a boring person."

"You are not boring at all." I walked towards the bookcases and scanned the titles of the books. "How many of them have you read already?"

"Probably one-third…" He leaned against the doorframe, touching his chin, scanning the books. "Maybe half. My parents read a lot. You will be impressed by their home library."

"Are these duplicate copies of what they have in their home library?"

"Hmm…" He gave my question a thought and said, "I would say no because I have yet seen any duplicate copy. I usually take one or two books with me, and when I am done, I leave them where I am and pick another one or two to take with me. Therefore, the books are circulating. All over the world, I should say."

"That's very interesting." I walked past him, leaving the room. "Not boring at all."

He followed me down a narrow hallway. "There are five bedrooms here," he said and opened the first door. "This is my room."

I stood in the doorway, surveying the room, which was well furnished and had a sliding door open to a small terrace.

"What do you think?" he asked, standing behind me.

"Very nice," I replied. And I turned around and asked, "In which room will I be sleeping?"

"You can pick any room, but I would very much prefer you to sleep in this one," he whispered in my ear.

I could feel his warm breath right by my neck. I tilted my head slightly, enticing him.

Just as his lips touched my skin, the doorbell chimed.

"Must be Chase," he said and placed a kiss on the crook of my neck.

THOMAS went to his first meeting after Chase left, and I made myself at home and unpacked our suitcases in his room. When I opened the closet, I noticed there were just three suits, a few shirts and jeans hung there.

Of course, he's traveling. I closed the closet, letting out a downhearted sigh. The thought of our time together coming to an end soon saddened me.

To lighten my mood, I connected my phone to the Bluetooth speaker in the living room and played my playlist, letting my favorite songs occupy my mind and my saddened heart while I wandered around this huge hotel suite.

"Anybody home?" Thomas' soft and low voice was at the door.

I walked briskly out of the study and jumped right into his open arms. He was only gone for less than two hours, and I did not like it at all. How would I feel after he left?

"This is nice," he said and kissed my forehead. "I would like to show you something." His voice sounded excited. "It's for tonight's gala." He opened the thick folder in his hands after we sat on the sofa.

The title, Elizabeth and Laila Foundation, on the cover page struck a strong emotion in my heart. I ran my fingers over it, feeling overwhelmed.

"Elizabeth is my mother," he said, his voice sorrowful.

I gazed at him, reaching my hand to touch his cheek.

He leaned into my hand, closing his eyes and inhaling deeply.

My heart was aching as he looked so hurt, somehow powerless.

He opened his blue eyes again, glinting with adoration. He took my hand and kissed its palm.

I drew in a deep breath, moved by his affection.

"My father…" His voice was full of emotions. He cleared his throat and continued, "My father could not recover from losing my sister and mother in such a short period of time. He buried himself in work for years." He looked down at the folder. "Eva and Louis—" He paused and looked at me as if pondering what to say. "Eva… She's my sister-in-law. They proposed a charity foundation idea to my father, and he jumped right into it. It really helped him because he believed he finally was able to do something for them. Give me a second. I will be right back." He got up and walked into the study.

He soon came back with some photos in his hands. Sitting back down by my side, he showed me the photos. "My mother and sister," he said, his voice full of love.

They were so beautiful, and their smiles were so sunny…

Both of them had rich dark curly hair with golden highlights, diamond shaped faces, and big brown eyes. In one photo, his mother and sister were facing the camera and making faces together; in another one, his sister wrapped her arms around his mother, kissing her cheek; and in the last one, they were sitting on a park bench arm in arm, and his sister had her head on his mother's shoulder.

Thomas fixed his eyes on the photos, which was reminiscent of his beloved mother and sister. He looked lost in thought, in those beautiful memories he had with them.

Gently, I touched his hand.

"Now you know I look like my father. I don't have my mother's beautiful features." He chuckled.

I think you are beautiful... I gazed at him.

He sat closer and started explaining the pages in the folder to me: Reports of contributions and prospective contributions, event proposals, details of anti-human trafficking and cancer research organizations...

Tears welled up in my eyes, and I found myself short of breath.

Thomas held me in his arms, kissing my temple and stroking my hair.

And for no reason, or too many of them, I broke down and cried in his embrace.

"I...I am too luc...lucky... compared to...to so many victims," I said, choked with emotion.

I had been trying to be strong and put everything behind me, but the overwhelming emotions and horrific memories always came back when I was least expecting them. So I suppressed them and refused to remember and talk about the details because they still frightened me.

Thomas cuddled me in his arms, whispering sweet and comforting words.

No one could comfort me like he did because he knew exactly what I had been through. Furthermore, he also understood the unspeakable suffering the victims' families had because he had experienced it himself.

"I am fine..." I breathed out the words, still sniffling.

"I thought these would help you." He gazed at me, wiping my tears with his thumbs.

"They do, Thomas. They do," I said, looking at the folder again. His family's story made me think about mine. My parents and DD looked so thin and pale when they arrived at the embassy. I later learned that they had reached out to all the U.S. embassies in Europe, the press, social media, etc., trying to find me.

"By the way, we will be sitting at the same table with my uncle —"

Speaking of changing the subject…

"What?" I interrupted him.

"The dinner." He looked amused by my reaction and added, "We are seated at the same table with my uncle and aunt and some of my father's friends."

"I…I didn't expect to meet any of your family…" I frowned.

"Just my Uncle Alain and his wife Nora. I promise you they are a very delightful couple."

"Okay…"

"We need to get you the gown," he changed the subject. Again. "I am not sure if they are ready or not…"

"They? What do you mean? Do I need more than one?" I was confused as we had not talked about this since last night.

"The boutiques will put together several outfits for you. You can try them on and choose one."

"Oh…" I was not expecting such special treatment. I guessed that came with being the date of the owner's son.

"I will bring them here after the next meeting, and you can pick one for tonight."

"That sounds wonderful," I said, trusting whatever he had prepared for me.

CHAPTER 21

> Odours have a power of persuasion stronger than
> that of words, appearances, emotions or will.
> ~Patrick Süskind,
> Perfume: The Story of a Murderer

THOMAS was gone again.

I decided to take a shower so I would have plenty of time to get ready later. My phone was chiming notifications of either missed messages or calls when I walked out of the bathroom.

I scampered to get my phone, thinking they were from Thomas.

Oh, from Antonio... I was disappointed.

Oh my god! What kind of friend am I? I already put Thomas before Antonio.

He called twice and sent three text messages. I tapped the screen to read his messages.

Antonio: Call me.

Antonio: Where are you?

Antonio: ???

I had never hesitated to call or text Antonio before. But I am holding the phone in my hand now, thinking about ignoring him. I was not ready to tell him and Jojo about Thomas yet, but I did not want to lie to them, either. He knew I usually stayed at the ranch over the weekends and would sometimes just drop by. I hoped he would not do it today. What if he did? What would DD and Janie tell him?

I groaned and quickly typed a reply.

Me: What's up?

I threw the phone on the bed and started getting dressed.

His reply came almost instantly.

Antonio: Need a place to hide tonight.

I rolled my eyes, typing my reply.

Me: I told you to get a hotel room and not to bring them home.

He was a woman-magnet and sometimes attracted pretty aggressive ones, although I still blamed him for giving out misleading signals.

Antonio: Carmella is here. My ears are on fire.

I laughed and sent him a laughing emoji. Carmella was his oldest sister. And she had been more of a mother than a sister to him after their parents got divorced.

Antonio: Not funny. I will be there before dinner.

Me: I'm not home. Make yourself at home.

He had my key, knew the security code, and never had a problem just showing up at my house anyway.

Antonio: I will meet you at the ranch. We can go home together.

Scheiße! What should I say now? I paced around the room for a couple of minutes and decided to go with the flow.

Me: I'm not at the ranch.

He did not reply right away, but the three dots kept blinking. And finally...

Antonio: What's going on?

I frowned, slumping into the sofa by the window. *Fine, here we go...*

Me: Remember the undercover agent I told you about? He is here. I am with him right now.

My phone rang, Antonio's goofy face appearing on my phone screen. He dressed as Freddie Mercury last Halloween, and the fake mustache still cracked me up.

"Hey..." I answered the phone, my voice calm.

"What do you mean *He is here, I am with him right now?*" Antonio's voice was serious and demanding.

"It means exactly what the words say." I could sound harsh as well.

"I am coming over right—"

"I just told you I'm not home," I cut him off, my voice annoyed.

"Where are you?"

"I am fine. He's not going to harm me. He saved me. Remember? My brother and Janie met him yesterday."

Then, he was silent. I waited and then started feeling uncomfortable. He was my best friend, and I was estranging him because of Thomas.

"You there?" I asked, my voice no longer harsh. He did not answer me, but I heard a noise sounding like he was pacing. I sighed and said, "He surprised me, Antonio. A very nice surprise… I will tell you all about it when I get home, okay?"

"Where are you?"

"In his hotel…" Somehow it did not sound quite right, so I added, "He invited me to attend a fundraising gala with him to—"

"A gala? And you are all right with that?" he interrupted me, his voice genuinely concerned.

"Yes, I am. I promise. It's a fundraiser for his family's anti-human trafficking and cancer foundation. It's very important to me. I…" I sighed. It was just so hard to explain everything on the phone now.

"Why am I not convinced? A gala? Seriously?" He was the one who sounded annoyed now.

"I am doing great. Really. Do you think my brother would let me come here if he doesn't trust him and doesn't think I can handle it?"

He let out a deep sigh and said reluctantly, "Fine."

"Hey, don't make me feel bad about stepping out of my comfort zone." I suddenly realized that I did not owe him any explanation. Yes, he was my best friend, but this was my decision. I did not need anyone's permission or approval.

"Iris…"

"I will talk to you when I go home. Say hi to Carmella for me."

We said goodbye, not pleasantly.

"Aaugh!" I exclaimed in frustration, running my fingers through my still damp hair.

Not wanting to dwell on the conversation with Antonio and feel irritable, I went back to the bathroom to dry my hair and do my skin care and makeup. I sprayed my favorite perfume, Quelques Fleurs, on the inside of my wrists and behind my ear lobes, inhaling the sensual floral scent. I let out a sigh of relaxation, my mood already lightened.

I decided to occupy myself by reading a book, so I went into the study to see if I could find a title that would catch my eyes. And... It was quite discouraging when I found that most of them were in either German or French. Then I saw *Perfume: The Story of a Murderer*, and my eyes glinted with excitement.

I tried to read this novel in its original language German once, but my elementary proficiency really ruined the fun. Hence, I watched the movie so many times instead.

Why have I never thought about reading the English version?

Sitting on the sofa by the window, I dived into the story instantly. In the fourth paragraph of chapter one, I was traveling to the filthy city full of rotten and putrid smells, where Jean-Baptiste Grenouille was born...

Suddenly, a chime of the doorbell startled me, and it was followed by Victoria's voice.

"Ms. Iris, Victoria here." Her soft voice was behind the door. "I have the gowns for you."

But... Thomas told me he would bring the gowns back here. I slowly walked out of the study and stood by the corner of the foyer, not sure what to do. He emphasized he would not send anyone else but Chase.

Maybe he thought I met Victoria already...

She rang the doorbell again, a really loud peal.

I knew the sound was not really louder. It was me... It was all in my head and was giving me a headache. I decided to ignore her. She could call Thomas if she wanted to. I walked back to the study, closed the door, and settled myself on the sofa again. Picking up the book, I was back in eighteenth century Paris...

The closed door did not block the doorbell; and she was pretty persistent.

What's her issue? I started to feel annoyed, so I put on my AirPods.

She's just doing her job... Feeling guilty for not wanting to answer the door and also not wanting her to get into any trouble, I texted Thomas and apologized to him.

The doorbell soon stopped ringing.

That's fast, I thought and went back to the story.

Before my mind could travel back to Paris, where fireworks were set off to celebrate the anniversary of the king's coronation, my phone started to sing Calum Scott's *You are the reason*—the special text tone for Thomas. I checked the message right away.

Thomas: Don't worry about it. Meeting just ended. I still need to speak with the managers. Be back as soon as I can.

I would not worry about it because I was going to find out what was the scent that Jean-Baptiste had never smelled before…

I had moved from the study to the dining area, then from the dining area to the living room. Now I was lying on the sofa, deeply involved in Jean-Baptiste's journey and completely lost track of time.

And then I heard voices outside the door.

"Thank you, Chase. I can bring them in myself."

Thomas' voice made me throw the book on the coffee table and sprint towards the door. I hastily opened the door.

"Hello." Thomas gave me a broad smile, and the smile spreading across my face was as bright as his.

"Ms. Iris." Chase gave me a respectful smile.

"Hi Chase," I replied perkily. This was the third time I saw him today, so I was not nervous anymore; and besides, my focus was on Thomas.

"Thank you, Mr. Torian." Chase accepted the tip from Thomas and gave us a nod before walking away.

"Those are for the gala?" My eyes were on a hotel luggage cart parked against the wall.

"My tuxedo and your gowns," he said and pushed the cart into the room. "And some accessories."

I helped him push the cart in and closed the door behind us, thinking about Victoria being here with all these earlier. Now I really felt bad for not answering the door earlier.

"What were you doing when I was gone?" He leaned in and gave me a kiss on the cheek.

I tugged the lapels of his suit jacket and pulled him back for a real kiss—a toe-curling one. I could feel his muscles tensing up, his hands roaming over my back and one moving lower to palm my buttock.

I had to push him away to get air but only managed to press my hands on his chest as he held me tighter. My eyes were glinting with mischief.

"I can really get used to this." He leaned into the crook of my neck and drew in my scent audibly. "You smell so wonderful." He gently squeezed my butt.

My gaze was fixed on his twinkling blue eyes, debating if I should keep going or put out the fire.

"Did you have lunch yet?" he asked tenderly, his hands moving from my butt to my arm—putting out the fire.

Dang it!

"Lunch?" I glanced at the clock on the wall. It was already after two o'clock. "Wow, I didn't realize it's so late."

"Do you want to order room service?" he asked, one hand moving to my lower back as he steered me back to the living room.

"No, I'm not hungry. I will have some fruit in a bit." I said, leaning against him.

"Das Parfum…" He mumbled, picking up the book from the table. He sat down on the sofa, holding my hand with his free hand and pulling me down to sit on his lap.

"I am hooked!"

"I am glad you found something interesting to do." He glanced at the front and back covers of the book. "I was worried you might be bored."

"I am pretty low-maintenance," I said, giving him a wink.

"Speak of that," he said, putting the book back down on the table. "I hope those can satisfy your demands if you are low-maintenance." He tilted his head towards the luggage cart, giving me a one-sided grin.

I turned my head to look at the loaded cart, wondering what was in those garment bags and boxes. I had been to many fundraising events before but never a black tie gala.

His hand gently stroked my hair, causing me to turn my head back to look at him.

He furrowed his brow and said softly, "I apologize for Victoria. She shouldn't have come here."

"No, please. No need to apologize for her." I mirrored his burrowing brow. "She just tried to help."

He casted his eyes down, not saying a word.

I did not like it, did not like that he thought he needed to apologize for his assistant, and did not like that his mood had changed because of her. Our time together was limited. I did not want to waste it on any other person.

"Can I look at the dresses?" I asked, my voice excited, hoping to lighten the mood.

"Of course!" His face lit up.

I stood up from his lap and walked briskly towards the cart.

He followed me and helped unzip the garment bags.

These are beautiful... I stroked the soft chiffon, laces, and silk. "Did...did you pick out all of these yourself?" I asked, hoping he did not give Victoria this task. Maybe I was jealous of her because she got to work by his side, and because I was rather insecure now.

"I gave Eva some ideas last night, and she managed to have those ready for you."

"All the way from Switzerland?" I asked in astonishment.

He nodded and asked, "Do you like them?"

"They are so beautiful. Your sister-in-law has a very sophisticated and elegant taste." Looking up at him, I wrapped my arms around his waist, my head leaning against his chest. "It's so sweet of her. Thank you and please thank Eva for me."

"You are more than welcome." He placed a soft kiss on my forehead. "Would you like to try them on now? There is still time if you need any adjustment."

I nodded enthusiastically.

We pushed the cart into the bedroom together.

"I will take these," he said, picking up a garment bag and a shoebox from the cart. "I will put them in another room and get ready there later. Call me when you are ready to show me the dresses."

I nodded and closed the door after he stepped out of the bedroom. Looking at those trendy and elegant dresses, I started to feel a little panicky as there was no way out of this now.

The first dress I tried on was Oscar de la Renta's sleeveless black velvet dress with a deep-v neckline. Eva even chose a pair of four-inch black Jimmy Choo sandals topped with a crystal knot for this dress. I fell in love at first sight with the shoes—me and my shoe obsession.

"Thomas?" I opened the bedroom door and walked out in the first dress.

"In here," he replied, his voice coming from the living room.

I walked towards him and stopped when I saw him.

Standing from a distance, he gazed at me in admiration. "How do you like it?" he asked.

I looked down at the dress and said, "It was very flattering. It's just…" I looked at my chest and sighed. "I wish I had bigger boobs."

He chuckled. "I like your—"

"Don't say it. Next one!" I interrupted him, whirling around, and headed back to the bedroom.

Second dress was Tony Ward's champagne tulle dress embroidered with beaded gold and silver lines and embellished with gold and silver sequins on the long sleeves and waistline. Eva matched it with Valentino Garavani nude sandals with pop gold flowers. Even though I had never met Eva, I knew already we were going to be best shoe-friends!

I really like this one… I thought when studying the dress in the mirror.

"What do you think?" I slowly walked up to Thomas, the tulle skirt billowing in the movement.

"Iris… You look fantastic." His eyes brightened up when he saw me. "You seem to fancy this one," he said and walked closer.

"I do. Very much." I twirled to show off the flowing gown.

He gave me a radiant smile.

"Okay, two down and one more to go," I said and headed back to the room.

The third one was Elie Saab's long sleeve blush hue gown with luxe lace top and chiffon flowing skirt. It looked too much like a wedding dress to me. When I put it on, the back buttons were hard to get to. Someone would have to help me with this dress; and I only have one person to help me here.

"Thomas, can you lend me a hand, please?" I placed my hands on my chest to hold the lace top in place and called for his assistance.

"At your service." He appeared by the door right away, holding a half-empty beer bottle in his hand.

"This one is a bit tricky." I turned around and showed him my back.

He walked in, put the beer down on the dresser, and stepped close to me. He ran his fingers on my bare back softly, my skin tingling all over from his touch.

"Up or down?" he asked softly.

"Up please," I replied in a playful tone.

"Are you sure?" he asked and slowly pulled the lace down, dipping kisses on my bare shoulders. And he slowly removed the lace top and lowered the dress. And I did not stop him...

I folded my arms over my chest to cover my breasts. Holding my breath, I stepped out of the dress. Now I had nothing but a nude silky thong and high-heel sandals...

I could hear him breathing heavily, his warm breath inches away from my neck. When his hands gently and slowly roamed along my back, all the hairs on my skin became erect to his touch.

He slowly walked around me and stopped in front of me. He lifted my chin so I could look at him, his direct gaze making my heart palpitate.

"You look amazing," he whispered.

I bit my lips so I would not say something witty like *I am practically naked.*

"You are such a distraction..." he said softly.

I blinked my eyes, grinning.

"I could not focus at work. Neither in my office, nor in the boardroom." His eyes glinted seductively. "All I have been thinking about is you." He leaned in and gave me a tender kiss, sending heat through my body.

Keeping one arm over my breasts, I reached one hand to touch his cheek. I closed my eyes, enjoying his alluring kiss.

I knew exactly what was going to happen, and I wanted it so badly. This man not only gave me an emotional refuge but also ignited the fiery passion that I did not realize I had ever had.

He took my hand from his cheek and placed a kiss on the palm. I opened my eyes when he placed one hand gently on the small of my back and guided me towards the bed. His sapphire gaze never left my eyes.

He helped me sit on the edge of the bed and knelt down in front of me. My legs parted as he moved closer in between them.

"I want to pleasure you," he whispered in my ear.

My heart rate was rising, anticipating what he meant by *pleasuring me*.

He removed my arm that was covering my breasts and leaned in. He kissed my cleavage first and then trailed kisses to my breasts.

I moaned aloud when he took one nipple in his mouth, tingles spreading through my body.

Unashamedly, I watched him licking and sucking me, my fingers threading through his thick dark hair.

"You like that?" he whispered, looking up and meeting my blatant gaze.

"Yes..." I breathed out the words.

I was never good at verbal expression during intimacy. As a matter of fact, I had never done it before. However, this man just naturally brought it out of me.

"And this?" he whispered again, his mouth back on the nipple, and one hand playing with the other aroused peak.

"Mm-hmm... Yes..." An affirmative response escaped from my throat.

His lips moved up, trailing kisses up to the crook of my neck and then my sweet spot.

I moaned, basking in the pleasure of his kisses.

He held me and slowly laid me down on my back. He pushed himself up with one arm, caressing my cheek with one hand, his gaze alluring.

"Thomas..." I whispered his name with lust.

He leaned in and slowly and tenderly trailed his kisses on my lips, chin, cleavage, stomach, and navel. His hands rested on my hips, his fingers playfully tugging my thong. Slowly, he removed the only covering I had and revealed me completely.

I inhaled sharply.

He gently lifted my left leg onto his shoulder. His fingers found my erogenous spot and gently moved in a small circle while he kissed my inner thigh softly.

My lustful thirst wanted him, more of him, but my instinct was to close my thighs.

He then moved his kisses lower, urging me to open myself wider for him. A soft crying sound escaped me when his fingers were replaced with his soft and warm lips.

I grasped the duvet underneath me, lifting my hips instinctively. My breathing picked up, and a rush of arousal ran through me.

He sucked and licked me hungrily. The sensation of his lips and tongue on me was nothing I had ever had before, my body responding to him in its own keenness. I murmured incoherently, my hands fondling my breasts, my hips writhing.

"*Tu es si belle*," he whispered something in French, something pretty or beautiful, but my mind was completely boggled by his *pleasuring* and did not really care what it meant.

Both his hands moved underneath my bottom, lifting me higher and closer to him. His mouth was back on me, devouring me.

My mouth half opened, drawing in air, my heart rate quickening. I felt all my muscles tensing up...

He sucked my erogenous spot keenly while slowly entering a finger in me.

"Thomas..." I moaned his name. It was so intense that I reached for him, not sure if I needed him to stop or give me relief. I tugged at his hair, my hips thrusting in its own eagerness.

I cried out when a forceful spasm took over my body. He sucked me harder, all my sensations intensifying. Crying out again, I had never had an orgasm so vigorous and seemingly going on forever.

When my body finally started to relax, I felt Thomas moving atop me. I opened my heavy-lidded eyes and met his conceited smile. He lifted himself up on his elbows so he would not put his weight on me, but his erection was hard against my inner thighs.

"Did I pleasure you?" he asked.

My face heated up. I bit my bottom lip, nodding.

Although my heart was still pounding, my chest heaving, I reached my hand between us to touch him.

"Mmm…" He shut his eyes for a moment, his manhood twitching in my palm. "Much as I would love to continue this, we don't really have time…"

"We don't?" I gently gripped him, making him chuckle.

"The dress needs alterations. We need to get re—" He groaned as I stroked him through his trousers. "You do understand that we are the guests of honor at the gala this evening, right?" He gave me a rueful smile.

Pouting, I withdrew my hand.

He kissed my forehead and the tip of my nose before pushing himself up and said, "I am going to take a cold shower now."

I burst out laughing.

CHAPTER 22

> Believe you can and
> you're halfway there.
> ~Theodore Roosevelt

PUTTING on the final touch—my white gold Caresse d'Orchidées earrings with which I rewarded myself when I finished a New York penthouse project a few years ago. I brought them with me because I knew its classic motif, delicate design, and feminine appeal would match everything I wore. I stood in front of the full-length mirror and was pleased to see that my precious collection complemented the Tony Ward dress beautifully.

I opened the bedroom door, feeling excited and anxious.

Thomas was standing behind the sofa reading an index card, probably notes for his speech. He put the index card down when he saw me. If his smile could make my heart skip a beat, the look of him in that tailored-fit black tuxedo would stop my heartbeat completely.

"You look..." he said, holding eye contact with me. "Perfect." Slowly, he walked towards me.

"You look dashing..." I repaid the compliment.

Is that a faint blush flashing across his face? My heart was warmed by these rare moments when he showed his shyness.

He held my left hand with his right hand and put his other hand on my waist, gently pulling me closer.

He smells so alluring... My gaze was fixed on him, draping my right hand on his shoulder.

He started to sway slowly, even though there was no music. I let him lead, feeling content.

"I asked the event manager to host the gala tonight," he said softly. "So I will be by your side the entire evening,"

"You don't have to do that."

"I want to," he said, holding me closer to him. "And I will make my speech where we sit. Please let me know at once when you start feeling anxious. We will come right back here."

I gazed at him, suddenly feeling emotional.

"Let's just enjoy each other tonight..." He leaned in and kissed my forehead.

I nodded and leaned my head against his chest, slowly swaying with him.

WE took the employee elevator down to the ground floor. He led us through a narrow hallway and came to a set of metal double doors.

"Ready?" He looked at me.

I would be lying if I said I was not nervous and tense. But he had done so much for me... I would try to manage my anxiety and go through the night with him.

"Yes..." I gave him a forced smile.

He kissed my temple and interlocked our fingers. Giving me a skeptical smile, he opened the door to a bustling pre-function area.

Instinctively, I stepped back, my heart palpitating.

Thomas let go of the door. Smoothly, the heavy duty door swung back and closed with a clang, immediately muffling the babel of voices.

"Are you all right?" he asked, his voice soft and concerned.

I can do this... I took a deep breath, giving him an apologetic smile. "Can I have a minute, please?"

"Of course. Take as long as you need," he said, turning himself to face me. His ultramarine eyes spoke of apprehension.

I shouldn't worry him... I reached my hand to cup his face, my head tilting to a side, my brow furrowing. "I am sorry..."

"Don't be. We don't have to do this. Let's go back upstairs."

"No." I drew in another deep breath and put on a bright smile. "I can do this... I have my personal bodyguard with me." I leaned in and gave him a kiss.

He did not look convinced. Taking my hands, he placed kisses on them.

"Thomas, I know I can do this," I reassured him.

"All right. But if anything bothers you, you must tell me immediately." His voice was dominant.

"Yes, Sir." I gave him a witty response, wanting to lighten the mood. And it successfully made him smile.

He held my hand and pulled the door open again, and we stepped into the pre-function area together.

People in formal attire were flowing towards the grand ballroom. Thomas deliberately walked us along the wall to avoid meeting anyone he knew. As we approached the already-crowded ballroom foyer, he stopped and turned to me.

"Are you doing okay?"

I nodded nervously.

He placed a kiss on my temple, wrapped his arm around my waist, and guided me across the pre-function area and into the ballroom foyer.

First person to greet us was Victoria who seemingly was expecting Thomas' arrival. She was dressed in a stunning bright red strapless mermaid gown. She gave me a Pan Am smile and started to address issues regarding the evening to Thomas.

I was listening to them first since they were speaking in English. All issues sounded really minor, but I assumed it was her duty to inform Thomas of all the details. Many people walked past us, some stopping to greet Thomas and Victoria. I squeezed his hand tightly when some people brushed past me. The voices around me started becoming waves of buzzing noise.

Oh no... I took several short breaths, trying to suppress a surge of anxiety.

Thomas pulled me closer to him, interrupting the rising panic in me.

I gazed up and met his doting eyes, my accelerated heartbeat slowing down.

"I am sorry about that. I promise I am all yours this evening," he said softly.

I broke our eye contact and looked around, realizing Victoria was gone.

"Should we?" he asked.

I nodded, and we strolled into the ballroom.

The ballroom was splendid, and the atmosphere was sophisticated. The theme tonight was Secret Garden, and the room was decorated with fresh flowers and greenery. Thomas told me all the plants and supplies would be donated to the local shelters, nursing homes, and hospitals after tonight's event to make the best use of everything.

"Thomas." A lady in a black lace gown approached us.

"She's our event manager Mrs. Alyssa Parker," Thomas whispered to me.

I gave him an appreciating smile, preparing myself for the introduction.

"I tol—" Thomas stopped mid-sentence as the event manager walked up to us. "Alyssa," he greeted her. "Please let me introduce you to Ms. Iris De Waal." He then faced me and said, "Iris, this is Mrs. Alyssa Parker. Our event manager."

"It's my pleasure to finally meet you," she said in an enthusiastic voice.

Finally? Has he mentioned me to her?

"Nice to meet you, Mrs. Parker," I responded, anxiously expecting she was going to shake my hand or cheek-kiss me, but she did not do either.

"I just came over to meet you and also let Thomas know that everything is in place," she said and gave us a warm and sincere close-lip smile.

"Thank you, Alyssa," Thomas said with a nod of appreciation.

"It's my pleasure," Alyssa said, holding her palm over her chest. "Enjoy the reception. I will see you later." She then walked towards the stage.

I wondered if Thomas had mentioned my condition to her. I did not mind if he did, but I would really appreciate it if he would ask me first. After all, it was my privacy.

Thomas cleared his throat after Alyssa walked away and whispered to me. "I hope you don't mind that I told her you were sort of a germaphobe and preferred not to be touched."

This man... I covered my mouth, trying to contain my laughter. "Not at all..." I chuckled.

He grinned and said, "Would you like to walk around before the seated-dinner starts? There is a silent auction room."

"Sure, although I'm not touching anything because I am a germaphobe." I winked at him.

He laughed and gave me a gentle hug.

Walking by the cocktail bar, he took two glasses of champagne for us before we entered the auction room.

The donations were impressive, as grand as a Mercedes Benz SUV and a luxurious trip to Fiji Laucala Island. I was not loaded, but I was sure I was able to make a contribution to such a good cause, but of course, not the Mercedes Benz or the hundred-thousand-dollar vacation.

We slowly walked through the room. He either wrapped his arm around my waist or held my hand. I really appreciated his thoughtfulness in making me feel safe in such an environment that I thought I could not handle anymore.

Was I anxious? My heart had been racing since we stepped out of his hotel suite. But I wanted to do this for him, and I knew I could do it as long as he was by my side.

I stopped at an elegant dinner-table-setting display and read the information. It was a certificate for a full-course dinner for two in the stylish Italian restaurant right here in DeMont.

"If I win the bid, I will take you out to dinner," I said.

"Deal." He smiled.

I wrote $2,000 on the bid sheet.

"Fantastic." He placed a light kiss on my hair.

We continued to browse around, commenting on some unique items screaming California, such as pet sitting and boarding, personal surfing sessions, private boat cruise with cocktails, etc.

"Excuses me, Tom." Suddenly, a familiar and honeyed voice startled us.

Both of us turned towards Victoria, and Thomas' hand was on my waist almost instantly.

"I was hoping to find you here," Victoria said, a radiant smile spreading across her flawless face. She then gave me a polite nod, but her gaze was back at Thomas right away. "Can I borrow you for a moment? I just received a call from Mr. Nelson's attorney, Mr. Durand." She turned towards me again and gave me an apologetic smile, which never reached her eyes.

An attorney? That sounds serious. I suddenly felt uneasy, worrying about being left alone since Thomas needed to discuss business with her.

"They can give me the answer on Monday." Thomas' tone was grating.

"He's requesting to discuss a few details before Monday." She stepped closer and spoke to him in a very soft voice, which bothered me a little. Well, maybe a lot.

Fine, it bothered me a lot. Her voice sounded too intimate. I leaned into his embrace, claiming what was mine.

"I already gave them my answer. You can tell him there is no room for negotiation," Thomas said to her with a straight face, which reminded me of the expression Max always had.

Victoria responded back in French.

That's kind of rude. I was pretty sure it was because she did not want me to hear it, so I averted my eyes, pretending I was not interested in their conversation.

"I wish to enjoy the evening and the rest of my weekend," Thomas replied in English, respecting my presence.

"Of course. I will let Mr. Durant know. Enjoy your evening." Victoria switched back to English. She gave us a nod and walked away gracefully.

"Everything all right?" I asked.

"I apologize for all these interruptions." He sighed.

"No apology necessary. She's just doing her job," I said to him. "It sounds pretty serious. I mean... An attorney is trying to talk to you."

"Not serious at all." He gazed down at me. "Just a business deal."

"Are you sure you don't need to attend to the business? Am I… Am I holding you back?" I did not know why I said that, but that was how I felt when he told me he was not going to host the event and would be by my side all evening. Basically babysitting me.

"Of course not. Iris…" He frowned, looking at me sincerely with his beautiful blue eyes.

"But I—"

He put his finger on my lips, stopping me from talking. "I told you I would be by your side the entire evening, didn't I?"

I nodded.

He leaned down and gave me a kiss on my lips, not shy about public displays of affection at all.

"Let's go and bid on more items." Wanting to lighten our moods, I changed the subject. "I am going to bid on some more items on behalf of my parents and DD."

"Laucala Island is a great holiday destination," he said.

"I am going to enjoy it on behalf of them also if they win the bid." I chuckled.

After we circled around the auction room, Thomas led us to our table, which was right by the stage. Two people were already seated when we arrived.

An old gentleman spotted us before we approached the table. He stood up, opening his arms and called Thomas, "Tommy!" And the lady sitting next to him turned around, a huge smile spreading across her beautiful and elegant face.

Tommy?

Thomas' eyes glinted with contentment when he greeted the old gentleman with cheek-kisses. He leaned in to cheek-kiss the lady right after. They then exchanged some words in French.

"Iris, let me introduce you to my Uncle Alain and Aunt Nora." He held my hand and pulled me closer to him.

I put on a big smile, my heart racing.

"*Oncle* Alain, *Tante* Nora, this is my dear friend, Ms. Iris De

Waal," he said to the couple and then faced me. "This is my Uncle Alain and his wife Nora."

"Lovely to meet you." Aunt Nora stood up from her seat, stretching out her hand.

"Nice to meet you." I nervously took her hand and shook it, my voice trembling a bit.

Thomas gently caressed my back, calming me.

"How do you do, Ms. De Waal?" His Uncle reached out his hand, his blue eyes identical to Thomas gazing at me with kindness.

"How do you do?" I shook his hand and said. "Call me Iris, please."

"What a beautiful name," Aunt Nora said.

"Thank you," I replied.

"Iris lives in Laguna Beach. I am absolutely delighted that she's joining me tonight," Thomas said to his uncle and aunt, but his eyes were fixed on me.

I could feel my face heating up.

"We are pleased to have you as well." Aunt Nora gave me a tender smile, her eyes darting between me and Thomas.

"We have been to Laguna Beach a couple of times. Such a beautiful and artistic city," Uncle Alain said.

"It is. I was born and raised there," I responded, wondering if they traveled here often, but decided not to ask any questions as I was still too nervous to socialize.

"We live in Santa Barbara," Uncle Alain said effusively.

"Really? You live here? I mean…in the States?" I was surprised to learn Thomas had relatives here.

My reaction caught Aunt Nora's attention. She gave me a broad smile and said, "I was born and raised in Seattle."

"Really?" I should have noticed that she did not have an accent like Thomas' or his uncle's.

"She moved to Switzerland with me for…" Uncle Alain gazed at his wife with his doting eyes. "Fifteen years?"

"Yes, *mon amour*." Aunt Nora returned his gaze with a content smile.

"My dove got homesick and wanted to move back here." Uncle

Alain leaned in and placed a kiss on his wife's cheek.

They are so loving... I could not move my eyes away from them.

"Alain." "Nora." "Tommy."

We were interrupted by other guests now standing by our table.

The ballroom suddenly felt boisterous and lively, and my anxiety level escalated as well.

Instead of greeting other guests, Thomas wrapped his arm around me as if he could sense my uneasiness and whispered, "Are you all right?"

I nodded, taking a deep breath.

"All other guests sitting at this table are my family's close friends. I would like to introduce you to them."

"Of course!" I said eagerly, even though my heart was still pounding heavily.

He kissed my forehead and steered me towards other guests.

All of them were his father and uncle's close friends who had been very supportive of the foundation for years. And I was surprised to learn that some of them flew here from Chicago and New York.

I felt so proud when Alyssa introduced Thomas, and the room gave him rounds of applause. As he had promised me, he stood right by me and gave an inspiring, humorous speech. After he finished, he received another round of applause.

"You are amazing," I said to him when he sat down.

"Thank you." He leaned in and gave me a kiss on my cheek.

Now and then, he would touch or hold my hand underneath the table, making sure I was doing okay.

As the evening went on, I managed to have casual conversations with other guests sitting at the table. This was quite significant as I had been avoiding meeting new people for over a year, not to mention having such an enjoyable time.

Everything went so smoothly until Uncle Alain asked us with a radiant smile, "So, where did you two meet?"

I choked on the water I just drank. Covering my mouth, I tried to cough as quietly as I could. And I heard a clink as Thomas accidentally dropped his steak knife on the china plate.

We looked at each other, eyes widened.

"Must be a fun story. Look at you two…" The gentleman, who was introduced to me as Uncle Alain's best friend Mr. Laurent, contributed to our awkwardness. He reminded me of French actor Gérard Depardieu, making me just want to smile at him.

Thomas picked up his napkin and patted his mouth, a furrow appearing in his brow.

"In Paris!" I burst out the words, forcing a smile. I was not lying because we did meet in Paris, or should I say he saw me in Paris.

Thomas blinked his eyes several times.

"The city of love. How romantic!" Mr. Laurent's wife joined the conversation.

I was so sure Thomas and I must look very uncomfortable because Aunt Nora looked over at me and said, "Excuse us, darling. We did not mean to pry. We just… We haven't seen Tommy for years." Her gaze flitted to Thomas. "We are just so glad that he's around and looks so happy now."

"It's not a problem." I returned her thoughtfulness with a smile.

"I…" Thomas cleared his throat, announcing to the table. "I saw her, and I just knew I must meet her…" He smiled at me, sneaking a hand under the table and gently squeezed my hand.

I was lost in his blue eyes tinged with wintergreen from the tea lights on the table.

"I believe that runs in the Torian family," Mr. Depardieu… Ahem… I meant Mr. Laurent, turned his attention to Uncle Alain. "You were basically stalking Nora when you first met her."

A ripple of laughter ran round the table.

I felt a rush of relief, and I heard Thomas breathing a sigh of relief as well.

After the dinner came the silent auction. I was out bid by a $5000 bidder—there went our dinner date. My father was also out bid, but DD was the highest bidder for a landscaping oil painting. Although I was disappointed that our dinner date was off, I was glad my brother was able to make a small contribution.

Live music started after the last winning bidder was announced, and people started to head to the dance floor. Uncle Alain and Aunt Nora could not be on their feet fast enough.

"They are so cute…" I said, watching them walking away arm in arm.

People also started circulating the room, socializing. I wondered whether Thomas would be mingling and associating with other guests if I was not here. I turned my head to look at him and met his gaze.

"Did you enjoy yourself tonight?" he asked.

"Very much…" I said, squeezing his hand. "Thank you for being so attentive."

Just as he was leaning in for a kiss, a man approached us. This man was introduced to me earlier, but I could not quite remember who he was.

"Mr. Bailey." Thomas stood up.

"Mr. Torian, Ms. De Waal." He gave us a polite smile and said, "I have to catch a flight back to New York now."

Ah… He is the general manager of DeMont New York.

"I am looking forward to your visit next week," he said to Thomas, extending his hand for a handshake.

Next week? He's leaving… Suddenly, the din of the crowd and music became silent to my ears. I felt completely lost and inundated by the very reality that he was leaving soon. He told me he was not sure when he was heading to New York, but apparently he was scheduled to be there next week.

I had known all along he was not here to stay. Would he visit me again next time he traveled here? Was I supposed to wait around for his visit? I was so high on him now. Could I handle the withdrawal after he left? What was it that we had? Oh god, I should not—

"Iris," Thomas' calling pulled me out of my dispirited mind. He must have called me many times because he looked so worried.

I forced a smile but could not hide my dejection.

"Love, are you all right?" he asked softly.

"Yes…" I tried to reassure him, but my mind was still occupied by one thing: He was leaving next week…

He held my hands and asked, "Do you fancy a dance with me?"

Looking at the crowd, I was not sure if it was a good idea.

"Trust me?" Same doting eyes were looking at me every time he asked me that.

How can I say no to those eyes? I nodded.

He walked us to the corner of the ballroom foyer instead of the dance floor. He pulled me closer, wrapped one arm around my back, and held my hand against his chest with the other hand.

I rested my head on his chest, slowly moving to the music with him.

He must have perceived my despondency and quietness as he stopped moving and said softly, "You are tired. Let's go upstairs…"

"Can…can you leave now?" My voice was small and hesitant.

"Of course," he said and kissed my forehead.

CHAPTER 23

> Love is taking chances when
> every rational part of you screams,
> "Don't risk it."
> Because it's only when
> your heart has been ripped open that
> you get a chance to find the one person
> capable of making it whole.
> ~Sabrina Jeffries

AS soon as we walked into his suite, I headed out to the terrace right away. I leaned against the iron railing, gasping for air. My body was trembling, and my breathing was becoming shallow and brisk as if I could not get enough air.

"Iris..." Thomas was standing right by me, gently rubbing my back.

It's harder than I thought... I had convinced myself that what was between us was just a fling, and I could easily go back to my self-pity life once he left.

"I am so sorry," he apologized, assuming my anxiety was caused by the gala.

"Are you leaving next week?" I asked, my voice quivering.

He did not answer me. His silence was a confirmation.

"It's harder than I thought, Thomas..." I felt so heavy-hearted.

He put his warm hands on my shoulders and gently turned me around to face him.

I looked into his eyes. They were worried and confused. I could not tell him how I felt because I did not understand it either. It just...

hurt so much, tears fighting to emerge.

Not wanting him to see my vulnerability, I grasped his tuxedo lapels, pulled him down, and kissed him recklessly.

I wanted to remember every minute with him, no matter what was going to happen after he left. I wanted to remember our laughter, banter, and heart-to-heart chat. His endearing smiles and captivating blue eyes would be imprinted indelibly on my mind. And our gratifying lovemaking... The thought of it made my heart ache, tears seeping out of my closed eyes and flowing down my cheeks.

Ignited by my fervor, he kissed me back fiercely. He cupped the back of my head with one hand, deepening our kiss.

When we finally broke apart, our eyes locked. He wiped away my tears with his thumbs and scooped me up. I buried my face in the curve of his neck while he walked us back inside and towards his bedroom.

I did not know how we got out of his tuxedo and my gown. It all happened so fast after he put me down. We were now on the bed, and our legs and arms were twisting around each other.

Thomas reached into the nightstand drawer for a condom while I was trailing kisses on his neck, shoulder, and chest. I heard him tearing the foil, but I did not stop kissing him. I could not. I was too eager to hold on to all the sensations I was feeling.

Facing me, he lifted himself up on one elbow.

I bit my bottom lip, gazing at him with anticipation.

"*Ma chérie...*" he whispered, stroking my cheek with his hand. He leaned in and pressed his lips on mine tenderly. His hand roamed over my shoulder, down my arm, and to my buttock. He brought me closer to him and continued to move his hand lower to my thigh. Gently holding the back of my knee, smoothly he rolled me on top of him.

I lifted myself up as he reached between us and placed himself at my entrance. I slowly lowered myself, sliding him inside me.

He pushed his upper body upward and sat up, filling me completely.

I moaned as the euphoric pressure was becoming more and more intense.

He put one hand on my back, holding me closer, as I slowly rocked my hips. He fondled my breasts with the other hand, trailing his kisses over my breasts. He looked up, locking eyes with me, as he tasted my pink peaks. He then kissed his way up to the crook of my neck, gently biting and sucking me.

It aroused me madly that I started moving my hips faster, gratified by the caress of his manhood.

"Move with me, *mon amour,*" he whispered, leaning back on the pillows. Both of his hands gripping my hips, he thrust harder.

Our eyes locked again. I was so enraptured by his gorgeous face and spellbinding blue gaze. The heat was traveling through my body, stirring up all my senses. As our movement was quickening, I was overwhelmed by so many emotions... I could no longer tell the difference between sadness and happiness. Overwhelmed and clenched by emotions, I felt I could give all myself to him. My body and soul...

"*Je t'aime...*" He said he loved me in a husky voice.

What? Did I just hear what I thought it was? My mind wanted to analyze, to understand why he said that, but my body was chasing the blissful relief.

The fervor was building up, higher and higher. My body started moving frantically.

And then, the heavenly ecstasy erupted in every cell of my body. I was spasming around him, his thrust intensifying. Together, we reached that dramatic finish.

I collapsed on top of him, and he tightly enfolded me in his arms. My heart was pounding violently, and I could hear his heartbeat thundering.

His chest undulated. The up-and-down motion was so soothing that I shut my eyes and let the exhaustion wash over me...

I awoke abruptly...

No... I felt so downhearted as I had not had disrupted sleep for months. I sat up, blinking my eyes to adjust to the dimmed light in the room. Thomas was sound asleep next to me. The corners of my lips lifted, remembering our fervid lovemaking...

I slipped out of bed and padded to the bathroom. I quickly brushed my teeth and washed my face, making as little sound as possible. Putting on a bathrobe, I walked quietly out of the bedroom and to the kitchen to get a glass of water. With the glass in my hands, I headed out to the terrace to get some cold air.

It was two in the morning, and I was sleepless. Putting the glass on a side table, I curled up on the outdoor sofa and held my knees on my chest, wondering about so many things...

Why did he say that? He must have said that in the heat of the moment, right?

We had never talked about what *this* was between us. It felt as if we were just picking up where we left off in Bern.

My condition was too complicated and unpredictable. Who would want to babysit me day and night?

Who would want to be with me?

These thoughts saddened me. Feeling so broken and helpless, I embraced myself, tears drenching my eyes.

"Hey..." A tender voice startled me. I quickly wiped the tears with my hands.

He sat down next to me.

Not wanting him to see my crying face, I turned away and kept my head down. Then, I heard him sighing...

This was what I hated the most—the sigh.

Here I was, becoming all emotional, and then he was going to run away as fast as possible. What was I doing? Crying was not going to make him stay. Crying was only going to make him feel sorry for me. And his pity was the last thing I needed.

I drew in a deep breath and forced a smile. "I really miss my parents...very much." I lied. And it sounded so stupid.

He did not say anything but wrapped his arms around my shoulders, my body tensing up. And he sighed again.

I had an urge to pull myself farther away from him.

He turned and faced me, but I looked away, not able to look into his eyes, from which I was not able to look away just hours ago.

"Iris…" He paused and let out another deep sigh.

There you go. The departure statement…

"I… I meant what I said earlier," he said softly, interlocking our fingers.

I turned to look at him, my brow furrowing.

"Is that what is bothering you?" he asked.

"I don't know what you are talking about." I turned away again.

"Je… I love you," he said, his voice deep and tender.

My eyes suddenly became blurry with tears. My head whipped around to face him. "Why? Why are you doing this?" I glared at him. "You are leaving."

"Come with me." His response was immediate, no hesitation and no apprehension in his voice. "To New York and then back to Switzerland with me."

I widened and blinked my eyes in disbelief, looking at him to make sure I had heard him correctly. His earnest expression and those captivating eyes showed me that I had.

I could not speak. I just held his gaze, could not be more baffled.

"Can we talk inside?" He broke the silence. "Or I would need to put on a shirt or something."

I just now realized he was only wearing pajama pants. "Of course…" I held his hand and headed inside.

What just happened?

Thomas held my hand firmly and closed the door with his free hand. Then he pulled me towards him and embraced me in his arms. "I know it sounds crazy," he said, letting out a deep breath. "I… I…" He became speechless.

I hoped he was not waiting for me to say anything because I was as speechless as he was. I could hear his heartbeat drumming. *Is he nervous? Anxious?* I enclasped his waist, wanting to comfort him.

"You don't need to give me any answer now," he whispered. "But please say something. Anything… So I know you are—"

"Do you want hot chocolate?" I interrupted him, looking up.

He loosened his embrace, gazing down at me, looking amused.

"I didn't really eat much today," I said, not making excuses or changing the subject. I was hungry as I did not have lunch and was too nervous to enjoy the gala dinner. "I am going to make hot chocolate. Would you like to have a cup?"

"Yes... Please." He looked completely bewildered.

I gave him a broad smile and turned towards the kitchen. He followed right behind me.

Milk, whipped cream, cocoa powder, chocolate, sugar... I gathered whatever I could think of to make hot chocolate. He really had the kitchen stocked to my liking.

How could you fall in love with me in four days? I frowned at him and put the saucepan on the stove and poured in the milk.

"Can I help?" His voice was nervous, probably because of my frowning and sighing.

I shook my head and started chopping the chocolate into fine pieces while the milk was simmering, although I glanced at him periodically.

It's okay to use terms of endearment to me... Frowning, I stared at him while I was whisking cocoa powder, chocolate and sugar into the milk. *But it's not okay to just burst out 'I love you.'*

He focused on the saucepan to avoid my stare.

"The, the..." he pointed at the saucepan as the hot chocolate was boiling.

I quickly turned down the heat.

And you just want me to give up my life here... I stared at the mixture in the saucepan and whisked more until it was smooth and creamy.

He walked closer to me with two white mugs.

"Thank you..." I tried to keep my tone as untroubled as possible.

He put the mugs down and wrapped his arms around my waist from behind. "Je t'aime," he whispered in my ear.

Stop saying that... I shut my eyes, letting out a deep breath. The truth was I should be mad at myself because...because I felt the same way...

"It looks delicious," he said, his warm breath tickling me.

"It tastes better than it looks." I smirked in triumph and started to scoop the hot chocolate into the mugs. I topped them with whipped cream and then dusted cocoa powder on top.

"Voilà!" I smiled at the masterpiece with satisfaction.

"Let's enjoy it," he said, picked up both mugs, and headed out to the living room.

I grabbed a couple of napkins and followed right behind him.

He handed me a mug and settled himself down on the sofa, inviting me to sit by him.

Sipping the creaming rich hot chocolate, I felt calm already.

"This is the best hot chocolate I have ever had," he said after taking a big sip.

I reached out my hand to wipe the whipped cream and cocoa powder on his upper lip. *Why are you so charming?* My thumb might have lingered on his lips a bit too long.

He put his mug down and took my free hand. "Iris, I am not good at expressing myself…"

"Are you sure you are not? You have told me that you love me at least three times."

"And I meant it every time." His blue eyes glinted with affection.

I looked away, taking a sip of my drink.

"How about you ask me questions or tell me what is on your mind instead?" He sank into the sofa, his thumbs idly stroking my hand. "Ask me anything you want to know. Tell me what you want."

I looked at him sideways. "Anything?"

"Anything."

I took his hand and moved it around my shoulders, nestling myself in his arms.

Silence enveloped us… There was not any awkwardness but only contentment.

What do I want? That is a million-dollar question…

I wanted to forget what had happened ever since I set foot in the U.S. Embassy in Bern.

I wanted to erase, delete, wipe out those 178 days of my life.

It had been 448 days since Thomas saved me.

I counted the days when I was in the mansion, and I became obsessive about knowing how long I had been freed.

448 days… It was two and half times longer than the period I

was in captivity, and I was still a mess. It felt like I would never be able to recover from it. How unfair was that?

I thought it would be easier to leave everything behind and dive into a new life after coming home. The truth was it was not easy at all. Dr. Warren encouraged me to talk about it, but I was never ready. And every time I decided to give it a try, I would be inundated with *what if* and *I wish* and then feel completely defeated by regrets, resentment, and sadness.

It would be nice if I could just push a reset, delete, or undo button.

And this man... I peeked at him from the corner of my eyes. *An inexplicable miracle of my misfortune. And also a reminder...*

Perhaps...

He was here to bolster my morale, to help me recuperate from the trauma, and to guide me through it.

I think I am ready...

"You have only been with me for four days..." I said, my emotions much calmer now—thanks to the hot chocolate.

He smiled at me and looked as if he was contemplating what to say. Then he took the mug out of my hands and put it on the table. He held both of my hands and said in a very solemn voice, "Max was deeply in love with you."

"What?" My brow burrowed, my voice small.

"When we met, I had been involved with that particular operation for more than two years," he said, his forehead crinkling in tension as he was recollecting the unpleasant past.

"More than two years..." I murmured. *How horrible was that?*

"At that point, we were able to transport some women to safety already."

"What do you mean?" I was told those women were sold to the procurers.

"We cracked down two traffickers working with Vera and posed as them to continue carrying out the deals with her. So when she sold those women to the traffickers, she actually was dealing with our agents."

"So... Those women were saved... I...I was told..." A thrill of astonishment and dismay ran through me, my voice quivering.

Thomas leaned in and pressed a kiss on my forehead.

"I wish…" I murmured but immediately shoved off the thought. No *I-wish* or *what-if.* Not today. Not now.

He sank back on the sofa, seemingly walking down memory lane.

What did he go through all these years? The thought made my heart hurt.

"I…I witnessed how they disposed of the women whom they considered of no value," he said cautiously, looking into my eyes and making sure I was okay.

I could feel my heart suddenly beating rapidly, wondering what if he were not there? What would I have become?

What's wrong with me! No what-if, remember?

"Are you all right? He asked softly.

"Yes, I am." I gave him a smile. "Tell me… Tell me how Max fell in love with me." My face heated up, but I was not shy or embarrassed. I was feeling nonplussed and also indulged in the idea that the stern and cold Max, who had most of the women in the mansion drooling over him, loved me.

He held me tightly in his arms, drawing a deep breath, and said, "When I saw you in the recovering house, I was astounded how much you reminded me of Laila." His deep blue gaze was fixed on my face, searching for something.

But, I don't look like his sister at all. I locked eyes with him, feeling uneasy because his reason for falling in love with me might be what I was afraid of… By rescuing me, he could heal from losing Laila.

What about my feelings for him? Is it just my gratitude to him for saving me? No… I knew it was so much more than gratitude.

"You talked like her, and your attitude…" He let out an amused sigh. "Your attitude was just like hers." A radiant smile spread across his face.

So… He does only see me as Laila… My heart was saddened.

"Thomas… I…" I slowly pulled away from him. "The love you have for me is for your sister. I can't—"

"No, it's not like that," he interrupted me, eager to explain. "I mean I *was* drawn to you because you reminded me of Laila. I felt strongly protective towards you."

"Because you wanted to protect Laila…" I murmured. What he felt was so righteous, but why did I feel disheartened?

"I did," he said. "Then I… I became so distracted. It killed me when you were sent to entertain anyone. That's why I made sure I was on duty when and wherever you were."

A burning sensation stung my eyes. The images of all those depraved patrons and dissoluteness in that mansion were still so vivid in my head. I tilted my head down, not wanting Thomas to see my misty eyes.

"But there were times I could not be there, so I started to interfere. I criticized your behavior, hoping Vera would think less of you. I warned you about the upcoming parties so you could prepare yourself for them."

"You… You knew I understood some German then, didn't you?" I casted my eyes in his direction and found him lost in thought.

"Soon after you arrived at the mansion…"

"And you purposely talked to the guards about the parties when I was around so I could hear you…"

"I was hoping you would perceive that and find a way to get out of those functions."

All those times he was trying to protect me and watching over me when I derided him as incompetent. I was such a fool…

I nestled myself closer to him, in desperate need of his closeness. He enclosed me, resting his head on mine.

"How could you love me when I was so…so broken?" Tears scalded my eyes. I quickly wiped them away and took a deep breath.

"Iris, you were courageous." He let out an audible sigh and continued. "My feelings for you became so strong that I was not sure Laila was the reason anymore. And getting you out of there was my priority at that time, so I did what I had to do."

I swallowed hard, remembering that dreadful day.

"I know I had frightened you terribly that day. I have never had a chance to tell you how sorry I—"

I turned towards him, reaching my hand to press my fingers over his lips. "Don't…"

He took my hand and placed a kiss on my palm. He locked his eyes with mine, his sapphire gaze affectionate and loving.

"Go on…" I said softly..

"After you were safe, I thought I could continue to carry out my duty without any distraction. But I could not get you out of my mind and could not focus on my job. I…" He hesitated for a minute and continued, "Then the team decided it was time to clamp down on Vera."

I did not press on what happened after that as Julia had already shared with me enough information, and I was not really interested in what happened to Vera's gang, either.

"Julia told me you were doing fine, but I had to see it with my own eyes. I had to see you…"

"I am glad you did…"

"So am I." His gaze intensified. "That ride was fantastic. I had not felt so happy and at ease for a very long time…"

An intense sentiment of warmth, or understanding, or possible *love* rushed through me. I moved to sit on his lap, wrapping my arms around his neck.

"This is encouraging…" He smiled.

"Tell me more…" I leaned against his chest.

"I…I talked to my psychologist about you."

"Psychologist?" I did not expect to learn that, my brow furrowing.

"Undercover officers are trained to manipulate our targets' emotions, so looking after officers' mental health is absolutely essential for the agency."

"I just thought you must be a very good actor…" I joked.

He chuckled and continued, "Undercover policing is an extremely complex process. Mental health professionals are involved in the team formation, the selection, and training. They also monitor undercover officers' health and welfare during and after the operations. There are many officers suffering psychological or psychiatric sequelae. Unfortunately…"

"Wow... Really?"

"I am fortunate to have all the support I need from fedpol and my family. Eva is a brilliant psychiatrist." He then paused, giving me a contemplative look.

"Is she your psychiatrist?"

"She used to..." He stopped, seemingly to reorganize what he wanted to say in his head. "Eva was one of the counselors who helped us after Laila was back and...and also after she was gone." He took a deep breath.

I moved one hand to his chest and gently rubbed it, wishing to comfort him...and myself.

"She became very close to my family after my mother passed away. So close that Louis decided to marry her." He chuckled.

"I get it. She couldn't maintain objective anymore."

"Right. So we were referred to her colleague. I like her better as a sister-in-law though. She keeps Louis out of trouble." His gleeful laugh put a smile on my face.

"How come..." The words stuck in my throat as I did not want to sound pathetic, but I really wanted to know one thing...

"Yes?" he asked. "Don't be hesitant. I want you to make the decision without any doubt and concern."

"Okay... Why did you just... I mean... I hadn't heard from you for months?" My voice was both shy and anxious. Eleven months was a long time. I needed to know why he did not reach out for me if he really had the affection for me like he just said.

"Believe me. I wanted to." He kissed my hair. "But there were so many things that needed to be properly thought out. It was quite complicated."

"I like *complicated*," I said, grinning. "We have the time and hot chocolate." I leaned towards the coffee table to reach for my mug.

"Let me warm them up first." He pulled me back and moved me to sit on the sofa. Grabbing our mugs, he said, "I will be right back." He stood up and walked into the kitchen.

I watched him walking away and then glanced at the clock on the wall. It was already four in the morning...

A couple of minutes later, he came back with our hot chocolates, warm once again. He handed me mine and sat back down right by me.

"So where were we?" he asked and took a sip of the drink.

"Something complicated..."

"Right... I am not a very good story teller, but I will try my best." He wrapped one arm around me and continued, "I was called back to the headquarters after I dropped you off at the embassy that day."

"Urgent?"

"Yes, it was urgent." He frowned. "I had to travel to Italy the same night."

How petty I am! I felt ashamed for bearing a grudge against him while he was on a dangerous mission.

"I was on that undercover assignment for a couple of months." He took a sip of the hot chocolate. "Almost the same time, Louis reached out to me. I had to go home right after the case reached a point."

"Everything okay...with your family?"

He smiled, nodding. "My father decided to dedicate all his time and energy to the foundation and requested Louis to take over his position at the company. He wished I could help Louis. That was when I reassessed everything. What I was doing, what I was actually good at, and what I wanted in my life."

I wonder where I fit in his life?

"Remember I told you I only decided to be a police officer because of Laila's death."

I nodded.

"I am a philomath." He looked at me, one corner of his mouth tilting up.

"You what?" I raised my eyebrows.

"I majored in economics and management and minored in philosophy, politics and economics at the University of Oxford." There was a hint of pride in his voice. He looked at me, seemingly waiting for my response.

"So... You are telling me that you are a nerd..." I joked.

A man with a brain... I am in so much trouble now.

"Pretty much." He smiled, a faint blush flashing across his face. "After several serious conversations with my father and Louis, I resigned from fedpol."

"To work for your family?"

"Not quite yet..." He sighed. "Going undercover took a toll on me, mentally. I started psychotherapy with my psychologist while shadowing Louis to take over his duties."

"Do you...do you like it? I mean the hotel business," I asked.

He gazed at me with a very pleased smile. "I do. You know... No one has ever asked me if I like it or not," he said. "Friends and families sort of just expressed how fantastic it was that I finally decided to work for the family."

"Do you enjoy what you are doing now?"

"Very much." His voice had a hint of excitement. "I initially went to school for that. And now, I have proven that I am actually very good at it." Then his voice suddenly became doleful. "Being a police officer was something I felt I had to do at that time of my life, to do something for Laila."

"You are still doing so much for her now. I mean...with the foundation."

He kissed my forehead. "Thank you."

"And safer, too..." I said in a very low voice.

"Exactly." He heard what I said and concurred with me. "Having a safer career concerns the most important thing I want in my life."

"Helping your family?" I asked, blinking my eyes. *What else will be more important than helping his family and doing what he likes?*

"No..." He looked at me with his alluring eyes. "You. I want you in my life."

I became speechless, my eyes fixed on his.

He took my mug and put both mine and his on the coffee table. He held my hands, his eyes full of emotions. "I worked with my psychologist because I needed to know what I felt for you was not sympathy and was not because of Laila. And the distance and time was the best test for myself and for...us." He looked into my eyes earnestly while saying the last word.

Us…

"Max was madly in love with you…" He stroked my face with his hand tenderly. "It was nothing to do with Laila or sympathy. And I know I am in love with you because you filled the void in me the moment I saw you last Wednesday."

My vision was buried with happy tears.

"My Love," he said in an agony tone. "Don't you know my affection for you by now?"

Leaning forward, I cupped his face and gave him a passionate kiss. He wrapped his arms around me, kissing me back.

"But…" I said when our lips parted. "What about my condition?"

"What condition?"

His eyes were so sincere, honest, and loving. I would be a fool if I turned away from them. In the past four days, he had shown me that I was capable of overcoming my fears. And he was always by my side, enfolding me in his massive invisible wings like a guardian angel.

What am I afraid of? I knew my parents would be happy for me, and DD and Janie liked him very much.

How about my work? I still wanted my independence. I supposed I could discuss that with Jojo and Antonio.

"Can we… Can we give it a try?" he asked since I had been so quiet. "And then you can decide if you want to be with me…"

How could I say no to him?

CHAPTER 24

> Being deeply loved by someone
> gives you strength,
> while loving someone deeply
> gives you courage.
> ~Lao Tzu

AFTER I called my parents early Saturday morning and told them about Thomas and the gala, they drove all the way to Laguna Beach the same day. And my mother demanded to host a small gathering for Thomas at the ranch Sunday afternoon.

So here I was, introducing the man who saved my life to my parents.

"Mrs. De Waal," Thomas greeted my mother and presented her with a bouquet of peonies, which were her favorite flower, and the biggest box of chocolate he could find.

"Thank you so much. Please, call me Koto," my mother replied and embraced him in her arms for the longest time, refusing to let go of him.

"We can't thank you enough!" My father firmly gripped Thomas' hands after my mother finally freed Thomas.

Thomas seemed a bit overwhelmed, but he had been looking forward to meeting my parents since…since I told him about them in Bern.

I was pretty sure my brother and Janie had already told my parents everything they knew and thought about Thomas as my parents were talking to Thomas like they had already known him.

"Daddy, Thomas' eyes lit up when he saw your Bentley earlier,"

I said to my father, knowing he would be excited about the topic. "He has a white one. He just told me yours is a much newer model."

Just as I had expected, all three men headed out to talk about cars. I actually did this on purpose because I needed my time with my mother and Janie. I needed their thoughts and advice.

"Honey, didn't you invite Antonio and Jasmine?" my mother asked.

"I did. They should be here soon." I looked at the clock on the wall. Since I was going to break the news about my decision to go to New York with Thomas, I might as well tell everyone at the same time.

But the thing was... How?

This morning I told Thomas I would go to New York with him first, and then we would go from there. I was not sure about going back to Switzerland with him. Yet. I trusted him, but I needed to know with certainty that I...I loved him, and that I did not just have an infatuation with him.

"Mommy." I sat down by my mother on the sofa, linking my arm with hers and resting my head on her shoulder. "I need to tell you something."

"Everything all right?" she asked, turning towards me.

"Janie," I called Janie, who was refilling chips and dips. "Can you join us, please?"

"Of course, hon." She hastily put down the bag of chips and joined us on the sofa.

I linked my other arm with Janie's, feeling cherished and loved.

Can I leave my family and move six thousand miles away to be with Thomas?

The old impetuous Iris would have started packing already, but the new Iris was uncertain and conflicted about everything.

"He's a very charming young man," my mother said. "Is it about him?" She could read me like a book.

I nodded.

"Did you have a wonderful time at the gala?"

I nodded again.

"I still couldn't believe you attended a gala." My mother's eyes turned misty.

"Mommy…" Seeing her so emotional saddened me.

"He's like a miracle worker. Jane told me you went to the beach as well." She stroked my cheek. "And you look…happy."

"I am…"

"How long will he be here?" Janie asked.

"That's what I need to talk to you about. He's leaving this week…"

"Oh… Are you all right?" Janie asked with so much concern.

My mother looked worried as well.

"I am great. But I… He…"

"What is it, honey?" My mother wrapped her arm around my shoulders.

"He… He told me he loved me and asked me to…to go to New York with him. And if things work out between us, he wants me to go back to Switzerland with him." I hastily let it all out before I lost my nerve.

"Oh, honey…" Janie squeezed my hand.

My mother was quiet, and it made me nervous. I wanted, no, I needed my parents' support.

"How about you? Do you love him?" After a moment's silence my mother asked, tugging a strand of hair behind my ear.

"I think so…" I murmured.

My mother smiled. She paused for a moment and asked, "And?"

"Mommy, he wants me in his life. But he lives six thousands miles away."

"Why *but?*" Janie asked?

I widened my eyes, staring at her. "It means either I move closer to him or…or we have to travel across the ocean back and forth to see each other."

"You always love traveling," Janie responded.

"Used to," I said, my tone harsh and dry. How could she forget about my conditions?

Janie let out a sigh, looking away.

My mother held me tightly in her arms and said, "Jane is right, honey. And you know it."

I glanced at Janie and saw her watery eyes. I reached my arms to wrap around her neck. "I am sorry. I didn't mean to snap at you..."

"Iris..." She hugged me back. "I love you so much. I've known you since you were a little girl. Not a second I don't think you are still the same witty, smart, and brave little girl David introduced me to."

"Princess Ariel..." I called her.

"I still missed that nickname." She chuckled, so did my mother.

I used to call Janie *Princess Ariel* because of her beautiful red hair. Well, I was only eleven then, and my life was nothing but Disney princesses. After I turned into a teenager and grew out of Disney, I *upgraded* Jane's nickname to Janie.

"But... What if—"

"Iris..." Janie interrupted me. "You've talked about this with Dr. Warren too many times. *What ifs* are not going to change the past, and they certainly are not going to dictate your future." Her voice was firm and encouraging.

"Honey, are you happy with him?" my mother asked.

"Very much." I faced my mother. "He might look serious, but he's funny and makes me laugh all the time," I said, recalling the time we had in Bern and the last five days. "He's also very attentive. I feel so safe, content, and happy when he's around."

"You have your answer then," my mother said, smiling.

"Oh..." My eyes casted down. *I love him?*

"Don't be afraid, honey." My mother cupped my face with her warm hands. "I took a chance with your father and moved across the Pacific. And I was rewarded with a loving husband and two beautiful children. I'm not saying you should marry him. What I am saying is you would never know if he is the one if you don't give yourself a chance."

"Even if I move six thousands miles away...from you?"

"Of course I want you around. All of you..." She smiled at Janie as well. "But my love for you shouldn't hold you back. You always have a home with us, like a safety net." My mother fixed her eyes on me and added, "Sweetie, after what had happened—" She paused, her gaze becoming sad and concerned. "I...I'm not sure..."

"Mommy?" I murmured. *Is she changing her mind?*

"I mean... I'm not sure I will be at ease with the idea of you being with anyone but Thomas."

My brow furrowed, "What...what do you mean?"

"I mean..." She stroked my hair. "I am absolutely confident of your decision. I haven't—"

"Hello~" Jojo's cheerful voice traveled to the family room from the front door, interrupting my mother.

"Let's talk more later," my mother whispered and kissed my forehead.

"In here," Janie called out.

Jojo scurried in, her golden ponytail swaying behind her. "Is that hottie Thomas?"

"That's my first thought, too," my mother said.

"Mom!" My voice was high-pitched.

"Being a mother doesn't mean I can't appreciate beautiful men, does it?" Her eyebrows arched, sounding all serious.

"Of course not!" Jojo walked towards us and leaned down to give my mother a hug. "Hi Koto... You look great!"

"Thank you, sweetie." My mother gave Jojo a heartfelt hug.

Jojo leaned in and gave me a bear hug. "He is so cute!"

I grinned.

"Hi Janie... How are you? Where are the kiddos?" Jojo moved on to give Janie a hug.

"Hi sweetie, I am doing great. The kids are in their rooms playing video games. How's life treating you?"

"Life has been treating me wonderfully," Jojo replied, a radiant smile spreading across her face.

"So, Mr. Viking has been treating you wonderfully," I teased her.

"Mr. Viking?" My mother and Janie asked in unison.

Jojo's smile became even brighter when she slumped onto the sofa across from me.

"She has a hottie herself," I whispered to both my mother and Janie loudly.

"A hot viking?" Janie widened her eyes. "Do tell!"

"Yup! Long hair, long beard, all that sexy stuff. But she asked him to shave his beard though." I winked at Jojo. "Not sure why though…"

"Don't you make fun of me." Jojo pouted. "He went home last week."

"Where?" my mother asked.

"Paris…" Jojo let out a sigh of disappointment.

Suddenly, my mother and Janie's eyes were all on me.

"What did I miss?" Jojo asked, sitting up straight.

I sighed and looked at Jojo. "Thomas asked me to go to New York with him this week. And—"

"New York? I thought he lives in Switzerland," Jojo interrupted me.

I spent the next half hour explaining everything to Jojo and also shared my thoughts on getting out of my comfort zone to go to New York with them.

"I want to travel again…" I said, my voice small.

"Of course you do… That's in your blood." My mother leaned her head against mine. "And I think Thomas is the perfect person to be by your side."

"What about after New York?" Jojo asked. Letting out a dispirited sigh, she added, "I must warn you that long distance relationships suck."

"He wants me to move to Switzerland with him, but I'm not sure. Not yet… I don't know…"

"Don't overwhelm yourself. One day at a time. Remember?" Janie said.

I nodded in agreement and turned to face Jojo. "Who knows what will happen after New York? I might find it to be just a fairytale fantasy."

"Our men should meet," Jojo said.

Now three pairs of eyes stared at Jojo.

"They both live in Europe and travel a lot. Iris, we can travel together!" She was all excited now.

"Travel where?" Antonio's voice made us all turn towards the front door.

"Carmella!" I jumped out of the sofa and scampered towards Antonio's sister.

"Hi sweetheart." Carmella held me in her arms tightly. "You look great!"

"I am so glad you could come." I linked my arm with hers and guided her to the sofa.

"Hi Koto, how are you?" Antonio kissed my mother's cheek and waved to Janie. He then faced me and said, "How come I don't get that kind of welcome?" He sat down on one of the single seat sofas.

"I am sure your harem gives you plenty of that." Jojo chuckled.

"They certainly do. Thank you very much." Antonio grinned at her.

Carmella exchanged pleasantries with my mother and Janie before she said to me, "I met the guest of honor when we got here. It's amazing that he came all the way here to visit you."

I smiled, realizing all Camarillo knew was what Antonio had told her. And Antonio did not know *Scheiße!*

"Thomas is a wonderful young man," my mother said to Camarillo, but her eyes were on me. "Iris is going to New York with him this week."

"What?" Antonio exclaimed.

"I am going to talk to you and Jojo about it so we can figure out a way to work on the projects while I am in New York."

"You've already worked from home for months, and it works perfectly," Jojo said, her voice encouraging.

"A word, please." Antonio stood up, tilting his head towards the kitchen.

"Sure." I stood up.

Jojo was standing up as well, but Antonio motioned her not to. "Fine," she said, sitting back down and rolling her eyes.

Antonio walked into the kitchen, and I followed him.

"So, when did you start to exclude me from all this...this nonsense stuff."

"Since you think what I am doing and want to do is nonsense!" I raised my voice.

He paused a minute to calm himself and asked, "What's the deal with New York?"

"He is traveling to New—" I stopped, realizing I needed to at least explain why Thomas was going to New York. "Thomas is no longer with fedpol and is working for his family now. His family owns DeMonte Hotels."

"*The* DeMonte?" His brows arched.

"Yes, *the* DeMonte." I stressed the word *the* as he did. "He's visiting all locations to conduct assessments of the management and the properties. His next stop is New York. He invited me…" I trailed off because his jaw looked really tense, and I might have seen smoke coming out of his nostrils.

"And just like that? You are all happy and ready to go?" His voice was higher than his usual tenor tone.

"What do you mean *just like that*?"

"We have all been sheltering and protecting you since you came home. And suddenly, this guy just showed up and ask—"

"This guy…" I cut him off, feeling steam was coming out of my ears. "This guy saved my life! Without him, I wouldn't be here for you to shelter and protect!" I practically yelled at him at this point.

"Chill, Iris," he said, frowning. "I know he saved your life. And I am grateful for that." His voice sounded calmer than earlier, and I assumed my yelling did the trick. He leaned against the kitchen counter, deep in thought.

I let out a deep sigh and moved closer to him. "Why are you acting like this?"

He gazed at me with his deep black eyes, his brow furrowing. "I just don't want you to make any mistakes. He did save you, but it's his job."

I could not argue with him about that as he was right. But he did not know the rest of the story, and I was not going to share the private and intimate conversations Thomas and I had with anyone.

"And saving you doesn't mean he has the right to demand you to do anything," he continued as I was quiet.

"He is not demanding me to do anything!" I raised my voice again. "Can you not assume things like that? And do you seriously think I am that weak?"

"I don't think you are weak, Iris. Never. But I thought... Didn't we just joke about maybe I should move into your place? And now, you are traveling to New York. What am I supposed to think?"

"Antonio. We joked about it." I was getting frustrated. "There is no way I am letting your butt-naked women walk around my house."

"What are you talking about? Don't you change the subject." He then pointed his finger in the direction of the front door. "You've never mentioned him to me since you came back. Not once," he said. "So, if this is not nonsense, what is?"

I bit my bottom lip, my brow arching in frustration.

"You can bake cookies for him to show your gratitude."

I chuckled, giving him a dirty look.

"You don't owe him anything just because he saved you," he added.

"He loves me..." I said calmly.

"What?" He looked shocked.

"It's... We reconnected over the last few days. He...he told me he's been in love with—"

Antonio busted out laughing, cutting me off, and that really angered me.

"You are such a jerk!" I snapped at him. "You think it's funny that he loves me?"

"I love you, too," he responded right away, stepping closer.

Now I laughed out loud and replied, "I love you, too, Antonio. But as a friend, a sister, a—"

Suddenly, he pressed his lips on mine, my eyes bulging.

It took me a second or two to react—swinging my fist and punching him in the jaw.

"What the..." Antonio cried out, cupping his jaw.

"Yes, what the hell, Antonio!" I exclaimed.

"Calm down, it's just a kiss." He was rotating and rubbing his jaw.

"A kiss I did NOT ask for and did NOT want!" I ground my teeth.

"Fair enough..." He looked away.

"Why are you ruining everything?" I was choked with emotion, feeling that I was losing my best friend.

"I...I do love you."

"It's a different kind of love, Antonio."

"But..." He casted his eyes down. "You are the only person who understands me, keeps me grounded, and..." His gaze moved up at me and continued, "...never thinks I am cute."

I chuckled, walking up to him and hugged him. "It's because you are not that cute."

He let out a heavy sigh and wrapped his arms around me.

"I love him, Antonio," I said, feeling emotional. "He makes me so happy."

"Don't I make you happy?"

"Stop comparing yourself with him!" I squeezed him hard.

"Fine. But if he ever—"

"He won't," I cut him off. "And I want you to like him."

"Fat chance," he said.

I knew Antonio too well to know he meant he would.

"Thank you..." I said, burying my face in his chest.

"What's the deal with you two dating European men now?"

I laughed.

"Wait... I am half Italian. Shouldn't I be considered as a European man?"

"Of course, *Signore*." I laughed even louder. Linking his arm. "Let's get back to the party."

When we were back to the family room, Thomas was already back. I immediately walked up to him and wrapped my arms around his waist. He enclasped me, kissing my hair, as if I had been gone for a long time.

DD fired up the grill for a backyard barbecue, and the kids finally came out of their rooms and joined the party. The afternoon and evening went pleasantly, better than I had expected.

Thomas seemed to enjoy himself and stayed by my side the whole time. That made me wonder if he was overwhelmed by the hospitality. It was hard to believe a once undercover police officer would feel nervous around my family and friends.

When my parents were in town, they usually stayed with me. However, they decided to stay at the ranch this time. My mother said she wanted to spend more time with her three little Js: Jake, Johnny, and Jenny. But I knew she and my father wanted to give me and Thomas privacy.

On our way home, I asked Thomas what he thought about the party, wanting to know if he was overcome by my overly diverting family and free spirited friends.

As it turned out, when I was talking to my mother and Janie about him, he was talking to my father and brother about me. And according to Thomas, my father told him that although he was not thrilled about me traveling across the country, ultimately, it was my decision. Thankfully, all of them were civil to each other.

I had decided to go to New York, and talking to my mother and Janie had only made me feel more certain it was what I wanted and needed to do. I would like to spend a couple of more days with my parents to make sure they completely understood how I felt about Thomas. I was not going to elope with him. Marriage or not, I wanted this chance with him and needed to know I could still love and be loved.

I disarmed the security after walking into the house. As I was reaching my hand to turn on the living room light, Thomas surprised me by holding my waist and whirling me around to face him. His brow furrowed, looking somehow worried and troubled.

My heart palpitated as I trusted his instinct for sensing danger. "Something wrong?" I whispered.

His gaze was intense, and his breathing was picking up. "Are you having second thoughts?"

"What?"

"To be with me?" His voice was soft but sad.

"Where does this come from?" I cupped his stubbled jaw, gently rubbing his chin with my thumb. "What makes you think I am having second thoughts?"

"I... I saw Antonio kissing you..."

"You did?"

"We were walking back to the house from the back, going to go through the kitchen. I saw you two were talking. And then..." he trailed off.

"Did you see me punching him?" I asked, my eyes glinting with mischief.

"Yes. That's why I did not storm into the kitchen."

"How come you didn't come in?"

"David pulled me aside and told me to...to let you two figure things out," he said, sounding defeated. "Did you?"

"We did," I replied, locking our eyes. "Antonio is my best friend. We grew up together and did crazy things together."

He sighed and said, "That's what David told me."

"Don't be jealous," I teased him. "I do love him but like a brother. Plus, he's a manwhore. I don't even know how I manage to tolerate that."

"So... You are still going to New York with me."

"Absolutely."

He leaned in and kissed me. "*Je t'aime...*"

"*Ich liebe dich auch...*" I replied *I love you, too* in German.

His eyes widened, a radiant smile spreading across his face. "You do?"

It just hit me that this was the very first time I said *I love you* to him. I nodded bashfully and wrapped my arms around him, burying my face in his chest.

"*Je t'aime comme un fou,*" he whispered in my ear.

"Huh?" I looked up at him.

"I love you like a fool..." His gaze was alluring, his voice smooth like velvet.

"*Ich liebe dich wie eine Närrin?*" I repeated in German with uncertainty as it sounded so unromantic and burst out laughing. "I think I am going to stick to English."

He cupped my face with his big warm hands and said, "I love hearing you say it. It doesn't matter which language you use."

"*Wo ai ni...*" I whispered in Mandarin Chinese.

"Mmmm..." He dipped a kiss on my lips. "Say it again..."

"*Wa ai li...*" I switched to Taiwanese.

He dipped another kiss on my lips. "Charming…"

"*Ai shiteru…*" I said in Japanese this time.

"There are roughly 6,500 spoken languages in the world. We can do this for years," he said softly and gave me a kiss that made my toes curl.

"You are such a nerd. How do you know there are that many spoken languages!" I chuckled.

He winked and said, "I am ready to leave when you are. Take as long as you need to talk to your parents and friends. And if you don't want to bring too much stuff with you, we can always pick up whatever—"

"Shh…" I looked up at him, interrupting him. "Aren't you scheduled to be in New York this week?"

"This is one of the benefits of being the boss. I can decide when I will be there." He smirked.

Of course I was not going to let him delay his schedule. "How about no later than Thursday? I…I really want to talk to my parents, especially my dad."

"Fantastic. I will arrange everything." He looked really pleased.

CHAPTER 25

> Love meant jumping off a cliff and
> trusting that a certain person would
> be there to catch you at the bottom.
> ~Jodi Picoult

WHEN my parents insisted on going to the airport with us, I asked them not to treat me like a child or a wounded adult child. And I promised them if I decided to go to Switzerland with Thomas, I would definitely come home first.

Thomas' suitcases were delivered to the airport directly from the hotel, so we were on our way to the airport straight from my house early Thursday morning.

When we were approaching John Wayne Airport, my breathing picked up.

"How about the car?" I asked, needing a distraction.

He arched one eyebrow, not sure what I was talking about.

"This car. Will someone be here to pick it up?" I knew it belonged to the hotel, and I did not even know why I was concerned about this car when I was about to walk into the crowded check-in counters and face the chaos in the terminal.

"Yes." He reached his hand over to hold mine. "Are you all right?"

"Sure." My hand started trembling.

Then Thomas turned into a private aviation parking lot instead of heading towards the airport terminal.

"Hmmm…" I made a sound, expressing my concerns and curiosity.

He pulled up to a small office building adjoining a big hangar and turned towards me. "Here we are. Ready for New York? Wait… I did not tell you we are flying private, did I?" His voice changed from excited to concerned when he saw my expression.

I shook my head, pouting "No. You could have mentioned this so I wouldn't have nightmares, worrying about getting on a plane with hundreds of strangers."

"I apologize, love. I…" He sounded worried. "I have been flying private for the past seven months. It did not—"

"I'm just joking," I interrupted him, feeling bad about making him so worried. "Don't worry about it."

"Forgive me." He stroked my cheek with the back of his fingers.

"There is nothing to be forgiven." I leaned in and hugged him.

He hugged me back and whispered in my eye, "Shall we?"

"Yes, we shall," I whispered back.

Looking out the window. I immediately spotted Victoria chatting with two men in pilot uniforms.

Thomas quickly got out of the car and opened the door for me. "Our pilots. The older gentleman is Captain Christen, and the other is Mr. Rey," he said to me while all three of them were walking towards us.

"Thank you." I held his hand tightly.

"Mr. Torian," the captain greeted Thomas first and gave me a pleasant nod. "Ms. De Waal." And the co-pilot followed suit.

Thomas introduced them to me and then conversed with them about the details of the flight.

After the gala, meeting new people had become much easier, especially, when Thomas was by my side. But just as I thought I was doing quite well, someone behind us opened the trunk of the car. I grasped Thomas' hand and whirled around in panic.

"They are just getting your luggage from the boot," he whispered, holding me closer.

I forced a smile, feeling embarrassed. And then I saw Victoria's expression of sympathy, annoyance, or probably aversion. I believed it was all in my head as she had been polite and nice to me since we met. It was my prejudice against her because of my silly insecurity.

"Are you all right, Iris?" she asked and turned towards the person carrying my luggage. "Please be more careful," she told him, her tone disapproving and harsh.

I wished I could dig a hole and bury myself in it.

"She's all right," Thomas answered for me, wrapping his arms around my waist. He then escorted me into the hangar and stepped up to the jet.

I was on the verge of tears, mad at myself for being so jumpy and for embarrassing myself in front of Thomas.

"Mr. Torian. Ms. De Waal. Welcome aboard." A soft voice pulled me back from my one-person pity party. A cabin attendant with a very familiar friendly smile was standing inside the jet.

Do I know her from somewhere?

My eyes were fixed on her when I walked past her. I knew it was rude, but she just looked so familiar to me. Big honey eyes, golden brown hair... I knew lots of women had honey eyes and golden brown hair, but not all of them had an earnest, caring, sincere, and memorable smile like that.

"Good morning, Emma," Thomas greeted her.

Emma? It doesn't ring a bell... Had I ever mentioned that I was hopelessly terrible at remembering names? This would be the time I wished I was good with names.

Thomas put his hand on the small of my back, steering me towards the back.

This cabin... My eyes were immediately drawn to the stylish space. It... It looked just like the jet bringing me home from Bern last year.

I did not take a tour of that private jet and also slept through that long-haul flight on the sofa, but I remembered I was very impressed by the design when I first walked into its cabin. Although I was not good with names, I was brilliant with identifying interior design styles and materials. And this plane had the same beige, diamond pleated leather club seats, divan, and sofas with dark brown welt, ebony credenzas, tables, and cabinets...

We stopped at the middle section of the plane. There was a seating area with one L-shape sofa and six bucket seats. Thomas motioned me to the sofa. I took the seat, still scanning around the space, frowning.

The friendly attendant followed us and took our refreshment order.

"Something bothering you?" Thomas asked.

"I...I think I was in this plane before."

"Are you sure?" His brow furrowed. "I don't believe our corporate jet was ever for hire."

"Corporate jet?"

"This jet belongs to our company." He scanned the space. "Maybe the one you flew had the same interior?"

"Silly me. It's over a year ago. I probably remember it wrong. It's no—"

"Excuse me." Emma walked in with our drinks. She put our sparkling water and a small plate of mixed nuts on the coffee table. "Is there anything else I can bring you?" she asked, her smile warm.

"No, thank you." I picked up the water, mirroring her smile.

Thomas gave her a nod of appreciation.

"Excuse me. Tom, Captain Christen would like to have a word with you." Victoria walked in while Emma was leaving.

"I will be fine. I promise I won't escape. There is no way out of here anyway," I joked, sipping my water.

"I will be right back." Thomas kissed my forehead and then left the room.

My mind was still wondering about the resemblance between the two planes.

I am going to call James once I get to New York.

The soft background music gave the cabin a relaxing and peaceful atmosphere. I took the book *Perfume* out of my bag and made myself comfortable in the corner of the sofa.

It did not take long before I heard clearer voices of Emma and Victoria behind the partition chatting friendly about Emma's friend. I didn't mean to listen in but it was impossible to mute them. It was very interesting that both timbres were sweet like honey, but each of them revealed the character I presumed: Victoria was authoritative and intimidating, and Emma was courteous and soft-spoken.

My ears pricked up when I heard my name, but Thomas walked in at this very moment, distracting my eavesdropping.

"Love, we are ready to take off," Thomas said, sitting down next to me. He gave me an adoring smile, his blue eyes looking so happy.

My heart suddenly palpitated. I was not sure if it was because of his enchanting gaze or the unknown future. I reached for his hand and interlocked our fingers, looking out the window.

After the jet reached its cruising altitude, Emma closed the curtain to give us privacy. Thomas gave me a tour of this luxurious plane.

There was a master suite in the tail section!

Seriously? I stared at the king size bed.

Thomas explained that they often had to attend meetings and take care of business soon after they landed, so having a good rest and feeling recharged and ready to go was important. They usually did not have time to recover from the journey.

I took another look at the bedroom before we moved on to other on-board amenities.

The flight was very smooth. While Thomas was on his laptop working, I spent a couple of hours reading and a great deal of time staring out the window, into the infinity of the sky...

Just last Wednesday, I was still hiding in my house, having no prospect of having a normal life. And then this man sitting next to me walked into my life, again, and I fell head over heels in love with him. My life took a dramatic turn, and I was flying across the country with him now.

Was I scared of all these changes? I was terrified!

I used to love visiting New York and was actually in the process of purchasing a property in the big apple since I traveled there so often for work; plus, I used to love the crowds and the fast tempo of the city. I found a waterfront apartment in Battery Park and planned to put in an offer once I returned from Paris. And, of course, things did not go as planned.

DeMont New York was located in the heart of Manhattan, which was the most densely populated district. The old Iris would be jumping up and down now and planning her trips to the Metropolitan Museum of Art, Guggenheim Museum, and all the boutiques on Fifth Avenue. But the current Iris just wanted to skip the ride into the city, stay in the hotel room, and put the do-not-disturb sign on the door.

How sad is that?

"Are you all right?" my newly-admitted boyfriend asked as I was staring aimlessly out the window.

"I guess…" My voice sounded downhearted.

He brushed my hair aside and nibbled my sweet spot.

"Don't start something if you cannot finish…" I joked.

"I certainly can finish it…" he whispered in my ear.

I chuckled and pulled away from him, pointing my index finger towards the front of the plane.

"If we keep it quiet," he said.

"You know I can't keep quiet," I teased him and was rewarded with his fruity laugh. "How long do you think we will be in New York?" I changed the subject, not ready to join the mile-high club….yet. I could not believe I did not ask him this question before getting on the plane with him.

"According to my schedule, approximately two weeks. Too long?" He pulled me back into his arms.

"No… You are there to work. Your schedule is my schedule."

He chuckled and added, "There are several business proposals I have to handle. I will be working a lot. Will you be all right?" He leaned in and nibbled my earlobe again.

"I also have work to do. Remember?" I wrapped one arm around his neck, bringing him closer.

"That's right…" He moved his warm lips down to my neck. "Would you like to stay longer?"

I could not answer his question because I was so distracted by his kisses. "I guess… I think we can make out a little, but we just have to keep it quiet," I whispered to him.

IT was such a rush of relief when I saw a limousine with black-tinted windows waiting for us after we stepped out of the jet. That meant I could hide in that limousine from the airport to the parking garage of the hotel.

I gazed at Thomas, appreciating how thoughtful, attentive, and understanding he was.

"Yes, love?" He caught my gaze.

"Thank you." I leaned my head against his chest.

He replied to my appreciation by wrapping his arms around me and kissing my hair.

We got into the limousine and waited for our luggage to be loaded. Then the car door was opened again, and Victoria got in and sat down across from us.

I completely forgot that she would be riding with us. The air felt a bit tense after she sat down and gave us an awkward smile.

Maybe I was the only person who thought her smile was awkward. I really needed to get over my low self-esteem.

I turned my face towards Thomas and met his doting smile.

He took my hand and intertwined our fingers, dipping a kiss on my hair.

I loved when he showed me his affection, but I felt extremely uneasy when he did that right in front of Victoria.

Does Victoria desire Thomas? A thought suddenly popped into my head.

He mentioned she was from London and was Louis' assistant for three years before becoming his assistant. She had been very helpful since he became involved with the family business, and they had been working together for over seven months now.

I wondered would she be sitting by Thomas now—not holding hands I hoped—if I were not here with him?

The gala... I was sure she would have sat next to Thomas at the gala if I were not his date...

Stop! My pragmatic voice snapped me out of my conjecture.

Thank you Miss Pragmatic!

Victoria should be the least of my concerns since I had enough on my plate now. Leaning my head against Thomas' shoulder, I closed my eyes.

It was two in the afternoon when we arrived at the hotel.

The *home* Thomas had here was on the penthouse floor. The design was contemporary and sophisticated. The living room with double-height ceilings and a grand spiral staircase astonished me.

Thomas had meetings lined up in the afternoon, so he promised me a cozy dinner right here at home tonight.

After Thomas left, I called my parents as I had promised. Their support was more than I could ask for. I also called Janie, Jojo, and Antonio. For a moment, I actually felt like the old me, who used to travel here for business and chatted with my best friends on the phone.

Should I call or not? I stared at my phone.

It was one o'clock in the morning in Switzerland. James always stayed up late when I was there.

I am calling! I tapped the call icon below his picture.

"Hi sweetie," James answered after just one ring.

"Hi darling, did I wake you?" I asked softly.

"No, we are just lying in bed watching a movie.... Never mind. He's already asleep. How are you?"

"I am great. You? Tim?" I wanted to skip the pleasantries and get to the point.

"Tim and I are fine, but we really are due for a vacation."

"Come visit me. Come back to your home country and visit me. Enjoy the California sunshine and the beaches," I said and continued before he said anything, "James, I need to ask you a question, and you have to promise me that you will be one-hundred percent honest with me."

"Of course, sweetie." His voice sounded serious and no longer sleepy. "You know I am always honest with you," he said.

"I know... And I thank you for that."

"Is everything all right?"

"Yes, everything is great. I just... I... Who arranged the private jet for my family and me last year?"

He became silent.

"James…"

"Why do you want to know that now?"

"James…"

"Seriously. Why are you suddenly curious about it now?"

"Well…" I cleared my throat. "Remember Thomas? I am with him now. And we—"

"Thomas is there in the States?" he interrupted me.

"Yes, he came to see me. And I am *with* him now," I said, the stress falling heavily on the word with, hoping he got the hint.

"Oh, sweetie. I am so happy for you." He sounded joyful. He got the hint…

"By the way…" My voice became soft and shy. "Thank you for giving him my contact information. I…I'm glad you did."

"I get to have the credit?" He chuckled, and then his voice became solemn. "I… I still have to apologize to you for giving him your phone number and address without your permission. He told me he wanted to surprise you. He was very persuasive *and* very cute, you know."

I laughed and said, "Oh, I know."

"Let me go outside first so I don't waken Tim."

"Okay…" I waited, hearing the shuffling noise and door closing sound.

"So, how does Thomas have anything to do with the private jet?" James asked.

"Well… We flew private from California to New York this—"

"You are in New York?" he interrupted me again.

"Yes, just got here."

"Sorry for interrupting. I miss New York! Please continue."

"No problem. The jet we were on today belongs to Thomas' company—"

"Wait… Thomas' company?" He interrupted me again.

Oh, right… He has no idea about that.

"Well, yes. Here is the story…" I recapped briefly on Thomas' new occupation.

"Wow… That's… It's great, isn't it? A much safer job and…

Well, it's not like being rich is important, but it's kind of nice." James chuckled.

"So, can I continue?"

"Oh, sorry. Please…"

"The cabin interior looked just like the one flying me home last year. I know I was not in my best condition then, so I probably remembered it wrong. But… I just have this crazy idea…"

"Sorry to disappoint you, sweetie. Thomas is not the one arranging the jet," James said before I finished my sentence.

"Hmmm… I don't think so either because he told me he was on an assignment in Italy then."

"There you go."

"Can you tell me who did that for me? Please"

James let out a deep sigh and said, "It has been almost a year. I hope she won't mind me telling you this."

"She?"

"Dr. Thompson…"

"Dr. Thompson?" I exclaimed. "She did that for me?" *Why would a psychiatrist go that far for a patient?*

"Yes, she arranged everything…"

"Did…did she also cover all the costs besides arranging the plane?"

"Yes, she did. I was very surprised when she called me and told me it was all taken care of. All I needed to do was get the paperwork done and get you all on the plane."

"Why didn't you tell me?"

"She asked me not to mention her name. She simply said it was the least she could do to help you go home safely and peacefully."

"The least she could do? She has done so much for me." My voice was suddenly choked with emotion.

"Iris…"

"I am fine… I need to thank her, James."

"No! Then she will know I told you. I did promise her not to tell you, and she asked me to swear on my first born."

"No, she did not." I laughed.

"No, she didn't. Maybe an opportunity will arise, and then you can thank her."

"Fine," I said reluctantly. "So… I guess it was just a coincidence that the two planes are alike."

"It has to be, right?" James' voice was comforting. "Don't fuss over things like that. Now tell me how did it get so fast between you and Thomas?"

"What do you mean?"

"He called me… Last… Wait, no. Yes. Last Monday. And now you are with him in New York. That is pretty fast, hon."

"I've known him for a long time, James."

"Since he needed to obtain your contact information from me, I doubt you two have been keeping in touch."

I knew I could never fool James. "It's a long story…"

"I always have time for you. And since I am not going to sleep anytime soon, I am all ears. Just let me get comfortable on the sofa now…"

It was so nice to tell someone who knew everything I had been through and never judged. He patiently listened to me telling him what Thomas had told me and what had happened in the past eight days, minus the intimate moments, of course. James just listened. He did not interrupt or ask any questions and only responded with mhm, uh-huh, and wow.

"So here I am…" I finished the story telling.

"Thomas just goes from cute to hot now, " James said.

"Honestly, I am still digesting all of this."

"I would get heartburn if I were you," he joked, and I burst out laughing.

How much I miss James! He would be one of the reasons if I decided to go back to Switzerland with Thomas.

"So… We are talking about *die Liebe* here," he said, emphasizing *love* in German.

"*Ya, Ich bin total verliebt in Thomas,*" I replied in German, telling him I was totally in love with Thomas.

When I was going to tell James more about how I felt about Thomas, the subject of our topic opened the door and walked into the foyer. "He just came back," I said to James.

"Hi Thomas," James greeted.

"James said hi," I said to Thomas, who just walked into the living room.

Thomas was caught off guard, his brow furrowing. He walked up to me and leaned down to give me a kiss on my cheek.

"Hi James," he said to the phone in my hand. Then he whispered to me, "I am going upstairs to change." He kissed my forehead and then walked towards the stairs, dragging his feet a little, looking tired.

"I am back…" I said to James.

"Honey, enjoy yourself. I am certain that he's a good man and the right one for you. Do what Janie has been encouraging you. Take a leap of faith! If you love him, then trust him," James said in a very sincere voice. "Sweetie, I am going to bed now…"

"Oh, okay. I will talk to you soon. Love you."

"Love you, too."

Hanging up the phone, I did feel much better. James was right. If I love Thomas, I should trust him wholeheartedly, knowing he would catch me if I took the leap…

CHAPTER 26

> You may be deceived
> if you trust too much,
> but you will live in torment
> if you don't trust enough.
> ~Frank Crane

AFTER Thomas left for work, staring out the window overlooking the breathtaking panoramic view of Central Park had become something I did everyday now if I was not working, reading, or watching TV and movies. And I would daydream about taking a walk to the Metropolitan Museum of Art and Guggenheim Museum, or simply strolling through the park.

However, I started feeling bored after almost a week, especially when Thomas had to work both Saturday and Sunday. If I were home, I could kill time in the fun room, friends and family would visit me, or I would be on my way to the ranch right now.

Thomas must have sensed my boredom because he asked me this morning if he could take me out for a dinner date tonight. I immediately said yes, not caring how he was going to arrange it. I just had to get out of this place.

"...How wonderful life is while you're in the world..." My phone started singing Thomas' new text tone.

Thomas: Love, dinner reservation at 8. Miss you.

I replied to his text with a heart-emoji, wondering where he was taking me...

Being in a relationship again was…amazing! And I jumped into this one with Thomas by flying across the country with him and practically living with him right now. I loved every minute of it. We could not keep our hands off each other when he was home, and I missed him terribly when he went to work. He would text or call me from wherever he was, either in the hotel or somewhere in the city. And I would smile like a silly fangirl while reading his sweet messages or on the phone with him.

It was three o'clock in the afternoon now. I bet Thomas needed a caffeine boost. Staring at the caffè mocha I just made, I was persuading myself to bring it to him.

He shared his schedule with me every morning, so I knew he was in his office now. However, the problem was his office was on the third floor of the hotel. I had been wanting to surprise him at his office many times, but the possibility of running into the staff whom I had never met scared me off.

"I have met most of the staff on the third floor," I said to myself. "Plus, only authorized personnel have access to that floor. It's safe."

Honestly, I was simply looking for excuses to get out of this penthouse suite.

"It will be a nice surprise," I continued to talk to myself. "The worst case is I panic and run all the way back here. Right?"

Right. I answered myself in the head and picked up the coffee mug.

There was no sight of any staff in the corridor when I stepped out of the elevator. I could hear faint voices coming from the offices.

I moved slowly towards Thomas' office, which was located at the end of the corridor. And then my heart sank when I reached this office and heard Victoria's voice behind the closed door.

Bad timing…

Just as I was ready to turn around, Victoria's saddened tone stopped me from doing so.

"Tom, you know me… I…I just thought…"

"Vic…" Thomas sounded hesitant.

"Aren't you surprised and excited?" She sounded eager and yearning.

Surprised and excited? I moved closer to the door.

"I didn't ask you because I wanted it to be a surprise. We had so much fun at the London jazz festival last year. I know—"

"I cannot go," Thomas cut her off, his tone harsh.

"You enjoyed the festival so much last year. I thought… I thought you would be thrilled." She sounded as if she was about to cry.

"You thought wrong, Vic." His voice became s little softer.

I hoped he was speaking softly to prevent her from crying because his harsh tone was intimidating. I had first-hand experience of that, and the thought of Max's vicious voice *and* look gave me chills.

"Then, tell me why…" She was choked with emotion.

She sounds so vulnerable. Oh… Wait… She wants him…

"I just want us to have some fun while we are here. I have been with you—"

"Working with me," he corrected her.

Have some fun? What kind of fun?

"Tom…" His name rolled off her tongue, her voice so seductive. "Yes, working with you, day and night. Don't you remember those late nights? You are always so thoughtful, so chivalrous."

Late nights? Chivalrous? I had an urge to go inside and tell her that he was mine. But… I was eavesdropping. Maybe I should leave now as curiosity killed the cat.

Iris, wait. A cat has nine lives. For three he plays, for three he strays, and for the last three he STAYS. Miss curiosity stopped me from leaving. And I moved closer to the door…

"It's enough, Vic." He surely sounded irritated.

I heard a shuffling noise. It sounded like he stood up, or someone did.

"No, it's not. Not until I talk some sense into you. I care about you, Tom…"

Oh, I hated the way she called his name.

"While we traveled to different cities, you enjoyed local cuisines and loved exploring their cultures. You told me you couldn't wait to travel the whole world. Just last month in Tokyo. Don't you remember?"

Do I want to hear this? Did they date before? Are they not together because of me? My chest suddenly felt heavy, my hands trembling. I quickly held the mug with both hands.

"I don't understand, Tom." Her saddened voice pulled me back from my thoughts. "You have changed since we arrived in California. First, you missed many meetings, and then you disappeared for days—"

"My whereabouts are not your concern," he interrupted her.

"I manage all your affairs, personal and business, when we are on the road. They are my concern."

Wow, she's tough. My brow furrowed.

"How am I supposed to do my job if you don't…" She paused.

Is she crying? I leaned my ear against the door.

"It's okay if you meet someone and want to have fun with her instead…"

Wait… Is she talking about me? Instead? What does that mean? My mind started surmising that there must be something between them before Thomas and I started dating.

"Tom… I'm not criticizing her," she continued. "But being with such a timid person is totally out of character for you. You are stuck in the hotel with her because she doesn't want to go out. Why are you doing this to yourself?"

He's stuck in the hotel? Because of me?

And then there was silence. None of them were speaking.

Why doesn't he defend me? Is he ignoring her or considering what she just said? My heart was palpitating, a burning sensation in my eyes.

"We can fly out in the evening just to see a couple of performances and come right back. Don't I deserve some attention from you?" Her voice was so tender, and it made me nauseous.

"I have already told you I cannot." His voice was harsh again.

"Nobody has to know. She doesn't have to know…"

"But I know," Thomas said with a very firm voice. "Iris…"

My heart nearly stopped when I heard my name. I could not bear to hear another word…

I have to leave now. I turned around and scampered towards the elevator.

Back in the suite, I put the mug back in the kitchen and headed upstairs to the bedroom.

Hastily, I undressed myself and jumped in the shower. I needed the gushing water enveloping me completely and the splashing sound blocking me from the outside world. All I needed was a few minutes of serenity to forestall an anxiety attack, a wave of depression, and intrusive thoughts.

Antonio was right… I had been sheltered and protected ever since I came home. Everyone around me was specially, or unusually, nice and attentive, to make me feel comfortable and good about myself. I was shielded from all negative opinions…

My eyes were burning, tears streaming down along with the warm water.

I am not timid… My whole life I had never been timid. I wanted to go out, and I wanted to travel the world, but only if I could stop the *damn* panic attacks.

Victoria was right about all the abnormal behaviors I had. And she was right about me holding Thomas back.

What should I do? I loved him too much to walk away. I was not a saint, and I did not know how to sacrifice my own happiness for his… Freedom? Did he feel stuck in the hotel with me here? What was our prospect after New York?

We needed to have this conversation before going any further in our relationship.

———

THOMAS came back a little after six-thirty. He walked up to me and embraced me in his arms, his smile wiping all my concerns away.

"You look so lovely. Looks like you are ready for our date night." He eyed me up and down, but his eyes lingered a little longer over my puffy eyes, which I covered with smokey eye makeup.

"I don't get to dress up to go out often now," I said eagerly, trying to distract his attention. "So, tonight is really a treat for me." I picked a black cocktail dress for our date, curled my hair, and put on heavier makeup.

"You can dress up for me anytime." He cupped my face and kissed me passionately, making my knees buckle. "I am going to take a shower and get ready," he said after parting his lips from mine.

I blinked my eyes, feeling woozy from the kiss. "I will be right here…" I whispered, drowning in his blue gaze. Now I was even more certain that I would do my best to make this relationship work.

He dipped a kiss on my forehead before heading upstairs.

When I found out he was not available this afternoon, I should have just come right back. Their conversation had been playing over and over again in my head now, making me wonder if he had given up the things he enjoyed because of me, if he felt he was stuck here with me, and if I was holding him back?

Standing by the window, I stared out at the skyline over Central Park. It was such a magnificent view, but I was in no mood for it. My mind was going crazy about what Victoria said. Apparently, Thomas never told her how we met and never mentioned my condition to her. And… There was another thing troubling me: What kind of attention did she want from him?

Affection or just phy… I quickly shook off the thought because what Thomas and I had was so special. I refused to let this thought contaminate it.

Nobody has to know. She doesn't have to know… Victoria's voice popped in my head again.

"She always knows!" I thought aloud.

Where is Miss Pragmatic? I needed her to snap me out of my insecurity and paranoia.

I trusted him, and I did not care if he had ever been with her before. Everyone would easily fall for him. He was very attractive, obviously, his heart so beautiful and his bravery admirable. Everything about him was…breath-taking. So perfect that my heart ached when he told me that he loved me.

What I really cared about would be how he responded to the temptations of other women. If he decided to take Victoria up on her offer, whatever it was, I would leave right away, even if I had to walk on the busy streets of New York City.

Why do you even think that is a possibility? Miss Pragmatic made her appearance.

Now you are here! I berated Miss Pragmatic. If she were here earlier, I would not be thinking about whatever I was thinking about now.

If you trust him, then don't doubt him, Miss Pragmatic stated.

"Iris…" Thomas' voice startled me. He then wrapped his arms around my waist from behind and whispered in my ear, "You are deep in thought…"

I turned around and wrapped my arms around his neck.

He was wearing light grey slacks and a white linen button-down shirt, top two buttons undone. He smelled and looked so yummy. I didn't mind skipping dinner and having him instead. Looking into his brilliant blue eyes, I was falling in love with him deeper and deeper everyday.

Raising my heels, I gave him an amorous kiss.

He was definitely aroused by the kiss. He picked me up and carried me to the sofa.

"It's already seven-thirty," I reminded him while he sat down on the sofa with me in his arms. "We will be late for dinner."

"I don't care…" He nibbled my neck.

I chuckled, moving to sit astride his lap. Cupping his face in my hands, I said, "The anticipation might stimulate the excitement. We can skip the desert…"

"How about skipping the dinner all together?" He sneaked his hands underneath my skirt and palmed my bottom.

Wasn't I just thinking about skipping the dinner earlier?

"Very tempting, Mr. Torian. But you promise me a night…out of this suite." I pouted my lips.

"I did indeed promise you that…" he said, sounding unenthusiastic.

"How about I promise you a great night after dinner," I whispered in his ear.

"Let's go then!" He gently spanked my buttock.

I laughed, getting off his lap.

He put on a black suit jacket that he had by the door. Now he looked perfect and totally matched my dress.

We left the suite and took the employee elevator all the way to the ground floor. He wrapped his arm around my shoulders before the elevator door opened as more employees and staff were here in New York than Los Angeles. And I made sure to focus on him instead of my surroundings.

We arrived at the entrance of *Dine*, which was a French restaurant owned by acclaimed French chef and restaurateur Claudine Aveline and housed in DeMont New York. I read the hotel booklet and learned that the name Dine was not the verb dine but the short form of Chef Aveline's given name Clau-dine. How interesting was that! Just like I was not named after the flower—laughing inwardly.

"Good evening, ma'am, Mr. Torian," a very pleasant host greeted. "We have your table ready. This way, please." He led us towards the restaurant staircase, which was right by the host stand, and up to the second floor.

The staircase was absolutely elegantly crafted with a long crystal raindrop chandelier, vintage mirrored walls, and delicate wrought iron railing. My enthusiasm for great designs completely distracted my attention away from strangers around us. A much warmer lighting and soft atmosphere welcomed us when we arrived at the second floor landing. This floor was definitely a much more exclusive dining area. We followed the host to the furthest corner of the room. A table-for-two, separated from the rest of the dining tables by delicate floor-to-ceiling crystal beaded curtains, was by the windows overlooking Central Park.

"I feel so… special," I said to him after the host left us.

"You are special." He leaned in and gave me a kiss on my cheek.

"Thank you," I said bashfully.

I noticed Thomas was looking out the window, so I turned my head towards the same direction and saw the sunset shading Central Park with its golden rays.

"Did you make the reservation at this time on purpose?" I asked in astonishment.

"I am glad you have noticed that," he said, a smile spreading over his face.

The truth was the smile on his face was more magnificent than the sunset.

"Love, Chef Aveline is walking over here," Thomas said. "She's a friend of my family and is as wonderful as her culinary skills."

I looked through the curtain opening and saw a tall lady walking towards us. She was not in a chef uniform but an elegant black suit.

"*Bonsoir,* Claudine." Thomas stood up.

"*Bonsoir*, Tommy." Chef Aveline's smile was cordial.

They greeted each other with cheek kisses.

"Claudine, this is my girlfriend, Ms. Iris De Waal. Iris, this is Chef Claudine Aveline."

"So nice to meet you, Ms. De Waal." Chef Aveline sounded absolutely pleasant.

"It's a pleasure meeting you as well, Chef Aveline. Call me Iris, please," I replied.

"Iris, then you must call me Claudine," she said, smiling broadly. "It's so wonderful to see Tommy dining with someone so special like you."

"Thank you…" I blushed.

"I will have Adam bring the wine. Château DeMont 2003?" she asked Thomas.

"Excellent choice," Thomas replied.

"Fantastic! Enjoy the wonderful evening." She patted Thomas gently on the shoulder, smiling at me. Gracefully, she turned around and left.

"Tommy… I noticed the whole table at the gala called you Tommy, too."

"A childhood nickname." He gave me a one-sided smile, shrugging.

"Who else calls you Tommy?" *Honestly, he didn't look like a Tommy.*

"Close friends and families…"

"Hmmm… I am happy to stick with Thomas."

"Wonderful choice," he said and gave me a charming wink. He picked up the menu and said with avidity, "Let's see what is good today."

"Surprise me." I ignored the menu, giving him a playful smile.

"Trust me?"

"Always."

"Fantastic!" He sat straighter, staring at the menu as if he was accepting it as a big challenge.

I just fixed my eyes on him, enjoying my view—forgetting about the sunset.

All of the dishes were exquisitely garnished as works of art, and they tasted absolutely divine. It was a perfect night out for me. I could feel the good wine slowly working its magic on me. It was making me feel both relaxed and cheerful and also boosting my courage to be honest with Thomas. What was the point of being together if we could not be completely honest with each other?

"I have a confession to make... Tommy," I said to him, my expression solemn.

He chuckled, presumably at me calling him his nickname. "I am listening," he said, his voice *seductive*.

Must be the wine... It was making him sound so enticing.

I took another sip of my wine and said, "I made a cup of coffee for you and brought it to your office this afternoon."

"You did? I am sorry that I missed you." He reached for my hand—the one not clasping the wineglass—and said softly, "I would have enjoyed your coffee very much. You must have come when I was at the lobby for—"

"You were at your office, and so was Victoria," I interrupted him, my voice casual.

"Why did you not come in?"

"I didn't want to intrude. It sounded like you two were having a serious conversation." I took another small sip of the wine and added in a very low voice, "I didn't mean to eavesdrop..."

He smiled, his sapphire gaze gleaming, and he had not let go of my hand.

"I... I heard just a little part of the conversation." I observed his expression, but all I saw was his charming smile. "I think... I think..."

"Love, that is a lot of thinking." His smile became *really delightful*.

Or maybe it's the wine... It made him look so charming.

"I am... I am sure many women are attracted to you..."

He raised one eyebrow and took a sip of the wine, one hand still holding mine. He put down the wine glass and reached the free hand out to touch my warm, wine-flushed cheeks, smiling in amusement. "Your checks are so red now..."

"Focus." My brow furrowed. "I am a woman, I know why they are attracted to you."

He tilted his head, narrowing his *gorgeous* blue eyes.

Maybe it's not the wine... His eyes were always so captivating.

"You cannot stop or change the way they feel about you..." I paused to take a deep breath—the wine was really getting to me now. "But you are the one who can decide how to respond to their affections. Don't you agree?"

"Totally," he said, nodding his head.

I took another sip of wine to give myself another boost of courage. "I...I don't know how she—"

"Who?" His brow furrowed deeply.

"Victoria. I only heard her suggesting that you two flew somewhere together..." I stared at my wine glass, my fingers idly running along the rim of the glass.

"Ah, that..." He let out a sigh, holding my hand with both of his warm, big hands. "She invited me to the Newport Jazz Festival in Rhode Island."

Jazz Festival? Suddenly, I felt downhearted because it was not something I was able to have fun with him. I pulled my hand back, picked up the wine, and took a gulp of it.

"Do you really think I would consider it?" He sounded slightly offended and hurt.

"No, I don't." I looked into his eyes. "I am just...sad." My gaze dropped down, staring aimlessly at the water glass in front of him. "I wish I could go to a jazz festival with you, but I cannot even walk into the hotel lobby by myself…" I forced a smile and moved my gaze back at him. "Can I ask you something?"

"Anything, love." His expression was now concerned and adoring.

"Do you feel stuck in the hotel with me?"

His expression was now gradually turning angry, or maybe annoyed. "You heard that…" His voice was harsh.

"I am sorry. I didn't mean to eavesdrop…" I averted my eyes.

"You have nothing to apologize for, love." He reached for my hand again.

"But… Why…why do you look so mad?"

"Not at you." He held my hand up and leaned in to press a kiss on my fingers. "And to answer your question. No, I don't feel stuck in the hotel with you. Or anywhere."

"But I'm not able to—"

He held up a finger to stop me from talking. "You flew across the country with me. That is a huge step, my love. Do you know how thrilled I was when you decided to give us a try? To take a chance with me. To trust me…"

"I do trust you…"

"Then don't ever doubt yourself, or me."

I bit my lower lip, my eyes brimming with tears.

He stood up and leaned over the table to kiss me. "*Je t'aime,*" he whispered he loved me when he parted his lips from mine.

Honesty was always the best policy. I was just awarded with an honest answer and an affectionate kiss.

"Ex…excuse me…" Adam appeared outside the crystal beaded curtains.

"Yes, Adam?" Thomas asked, his eyes still fixed on me.

Adam parted the crystal strings and walked into our little secluded corner. "Would you like to look at the dessert menu, Ms. De Waal, Mr. Torian?" he asked.

Thomas looked at me, wiggling his eyebrows.

I nodded in enthusiasm.

"We are done here, Adam," Thomas replied, holding my hand,

eager to head back upstairs. "We have to go now."

"Yes, of course, Mr. Torian." Adams stepped aside, holding the curtain open for us.

Instead of going downstairs to take the elevator, Thomas took me through a hidden door leading to a narrow passage and then through another door opening to the employee elevator on the second floor. Sometimes I forgot his family owned this place, and he probably could walk around this building blindfolded.

Once we stepped into the elevator, he pushed the button and immediately sealed my lips with his before the doors even closed. I could smell the alluring wine in his breath.

Out of the elevator, we walked towards the suite briskly. He already had the key in hand, wasting no time to open the door.

And then, I stepped on something when I walked into the foyer. An envelope… Someone slipped it under the door while we were out.

We both looked at the envelope, bewildered.

I picked it up and saw it was addressed to me. "Nice handwriting," I commented.

"Unbelievable…" Thomas murmured when he took a look at the handwriting. The amorous expression disappeared from his face.

An ostentatious greeting card was revealed when I opened the envelope.

Dear Iris,

Thomas' favorite musicians will be performing at Newport Jazz Festival this Friday evening. Enclosed are the tickets for the event. I hope you will enjoy it.

It would also be my pleasure if I can accompany you to explore this fabulous city. I can also make arrangements to have personal sales associates for you in any boutique you desire. I promise you will enjoy my company and the city. You can give me a ring at my room 1206 or the office.

Sincerely,
Victoria Nilsson

I showed Thomas the tickets, feeling uneasy.

"I am going upstairs." He glanced at the tickets and gave me a kiss on my forehead.

What made her decide to give me the tickets and invite me to tour the city? I did not hear how their conversation ended. I hoped it did not end awkwardly as they still had to work together after all.

Letting out a sigh, I left the card and tickets on the foyer table and headed to the spiral staircase. Victoria's good intentions, at least I thought it was good, completely spoiled our mood.

Thomas was in the bathroom when I walked into the bedroom. He was either very tidy or well trained by the police academy. His wallet, watch, and keys were neatly placed on top of the dresser, and his suit and shirt were hung in the closet.

He was brushing his teeth in his pajama pants, topless, when I walked into the bathroom.

I stood next to him and reached for my toothbrush. He immediately wrapped his arm around my waist with his free arm. Even when we were alone, his affection was never absent...

When he was done, he gave me a kiss on my hair and walked back to the bedroom. He was quiet, and I could feel that something was bothering him.

I decided to put on one of the gifts he had showered me with since we arrived in New York to redirect our mood back to before discovering the envelope. This *Agent Provocateur Christi* nude-and-red, short slip had better work its magic.

He was sitting on the end of the bed, flipping through TV channels, and he stopped when I walked into the room.

I sat astride his lap, resting my arms around his neck.

He palmed my buttock and wanted to pull me closer, but I stopped him and sat where I was.

"If we want to make this work, you should be able to tell me what is troubling you, and I should do the same. Not necessarily at this very moment, but whenever you are ready," I said in a very soft voice.

Gently, he stroked my hair, his blue gaze flicking between my eyes.

"Something is troubling you…" I continued, "I know you want to take care of me and protect me as meticulously as possible. And I wish to do the same if I can…"

"There's nothing between Victoria and me," he said, sounding frustrated. "I see her as a colleague, maybe as a friend because she has worked and known my family for years."

"That's understandable…" I ran my fingers through his black mane.

He let out a heavy sigh, averting his eyes. "I sense and know she wants more…"

I could tell he did not even want to talk about it, so I whispered softly to him, "Hey… I know…" I cupped his face, making him look at me again. "And you have been a perfect gentleman."

He leaned in, wanting to kiss me, but I tilted backward because I wanted our intimacy to be carefree and worry-free.

"I know taking care of me is not an easy task…" I felt a lump in my throat.

"Iris…" He looked at me with his doting eyes. "Don't say that."

"I am embracing what I am now. I can't deny it…anymore," I said with a heavy heart and then quickly put on a smile. "I don't want you to fit in with my needs and babysit me. If you want to do anything, you should go and enjoy it. I am a reasonable person." I dipped a kiss on his lips. "If you will enjoy the festival, you should —"

"Honestly, I don't," he interrupted me.

"Oh…" I widened my eyes because it was not what I heard this afternoon.

"She invited me to the London Jazz Festival last November after I mentioned I enjoyed jazz. I went because she also invited Louis and Eva. My favorite singer Max Raabe is not even a jazz singer."

That made me chuckle. "Max Raabe?" I asked, still chuckling because his frustrated and annoyed expression really did not suit him.

"He's a talented crooner from Germany. I would love to take you to one of his concerts." Gently rubbing my arms, he said, "I enjoyed many things. And I will enjoy them even more if I can have your company."

This man... I cupped his face and kissed him passionately.

He held me closer and deepened our kiss. I could feel he was getting his mood back as his erection was getting profound.

I pulled myself away from his warm lips—reluctantly—and said, "I will write a nice note replying to Victoria's card. And it will be very kind of you if you can drop it off for me."

"Mmmm..." He did not sound like he heard me as he leaned in and trailed the kiss down my neck.

"And... Would you like some dessert now?"

"Yes, lots of it." He tugged me closer and groaned.

It was still dark when I woke up in the morning. Not wanting to disturb Thomas, I padded out of the bedroom and did my morning business in another bathroom. I made a cup of coffee in the kitchen and then went to the home office as I remembered I saw the hotel stationery in one of the desk drawers.

I started to compose my reply and realized it was harder than I thought. I wanted it to be polite and respectful, but at the same time I did not want to share too much with her, either...

Dear Victoria,

Thank you for the tickets. However, Thomas and I are not able to attend the festival due to a prior engagement. Enclosed are the tickets. Perhaps you can offer them to your friends instead. Your kindness is greatly appreciated.

New York is a fabulous city. I had the opportunity to work here years ago and enjoyed its culture and lifestyle very much. Unfortunately, I have to decline your invitation as I have a project deadline to meet before going back to LA next week. Thank you for your understanding.

Sincerely,
Iris De Waal

CHAPTER 27

> Be curious, not judgmental.
> ~Walt Whitman

"**IS** it because of me?" I asked. "Is my reply too harsh?"

"Not at all, love. It's polite and perfect."

"Then, why did she suddenly quit?" I asked, feeling panicky and guilty.

Thomas just told me that Victoria handed in her resignation letter today, and I really thought it was all because of me.

"Was she upset? Did you talk to her? Did you ask her why?" I asked eagerly, following behind Thomas who was walking towards the bedroom to change. And I walked right into him when he stopped abruptly.

"Iris…" He turned around, gazing down at me.

I rubbed my forehead as his back muscle was really hard.

"She handled everything professionally." He moved my hand away and pressed a kiss on my forehead. "She already hired a temporary assistant for me and detailed all the job descriptions for her replacement."

"Just like that?"

"Just like that." He wrapped his arm around my waist, and we walked into the bedroom together.

"Is she going back to Bern? Or back home. London, right?"

"I don't know." He started to remove his phone, wallet, and keys from his pockets and neatly placed them on top of the dresser.

"Can I talk to her?"

He turned to me, his brow furrowed.

"Just a chat. No big deal. I will be right back." I ran downstairs to retrieve my phone.

I was not crazy or so masochistic that I wanted to talk to the woman who wanted my man in a romantic way. But she just did not appear to be that kind of person who would throw a tantrum and quit her job when someone rejected her. Since I met her, I had held a prejudice against her because of my stupid insecurity. Now I was really curious about her.

"Can I have her number, please? *Mon Chéri*..." I asked when I walked back to the bedroom.

I whistled at him when I saw he had already stripped down to his brief.

"Like what you see?" He winked at me, opening a dresser drawer for a t-shirt.

"Very much..." I walked up to him and wrapped my arms around his waist from behind. "Since we are not going anywhere, why don't you just walk around like this?"

"Hmmm..." He sounded like he was actually considering the idea. "Well... Will you join me?"

"What? In my thong?" I laughed, leaning to one side to look at him.

"I am picturing it now..." He closed his eyes, smirking. "Wow..."

"Stop it..." I looked at his handsome face and asked. "So... Can I have Victoria's number, please?"

He looked at me, frowning. "You really want to talk to her?"

I nodded and said, "Just something I feel I have to do. *Je t'en prie*..." I begged him in French, and that made him smile.

He grabbed his phone on the dresser and handed it to me. "Passcode is your birthday. Day. Month. Year," he whispered in my ear. Then he kissed my forehead and walked into the bathroom.

My eyes widened in surprise, watching him walking away. My gaze slowly focused on his backside. *Yummy*... Then I let out a sigh of disappointment when he closed the door.

My birthday? I stared at his phone. *Maybe I will change mine to his birthday.* I unlocked his phone and opened the Contacts app. I quickly scrolled the list down, found Victoria's information, and shared it to my phone. Then I continued staring at his phone.

No, Iris. Do not snoop through his phone. Miss Pragmatic said rigorously.

No, I'm not snooping. But... Can I look at the photos? My index finger paused on top of the phone screen.

Absolutely not! Miss Pragmatic rebuked.

Fine! I pushed the side button to turn off the phone. Miss Pragmatic was right. I should not misuse his trust. I put his phone back on the dresser and went downstairs to make the call.

Not sure if she would answer an unknown call or not, I decided to send her a text first.

Me: Hi Victoria. This is Iris. Are you available? Can I give you a call now?

Victoria: Yes & Yes

She replied to my text almost immediately.

I tapped the phone icon, and she answered the phone on the first ring.

"Hello Iris," her usual low and sweet voice greeted me.

"Hi Victoria."

"What a surprise! How can I help you?" She sounded cheerful.

Is she being sarcastic?

Stop this bias if you still want to chat with her! Miss Pragmatic yelled at me.

Right... Okay. Here we go. I took a deep breath. "I am wondering if we can talk over a cup of coffee? Or tea? I mean whatever you like to drink... Whenever you have time..." I started babbling.

"Of course. I would love to."

"You would?" I thought out loud. I smashed myself on the forehead. "Great! When would—"

"How about now?" she interrupted me.

Huh? Now? I didn't even know what I was going to say or ask.

"I am going somewhere in a couple of hours. And tomorrow is going to be crazy since it's my last day. Would you like to grab a drink in the bar?" Her response was so casual as if she did not just quit her job today.

Will Thomas be okay with this? I looked up, staring in the direction of the bedroom. *He can have dinner without me for one night.*

"Sure," I said and added. "But…but not the bar though."

"We can go to the coffee shop if you really want coffee?" she asked.

"Here is the thing…" I hesitated but believed it was best just to be candid. "Vitoria, I have this issue with crowd and strangers—"

"Oh my god!" she exclaimed, interrupting me.

"What happens? Are you all right?" I jumped on my feet, frantic with worry.

"I am so sorry, Iris. I didn't know… Otherwise I wouldn't have given you the festival tickets and invited you to go shopping." Her voice sounded regretful.

"Please. It's all good." I sat back down. *Is she always this dramatic?*

"I feel so silly, Iris. You have no idea…"

"Don't worry about it. No harm done," I said but regretted it immediately. *No harm done? She quit her job!*

"Would you like to come to my room?" she asked frankly as if we knew each other very well.

"Oh… Are you sure?"

"Absolutely! If you don't mind me getting ready while we talk."

I looked down at myself and said, "If you don't mind me in shorts and a t-shirt."

"Of course not, silly." She chuckled. "I am in Room 1206. See you later."

"See you later."

I ended the call, feeling both relieved and nervous at the same time. The tone in her voice sounded almost jolly, and she also sounded like she actually liked me.

What do I want to say to her? Why do I even want to talk to her? Honestly, I had no idea.

"Are you all right?" Thomas asked, walking downstairs in rustic blue jeans and a white t-shirt.

I gazed at my man, nodding and smiling like a silly fangirl—I was his silly fangirl.

"Room service should be here soon. I will get the wine," he said, walking into the kitchen.

"About that…" I got up and followed him. "Do you mind…"

"Yes?" He opened the wine cooler and pulled out a shelf, scanning the bottles.

"I called Victoria earlier," I said, waiting for his reaction.

"Hmmm…" He seemingly did not care. Picking up a bottle, he carefully read the label.

"She invited me to her room to chat." I leaned against the cabinet by the cooler, looking at him. My hand reached out on its own to comb his hair back with my fingers. He probably needed a haircut soon, but I liked it. I liked that I could run my fingers through those dark strands and gripped them when I came…

He gazed moved from the wine label to me.

Grinning, I pulled my hand back and put both hands behind me so they would not touch him on their own.

"Now… I mean to her room now. Do you mind eating dinner without me?" I asked.

He raised one eyebrow, closing the cooler door. "Of course not," he said, opening a drawer for the wine opener. "If that is what you want to do."

"Sort of… Yes." I nodded.

"Should I keep your dinner warm or put it away?" He started opening the bottle of wine he just chose.

My dinner was his concern, not his girlfriend going to chat with his soon-to-be-former assistant who had a crush on him.

This man… I walked up to him and wrapped my arms around his neck.

He put the half-opened wine down and wrapped his arms around my waist, giving me his full attention.

"I will be back in a couple of hours. I promise." Raising up my heels, I gave him a kiss.

"I can wait for you."

"No. You had worked all day and must be tired and hungry. Just enjoy the dinner and wine."

"Okay…" He leaned down and kissed me passionately, making me want to reconsider my plan.

"I…" I spoke against his warm lips. "I should go now…"

He gave my bottom a gentle squeeze before letting me go.

"*Je t'aime,*" I said, winking at him before I left the kitchen.

I grabbed my phone, not bothering with the key, and left the suite. I took the employee elevator down to the twelfth floor to avoid the possibility of running into strangers. Following the sign, I quickly came to Room 1206 and knocked on the door before losing my nerve. Music was playing behind the door. I hoped she heard the knock.

"Coming!" Her voice sounded muffled.

And soon the door was opened. Victoria was in a hotel bathrobe, her hair wrapped in a towel. She had no makeup on and looked so much younger.

"Hi! Come on in, please." She smiled, motioning me to the room.

I stepped into a spacious living room elegantly furnished with camelback sofas and marble top coffee tables.

"This way." She led me through a sliding door and into the bedroom.

I felt very uncomfortable when I walked into the bedroom as we did not really know each other. At all.

"I usually go to the club whenever I am ready, but today I am supposed to meet someone there."

"Oh, I am sorry. We can chat some other time."

"No way. I am so glad that you called," she said, walking into the bathroom. "Would you like something to drink?"

"No, thank you." I quickly scanned the room: King size bed, chaise lounge by the window, TV on the wall… I walked towards the bathroom and stood outside. "So, you are going to a club?" I asked, making a conversation.

"Yes—" she said and turned on the hair dryer.

Yes was all I heard, and everything else she was saying now was quelled by the hair dryer. She smiled at me from her reflection in the mirror.

I smiled back, deciding not to ask her to repeat what I had missed but get to the reason why I was here. "Victoria..."

She shook her head, her free hand pointing at her hair. "Give me two minutes!" She shouted over the hair dryer.

Okay... I have two minutes to compose what I want to say. I nodded, sitting down on the bench by the bathroom door.

What I really wanted to know was... Seriously, I should not feel guilty if she quit because Thomas rejected her.

Then, why am I here? Well... I simply wanted to ask her if she was all right...

The sudden silence—actually, not really silence as the music was playing in the living room—pulled me back from my thoughts. She was done with drying her hair.

"I am sorry. What did you want to say earlier?" she asked, running her fingers through her silky blonde hair.

"I... I was..." I let out a deep sigh and asked, "Are you all right?"

She looked surprised, frowning, and then a faint smile spread over her face. "I am great, Iris." She walked out of the bathroom and sat down on the bed facing me. "You want to know why I quit my job..."

Wow, she's straightforward. I considered my answer and said, "Yes."

"I will need a glass of wine for it," she said, standing up and walking into the living room.

I followed her, my eyes widened. *Is it that bad?*

She poured herself a glass of white wine and turned back to me. "Can I offer you one?"

"No, thank you." I was surprised as her smile was radiant. "But... But... Water, please, if not too much trouble."

"Sparking?"

"Even better."

She handed me a bottle of San Pellegrino and walked to the desk to pick up her phone. She stopped the music, put the phone back down, and walked to the sofa, sipping her wine in the entire process.

She really needs that drink...

She sat on the three-seater sofa, giving me a bright smile. "Please have a seat."

She looks happy though... I took the one seater sofa across from her.

"I really, really fancy Tom," she said almost right after I sat down.

"I know," I replied. I could also be straightforward.

She seemed to like my answer as her smile became even bigger. She took another sip of the wine and said, "But he loves you."

My heart palpitated, wondering if this was a bad idea and I should leave now.

"This whole thing between you two is such a wake-up call for me," she said, letting out a soft sigh.

"What...what do you mean?" I suddenly felt nervous and even a bit nauseous. *What does she know?* I knew Thomas would never share my story. Maybe I should leave...

"I was told Louis had a younger brother after I started working as Louis' PA," she started to explain.

I think I am staying...

"However, the whole family had never talked about him. Actually, now I think about it... I think they avoided talking about him. Anyway, I thought they probably weren't close. And then one day, out of blue, Louis told me his baby brother was going to take over his position. Tom has been such a mysterious man, from the very beginning."

Tell me about it... I smiled inwardly.

"Maybe that's the reason I am so attracted to him," she added.

It started to bother me that she was using present-tense: I *fancy* Tom. I *am* so attracted to him.

"And the longer I worked with him, the more I fell for him," she added more.

Past-tense? That's better...

"He's always so serious and gentlemanly. Once I told Louis that I thought Tom should be the older brother." She chuckled.

For some reason I felt jealous of her. She knew his family and worked with him longer than we had been with each other.

"Then, he completely changed after we arrived in California."

Okay... This is what I heard the other day...

"You've changed him." She pointed her index finger at me.

"Have I?" I sank deeper into the sofa, feeling I should justify myself.

"In a very good way though..." she quickly added.

"Oh..."

"You have made him even more attractive and desirable."

"Victoria... Darling... You need to stop using *attractive* and *desirable* to describe my boyfriend." I took a sip of the water, hiding my grin.

"Why? He *is* attractive and desirable. You should be proud," she said and downed the rest of the wine. "I would feel great satisfaction if my man attracts all the women who lay eyes on him."

She is right...

She stood up and walked back to the minibar for a refill. "He became exuberant and cheerful."

He made me exuberant and cheerful. I smiled at her comment. Thomas and I had changed each other.

"I wanted him more than ever, Iris." She walked back, giving me a serious look.

Oh my...

"I always go for what I want. And I always get what I want." She winked at me and sat back down, crossing one leg casually over the other. "Except Tom," she added.

She had such a straightforward and honest personality, and I really admired her for it.

"It feels so good to talk to you about it." She raised her glass to me and then took a hearty sip. "I am so jealous of you, Iris. Hmmm, I think I hate you." She chuckled.

"Victoria..."

"Honestly, that boy is crazy about you."

My cheeks burned with diffidence.

"I want someone like that." She tried to sound like a spoiled brat.

"When the right one—" I tried to encourage her but was cut off by her palm facing me, asking me to stop, or shut up.

"Don't tell me you really believe in that sort of cliché." Her eyebrows arched.

I shrugged, not sure what to say.

Knowing Thomas was like a fairy tale, but where I met Max was a nightmare. What if Thomas and I were destined to meet under *that* circumstance? If I had a choice, would I go through everything just so I could meet him?

The thought sent a chill down my spine. I would definitely run towards the opposite direction despite not having Thomas in my life, and I knew he would not want that, either.

But... The thought of having a life without him hurt so much. Tears threatened to spill from my eyes.

"Iris. Are you all right?" Victoria's concerned voice pulled me back to the present.

I blinked back my tears, smiling at her, and said, "Thomas and I have a history."

"I thought... Oh, forget about what I thought. So this is the second chance for you two." She widened her big light blue eyes, enthusiasm in her voice. "I don't know what happened to your first chance, and I am not going to pry. But if I were you, I would not let him slip through my fingers again." She sighed. "Who am I to give you love advice? I am a hopeless romantic, and that gets me nowhere."

"Why did you quit? Just because he rejected you?"

"Like I told you. Your relationship has inspired me. I am thirty-two already. I want and need stability. I want a real relationship, not just fantasizing that my boss would fall in love with me."

I laughed, really enjoying her humor and candidness. I liked her, truly. "Are you going back to Bern?"

"I am going to stay here in New York for a while. I inherited a brownstone in the Upper West Side from my father years ago."

"Oh... I am sorry." I could not imagine losing my father at such a young age.

"Don't be. He had a fling with my mother, and I was the product of the affair," she said casually.

"Oh…" I was speechless.

"Look at your face!" She laughed. "I was joking. My father met my mother when he was working in London. They fell out of love faster than they fell in love and got divorced soon after I was born."

Her openness really caught me off guard here.

"Anyway, I didn't really care for that property when I got it. My plan now is to fix up that place while I am figuring out what I want to do next."

"That sounds like a great plan. And, a brownstone…" My passion for architecture kicked in. "Do you plan to do something dramatic with that property?"

"I am going to gut it!" she said, excitement in her voice. "Would you help me?"

"What?"

"Tom told me you are an interior designer. You can design the whole place for me. We can go take a look at the place, and you can tell me what you think about it." She widened her eyes.

Oh my… Only if she had known… I've never been to any site for almost two years. I stared at my water bottle, debating if I was able to be as open as she was and share my story with her. Then I decided against telling her as it was not a story worth sharing. To her, I was simply an interior designer whom Thomas met in California.

"Are you too busy or you don't want to?" she asked frankly.

I really loved her personality. She said what she thought and did what she wanted.

Just as I was going to suggest some ideas to her, a loud French song started to play. It was coming from the desk by the window. Her phone was playing the song.

"Excuse me." She jumped up and scampered to the desk. She grabbed the phone and made a face. "Oops!"

I assumed it was a text message as she was reading her phone.

"Come!" She beckoned to me and headed back to the bathroom. "I need to get ready."

"We can chat some other time…"

"I love talking to you," she said. "Yes, we must meet again. But how about my house?"

I followed her back to the bathroom.

Wow... Pink lace corset and matching thong. She had already taken off her robe, standing in front of the vanity.

I quickly averted my eyes.

"You can look," she said with both sensuality and sincerity in her voice.

Who is this woman? I put on a smile and moved my gaze back to her. "I am going to share my partner Antonio's contact information with you now." I started tapping on my phone, and her phone chimed soon after. "He's our business mastermind. He can definitely give you some professional and useful advice before you start the project."

"Fantastic!" she exclaimed. "Is he in New York?" she asked, opening a delicate jewelry box.

"No, but he—" I suddenly became speechless when I saw the necklace she pulled out of the box.

"He what?" she asked, putting the necklace on.

My eyes were glued to the pendant—a white diamond star surrounded by black gemstones.

I've seen the same design somewhere...

"Are you all right?" she asked, turning towards me.

"I... I've seen that star, that design before." My eyes were still fixed on the pendant setting elegantly between her ample bosoms.

"Really?" She tilted her head, looking skeptical.

I nodded, my eyes still on the star.

Her fingertips gently touched the star, but her eyes were on me. "Are you sure?"

I nodded again and moved my eyes up to hers. "But it's not a pendant..." I trailed off, trying to remember what I had seen and where I had seen it.

"Cufflink or ring, perhaps?" she asked. She completely turned towards me, seemingly very interested in the fact that I had seen the star before.

Cufflink or ring? My brow furrowed, and my eyes were on the star again. And then, an image flashed in front of me: Mr. Viking standing in front of Étoile.

"A ring," I mumbled, remembering Marcus had the ring when I met him at Étoile, although he did not wear the ring when I met him last month. I would have noticed since it was such an eye-catching piece of jewelry.

"A ring?" Victoria's voice sounded a bit too surprised.

"Yes," I replied with confidence. "My best friend's boyfriend has a ring with the exact star."

Victoria grinned and turned back to look at herself in the mirror, continuing to work on her already perfect makeup. "Boyfriend? Your best friend is very lucky." She winked at me in the mirror.

"Huh?" What she just said completely baffled me.

Then, she changed the subject as if I had never mentioned anything about the pendant. "Will your partner fly here to meet me?"

"Huh?" My brain had not caught up with her.

"Antonio is it? Will he come to New York?"

"Yes, of course. We've done many projects here." I took a step back, smiling at her broadly. "I should go now. Enjoy your night out. You have my number. Please text or call me if you like to chat again."

"I would love that." She stepped forward and hugged me. "I am so glad that we could connect. You are so nice. I've decided I don't hate you at all." She laughed.

"You've spoken for both of us." I chuckled. "I will let myself out."

"You hang onto that man of yours, Iris!" She gave me a squeeze affectionately before letting me go.

I headed out of her room, feeling relieved.

You hang onto the man of yours. Her words were echoing in my head as I wandered the corridor.

The chime of the elevator startled me, and I heard people chatting. My first instinct was to run in the opposite direction.

Where am I? I spotted an exit sign and headed towards it. Pushing the door open, I stepped into the emergency stairwell. Letting out a sigh of relief, I decided to take the stairs to avoid running into strangers.

What is stopping me from going to Switzerland? I had been

working so hard to have my life back, to have the old Iris back, and I knew the old Iris would scream *yes* when Thomas asked her.

What am I afraid of?

My career? I owned half of the company. The new arrangement with Antonio and Jojo worked perfectly, and we could always hire new designers.

My family? I lived alone, my parents were traveling around the world for the hundredth time, and DD and Janie were raising the most beautiful and smartest kids in the world—proud to have the auntie syndrome.

Being cheated? Once bitten, twice shy. But I trusted Thomas, and I should not even worry about it.

Being abducted, again? Suddenly, my pace slowed down, and my heart palpitated with fear. *Am I really afraid of being abducted again?*

Human trafficking took many forms and occurred across the world in countries rich and poor. I would be imprisoned myself if I lived in fear. And, I had Thomas, my guardian angel and safe haven.

I know my answer! I picked up my pace because I could not wait to tell him that I decided to go to Switzerland with him.

When I finally arrived at the twentieth floor, I was short of breath. What was I thinking when I decided to climb eight flights of stairs? I reached for the door handle and... It was locked!

"*Scheiße!*" I swore in German, pulling the door a couple of more times.

I called Thomas, hoping he was close to his phone.

"I have been missing you," he answered.

"So have I."

"Are you coming back soon?"

"If someone can open the door for me..."

"Why did you not ring the doorbell? Let me get the door," he said.

"Not that door..."

"What are you talking about?"

I could hear him opening the door.

"Where are you, love?" he asked, his voice worried.

"Grab your room key so we don't get locked out."

"Iris…"

"I am in the emergency stairwell now. The door—"

"You what?" he exclaimed.

"It's a long story, *mon chéri*."

"Which staircase?" he asked, his voice so worried. "I am coming now."

"There is more than one? Double *Scheiße!*" I swore aloud.

"What?" He laughed.

I loved his laughter so much… I smiled.

"Iris?"

"I don't know which one. I was going to walk to the employee elevator but walked in the wrong direction. I think… Then I heard the guest elevator chiming, I just ran and pushed open an exit door and got out."

"I know where you are. I will be right there," he said and hung up the phone.

I almost forgot he knew the hotel inside and out. Soon I heard knocking on the door. "Iris?"

"I am here!" I struck the door.

The door was opened with a loud click, and Thomas' handsome face appeared.

I wrapped my arms around him immediately.

He laughed, embracing me. "Are you all right?"

I did not answer but grabbed his hand and walked out of the staircase.

CHAPTER 28

> Throw your dreams into space like a kite,
> and you do not know
> what it will bring back,
> a new life, a new friend,
> a new love, a new country.
> ~Anaïs Nin

A life changing decision was made. I was now on my way to Switzerland with Thomas.

The last two weeks went by in a blur. It was surreal...

After Thomas finished his business in New York, we flew back to California. We broke the news to my family and friends and received warm wishes, even from Antonio.

Thomas told me the jet had enough cargo space if I wanted to ship all my stuff to Bern. But three large suitcases were all I decided to bring with me.

It was late in the afternoon when we arrived in Switzerland. The anxiety and excitement were beyond my imagination...

Eleven months ago, I was staring out the window when the plane was taking off, feeling relieved and free, and believing I would never come back here again. Now I was staring out the window when the jet was taxing towards its designated hangar, feeling loved and excited, and believing my future with Thomas was going to be bright.

Thomas gently put his arm around my shoulders, pressing a kiss on my temple.

I turned my face to give him a loving smile. Our eyes locked.

This is it. A new chapter of my life, our life, has begun.

When the jet came to a complete stop, my heartbeat suddenly sped up. *I can do this...* I took several deep breaths, calming myself.

"Are you all right?" Thomas stroked my back.

"I am great, just a bit anxious."

"We will go straight home. No more traveling." He pressed another kiss on my forehead.

I nodded, grabbing my tote bag, while he reached for his travel briefcase. We said our farewell to our flight crew, and Thomas steered me towards two large SUVs parked by the hangar. I saw a couple of people loading our luggage into one of them.

The ride to Thomas' place took less than thirty minutes. It was located in Weisses Quartier, an old classic area in Bern. I was surprised how close it was to the U.S. Embassy.

It was not an apartment I had expected. It was a huge loft on the top floor of an old four-story modest Heimatstil style building at the outskirts of the old town.

It's an interior designer's heaven... I scanned the space slowly.

An Eames lounge chair and ottoman by the corner window was a perfect reading spot.

A large black-leather sectional sofa leaning against the accent red brick wall, two Barcelona chairs, and a Noguchi table, which gave the black-leather and stainless steel chairs and sofa a soft touch. The furniture created a both relaxed and suave seating area.

A rectangle live-edge oak-slab dining table was matched with four black flat-bar Brno chairs. It was another softness meeting hardness concept.

Dark hardwood floor ran through the entire space.

Bookcases stood tall against almost every wall between the windows, decorating the off-white walls with colorful spines of the books and some decorative statues.

The open kitchen with stainless-steel appliances, Calacatta sky-grey marble countertop, and black cabinets was spotless.

"Do you like it?" Thomas asked, walking in behind me.

"It suits you perfectly." I gave him a broad smile.

"Louis and Eva were here yesterday to stock up the refrigerator and pantry," he said.

"That's so nice of them," I said while I walked towards the window by the seating area. Looking out the window, I saw the same style of buildings on every corner and few people strolling on the street, so calm and peaceful. But... I sort of missed my ocean view...

"Sorry. This place does not have an amazing ocean view..." he said, wrapping his arms around my waist from behind.

I chuckled as he just read my mind. "How do you do that?" I murmured.

"Do what?"

"Nothing... This is perfect." I turned around and wrapped my arms around his neck, asking for a kiss.

He leaned in and gave me an alluring kiss.

"So, what's next?" I asked when our lips parted.

"I can give you a tour to the master bedroom if you fancy that," he said in a seductive voice.

"That sounds very tempting." I winked. "How many days will you be off from work?"

"A couple of weeks," he said. "Why?"

I shook my head, not wanting to tell him that I was not ready for him to leave me here alone, not yet. "That's good..." I mumbled.

"Actually..." He gazed at me. "I would love to take you to visit my family."

I blinked my eyes rapidly, not sure how to react. We did not even know if our relationship was going to work, or if I was going to survive in this new environment.

Thomas looked a bit concerned. "Do you not want to?"

I leaned my face against his chest. "Please give me just a little bit more time," I said in a very low voice. "I would love to, but I am not sure I can handle all these changes, the new environment, and meeting new people all at once."

"Of course. We just came home." He embraced me. "I am sorry for rushing you."

Home... I grinned in his arms.

"I am just eager to introduce you to my family. They have heard so much about you."

"They have?" I looked up at him.

"I could not stop talking about you," he said, chuckling. "They are looking forward to meeting you."

"Seriously? I...I don't want to embarrass you if I can't control my anxiety..." My voice was nervous and trembling.

"*Ma chérie,* you can never embarrass me." He held me tight and gently rocked me like a baby. "I promise you are going to be fine around them," he said and loosened his arms. "Look at me..."

I gazed up at him, admiring his serene blue eyes. Those were my amazing ocean views now.

"Let's not think about that right now. We are going to settle you in first. There are three bedrooms here. I am going to put all your suitcases in one room, and you can take your time to unpack. But first, I am going to make us something to eat. I am hungry," he said and steered me towards the kitchen.

FOUR days later, we were on our way to visit his family on the shore of north Lake Geneva. After about an hour and a half drive, he turned into a gravel road. I was speechless when a sumptuous château came into sight. It was a two-story manor house with light brown stone exterior walls and chocolate Mansard roof sitting on a plateau overlooking Lake Geneva. The property was surrounded by flourishing greenery, and in a near distance I saw pastureland and an equine facility.

"You grew up here?" I said in astonishment.

"Yes," he said proudly. "My families have been living in this area for many generations. Make sure you ask my father about the story of DeMont Hotels."

Soon he pulled up to the manor house's grand, ornate wrought iron double doors with frosted glass.

"They are waiting for us." Thomas got out of the car and walked briskly to my side to open the door for me.

I took his hand, drawing in a deep breath, and stepped out of the car.

His family must have heard our arrival as I saw shadows behind the frosted glass. When the door was opened, I froze on the spot as I saw Dr. Thompson appearing in the doorway.

"Hi, Iris." Dr. Thompson's voice was still so gentle and comforting.

"Welcome, Iris." A male voice snapped me out of the overwhelming surprise. My eyes flung to the man standing behind Dr. Thompson. He must be Louis as he really resembled Thomas.

I became speechless, not able to respond to their greetings.

Thomas squeezed my hand, drawing my attention to him.

I turned to look at him, my brow furrowed.

"I know what you are thinking, love. Eva will explain everything to you later. I promise," Thomas said, his voice soothing.

I turned my gaze back to Dr. Thompson, a smile breaking out. I walked up to her and wrapped my arms around her to give her a hearty American hug instead of Swiss cheek-kisses.

I became so emotional, my eyes brimming with tears.

"Thompson is my maiden name," she said, hugging me back. "It's easier for my patients."

After I finally let go of Dr. Thompson, she gently put her hand on the arm of the man standing right next to her and said, "This is my husband, Tommy's big brother, Louis."

"Pleased to meet you, Iris." Louis leaned in and gave me cheek-kisses.

I was expecting a handshake as we were meeting each other for the first time, but at this point the Swiss social etiquette I had learned was forgotten.

Louis was as dashing as Thomas and very sophisticated. I thought he looked like his mother because of the dark brown hair and eyes.

Thomas was now by my side. He put one arm around my waist, seemingly relieved and pleased.

"Let's all go inside," Eva said. "Mr. Bernard will get the bags later."

"Where is papa?" Thomas asked, ushering me into the foyer.

"He's in the garden with Adeline," Eva said, walking arm in arm with Louis behind us. "He asked me to fetch them when you two arrived. I will be right back."

I assumed they all spoke English because of my presence, and I really appreciated their thoughtfulness in making me feel as comfortable as possible.

"Eva, wait. We can go to the garden," Thomas said and held my hand, starting heading to the back.

"Who is Adeline?" I asked in a very low voice.

"She is the advocacy director of the foundation. They started dating just in recent years."

I did not ask more questions as I was becoming anxious when we walked through a room that looked like a sunroom and then out to an outdoor porch. A magnificent garden came into sight. And I immediately saw a lady with a beige sun hat standing by a man who was kneeling on the ground, packing soil around a small plant.

"Papa," Thomas called.

When the man turned around, I definitely saw the resemblance between the father and son, notably the brilliant blue eyes.

"Tommy!" he exclaimed.

He quickly got on his feet, brushed off dirt on his pants, and took off his gardening gloves.

Thomas walked up to them and greeted them with cheek-kisses. He then put his hand on the small of my back, rushing me closer. "Papa, Adeline. This is Iris. Iris, my father Florent and Adeline."

"How do you do?" Adeline quickly removed her gardening gloves and extended her hand for a handshake.

"How do you do?" I shook her hand.

"Iris…" Florent gazed at me, his voice low and soothing.

The way he called my name warmed my heart because it sounded as if he had already known me for a long time.

"I have heard so much about you." He extended his hand for a handshake as well.

"Mr. Torian. Nice to meet you." I reached my hand to shake his.

"Call me Florent, please." He smiled broadly, holding my hand with both hands, squeezing it gently.

I responded with a beam, my heart pounding.

"Should we go inside?" Thomas walked behind me, putting his hands on my shoulders.

"Yes, of course." Florent let go of my hand and extended one hand to Adeline. She walked closer to him and held his hand.

Florent motioned Thomas and me to the house, but Thomas gestured for him and Adeline to go first. We followed the couple back to the house and walked into the room we walked through earlier. Eva and Louis were cuddling on one of the luxurious velvet Chesterfield sofas.

I was a nervous wreck earlier and could not pay attention to this bright and spacious sunroom. Polished parquetry ran through the entire room, two chandeliers were suspended from the high ceiling, the off-white walls were decorated with elegant mouldings, and three arch French doors opened to a terrace sitting area.

"Allow us to clean up first. We will be right back," Florent said and left the room with Adeline.

"Please have a seat." Eva gestured for me to sit on another plush sofa. "Would you like something to drink? Maybe some light refreshments?"

"Just water, thank you," I said.

Thomas steered me towards the sofa and sat down next to me.

"Want a beer, Tommy?" Louis asked, tilting his head towards the door, while Eva walked towards a wet bar.

"Yes," Thomas nodded to his brother and turned to me to give me a kiss on my forehead. He then headed out of the room with his brother.

Eva walked back with two water bottles and handed one to me. Smiling at me, she sat down on the single seater next to me.

I had a feeling that the Torian brothers left the room on purpose so Eva and I could talk.

"I am sure you have many questions," Eva said.

I furrowed my brow, suddenly speechless. I did have many questions, but I was not sure how to start.

"Iris, I am just Eva here, not Dr. Thompson." She took a sip of her water, seemingly thinking or considering something. "How about let me start first?" Her comforting smile reminded me of the sessions we had.

I nodded.

"Tommy called me after you were brought to the U.S. Embassy," she said. "We hadn't heard from him for over two years then, so it was absolutely unexpected. He told me about you."

I smiled, blinking back my tears as those memories still affected me deeply.

Eva extended her hand to hold mine, squeezing gently. "He asked if I could reach out to the counselor in charge of your case and help you."

"He... He's never told me..."

"I am sure he has his reason."

I tilted my head to one side, bewildered.

"His job, I mean the previous job, was very dangerous and complicated. And he had never reached out to me for help until he met you. I should have declined his request because of our relationship, but he was so desperate..."

"He was?" I whispered.

Eva nodded. "He told me he made a judgment call based on his personal feelings for you and had to take care of the fallout."

"Fallout?" My breathing was picking up. "But he...he told me..."

"Iris... Breathe, please." Eva gently squeezed my hand. "There is no need to wonder about anything. Tommy did what he had to do. Okay?"

I nodded, taking in deep breaths. "I am sorry... Please continue."

"No apology necessary, Iris. Your reaction is absolutely understandable," she said, giving my hand another squeeze, and then leaned back into the sofa. "He told me he would not be able to watch over you anymore and pleaded for my help. So I agreed to help him under certain conditions."

I probably still looked confused as Eva gave me an understanding smile and continued, "I told him I would take your case but he could not ask me about you or tell me his personal feelings for you."

I drew in a breath when I heard that.

"And he could not disclose our relationship to you," she added.

"But...but why?"

Eva let out a deep sigh. "I needed to be absolutely objective when I met you, and I needed to gain your trust as well. Tommy's job was to eradicate those criminal organizations and save those victims. And my job is to help those victims recover from all sorts of traumas."

"You save...save us, too." My voice was trembling, especially when I just acknowledged myself as one of the victims.

"Thank you. *Save* is a very heavy word..." Eva's eyes casted down, seemingly lost in her thoughts. Then she quickly put on a smile and faced me again. "When we first met, I needed you to trust me as a psychiatrist who had years of experience and whom you could trust. Anything more than that was unnecessary and a distraction. Tommy was still undercover then. It would only make you feel more bewildered and distrustful. And as for Tommy..." Eva paused, fixing her eyes on mine. "It was...it was not easy for him as well."

"He...he shared something with me after he came to visit me," I said, my voice timid.

"About Laila?"

I nodded, my heart aching just thinking about how tragic it was for his family.

"He was only eighteen when I met him."

He was still a kid then...

Eva paused, seemingly deciding what to say. "I think he should be the one who tells you his own story."

"I understand that..."

"Do you have any questions?"

I shook my head, still feeling speechless, then I remembered what James told me. "Oh... I want to thank you for arranging the private jet to fly me and my family home. You've done so much for me..."

She gave me a broad smile. "Don't mention it, Iris. I want you to know that I am here for you and Thomas, not as a psychiatrist but as a family. We are all here for you both."

"Thank you…" My eyes brimmed with tears. I quickly looked down to hide my emotions.

"Speaking of family. I think all of them are hiding from us." She chuckled.

I laughed, quickly wiping away my tears.

CHAPTER 29

> Happiness is having a large, loving,
> caring, close-knit family in another city.
> ~George Burns

"**THIS** very location is where DeMont Enterprise started..." Florent began to tell me the story upon my request. "Our ancestors grew grapevines and made wine on the hill, right behind the château."

The seemed-endless vineyard we drove by earlier. Wait... "Château DeMont?" I looked at Thomas.

He nodded and said, "Best wine."

"DeMont Hotels. Château DeMont. How did I not make the connection between them?" I widened my eyes.

Thomas pressed a kiss on my temple and whispered, "Cause I am a very good distraction,"

My cheeks burned, hoping his family did not hear that.

"Tommy, you must show Iris the vineyard." Florent pointed at his son and then turned to me. "This boy is our sommelier."

"Why am I not surprised?" I gave him an admiring smile.

"The vineyard is on our itinerary." Thomas held me closer and interlocked our hands.

"My third great grandfather Gefrei Ewart Torian built a small cottage right here and ran an inn." Florent continued the storytelling. "Back then, it was just a small lodge. It had a great reputation for good wine and hospitality. They called it DeMont Inn," he continued. "They worked hard and also sold their wine in many cities."

Florent's Second Great Grandfather Peire Gefrei Torian built more lodges in different cities where their wine was sold. And his Great Grandfather Lucus Peire Torian rebuilt this cottage into a private château. DeMont Hotel was not established until his Grandfather Henry Lucus Torian had a vision of running a worldwide hotel chain offering the best quality and services. Henry worked with his son Michael Henry Torian and founded the acclaimed international hotel chain DeMont Hotels.

"We are one hard-working family." He chuckled. "Never rest."

"I think it's amazing," I said, giving him an appreciative smile. "Thank you for sharing your family story with me."

"Now Louis and Tommy are running the show now." He looked at both his sons with pride.

I looked at Thomas, feeling proud as well, and also admired how humble and sincere his family was.

"Dinner will be ready soon. Maybe we should unpack first," Thomas said to me and turned to his family. "Excuse us."

"Of course…" Florent said, smiling.

"Mrs. Carson is cooking your favorite dish for dinner tonight," Eva said to Thomas, her smile so adoring.

"I tried to sneak into the kitchen earlier, but she caught me at the door. But I could smell it." He wiggled his eyebrows and said to me, "Best bouillabaisse."

"I can't wait." It was my favorite, too.

Although I could not—hope one day I could again—just go to any restaurant to enjoy gourmet food with Thomas, we still found a way to enjoy great food. And after we found out that both of us were seafood lovers, ordering seafood from different restaurants and trying different seafood recipes became our go-to dinner plans.

I gave his family a small wave before we left the room. He led me towards the back and stopped in front of a hidden door.

"Where are we?"

"Secret escape route," he said, pushing the door open and flipped the light switch.

"Huh?"

He held my hand and walked through the door. We walked into a narrow well-lighted spiral staircase and headed upstairs.

"Where are we escaping to?" I whispered.

He laughed and whispered, "You don't need to whisper."

"Okay…" I whispered back again. "So, where to?"

"To Tommy's childhood bedroom."

I grinned, following behind him. "What's in Tommy's room?"

"All kinds of fun." He squeezed my hand.

After two flights of stairs, he opened a door, and we exited the staircase and walked into a huge bedroom. Our bags were on the end-of-bed bench.

"This is your childhood bedroom?" I scanned the room: A king size bed with black leather headboard, a set of matching leather sofa by the windows, a gas fireplace with black marble surround… So modern! I had assumed all the rooms were the same country aesthetic style like those I had seen so far. The foyer, the corridors, and the sunroom still carried the historic and intricate details and were decorated with chenille jacquard fabric, luxurious furniture, and art objects. But his room… It was so Thomas.

"It was remodeled a couple of times," he said casually, closing the hidden door.

I whipped around when the door was closed, pointing at the door. "I love that staircase!"

"Me too!" Thomas mimicked my excited voice. "When we were kids, Louis and I fought for this room because of it."

"I assumed you won."

"No, Louis did because he was older and bigger." He walked behind me, gently moved my hair aside and kissed my neck.

I let out a soft moan.

"I stole it from him," he whispered in my ear.

"How? Switching the room while he was not home?" I said, but my mind was pretty occupied by his alluring kisses.

"Precisely…" He kissed my sweet spot.

"Seriously?" I chuckled.

"My parents sent him to a boarding school. Since he was not home to use it, I switched rooms." He let go of me and walked towards where our bags were.

"Boarding school? Did you all go to boarding schools?" I

followed him and sat on the bed, watching him unpacking. Not that I did not want to help. He was just a much better organizer.

"No, just Louis. He was the wild one." He unzipped the bags and started to take out the contents and lay them neatly on the bed.

"He still came home for the holidays, right? Did he want his room back?"

"He did." He smirked. "He broke my nose."

My jaw dropped. "I guess the boarding school didn't tame his wildness." I murmured.

"Nope. And he was not allowed to have this room because of it." He scanned the room. "I got it with a bloody nose."

I got on the bed and walked towards him on my knees. And I cupped his face, studying him carefully. "I am glad he didn't disfigure your face."

He leaned in and gave me a kiss. "Are you going to wear this for me tonight?" he asked.

I looked down at his hands which were holding the black babydoll lingerie and the matching g-string thong I packed. I was not sure if we were going to fool around here or not, but I packed them anyway—just in case.

I wrapped my arms around his neck and whispered, "We will see…"

MY favorite spot in this enormous château was the outdoor seating area by the edge of the back yard looking onto Lake Geneva. The view was insanely beautiful.

There were no strangers nearby, therefore I felt so carefree and was able to really enjoy myself. It felt like being in the ranch but timed a thousand times because this estate was huge.

The only non-family members were the butler Mr. Bernard, the cook Mrs. Caron, and Mrs. Brun, who sort of did everything else. I was told they had been with the family for a long time and went through the heartbreak with them when Laila and Thomas' mother passed away. They basically were family. They were amazingly nice and attentive to me, and I felt they had spoiled me too much as I usually did my own cooking, dishes, and cleaning.

Breathing in the fresh Lake Geneva air, I was lounging on the grass.

"Iris!" Thomas called.

I turned in the direction of his room. *There he is, standing at the open window overlooking the garden.* He gave me a smile when our eyes met.

"I am coming down now!" he yelled from where he was.

"Okay!" I yelled back.

Florent told me that Thomas and I had made the whole place feel so alive. I believed it was because we were frisky and loud all the time.

I turned around to face the lake again. A content smile had been lingering on my face since I arrived. And I also noticed Thomas was more relaxed, happier, and really playful. I saw him at the stable humming softly and talking to the horses, and he chatted and laughed with his brother like they were best friends—maybe they were. And he had so much fun cooking with Mrs. Caron.

Being with him makes my life so perfect... I closed my eyes, taking a long, deep breath.

"My love." His charming voice made my smile become brighter.

I looked up at him and invited him to sit down with me.

He laid down and rested his head on my lap. "I have to go into the office tomorrow."

"Tomorrow?" I frowned. I thought he did not have to work for another week since he had been on the road for months.

"Several interviews were scheduled. I have to hire an assistant before my next trip."

That's right. The temporary assistant only worked for him in New York. I gently brushed his thick dark hair with my fingers and kneaded his temples and scalp. "Should we leave this afternoon?"

"Probably after dinner or tomorrow morning. My father likes us to stay a bit longer," he said in a lazy voice, enjoying the head massage.

I did not say anything, just enjoying the quiet moment with him.

"Will you travel with me next week?" After moments of silence, he asked.

"Next week?" I was surprised. I did not expect he had to leave so soon. "Yes, of course. Don't leave me home alone...." After I said that, I realized I sounded a bit panicky.

"I will never leave you alone." He raised his hand to grab mine and rested it on his chest.

"Where are we going?" I was actually feeling excited to be able to travel to places, with him of course, even just staying in the hotels.

He looked hesitant.

"Are we going to the Arctic or Antarctic? I didn't pack any winter clothes," I joked.

He laughed and kissed my hand. He opened his eyes and gazed at me.

I leaned down and gave him a kiss.

He looked into my eyes deeply and finally asked, "Would you go to Paris with me?"

Suddenly, my heart was pounding violently, and I became silent. No wonder he was hesitant.

I looked up and stared at the surface of the lake...

What is wrong with me? He was asking me to go to Paris, the city of love, with him, and I was afraid to say *yes*.

In the past two years, my mind was constantly occupied with *what ifs*. What if I did not walk into the lady's room? What if I just stayed close to my friends? What if I did not drink that night? What if I did not go to that nightclub?

What if... What if I did not go to Paris? Then, my life would not have been hijacked, I would have relocated to New York, and I would have been living my life the way I had planned.

I looked down again at his beautiful and slightly squinted eyes. Then, I wouldn't have met him and fallen madly in love with him.

"Of course, I would love to go to Paris with you," I said, hoping that I would not regret this, and he would not regret asking me.

He touched my face, reading my expression, and looked pleased. Turning his body towards me, he wrapped his arms around my waist and closed his eyes again.

I could feel his breathing become slower and calmer. This was the time he was not the tough, protective, and vigilant Thomas, but the one who wanted and needed comfort, support, and…maybe a break from taking care of me.

During dinner, the father and sons were casually chatting about the business, such as new menus in the restaurants and the harvesting of the wine grapes next month. Even though they were all speaking in English for my benefit, I still felt lost and could not quite participate in their conversations. And also, I was still preoccupied by the upcoming trip to Paris, feeling nervous and even a bit fearful about it.

The delicious sole meunière prepared by Mrs. Caron was a great distraction. It was so buttery but light. She had cooked seafood for the last few days especially for me after she learned that I loved seafood.

I am going to ask for her recipes before we go home! I took another bite.

"…Iris?"

The calling of my name interrupted my thought. I turned to Thomas, bemused, and then I scanned the table and noticed all five pairs of eyes were looking at me.

"Pardon?" I asked, not knowing what they were talking about.

"Paris. I hope you will enjoy Paris," Thomas said, his doting eyes making me smile.

Paris… That's right… My smile faded a little.

"That is wonderful! *Mon cheri,* Can we join them?" Eva asked Louis.

I looked at Eva, not sure if she had sensed my hesitation or really wanted to go to Paris. It would be great if she was around, just in case I had nonstop panic attacks.

"Of course." Louis gave his wife a loving smile.

She kissed and said to us, "It's going to be a wonderful trip."

"Why don't we join them?" Florent joined the Paris topic and asked Adeline.

Thomas told me Adeline was a breast cancer survivor and was

heavily involved with the foundation since it was established. Thomas was truly grateful to her as she was by his father's side when he was away, committing himself to his police duties, and trying to deal with his own grief.

Adeline gazed at Florent and nodded.

"Fantastic," Florent said in a low and bright voice, holding Adeline's hand. "We have not made a family trip for years."

"Woohoo!" Thomas raised his wine glass and took a big sip. He leaned over to me and kissed my cheek while I was still processing the whole thing.

A family trip? I am a member of this family? Looking around the table, I saw cheerful Thomas toasting his father with the wine, Florent returning Thomas' toast with a broad smile, thoughtful Eva smiling at me, loving Louis gazing at his compassionate wife, and lovely Adeline giving me a motherly smile.

This family was full of love and compassion. And they considered me as one of them.

CHAPTER 30

> Love is that condition in which
> the happiness of another person
> is essential to your own.
> ~Robert A. Heinlein

WE decided to stay another night and leave early the next morning. The whole family was up early to have breakfast with us and saw us off. And in three days, we would travel to Paris together.

"Can we invite James and Tim over for dinner tonight? Or tomorrow night?" I asked Thomas.

Thomas glanced between me and the road. "Of course," he said, reaching his hand to hold mine.

"Thank you," I gazed at his handsome profile.

"Would you like me to pick up takeaways?"

"No... I like to cook."

He gave me another glance with a sweet smile. Holding up my hand, he gently dipped a kiss on it. "Let me know if you would like me to pick up anything after work."

"Probably just fresh baguettes," I said, turning my eyes to the road again.

An hour and a half later we were back at Thomas' apartment.

"I have to go now," he said after putting our bags in the bedroom. "Are you going to be okay?"

"Of course," I said, grinning. "I am going to call James to see if they can make it today or not since it's such a short notice. I will let you know."

"Okay," he gave me a kiss, holding me tight. "I should be back around two if not sooner."

"Go. To manage some hotels or wine or something," I joked, trying to conceal my anxiousness.

Interlocked our fingers, I walked him to the elevator. When the elevator doors closed, I suddenly felt so lost. I dragged my feet back to the apartment, locked the door, and headed to the kitchen to make myself a cup of coffee.

This was not the first time I said goodbye to him when he went to work. I did it so many times in Los Angeles and New York. However, it just felt so different here. Maybe it was because I was so far away from home, or maybe it was because this was not just a hotel room but his apartment. It had been a week, but everything was still so strange and unfamiliar.

I finished making my coffee and headed to Thomas' study, where he let me set up my workstation. Doing something I was familiar with would be a good distraction. Putting the coffee mug on the desk, I turned on my laptop and opened the work folder.

"Oh. Right. James. My phone." I walked back to the kitchen where I left my phone.

Chatting with James is a better distraction...

I was in the bedroom unpacking when I heard the door open.

"*Ma chérie?*" Thomas' calling made my heart palpitate.

I scurried out of the room.

This man...

He had fresh baguettes in one hand and a bouquet of red roses in another, smiling broadly. Although my name was Iris, my favorite flower was rose. I loved its delicate fragrance and was always fascinated with its intriguing spirals.

I scampered towards him and got on my tiptoes to wrap my arms around his neck. "I miss you..." I whispered.

"I miss you, too." He embraced me, leaning in to kiss me.

I could smell the mixture of the roses and baguettes...and him. Intoxicating...

Letting go of him, I received the roses and held them to my chest to inhale the alluring scent. "Thank you," I whispered into the red velvet beauties.

"You are welcome," he said and gave me another kiss on my cheek, putting his free hand on the small of my back. "There are several vases in the cupboard. Let me get one for you."

"Thanks." I held the bouquet like a baby, smiling broadly at him.

"I will buy you flowers everyday if they can make you smile like that," he said, putting the baguettes down on the island counter.

A big grin spread over my face.

He took off his suit jacket and hung it over the back of one of the stools. "Are you ready to host our very first dinner?" He walked into the pantry and soon came out with a crystal vase.

Host our first dinner... Wow, I did not think about that. "We are hosting a dinner as a couple for the very first time," I said to him, my eyes widened. "Good... I can practice this hosting thing on James."

Thomas laughed, handing me the vase. He took his phone out of his jacket pocket and plugged in the phone charger on the kitchen counter. He picked up his jacket and walked back to me. "I am going to change," he said, kissing my hair.

"Sorry. I was unpacking before you came home. There are some clothes on the bed. I will put them away later."

"Don't worry about it," he said, walking away.

My eyes were fixed on the beautiful roses, arranging them to my liking. And suddenly, Thomas' phone vibrated, dancing on the marble countertop. I ignored it, and it stopped soon after.

Just as I was picking up the vase, the phone buzzed again and startled me. Fortunately, I did not drop the vase. Ignoring the ringing phone once again, I brought the flowers to the dining table and set it down as a centerpiece for tonight and rearranged the table setting to coordinate with the flowers. Thomas' phone finally stopped but buzzed again right away.

Maybe it's urgent... I walked over to the phone and saw the name Anna Haller on the screen. I was not going to answer the call as I believed we should still respect each other's privacy. I unplugged the phone and took it to the bedroom. It stopped buzzing, and I saw three missed calls notifications all from the same person.

"Your phone rang three times. Maybe it's urgent." I handed the phone to Thomas, who was standing in front of the tall dresser and in just a pair of blue jeans.

"Thanks." His eyebrow arched, and then his brow furrowed when he looked at his phone and tapped it several times. I thought he was going to call this Anna Haller back, but he walked towards his bedside table and plugged in the charger instead.

"Not urgent?" I asked, although what I really wanted to know was who Anna Haller was.

"No." He walked towards me, all smiling and seductive. Wrapping his arms around my waist, he leaned in and kissed my neck.

I giggled as his stubbles were tickling me.

"Do we have time for a quickie?" he asked, breathing down my neck.

"We can do better than a quickie..."

While I was boiling water for linguini and defrosting the shrimp for shrimp scampi, Thomas was preparing a cheese platter and wine.

He dipped a kiss on my head when he walked by me to get a bottle of wine from the wine cooler. Intensively, he scanned the six-feet-tall cooler just to pick the right bottle.

I wished I could talk about wine with him. I mentioned that to him once in New York, and he told me that he would enjoy tasting wine with me very much, but comparing notes or discussing a wine's vintage would bore me.

The doorbell chimed.

"I will get it," Thomas said as he grabbed a bottle of wine. He placed it on the island counter and marched towards the door.

Just a couple of hours ago, I learned from him that pinot grigio paired very well with creamy cheese varieties he had prepared and the shrimp scampi I was cooking. So out of curiosity, I glanced at the front label of the black bottle.

Gravner. Hmmm... The name did not help much, so I picked up the bottle and read the back label: Venezia Giulia / Indicazione Geografica Tipica / Pinot Grigio / 2007.

Hmmm... All I understood was Pinot Grigio, and my only

thought was the label and bottle were very modern.

I used to only buy wines with unique or pretty labels and bottles because I could not really tell the difference. However, I had learned from my personal wine steward that I enjoyed late harvest wines because they were sweeter, but I was still useless at describing taste.

I resumed my food preparation and put the linguini in the boiling water before joining Thomas. He buzzed the ground floor entrance door and opened the loft door waiting for our guests.

When I heard the elevator, I scampered towards the hallway.

"James!" I screamed when our guests walked out of the elevator.

"Hi honey." He embraced me in his arms so tightly.

"Hi Tim," I greeted Tim after I let go of James and exchanged cheek-kisses with him. "This way…" I ushered them to where Thomas was standing.

"Honey, you look great and smell so good." James held his arm around my waist.

"Thank you." I leaned in, wrapping my arm around him as well.

"James, Tim," Thomas greeted.

"Thomas." Both of them shook Thomas hand when they walked into the apartment.

"What a beautiful place you have," James praised when he scanned the room, just as how I reacted when I first walked in here.

"Thank you," Thomas said, closing the door.

"This is for you." Tim handed me a large box.

"Thank you!" I received the box with anticipation.

When James asked me what they could bring, I suggested dessert and told him not to bring wine because he would be enjoying Thomas' collection. I took a whiff on the box and exhaled with a satisfied smile. "I knew it!" I exclaimed and strolled down memory lane…

~ ~ ~

Over a year ago…

"Black forest gateau will go so well with this coffee now," I said to James one day when we were drinking coffee in his office.

And the next day, I received a beautiful small box with a red ribbon on top from him and Tim. I could smell the sweet creamy chocolate before I opened the box.

~ ~ ~

Thomas looked curious and guessed, "Black forest gateau?"

I nodded with a broad smile, walked away with the box, and put it in the refrigerator. Thomas followed me back to the kitchen to open the wine.

"Look at you two." James walked into the kitchen and sat on one of the stools, smiling.

I turned around and gave him a wink, quickly glancing at Thomas.

"Wine?" Thomas asked James and looked at Tim who was walking around, admiring the loft.

"Yes, please," both answered in unison and gave each a doting smile.

Thomas poured everyone, except me, a glass of the white wine and brought his glass to me. "Babe, do you like to try it first to see if you like it or not?" He knew I enjoyed sweeter wine.

After putting the cooked pasta aside, I took a sip and nodded with a smile. He then poured me a half glass while I started melting butter in a large skillet and adding marinated shrimp.

Tim took a seat next to James and picked up the wine. He gazed at the content first and then swirled the glass. He tilted the glass and took a quick, short sniff before taking a small sip.

I stared at him because he was doing what Thomas did every time he opened a bottle of wine.

"This is delicious," Tim praised after he took another sip.

"If he approves it, I'm all for it. He's my wine guy." James took a sip of his wine.

"Please." Thomas gestured to the cheese platter.

"Can you open a bottle of wine for me? For the sauce," I whispered to Thomas.

He picked up the bottle we were drinking and handed it to me.

"Are you sure?" I asked as it looked and tasted too expensive for cooking.

"Of course. I will open another bottle."

I shrugged and took the bottle.

"It smells divine, Iris," James said, sipping the wine.
"I promise you it tastes even better," Thomas said with pride.
I grinned.

Dinner turned out great and all three boys could not stop telling me how delicious it was.

We were now sitting at the dining table, chatting and enjoying coffee and the black forest gateau.

Thomas rested his hand on the back of my chair, gently rubbing my back with his hand. His touch always made me feel so content.

"I saw you have many books by Dr. Noam Chomsky, Dr. Tyler Burge, and Alain de Botton," Tim said to Thomas. "Did you study philosophy?"

"Yes, I did."

"May I take a look at them?" Tim asked.

"Of course." Thomas stood up, motioning Tim to the bookshelf in the living room.

"Oh, my handsome nerd…" James emptied his coffee.

I chuckled over his reaction.

"I will help you clean up since our boyfriends are drawn to the books," he said.

"Thank you." I started collecting cups and plates.

James followed me with the rest of the dishes to the kitchen.

After putting the dishes in the sink, we leaned against the kitchen counter and stared at our men.

"Are you doing okay?" James asked in a very soft and concerned voice.

"I think so," I said and took a deep breath.

"Iris?" He wrapped his arm around my shoulders. "What's the matter?"

"Everything is too good to be true…"

"And?" he prompted.

I took another deep breath and turned to face him. "I feel…I feel he's stuck with me."

He frowned, one eyebrow arched, just staring at me. Finally, his perplexed expression subsided and said, "Tell me why you feel this way."

I rested my head on his shoulder, letting out a deep sigh. "He has been by my side since we reconnected. When he has to work, I am tucked safely in the hotel rooms or here, like today."

"Okay…" He sounded bewildered. "He still goes to work. What do you mean he is stuck with you? What is the problem?"

"I am so grateful that he is so protective and attentive. But… But I think he feels he has to take care of me instead of living his *normal* life." I even used air-quotes when I said the word normal.

"Well, he did bring you all the way here. He should take good care of you," he said matter-of-factly.

"No, he shouldn't. I want a boyfriend, not a babysitter." I crossed my arms across my chest, looking at Thomas chatting enthusiastically with Tim. "I overheard him on the phone the other day. He kept apologizing and said he really could not join them and wished them a good time." I turned to face James again. "That call was in English. Now I wonder about other calls when he spoke in French, German, or Italian!"

"I am sure they are not all social invitations."

"He has to decline stuff like that to be with me…" I trailed off. "Because he can't introduce me to his friends at *normal* gatherings." I used the air-quotes again.

"I thought you went to the gala and just came back from visiting his family."

"Those were not the causal gatherings, James. The gala was in his hotel, and he never left my side. Not for a second. And his family was in their country estate—"

"I still cannot believe Dr. Thompson is his sister-in-law," James interrupted me.

That was the first thing I told James when I called him this morning.

"His whole family is…is just amazing."

"I am here visiting you. This is a casual gathering, isn't it. I think —"

"Here, James. His apartment, a safe zone," I cut him off. "He can't invite all his friends or colleagues here to meet me, can he?" I sighed and murmured, "Maybe he doesn't even want me to meet his friends…"

"You remove that thought out of your head at once!" he snapped at me, sounding really upset.

"James… You saw the worse of me." I wrapped my arms around his waist.

"Not the worst. The most vulnerable," he said and kissed my hair. "But you are so much better now."

"Not enough, James. I got myself locked in the hotel emergency staircase in New York!"

"What?"

"Long story short. I panicked and ran into the emergency staircase. Then I decided to walk all the way to the penthouse level, not realizing the door could only be opened from the other side. And I was afraid to go back down." I sighed and added, "I had to call Thomas to rescue me. It was so embarrassing."

I glanced at James and found him rolling his lips and trying to suppress a laugh.

"It's not funny!"

"No, it's not. It's hilarious!" He chuckled. "But seriously, don't be too hard on yourself."

"I want our relationship to work. I really do. But I don't want to be his burden. I am afraid he might get tired of me being so…so emotionally fragile and tired of taking care of me."

"He loves you, Iris."

"People fall in love and also can fall out of love, once…once…" I was suddenly choked with emotion.

"Honey, I truly believe he's not a person who would fall in and out of love so easily." James lifted my face to look at him. "And you, Iris. Do you know how brave, amazing, and beautiful you are? If I were not with Tim, I would fall madly in love with you."

I gave him a much appreciative smile. "In that case, Thomas would not stand a chance." I buried my face in his chest.

"I am glad you said that because I am a bit worried now." He paused momentarily and said, "Your man is getting too close to mine."

I turned in the direction of our boyfriends, who were standing quite close and holding a book. I burst out laughing.

My laughter caught both Thomas and Tim's attention. They turned their heads in our direction.

I blew them a kiss and leaned my head against James' shoulder. Both men smiled at us and resumed their attention back to the book.

James held me even closer and kissed my hair. "The way he looks at you has never changed since the day I met him," he said softly. "There is no room for anyone else in his heart, trust me. And my advice is…" He paused, staring at Thomas, or probably Tim, and continued, "Talk to him about it."

OUR guests were gone, and we did the dishes and the cleaning right after, not wanting to wait until tomorrow.

"What are you thinking?" Thomas asked when he came back from taking the trash out and perceived I was sitting on the sofa, staring out the window aimlessly.

My gaze followed him to the kitchen. He washed his hands and poured himself another glass of wine. He walked towards me, gazing at me with those alluring blue eyes of his.

"Thank you," I said to him when he sat down next to me.

"What for? You did all the cooking." He settled me in his embrace.

"Having guests here at your place," I said, and then I saw the smile on his face vanishing.

"This is your home now," he said so tenderly. "I know it will take some time for you to feel at home here. Do it at your own pace. I just want you to be happy. And if you feel homesick, we will fly back to the States right away."

"Thomas… I…I want you to be happy, too. You can't just change your life to suit my needs." I reached my hands to cup his face. "I have lived with my stress disorders for over a year. I…I know how hard it is for the people around me…" I trailed off.

I knew all too well how my condition had impacted the lives of all my friends and family. They had to constantly manage my unpredictable symptoms, which might be triggered by a sound, a sight, or even a smell. I was not only a burden but also an ungrateful bitch sometimes. I hated how people around me treated me differently, and then I accused them of not being able to relate to what I was going through when they simply encouraged me to overcome my fear. And I also resented the whole universe for my misfortune sometimes. Fortunately, I did not do well with alcohol and drugs, otherwise I would have become an addict.

"Iris..." His gaze flipped between my eyes, both devoted and intent. He put the wine down and held my hands with his and brought them to his chest. "I was eighteen when Laila was taken."

"Thomas..." My heart ached. I wanted to know his story, but was he ready to share with me or did my self-pity coerce him to do it? "You don't have—"

He silenced me by placing his finger on my lips and continued, "We thought she was kidnaped for ransom at first, but no one contacted my family. Two months went by, and I knew in my heart that she was abducted and trafficked." He let out a deep sigh. "I started reaching out to organizations fighting against human trafficking and supporting survivors, not knowing what I was doing. That was when I met Eva. She worked for FIZ then. FIZ is an organization that offers direct support for victims of trafficking."

That's what Eva said...

"Laila was missing then. There was no proof or evidence of her being abducted and trafficked, but Eva still helped me cope with the loss and understand the unspeakable traumas those victims had been through."

"Oh Thomas... You were still a child then."

"An ignorant eighteen years old..." He shook his head slightly and continued, "Three years later Laila was found. I deferred university for a year and moved back home so I could be by her side." He let out another deep sigh. "She was...she was..." He was struggling to continue, his face in pain.

I cupped his face and gave him a soft kiss. He requited it with an appreciative smile and held my hands.

"She would not talk, so we couldn't find out what had happened to her. However, her physical exam gave us a clear picture. She could not... She could not bear children anymore..." He clenched his jaw, his grip on my hands tightening.

What happened to her? I gasped in horror, my eyes widened. *Do I dare to know?*

"She was... They had..." His eyes were turning pink, tears emerging.

"Shh..." I kneed on the sofa and enfolded him in my arms. I had never seen him so emotional. "Shh... Thomas, I don't want you to remember those horrible things."

"It has been more than ten years, and it still hurts."

I gently rubbed his back.

"When I went undercover, I witnessed the unspeakable Eva had told me about." He sighed and gazed at me. "So you see... You are not going to scare me off."

I felt a lump in my throat, tears scalding my eyes. We held each other in silence, calming down our emotions.

"Can I ask you a question?" My voice was timid.

"Of course." He caressed my face with the back of his fingers.

"Eva told me you made a judgment call to save me and had to take care of the fallout. What fallout? Did I... I mean... Were you in trouble because of me?"

Did Vara find out he was a police officer?

He frowned, apparently surprised by my question, or maybe he was not supposed to talk about his mission.

"Forget what I asked..." I averted my eyes. "Maybe there are some top secrets I shouldn't know anyway," I joked.

"I broke the protocol," he answered.

I flung my eyes back to him, my brow burrowed. "What? The protocol didn't allow you to save me?"

He sighed and said, "I was supposed to wait for other officers to pick—"

"You mean those who posed as traffickers?" I interrupted him.

"Yes..." He held my hand and squeezed it tight. "But it could take days, and Vera was too unpredictable. She..." He trailed off, seemingly searching for words that would not frighten me.

Did The Vixen plan to harm me?

"Anyway, the fallout was that Vera suspected my motive."

"Oh no…" I murmured.

He smiled, cupping my face. "There is no *oh no*. It's all over now. You are safe, and I am here with you." He tenderly pressed a kiss on my lips. "Your happiness is my happiness, Iris. And I am not changing my life to suit your needs because…" He fixed his doting eyes on mine and said, "You are my life now."

CHAPTER 31

> Your past history and all of your hurts are
> no longer here in your physical reality.
> Don't allow them to be here in your mind,
> muddying your present moments.
> ~Wayne Dyer

PARIS, the city of love…

When the jet landed, I grasped Thomas' hands and looked out the window.

I was back, and this time I was the one with my own personal bodyguard. How I wished I could say that to Vera's face!

It was late in the afternoon when we arrived at DeMount Paris located at the center of the luxurious and elegant Chaillot Quarter. It was a breath-taking Second Empire architecture and much richly decorated with sculptures.

Thomas told me that this building was built in the late nineteenth century and was originally a private residence of a Parisian merchant. Thomas' Great Grandfather purchased the property and opened the third DeMont Hotel. Rooms for the family members were different from those in the States. Instead of sharing a big apartment-style space, here they had suites on both sides of the corridor on the top floor of the east wing. And the elevator lobby was converted into a large seating area looking onto a large private rooftop terrace. I assumed, since I did not ask, they decided to keep the original layout because this was an old and historical building.

I felt anxious when I stood by the balcony glass-folding doors of our living room, looking in the direction of the Eiffel Tower. I knew

Shangri-La Paris, where I stayed last January, was just a five-minute walk away, and Étoile nightclub was farther south along the Seine.

Thomas approached me from behind and wrapped me in his arms. "*Je t'aime,*" he whispered in my ear.

I turned around to face him and said, "Thank you for bringing me back here."

He scanned my face, searching for traces of apprehension. Gently, he brushed the loose hair on my face behind my ears and gave me a soft kiss on my lips. "I will take you anywhere you desire."

To soothe my anxiety, I leaned against his chest and listened to his mellow heartbeats. "I am happy where I am now…" I whispered. "With you…"

"We can stay here for the rest of the day and have room service. Or, we can walk around the hotel if you like. It's quite hot outside, so I won't suggest going to the terrace now." Thomas sounded eager to plan our stay and make sure I would not be bored.

"How about your family?" I wondered if they planned to do certain activities together or at least to have dinner together like my family would do.

"Eva did mention if we like to dine with them. She suggested our own restaurant Prévost. Have you ever dined there before?"

I shook my head as I had never been in this area at all, not to mention eating at DeMont.

"Or we can try L'Orangerie, which is very quiet and unique. It's in the courtyard of the Four Seasons, not far from here."

I drew in a deep breath and gave him a half-smile. "You decide," I said, not wanting them to accommodate me.

"Okay, let's dine at Prévost. I will make the reservation and let everyone know," he said, letting go of me, and walked to the desk behind the sofa to use the hotel phone.

I was so glad he chose Prévost as it was just on the ground floor. And I had a feeling he did that for me. I sat on the sofa, hugging my knees and wondering how far I would test myself on this trip. I wanted to go back to Étoile to overcome my fear and nightmare. I had not talked to Eva about it. Yet. Maybe I should, so she could give me some advice or simply tell me not to go. But, what if Étoile was the underlying cause of my anxiety? I would never know if I did not face it again...

"Ma chérie?" Thomas called softly and sat by me. "Are you sure you are all right? You have been like this for several days." He looked worried.

"What do you mean?" I frowned.

"Like this," he said, pointing at his frowning brow.

I smiled at his imitation of me.

"Do you want to talk about it?" He held me in his arms.

"I..." Now I could feel my brows were burrowing. I rubbed my forehead with my hand, remembering how my mother used to smooth my forehead with her hand when I was just a teenager as I frowned a lot.

"Paris?" he asked.

I fell deep in thought again, nodding my head unconsciously.

Should I ask him? I gazed at him.

He was there when they abducted me. I wanted to know how they did it and all the details so I could fill the blanks in my memory and know that there was nothing I could have done to prevent it from happening. Tears were running down my cheeks before I could stop them.

"I am sorry..." I hastily wiped them away.

Kissing my temple, he held me tight and asked, " Would you like to talk to Eva?"

I shook my head and wrapped my arms around his neck. "I'll be fine. Just need a moment..."

After dinner, Thomas and I did not join the other two couples for a sunset stroll. How much I wished we could and wished we were able to enjoy just a normal walk in a park one day.

Thomas seemed to perceive my regret. He walked me out to the rooftop terrace after we stepped out of the elevator. I was drawn to the magnificent view of the sunset.

The daylight was fading, and the sky was changing to bright orange. The silhouette of the Eiffel Tower was becoming more distinguished by the second. Leaning against Thomas' broad chest, I breathed in the cool breeze and fixed my eyes on that yellow ochre iron structure.

The last time I was here, I was standing on the terrace of Jojo's suite admiring the Eiffel Tower sunset. We were drinking champagne and bantering with each other, having no clue that in less than six hours my life would be stolen...

What are you doing, Iris? Snap yourself out of the slump! Miss Pragmatic scolded me because I was supposed to make new memories here with Thomas.

I closed my eyes and drew in a deep breath, bringing myself back to the present.

Wow... When I opened my eyes again, I was astonished by the spectacular sight in front of me. The tower was illuminated after the golden sun made its grand exit.

Thomas gave me kisses on my sweet spot, showing me his attentive affection.

He's right. It has been days... Ever since he told me about this trip, I had been distracted and preoccupied by awful memories and uneasiness.

I turned around and looked up at him. I cupped his face in my hands and brought it down to requite his patience and thoughtfulness with an impassioned kiss, tasting his full lips tenderly but yet eagerly.

He returned my ardor first with caution, and then his kiss became lustful and hungry. He placed his hand behind my head, bringing me closer, deepening our kiss.

I had to pull myself away from him to catch my breath. His please-don't-stop pleading look made me want him more. Giving him a smile, I held his hand and started walking back inside, back to our suite.

He whirled me around and caught my lips again after he closed the door. My poor Thomas had suppressed his libido as I had been feeling anxious and even a bit depressed for the past few days. My enticement now completely released his lust for me.

I clung on to him, leaving no space between us. I could feel his hardness pushing against my stomach.

He picked me up and carried me to the sofa—the bedroom was too far at this moment. Gently, he laid me down and lay right next to me, trailing his kisses slowly to my sweet spot. His hand was underneath my short sundress, roaming along my thighs and up where he soon was going to fulfill my desire.

I pulled his silk-knit polo shirt up, wanting to take it off, so I could kiss and feel his toned chest muscles.

He pushed himself up and kneed astride my thighs. He hastily removed his shirt and tossed it on the floor while I unfastened his belt and unbuttoned his jeans. He then got to his feet, kicked off his loafers, and took off his jeans while I was busy unbuttoning my dress. He was soon back on top of me. He pulled down one cup of my lace bra, revealing my breast. He bent down and sucked my nipple, one hand fondling the other breast.

I moaned, my hands tugging the waistband of his brief.

We were eager to satisfy each other, skipping the intimate foreplay and forgetting about the protection…

Wait… You cannot forget about the protection. Miss Pragmatic was shouting.

I knew we both were clean, but I was not on the pill. Maybe I should start considering that option.

"Condom…" I whispered in his ear.

He uttered a deep groan and gave me a bittersweet smile.

"Night stand?" I asked as he was the one who unpacked our bags.

He buried his face in the crook of my neck, nibbling and tickling me.

I laughed, trying to push him away. "Still need a condom…" I screamed out the words, laughing at the same time.

He pushed himself off me, got off of the sofa, and scooped me up in his arms. "I am not leaving you here." He then marched towards the bedroom.

Wrapping my arms around his neck, I leaned my face against his cheek, inhaling the alluring and elegant Duc de Vervins he was wearing.

First time I caught this scent was when he visited me at the embassy. I thought I was attracted to his cologne and not to him. I remembered Max always smelled soapy fresh only, but I was probably too busy loathing him to notice what cologne he was wearing then.

Thomas gently put me down on the bed and lay down next to me. He lifted himself up on one elbow and placed his lips on mine, his other hand roaming along my thigh. His lustful kiss and loving caress were intoxicating. I felt so drunk, even though I did not drink anything but water at dinner tonight.

Suddenly, he pulled away and got out of the bed, his gaze fixed on me.

"Don't go…" I entreated, pouting.

His amorous smile made my heart palpitate. He winked at me and walked out of the room.

I sighed in frustration. These interruptions felt like a cruel foreplay.

And then, Jon Batiste started crooning *The very thought of you*, making me smile in contentment, '… *It's just the thought of you, the very thought of you, my love…*'

I love him so much… I jumped out of the bed, grabbed the throw on top of the bed to wrap around myself, and sauntered back to the living room.

There he is… He stood by the desk, wearing nothing but a black brief, his blue gaze fixed on me.

I tossed the throw on the floor and walked up to him. He enfolded me in his arms, burying his face in the crook of my neck.

We swayed to the music, half naked.

It was amazingly romantic.

AFTER Thomas went to the office the next morning, I invited Eva to our suite as I really needed her professional advice.

"So, what do you think?" I asked Eva after I shared my thoughts about revisiting Shangri-La Hotel and Étoile.

Eva was silent, her brow furrowed.

"You don't think it's a good idea..." Her silence discouraged me. "I just thought... I just thought if I...if I..." Suddenly, I was choked with emotion. "I thought maybe after revisiting those places I can finally talk about it..."

"Iris..." She held my hands clasped on my lap. "Returning to the scene of the trauma is often recommended as part of therapies for PTSD."

The scene of the trauma... But where would be *my* scene of the trauma? Étoile? The recovering house? The mansion? Or all of them?

"Iris..." She squeezed my hands. "I am not your therapist anymore. You should seek advice from Dr. Warrens, or I can recommend you to a wonderful psychiatrist in Bern."

"Why can't you be my therapist again?"

She gave me a caring smile and said, "I care for you too much to be objective."

Although disappointed, I was moved by what she said.

"I have read several academic journals and articles regarding this form of therapy published by Cambridge University Press and other institutes and organizations, such as your country's Department of Health and Human Services. But..." Her voice became hesitant. "I have never carried out site visits with my patients. Therefore, it's hard for me to give you any practical advice."

Eva's answer made me feel utterly deflated, my eyes staring at my hands idly.

"Would you mind sharing with me what you are thinking now?" Eva asked in a calm and sensible voice as she perceived my downhearted expression.

I looked up at her, my eyes brimming with tears. "I...I don't want Thomas to miss out on the fun of his life because of me..."

"Iris..." Eva stroked my cheek with her soft hand. "This is why Tommy fell for you. You are trying to overcome your fear here, and you still put him before you."

"He has done so much for me." My eyes were stung by the hot tears. "I know those recurrent memories and nightmares are never going to go away." I sighed and continued, "Eva, I am not wishing for a miracle. I just thought if I could fill in the blanks, maybe… Just maybe, I could finally stop asking myself *what if* I had never come to Paris in the first place."

Eva wrapped her arms around my shoulders and kissed my temple. "As a psychiatrist, I am so sorry that I could not be of much help. But as a family—"

"Family?" I gazed at her, tears rolling down my cheeks.

"Yes, you are our family, love." Eva squeezed me tighter. "When Tommy called me and insisted I must take your case, he told me you were very special to him. And I saw his reason after I met you." She leaned her head against mine. "Therefore, as a family, let's take some time to think it through and talk to Tommy together. I am sure he will have a very strong opinion about it."

"NO. Absolutely not!" Stubborn Thomas said in a low and authoritative voice and started pacing the room. He was frustrated because he knew he could not stop me if I insisted on going. And I could see his pleading in those blue eyes.

"I called Jojo's boyfriend Marcus. I told you about him. Remember?"

He gave me a sideways glance, frowning. "The club owner?"

"Yes." I walked up to him, stopping him from wearing out the carpet. "He will meet me, us, there. You are going with me, aren't you?"

"Of course I am! Wait…" he exclaimed and then realized he just gave in to my idea.

"Thank you." I wrapped my arms around him. "I can't do this without you."

We did not tell Florent and Adeline where we were going as we did not want them to worry about me. Eva and Louis insisted on driving us there and being with us to show their support.

So, here we were, approaching the nightclub where I was

abducted.

Looking out the window, I stared at the sidewalk, remembering I was screaming how cold it was that night. Farther down the sidewalk, I could see a crowd gathering outside a building. A sudden sickness swept over me, making me nauseous.

"Stop... Stop, please," I gasped out.

Thomas held me tight in his arms, gently rubbing my arm. "Breathe, love. Breathe," he whispered.

Louis quickly pulled up to a curb by the Seine, and all three pairs of concerned eyes were focusing on me.

"I am sorry..." I whispered.

"Don't be, love." Thomas kissed my temple, enfolding me tighter.

"I...I don't think I can..."

"That is all right, Iris," Eva said, her voice soft and comforting. "Don't force yourself."

Feeling defeated, I looked in the direction of Étoile. I was so certain that I could step into that club with Thomas, Marcus, Eva, and Louis by my side. However, the fear of something bad might happen to me again haunted me.

"Would..." I turned to face Thomas. "Would you call Marcus for me?" I handed him my phone. "Just..."

"Don't worry. I got you." He kissed my forehead and tapped my phone to call Marcus.

Looking out the window again, I regretted not having the courage to walk into my first scene of the trauma.

"*Bonsoir, c'est Thomas. Ça va?*" Thomas greeted Marcus good evening and identified himself on the phone.

Marcus probably thought we had arrived at the club.

"*Elle s'en sort bien.* I am afraid we are not going to make it tonight," Thomas told him I was doing well and then switched to English. I was certain he did this for my benefit. He gently stroked my hair while listening to Marcus. "Let me ask her..."

I turned and looked at Thomas again as I assumed the *her* was me.

"Marcus would like to visit you tomorrow if it's okay with you?

He said Jasmine demanded that."

I smiled, missing my dear Jojo, and nodded.

"She's looking forward to your visit." Thomas was back on the phone. "I will text you my number." He then listened to Marcus for a few more minutes. "*C'est très bien. À demain,*" he acknowledged whatever Marcus said about tomorrow and ended the call. Then he put my phone in his breast pocket.

"I assume everyone is pleased with this adventure," I joked, looking at everybody.

"It's the highlight of my day!" Louis grinned cheerfully, and we all burst into laughter.

"Ready to go back?" Thomas asked.

I nodded and looked at Eva and Louis. "Thank you for being here for me."

"You are very welcome, love." Eva gave me a heartwarming smile.

Louis nodded at me with his usual lighthearted smile and started the car.

I cuddled up to Thomas, feeling much calmer and more relaxed.

The ride was peaceful, but I hastily sat up when I saw a familiar iron gate. Louis drove through it and pulled up to Shangri-La Hotel's front entrance, right underneath its ornate wrought-iron glass awning.

Two liveried doormen opened the car doors for us after we came to a complete stop.

This Torian Family is full of surprises…

"Thank you," Thomas said to Louis and Eva and stepped out of the car. He came around to my side and reached for my hand. "Join me, mon amour."

I looked at Eva and Louis, speechless.

"Enjoy," Eva said to me.

Holding on to Thomas' hand, I slowly stepped out of the car.

He put his hand on the small of my back and ushered me into the lobby. I remembered how impressed I was with their perfect blend of European intricacies and Chinoiserie furnishings the last time I was here.

"*Bonsoir, Monsieur Torian,*" the concierge greeted when we walked past the lobby. "*Bonsoir, Madame.*" He gave me a courteous smile.

"*Bonsoir,*" Thomas responded and continued to lead me towards the elevator.

I guess we are already checked in.

We rode the elevator all the way to the sixth floor and walked into a suite with a corner terrace looking onto a stunning view of the Eiffel Tower and the Seine.

"I wanted to reserve La Suite Shangri-La on the seventh floor, but it was not available," he said when I walked out to the terrace.

I was speechless. I did not need the lavishest or the biggest room. All I wished was to wake up in the morning next to him in this very hotel. I wanted to make new memories.

I turned around and gazed at him with my misty eyes. "*Je t'aime...*"

He walked up to me and cupped my face in his hands. "*Chaque jour je t'aime davantage.*"

Whatever he just said—I only understood *je t'aime*—was like a magic spell, which completely, thoroughly, and utterly enchanted me.

"I have other surprises," he said, steering me back to the room. He walked to the wet bar and took a bottle of wine out of the refrigerator.

I walked closer to and saw the label Moscato d'Asti.

"I hope you will like it," he said, opening the bottle.

Does he remember everything I've told him? I looked up at him in astonishment. After our sweaty and gratifying lovemaking the other night, I told him I wanted to make new memories with him here in Paris, and it would be even better if I could overwrite the old ones. I did not know he would go to great lengths to do all this for me.

"Come." He took the wine and two glasses, gesturing me to the sofa.

We cuddled together, drinking to our new life together.

"Can I ask you something?" After about half a glass of wine, I built up the courage to ask what was in my mind.

"Of course, love." His blue gaze was alluring.

"But you have to promise me that you will tell me whatever I want to know."

"Iris…" he looked concerned.

"Please… I need to know."

He let out a sigh and nodded reluctantly.

"Can you…can you tell me what happened to me that night?" I asked and took a gulp of my wine.

His smile disappeared, deep furrows appearing in his brow.

"Please…"

He sighed with distress and nodded. He held me closer and said, "Vera contracted with a wide range of people to abduct their targets."

"What…what do you mean *contracted*?"

"Human trafficking is like a chain…" He paused, seemingly considering an easier way to explain things to me. "Every piece is an organization, a group of criminals, or a procurer. They are individually operated but linked together. Does that make sense to you?"

"I guess…"

"Those people who abducted you are criminals specializing in kidnaping, abduction, and contract killing…"

Contract killing? What he just said sent a shiver down my spine.

Thomas took a sip of wine and continues, "Vera's organization worked—"

"Organization? Vera had an organization?" I interrupted him as I always thought Vera was just a madam running a brothel and finding women for her rich and important clients.

"She belongs to an Italian crime organization."

Belongs? Present tense… I took another gulp of wine, trying to wash down the knot forming in my throat. "Isn't she in prison now?" I whispered my question.

"She is, but unfortunately that does not cut her ties with the organization. And…" He frowned at me. "You should take it easy on the wine."

I looked at my glass and found it was empty. I motioned him to pour me more. "Please..."

He shook his head and poured more wine into my glass.

I stared at the bubbling liquid slowly filling the glass while my mind was going a thousand miles an hour...

Italian crime organization... He said Laila was found in Italy. Was it possible that...? No... It was too much of a coincidence. Should I ask him? No... I did not want him to re—

"Are you all right? Is it too much for you?" He interrupted my thoughts, his voice concerned.

"I am okay..." I gave him a reassuring smile and asked, "Why... why was Vera in Paris if she had other people doing her dirty work?"

"To inspect the merchandise..." It was his turn to take a big gulp and finish his wine. He poured himself another glass as well.

Merchandise... I was just a merchandise. The fact nauseated me. "What did they do to me?" I asked, afraid his answer was going to make me sick.

He fixed his eyes on mine. "They watched and followed you surreptitiously, just waiting for the right opportunity. There was a group of people following you into the nightclub."

Frowning, I tried to recall if I noticed anything suspicious that night. Nothing. I was having so much fun with my friends.

"Those criminals circle around their targets without them knowing. And they create their opportunities to drug them. Drink or needle spiking. Whatever is easier..." Thomas let out another deep sigh and added, "And then they wait for the drug to take effect."

"We drank the same bottle of champagne, so it was definitely not spiked. Then I went to the restroom by myself. That's all I remember..." I looked at him, feeling frustrated.

"Did you talk to someone on your way to the restroom?"

I shook my head. "I was the only person in the restroom. And I did find it very strange since the club was packed."

"They had their way to isolate—"

"Wait! A woman was coming out from the restroom when I was going in. She was the only person I saw there."

Thomas frowned, sipping his wine.

"Do you think that woman drugged me?"

He shrugged, not saying anything.

"Tell me what happened after you got there."

He gave me a concerned look first and said, "The pickup location was in an alley a block away from the club. When we arrived, you were in a cargo van already. You are... You are unconscious..."

A sickness washed over me, making me tremble.

"My love..." His voice was so sad. And I could sense his regret.

"And?" I prompted because I had to know...

Furrows on his brow deepened. He took another gulp of wine and said, "After Vera gave her approval, you were driven across the border to a recovering house in Switzerland."

"I have... I have fragments of that." I stared aimlessly at my wine glass. "Waking up and then falling back to sleep, again and again..." My eyes were submerged with tears. "So, it didn't really matter if I was at Étoile or any other club..." I felt so violated, and my chest was filled with indignation and resentment.

"Or any city or country..." Thomas added.

I looked at him, perplexed.

"She had scouts in almost all major cities to find her targets. You could be in Rome, Tokyo, or even New York."

"New York? In my own country?" I almost shouted.

"*Mon amour*, it's all over now," he comforted me.

"So, it's nothing to do with Paris..." I trailed off. All this time, I had been blaming myself for ever being in *this* city.

Thomas held me closer and kissed my hair.

CHAPTER 32

> I love you
> not only for what you are,
> but for what I am when I am with you.
> I love you
> not only for what you have made of yourself,
> but for what you are making of me.
> I love you
> for the part of me that you bring out.
> ~Elizabeth Barrett Browning

MY new life in Bern was *amazing!* I had been doing very well by myself when Thomas was at work. I spent most of the time working on the projects Antonio and Jojo had emailed me, and reading had been keeping me occupied as well. So far, I felt content and enjoyed my life here with him very much.

He had been working in the Bern office for almost a week now and was scheduled to travel to Oslo, Stockholm, and Helsinki next week. He promised me he would only be gone for less than ten days, and I was sure I would be fine here by myself; and plus, I had James, Tim, and his family around. This arrangement might actually work.

Stepping off the treadmill, I was ready for a shower. I plugged my phone into the charger on the kitchen counter and scurried into the master bathroom.

This bathroom was like a getaway, a superb, spacious, and spa-like place to unwind. It had a huge enclosed shower with overhead rainfall shower-head and wall-mount body sprays, a double-ended soaking bathtub, and a big leather chaise lounge.

I turned on the shower first to get the hot water, quickly got undressed, and then went back into the shower.

Before Thomas left for work this morning, I promised him his favorite chicken dish for dinner tonight. He would be home in less than two hours, so I had better hurry up.

Five minutes... I turned on the body sprays, and enjoyed the pressurized jets massaging my muscles. *I need more than five minutes...*

Wow... I let out a satisfied sigh after turning off the water. And when I walked out of the shower, I heard music outside the bathroom.

Oops, he is home early. I haven't started cooking yet. Quickly, I put on a bathrobe and headed out to greet him.

"You are ho—" I stopped in mid-sentence because it was not Thomas but a woman, whom I had never seen before, standing in the kitchen. And she seemed in shock as well when she saw me.

"*Wer sind Sie?*" the woman asked me who I was in German, her eyes widened. And then she started walking towards me.

Instinctively, I ran back to the bedroom and shut the sliding bedroom door, and I hastily locked the door because she was after me.

"*Wer sind Sie?*" she yelled, pounding on the door.

I glanced around the room looking for something to block the door, my heart beating so fast and hard. I started to push the heavy, tall dresser by the door towards the door, but the stubborn dresser would not budge.

"Dammit!" I growl.

Her yelling was becoming aggressive, and I could not understand what else she was saying. And suddenly, I heard a key jingling in the door lock.

She has the bedroom key? I pushed the dresser in panic, and with a big adrenaline rush, I propelled it to the door. I whipped around, looking for other furniture, and then the key unlocking sound startled me.

I ran! I ran into the bathroom, shut the door, and locked it right away. I leaned against the door, panting and trying to think.

However, the sound of her pounding on the bedroom door seemingly became louder.

"Stop it!" I screamed, covering my ears as the banging started giving me a throbbing headache.

Glancing around, my eyes landed on the big leather chaise. I darted across the room and started pushing it towards the door.

Once it was in front of the door, I backed away until my back bumped into the shower glass wall. Sliding down, I fell onto the cold tile floor. Tears started gushing down, and I was so lost that I could not think straight.

I have to call Thomas...

"Shit!" I bellowed in agony because my phone was in the kitchen.

What am I going to do now? I wiped the tears with the bathrobe sleeves, trying to make sense of what was happening. *Who is she? How did she get in?*

Regardless of why this was happening, I needed to protect and defend myself. I got up and went through the drawers to find something I could use. When I saw a pair of first aid scissors, I grabbed them and sat back down where I was, my eyes fixed on the door blocked by the leather chaise.

I could still hear voices and noises, but they were not close. That meant she did not get into the bedroom. Thomas should be home soon, and then I would be safe. My knuckles turned white as I was gripping the scissors tightly.

"Iris!" Thomas' voice made me jump on my feet. It sounded like it was outside the bedroom.

"Thomas!" I tossed the scissors, scurried to the door, and started pushing the chaise away from the door, but it was not moving. "Thomas! I am in the bathroom!" I screamed.

"Iris!" His voice was much closer now, right outside the bathroom.

"The chair won't move!" I cried out devastatingly.

"*Mon amour*, I am here now... Don't worry. Unlock the door first, okay?" he said calmly.

"Right, the lock…" I quickly unlocked the bathroom door and tried to push the chair again, but it still would not give an inch. "It still won't…" I burst out crying.

"Step back now. I am going to push the door open."

"Oh… Okay…" I stepped back, wiping the tears away.

The door was slowly pushed open, and the high-pitched sound of the chaise's legs scraping against the tiled floor was deafening.

My heart sped up when I saw his face. I moved towards him instantly.

"Wait…"

I halted on his command, my breathing hasty, and watched him pushing the door wider and squeezing through the gap. I launched myself at him. He caught me in his arms, enfolding me tightly.

I sobbed uncontrollably, my knees giving out.

Thomas picked me up and sat down on the chaise, placing me on his lap. He held me close, gently stroking my hair while whispering endearments.

"I…I didn't…didn't know…know wha…what to do…" I said between sniffling and hiccuping.

He cupped my face in his hands and kissed my forehead, my nose, and my eyes. He then wiped my tears away with his thumbs. "You could call me…" he said.

"My phone is in the kitchen…" I broke down and sobbed again.

"There, there. It's all right now."

I nodded, trying to contain myself. And when I was finally feeling calm, I glanced over his shoulder, frowning at the half-opened door.

"Feeling better?" he asked, stroking my cheek.

"I don…don't know why I… I couldn't mov…move the chair…"

"Don't worry about it." He kissed my forehead. "I will move it back."

I nodded and moved my legs off his lap to stand on my feet. He stood up as well and wrapped me in his arms again.

"I am so sorry," he whispered.

"That's o…okay. You are here now…"

He let go of me and turned around to move the chair away. It was an oversized seating with leather upholstery and solid wood. It weighed a ton.

How did I move it earlier?

"There." He moved it back to where it was. He turned around and looked at me, seemingly feeling as surprised as I was.

"I just did it. I don't know how..."

"You must be very scared," he said, wrapping his arm around my shoulders.

"I am..."

"It's all right now." He kissed my hair, steering me out of the bathroom.

But I pulled back, tugging his suit jacket. "Is that woman still out there?"

He sighed deeply and shook his head.

I wanted to ask him who she was but decided to wait.

"How... How did you get in here?" I asked in astonishment when I saw the tall dresser still blocking the doorway, although the sliding door was opened.

"I climbed over the dresser."

Scheiße! I forgot it was a sliding door. Blocking it was useless.

"Do you know how heavy that dresser is?" he asked, his eyebrows arched.

I bit my trembling lower lip, feeling sad and anxious again.

"*Mon armor...*" He embraced me. "I am so sorry... Why don't you get dressed while I move the dresser back. Okay?"

I nodded in his arms.

He lifted my face to look at him and said, "I promise I will explain everything later."

I stood on tiptoes and gave him a kiss on the cheek.

———

WHEN we walked into the kitchen, I saw a bag of groceries on the island. I wondered if Thomas had gone to the store, but he grabbed it and tossed it in the trash pin.

"Do you still want the lemon chicken?" I asked, pretending I did not see him throwing away the bag.

He shook his head, opening the wine cooler. "How about just fondue tonight? It's easier," he said, grabbing a bottle of white wine out of the cooler.

"Sure…" I walked up to the cabinet to get a caquelon and a small burner out and then started to prepare bread cubes while Thomas prepared the cheese mixture.

I could sense the tension and his gloomy mood, and I was still feeling on edge myself. However, we managed to get the food ready. The bubbly gooey cheese infused with white wine and garlic was cozy and solacing, a perfect comfort food to ease the stress and strain.

Thomas took a big sip of his wine and gazed at me in rue.

"What's the matter?" I asked, putting down my fork.

He held my hands, his thumbs idly rubbing on my palms. Cleaning his throat, he said, "Her name is Anna. She's my ex-girlfriend."

Instinctively, I pulled my hands back, but he held them tighter.

Anna… Anna Haller? The missing calls…

"The door was locked. She must have your key," I said coldly, my brow knitted. I tried to pull my hands back again, not wanting him to touch me.

"Will you give me a chance to explain before getting mad?" He gently squeezed my hands.

I tugged my hand back, feeling sadness in my chest and a burning sensation in my eyes.

He let out a deep sigh and continued, "I told you I was in a relationship for years…" He paused, probably waiting for my reaction.

I just stared into the distance, blinking back my tears and wondering what I was doing here in Bern with him.

"I… We met when I worked in the federal office. She was an administrator there. She still is."

"You did break up, right?" I asked, my voice small. I did not care when or where they met. I only cared if they were still seeing each other.

"Of course, we did. It ended three... No... Four years ago. I am not with anyone else but you," he explained eagerly. "*Je t'aime,*" he said. His voice was so tender and...hurt.

I looked at him, nibbling my bottom lip. "You lived together? Here? She still has your key..." I trailed off, feeling nauseous.

"No, we had never lived together. She had my key because she checked on the apartment for me while I was on assignments."

"I locked the door. She must have a key." I repeated my statement, my voice trembling and sad.

They must be very close for her to still have his key. And I hated liars and loathed cheaters.

Trust him, Iris. Miss Pragmatic whispered in my ear.

I do trust him. With all my heart... That's why it hurts so much. I looked into his eyes, afraid to see any sign of lies and deception.

"She gave me the key back when she called off our relationship," he said, his gaze earnest.

"She broke up with you?" My voice might be a bit too high.

He nodded. "She couldn't handle the nature of my assignments. She thought they were too dangerous and asked me to pursue a management position in fedpol, but I refused because I had completely dedicated myself to the operations then."

I don't think I could handle that, either...

"Anyway, earlier she admitted to me that she took the key back when she was here the last time."

"Last time?" My eyebrow arched all on its own.

He reached for my hand again, and I let him hold it, needing to bring my jealousy down a notch. They were in a relationship for years, and we just started dating. It was not my place to question whatever they did before we reconnected.

"Okay... Go on then... I am listening," I said, trying to make my voice as calm as possible.

He leaned in and kissed my forehead. Then he sat back, looking more at ease now. "We ran into each other at a formal colleague's new year's party. We sort of got on again..." He paused again, probably worried about my reaction.

I gave him a reassuring smile, mentally reminding myself that it was months ago.

"She and several friends came back here after—" He stopped mid-sentence when he saw my knitted eyebrows. "No. I did not sleep with her if that's what your pretty little head is thinking about." He squeezed my hand and added, "And that was the last time I saw her before today."

I *was* thinking about if they slept together, but he had all the right to sleep with anyone he wanted to then. "You... We...we weren't together then. It's not my business…"

"I could not do it because I couldn't stop thinking about you."

"Really?" My gaze was fixed on his doting blue eyes.

He pulled me in and pressed his lips on mine.

He loves me... That's all that matters. I wrapped my arms around his neck, deepening our kiss.

After a passionate kiss, the tension between us was gone. I leaned against him, reaching for my fork to have more fondue. "Why did she come here today?" I asked.

He finished the wine in his glass and poured more in. He took another sip before he answered, "She has been texting and calling me since we came back, wanting to get together. I was too preoccupied to acknowledge her. It's my fault. I should have told her about you."

I rested my head on his chest, idly stirring the melted cheese with the fork.

"She called me earlier. I almost did not answer her call, then I thought it was time to be frank with her. When I answered the call, she was frantic and told me someone had broken into the apartment." He stopped to take a sip of the wine. "I tried to call you, but you did not answer."

Our eyes moved to my phone sitting on the kitchen counter.

"I just rushed back," he continued. "When I got here, there were two police offices—"

"What?" I interrupted him, exclaiming. "She called the police on me!"

He tightened his embrace and kissed my temple, calming me. "Love, it's simply a misunderstanding."

"Fine... Go on."

"I rushed in here, asking *Where is she? Where is she?*"

I chuckle at his change of tone, how he was trying to sound urgent and worried. My mood was finally lightened up.

"She told me the intruder locked herself in the bedroom. She took the bedroom door key from the drawer to open the door, but the intruder blocked the door with a dresser."

"An intruder, huh?" I scoffed.

"That was when I realized what a mess it was. So I told the police officers it was a misunderstanding and asked them to leave."

"How about your *ex*-girlfriend?"

"I asked her why she was here, of course. She told me she could not get hold of me, so she decided to surprise me by coming over here to cook dinner for me."

"How nice of her," I said sarcastically. *That's why there's a bag of groceries...*

"Like I said, it was my fault. She wanted to get back together, and I had been avoiding her."

"Does she know who I am now?" I tilted my head to look at him, my voice was small.

"Yes, she does now. I told her you were my girlfriend and lived here with me."

"Was her reaction rational?" Last thing I needed was a crazy ex-girlfriend of his.

"I believe so. She apologized and left. And left the key." He tilted his chin in the direction of a key laying on the kitchen counter.

Wow... It must be hard. Although I felt sorry for her, I still thought she shouldn't have taken the key without his knowledge in the first place. Then, this whole thing...

"I am sorry..." I buried my face in his chest.

"For what?"

"If I had reacted like a normal per—"

"Stop," he interrupted me. "You are normal."

"Thomas." I looked up at him. "A normal person would have asked your ex-girlfriend who she was and how she got in here. A normal person would have told your ex-girlfriend that she should come back later or call you."

He held me tighter.

"And a normal person wouldn't have hidden herself in the bathroom, thinking she could defend herself with first aid scissors." I chuckled.

"You are so brave, *ma chérie.*"

"*Allons bon?*" I asked if he really thought so. "I stampeded like a wild animal!"

"*Bien sûr,*" he said of course and added, "You acted and got away from people you thought might be dangerous to you. Like a normal person."

I guessed he was right. I did not freeze or get too panicky to act. I nestled in his embrace again, appreciating his presence.

He stroked my hair and said, "I want you to travel with me."

I looked up at him, not sure what he meant.

"Even though my family and James are around, I cannot leave you here by yourself. I need you to be by my side."

"Thomas, you just told me I am brave."

"You are, but I am not."

"What?" This man was confusing me.

"When Anna called and said someone had broken in here, I...I had never felt so frightened before. I couldn't rush back here fast enough. I cannot imagine..." he trailed off.

"Silly, you can't watch me every second," I said, although I was deeply moved by his sentiment.

"I would put you in my pocket if I could."

I reached out and touched his stubble chin, holding his gaze, and said, "Just tell me when to pack." And I pressed my lips on his.

CHAPTER 33

> "What day is it?" asked Pooh.
> "It's today," squeaked Piglet.
> "My favorite day," said Pooh.
> ~A.A. Milne

THIS was my fairy tale: Meeting the love of my life and traveling around the world with him. And, I was getting married today!

One would think my lover boy would have planned a grand marriage proposal.

No, nein, non!

There was no beautiful sunset, no airplane banner message, no red roses, and no getting-on-one-knee-and-opening-a-ring-box...

~ ~ ~

Four months ago...

We were supposed to fly to Riyadh for a week, but a serious stomach flu that had made me sick for more than a week completely messed up our travel plan. Hence, Thomas had to go alone. It also meant that he would be traveling without me for the very first time since we started dating, and we would not see each other for a week. I was devastated—probably not that dramatic but definitely *very* disappointed—and insisted on accompanying him to the airport.

When he walked up to the jet after our passionate-kiss-goodbye, he suddenly turned around, his blue eyes glazed with anticipation, and said to me, "Let's get married when I come back."

He *said,* not *asked.*

"Okay." I grinned like a silly fangirl.

"Fantastic..." He gave me a wink before walking into the plane.

What just happened? My eyes were fixed on the jet door.

Emma appeared in the doorway, waving at me.

"Take care of him for me, please…" I said.

"Absolutely. I hope you feel better soon, Iris." Emma gave me her trademark smile.

"Thanks." I waved goodbye and stepped back several feet away. My eyes moved to the windows, hoping to catch a glimpse of my man. And I found him looking at me through a little window.

I love you. I mouthed the words, waving at him.

He replied with the same words, and then he turned away as someone needed his attention.

I sighed and turned towards the car driving us here. Then a rush of nausea suddenly hit me. While I rushed to the restroom, I heard the jet engine roaring behind me.

When I finally came out of the restroom, the jet was already gone. I ran out of the hangar and saw it taking off on the runway, heading to Saudi Arabia without me.

Thomas cut his trip short and came home in three days because I had become too frail from all the nausea and vomiting. Even though James and Eva had checked on me everyday, he still insisted on coming home to take care of me.

"I am taking you to the hospital now," he said when he saw me lying on the bathroom floor after spewing my guts all morning.

"I just want to go to sleep." I covered myself with a big bath towel, feeling tired and enervated.

He scooped me up and carried me to the bed. "I am going to change you now."

"What?"

"I am taking you to the hospital. Now." He sounded unyielding.

I did not have any energy left to argue with him, so I got out of the bed and dragged my feet to the closet to change.

An hour later, we were sitting in an exam room waiting for the A&E doctor and my lab results. I leaned against Thomas' chest, ready to fall asleep.

A knock on the door startled me, and the doctor who examined me earlier walked in, a big smile on his face. I guessed it was not serious, otherwise he would not smile like that. Feeling relieved, I sat up straight on that very uncomfortable hospital chair. Thomas wrapped one arm around my shoulders and dipped a kiss on my temple.

"Your lab results came back normal..." He paused, his eyes flicking between me and Thomas.

"Great!" Thomas gave me a comforting squeeze.

But why am I feeling so sick? I frowned. *I am...*

"Congratulations, Ms. De Waal. You are pregnant," the doctor interrupted my thoughts.

What? My eyes blinked rapidly.

Thomas and I turned our heads and looked at each other, our eyes widened, smiles spreading across our faces.

"I will leave you now. Take your time." The doctor stood up, apparently sensing that he just gave us some unexpected news. "The nurse will give you a list of supplements I recommend before you see your ob-gyn. They will—"

I raised my hand like a student asking permission to ask questions.

"Yes?" The doctor chuckled.

"But I am sick all day..."

"Morning sickness is incredibly varied, despite its name. Some people are sick in the morning or evening, some are sick all day, and others are sick if they have not gotten enough rest. Don't worry about it. Some of the supplements can alleviate the symptoms. But I recommend you see your ob-gyn as soon as possible since your symptoms are quite severe."

I nodded, my brow furrowed.

"Thank you, doctor." Thomas stood up to shake the doctor's hand.

Pregnant? How did it happen? Of course I knew how people got pregnant. I meant how did we get pregnant? We always used condoms; even when we realized we had run out of them in the middle of action, Thomas would get dressed and rush to the drugstore.

"Iris?" Thomas' voice pulled me back from my thoughts. His blue eyes were glazed with excitement but immediately became worried when he saw my eyes brimming with tears. "Are you... Are you not ready for this?" He sounded so worried.

I was ready to have his baby. I wanted his baby. But this was not what I had imagined and planned. I wanted to get married first and be Mrs. Torian for a couple of years before becoming Mama Torian.

Suddenly, I began to sob, tears gushing out.

"Oh, Iris..." He held me in his arms. "What...what can I do?"

I want to be Mama Torian...

"They...they are happy tears." I sniffled. "And..." I hastily stood up. "Excuse me, love. I need to use the..." Covering my mouth, I rushed out of the room before finishing my sentence.

About two months after we found out the stomach flu I had was actually morning sickness, Thomas suggested we went for a ride. Without a second thought, I gladly accepted his suggestion as I had been stuck in the apartment forever.

He drove us to Lake Neuchâtel and parked outside a contemporary waterfront apartment building. A nicely dressed gentleman greeted us when we got out of the car.

"Good day, Mr. Torian, Ms. De Waal." He spoke in English and knew our names. He extended his hand towards Thomas for a handshake.

"Iris, this is Mr. Lorenz. Our real estate agent," Thomas said to me.

"Real estate agent?" I murmured.

Mr. Lorenz, who did not reach his hand to shake mine, smiled at me broadly. Thomas must have told him that I was a *germaphobe* and preferred not to be touched. I suppressed my mirth and smiled at him respectfully.

"I have a surprise for you," Thomas said in an enthusiastic voice, wrapping his arm around my waist.

"Are we moving?" I asked.

Thomas did not answer me, his smile broadening.

"This way, please." Mr. Lorenz motioned us to the opened glass front entrance.

We followed him into a white lobby with very minimal decorations. Three pairs of red, cream, and black Swan chairs were placed against the windows, and a large, same color tone, abstract painting was hung on the white wall. We walked through the lobby and towards the elevators, which were right behind the seating area. Mr. Lorenz pressed the button and one elevator opened right away. It took us all the way to the fifth floor, which was also the top floor. The elevator door opened to a bright lobby. We followed Mr. Lorenz and walked through a narrow hallway. I saw two big black doors at both ends, and one was already opened.

Mr. Lorenz led us towards the opened door.

"I thought you might like to have another home with a waterfront view," Thomas whispered in my ear while we walked through the opened door.

I was speechless. This spacious apartment was so bright and had sweeping views of Lake Neuchâtel.

"I looked at several properties and found this one—" Thomas was following me towards the balcony.

"Is perfect," I finished his sentence.

Mr. Lorenz opened the glass sliding door to the balcony for us and excused himself. "Call me if you need me."

I closed my eyes and inhaled deeply... The air did not smell salty and sunny like California, but it was fresher and greener. The crashing water did not roar as loud and long as the Pacific Ocean, but it was soothing and comforting. I could sense a small hint of my childhood...

"And... I have this for you," he said, his voice right in front of me.

I opened my eyes and saw a white gold, solitaire ring set elegantly in an opened, deep-red box with black velvet interior.

"If you have not changed your mind," he said. "I like to give you this." Then he got on one knee.

He got on one knee... My heart was melting.

I blinked back the tears, giving him my left hand.

Am I too fortunate to have all of these and too greedy to want them all? I watched him take the ring out of the box and put it on my finger. I leaned in and wrapped my arms around his neck.

He stood up, holding me in his arms. "You can start to plan our wedding or wait…"

"I don't want year-long-wedding-planing and trying on hundreds of wedding dresses."

"Anything you want, *mon armor*."

"I…I want to get married before the baby is born," I added.

"My bride can do whatever she desires…"

A week later, we broke the news to our families and friends: We were engaged, expecting a baby, moving to Lake Neuchâtel, and getting married in April. In that exact order.

~ ~ ~

All of these happened in the last four months. And let me announce it again: I was getting married today!

THOMAS managed to fly my family and close friends here last week. They got to sightsee around the incredibly beautiful Bern and Lake Geneva before they arrived at Thomas' family château today to attend our wedding.

Here was the secret just a few people knew—I became Mrs. Torian last week as we were obliged by the law to marry at a registry office first. Therefore, I was just here to enjoy the party!

After Julia received our invitation, she called Thomas to congratulate us and also to give him a message from fedpol requesting him not to put our wedding announcement and photos in any media because a couple of police operations in which Thomas was involved were still ongoing. And for that very reason, we asked all our guests not to post anything on their social media as well.

Last night, I stayed with my family and friends at a nearby hotel and arrived at the château several hours ago. We would have stayed at a Hotel DeMont, but the closest one was in Geneva, which was an hour's drive away.

Jojo, my maid of honor, was helping me get ready in Thomas' room while guests were arriving and gathering in the magnificent lake-view garden.

"Are you ready?" Jojo asked me.

"I think I am…" I looked into the mirror, gently rubbing my sixteen-week baby bump. It started to show now but was still pretty unnoticeable under my elegant Jenny Packham a-line wedding dress.

"You look so amazing…" Jojo stood next to me, looking into the mirror as well and holding a flower crown matching the floral appliqués of my dress.

I grinned at her.

Carefully, she put the crown on top of my head and used hair pins to secure it in place.

Suddenly, I noticed a glint in the mirror on top of my head. I looked up at Jojo's hand and shrieked with surprise. "What is that?" I grabbed her left hand and saw a round diamond ring on her ring finger.

Her face turned crimson.

"When? How come you didn't tell me?" I was jumping up and down, staring at her delicate ring.

"The baby! Stop jumping!" She looked all horrified.

"When did he propose?" I ignored her, still bouncing on my feet.

"Last week… I was going to tell you after the wedding. I don't—"

"Congratulations!" I wrapped my arms around her.

"Thank you, honey." She hugged me back.

"Who else knows?" I asked eagerly, grabbing her left hand up to examine the ring again.

"I haven't told anyone yet. Not even my parents."

"Yay! I am the first one!" I raised one arm in a winning gesture. "How did you walk around with this huge rock and no one noticed it?" I tilted my head, gazing at her round, brilliant diamond stone framed by micropavé diamonds and set on a micropavé band. "This ring is so…you!"

"I…I hadn't been wearing it since we got here. Marcus was a bit upset, so I put it on this morning."

"Why do you want to hide such a beautiful ring?" My eyes flicked to her.

"I don't want... You know, it's your day."

"You, silly." I hugged her again. "I would—"

I was interrupted by a knock on the door followed by Eva's voice. "May I come in?"

"Yes!" We answered in unison.

Eva opened the door. "Oh, love. You look beautiful."

"It's time?" I asked.

She nodded with a radiant smile.

"One second!" Jojo double-checked the flower crown. "All set!" And she picked up the bouquet consisting of fresh champagne and blush roses on the coffee table. "Should we?" she asked, handing me the flowers.

I nodded.

Slowly, we walked downstairs, through the sunroom, and out to the garden.

We only invited close families and friends to our ceremony, but I was surprised to see so many people were here. Many of them traveled here from the States and Asia. I felt so blessed but was anxious at the same time because of the crowd.

I sneaked a peek at the crowd and spotted my grandparents, my mother, Jake, Marcus, and Carmella sitting at the very front. Victoria caught my attention—as always—and an equally strikingly beautiful man was standing right next to her, his hand resting on the small of her back. I felt so happy for her, a smile spreading across my face.

My father was waiting for me at the end of the aisle.

"You look beautiful, honey." He leaned in to kiss my cheek, and I saw tears in his eyes.

"Thank you, Daddy." I held on to my father's elbow, taking in deep breaths to ease my anxiety.

The live music stopped, and the pianist started to play my walk-down-the-aisle music *The very thought of you.* Our bridesmaids and groomsmen Eva-and-Antonio, DD-and-Janie, James-and-Tim started walking down the aisle, and they were followed by Jojo and Louis, our maid of horror and best man. Johnny, the ring boy, and Jenny, the flower girl, were right after them.

At this moment, the only person I wanted to see was Thomas. I looked in the direction of the altar, which was decorated with different shades of roses, and met his adoring eyes right away. Our eyes locked, and mine immediately brimmed with tears.

My father started walking me towards Thomas.

Everything around Thomas became blurry... He was the focus of my vision and my life.

"Thank you," Thomas said to my father when he received my hand from him.

My father is giving me away to Thomas... My hand was trembling. I was not sure if I was sad because given-away-by-my-father was quite dejected, or if I was too happy as I was given-to-Thomas.

My father gently kissed my cheek and walked back to his seat.

Thomas squeezed my quivering hand tight and whispered, "You take my breath away..." He then walked me closer to our officiant.

An unexpected rush of intense anxiety nauseated me. I started taking deep and short breaths, trying to calm it down.

This is not happening! I am not having a panic attack. I cannot have a panic attack now.

Thomas' arms gently wrapped around me, turning me to face him. He kissed my hair and pressed his forehead against mine.

"*Je t'aime à la folie,*" he said he was madly in love with me. "Having you and the baby..." He paused and placed his hand on my baby bump before he continued, "...in my life is the best thing that has ever happened to me."

My heart rate was slowing down...

"*Mon amour.*" He caressed my cheek with his fingers. "I think of you in my waking hours, and I dream about you when I sleep."

My breathing was becoming calmer, tears filling my eyes.

"*Mon ange...*" He held my hands, calling me his angel. "Legally, we are married, so you cannot back out of this now."

I laughed, tears rolling down my cheeks.

"Feeling better now?" he asked, his voice loving and tender, and wiped my tears away with his fingers.

I nodded bashfully.

Suddenly, loud applause erupted. We both turned towards the crowd and found our guests cheering. Apparently, all of them heard Thomas' confession. I saw my parents having tears in their eyes.

Not everyone here knew about my abduction. For those who did not, they might think Thomas could not wait to recite his vow. As for those who knew our story, they knew Thomas was trying to mollify me and knew he was my anchor.

"I think I officially approve of you now," Antonio stated loudly.

Our guests erupted in merry laughter.

Today is my favorite day...

CHAPTER 34

> Some things are so unexpected
> that no one is prepared for them.
> ~Leo Rosten

BEING pregnant did not stop me from traveling with Thomas. I would rather feel sick than not see him for days, or worse, weeks if he traveled to Asia or America.

We arrived in Los Angeles last week. And since Thomas was here for work, it was much more convenient for him if we stayed at the hotel until he was done. After that, we planned to stay in Laguna Beach for at least a week before heading to New York.

My parents arrived at the ranch yesterday, so we were going to have dinner with my family today.

It was getting harder and harder to get in and out of the car with my thirty-week belly. Thomas helped me settle into the car before he took the driver's seat. He just finished all his meetings, and we were on our way to the ranch.

Chase was waving goodbye to us while Thomas slowly drove out of the parking garage and turned onto the main street. He reached for my hand and brought it to his lips. He pressed a kiss on the back of my fingers while keeping his eyes on the road.

I gazed at him, admiring his sexy new look. He had grown a beard, which reminded me of the British model David Gandy's circle beard. I smiled, thinking about how much I liked it when he went down on me. His short hair felt so rough on my delicate skin…in a very, very good way. The thought made my lady part throb. This pregnancy hormone really increased my libido big time. And having a husband so sexy made me want him all the time.

I uttered a sigh of satisfaction, not able to wipe the silly smile on my face.

Suddenly…

A loud crashing sound… A violent impact…

Thomas reached over, trying to shield me and our unborn child.

My body was flung to the left towards Thomas, but a sudden tight hug from the seatbelt held me in place.

A deafening bang burst right in front of me, a blow punching my face and chest.

I smelled smoke and felt dizzy. I was surrounded by airbags.

I heard many different voices around me

"Thomas?" I tried to turn towards him, but I could not. I could not turn my head, and my eyes were blurry…

CHAPTER 35

> It's been my experience, Charlotte,
> that the crisis never comes
> as or when you expect.
> ~Alice Duer Miller

DEMONT Beverly Hills...

"What the...?" Chase was walking back to his post when he heard the thunderous crashing sound coming from the parking garage entrance. He immediately started running out of the building.

Several people in the garage were heading towards the entrance as well when many of them stood where they were, looking shocked and confused.

Chase ran out of the parking garage and turned towards the main street.

"Oh my God!" he exclaimed when he saw the wreckage of Mr. Torian's car.

Many bystanders were on their phones, and some were taking pictures or video.

Chase quickly took his phone out and dialed 911 while starting to run towards the hotel lobby.

"There...there is an accident. Please help!" He was running and talking to a 911 operator at the same time. He gave the operator the address and was told the help was already on its way.

"Mr...Mr...Mr. Pattillo..." Chase called when he rushed into the hotel front entrance.

"Chase." Chief concierge Mr. Pattillo, who was on his way out after hearing the appalling sound, gave Chase a stern look as Chase's behavior was disturbing the guests in the lobby.

"Mr. Torian... Mrs..." Chase said, trying to catch his breath. "Accident... Car accident! Outside! Hurry! I...I called...called 911 already."

Mr. Pattillo's expression turned from annoyed by Chase's behavior to shocked and worried. He hastily rushed to the closest hotel phone and dialed the general manager Mr. Williams' office. "Mr. Williams, there was a car accident right outside the hotel. I am afraid Mr. Torian and his wife are—"

"I will be right there," Mr. Williams cut him off and hung up the phone.

THE scene of the accident...

"Ma'am, can you hear me?" a fireman asked Iris, who was slowly regaining her consciousness.

"Ow..." She groaned in pain, hearing sirens and many voices.

"Ma'am, can you hear me?" the same fireman asked again.

She nodded...

"She's conscious," the fireman said to the paramedics, who just approached Iris. "And she's pregnant."

"The... " Iris tried to talk, but the pain in her chest was unbearable.

"Yes, ma'am?" A paramedic asked, taking over the spot occupied by the fireman just a moment ago.

"Baby..." she whispered.

"We will take good care of you," he said to her, his voice calm.

"Tho...Thomas..."

"Thomas? Who is Thomas?" he asked.

"Hu..." She drew in a painful breath and tried again. "Hus... husband."

"Don't worry. We will contact your husband right now," he comforted her.

Contact? What does he mean? Iris frowned.

She then found herself surrounded by so many different voices and noises…

"Let's get her out first."

"We need to cut—"

All the sounds and voices were becoming muffled to Iris' ears.

She felt the air becoming thinner…

She started gasping for air…

To be continued…

What is going to happen to Iris and her unborn child? Where is Thomas?

Get your copy of The Very Thought Of Us, which concludes the story.

BOOK 2
The Very Thought of Us

CHAPTER 1

Day of the accident

IRIS regained consciousness slowly, but the excruciating pain throughout her body was so unbearable that she screamed in agony. She felt hands on her head and arms. Instinctively and frantically, she waved her arms around, wanting to knock those hands off her.

"Ma'am," one paramedic said to her, holding her still. "You need to calm down."

The ambulance with blaring sirens was racing through traffic, and every jolt and bump was making Iris feel as her bones were being crushed over and over again. The swerving movements were adding nausea to her already insufferable affliction.

"Roll her onto her side!" one paramedic shouted.

Just as the paramedics were unbuckling the gurney straps, an involuntary and forceful contraction of Iris' stomach caused her to throw up. She coughed violently, choking on her own vomit.

The paramedics hastily removed the oxygen mask and rolled her on her side.

Tears gushing out of Iris' eyes, she wailed.

"Ma'am, it's going to be all right," a female paramedic said to Iris while making sure her airway was clear before rolling her on her back again. "Think of the baby," the paramedic added.

"**THANK** you, Mr. Williams." David ended the call and turned to face his parents and Jane. "She is taken to Cedars-Sinai Beverly

Hills," he said, his voice trembling.

"Thomas, too?" Jane asked.

"He doesn't know. He is still trying to find—" David was interrupted by his mother.

"Let's just go!" Koto was already at the door.

"I will call Eva now," Jane said as she walked out of the door.

It was three in the morning in Switzerland, but Eva answered the call after just two rings. Louis already received a call from Mr. William, and he and Eva were getting ready to fly to the States.

"Louis and Eva will be here tomorrow evening," Jane said after hanging up the phone. She stared out the car window, trying to hold herself together.

No one said anything…

David's hands tightly gripped the steering wheel, his knuckles turning white.

Lucas wrapped his arms around his wife's shaking body. He was not able to say anything to comfort her as he was also in shock, still trying to process everything.

The ride to the hospital was intolerable. When they finally arrived at the emergency room entrance, David dropped off his parents and Jane first. They rushed through the sliding glass doors, not knowing what to expect.

"Iris and Thomas Torian. They… Um… They were brought here. It's a car accident." Lucas checked with the front desk.

The nurse typed on the keyboard and stared at the screen for a couple of minutes. "Iris Torian is in surgery now," she said. "Did you say Thomas?"

"Yes."

Furrowing her brow, the nurse typed on the keyboard again. "Hmm… No one named Thomas Torian was brought in. We only had one car accident patient in the last few hours. And that's Iris Torian."

"Thank you," he said and looked at his wife and Jane, surprised and baffled. They all wondered the same thing: Where was Thomas?

"Excuse me," the nurse tried to get their attention.

Lucas hastily turned back to the nurse, thinking she might have located Thomas.

"You can wait in the waiting area." She gestured him to the area right across from the front desk. "A doctor will give you the updates as soon as possible."

THOMAS was awakened by a sharp pain in his chest. He opened his eyes and found himself inside a moving cargo van. Keeping his body still, he scanned the space and saw five vicious looking men sitting on the benches on both sides.

His police training and experience told him to remain calm. He closed his eyes again, trying to remember what had happened before he lost consciousness…

He was turning onto the main street…

In his peripheral vision, he saw a van heading towards them from the right…

And then it crashed head-on into the passenger side…

Iris… His heart sped up at the thought of his wife and unborn child.

He remembered he extended his right hand out to shield Iris, but the forceful impact threw him towards the opposite direction. He must have hit his head then and lost consciousness…

Those fragments were all he remembered.

How long have I been out?

Another sharp pain in his rib cage hit him hard when he tried to take a deeper breath.

Fractured ribs?

Resuming taking shallow breaths, he remained calm and waited for what might happen next.

The van finally stopped. All five men jumped out of the van, chatting about another van and a building. Then two men came back and roughly grabbed Thomas arms from both sides.

"I think my ribs are broken…" Thomas groaned in pain.

They gave him no sympathy and dragged him out of the van. And before he could stand on his feet, they tossed him into another van and jumped in. The other three men were already in the van.

This is not good. Not good at all... It was obviously premeditated. Thomas had a really bad feeling about it.

Iris... Do they have her?

"Where is my wife?" he asked.

"Shut up!" one man shouted and shut the doors of the van. And the van started moving almost instantly.

Thomas kept quiet as he knew there was nothing he could do with the broken ribs in this moving van while five men were staring down at him. So, again, he remained calm and waited for what might happen next.

He sensed the van was on a freeway for a while and then made many turns after that. He slid towards the front and bumped into the metal wall when the van came to an abrupt stop.

"Putain!" he swore, groaning in pain.

The doors were opened, and two of the men dragged him out of the van. It took him some effort to stand still, left hand gently pressing against the left side of his rib cage. He glanced around and found they were inside an empty warehouse. He did not see other vans or cars around.

Iris is not here...

A big, bald man walked up to him, his fierce eyes fixed on Thomas. He tapped on the phone in his hand and then held it up to his ear.

"Tell her we got the guy," the bald man shouted into the phone in German. "And the price is higher now."

Frowning, Thomas listened to the conversation carefully.

"Okay, I will wait for her answer," the bald man said and hung up the phone. He switched to English and asked Thomas, "What did you do to piss off a woman like that?" It sounded more like a sarcastic comment than a question.

A woman? Thomas frowned. "Well, if you want to get paid, you had better patch up my broken ribs first," he said to the bald man in German.

"Fuck!" The bald man turned towards the rest of the men in the room, "You morons! Didn't I tell you not to damage the goods? Call

Dr. Smith now!" Then he turned back and reached for Thomas' left forearm.

Thomas groaned in pain, not sure what this guy was going to do.

"This is worth at least twenty grand." The bald man forcefully removed Thomas' watch.

Thomas was annoyed by it, but he was not going to risk his life for a watch. Then the bald man reached for Thomas' left hand, attempting to remove his wedding band. Thomas instinctively clenched his left hand into a tight ball to protect his ring and punched the bald man on his chin. The excruciating pain in his rib cage was suddenly insignificant.

"You. Mother fucker!" The man swung his arm, aiming at Thomas' abdomen.

Thomas bent down and turned around, letting his shoulder and upper arm take the blow.

Two henchmen grabbed hold of Thomas' arms, forcing him to stand straight.

Thomas howled in pain, left hand clenching even tighter. He glared at the bald man and said, "You will have to kill me first before you can touch this ring. I don't think you will get paid if I am a dead man."

CHAPTER 2

Three days since the accident

IRIS was gaining consciousness. She heard beeping sounds, just like the hospital vital monitor but a little too fast and busy.

"She is blinking her eyes," Jane whispered to David, her voice excited but nervous.

"Honey," David called his baby sister softly.

Iris groaned in pain when she tried to move.

"Honey, can you hear me?" David asked, gently stroking Iris' hair.

Iris blinked her eyes several times, trying to open them. She turned her head towards her brother's voice on her left and raised her left hand to reach for him. Then she saw an IV catheter taped on the back of her hand. A horrible thought struck her. It was a nightmare she had a long time ago.

"I am not going back!" With a big adrenaline rush, she screamed and tried to rip the IV off.

"Honey, honey…" David held her down while Jane buzzed the nurses.

"Get off of me!" Iris yelled, fighting even harder despite her physical pain.

"Honey, it's me. DD," David said with a soothing voice.

"I'll call mom now," Jane whispered, holding back her tears, and stepped out of the room.

Soon after Jane left, two nurses and a doctor rushed into the room. David stepped aside so the doctor and nurses could do their job.

"Wait, no..." Iris said in a weak voice when she saw a nurse injecting medication into the IV. "No, please. It will hurt my baby," she begged, her eyes brimming with tears.

"Mrs. Torian, don't worry. It is safe for the baby," the doctor reassured her.

"No... I...I..." Iris started to feel drowsy. "I beg..."

The doctor turned towards David. "The fetal monitor is still showing signs of distress. Keeping her calm is the best thing for the baby now."

David nodded, his eyes fixed on Iris, who was slowly falling back to sleep.

"I will check on her later," the doctor said and left the room with the nurses.

David walked back to Iris' bedside, feeling helpless and useless when he gazed at his precious sister, who was covered with cuts and bruises.

"They are on their way." Jane walked in and wrapped her arms around David.

David embraced her, letting out a sigh of distress. "Should we call Eva and Louis?"

"I already did. They are also on their way here."

David turned to Jane and placed a kiss on her forehead.

"**HOW** is she?" Koto walked into the room, followed by her husband.

"Drifting in and out of sleep." Jane stood up from the chair. "David just went to get coffee."

"We ran into Eva and Louis downstairs. They are in the waiting area now," Lucas said to Jane.

Koto walked closer to her daughter, tears in her eyes. Gently, she touched Iris' hand.

"Mommy?" Iris believed she just heard her mother's voice. She tried to open her eyes, but her eyelids were so heavy.

"Yes, my baby..." Koto held Iris' hand with one hand and

caressed her cheek with the other. "Mommy is here."

Iris smiled in relief, but it hurt so much when she moved her lips. She reached her hand up, wanting to touch the painful spot but moaned in pain as her arm and whole body hurt. She dropped her hand and shut her eyes, her breathing sped up.

"What...what happened to me?" she asked in agony.

"Honey, you were in a car accident..." Lucas answered her as Koto was too emotional to speak.

"Right..." Iris breathed out the word. She had some vague memories. And then... She fell asleep again.

"I am going to stay," Koto said to her husband. "Why don't you talk to Eva and Louis without me."

Lucas nodded and placed a kiss on his daughter's forehead. He then kissed his wife's hair and headed out the room with Jane.

David was leaning against the wall and sipping the vending machine coffee when Lucas and Jane walked into the seating area by the elevator lobby. Jane walked up to him and wrapped her arms around his waist, leaning her head on his chest.

"Still nothing?" Lucas asked Louis.

"No..." Louis shook his head. "Julia is working very closely with the FBI. They found the van but nothing else. There is also no phone call asking for ransom."

"What should we tell her if she asks?" Jane asked.

Even Eva was speechless. It was her profession to help people in crisis, but now she was too close to the crisis herself. Thomas was missing, and Iris was fighting for her and their baby's life.

"Are you okay, dad?" David asked.

"I'm fine," Lucas replied and sat down on a chair, feeling unsettled and dejected.

A light chime of the elevator caused them to glance at the elevator. Antonio walked out of the elevator, looking distressed. Jane also called him earlier after Iris awoke.

"How is she?" Antonio saw Jane and David right away. He walked up to them and saw Lucas and Thomas' brother and sister-in-law. He gave them a nod and leaned down to give Lucas a hug.

"Falling in and out of sleep…" Jane said, her voice quivering.

David held her tight, kissing her forehead.

"Can I see her?" Antonio asked, looking between Lucas, David, and Jane.

Lucas nodded. "Koto is in the room with her."

Antonio nodded and added, "Jasmine is catching a flight back later today."

Antonio patted David on his shoulder before heading towards Iris' room.

THOMAS was locked in a small room with an adjoining half bath size of a closet. A dirty mattress was on the floor against one wall.

A doctor did come to check on him and just told him the ribs would heal on their own. He gave him a bottle of pain killer and instructed him to breathe deeply to prevent developing pneumonia. Different men brought him food in the past three days, and nothing else had happened. Lying on the mattress, he was becoming more and more frustrated as he did not know what had happened to Iris.

Suddenly, the door was opened, and the bald man walked in followed by two henchmen.

"Today is my payday," he said with a smirk. "Get him in the van."

What? Thomas was caught off guard.

The two stooges reached down to seize Thomas' arms before he could react or say anything. They dragged him up from the mattress and out of the room.

Thomas clenched his jaw, enduring the pain. He stumbled a couple of times on concrete cracks, but those men's tight grip on his arms had kept him from falling over.

"Get in there!" one man commanded in a gruff voice.

Thomas was glad they did not just toss him into the cargo van this time. He slowly stepped into the van and sat on one bench. He shut his eyes, remaining calm. Obviously, they were handing him over to whomever paid them to kidnap him.

Who ordered my kidnapping? He had been contemplating the answers to that question for days.

"Let's go!" the bald man shouted, interrupting Thomas' thoughts, and the van took off at a high speed.

Thomas sensed they were on freeways for a while, then he heard airplanes taking off and flying. *Airport?* He opened his eyes and found all the windows were sealed. He could not confirm his suspicion.

"Cover your eyes," one of the men said, throwing a piece of thick black cloth on Thomas' lap.

Thomas frowned, unwillingly picking up the cloth, and tied the cloth around his head to cover his eyes.

And suddenly, someone grabbed his hands. He flinched, not knowing what was going on as he was now blindfolded. One man yanked his hands together in front of him and another bound them with a zip tie.

"Is this really necessary?" Thomas growled.

They ignored him.

When the van made a complete stop, Thomas was manhandled out of the car. One man seized his upper arm and steered him towards…somewhere. Thomas tried to use his other senses to figure out his whereabouts. He heard louder airplane noises, smelled burnt fuel, and—

"Steps!" One man walked by Thomas said aloud, startling him. Then Thomas was pushed up several steps before he reached a landing.

I am boarding a jet… His perception gave him all the indications. He was too familiar with all those smells, sounds, and vicinity because he had been flying all over the world for a couple of years now.

"Keep moving!" the same man yelled, shoving Thomas.

Thomas couldn't see where he was going. He stumbled forward and bumped into a seat. "Putain!" he cursed, groaning in pain. He reached his bound hands out in front of him, trying to regain his sense of direction.

"For fuck's sake!" The man behind Thomas seized Thomas'

upper arm and steered him towards the back of the cabin. When they arrived at the last row of seats, he pushed Thomas roughly down on a seat and buckled him up.

Still blindfolded, Thomas pricked up his ears, trying to catch any conversation that might give him a clue as to where they were taking him, although all he heard was vulgar talks in…German.

However, that still did not indicate they were taking him to Europe.

Letting out a sigh, he leaned back in the chair when the jet started to taxi to the runway.

He wondered if this had anything to do with any of his assignments as an undercover agent. As far as he knew, his real identity was sealed. For ransom? His family had money, but it was nothing compared to Global 500 companies.

Iris… Are you safe? His heart started beating faster at the thought of his wife. He still remembered the fear in her eyes when they were hit.

It felt like hours since the jet took off, and no one had yet removed his blindfold and zip tie.

"Entschuldigung…" he said 'excuse me' in German, trying to get those men's attention, assuming they knew he understood the language they were speaking. "I really need to use the lavatory."

"Raise your hands," one man said to him.

Thomas raised his bound hands and heard a sudden sharp snapping sound. His hands were free instantly. He immediately removed the blindfold himself.

A man holding a pocket knife smirked at him and walked back to the front.

Thomas looked around the cabin and saw only two men he had never seen before sitting several seats away from him. He stood up and walked into the lavatory which was right behind his seat.

Staring at the mirror, he almost could not recognize himself.

He was bruised, scratched, and covered with dry blood and dirt. And he had not shaved and showered for days, so unkempt that he quickly turned away and started checking all the cabinets and drawers to see if he could find anything to use.

Well, better than nothing. He saw some travel size hygiene products in one of the drawers.

He brushed his teeth first and tried to clear the dry blood and sweat. And the travel size deodorant was a lifesaver.

CHAPTER 3

Five days since the accident

IRIS tried to open her eyes. Her eyelids felt lighter now, and so did the pressure in her eyes. Blinking several times, she was able to open her eyes completely, but her body was still aching.

She moved her eyes towards the continuous beeping sounds and saw a monitor above her head and a printer looking machine next to her.

Baby monitor? She frowned and continued to scan the room. Then she saw her mother sleeping on the sofa and her father reading right by her bedside.

She tried to call her father but her throat felt too dry to make a sound.

"Daddy…" she whispered.

Lucas' eyes flung to his daughter. He quickly closed the book and leaned closer to her. Gently, he stroked her forehead. "Sweetheart…"

She pointed at her throat and licked her lips.

Lucas quickly grabbed the water cup on the bedside table and gently brought the straw to her mouth.

Slowly, Iris took a couple of sip and then cleared her throat.

"Where is Thomas? Is he all right?" she asked.

Lucas became silent. He did not know what to tell her.

"Daddy?" Iris frowned, all sorts of bad thoughts going through her mind. "Oh, no… Daddy, please tell me he is all right…" she pleaded, tears welling in her eyes. Her vital monitor started beeping faster.

"Shh... Sweetheart." He stood up from the chair and leaned against the bed rail. He caressed her face and said softly, "Every... everything will be all right."

"Oh, honey..." Koto was awakened by her daughter's feeble voice. She scurried towards her bedside.

"Mommy... Where is he?" Iris turned to face her mother.

Koto looked at her husband, feeling lost.

"Sweetheart..." Lucas tried to keep his voice calm. He had to be sensible, strong, and calm for his daughter and wife. "Thomas... He is missing."

"Missing? What...what do you mean?" Iris asked, wanting to sit up but her aching body pulled her back. She moaned in pain. Her vital monitors sounded a warning, reflecting her palpitating heart rate and startling all of them.

And another alarm coming from the fetal monitor shocked them all.

"What...what is happening?" Iris asked panically, staring at the printer-looking machine.

Two nurses rushed in. Lucas and Koto hastily stepped aside so the nurses could attend to their daughter. Lucas walked up to Koto and held her in his arms.

One nurse turned off both alarms and checked all wires connecting to Iris, especially those around her belly, while the other checked Iris' IV.

"Is the baby all right?" Iris asked the nurses.

Both nurses smiled at Iris kindly, and one said, "Your baby is stressed."

Iris frowned, tears rolling out of her eyes.

"It can feel how you feel..." Another nurse tried to be sensitive and delicate. "So stay calm for the baby, okay?"

Iris nodded desperately, wiping her tears away.

One nurse turned to Lucas and Koto. "I will tell the doctor she is awake."

"Thank you," Lucas said.

Both nurses soon left the room.

Iris was taking deep breaths to calm herself, a breathing exercise she was too familiar with.

Lucas and Koto walked back up to their daughter's bedside.

Iris looked at her parents with her watery eyes. "What…what…" She paused to take another deep breath and continue, "Missing? He…he was right…right there next to…to me…"

"Honey…" Koto pointed to the fetal monitor. "Look at this…" She tried to distract Iris' attention. "Your baby needs you now. You have to stay calm and rest so the baby will stay safe."

Iris drew in a deep breath, staring at the monitor. "Okay…"

"Daddy will tell you everything we know so far—" Iris' pained expression stopped Koto from continuing. "Oh honey…" She caressed her daughter's cheek.

"Sweetheart, why don't you rest first…" Lucas said.

"Tell me now… Please, Daddy."

Koto nodded at Lucas, encouraging him to explain the situation to their daughter.

Lucas sighed and said, "According to the witnesses, a group of men put Thomas in a van and fled the scene."

Iris could feel her breathing becoming harder, and her vital monitor showed her heart rate was rising. She turned her head to her baby's monitor, reminding herself to stay calm.

"Eva, Louis, and Julia are here," Lucas added.

"Julia?" Iris turned her face back to her father.

"She is working with the FB—" Lucas explained

"Do they know where he is?" Iris interrupted him.

Lucas and Koto looked at each other, speechless.

"So, no…" Iris murmured. "What day is it today?"

"Monday…" Koto replied.

"That's… I was out for that long?" Iris murmured, frowning. "That means…" She looked at her parents, her eyes widened. "He… he has been missing for four…five days." Tears were running down her cheeks. *Thomas, where are you?*

THOMAS woke up from a very deep sleep. The seat of the jet was much more comfortable than the old mattress. Since they had been in the air for so long, he was very sure he was no longer in the States.

Where can they take me without my passport? He wondered but then chuckled as after years of undercover experience, he knew just how easy it was to smuggle a person in and out a country.

Lifting the blind, all he saw was hollow darkness. He was thinking about his Iris again. *Is she injured? Is she safe? And is the baby all right?*

Hours later, Thomas noticed the plane was descending.

What did you do to piss off a woman like that? What the bald man said to him played in his head again.

A woman like that... Who? He assumed she must be related to the cases he was involved in before. However, he could not recall any woman having such kind of power and ability to orchestrate this.

Vera? He knew for certain she was found guilty and locked in a prison now. Although the evidence showed that she was controlled by the Italian and once a victim herself, she was still guilty for what she did.

The jet landed smoothly. He looked out the window and saw nothing but runway lights. Then the jet made a turn, and he saw some lights by the runway. The jet was taxiing towards those lights, and it made a complete stop near two black SUVs.

"Let's go!" one of the men shouted from his seat when the cabin door was opened.

Thomas complied, walking towards the door and off the jet. He was immediately hustled into one of the SUVs by two brawny men waiting outside the jet. Compared to the bald guy and his gang, these two stern men were calm and trained. Thomas was on high alert if he wanted to stay alive.

He glanced at the infotainment system of the car, and it just gave him the clue to his whereabouts.

German... I am back in Europe...

The ride was pretty rough, and all Thomas could see was the gravel road shone by the headlights.

An hour and fifty-two minutes from the airport... He took a look at the clock on the infotainment system screen when they finally arrived at a dilapidated farmhouse.

He was pushed out of the car, towards the farm house, and through an open rusty gate. One man walked past him to open the front door of the house.

The door opened into a luxurious living room. And sitting on one of the sofas was the woman he believed he would never see again.

"Hello Max," Vera greeted. "Or should I call you…Thomas?" she asked, giving him a seductive smile.

He was absolutely surprised, but he kept a stern expression. Years' training and experience alerted him to stay calm and collect information first.

Does she know? He wondered if she had discovered his true identity and was now seeking revenge. If that was the case, he might not walk out of here alive. And if not, then why did she have him kidnapped and brought here?

"Not even a hello?" With her alluring eyes, she signaled the two men standing by Thomas to bring him closer to her. She picked up the wine glass on the side table and took a sip, fixing her eyes on Thomas.

The two men jostled Thomas to move forward.

"Have a seat, darling." Vera gestured to the single seat sofa by Thomas. "I am sure you are very surprised to see me."

He quickly scanned the room before sitting down. There were at least a dozen guards in this room, and they reminded him of the security team he led when he was undercover. He knew for certain there were at least another dozen on this premises.

Vera took another sip of wine and rolled the stem of the glass between her fingers. "It was not difficult to play the victim. The sympathies I received…" She laughed, slightly shaking her head. "And of course, having money and excellent lawyers made a big difference as well." She smirked. "I am sure you agree."

Thomas made a swift decision, assuming she did not know he was a police officer. He sank into the sofa, relaxing his body and nodding his head in agreement.

"I knew you would." She laughed again. "Care for a drink?" she asked, raising her glass in his direction.

He shook his head.

"Suit yourself." She took a sip and continued, "I was told you pleaded guilty and worked out a deal. And... You had the best lawyers in town. I was curious how you could afford them." She gazed at him. "I was intrigued by you, Thomas. Still am, actually. So I did a little digging."

She bought the cover story. But what else did she find out? He fixed his eyes on her.

"A trust fund kid. You come from money, Thomas. However, your father disowned you because you broke some laws after you graduated from university. Then... You vanished and resurfaced years later with a new identity. Where did you go?"

Thomas shrugged, but inwardly, he was relieved she only had the cover story.

"By the way, congratulations on your wedding!" She toasted him and took a sip. "Thanks to Instagram and Facebook, otherwise I would never know the good news."

Social media... They specifically asked their guests not to post anything on social media. Apparently, some people still did.

"I am so disappointed that I was not invited to your and *my* precious Iris' wedding."

Thomas clinched his jaw when Vera emphasized Iris was hers.

"My feelings are hurt, Max. I thought we were a good team." Vera gazed at him, slowly crossing her legs, revealing her black lace panties to him on purpose.

Thomas fixed his eyes on her eyes. He knew this woman was a skilled seducer.

"Instead of stealing her from me, you could have told me you fancied her," she said, frowning. "I would have made sure she was for the exclusive use of you."

He felt an uncontrollable anger surfacing, remembering Vera had instructed him to let the guards have fun with Iris before handing her over to a souteneur. He forced himself to contain his anger because he had to get out of this place alive for Iris and for their unborn child.

"Those Americans took it a bit too far. However, I can assure you Iris is surrounded by her family and receiving proper treatments in the hospital now."

He gave her a blank expression, but his heart was palpitating. He wondered if he could believe her. He wanted to because that meant Iris was safe.

"Congratulations on the baby making, too," she continued since Thomas did not give her any response. "She looked like she was seven or eight months pregnant. Right?"

She saw her? Thomas frowned and immediately regretted showing his concern.

Vera watched him carefully and caught a flash of furrow appearing on his brow.

"Did you plan it?" She sipped her wine. "Knocked her up first and then married her. Or…" She looked at him with a dramatic expression, her eyes widened. "Are you entrapped by her?"

He kept a stern expression this time.

"Still not talking to me?" Putting down her wine glass, Vera stood up and walked towards Thomas. She elegantly sat down on his lap.

Thomas leaned backward and kept his hands on the armrests. "I don't think my wife will appreciate this."

Running her slender fingers across his chest, she said, "I am just trying to refresh your memories…" She leaned in to kiss him, but he closed his eyes and remained still. She slowly trailed her lips over to his ear and whispered, "I will forgive you if you work for me again. Or even better, we can be partners. I really think we are perfect for each other."

"I am married," he said indifferently.

She laughed, wrapping her arms around his neck. "Does that even matter?"

Thomas looked straight ahead, ignoring her.

Vera stood up and walked around him, running her fingers across his shoulders. "What a shame, Thomas. You are always my favorite," she said, walking back to where she put her wine glass. "I guess I will go for Plan B then." She picked up the wine and took a sip.

Plan B? Thomas glared at her.

"I am sure the Torian Family will be willing to buy you back."

She wants money. That's good. Thomas finally felt a bit relieved since he awoke in a van because she would have to keep him alive for ransom.

"I am tired." She turned around and headed towards the corridor. "We will catch up tomorrow."

One of the guards seized Thomas' arm, pulled him up from the sofa, and manhandled him towards the same direction.

Vera walked through the double doors at the end of the hallway. She turned and gave Thomas a seductive wink before closing the doors.

"Get in!" the guard commanded, pushing Thomas into a room next to the closed double doors, and shut the door.

The room was dark.

Thomas extended his hands out to reach for a light switch by the door and found it right away.

Definitely better than the warehouse dump. He scanned the room. He was surprised to find several clothing items hung in the open closet. And when his eyes landed on the en suite, he dashed into it.

CHAPTER 4

Nine days since the accident

IRIS had another abrupt awakening. When she opened her eyes, the realization of why she was in the hospital saddened her. She felt empty and lost without her Thomas…

It had been almost a week since she learned Thomas was missing. She had tried her very best to stay calm and stay positive for their baby. She was free from the IV and all the monitoring now. Other than some minor bruises and cuts, her physical condition was good enough to be discharged. However, the doctors insisted on keeping her in the hospital because of her baby's unstable stress level.

Carefully, she sat up, moved her legs to the edge of the bed, and lowered them to the floor. Holding on to the bed rail, she stood up, and after she balanced herself on her feet, she walked towards the windows slowly and quietly, not wanting to disturb Jane who was sleeping on the sofa.

My love, where are you? Iris looked out the window, hot tears dripping on her hands, which were placed gently on her belly. *Who took you? Why?* She was told fedpol was looking into all his assignments, but there were no updates.

What if… Horrible thoughts popped into her head many, many times. And it was getting worse with each passing day. She felt hopeless and fearful. What if… What if her guardian angel would never come back to her?

Suddenly, she felt the baby kicking. She gently rubbed her belly, wishing to soothe her *little one*.

They decided not to know the gender of their child, so Thomas called the baby *ma puce*, and Iris called the baby *little one*.

"I know, little one. I know…" she whispered to her baby, more tears welling in her eyes. She believed her little one was trying to remind her that he or she was still with her and was her little guardian angel…now.

They were still working on turning the den into a nursery. It was still an empty room with paint sample cards taped on the walls because they had been traveling. However, she had already had a perfect image of the nursery in her mind: Beach sandy color carpet, walls and ceiling painted with blue sky and many hot-air balloons, a small hot-air balloon basket filled with stuffed animals hung from the ceiling…

"We have time," she told Thomas just before they left home.

Now she wished she had spent more time in that room with him.

"Sweetheart…" Jane whispered, walking up to Iris.

Iris turned and looked at her dear sister-in-law with her watery eyes.

"Oh sweetie…" Jane embraced Iris in her arms. "Would you like to talk to Eva or Dr. Warren?"

"No…" Iris breathed out the word. "I…I just…I just want him back."

"I know, honey. I know." Jane gently stroked Iris' back, soothing her.

"Baby…baby is…is kicking…again," Iris said between snivels.

Jane leaned her head against Iris' temple and gently put her hand on Iris' belly. "Active little one!" She chuckled.

"I…I think it's…it's a…a boy," Iris said, a small smile spreading across her face, but big fat tears gushed out almost at the same time. "A…a mini…mini Tom…Tommy."

Jane placed a kiss on Iris' temple, not sure what she could say to comfort her…

THOMAS was sitting on the bed, sighing in frustration. Vera had not talked about her Plan B since the day he arrived. She demanded him to dine with her and acted as if they were two old friends. She eagerly talked about her new business plans with him as if he had already agreed to partner with her. And then after each meal, he was escorted back to this small bedroom right next to Vera's suite. Other than walking to and back from the dining room, he was confined in this small space.

The fractured ribs had limited what he could do to stay active, so he often paced around or slowly jogged if the pain was tolerable. And being active could also help him stay positive, and he needed to do that for Iris and *ma puce*.

"Yes… Aaah…" Vera's moaning came through the thin wall between the two rooms.

Thomas gave a groan of disgust. This happened nightly and had made him all the more regard her in disdain.

He stopped his routine light jogging and stepped into the bathroom. He turned on the shower first to get the hot water and then shut the door to block the noise. He knew all too well what Vera was trying to do because she had tried to seduce, lure, and bribe him into being her partner of business *and* pleasure for the past five days.

When he first worked for her, she made it clear that she wanted him in her bed. And after he stated that he had never mixed business with pleasure, she desired him even more and valued him as a hardcore loyal guard, whom she could trust with her life. She demanded him to be her personal bodyguard when she traveled and soon made him the foreman of her security team.

Was she not attractive enough for him? Yes, she was. She would definitely capture his attention with her unspeakable beauty. She was absolutely a temptation for many men—perhaps women as well. Her stunning quality of physical appearance was indisputable, and the way she carried herself—a mixture of innocence, confidence, and sexiness—would make men and women become submissive. But Thomas despised the business she had conducted and her lack of morals, and that had made her the least desirable woman he had ever met.

Thomas stripped down and got in the shower. The sound of

falling water soothed him, but the unsettling feeling in his chest could never go away, not until he knew Iris and their unborn child were doing well.

He missed Iris desperately. They had not been away from each other for this long since he showed up at her house unannounced last year.

He smiled at the thought of his beautiful Iris, strolling down memory lane…

~ ~ ~

He had been thinking about visiting Iris after he left fedpol. Therefore, when he knew he was scheduled to visit DeMont Beverly Hills, he called James at the U.S. Embassy and invited him for a drink.

"I will give you her contact information, *but* I will hunt you down if you hurt her," James said to him after he explained his intention.

It was late at night when he arrived in Los Angeles. He tossed and turned all night and hit the hotel gym early in the morning to relieve the apprehensive feeling he had since he decided to visit her. He was not sure how she felt about him now as it had been almost a year since they last saw, or talked to, each other.

After his morning meeting with the hotel manager Mr. Williams, he jumped into the car and headed south. Instead of taking the freeways, he took the Pacific Coast Highway, a longer and more pleasant route, because he needed a bit more time to think and to prepare himself…mentally.

He stood in front of her house and gave himself a serious pep talk before he finally took the courage to call her. After three rings, the call went to the default voicemail.

She declined the call… He assumed she probably did not answer unknown callers, so he tapped the call icon again. And this time it rang more than three times… Just as he was anxiously waiting to hear Iris' delightful voice, which he still remembered, the default robotic voice answered, "Please leave your—"

He ended the call.

I shouldn't have come here.… He slowly walked away, feeling stupid and despondent.

Then his phone rang, and her name was on the screen.

She is calling me back! He stared at his phone, feeling like a teenage boy finally getting his crush's response. "Torian," he answered after two rings.

"Hi, you called me twice. I believe you had the wrong number," she said, her voice euphonious.

"Iris?" He was so nervous.

"Yes, this is she. May I ask who's calling?"

"This is Thomas."

"Thomas..." She murmured and was silent for a minute too long. "Mr. Thomas Dwell?" she then asked.

It was really a blow to his confidence as she did not recognize his name and voice. He sighed, not sure what to say.

"Hi Thomas..." Her voice changed, sounding like she did recognize him.

Thomas let out a sigh of relief, turning around to face Iris' house again.

She agreed to see him. And the moment he saw her appearing in the doorway, he knew he would never let his chance slip away again. She was as beautiful as he had always remembered, and he noticed her long wavy hair was cut short above her shoulders.

She agreed to see him again the next day, so he cleared his schedule to be with her for as long as she allowed him. He needed to explain himself to her, had too much to tell her, and was eager to confess his feelings for her. It was encouraging when he felt that she was as attracted to him as he was to her, and the sexual attraction between them was undeniable.

~ ~ ~

An image of Iris from her birthday last December appeared in his mind and it made him hard almost instantly.

~ ~ ~

He took her to dinner at a restaurant in DeMont Bern and told her he had reserved the penthouse for the night, but she told him she wanted to go home. After they got home, she asked him to change into something comfortable. He was not going to argue with the birthday girl, so he did as he was told.

When he walked out of the bedroom, he was astonished by what was in front of him...

Candles were lit and spread out across the living room. Iris was leaning against the floor to ceiling window, her hands pressing on the glass, which was fogged up by her body heat. Her *naked* body was illuminated by the flickering candle lights, and the dancing snowflakes glinting in the streetlights was a perfect backdrop.

She glanced over her shoulder at him with a luscious smile when she heard him.

"I thought today is your birthday, not mine." He stopped to admire the view.

"I thought I would share my present with you," she said, her voice sultry. "Come here..." She beckoned to him with her index finger.

He did as the birthday girl asked, locking his eyes with hers. He leaned in and placed a kiss on her shoulder, his hands caressing her arms gently.

A soft moan escaped from her when he pressed his body against her, embracing her from behind.

~ ~ ~

The memory was so vivid. Thomas braced a hand against the tile and gripped himself with the other, water flowing over his head and down his body.

CHAPTER 5

Eleven days since the accident

IRIS was startled by a gentle knock on the door. Her reaction pained her mother.

Koto reached for Iris' hand and squeezed it tenderly, comforting her.

The door was opened, and Eva and David walked in.

"What is it?" Iris asked because they looked at her differently. She knew they would do everything to shelter her, but if they knew anything about Thomas, good or bad, she had to know. "Just tell me," she said before either of them spoke.

Eva walked closer and held Iris' other hand. "Louis got a call last night. It was from the kidnappers," she said.

Kidnappers... Iris blinked back her tears. "That means Thomas is alive," she murmured, her body trembling.

"Love... Yes, he is." Eva squeezed her hand.

"Is he all right? Where is he now?" Iris' voice was quavering.

"We...we don't know yet," Eva said and let out a sigh. "That person on the phone asked for one hundred million Euros and said he would keep in touch to arrange the details. Louis is on his way back home now."

"So, let's...let's get the money ready." Iris looked between Eva and David. "I...I can sell the beach house here and...and...and the two apartments back home. We have...we have savings." She was on the verge of breaking down, tears submerging her eyes. "Do you... do you think it's...it's enough?"

Koto embraced Iris, trying to calm her down. "We want to help."

She looked at Eva.

"Don't worry about it. Louis will take care of that." Eva patted Iris' hand gently and gave Koto an appreciating smile. "He is communicating with a negotiation agency now."

"What?" Iris looked bewildered. "I don't…I don't understand."

"This agency is highly recommended and has worked with fedpol for many years. They will speak with the kidnappers next time to make sure they really have Tommy."

"What do you mean to make sure they really have him?" Iris asked in frustration. "They…they have him. He is alive." She looked between her brother and Eva. "Will the negotiation put…put him in…in danger? Can't…can't we just pay, so…so he can come back now?"

"Honey…" David walked up to the bedside. "We have to trust fedpol and the negotiation agency. Thomas used to be one of them, so they take this case very seriously."

"I…I just want him back…" Iris mumbled, tears streaming down.

"Sweetheart, we know…" Koto enfolded Iris in her arms.

"Where is he now?" Iris asked.

Eva and David looked at each other, not sure how to respond.

Iris looked up at them. "Just tell me." She raised her voice. Her breathing became labored as she suddenly had discomfort and stress sensations in her belly.

"Are you all right?" Koto asked.

"Mommy, I am fine. Just tell me, please…" She wiped her tears away, taking in a deep breath.

"Fedpol did pinpoint the location of the call. It was in southern Europe," David said.

"I am going back," Iris said immediately. "I have to be there for him."

"Fedpol doesn't have the exact lo—" David said.

"I don't care…" Iris cut her brother off.

"Honey…" Koto gently stroked Iris' hair. "Don't rush. Let's talk to your doctor first."

"Now that I know Thomas is in Europe, I have to go back. I will go crazy if I stay here. It's not good for me and the baby. Please," Iris pleaded. "Please... Help me. I have to go home now." She looked between David and Eva.

Eva sighed, squeezing Iris' hand tight. She turned to look at Koto and David, hoping they would know what was better for Iris.

Koto gazed at her daughter, tears flooding in her eyes, and David shook his head, feeling a great deal of ambivalence about what Iris was asking.

Letting out another sigh, Eva turned back to look at Iris. "Okay..."

All three pairs of eyes were on Eva.

"But you must talk to your doctor first," she continued. "And be patient. Give me enough time to arrange everything. We need at least one fertility nurse accompanying you."

Three days later, Iris was flying back to Switzerland.

Although her parents, Jane, Jasmine, and Eva were by her side, she still could not shake off the apprehensive feeling in her chest. Without Thomas, everything was so different. She felt anxious, empty, and lost.

"Can I come in?" Jasmine asked after knocking on the master suite door.

Iris was on the bed resting, and her mother was sitting on the sofa keeping her company.

"Yes," Iris replied.

Jasmine walked in, a tender smile on her face.

"Why don't you girls catch up?" Koto stood up and leaned in to place a kiss on the top of Iris' head. "Call me if you need me..."

"Thanks, Mommy."

Koto left the room and closed the door behind her.

"Are you doing all right?" Jasmine sat down next to Iris.

Iris nodded and rested her head on Jasmine's shoulder. "I am sorry..." she whispered.

"What for?" Jasmine intertwined her fingers with Iris'.

"You...you have been flying back and forth because of me..." Iris suddenly felt emotional.

"Silly…" Jasmine squeezed Iris' hand. "You've nothing to apologize for."

"Are you heading to Paris after we arrive?"

"No, I am staying with you until everything is over. Marcus will be in Lausanne in a couple of days."

"He is?"

"Girl, you need all the support you can get."

When Iris first moved back to Switzerland and needed an obstetrician-gynecologist, Eva referred her to her own doctor Dr. Édith Beaumont. And because of her mental health condition, Dr. Beaumont had been monitoring Iris' pregnancy very closely. It saddened her when she learned about what had happened to Iris and Thomas in the States.

Iris' medical records from the accident had been sent to Dr. Beaumont prior to her arrival. And per Dr. Beaumont's order, once Iris arrived in Lausanne, she would check into Lausanne University Hospital, known as CHUV—*Centre Hospitalier Universitaire Vaudois,* straight away. CHUV was ranked the best hospital in Switzerland and was only twenty minutes away from the Torian's family château.

While Louis was at the hospital preparing for Iris' arrival, Florent and Adeline were waiting for her at the airport.

He looks so aged... Iris' heart ached when she saw her father-in-law.

Despite being devastated by the situation, Florent was still standing straight and tall, greeting Iris and her family and friends in a dignified manner. He kissed Iris on her cheeks and held her in his arms for a long time without saying a word.

She looked up at him, and her legs weakened when she saw his blue eyes identical to those of Thomas. She could not imagine what her life would be if she was not able to see Thomas' beautiful blue eyes again.

Florent felt her frail body in his arms. He held her tight and slowly walked her to the waiting car. Lucas quickly stepped up to give him a hand.

"I will see you at the hospital," Florent said to Iris before he closed the car door.

After Iris was settled in the hospital room, she insisted on knowing everything.

"Mr. Marseille is our crisis negotiator," Louis said. "He specializes in hostage negotiation."

Hostage... Iris felt her heart pounding rapidly.

"He had another contact with the same kidnapper two days ago —" Louis continued but was interrupted by Iris.

"Is Thomas all right?" Iris asked hastily.

"We will know soon," Louis replied, giving her a reassuring smile. "The kidnapper agreed to give us a video or audio recording that proves they really have Thomas."

"When?" Iris asked eagerly.

Koto wrapped her arms around her daughter gently, calming her.

"They will contact Mr. Marseille again for more information," Louis answered.

"So...so we just wait? Not knowing if he's all right?" Iris sounded frustrated.

Louis nodded, not able to give Iris a better answer.

"Honey, stay positive," Koto whispered to her daughter. "This means he is a...a..." Koto hesitated to use the word alive. "I'm sure we will hear from them soon if they want the money."

He is fine. He has to be fine. Iris' heart was pounding even harder now as she could not stop worrying about *what if* something went wrong.

"Love, why don't you rest first?" Eva perceived Iris' fearful expression. "I will stay with you tonight." She turned around and looked at Iris' parents, Jane, and Jasmine. "You must be tired. Why don't you go home with Louis first, and we can all have a fresh start tomorrow?"

"I like to stay," Koto said, not wanting to leave her daughter.

"Me too," both Jane and Jasmine said in unison.

Eva gave them a thoughtful smile and said, "We all need a good rest as well. We will take turns like we did in the States."

"Honey..." Koto gazed at Iris, who looked so preoccupied and exhausted.

"I am fine, Mommy." Iris gave her family and Jasmine a reassuring smile. "Eva is right. Let's all have a good rest first."

THOMAS sat down for dinner, ignoring Vera, who was sitting at the other end of the table.

"I have good news for you," Vera said, waiting for Thomas' reaction, but he gave her none. "I have informed your family you are still alive," she added.

Finally... Thomas glanced at her, showing no emotion. He placed the cloth napkin on his lap, picked up the wine glass and took a sip, and started eating without waiting for Vera. He could not care less about table manners under this circumstance.

"How about I cheer you up by giving you an update on your wife's condition?" she continued, still trying to stimulate a reaction in him.

His hands started to shake slightly. He put the cutlery down and stared into her eyes.

Vera gracefully picked up her wine glass and took a sip. "She is doing fine," she said, putting down the glass and picking up a fork. She played with her food, smirking in conceit.

Thomas tried to calm his rising anger by taking a deep breath. Since Vera did not say more, he picked up the cutlery again and resumed eating.

"I was told she was having a hard time with that baby of yours..." She tried to elicit a response from him again.

Thomas did not give her the satisfaction this time, not wanting to play her devious game. He focused on his food and wine, but his heart was aching. He regretted he could not be there for Iris if what Vera said was true...

The pregnancy was not quite smooth as they expected. The never-ending morning sickness had almost drained Iris' energy empty; the irregular light bleeding had contributed to her anxiety disorder; then she was diagnosed with anemia. It was hard for her, but at least he was by her side.

He could not imagine what level of physical injuries she might have after the car accident and how she was doing after knowing he was abducted.

Letting out a deep sigh, he picked up the wine glass and took a big sip to help conceal his perturbation.

Vera started feeling exasperated by his silence and coldness. "I can delay your release if you wish to stay here longer," she tried to provoke a reaction from him.

Putting down the cutlery, he looked at her with his piercing eyes. "Thank you for the information," he said.

"I am happy to find out more information for you if you like. With a price, of course." She gave him an alluring smile.

"What might that be?" he asked politely.

"Just enjoy the meal with me," she said, her voice somehow sounding dejected.

"I am enjoying the meal." He raised the wine glass in Vera's direction.

Vera waved her hand, motioning the guards to leave them.

Four guards at the four corners of the dining room stepped out of the room immediately.

"Better?" she asks.

"Sure," he answered, not sure what she was plotting.

"Good..." She picked up a fork and took a small bite of her salad. However, she was not hungry for the food. She was hungry for the affection from the man sitting right at the table with her.

She put down the fork and picked up the wine glass. She stood up and sauntered towards him, her red, chiffon, long dress flowing gracefully on her curvy body.

Thomas sat back, leaning against the dining chair backing. He did not like what she was doing, but he just had to play by her rules now if he wanted to know Iris' condition.

She took a sip of the wine and put the wine glass on the table before she sat astride his lap.

Thomas frowned.

She held both his hands and placed them on her thighs, but he lifted his hands the moment she let go of them. She scowled at him as no man ever showed her such bitterness or resentment.

"I have everything she has, and I am more than you can handle," she whispered in his ear.

"But you are not her," Thomas said in a tender voice, not wanting to upset her. "I love my wife."

"More than this?" she asked, gently moving her hips, wishing to arouse him.

"Yes," he answered in frustration. "This is not going to work, Vera."

He seized Vera's upper arms and stood abruptly. Vera fell off from his lap, but his hold on her arms had prevented her from falling onto the floor. The chair was tipped over and hit the floor with a loud thud.

Vera was shocked by his sudden action. Blinking her big enticing eyes, she intentionally fell onto his chest, but he grabbed her arms again and held her back, keeping an arm's length distance.

"Why?" She felt humiliated.

"You can lock me up for as long as you want." He had enough of her preposterous exhortations. He would not explain himself to her, would not please her, and absolutely would not satisfy her sexual need. Turning on his heel, he stormed out. He heard the glass-breaking sound echoing in the room behind him, but he really did not care.

CHAPTER 6

Eighteen days since the accident

IRIS had slowly regained her strength and was able to move around without much help. Because her baby's distress level was still concerning, Dr. Beaumont insisted on keeping her in the hospital for close monitoring.

She stood in front of the bathroom sink washing her hands, her mind wandering...

The kidnappers agreed to send proof more than a week ago, but they had not contacted either the crisis negotiator or Louis again since then. She feared the reason they had not sent the proof was that they either did not have Thomas or...or...

No... He is alive and will come back to me. Iris violently shook her head, dismissing the dreadful thought.

"Love, are you all right?" Eva gently knocked on the bathroom door. She was worried as Iris had been in the bathroom for a while.

Eva's voice interrupted Iris' brooding thought. "Yes..." she replied in a weak voice. "I...I'll be right out."

She turned off the water and dried her hand. While she was reaching for the door handle, she suddenly felt severe cramps in her belly. She held onto the vanity countertop to prevent herself from falling to the floor and put one hand underneath her belly. She took several deep breaths, trying to ease the pain, but the cramps were only getting worse.

"Eva..." She tried to call Eva, but she could hardly make a clear sound as the pain was like a knife cutting into her flesh. Then she felt warm fluid running down between her inner thighs.

Did my water just break? She looked down in panic and saw blood dripping on the floor. She froze, her eyes fixed on the pool of blood.

"Iris?" Eva knocked on the door again. Her voice pulled Iris back from her shock.

"Eva…" Iris called in fear, her voice weak and trembling.

Eva hastily opened the door when she heard Iris' calling and saw Iris standing by the sink, her face pale as snow.

Iris gave Eva a fearful look and then looked down at the floor. Eva's eyes followed Iris' gaze, and she immediately pushed the call button by the bathroom door and rushed towards Iris.

"Eva…" Iris' voice was quavering.

"Don't worry, love." Eva wrapped her arms around Iris. "Nurses are coming."

Wanting to step away from the blood on the floor, Iris took one small step and immediately felt warm fluid gushing out of her body. "No…" Tears were rolling down her cheeks.

"That's all right," Eva said in a very calm and soft voice. "We are going to stay right here and wait for the nurses."

"Eva. I…I…"

"Yes, love?"

"I can't…" Iris felt her strength leaving her body. "Please, don't let me fall…" She leaned onto Eva. "Don't let anything happen to my baby, please."

"Love, nurses are coming.…" Eva held Iris tight.

A nurse knocked and walked into the room.

"*Ici!*" Eva shouted *in here* when she heard the knock.

Shocked by the scene in front of her, the nurse quickly pushed the call button by the door a couple of times and rushed over to Iris.

Iris felt an instant relief when she saw the nurse. "Hang in there, little one…" she mumbled.

"Mrs. Torian, we will take good care of you. Don't worry…" the nurse said to Iris.

Soon four more nurses rushed into the room. Eva stepped aside so the nurses could help Iris. They carefully moved Iris out of the bathroom and onto the bed while one nurse left the room to fetch the on-call doctor.

"Eva..." Iris called.

"I am right here," Eva walked closer and stood near Iris' shoulder while the nurses were trying to take care of Iris.

Iris reached for Eva's hands. "Please don't leave me."

"I won't, love." Eva gave Iris' cold, trembling hand a gentle squeeze.

Dr. Heinrich walked into the room briskly. He had known Iris since the first day she arrived and was familiar with her medical records as well as Dr. Beaumont. He kept a smile on his face when he approached Iris.

"Iris," Dr. Heinrich said softly and calmly. "I have already called Dr. Beaumont, and she is on her way here. I am going to examine you now. All right?"

Iris nodded and turned to look at Eva, seeking comfort.

"Love, focus on your breathing," Eva whispered to Iris.

Iris fixed her eyes on Eva, inhaling and exhaling deeply.

"Wonderful..." Eva gave her an encouraging smile.

Dr. Heinrich instructed the nurses to prepare the operating room and then said to Iris, "The baby is ready to meet you."

"It's too soon," Iris responded in panic.

"The baby has to come out now so we can stop your bleeding. We will perform a Caesarean section to deliver the baby first and then take care of you," Dr. Heinrich explained in a comforting voice.

"Eva..." Iris was gasping for air, a surge of overwhelming anxiety erupting.

"Love, I am right here," Eva said softly to Iris and then asked Dr. Heinrich, "Can I stay with her?"

"Only during the delivery," Dr. Heinrich answered Eva and looked at Iris again. "Iris, I know you are scared. Thirty-week is early, however the baby is fully developed already. Dr. Beaumont will be here to deliver your baby, so don't worry. And I will be there to assist her."

Iris only cared if her little one was safe. She vigorously nodded her head and grasped Eva's hands tight.

Dr. Heinrich instructed the nurses and proceeded to push the bed towards the operating room.

Iris closed her eyes, focusing on her breathing just like Eva had been reminding her to do since the first day they met…

~ ~ ~

"Iris, this is Dr. Eva Thompson," James introduced the lady sitting at the conference table to Iris when they walked into the room.

She is so petite… That was Iris' first impression of Eva, the psychiatrist of whom James spoke highly.

"Hi Iris," Eva greeted her but did not reach her hand out for a handshake. She stayed where she sat, smiling broadly at her.

Iris gave Eva a timid smile and averted her eyes right away. She followed James and sat down next to him. A jar of pink M&M's on the table caught her attention.

"I had the pink ones when I was at a friend's wedding and became addicted to them," Eva said.

Iris moved her eyes to Eva, finding how she started their session interesting. She had dark brown curly hair and light brown eyes.

She is so pleasant to look at… That was Iris' second impression of Eva. She was one of those people who would make you smile unconsciously when you looked at them.

"I always have a jar of those cuties with me if you are wondering." Eva reached for the open jar and took some chocolate candies. She tossed a coupe in her mouth and continued, "You are welcome to have some. One can never have enough chocolate." She grinned.

A small smile appeared on Iris' face …

Before their first meeting ended, Eva said to her, "If you start feeling anxious or uncomfortable in any situation, focus on your breathing. Slowly take a deep breath and let it out slowly. Let's practice. Inhale… and exhale…"

~ ~ ~

"Iris…" Dr. Beaumont's voice brought Iris back to the present. "Are you with me?" she asked Iris.

Iris opened her eyes and nodded, feeling relieved to see her doctor.

"The nurses are going to prepare you now. Eva needs to change so she can stay in the operating room with you." Dr. Beaumont held Iris' hand, replacing Eva's.

A nurse placed an intravenous line in her arm while Dr. Beaumont was talking to her.

"Love, I will be right back." Eva kissed Iris' forehead before she followed one nurse and left Iris with Dr. Beaumont.

Dr. Beaumont nodded at the nurses around them and proceeded to push Iris into an operating room, she never letting go of Iris' hand.

Once they settled Iris on the operating table, Dr. Beaumont sat down on a stool right by Iris and said to her in a soothing voice, "Iris, I am going to explain everything to you now. Okay?"

Iris nodded, blinking her tears back.

"A neonatologist, Dr. Hunziker, will join us later to take care of the baby."

Iris nodded again.

"Dr. Kuhn here," Dr. Beaumont gestured in the direction of a medical personnel, who was standing on the opposite side of the operating table.

Iris fixed her eyes on her doctor, not able to look at the other one.

"Hi Iris," a safe male voice called her name. "You are in good hands."

"Dr. Kuhn is our anesthesiologist. He is going to put you under regional anes—"

Iris' body suddenly started to tremble involuntarily. She was not sure if the room was too cold or her anxiety level was elevating. She grasped Dr. Beaumont's hands tight, her eyes widened.

"Relax, Iris. It will be all right. We are all here for you." Dr. Beaumont smiled and continued, "The regional anesthesia will numb only the lower part of your body and allow you to remain awake during the procedure. Any question so far?" She needed to make sure Iris was still following her.

Iris shook her head nervously. The truth was she did not know what to ask. She made up her mind to have natural childbirth without an epidural in the very beginning of her pregnancy. She had read so much information about vaginal birth, even about how to make her vagina go back to normal, but she knew nothing about c-section.

"After the baby is delivered…" Dr. Beaumont continued. "Dr. Kuhn will put you under general anesthesia. You will feel as if you are in a deep sleep."

Iris nodded again, trying to be as brave as possible.

Dr. Beaumont gave Iris an encouraging smile and then looked up to give Dr. Kuhn a nod. Focusing back on Iris, she said softly, "I am going to turn your body to face me now. And once you turn towards me, try to curve your back as much as possible. And don't worry. I will help you."

With the help of the nurses and doctors, Iris lay on her side and tried to bend her body. "I can't…" she said, tears rolling down.

"That's all right. I will help you," Dr. Beaumont said. One hand on Iris' shoulder and the other on the back of her knees, Dr. Beaumont helped Iris curve her back so Dr. Kuhn was able to administer spinal anesthesia.

Eva walked into the operating room and stood by Iris, who was squeezing her eyes shut while Dr. Kuhn was giving her the injection. She saw tears running down from the corners or Iris' eyes, her own eyes flooded with tears as well. She could not imagine how scared Iris was…

Once Dr. Kuhn was done, they repositioned Iris on her back, and the nurses and Dr. Kuhn were all surrounding Iris, busy with the preparation.

"You are doing a fantastic job," Dr. Beaumont said, handing Iris' hand back to Eva and stepping aside.

"I am back, love," Eva whispered.

Iris opened her eyes and met Eva's warmhearted gaze. She heard Dr. Beaumont's voice and turned in her direction, but her line of sight was blocked by a blue surgical cloth hung above her baby bump.

Did she start the procedure already? I don't feel anything… She felt a surge of desolation washing over her. Shutting her eyes, she held Eva's hand firmly and resumed her focus back on her breathing.

This is not what I had imagined… Iris felt devastated as Thomas was supposed to be here and hold her hand while she was giving birth to their child. She was supposed to yell at him when she was having contractions, and he was supposed to tell her how brave she was, what a fantastic job she was doing, and how much he loved her.

Everything is wrong, so wrong now... Hot tears were running down from the corners of her eyes and soaking the blue surgical pillow underneath her head.

Although she could not feel any pain, she could still sense her organs being moved around, a peculiar sensation she had never experienced before. It was disturbing, uncomfortable, and troubling, so much so that Iris started gasping for air.

"Love, you are doing great," Eva whispered in her ear as she could feel Iris' hand trembling. "Breath…"

Iris started focusing on her breathing, and the nasal cannula set below her nose was supplying extra oxygen she needed.

Breathing in.... Breathing out... Breathing in.... Breathing out... Iris was concentrating on only these two things in her mind, blocking what was happening to her and around her.

"Congratulations, Iris. You have a baby boy," Dr. Beaumont announced.

Iris' eyes flung open, brimming with tears.

"Congratulations, love," Eva whispered in Iris' ear as tears were running down her cheeks as well.

Iris had imagined the nurse would bring their baby to her and Thomas, and then both of them would enjoy the very moment when they met their child for the first time.

But… Thomas is not here…

"I don't hear him crying…" Iris mumbled.

"Love, the doctor has to examine him first. Don't worry…" Eva comforted her. However, she felt absolutely perturbed when she saw the neonatologist and pediatric nurses rushing the newborn out of the operating room. She did not even catch a glimpse of the baby.

Drawing in a sharp breath, Eva suppressed her own emotions. She knew the survival rate for babies born at thirty weeks was quite high, so she was not going to consider any negative outcome.

"Ma'am," a nurse tried to get Eva's attention.

Eva blinked back her tears and looked at the nurse.

The nurse gestured Eva to the operating room exit.

Right... They did tell her she could not be in the room when they proceeded to the next step of the surgery.

"Love, I will be right outside," she whispered to Iris.

Iris nodded, feeling drowsy, her eyelids heavy.

THOMAS was roused by the noises outside the room. He got out of the bed and went into the bathroom to wash up.

"Come with me." Vera was marching towards Thomas' room, followed by four guards.

The guard by the door quickly unlocked and opened the door for Vera.

Thomas walked out of the bathroom when he heard the door being opened.

"Have the recording ready," Vera said to the guard holding a phone in his hands. She stared at Thomas and said, "I am going to show your family that you are still alive. But I am also going to let them know how serious I am."

Thomas frowned, not sure what was in her evil mind.

"Alive doesn't mean unharmed." She motioned to the guards behind her.

Two of them walked towards Thomas and seized his both arms.

Thomas did not put up much of a fight as he knew he was not able to defend himself against those bulky guards. He pretty much figured out what they were planning to do to him when he saw the brawniest guy was cracking his knuckles, waiting for Vera's command.

"Hmmm..." Vera walked closer to Thomas, scanning his face carefully and said, "It will be a shame if he leaves any mark on your pretty face." She turned towards the brawniest guard and said, "Darling Ben, I don't care if you break anything. Just make sure he is alive and we don't need to call a doctor."

Thomas glared at her, his nostrils flaring.

She turned back and stared at Thomas. "You are going to wish you had enjoyed dinner with me the other night," she said coldly. Giving him another piercing glare, she turned and walked out of the room.

Before Thomas could prepare himself, at least mentally, Ben punched him in his gut. Thomas doubled over, groaning in pain. He could feel that blow was very close to his fractured ribs. Both guards by his sides yanked him upward, and Ben's fist immediately hit Thomas' jaw before he was able to manage the pain from the first punch. He lost his balance and fell backward, but the two guards held him still. He could taste blood in his mouth. And then the third punch came, hitting him across his face...

At least they will keep me alive, Thomas thought.

Trying to distract himself from the intolerable pain and block the physical torture out, Thomas let his memories go wild...

~ ~ ~

He was such a late bloomer, always the smallest boy in his class before hitting his growth spurt at fifteen, and constantly harassed by those big guys at school and in the neighborhood.

One day, at the age of seven, he came home from school and was covered in dirt, and his shirt was torn. His thirteen-year-old sister Laila marched into his school the next day. She lectured not only the boys bullying him but also the principal and teachers. She was his super heroine.

"Tommy, they were big, but that's not a problem. Fight with your brain and skills because you are the smartest boy I have known," she said to him.

She taught him how to ride a horse—not a pony but a full-grown, fifteen-hands-tall Morgan horse—when he was only eight years old. He was too small and too scared to get on that giant, long-face animal, and Louis laughed and called him a weakling. Of course, Laila later gave Louis the consequences of laughing at their baby brother—cleaning all horse stalls.

She was tough and never stopped encouraging him to challenge himself.

~ ~ ~

After all these years, Thomas still missed Laila terribly. He smiled at the thought of his sister.

All four guards were baffled by his smile, wondering what kind of man would enjoying such torture.

"Wipe that smile off your face!" Ben shouted and kneed Thomas in his stomach, knocking the wind out of him.

Thomas coughed violently. He did not give them any response but tried to think about Iris so he could disregard the unendurable pain.

~ ~ ~

When he picked up Iris from the recovering house, she looked as terrified and apprehensive as other victims he had met. His job was not there to physically rescue those women but to locate the organization behind Vera's operation. It was never easy to watch them suffer, so he consistently had to remind himself to see the bigger picture because his mission was to take down the entire organization.

"Don't touch me!" Iris screamed behind him, causing him to turn around. He saw her yanking her arm away from one of the guards. She was not at all intimidated by the hefty man, who was almost double her size.

Just as he was surprised by her undaunted attitude, she lost her balance and fell backward. He lunged forward and caught her, keeping her from falling onto the concrete steps.

"Are you all right? Can you walk?" he asked her, gazing at her dark brown eyes.

"Of course I can walk," she huffed, pushing herself away from him.

At that moment, he saw Laila in her, incredibly plucky and fearless. He smiled inwardly, watching her getting into the van. That night he tossed and turned, wondering if she was all right. He did not think much about it and believed his sleeplessness was simply caused by his sympathy for another victim. However, he was eager to find out how she was doing the next morning. And since then, he had been watching over her from a distance.

He felt sorry for every single woman Vera had obtained and was able to contain his commiseration for their misfortune and execute his job as the amoral security foreman. Then something had changed after Iris arrived at the mansion. His chest felt tight when he saw her looking out the windows aimlessly and shedding dejected tears. And he had to restrain himself with gargantuan effort from punching everyone who touched her. He knew he was not supposed to feel this way, but he could not control his feelings towards her.

Although Iris was miserable, she still stood up for several timid women against the spiteful ones and bluntly chastised the patrons for being unethical. Despite his admiration for her, he was greatly worried about her as she constantly got herself in trouble with Vera because of her attitude, and he knew all too well how Vera would do to the women whom she wanted to discard. So when Vera asked him to contact one of her procurers to pick up Iris, he had to act and get Iris out of the mansion right away. His supervisor Julia rebuked him for being irrational and insisted that he must follow the protocol and wait for their agents, who personated the procurers, to pick up Iris.

"It will be too late. Vera is going to let the guards take turns raping her first. She intends to break her and punish her before she lets her go," he pleaded. "I cannot let that happen to her."

Julia realized they could not overlook the abuse and torture Iris was going to endure if they did not act on it, so she agreed to meet him halfway and take her to the U.S. Embassy.

When he introduced Julia to Iris, Iris shrank and hid behind him. He turned around and gazed at her, his heart palpitating. He wanted to hold her in his arms to comfort her and tell her everything would be all right, but his rational mind won the battle. He shoved his hands in his pockets, fighting the urge to take her into his arms.

"Will I see you again?" she asked him.

He had to force himself to walk away without turning back to catch another glimpse of her.

He believed once Iris was gone, he could continue to carry out his job like before. But no... All he thought about was her.

~ ~ ~

Mon amour... Thomas missed his Iris.

Suddenly, he collapsed onto the floor, his shoulder hitting the hard floor tiles and the pain bringing him back to the brutal reality.

The guards were done with him. They walked out of the room and shut the door behind them.

Thomas groaned in pain when he turned his body to lie on his back. The coldness of the stone tiles actually felt really good at this moment.

CHAPTER 7

Nineteen days since the accident

IRIS roused, blinking her eyes several times, and her mind was fuzzy.

"Little one…" she murmured, remembering the blood and the operating room.

"Honey…" Koto whispered when she heard her daughter's almost inaudible voice. She and her husband had been sitting right by her bedside since she was brought back from the surgery.

The room was cleaned, no sight of the horrific and anguish episode happening earlier.

"Where…where is my little one?" Iris asked.

"Sweetheart, he is in the nursery." Koto smiled at Iris, feeling both proud and downhearted.

When she and Lucas arrived at the hospital, Iris was already in surgery. They waited for hours before being informed that Iris had given birth to a baby boy, and they waited for several more hours until Dr. Beaumont came to the waiting room and told them that the surgery went well. The doctor also told them the baby was admitted to the neonatal intensive care unit and they were doing their best to take care of him.

"I want to see him," Iris said, her voice demanding.

Koto and Lucas looked at each other, not sure how to fulfill their daughter's request.

"Is he all right? Is there something wrong with him?" Iris panicked as her parents were quiet.

"He…he is in the intensive care nursery. They are taking good care of him."

"Intensive care?" Iris asked in fear. "What's wrong with him?"

"Honey," Lucas said. "He is a perfect boy."

"Yes, he is so beautiful," Koto said to her daughter. "He was just born prematurely. They have to keep him in the incubator for now."

"Can I see him?" Iris asked, choked with emotion.

"Of course," her mother replied. "Once you feel better and have your strength—"

"So I cannot see my baby now?" Iris snapped, tears streaming down her face. She was so tired of being patient and pretending to be brave when the unfortunate events kept happening one after the other.

Koto was silent, overwhelmed by her daughter's reaction. She quickly wiped away her tears.

"Honey, you just had a surgery," Lucas tried to calm his daughter. Seeing his daughter and wife in distress saddened him greatly. "Be patient. Once the doctor—"

Lifting the blanket over her head, Iris hid herself underneath it. Her baby had been keeping her company and making her life more tolerable while waiting for Thomas' safe return. The baby had been her consolation. And now… She was all by herself. She had never felt so lonely before.

Lucas gently embraced his daughter's trembling body. "Honey, the baby is in good hands. You can visit him as soon as the doctor checks on you…"

"Promise?" Iris lowered the blanket, blinking her tears away.

"Promise." Lucas gazed at his precious daughter.

Iris turned to face her mother and said, "Mommy, I am sorry…" As soon as she said that, she burst into tears.

"Oh, honey." Koto stroked Iris' hair tenderly.

"I…I miss Thomas. I want…want Thomas…" Iris cried in her parents' arms. "I thought…I thought I was…was going…was going to lose the baby," she said between sniffles.

"But you didn't…" Lucas kissed the top of Iris' head. "Everything will be all right… Everything will be all right…"

"HOW long has she been like this?" Eva whispered to Jasmine when she walked into Iris' room and saw Iris still covering herself underneath the blanket.

"All day, except when Dr. Beaumont and nurses were here to check on her." Jasmine sighed.

Eva walked up to Iris and said softly, "Love, I am here…"

Iris did not answer her.

"She has her AirPods on, " Jasmine said.

Eva nodded, giving Jasmine an appreciating smile. She sat on the chair by the bed and slowly lifted the corner of the blanket, making sure not to startle Iris. She looked underneath the blanket and met Iris' watery eyes. Her heart ached for her.

"I heard David and the kiddos are on their way here to see you," she said softly.

Iris did not respond. She turned her head and body towards the opposite side. She was tired of talking because there was nothing left to say. She felt she was all alone now and only wished to be left alone.

Eva let out a sigh and put the blanket back down. She wished she could bring her good news, but there was no further contact from the kidnappers and the newborn was still too fragile.

THOMAS finally got enough strength to get up from the floor and climb into the bed. If going through this torture could get him back to his Iris, he welcomed the pain.

He was not surprised at the way he was treated as he had seen too much when he went undercover. He knew clearly he was not born to be in this line of work when he was considering joining the police academy, but his anger, grief, and sense of responsibility made it all possible. Then Iris tumbled into his life in the most horrendous way. He could not imagine his life without her now, but if he had a choice which would alter Iris' misfortune he would snatch that choice in a heartbeat, even if it meant never having the opportunity to meet the love of his life.

Mon amour... Thinking about Iris surely made the pain a bit tolerable. A memory came into his mind, a smile appearing on his face.

~ ~ ~

When he was working undercover in the mansion, he could not have a break from pretending to be someone he was not until he was in his own room or reading in the library late at night. Alone.

One night, he was sitting on an armchair in the corner of the library when Iris walked in quietly. Since many women in the mansion often made up all kinds of excuses to strike up a conversation with him when they spotted him, he was debating if he should leave, stay, or ask Iris to leave. He really needed some alone time to feel normal and to stay sane. And just as he was ready to close the book he was reading and head out of the library, Iris hastily hid behind the bookcase when she saw him.

He smiled slightly and decided to stay. He resumed his reading, ignoring her.

Not until the night guard disturbed his peace by barking at Iris did he look up again and saw the shy and fearful Iris. The resolute façade she put on during the day was gone.

"Hurry up!" the guard bellowed out, making Iris flinch.

"Leon, leave us," Thomas said to the guard, his glare piercing.

"Mr. Martin," the guard greeted him, but he did not move. He was not supposed to let Iris out of his sight before he escorted her back to her room.

"I will walk her back. You can go back to your post," Thomas said, knowing all the guards took their duties seriously.

"Yes, Mr. Martin." Guard Leon nodded and left the library.

Thomas did not check on Iris. He went back to his book and tried to enjoy the quietness once again. However, he could not concentrate on his reading. Her presence had gripped his full attention. He looked up, his eyes searching for her, and found her browsing books.

Then she began to hum softly to herself like she did not even care that the ruthless Max was in the same room with her.

He watched her picking out books from the shelves gracefully and noticed she ran her slender fingers over their titles. She had her long, wavy, dark brown hair down and was wearing a t-shirt and leggings instead of the seductive and sexy sleepwear Vera had given to all the women here. Her cheeks were naturally glowing and blushing without any makeup. He was mesmerized by her upward-almond-shaped, dark brown eyes, which were mysterious and enticing.

What am I doing? He thought to himself when he realized he was staring at her. With a great effort, he tried to focus back on his reading again.

When he realized her soft humming sound was all he was focusing on, he decided it was time to send her back to her room.

"Are you ready to go back to your room?" he asked, his voice gentle.

She stopped humming, her brow furrowed. Letting out a deep sigh, she picked up two books she set on top of the shelf and nodded.

He was intrigued by her choices of the books—*Tarzan of the Apes* and *The Odyssey*.

"Why those titles?" he asked.

She looked at him, seemingly puzzled by his question.

"Fan of Tarzan?" he asked.

"Oh…" She looked down at the books in her hands. "I miss my brother…" Her voice was just above a whisper.

Brother? That's an odd answer. However, Thomas did not press on.

"And this…" She stared at the cover of *The Odyssey*. "It's always my favorite. I hope my journey home will be easier than Odysseus'…" she trailed off, not intending for anyone to hear.

But Thomas heard every single word. His heart sank and wished he could tell her not to worry and not to be afraid. He was standing less than a foot from her, so he had to suppress the urge of wanting to touch her hair and comfort her. When she looked up and looked into his eyes, he did not pretend or put on a stony face. He let her see his true emotions: Compassion and understanding.

Ever since that night, he was always looking for her face in the mansion.

When he was invited to David's ranch after he and Iris reunited, he was puzzled when Jane called David *John*.

"John?" he asked Iris.

Iris grinned and explained, "She is his Jane, and he is her Tarzan John Clayton. I will take the credit because I was the one calling them John and Jane when they started dating."

He then remembered their conversation in the mansion library and realized why she said she missed her brother…

~ ~ ~

Thomas was drunk in his memories. He missed Iris' smell, sweet kisses, and soft touches. The heartache of not being able to hold her and kiss her was more painful than the physical agony he was enduring now.

CHAPTER 8

Twenty seven days since the accident

IRIS had not spoken a word since she visited her baby over a week ago. She was so excited to meet him, and then what she saw completely broke her...

~ ~ ~

Iris was in a wheelchair pushed by a nurse heading to the neonatal intensive care unit. Her parents were with her, but they had to wait outside while a NICU nurse pushed her to meet her son for the very first time.

Oh my god, he is so tiny... Tears flooded her eyes when she spotted her son. Then when the nurse pushed her closer, she was perturbed and could not believe her eyes. Her baby was connected with so many tubes and looked so skinning and fragile.

A set of nasal cannula was connected to his little nose, so big that she could not see his nose. A feeding tube was inserted in his mouth, and a bandage was over his eyes. His whole face was basically covered.

An IV catheter was attached to his arm, as thick as his teeny fingers. One monitor wire was taped on his chest, and another one was wrapped around his little foot.

Iris was overwhelmed by guilt. She despised herself for not taking good care of herself, and now her baby was suffering.

She had been so lost since the moment she knew her savior, guardian angel, and the love of her life was kidnapped. She could not handle the stresses, could not deal with what was happening, and could not face the possibility that Thomas might never come back.

How was she able to take care of their son and raise him by herself? And what if… What if their son did not make it? Then she would be all alone, without her husband and son…

Iris burst into tears, burying her face in her hands.

The nurse gently rubbed Iris' arm, comforting her.

"Please…please take me back to my room," Iris whispered. She had no strength left to manage the heartbreaking sight of her son. She just wanted to hide, to avoid reality, and to block everything out.

~ ~ ~

Two weeks had gone by since Mr. Marseille spoke with the kidnapper, and he had not received any evidence proving Thomas was indeed their captive and still alive.

Iris became more despairing with each passing day. She tried to stay positive, but she found herself falling into a deep, depressing, black hole. So dark and so lonely…

What if they don't plan to let him go?

What if Thomas is…

She shook her head violently, tears gushing down her cheeks. She embraced herself, curling in a fetal position underneath the blanket, her body trembling.

"Sweetheart…" Koto whispered to Iris when she heard her weak sobbing noise. She gently touched her shivering body. "Everything is going to be all right…"

Koto knew Iris would not respond to her because she had been completely shut down after she visited her baby. She was either hiding underneath the blanket or staring out the window aimlessly, not even asking about her son or Thomas anymore.

But Koto had never stopped talking to her. She constantly updated Iris on her baby boy's progress and encouraged her with loving words, even though Iris had never given her any response.

Jane walked up to Koto and held her shoulders tenderly, giving her moral support.

David arrived with their kids soon after he learned Iris had an emergency c-section. He and Jane offered to take turns keeping Iris company in the hospital, but Koto refused to leave because her daughter needed her.

Iris knew her family and friends were trying to help her, but she felt she had hit the very bottom of this indescribable dark hole she was in now. She had no strength and no will to get out of it because she had no husband and no son now... Nothing mattered now...

He is not coming back. Iris was certain about that because Eva and Louis had stopped mentioning anything about Thomas when they visited her. She believed they were afraid to tell her the negotiations had gone wrong, and her mind started imagining many horrific scenarios.

He has to come back to me. He knows he has to or I will not survive...

Her mind drifted back to the moment when she ever really *noticed* Thomas, the foreman of the security Max.

It was not when she saw him for the first time in the recovering house, or when she caught him staring at her across the room in the mansion.

It was when she saw him in the mansion library one night...

~ ~ ~

One sleepless night, she persuaded the night guard to let her grab a couple of books from the library, which was her safe haven then. And as far as she knew, no one went there except her.

The lights were on when she got there, and she saw Max was sitting on an armchair, reading a book. Her instinct was to hide behind the bookcase by the door. She could not care less about him and never understood all the fuss over him among the other women. However, out of curiosity, she peeked at him from behind the bookcase.

He looks different. So tranquil... She was intrigued by his completely different mien since he was always scowling.

I guess he is kind of cute. She studied his face but still thought her brother David was the most handsome man she had ever seen though. *Sorry, Daddy,* she chuckled inwardly.

Maybe it's the hair and his clothes... She noticed there was something different about his hair and outfit, and that was why he looked so different. His wavy, shoulder-length, dark hair was down and slightly damp, and somehow that made him look less intimidating. He was wearing a white t-shirt and blue jeans instead of the all-black, security-guard outfit. He actually looked like a friendly, artistic, cute guy who would usually sit in a café, reading a book, in her Laguna Beach neighborhood.

"Are you done yet?" The night guard's loud bark just disclosed her presence to Max.

"Almost done…" Iris whispered and walked out from behind the bookcase. She glanced at Max, who was staring at the night guard, scowling, and then his piercing gaze turned towards her. She quickly averted her eyes.

There goes the friendly, artistic, cute guy and comes the grumpy Bossman. Iris rolled her eyes.

"Hurry up!" the guard bellowed out, making Iris flinch and scurry away from him.

"Leon, leave us," Max said to the guard.

What? Iris was shocked.

"Mr. Martin," the guard greeted Max.

Iris peeked through the gap between the books and the shelf and saw the guard still standing by the door. *Please don't leave…*

"I will walk her back. You can go back to your post," Max said, his voice deep and authoritative.

"Yes, Mr. Martin." Guard Leon nodded and left the library.

Shit! Iris sighed, wondering if Max was going to give her some kind of hard time like he always did.

But much to her surprise, Max just went back to his book and left her alone. She proceeded to browse books but was on full alert, just to make sure he stayed where he was.

I guess Mr. Bossman likes to read, too. She took a quick peek at him, who seemed to be enjoying his book very much.

She shrugged, feeling less nervous, and turned her attention back to the books on the shelves. Unconsciously, she started to hum Elton John's *Your Song*, which she sang to her niece and nephews all the time when she babysat them.

She finally decided on two books but was not ready to go back to her room yet. She wandered around in the room, browsing aimlessly.

"Are you ready to go back to your room?" Max asked. Even though his voice was soft, it still startled her.

Letting out a deep sigh, she picked up the two books she set on top of the shelf and nodded. She considered just leaving the library and rushing back to her room without dealing with Max. But when she saw him walking towards her, she abandoned the idea because she was not allowed to go anywhere by herself.

"Why those titles?" he asked out of the blue.

Huh? She tilted her head, puzzled by his question.

"Fan of Tarzan?" he asked, his voice playful.

She looked down at the books in her hands, suddenly becoming emotional. "I miss my brother..." she whispered, more like talking to herself than answering his question.

Max looked bewildered.

"And this..." She looked at the cover of The Odyssey. "It's always my favorite. I hope my journey home will be easier than Odysseus'..." she trailed off, not sure if it was a good idea to share her thoughts about her misfortune with Max.

Max became quiet and just gazed at her. Finally, he sighed and said in a very low and soft voice, "Let me walk you back to your room."

Iris looked up and found his deep blue eyes looking so dejected. She had an urge to ask him if he was all right, but he quickly turned away and headed towards the door.

She followed him out of the library. He slowed down his pace so he could walk right by her. His soapy fresh scent was so refreshing and made her feel sort of at ease and forget he was a bad guy for a moment.

~ ~ ~

A surge of despair was deluging Iris vigorously. She held herself tightly, hands gripped her arms, nails digging into her flesh. She could not even feel the physical pain as her heart was hurting too much.

Please come back to me... she pleaded silently.

LUCAS walked into Iris' hospital room quietly. He sighed when he saw Koto wiping tears and heard Iris sobbing underneath the blanket. He beckoned to Koto and Jane and tilted his head towards the door, asking them to head out with him.

"Everything all right?" Jane asked.

Lucas was silent, motioning them to follow him. He did not want to say anything until Iris was out of earshot.

"Eva has some news about Thomas," Lucas said to Koto and Jane when they turned the corner. He wrapped his arm around his wife and kissed her hair tenderly.

Koto took a deep breath and asked in a weak voice, "Good news?"

"I don't know. She thinks it's better we hear it first before breaking it to Iris. She is in the waiting room now," Lucas said.

"Oh god..." Koto had a bad feeling about it.

"Let's stay positive." Lucas gently gave his wife a comforting squeeze.

Eva was on the phone when they walked into the waiting room. She quickly ended the call and greeted Koto and Jane. She then gestured them to the chairs in the room.

Koto held Lucas's hand tight, hoping for good news.

"Mr. Marseille received a video from the kidnappers this morning. They do have Thomas," Eva said, going straight to the point.

All three of them let out a sigh of relief.

"Is he all right?" Koto asked, knowing that was what Iris would ask once she heard the news.

Eva frowned, seemingly having a hard time answering her question.

"Eva?" Jane was sitting next to Eva. She gently put her hand on Eva's shoulder. "Thomas is alive, right?"

Eva turned to Jane, nodding her head, her eyes brimming with tears. "He...he..."

Jane wrapped her arms around Eva, comforting her.

Eva took a deep breath and turned to face Lucas and Koto. "He is badly beaten. He was…" She was choked with emotion and had to take another deep breath before she could continue, "He was lying on the floor…unconscious at the end of the video."

Koto covered her mouth, trying to muffle her sobs.

"When will they release him?" Lucas asked, embracing Koto in his arms.

Eva sighed and said, "The kidnapers said they would contact Mr. Marseille for further instructions."

"So we just wait?" Koto sounded frustrated. "They are playing with our emotions!"

"What should we do if Iris asks to watch the video?" Jane asked.

"That's the reason I wanted to speak with you first. Letting Iris know we have the proof might help her with her depression, although I am worried the video is too…too much for her." Eva let out a deep sigh.

"I…I don't think she can handle that…" Jane said, her voice trembling.

"Is Florent doing all right?" Lucas asked, assuming Thomas' father had watched the video.

"He is hanging there…" Eva said, letting out a deep sigh. "He had to…had to walk away when those men started throwing punches at Tommy. He could not watch the whole thing…"

Lucas nodded, knowing exactly how a father would feel when he saw his children suffering. "Can I…can I help with the ransom? I can easily transfer the money to you."

"Don't worry about it. Louis has already taken care of that." Eva gave Lucas a grateful smile.

And then a dreadful silence fell over them. An update on Thomas was better than nothing, but knowing he was brutally tortured was unbearable. They did not know how serious his injury was, and they did not know when the kidnappers were going to release him. Could Iris handle the news and the unknown?

"Don't tell her," Koto broke the silence.

"Mom?" Jane looked at Koto with concerns.

"She…she is hanging by a thread. Her meltdown after seeing the baby almost pushed her over the edge. Let's wait… Let's wait until…" She became speechless, wishing she could say *Let's wait until Thomas is back in one piece.*

THOMAS had been locked in the room for days. He still had severe pain all over his body, and he believed they cracked his ribs again. The massive bruising forming underneath his rib cage concerned him. He hoped there was no internal injury.

Vera had stopped asking him to dine with her since the day he humiliated her. Even if she had, he would not make it as he was too weak to get out of the bed. The food was brought to him, and he forced himself to eat so he would have strength when Vera decided to release him.

When he was thrown onto the floor after almost being beaten to death, he nearly gave up. The only thing that made him want to stay alive was the thought of seeing Iris again and meeting their child.

Ma puce is more than thirty-one weeks now, Thomas wished he would be released soon and be there when their child was born.

When the doctor told them they were pregnant, he was thrilled, but the news also completely disrupted his plan of giving Iris a memorable marriage proposal, even though he had proposed to her on the spur of the moment before he boarded the jet traveling to Riyadh. And that was not even a proposal…

~ ~ ~

"Let's get married when I come back," Thomas said to Iris.

"Okay," she said, smiling radiantly.

"Fantastic…" He gave her a wink and then walked into the plane.

"Did I seriously just say that to her?" Thomas murmured, smacking his forehead.

"Is everything all right?" Emma asked him when she noticed his troubled expression.

He nodded and continued to walk to a seat by a window. He looked out the window and saw Iris scanning the jet windows, her brow furrowed. Then her pale face broke into a smile when she spotted him.

I love you, she mouthed the words exaggeratedly, waving her hands.

He did the same, missing her already…

I am such an idiot! She deserves better than that! He mentally scolded himself.

When he was in Riyadh, he made a trip to Cartier in Al Faisaliyah Center and found the perfect ring—a platinum Solitaire 1895 set with a brilliant-cut, two-carat diamond. He knew Iris preferred elegant and simple design to extravagant style, and this classic and refined ring was perfect as it reminded him of her.

Engagement ring, checked.

He planned to take her to Rosengarten Park, where he kissed her for the very first time, and have a picnic. And before the sun went down, he was going to get down on one knee and ask her to marry him. Again.

That was the plan, although Iris' morning sickness had chained her to the toilet twenty-four-seven.

Picnic and proposal in the park, scratched out.

He watched her vomiting and fighting nausea every day, wishing he could take her place, but she told him as long as the baby would be healthy, she welcomed the sickness.

He wanted to do something for her, giving her the world if he could, but nothing could express his love and gratitude for her.

Maybe I can give her something reminding her of her hometown? An idea popped into his head one day. He called their family's real estate agency right away and started working on the idea.

He was planning to show her three properties, but she immediately fell in love with the first one by Lake Neuchâtel. That modern, spacious apartment was his first choice as well.

Some might think his idea of giving Iris a property by the lake was over the top. As for him, bearing their child was priceless, their love was priceless, and building their future together was priceless. He knew she would still be happy and want to marry him without a two-carat diamond ring and a waterfront property, but he wanted to spoil her because she deserved the best and she was worthy.

~ ~ ~

A smile spread over Thomas face when he remembered the moment he slid the ring onto her finger.

Have we ever fought? He wondered because he could never be angry at her or even disagree with her when she gazed at him with her dark brown eyes, pouting her kissable lips.

Wait... He remembered they were indeed mad at each other once. Over his stupidity...

~ ~ ~

Often he would wake her up in the morning by burying his face between her thighs. Although that morning, she awoke him by getting on top of him, straddling his hips, and enjoyed his morning wood. After she came down from her high, he flipped her on her back and gave her another amazing orgasm.

He took a shower after their morning love-making and walked out of the bathroom, a towel wrapped low around his hips. He saw her eyes following his almost naked body and her smile brighter than ever. She often commented that his six pack and v-line were enthralling and...yummy, so he slowly and deliberately sauntered in front of her. He winked at her before walking into the closet to get ready for work.

"Oh, I will be home a bit late today," he said, picking out his outfit for the day.

"Busy day?" she asked, still smiling.

"No. I am having a drink with Anna after work," he said casually.

"What?" She sat up on the bed, her eyes widened. "Anna? You mean your ex-girlfriend?"

He walked out of the closet, clothes in his hands. And he noticed the smile on her face was replaced with a scowl.

"It is just a drink, love." He laid his clothes on the bed, removed the towel, and stood completely naked in front of her. However, his nakedness did not soften her expression.

"And...when did you make this plan?" she pressed on.

"She called me yesterday and congratulated us on our engagement," he said while he put on black boxer shorts.

"And you didn't think it's necessary to tell me about it when you came home yesterday?" Her voice became higher.

He frowned, not sure why she thought it was a big deal. He did not answer her and started putting on his shirt.

His silence only made her feel more irritated.

"Who else will be there?" she asked.

"Just two of us, I think. She didn't mention there would be anyone else joining us."

"You can't go," Iris blurted, but she immediately regretted her words because she always encouraged him to go out and hang out with his friends.

He looked at her, one eyebrow raised.

She did the same and crossed her arms over her chest to emphasize her behest.

"And may I ask why?" he asked, looking solemn.

She averted her eyes, seemingly trying to think of an excuse.

He sighed since she was quiet and said, "I understand you don't have a good impression of her. What happened that day was a huge misunderstanding. I've known her for a long time. She is a good person."

Initially, he did not think having a drink with Anna was a good idea either. Then he remembered the shock, hurt, and embarrassment on Anna's face that day when he told her Iris was his girlfriend living with him. She could not even look at him when she took his key out of her purse and set it on the kitchen counter. She whispered her apology and scurried out of his apartment. He thought he was at fault for not telling her sooner.

"She still wants you," Iris blurted. Again. And this time her expression was serious.

"That's absurd." He chuckled. "She knows we are engaged."

"Relationships, engagement, or even marriage doesn't mean anything to some people!" She was angry.

He immediately remembered what Iris had shared with him about her past relationship. She had first hand experience with cheaters. A formal employee of hers openly flirted with Iris' then boyfriend in the office and company functions, and he absolutely enjoyed the attention and responded to her flirting with coquetry of his own. Then their flirtation soon turned into copulation.

Thomas frowned, stopping getting ready. "You don't know Anna."

"No, I don't. Because the first time and the only time I met her and heard about her was when she thought I was an intruder. It's hard to know her when she was chasing after me and called the police on me. She scared the shit out of me!" Iris was enraged now. "Why are you defending her?"

"I told you it was a misunderstanding." His voice was loud like hers.

She stared at him, not able to believe that he just raised his voice at her. She got out of the bed and stormed into the bathroom. "Fine. Enjoy your lovely evening!" she said before shutting the door.

Thomas closed his eyes, taking deep breaths to calm himself down. He had never raised his voice at her, but he had never seen her reacting so irrationally, either.

Maybe it is because of the pregnancy hormones. He shook his head, resuming getting ready for work.

Iris still had not come out of the bathroom when he was about to leave, so he gently knocked on the bathroom door and said goodbye.

She did not reply.

He sighed and left for work.

Anna texted him to confirm the time and the place she had chosen. He was not surprised she picked Noumi Grill & Bar as they used to go there quite often, either themselves or with friends. It was one of his favorites. He would have brought Iris there if she would be comfortable dining out at different places other than the restaurants in their hotels.

Thomas: On my way.

He texted Anna after he left the hotel.

Anna: Find me at the bar.

Her reply arrived almost immediately as if she had been waiting for his text.

He spotted her right away after walking into the restaurant. She was sipping wine and chatting with a bartender.

"Hey..." He approached her.

"You are here!" She pivoted on the barstool, her voice enthusiastic.

They gave each cheek-kisses like a couple of old friends.

He took the seat next to her and ordered a beer.

"You look great! As handsome as always. Engagement suits you well." She gazed at him.

Her friendliness felt familiar to him as she was always confident, cheerful, and optimistic.

"Thanks." He gave her a smile.

They talked about their jobs and friends as if the last awkward encounter at his apartment had never happened. Until...

"Tommy, I...I really want to apologize for what I did..." She let out a sigh of relief. "Yes! I finally said it." She picked up her wine and finished it. Then she waved to the bartender for another one.

Iris is so wrong about Anna. He smiled at her, surprised by her confession and also wondering how many glasses of wine she had already had before he arrived. It had always been easy to talk to her, even before they started dating. He thought Iris would have liked her if they did not meet under that very unpleasant circumstance.

"I've never thought you are the marrying type." She picked up the wine glass that was just placed in front of her. She took a big sip of wine, seemingly trying to use alcohol courage to say what was on her mind.

He gave her a smile because she was right. He had never considered marriage until he met Iris.

"You were so dedicated to your assignments. I was so jealous of those criminals because they got to have you."

He was not sure how to react to her comment like that.

"I am so hungry," she suddenly changed the subject. "I was so nervous about our date today that I didn't have lunch."

Date? He raised an eyebrow at her.

"Can we get some dinner?"

"Sure..." He thought a light dinner should be all right, even though he only planned to have a beer with her.

She gave him a grin and pushed herself off the stool. "It is so nice outside. Let's get a table on the terrace." She walked to the hostess to request a table for them without waiting for his response.

He grabbed his unfinished beer and followed her. He was thinking about calling or texting Iris to let her know he would be later than he had told her. Then he remembered their conversation this morning and abandoned the idea because he knew she was only going to become angrier.

They were seated right away, and Anna continued their conversation—or just her unbosoming herself to him.

"She must be very special or you wouldn't have given up fedpol. You had so much passion for what you were doing. I am sure you still do. Don't you miss it? Where did you two meet?" She unloaded her thoughts and questions without much of a break between sentences.

He knew Anna did not know what had happened to Iris because her job did not allow her to view classified cases. He did not plan to share that information with her, either. And it was not really a comfortable conversation he wanted to have with Anna, or anyone.

"The States," he said, giving her the shortest answer.

She nodded slightly, and just as she wanted to ask more questions. A waiter came to take their orders, giving Thomas a chance to change the subject.

"How are your parents?" he asked before she could dig deeper into his private life.

"They are great. They miss you." She smiled, gazing at him. "When I told them you finally surfaced from the underground, they were thrilled."

He chuckled at how she phased his undercover missions.

"They will be so happy to see you." Her voice was tender.

He did not respond. Her parents were wonderful people, but he could not picture himself meeting them anytime soon.

"The traveling must be amazing," she swiftly changed the

subject again, seemingly noticing his uneasiness.

"Yes, that is the best part of the job." He immediately relaxed, a smile spreading across his face. He started telling her all the places he had visited, and she was listening to him with all her attention.

Thomas was well trained to read people, so her admiring gaze and the little hit of sadness in her eyes made him wonder if she had regretted her decision to end their relationship. But the ship had sailed. He could not picture himself with anyone else but Iris.

Food was amazing and the conversations were easy and pleasant. Thomas ordered cognac, neat, to go with thunfisch-tartar. And after he finished his drink, Anna got him another one. Even though the voice in his head was telling him he had enough, he accepted the drink since he knew he could hold his liquor.

"It's late," she whispered, her cheeks red from the wine.

He looked around, realizing it was already dark. He looked at his watch and was surprised that it was already after nine.

Iris has not texted or called...

"It is…" He got the waiter's attention, asking for the check.

Anna was quiet when she finished the last of her wine.

They walked out of the restaurant, both silent. And just as he leaned in to kiss her cheek, she wrapped her arms around his neck and kissed him on his lips.

He pushed her off him right away, staring at her in surprise.

"I miss you…so much!" She blurted out.

"Anna, I am engaged." He frowned.

She shrugged. "So? You don't even want to talk about her like… like you are not happy with her." Her head turned towards Hotel Bellevue Palace, which was right next to the bar. "Let's get a room. Spend a night with me."

Iris is right. He sighed. "You had too much to drink… Let me take you home."

"So, you want to come home with me?" Her eyes sparkled with hope.

"No, Anna. I am taking you home, *and* I am going home to Iris."

"But…why? You…you don't have to marry her if…if you don't

want to." She was slurring her words now.

"I love her, I want to marry her, and we are having a baby." He started to feel irritated by the way she was acting now.

She blinked when she heard the last part. "A baby?"

"Yes."

"So… You…you are marrying her because…because she is pregnant?" She tilted her head, looking at him.

He let out a deep sigh and took out his phone. He called his chauffeur and asked him to meet him outside the bar.

"You…you don't… You shouldn't…shouldn't marry her for that…that reason," she continued when he gave her no answer. "I will talk to her for you. Woman to woman…"

He looked at her, shaking his head. She was really drunk now. She was going to forget everything she was saying now when she was sober later, so there was no point in replying to her. He stopped listening or paying attention to her and only kept his eyes on her to make sure she did not fall.

Several minutes later, a black Bentley Flying Spur pulled up next to them.

"Leon, thanks for coming at this hour," Thomas said when the chauffeur got out of the car and walked around it to open the door for him.

"Not a problem, Mr. Torian." Leon held the back door open for Thomas.

"I need you to take Ms. Haller home. I will text you her address." Thomas put his hands on Anna's shoulders and steered her towards the back door.

"Wow, nice…" Anna stepped into the car, grinning.

Leon closed the door after Thomas stepped away.

"Wait!" Anna tapped on the window and tried to push all the buttons on the door to lower the window. "Aren't you coming?" She stuck her head out of the window.

"Have a good night, Anna. Leon is going to take you home," Thomas said to her while he stepped up to the sidewalk.

"Should I come back for you?" Leon asked. Both men ignored whatever Anna was trying to say to them.

"No, thank you. I will take a taxi. Thanks again, Leon." Thomas found Anna's contact information on his phone and texted the address to Leon.

The apartment was dark when Thomas got home. He spotted Iris sitting on the sofa looking out the window. He walked towards her, filled with guilt.

His footsteps announced his presence, but she did not turn around.

He sat down next to her, but she did not move.

He gently pulled her hair aside and placed a kiss on her neck, but she did not react to him.

"I am sorry," he whispered in her ear. "You are right."

She turned to face him, her eyes puffy and red.

His heart ached, regretting hurting and disappointing her.

~ ~ ~

Vera's voice outside the door pulled Thomas back from his memory. He shut his eyes in exasperation as Vera had purposely raised her voice to announce her presence to him when she walked in and out of her room and to remind him that she was in charge and she was the only person who could decide his fate.

He kept his eyes shut when he heard his bedroom door being opened and frowned when he heard clicking sounds of sharp stiletto heels coming closer.

"Leave us," Vera said to the guards.

He did not open his eyes, ignoring Vera, then he felt the bed gently dipped. He opened his eyes and saw Vera sitting right on the edge of the bed close to him.

"Ben really did a number on you, didn't he?" She gently touched a black-and-blue mark on Thomas' cheek, her voice soft and seductive.

Thomas grabbed her wrist and moved her hand away from him, giving her a piercing stare.

Instead of feeling offended, she smiled and leaned forward. "This is why I like you. I miss you, Max…"

~ ~ ~

Vera noticed Max almost immediately when he first joined her security team. Not only was he extremely handsome, but his serious and unrelenting manner was also incredibly charming.

She summoned him to her room one night soon after he started working at the mansion.

"Come in," Vera answered the knock on the door, her voice lazy and alluring.

Thomas opened the door and walked into the living room of Vera's suite. She was not in sight.

"In here," she said from her bedroom.

Thomas hesitated, knowing exactly what was going to happen. Having sex with the suspect was definitely not on his job description. Some of his fellow officers could not resist this type of temptation, and then they either jeopardized the operations or made their missions so much more complicated. He had finally infiltrated Vera's operation, one step closer to the criminal organization behind her, so he must handle this situation carefully. However, fucking Vera was never an option for him.

Slowly, he walked into the bedroom.

Vera stood by the foot of her enormous bed, wearing just a long black lace robe disclosing she had nothing underneath it.

She gave him a seductive smile, her hands reaching for the robe belt knot to untie it. She opened the robe and let it fall down to the carpet. She placed her hands on her hips, her head high. She was perfectly comfortable with her naked body.

Thomas stayed where he was, evaluating his options.

"Come closer…" Vera commanded.

He did not act, his eyes staying on hers.

"Did I misjudge your sexuality?" She sauntered towards him and then circled around him before standing right in front him. However, he kept his eyes straight ahead, unimpressed with her nudity and seduction. She looked up at him as he was at least a foot taller. She pressed her palm on his hard chest and whispered, "I hope not…"

He knew he had to say or do something to turn the table. He could not anger her and had to hold the interest of her if he planned to make this operation as productive as possible.

Unexpectedly, he slid his hand into her hair on the back of her head. He fisted her hair, holding her in place, and kissed her hard on her lips.

Vera was surprised but very pleased as his kiss felt so possessive. She kissed him back, her hands snaking up his back, wanting to hold him closer.

Just as she thought she was getting what she wanted, he pulled away, his hand still gripping her hair. He looked into her eyes and said, "I don't shit where I eat." He then let go of her hair and walked out of her suite without waiting for her response.

~ ~ ~

"I am not yours to touch," Thomas said, his voice low and stern.

"Hmm... Are you sure you don't want to reconsider this opportunity I am offering you?" Vera stood up, moving to lean against the wall. "Imagine all the women, money, and power you can have. We can be an amazing team. I can guarantee you that the board will forgive your past behavior and even give us a bigger territory to operate."

Thomas felt sick to his stomach. If he could get out of this alive, he would do his best to help fedpol shut down her operation.

"No?" she asked since Thomas was silent. "Well..." She walked towards the door and stopped halfway. She turned towards Thomas and said in an icy voice, "I think you and your precious whore were screwing under my nose and plotted her escape. And that had cost me a fortune. She was my star. Do you know how much those men had offered to fuck her?" She stared at him.

Thomas threw her a warning glare when she called Iris a whore, but he remained calm, not going to respond to her provocation.

"I am sure you know what a good fuck she is," she said with heavy sarcasm, deliberately provoking him.

Thomas stifled his fury, refusing to flinch at the acidity in her words.

She was frustrated by his equanimity and furious at his indifference to her. There was nothing she could say or do to make this man react to her. She turned and headed to the door. And before she opened the door, she said to him, "I am going to double the ransom, and you had better hope your family has the money."

CHAPTER 9

Thirty one days since the accident

IRIS awoke abruptly, covered with night sweats and feeling disoriented and confused. She had been having those nightmares that she used to have when she was imprisoned in the mansion. In those dreams, she was either lost in the woods, drowning in the ocean, or walking the streets alone at night...

The hospital room was dark, but a couple of night lights were on, illuminating the space. She saw her mother sleeping on the sofa.

Another day and another night... She let out a deep sigh, staring into the darkness. She had lost her sense of time, not sure what day it was. But she did not really care because...Thomas was gone, for good.

She had given up hope because her heart was so broken that she could not handle any disappointment any more. She was also too afraid to feel anything because any emotion would be too much to bear.

Will people die of a broken heart? She had been thinking about the question.

She had wished that she could deaden all her senses and that she could fall asleep and never wake up again. Those wishes were the reasons she welcomed all the medications given to her to numb all her feelings and emotions.

Little one... The image of her son lying in the incubator tormented her. *He doesn't even have a chance to meet his daddy... Will he be all right if he doesn't meet me, either?*

The thought of leaving their son behind and seeking her own

relief terrified her.

What kind of mother am I? She dug her nails into her arms, wanting to feel the pain because physical pain was much more bearable.

"Honey..." Koto whispered, and then her voice became panicky. "What...what are you doing?" She grabbed Iris' wrists and pulled her hands off her arms. Blood was slowly seeping through the small puncture wound. Koto grabbed some tissues from the side table and put them over those wounds to stop the bleeding. Fortunately, those were shallow cuts and already started to dry up.

"Honey..." Koto gazed at Iris, wishing her daughter would give her some responses.

Iris stared at those cuts for a few seconds and then lifted up the blanket over her head, burying herself underneath the blanket again.

Gently, Koto rubbed her daughter's shoulder, tears in her eyes. "Mommy is here. Everything will be all right..." she whispered.

This was not the first time Iris unintentionally hurt herself or did not care if she was hurt. A week ago, Jane spotted blood on Iris' hospital gown because her c-section incision had come apart, but Iris did not care at all.

"Are you in pain? I am calling the nurse now." Jane was so worried.

Iris just stared at her bloody gown, her eyes empty...soulless.

Dr. Beaumont had been working with a psychiatrist to help Iris cope with her depression. And since Iris had completely shut herself down, both doctors were not able to talk to her. They could only used medications to control her condition. And fortunately, Iris was willing to take her medicines.

"DAVID," Louis called before David and his father headed out the door.

"Morning, Louis." David turned around, giving Louis a gentle nod. "We are going to the hospital early today. My mother called. Iris is not doing well this morning."

Louis sighed, wishing what he was going to tell them would bring a little hope to everyone. "Mr. Marseille and his team left for the ransom exchange early this morning."

"Really?" David's eyes widened. He turned towards his father, who was already standing by the car waiting for him, and said in an excited voice, "Dad, Louis has news about Thomas."

Lucas quickly walked back into the house.

"He said Mr. Marseille left for the ransom exchange early this morning," David said to his father.

They knew the kidnappers had finally contacted Mr. Marseille just two days ago and demanded two hundred million euros instead. They were surprised the negotiation went so fast.

"That...that's great!" Lucas said.

Louis nodded at Lucas. "We told Mr. Marseille we would agree to any amount and condition as long as Tommy could be released immediately."

David gently patted his father's shoulder and asked Louis, "So... Do you know if Thomas is coming back today? Or..."

"Hopefully. If everything goes well," Louis replied honestly. "Mr. Marseille has a big team with him, and fedpol's team will be nearby—"

"Fedpol?" Lucas interrupted Louis.

"Tommy used to be one of them. They want to make sure of his safety," Louis said.

"Of course...of course." Lucas nodded.

"Morning..." Eva walked into the foyer, her eyes red. She was just comforting his father-in-law after they heard from Mr. Marseille.

"Morning," both Lucas and David greeted Eva.

"How's Florent? I am sure he is thrilled with the news," Lucas asked Eva.

"He is overwhelmed..." Eva replied, letting out a deep sigh.

"Should we tell Iris about this?" David asked, thinking Eva would know what was best for Iris.

Eva frowned at the question. She gazed at Louis, seeking for thoughts from him.

"I told them we are hoping Tommy will be back today...if

everything goes well." Louis returned her gaze, wrapping his arm around her shoulders.

Eva thought for a few seconds and looked at Lucas and David. "If everything goes well, Mr. Marseille will bring Tommy to the hospital directly. I suggest we wait until Tommy is back…safely."

ACCORDING to the kidnapper's instruction, there would be two black SUVs coming to the specified location after sunrise. Thomas would be in the first car with two armed men, and the second car would be parked fifty meters away with just the driver, who would be armed as well.

Mr. Marseille would receive a phone call instructing him to load the cash into the second car. He negotiated with the kidnappers to have one person from his team to be closer to Thomas, just to make sure the kidnappers would not harm Thomas after they got the money. The kidnappers agreed but stated that the person must stand at least fifteen meters away from Thomas.

After the money was loaded, the driver would check if the bills were authentic and unmarked and also detect tracking devices.

Mr. Marseille knew the kidnappers would be satisfied because he would never jeopardize his missions and his priority was always the safety of the hostages. Furthermore, Thomas' family only wanted his safe return. They did not care if they could get the money back or track down the kidnappers. Fedpol would take over once Thomas was under his protection, therefore his only task was to bring Thomas back to his family safely.

He had been in this profession for decades and had handled many cases that were more complicated and dangerous. However, he executed every operation as if it was the most threatening plight because every life was priceless.

Thomas should be released once everything was checked out and the kidnappers honored the deal without any further demand.

Mr. Marseille was warned the deal would be off and Thomas would get a bullet between his eyes if there was any sign of the police or if Mr. Marseille and his team attempted to ambush or take out any of their men. Mr. Marseille took those warnings seriously because those kidnappers were maniacs and unpredictable. However, he did not just take orders. He made it clear to the kidnappers that he would be prepared if they backed out from their deal or tried to harm or kill Thomas after they got the money. And the consequences were too high for both parties to dishonor their agreement.

Mr. Marseille and his teammates arrived near the specified location before dawn. Four of them, including Mr. Marseille himself, were in a black van with eighteen large duffle bags containing one hundred eighty million euros which was the amount that Louis would be able to amass within such a short period of time and was accepted by the kidnappers. The rest of his teams were spreading out in the surrounding area, out of sight.

Now they waited for the sun to rise.

THOMAS awoke with a start when three guards barged in. He blinked several times, trying to make himself aware of the situation fast.

One of them grabbed his clothes and loafers from the closet and tossed them at him. "Put these on and hurry up!"

Another guard gripped his arm and pulled him out of the bed when Thomas did not comply immediately.

Thomas winced at the sharp pain in his rib cage and slowly put on his clothes. He glanced out the window and found that it was still dark outside.

Where are they taking me at this hour? He wondered. *Execute me?* He shook his head, reminding himself to stay positive.

"Let's go!" One guard pushed him towards the door after he put on his shoes while the other two were walking out of the room.

Thomas followed them down the hall and out of the building through the side door. He did not see anyone around. The farmhouse must have been vacated overnight. He assumed Vera had taken the precaution before releasing him for ransom, in case her hiding location would be exposed.

There were two black SUVs, probably the same ones taking him here days ago, waiting by the door. Both guards walking in front of him took the driver's seats of both cars.

"Get in!" the guard walking behind Thomas commanded, jabbing him at his shoulder with a pistol forcing him towards one car.

Thomas looked over his shoulder and frowned at the handgun pointed at him. He then got into the car obediently.

The guard took out several thick zip-ties from his back pocket and tied Thomas' hands to the handle above the car door and then tied his ankles together.

Thomas took in several deep breaths as it was extremely painful to hold his arms up.

After the guard secured Thomas in place, he got in the car from the other side and sat next to him. And both cars took off at a high speed.

Thomas hoped he was on his way to his freedom and to reunite with his family. He wanted to stay positive but could not shake the fear of not being able to make it back to Iris alive.

They were on the road for quite some time. Dawn was breaking, so Thomas was able to see that they were in a remote area. The car stopped when they reached a hillside by the edge of a lake, but the other car continued going for a great distance before it stopped.

Suddenly, Thomas felt terror-stricken, wondering if they had driven all the way here just to kill him and dump his body in the lake. He tugged on the zip-tie to see if he could break free but was disheartened by how tight it had wrapped around his wrists.

The guard next to Thomas got out, walked around the car, and opened the door. He then pointed the pistol at Thomas.

Is he going to shoot me like this? Thomas stared at the guard, not sure what to expect as the guard just stood next to him.

"They are here. Let's move to the designated spot," Mr. Marseille said to his teammate in the driver's seat.

When their van slowly moved towards the edge of the lake, they saw two black SUVs waiting.

A sound of a moving vehicle caught Thomas' attention. He looked towards the source of the noise and saw a black van moving towards them from the opposite direction. Then it stopped closer to the other SUV.

Are they here for me? Thomas certainly hoped so, although it was still too early to be hopeful because he was not sure who was in the van and what was going to happen.

Through binoculars, Mr. Marseille saw Thomas sitting in the back of the first SUV and both arms were up, probably tied to somewhere in the car. A man was pointing a gun at Thomas, and the driver just stepped out of the car. Mr. Marseille turned his binoculars to the other SUV, about fifty meters away to his right, and saw a man sitting in the driver's seat. Everything looked as the kidnappers had said.

Right on cue, Mr. Marseille's phone rang.

"Talk," Mr. Marseille answered, his tone authoritative and calm.

"Load the money now. Don't play any game or your guy is going to get a bullet between his eyes." The kidnapper ended the call after he finished giving the thread.

Keeping his eyes on the guard pointing a gun at him, Thomas listened closely to what the other guard said on the phone. He immediately felt relieved despite the threat of a bullet in his head. That van was here for him. However, he was still on high alert and hoping the process would go smoothly because his life depended on it.

Mr. Marseille got out of the car and said to his teammates, "Go." He then slowly walked towards Thomas while his teammates drove towards the second SUV.

The driver of the second SUV got out, one hand holding a pistol, and walked around the car to open the rear door. He aimed his gun at the three men delivering the ransom, watching them moving the bags from the van to his car.

Mr. Marseille approached Thomas, keeping his eyes on the man pointing a gun at Thomas.

"Close enough!" the armed man yelled to stop Mr. Marseille from walking any closer.

Mr. Marseille stopped, holding both hands in the air, not wanting to provoke the kidnapper. He glanced at Thomas and could tell he was in bad shape. But there was nothing he could do to help him until he was released. He shifted his eyes back to the armed man and waited for his team to finish the job.

Once Mr. Marseille's team finished loading the money, they stepped aside as instructed.

The driver tucked his gun into the shoulder holster, took out a scanning device from his back pocket, and started to go through every single bag very carefully.

Everyone was quiet, waiting patiently for him to finish his job.

Finally, he zipped up the last bag and shut the door. He took out his phone and called his accomplice, smirking in triumph. "Good to go," he said to the phone. He gave Mr. Marseille's team a smug glare while he marched back to the driver's seat.

When Mr. Marseille saw the armed man taking out a pocket

knife, he drew his gun. He aimed at the man's head, confident that he would not miss his target, even though he was a hundred meters away from it.

Thomas thought they were going to kill him anyway after they got the money when the armed man waved a knife in front of him.

Why not just use the gun? He stared into the man's eyes, feeling defenseless as his hands and legs were tied up.

The man swiftly cut the zip-tie around Thomas' wrists and dragged him out of the car. Thomas' ankles were still tied together, so he tumbled from the car and onto the dirt ground.

The armed man shut the door and jumped into the passenger's seat. And the car took off immediately.

Mr. Marseille ran towards Thomas while his team jumped into the van and rushed to Thomas as well. He squatted next to Thomas and swiftly took out a Swiss knife to cut the zip-tie around Thomas' ankles. He carefully helped him sit up.

"Thomas, my name is Eric Marseille. I am the crisis negotiator working with your family." He introduced himself.

Thomas was still in shock. He breathed heavily, staring at Mr. Marseille, letting those words register in his chaotic mind.

"Than…thank you." Thomas was finally able to talk, his breathing slowing down. *It is finally over…*

"My wife… I have to call my wife," Thomas said, grabbing Mr. Marseille's forearm. He did not know what kind of deal was agreed on between his family and Vera as he did not see any police around. He surely hoped the police would be able to track her down.

Thomas held on to Mr. Marseille and tried to stand up. He winced when he pushed himself up. The fall earlier had worsened his injuries.

"Take it easy," Mr. Marseille said, gently holding Thomas' arm over his shoulder so he could help him stand up.

The van stopped right by them and all three team members jumped out and came to Thomas' aid. They worked together to help Thomas stand on his feet.

"Can you walk?" Mr. Marseille asked.

"Yes." Thomas sounded frustrated, annoyed by how much pain he had throughout his body. "Can I borrow your phone to call my wife?"

"Let's get you in the van first." Mr. Marseille avoided his question.

Thomas did not argue with him as he would not have any strength left to talk to Iris if he stood on his feet for a second longer.

"We are taking you to the hospital right now," Mr. Marseille said to him. He saw the video and knew how badly they had tortured him, so he was impressed by this young man leaning on him now. He had shown no sign of weakness or exhaustion.

"Your wife is in the same hospital. We are—" Mr. Marseille continued to say.

"Wait." Thomas faltered and looked at Mr. Marseille. "Where is my wife? Where are we exactly?" He was locked in that farmhouse for days, not knowing where he was.

"Lugano," Mr. Marseille replied. "Your wife flew back from the States as soon as fedpol pinpointed the kidnapper's phone call."

"I am in Switzerland all this time…" Thomas mumbled. "Let's go." He resumed his steps, eager to get in the van, but the broken ribs and the muscle pain stopped him from moving.

One of Mr. Marseille's teammates perceived Thomas' reaction and rushed to his side to assist him. Slowly, they helped Thomas get in the van.

"I need to call Iris to let her know I am safe now," Thomas said to Mr. Marseille once he sat down.

"Our plane is standing by at the nearest airport. You will be there in no time. And you really need some medical attention first," Mr. Marseille said, assisting Thomas to settle in the seat. He then walked rapidly around the van and sat by Thomas. Once they all got in the car, they were on their way, bringing Thomas back to his family.

Thomas was relieved when Mr. Marseille took out his phone, but Mr. Marseille did not hand him the phone. He made a call instead.

"He is with us now. Here he is," Mr. Marseille said to the person on the other end of the line and then handed Thomas the phone. "It is

Louis."

Thomas put the phone against his ear. "Louis?"

"Tommy…" Louis' voice was trembling. "Hold on. Dad wants to hear your voice."

Thomas was too overwhelmed to respond. He waited…

"Tommy…" Florent's voice was breathy.

"Da…" Thomas could not hold back his emotions when he heard his father's calling, tears scalding his eyes. "I am safe now. You don't have to worry about me anymore."

"That's good… That's good…" Florent had so many things he wanted to say to his son, wanting to tell him how proud he was of him and how much he loved him, but his throat was tight when he tried to control his emotions. "We…we will see you soon, my boy. Here is Louis…"

"Is Iris with you?" Thomas asked once Louis was back on the phone. He was grateful to his brother for everything he had done for his release and he could not thank him enough, but all he wanted now was to talk to Iris. "I need to talk to her now."

"I understand, Tommy…" Louis kept his voice calm, for himself and for his brother as what he was going to tell him might make his brother become more anxious. "She is here. We are all at CHUV waiting for you. Mr. Marseille is taking you here directly."

"I need to talk to her." Thomas could feel his brother was avoiding his request, just like Mr. Marseille had been doing.

Louis let out a deep sigh, knowing how stubborn his little brother was. "First of all, both of them are in good hands—"

"Both? What are you talking about?" Thomas raised his voice. A sudden sharp pain in his rib cage caused him to shut his eyes.

"Iris… She gave birth to a baby boy," Louis said, his voice hesitant.

"A boy… But she is only thirty… No, thirty-two weeks pregnant now." Thomas leaned his elbows on his knees. "A boy?" He suddenly felt overcome with a warm sentiment inside his chest.

"She had an emergency c-section about two weeks ago." Louis paused to wait for Thomas' reaction or question, but Thomas was silent, so he continued, "The baby is healthy and is now in the neonatal intensive care unit."

"I should have been there for them…" Thomas murmured.

"Tommy, you are coming to them now. That is all that matters."

"How is Iris?" Thomas asked.

"She lost a lot of blood that day, but the doctors took good care of her."

Thomas let out a sigh of relief, his hand gripping the phone tightly.

"There's something you need to know." Louis was considering how to tell his brother about Iris' current emotional condition.

"Just tell me." Thomas snapped. He did not mean to be rude to his brother. But the more cautious Louis was, the more frustrated he became.

"She had an emotional meltdown…" Louis trailed off.

Thomas started to breathe heavily. He could not imagine what Iris had gone through.

"She would not…" Louis sighed. "She shut herself off completely. Nobody can get through her. I am so sorry…"

"Did Eva talk to her?" Thomas asked, feeling helpless.

"She tried…" Louis let out another sigh, not sure how to explain to Thomas just how depressed and despairing Iris was.

Thomas suddenly felt worse than when he was almost beaten to death, worse than when the guard pointed a gun at him.

CHAPTER 10

Thirty one days since the accident

IRIS was sitting on the bed, staring out the window aimlessly.

Her insomnia was worsening. She had great difficulty falling asleep, and at the same time she was afraid to go to sleep because those nightmares were too vivid. Sleeping pills could give her dreamless nights, so her psychiatrist increased the dosage. However, the medication had caused her severe headaches, and the constant pain felt like a belt tightening around her head. But she would rather have headaches than nightmares.

The doctor also increased the dosages of her antidepressants because she would unconsciously harm herself. Even though they were never life threatening injuries, her behavior was alarming.

Now she finally felt some calmness as if her brain—or her heart—finally was able to take a break. Nothing saddened her, and nothing excited her either. And that was perfectly fine with her because she felt nothing and nothing was all she wanted now.

Her father and David walked into the room, but Iris did not turn her head. She just did not see the need to. Families and friends came and went. They expressed their sympathy when they first visited her, and then they had nothing else to say because there was nothing left to say.

Lucas leaned in and gave his daughter a hug and kissed her forehead. David followed suit.

Iris never moved her eyes away from the window. She was so tired and numb, and the headache was all she felt.

Lucas and David exchanged a look before Lucas held his wife's hand and led her out of the room.

"Thomas is on his way here," he whispered to Koto once the door was closed.

Koto's both hands flew to her mouth. She burst into tears and fell into her husband's embrace.

"Should we…should we tell her now?" Koto asked Lucas after she finally calmed down.

"I really don't know." Lucas gazed at Koto's watery eyes. "Eva suggested we should wait until Thomas is here."

"I agree…" Koto sighed. "The waiting and expectation are too much for her."

"His family was in the ER now. Jane will be here shortly after she settles the kids." And before Koto asked about their grandchildren, he added, "Mrs. Brun and Mr. Bernard will watch them."

Koto nodded, wanting to go back to the room to be by her daughter's side already. Every time she stepped away from Iris, she felt unsettled and anxious.

"Let's go back inside," Lucas said, knowing how his wife felt.

Koto gave her husband a loving smile and walked back into the room. She stopped when she saw her two children sitting side by side, tears flooding her eyes again.

David was sitting on the bed by Iris, humming a song softly. His arms were wrapped around her shoulders, and his head was leaned against hers.

Koto remembered when David first met his newborn baby sister, he was in tears. He adored her and often held her in his arms, humming songs to pamper her.

David noticed his parents were back in the room. He kissed Iris' temple and got out of the bed. When he saw his mother's watery eyes, he held her in his arms and whispered, "Everything will be all right now…"

Lucas and David left the room together, and Koto sat in the armchair by Iris' bedside. She gazed at her daughter, hoping today was also the day when Iris would come back to them.

Little did Iris know that their close families and friends had come to the hospital when they heard the news. They were now anxiously gathering in the emergency room, waiting for Thomas' arrival.

IT was twenty minutes ago when Mr. Marseille called Louis to let him know they had landed at Airport Lausanne, which was about ten minutes away from the hospital.

"He is here." Louis just received another call from Mr. Marseille. He walked out of the emergency room, followed by the rest of the families and friends. Two nurses and a resident had already stood by the entrance with an emergency room gurney.

A black town car slowly pulled up to the entrance.

Florent found himself trembling with emotion. His eyes were stung by hot tears when the back door was opened and his son saw him and gave him a warm smile. Then his view was soon blocked by the doctor and nurses assisting Thomas to step out of the car and get on the gurney.

Thomas was surprised to see his in-laws and some of their friends, but how much he wished his wife was here now.

Not all of them knew Thomas was brutally beaten, so they were shocked when they saw the bruises and cuts on his face and arms and how he limped heavily when he got out of the car. Louis and Eva had watched the entire video, so they were prepared. However, when they saw him, they were still overcome with emotion.

They all stood aside, giving Thomas supportive smiles, and let the hospital staff do their job.

Louis wrapped one arm around his father's shoulders and interlocked his hand with Eva's. "We will see you inside," he said to his little brother when he was rolled into the emergency room.

A detailed exam was followed by X-rays and a CT scan, and then Thomas was treated for open wounds. He was going crazy when he was told to wait for the results in the emergency room.

Iris and their son were just upstairs, but he could not go to them.

Eva came to see him and explained Iris' condition to him. She advised him how he should approach her and encouraged him to be patient.

And finally, after almost three hours since he was brought in, the emergency room doctor, who treated him earlier, came to his bedside to explain the results.

Four ribs had cracks, and his left jaw, left thigh bone, and several ribs had hairline fractures. The good news was the CT scan showed no internal bleeding. And the ecchymosis, the large deeply bruising area right below the rib cage, would need to be observed. More tests would be needed if it got worse.

"I want to see my wife," he said right away when the doctor finished, not caring about his own injuries at all.

"We will arrange that as soon as we move you to your room," the doctor replied. He knew what had happened to Thomas and was going to help him as much as he could. "Congratulations on your baby boy," he said to Thomas. "Dr. Beaumont asked me to tell you that your son is doing wonderfully."

"Thank you. Can I...can I see him?" Thomas' voice became soft.

"That can be arranged as well." The doctor gave him a smile. "I will have the nurses take care of that right away." The doctor nodded at Florent and Louis before he walked away.

"That little boy is a fighter," Florent said to Thomas.

"**ARE** you coming?" Jasmine asked Marcus.

Marcus shook his head and said, "Go ahead and spend some time with her." He gently gave her a hug and kissed her forehead.

He flew in two weeks ago after Jasmine informed him about Iris' emergency c-section. He wanted to be here for his fiancé. What Iris and Thomas were going through had made him realize how important it was to cherish what he had, and Jasmine was the most important thing in his life now.

Jasmine nodded and headed out of the waiting room. She walked past David and Jane and gave them both warm hugs before leaving the room.

The waiting room was crowded but quiet. Their families and friends had moved from the ER to the waiting room now while Thomas was being treated.

"He is visiting the baby now," Louis said to the crowd when he walked in with his father.

Adeline immediately walked up to Florent and embraced him.

Jane could not hold back her tears anymore. She buried her face in David's chest and sobbed.

Lucas pressed his clenched hand over his mouth, suppressing his overwhelming emotion. Marcus was sitting by Lucas. He gently patted his shoulder.

James leaned his head against Tim's shoulder, their eyes brimming with tears.

Thomas' close friends and formal colleagues let out deep sighs of relief, some hugging each other.

THOMAS put on an isolation gown and was wheeled into the NICU by a nurse. He saw his son right away because Eva was waiting for him by his son's incubator.

"He...he is so small..." Thomas was choked with emotion.

"Would you like to touch him?" the nursery nurse asked.

"Can I? I mean he is so small." He sounded hesitant as his son looked so fragile.

"Of course," the nurse gave him a bright smile and pulled out a pair of gloves by the incubator for Thomas. "You can talk to him, too. Let him hear your voice."

He put on the gloves and slowly put his hands through the two holes. Using just one finger, he gently rubbed his son's hand.

The baby responded to his touch. His tiny hand opened and closed as if he was trying to grab what was touching him.

Thomas moved his finger to his son's palm, and the baby immediately held on to it. His heart pounded violently in his chest, tears submerging his eyes.

How can such a little thing have this kind of impact on me? Thomas was in awe. He felt his heart was not big enough to hold the love he had for his son. He thought his love for Iris was so great and almost unbearable, but what he was feeling right now was extraordinary. *Love* was not enough to describe it. It was pride, a sense of contentment, and so much more.

"He was born underweight. However, over the past two weeks he has grown so much. He is a very healthy baby," the nurse said.

"*Ma puce...* Mommy did an amazing job, didn't she?" he whispered to his little boy, still not able to believe their son was right in front of him now. He remembered he and Iris had a conversation about their child just the day before the accident...

~ ~ ~

"Our child..." Thomas paused and placed a tender kiss on Iris' belly. "...will definitely be multilingual," he continued with an endearing smile. He was already in a loving and proud father mode, even though the due date was still more than two months away.

Tenderly rubbing Iris' growing belly, he added, "I will teach him or her French, German, Italian, and English. And you, my love..." He turned his head, winked at his wife, and continued, "...can cover American English." He gave her a mischief grin and added, "Your mother will be in charge of Chinese and Japanese. And... Oh wait. Your father speaks Norwegian or Swedish, eh?"

"Eh?" Iris chuckled. "Would you like to teach the kid Canadian English?"

It took him a minute to realize her sardonic remark.

"*Touché, mon amour. Touché.*"

~ ~ ~

"I need to see Iris now," he said to Eva.

Thomas was wheeled into the waiting room by a nurse, Eva right by his side.

Jane leaned in and gave him a gentle hug while Lucas and David patted him on his shoulders.

"Mom and Jasmine are in the room with her," Jane said to Thomas.

Thomas nodded and scanned the room, giving everyone a smile expressing his gratitude.

"May I?" Jane asked the nurse, wishing to take over the wheelchair.

The nurse nodded and stepped aside.

Jane slowly pushed Thomas towards Iris' room, which was at the end of the hallway. When they arrived at the very last door, she gently knocked on the closed door before she opened it slowly. She did not walk in but beckoned to her mother-in-law and Jasmine.

Quietly, Koto and Jasmine walked out of the room, and tears gushed out when they saw Thomas. Koto gently gave him a hug, her body trembling. Jasmine leaned in and gave him kisses on the cheeks.

"I would like to go in by myself…" Thomas said to Koto just above a whisper.

Koto nodded, a smile spreading across her face.

Jasmine held the door open for Thomas so he could wheel himself into the room. He winced when he placed his hands against the hand rims.

Koto stepped closer, wanting to help him, but he gave her a gentle smile and shook his head. He took a deep breath and pushed the wheels forward. Slowly, he pushed himself through the door.

Jasmine gently closed the door, one hand wiping tears off her cheeks.

Thomas slowly moved towards the bed. He saw a body shape curing up in a fetal position underneath a blanket. His heart was palpitating when he was moving closer to his Iris.

He parked the wheelchair by her bedside and reached his hand out, wanting to touch her. Then he stopped suddenly, his hand right above Iris' petite frame.

She is extremely fragile and easily startled. You must approach her with caution. Eva's words were playing in his head.

He pulled his hand back and whispered softly instead, "Mon amour…"

Thomas? Iris heard a voice. *Am I going crazy? I am hearing his voice…* She let out a deep sigh. *I think I've finally lost my mind…*

Thomas heard her sighing and saw a gentle moment underneath the blanket, but she was still in the same position and not responding.

"Iris..." He tried again, calling her in a soft voice.

Oh, god... No... Iris covered her ears, believing she was hallucinating, tears flowing down. She missed his voice so much, but at the same time she was so scared that she had gone insane and was fearful of being trapped in this dark hole forever.

Thomas saw her trembling, his heart aching. He gently lifted the blanket up and looked underneath.

There she is... He gazed at the love of his life and the mother of his son. Slowly, he pulled the blanket away, revealing her beautiful face.

Iris squeezed her eyes shut, spurning the bright light, and reached her arms out to pull the blanket back.

"Mon amour..." Thomas put his hand on her arm gently. "It is me, Thomas."

Iris froze. She opened her eyes and stared at the face in front of her. She blinked her eyes rapidly.

Thomas? She frowned.

But... The jaw is so swollen. The face is covered with cuts and bruises. She studied the face more carefully.

So scruffy... Then she recognized that pair of the most beautiful blue eyes she had ever seen.

Why are they filled with tears? She reached her hands out and gently cupped his face.

"Don't cry..." she whispered.

Thomas could no longer hold back his emotions. He leaped to his feet and embraced her in his arms.

Iris breathed sharply in his embrace.

Is this real? She froze.

Thomas completely forgot about the pain when he stood up so quickly and held Iris in his arms. When he slowly loosened his embrace, he groaned as painkillers could only do so much.

Iris frowned, looking at his painful expression. She moved her body backward and patted on the bed, inviting him. She was still in shock, her eyes fixed on his face.

He smiled, climbed onto the bed, and pulled the blanket over their bodies. He wrapped his arms around her while she nestled herself safely in his embrace. None of them said a word. They simply listened to each other's breathing and heart beats.

The past few weeks felt like a lifetime. They were both enervated.

Finally, they both drifted off to sleep peacefully.

CHAPTER 11

IRIS was sitting in a recliner in the NICU, holding their tiny pinkish miracle skin to skin upright on her chest. She was cuddling him and keeping his temperature with her body heat.

"*Je t'aime, je t'aime toujour.* I am forever yours. Sweet dreams, sweet dreams *mon cher...*" Softly, she was singing Kelly Sweet's *Je t'aime* to her baby boy, and the baby's eyes were wide open, seemingly focusing on his mommy's voice.

Sitting by his wife and son, Thomas felt content. He fixed his eyes on his son's adorable face, his hand gently caressing Iris' arm.

They were both discharged from the hospital more than three weeks ago. Initially, Iris refused to leave without their baby, but there was nothing she could do as her little one was still too weak to go home, and the hospital was not a hotel after all. They stayed in the château and went back to the hospital everyday to bond with their baby boy.

The baby was more than five weeks old now. Although he still had a breathing tube taped on his face, he was able to drink from a bottle already. When Iris fed him for the first time, she was so nervous that the nurse had to hold her hands. How much she wished she could breastfeed him, but her milk had dried up because she had never had a chance to do that after her little one was born.

"This little guy needs a name," Thomas whispered.

Iris looked at him, wondering if Thomas would like—or even approve—the name of which she had been thinking. Then she was captivated by his blue gaze, already forgetting what he just said. She still wondered from time to time if she was hallucinating and if he was really back....

~ ~ ~

That day when he was in her hospital bed, holding her in his arms, she had a dreamless and peaceful sleep. But when she awoke and felt arms wrapped around her, she flinched and instinctively tried to fight off whomever was holding her.

Thomas was woken by Iris' sudden and unexpected reaction.

"Shh... It is me..." He held her tight, whispering in her ear.

"Get off me!" She struggled.

"Look at me. Iris, look at me." He kept his voice calm. "It is me. Thomas."

"No..." She kept her eyes shut, her heart beating violently, "He is not coming back..."

"I am back." He moved one hand to her chin and lifted her face. "Open your eyes, my love."

She stayed still, refusing to open her eyes, her breathing heavy.

Is he really back? What if he disappears when I open my eyes? I cannot handle another disappointment... She shook her head, tears seeping through her closed eyes.

"That's all right..." He held her tight in his arms. "Whenever you are ready, my love. I am not going anywhere."

After moments of silence, she whispered in his arms, "Thomas?"

"Yes..."

"Will you leave me again?"

"Never..."

"Promise?"

"Promise..."

Her body started quivering. She broke down and sobbed.

~ ~ ~

"Would you like to share with me what's in your mind?" Thomas' voice brought Iris back to the present.

She blinked several times and smiled at him, hesitation in her eyes.

"Or should I guess?" He moved his hand to her face and stroked her soft cheek.

"I... What about..." She paused, deciding just to blurt it out. "Maximilien... Bébé Max..."

Thomas became still, surprised by the name she just said.

"You…you don't like it?" she whispered.

"Maximilien Thomas Torian." He turned to gaze at their little boy, mumbling the name.

"I…" Her eyes landed on their son as well. "Max is very special to me."

"I think it is perfect," he said, a smile spreading across his face.

Her smile matched his when she whispered to her son, "My Maxipoo…"

Thomas laughed quietly, amused that Iris had already nicknamed their son.

They spent another thirty minutes with their son before a nurse walked up to them. Reluctantly, Iris handed her Maxipoo to the nurse and watched her walking away with him and putting him back in his incubator.

Thomas reached for her hand and said, "He will be ready to go home soon."

"I know…" She took a deep breath and gave him a forced smile. "Shall we?" She stood up, reaching out for his hand.

He nodded and put his hands on both armrests to push himself up. He winced when he lifted his chest up high and engaged his abdominal muscles to ascend from the seated position.

Iris quickly stepped closer and wrapped her arm around his waist to be his crutch.

"Thanks," he whispered, putting one arm around her shoulder, and balanced himself on both feet.

Iris bowed her head to hide her sad expression from him. His doctor told them he would make a full recovery, but it still hurt to see him in pain.

"Hey…" Thomas whispered to Iris, knowing she was trying to be strong for him and she did not want him to see her watery eyes. "I am all right."

Iris nodded, remembering how shattered she was when she first saw his injuries…

~ ~ ~

The hospital put Iris and Thomas in the same room as they

refused to be separated. She could not handle him being out of her sight, even when Thomas needed to use the bathroom. She was too overwhelmed by his return to notice how badly he was harmed.

One evening, Thomas took a shower and stayed in the bathroom a bit longer. Iris started pacing the room, her eyes fixed on the bathroom door. She wanted to help him, but he declined.

She stopped her pacing when the water was turned off and stood in front of the door, waiting for him eagerly.

Why is he taking so long? She became impatient, so she knocked on the door. "Are you all right?"

"Ye...yes... Just a minute..." he answered, his voice a bit out of breath.

She frowned, worried about him. "Let me help you."

"I am... I am all right. Just giv—"

Iris could not wait any longer, so she opened the door. "Just let me—" She stilled, shocked by the massive bruising on his abdomen and left thigh.

He quickly dropped the bandage in his hands and grabbed a fresh patient gown on the shelves.

She slowly walked towards him, staring at his abdomen, while he was putting on the gown.

"It looks worse than it is..." He looked at her troubled face.

She put her hands on top of the thin fabric, afraid to touch him, afraid that she would hurt him.

"I am all right." He held her hands and pressed them down on his body. "See. It doesn't hurt at all."

She looked up and met his soft blue eyes. "How? These...these are not from the accident, are they?" It had been more than a month since the car crash, and her own injury had already healed. Either he was badly injured during the crash or... The thought of him being brutally tortured in captivity made her weak in the knees.

The desperation in her eyes pained him more than his own physical injuries. He caught her and held her in his arms. He could feel her body trembling. "Shh..." He kissed her hair and whispered endearments.

~ ~ ~

"Ready?" Thomas interlocked their fingers, bringing Iris back from her thoughts.

She nodded, pushing aside her low-spirited mood and giving him a bright smile.

He returned her smile and kissed her hair, and they slowly walked out of the NICU.

THOMAS walked out of the bathroom, a towel wrapped around his hips. Instead of walking into the closet to put on pajama pants, he walked towards Iris, who was reading on the bed. He sat down on the edge of the bed next to her.

Iris smiled, sensing his proximity, but her eyes stayed on the page.

He leaned in and kissed her cheek.

She focused on her reading, her smile broader.

He moved lower and placed a kiss on her bare shoulder. "We named our son today," he said, moving her hair aside and trailing his kisses to her neck. "We should celebrate."

She giggled, feeling ticklish.

He grabbed the book and tossed it away, nibbling at her earlobe.

"Hey…" She protested. "I am in the middle—" Her words turned into a moan.

His finger hooked one strap of her silk babydoll nightie and slowly pulled it over her shoulder.

"Wait…" she whispered, her hands pressing on his hard chest. "You…you…" She moved away from his kisses.

He frowned, giving her puppy eyes.

"You are still in pain…" She gently touched his freshly shaved face.

"Only when I put weight on my left leg." He leaned in, eager to catch her lips.

But she stopped him and sat up straight.

"Mon amour…" He was surprised as she had never rejected him before.

Seeing the disappointment and perplexity in his eyes, she quickly said, "I...I don't want to hurt you."

"You won't." He grinned. He took her hands pressing on his chest and kissed them.

"You just said it hurts if you put weight on your left leg."

"You can be on top..."

She blushed as that was her favorite position. She had craved sex more since she became pregnant, and Thomas definitely did not disappoint her. The last time they made love was that morning before he was kidnapped. She still remembered him scooping her from behind when she was half awake, caressing her baby bump. His hand slowly moved between her thighs and gently rubbed her, arousing her, making her wet. She put her hand over his and when he moved his hand away, she continued to touch herself. When he entered her, an orgasm happened almost immediately.

But now... Her sex drive was *non-existent*...

Is it because I already gave birth? She wondered so many times.

Thomas slid one hand behind her neck and leaned forward to kiss her.

"Let...let's wait..." She pulled back, averting her eyes. She felt so disappointed in herself. She missed their intimacy so much, but she was just not in the mood—or never was since the accident.

Thomas bowed his head, letting out a loud sigh.

"I am sorry..." she whispered. "It's just..." She had no words to explain her loss of libido.

He sat up straight and cupped her face with his hands, bringing her eyes to meet his. "Don't be," he said and placed a kiss on her lips softly. "We will get there..."

She could see his disappointment in his eyes and forced smile.

Thomas embraced her in his arms, inhaling her floral scent. The closeness only made him harder, made him want her even more. But she was not ready...for whatever reason she had.

"I will be back..." he whispered in her ear and dipped a kiss on her temple. He stood up, letting out a quiet sigh.

Iris bit her bottom lip, watching Thomas walk away. He might grimace with pain when he tried to stand, but he no longer limped when he walked. Although his movements were still slow, they were relaxed and assertive.

Thomas walked into the bathroom, closed and locked the door behind him. He stood in front of the vanity, both hands pressing on the countertop.

Is it because of her depression? Her PTSD?

He was able to talk to Eva a couple of times when Iris was sleeping. Eva was absolutely concerned about Iris' clingy behavior, and she encouraged him to be patient. Furthermore, she reminded him that while his police and undercover training had helped him handle all situations in captivity, Iris was vulnerable and traumatized by his kidnapping, the emergency c-section, and the possibility of losing both him and their baby. Her withdrawal was her way to protect herself from drowning in despair while her little family was being torn apart.

Thomas let out a deep breath, his hands clenched into fists. He would be patient for as long as it took, but he missed her so much. He missed her carefree laughters, sexy and adorable winks she gave him spontaneously, and her blazing passion that she had never shied away from showing him since they rekindled their attraction for each other.

When he met Iris, her strength and braveness had filled him with nostalgia for Laila. His inclination to protect her was so overwhelming that he had gone to any length to keep her safe.

When he saw the vulnerability in her eyes while they were enjoying the sunset near Rosengarten Park, it was clear to him that what he felt was not just an infatuation or compassion. He not only wanted to ease her pain and fear but also was eager to make her feel safe and happy.

When tears flooded her eyes and rolled down her cheeks while she was looking at him, his heart ached as he knew what she wanted to tell him. He understood why she was still feeling desolate even though she was physically safe. It was because she was still trapped in those nightmares, scared and helpless. He embraced her, wanting to forevermore keep her in his arms.

After she flew home and he started working for his family, the separation made him realize how much he wanted her in his life. He was determined to win her back, and the reward was more than he had expected. She brought happiness, excitement, and so much love into his life.

Thomas broke into a bright smile when he remembered what she did on his last birthday....

~ ~ ~

"Five hours top. I promise." Thomas could not take the day off on his birthday, but he promised his newly wedded wife that he would be home as soon as the meetings were over.

Iris pouted and kissed him goodbye.

After his assistant Travis, who he hired after Victoria resigned, briefed him on his schedule for the day, he dived into work right away with intent to leave work in just a couple of hours.

"Thomas." Travis knocked on the door.

"Come in," Thomas said, his eyes staying on the document on the computer screen.

Travis opened the door but did not walk in. "Everything is set up in the conference room for your ten-thirty."

"Thank you, Travis." Thomas turned his head to give his assistant an appreciative smile. He glanced at his watch and said to his assistant, "Please hold all the calls."

"Yes," Travis replied and closed the door.

Thomas resumed what he was doing, wanting to finish reviewing the proposal presented by Mr. Nelson, a hotelier who was eager to affiliate his New York hotel with DeMont Enterprise. Thomas rejected his proposition last year, and the new proposal was much more acceptable this time. It would be a good investment, and he needed to make his decision soon.

He was concentrating on the document and was startled when his phone rang. He was going to ignore it at first, but when he saw Iris' grinning face on the screen, he picked up his phone right away.

FaceTime video? He answered the call and saw her beautiful smile. "Ma chérie..." He smiled back.

"Hi..." She grinned, just like the photo on his phone. "Are you busy?" she asked, her voice a little shy.

"Never too busy for you," he said, leaning back in his chair.

"You alone?" she whispered.

"Yes…" he whispered back, not sure why she was whispering.

"Good," she said, blushing.

God, she is so adorable, he thought, wishing he could have stayed at home. "Why are we whispering?" he asked.

"I…" she seemingly moved around, but he could not see as she was holding the phone really close to her face. "I want to give you one of your birthday presents now."

"One of my birthday presents?" He was intrigued. "Now?"

She nodded, turning her head around as if she was trying to sit down.

"Okay…" He did not know what to expect. *Did she decorate the apartment?*

"You ready?" she asked, facing him now. Her expression was a mixture of excitement and nervousness.

"Yes…" He focused on the screen, ready to be surprised.

Iris slowly moved the phone away from her. It looked like the phone was on a stand or something and she was pushing it further away from her.

"*Je pense que j'hallucine!*" in French Thomas blurted 'I must be hallucinating.'

She was lounging on the bed in a black lace teddy, garter belt, and stockings. She licked her upper lip and winked at him.

He felt his pants becoming tighter. "I… Wow…" He brought his phone closer. "I really wish I could see this present in person."

"You will when you come home. But…" She teased him by quickly opening and closing her knees, flashing him what was between her legs.

"That…" He became speechless when he caught a glimpse of the crotch. It was crotchless.

"Do you like what you see?" she asked, moving her hand between her thighs.

He blinked several times before he was able to respond, "Give me a second. Don't move. Keep that thought. And…and the position." He put the phone down and heard Iris' surprised voice saying 'What? What are you doing?'

He got up and walked swiftly to the door. He locked the door and walked back to his chair. He picked up the phone again and saw her furrowed brows. "I had to lock the door," he quickly explained. "So... What's your question again?"

She burst out laughing and brought a smile to his face. As much as she was trying to act seductively in that sexy lingerie, she could not hide her playfulness.

"I love what I am seeing very much," he said to her, his eyes focusing on her face, which was turning rosy.

She gave him a bashful smile and lowered her eyes, avoiding his intense blue gaze.

"That's a good tease, Mrs. Torian," he said, ready to end the call as he thought that was all she had planned to show him. He wished he could rush home now and have all the fun he could have with her in that crotchless teddy.

She turned her face to look at him again. The playfulness in her eyes was replaced by an alluring expression with a little hesitation. She slowly opened her legs, her hand reaching between them.

"Ma chérie..." He could feel his heart beating harder and faster when he saw her starting to touch herself.

She shut her eyes, her hips synchronizing with her fingers.

Thomas unzipped his pants and tugged his brief down, freeing the painful erection he had. He started stroking himself, his eyes fixed on the screen.

"Thom...Thomas..." she whispered his name, her voice breathless. Her movement began to intensify.

"Yes, babe..." He responded to her moan, his eyes not able to move away from the screen or even blink. He watched her reaching her peak and letting out a loud moan.

He stroked himself faster and harder, shutting his eyes and finishing himself right after her. When he opened his eyes, he saw that Iris was lying on her stomach and smiling at him.

The entire experience was mind-blowing. He was so aroused and astounded.

"I assume you like your present..." she said, winking at him.

"You are killing me, *ma chérie*."

"Good," she said. "So, I will see you when you get home. Love you. Bye~" She reached her hand out to tap her phone and ended the video call.

"Wait—" He wanted to stop her, but she had disappeared from the screen. He shook his head when he saw the mess he just made. He got out of the chair and walked into the en suite.

~ ~ ~

Thomas still remembered Iris' mischievous expression when she ended the call and she was waiting for him on the sofa wearing the same lingerie when he got home that afternoon.

CHAPTER 12

IRIS was feeling restless as Thomas had been on the phone with his former supervisor—not Julia but Julia's supervisor—in the study all afternoon. She was getting worried about what fedpol would want from him and getting impatient as they were supposed to be on their way to the hospital to pick up their son already.

Bébé Max had responded well to all treatments and continued to gain weight like a champ, so his doctor decided to discharge him.

Iris and Thomas had first planned to bring their son *home*— their home at Lake Neuchâtel. And then they decided the family château was a better idea for the time being because not only was their home an hour away, but the nursery was also not finished. Furthermore, Thomas was brought back to the château after he was born, so bringing their son back to this family home was especially meaningful.

Finally, Thomas walked out of the study and into the sunroom, where his family and Iris were waiting for him.

Iris' family and friends flew back home more than a week ago as the crisis was over. Her mother had the hardest time to say goodbye, and Iris promised her they would visit them as soon as the baby was good for traveling.

"Is everything all right?" Florent asked when Thomas walked in.

"Yes," Thomas replied and sat down next to Iris, who immediately interlocked their fingers and nestled in his arms. He kissed her hair and then turned to his family. "They recovered most of the ransom and tracked down several men working for Vera," he spoke so calmly as if they were not his kidnappers and assailants. Then, he sighed and looked at Iris. "They did not catch her."

Iris frowned, burying her face in his chest. She loathed Vera so much, and after knowing she was the one behind Thomas' kidnapping, she hated her with a passion.

"Shouldn't you go to the hospital now?" Eva said, changing the subject to lighten up the mood.

"Are you sure you don't want us to go with you?" Louis asked.

Iris looked up at Thomas, giving him a smile.

"Let's bring him home," Thomas whispered to her and turned to his family. "We got this. Just have the welcome party ready for him."

They had been relying on Leon, their chauffeur, for weeks because of Thomas' injuries. However, bringing their son home was too personal and special, they wanted to do this themselves. And since Thomas had been back behind the wheels for almost a week now, it worked out perfectly.

They walked hand in hand towards his Bentley Continental. The top was on, and a black infant car seat was secured in the back seat.

Everything went smoothly at the hospital.

Thomas carefully snapped the infant car seat in which Bébé Max was cradled safely and comfortably onto its base. Iris got into the backseat and sat next to their baby. Thomas leaned forward to give Iris a kiss before he closed the door and got into the driver seat. He looked at his family from the rear view mirror, feeling content. The car crash, his kidnapping, and their injuries were all forgotten as if the past two and a half months had never happened.

When Iris noticed Thomas did not start the car, she raised her gaze from her Maxipoo to Thomas and met his doting eyes in the rear view mirror.

"*Je t'aime,*" she whispered to him.

As they drove past the front gate of the château, they immediately noticed that the trees on both sides of the road were decorated with baby blue ribbons.

They both laughed.

"Louis took the welcome home party seriously." Iris chuckled.

When they turned the corner and the manor house came into view, they saw its façade was decorated with different shades of blue ribbons and balloons and the front door was covered with a huge baby blue balloon arch.

"Wow…" Iris was astonished at the scene.

Thomas laughed out loud, surprised and touched by what his family had done to welcome Max home.

"Owh…own…" Suddenly, Bébé Max made some sounds, his face twisting, seemingly not happy about his sleep being disturbed.

"*Désolé, ma puce,*" Thomas whispered an apology to his son.

"Shh…" Iris gently rubbed the baby's chest with her fingers and started to hum the song she sang to him when she visited him at the NICU.

Bébé Max made a couple more sounds and fell back to sleep.

Thomas glanced at the rear view mirror and saw Iris' soothing expression, a smile spreading across his face but his brow also furrowing.

Now that the baby is home, maybe she will get better, he thought, turning his eyes back on the road.

He had witnessed how Iris continued to battle with her depression and anxiety. Her fear of losing him and the baby was still giving her nightmares even though he was right by her side and very much alive.

Dr. Fournier, the psychiatrist who had been treating Iris since she arrived at the hospital, was able to start psychotherapy since Iris was willing to talk now. And Thomas had been accompanying Iris to all her sessions because she refused to do anything without him by her side.

"Wow… Look," he whispered, not wanting to waken the baby again when he saw his family, the whole household, and many staff from the vineyard and stable were waiting outside the front door.

Iris moved her eyes away from her son and saw what had surprised Thomas. "Wow…" She let out a sigh of surprise as well.

Her maternal instinct kicked in immediately. She turned back her baby and gently tugged his little knit hat down to cover his ears and pulled the blanket over his ears as well to muffle the sounds that might disturb him.

When they pulled up to the front door, many of them started to clap their hands. Louis walked up to the car and opened the door for Iris, the cheering erupting.

Thomas jumped out of the car, giving the crow a radiant smile. He opened the back door and carefully took the infant car seat out. When the cheering was becoming louder, he quickly put his index finger on his lips, signaling the crowd to be quiet.

Instantly, everyone was silent, some covering their mouths with their hands, some clapping silently.

Thank you, Thomas mouthed his appreciation to the crowd while he slowly walked around the car and joined Iris.

This is what I have been dreaming of... Iris thought, looking at Thomas, a proud daddy, walking towards her with their son.

Florent walked closer to the couple and looked down at his grandchild. He whispered softly, "Welcome home, Bébé Max..."

"Salut pépère," Thomas replied 'hi Grandpapa' in French for his son.

Florent broke out in laughter, feeling proud, happy, and gratified.

"We have more people waiting inside," Eva said.

"More people?" Both Thomas and Iris responded in unison.

Eva did not say anything. She and Louis ushered them into the house and towards the sunroom. The rest of the household and staff followed them into the house and went into the kitchen and adjoining informal dining room to continue the celebration.

"Surprise!" Cheers came out from the surround sound speakers of the room when they walked into the sunroom.

Thomas and Iris looked around and were surprised to see Iris' family and friends on the big screen TV.

"How... I mean... Wow..." Iris stared at the TV, watching everyone waving at them.

"Auntie, I want to see the baby!" Little Jenny was jumping up and down in front of her parents.

"Hi Jenny... Okay..." Iris smiled at her niece. She did not expect them to arrange the video call to welcome Maxipoo home together.

"There he is..." Thomas lifted up the car seat and faced the TV.

The room was immediately filled with voices expressing

admiration.

"He is the cutest baby!" Jenny screeched.

Then suddenly, everyone became quiet when Bébé Max burst out crying. Thomas quickly put the car seat down on the coffee table and gently picked up the baby. He held him in his arms, slowly rocking and pacifying his son.

My most beautiful man and baby. And I almost lost them both… Iris was mesmerized by the image.

THOMAS nervously handed Bébé Max to his brother. "Be careful," he said. "Put…put your hand behind his neck and head. Like this…"

"I got it. I got it!" Louis was sitting on the sofa, gently holding the baby on his lap.

Eva gazed at her husband, trying to hold back a laughter by sipping her wine.

Florent and Adeline were cuddling on a sofa, watching the two brothers handling the tiny baby.

The celebration lasted for hours. The Torian household were enjoying a feast for dinner specially prepared by Mrs. Carson, and the faraway family and friends in the States were having an outdoor barbeque for lunch, chatting and laughter filling the air.

"I think I am going to lie down," Iris whispered to Thomas, her eyes fixed on her precious boy, who was pouting his tiny lips, grasping his Uncle Louis' finger, and looking adorable.

"Are you all right?" Thomas asked in a concerned voice.

She gave him a smile and a gentle nod and left the room without saying anything to the rest of the family, feeling sick with exhaustion. For some reason, the walk to the bedroom seemed so much longer. She dragged her feet and climbed the stairs with all the strength within her.

Dr. Beaumont ensured her that there was no permanent damage caused by the bleeding and told her *resting* was the best remedy. However, she felt otherwise…

She was tired all the time and had no energy or interest to talk or socialize, not even with her mother, who had been by her side since day one.

Maybe it was psychological stress, Iris wondered.

Dr. Fournier also told her to rest and prescribed several medications for her anxiety, depression, and insomnia. She felt like she was back in the time when she was first diagnosed with PTSD and all her progress had gone out of the window.

Finally, she reached her destiny. She went into the en-suite and took her medications first and then crawled into bed. She hid herself underneath the duvet, feeling exhausted and lightheaded.

Now that Bébé Max is home, maybe I can really rest and get better now…

"Mon amour," Thomas called softly, trying to wake up Iris.

She blinked her eyes several times and saw a pair of doting blue eyes. "Hi…" She gave him a smile and asked, "What time is it?"

"A little after eight."

"Eight in the morning?" She frowned.

Thomas chuckled, lying down next to her. "Yes, eight in the morning."

"Wow…" She was surprised that she slept through the night.

"You were in such a deep sleep when we came in last night. I didn't want to waken you," he said and leaned in to kiss her.

She turned her face and let him kiss her cheek instead of lips. "Let me brush my teeth first," she said, rolling away from him and getting out of the bed. Morning-breath had never been a problem for her, but she just…just… She did not know why she suddenly felt so self-conscious.

Halfway to the bathroom, she changed her mind and scurried towards the crib by the window.

Thomas narrowed his eyes, but he immediately pushed aside negative thoughts, got out of the bed, and followed her.

Maxipoo… Iris let out a sigh of contentment when she saw her baby sleeping quietly in the beautiful vintage crib, which Florent had placed in the room and told them that all his three children had slept in it. Iris gently caressed her son's cheek with a finger, a soft smile crossing her face.

Suddenly, she flinched when Thomas wrapped his arms around her.

"Are you all right?" he asked, stepping aside.

She took a deep breath and turned to face him. She gave him a forced smile and rested her forehead on his broad chest.

I am not sure... she thought.

He put his hand under her chin and lifted her face to look at him. "Je t'aime..." he whispered and bent his head to kiss her

She let his lips touch hers lightly before she pulled away, and the bewilderment in his eyes saddened her. Since they met, she had never rejected his affection, and they could hardly get their hands off each other...

What is happening to me? She buried her face in his chest. "I am sorry..."

CHAPTER 13

IRIS was checking over the murals she just finished in the nursery: endless vineyard, clear blue sky, and many colorful air balloons.

A small air balloon wicker basket filled with stuffed animals was on the floor, ready to be hung from the ceiling, where she had painted a huge air balloon.

They came back a week ago, and she regretted that she did not have the room ready before they brought their son home. So she jumped right in and worked on the room everyday to transfer the images in her head to the artwork in the room.

She took a long, deep breath and sat down on the carpet covered with plastic paint tarp, a lethargy lying heavily on her. She did not think she had worked that hard, but she felt her body and brain were going to shut down soon.

Dr. Beaumont and Dr. Fournier both told her to have plenty of rest, but she was just so sick of being tired and sleepy all the time.

Her phone dinged, indicating a text message. She wiped paint off her hands on her sweatpants before picking it up.

Walking into the kitchen, Iris said to Thomas, "Eva just texted me. She would like to pay us a visit this afternoon."

"Sounds great," he replied, busy warming up Bébé Max's formula.

"Should I reply to her text?" she asked blankly.

Thomas looked at her, frowning.

"Oh…" She did not know why she even asked him that. It was as if her brain was completely fogged up. "Of course…" she murmured, turning around and walking back to the nursery without offering him any help or checking on Bébé Max, who was in his rocking cradle by the kitchen island.

What am I doing? She halted, shaking her head, and turned around to attend to the baby.

"I like to feed him." She picked up Bébé Max, oblivious to her paint-covered hands and sweatshirt, and sat on a dining chair. She kept her eyes on her son, avoiding Thomas' puzzled—or maybe disapproving—expression.

He handed her the bottle and sat down next to the baby, giving his son a soft smile.

"Can you reply to Eva's text, please?" she asked impatiently.

Thomas gazed at her, furrows in his brow. He did not want to say anything that matched her tone or attitude. He understood she was still struggling with her PTSD, but sometimes he wondered how much longer he could patiently handle this tension between them.

When Thomas did not respond, she glanced at him. And then she became fully aware of the petulant tone in her voice and the look she just gave him.

"I am sorry. I…I am just mad at myself." She turned her eyes back to Maxipoo, who could always bring a smile to her face. Then her hands started to tremble when she noticed her son's onesie was covered with paint. "I…I am sorry.…" She was not sure she was apologizing to Thomas or her son, probably both.

"I will change him later. Would you like me to feed him?" he asked tenderly, touching her trembling hands.

"Yes…please." She put down the bottle and carefully put the baby in his caring daddy's arms, feeling completely useless.

Thomas cradled his son in one arm with so much joy in his eyes and picked up the bottle.

How come I don't have the patience like he does? She stared at the way Thomas adored their son. *How come I just want to get the job done so I can go back to bed?*

"Thomas…" she whispered.

"Yes?" He responded, his eyes never moved away from his beautiful son.

"Never mind. I'll text Eva back now." She stood up and walked back to the bedroom, feeling incompetent.

After Eva left, Thomas started putting away all the new toys and clothes Evan and Louis gifted Bébé Max, but Iris just wanted to close her eyes and do nothing.

"Why don't you call Louis now?" Iris asked because Eva asked him to do so earlier.

Iris also wished he could stop cleaning and tidying. She knew she had been…lazy since they came home. She really wanted to help but just not at this very moment.

He glanced at his watch. "Yeah… I probably should do it before he leaves the office."

Bébé Max decided to join the conversation. He made some *waah-waah* sounds first and then started crying and fussing.

"I got it." Iris leaped to her feet and scurried to her baby. She picked him up from the cradle and gently rocked him. "I know…I know… *Mon cheri*," she cooed. "I want to play with the new toys, too." She leaned Bébé Max's head on her shoulder and gently patted his back, slowly walking towards the bedroom.

She walked up to the window and leaned against it. "Can Mommy sing to you?" she said to her son tenderly and started to sing. "*Je t'aime, je t'aime toujour.* I am forever yours. Sweet dreams, sweet dreams *mon cher*. You're always in my prayers…"

She repeated the song again and again until the baby fell asleep. Slowly, she walked towards their bed and put him down.

Check on Thomas… Miss Pragmatic whispered in her ear.

Iris shut her eyes, eager to lie down next to her baby and take a nap.

Spend some alone time with him, Miss Pragmatic voiced again.

Letting out a sign, Iris opened her eyes and dipped a soft kiss on Maxipoo's forehead. She grabbed the baby monitor and tiptoed out of the room.

Thomas was talking on the phone on the balcony when she walked into the living room. Not wanting to disturb him, she lay down by the open sliding door. She rested her head on the armrest of the sofa and closed her eyes, listening to his rich and deep baritone as if it was a lullaby.

His voice was one of his charms. It was always level and calm, no matter if he was irritated, upset, or really pissed about something.

She had been living in Switzerland for more than two years now and had the opportunity to catch up her German and learn French. Even though carrying out a conversation in either language was still quite difficult for her, she was able to understand easy dialogues.

Huh? Need a break... What does he mean he needs a break? She tilted her head so she could hear him better.

I cannot leave her... What? Why did he say that? She frowned.

"Thomas," she called, sitting up.

"*Un instant, Louis.*" Thomas asked Louis to give him a moment and held the phone down. "Yes, *ma chérie?*" He turned to face Iris.

"You don't have to stay here," she said, not caring if she had interrupted their conversation. "Take the break you need. I can take care of myself and Max." Her heart was pounding.

"Louis, I will have to call you back," he said to his brother and ended the call. Walking in, he sighed and sat down next to her. "That's not—"

"I think you should go back to the office," she interrupted him. "I am perfectly fine and capable of taking care of Max while you are not here." She drew in a deep breath and continued in a calm voice. "Don't stay home because you have to."

"Iris..." He reached for her hand, but she stood up raptly and walked to the kitchen.

Iris knew she was the reason why Thomas had been working at home. She had been selfish and unreasonable for wanting him around twenty-four-seven. But she almost lost him and Maxipoo, and that reason alone was enough for her to justify herself. However, what he said to his brother really bruised her self-esteem.

"I...I think we should go back to a normal routine. It will be better for all of us..." She started to wash the dishes in the sink, making herself busy so she could avoid Thomas.

"You are upset." He followed her to the kitchen.

"I am not. Please, let's just—" She paused when Thomas put his hands on her shoulders and turned her to face him.

"Look at me," he asked.

She let out a deep sigh and looked up at him.

"You are upset."

"I am not!" she argued. "More like annoyed."

"All right. Annoyed. Louis asked if I wanted to grab a beer with him tomorrow."

"Then go grab a beer!" She raised her voice.

"Stop it," he said, his voice solemn.

"Stop what?" She widened her eyes.

He was silent, his eyes a bit too piercing for her liking.

"Stop what?" she asked again. "Stop talking?"

Thomas bowed his head, feeling defeated. "You know what I meant."

Iris shut her eyes, trying to calm herself, knowing he was right… She knew exactly what he meant. She had been so vexed with him when he had been nothing but patient, understanding, and loving. She wanted him around, but at the same time she wanted him to leave her alone. Did that even make sense? Nothing was making sense to her now.

Finally, she opened her eyes, but she turned away from his gaze. "Should I cook tonight or should we order takeaway?" she asked, completely changing the subject.

Thomas chuckled and pulled her into his arms. "*Je t'aime tellement,*" he whispered.

"I know…" She wrapped her arms around his waist.

"I miss your spaghetti," he said, but his voice still held some uncertainty, not quite convinced by her sudden change of mood. And attitude.

"Okay, spaghetti it is." She stood on tiptoes to give him a kiss on his cheek and then walked to the refrigerator.

"Can I—" Thomas was interrupted by a babbling sound coming from the baby monitor. "I will go check on him," he said, heading to the bedroom.

Iris sighed and opened the refrigerator, which was fully stocked by Thomas.

Before the kidnapping, Iris was doing so much better that she was able to go grocery shopping with Thomas. She enjoyed walking around the store with him so much. And now… She was back to square one, afraid to go anywhere and afraid to be around people. She was constantly having a tightness in her chest, scared that something horrible would happen to Thomas or their son, or both of them.

After several sessions with Dr. Fournier, she was calmer. Even though she still experienced separation anxiety, she did feel less stressed and less…everything.

She was not as sad and depressed as before, but at the same time she was not happy or excited, either. Nevertheless, it was better than being anxious and fearful all the time.

Thomas rejoined her in the kitchen with Bébé Max.

She walked up to them and kissed Maxipoo's chubby cheek. Then she suddenly felt self-conscious when she sensed Thomas' eyes on her. "Stop staring at me," she said, turning back to prepare dinner.

"Are you really okay with me going back to the office?"

"Yes, I am." She stopped what she was doing and turned to look at him. "Call Louis now and tell him that you are going to the office tomorrow."

He studied her expression with an amused smile.

"Do it now before I change my mind. And also…" She pointed the spoon in her hand at him and added, "Go grab that beer with him."

"Come here…" He reached one arm out and pulled her closer. "He invited me to have a drink after work, but I really don't want to go."

Pouting, she looked at him. "Then…then why did you say you need a break?"

A broad smile appeared on his face. "Your French has improved."

"Don't change the subject." She narrowed her eyes. "Do you need a break from me?"

"No, I don't. I've never needed a break from you." He kissed her forehead. "I just—"

She could hear the hesitation in his voice. Not wanting to press him for a meaningless explanation, she interrupted him, "Would you get Maxipoo's bottle ready while I prepare the dinner." She pulled away from him.

He kept his hand on her waist while she was pulling away, giving her an alluring smile. She used to leap right back to him and kiss him passionately when he did that, but now she just walked away from him.

THOMAS sat at the desk in the study after dinner, thinking about his conversation with Louis this afternoon…

~ ~ ~

"Are you doing all right?" Louis asked.

"Just tired," Thomas simply said, but he truly wanted to tell his brother that he would love to go back to work in the office as soon as possible and that he started feeling a bit suffocated at home now.

"I bet you are. You have a newborn, and Iris is still fragile," Louis said. "Maybe you just need a break."

"Yeah… Maybe I just need a break," Thomas echoed what Louis said but never meant it.

~ ~ ~

Thomas was surprised that Iris was upset about what he had said, and then she would not let him explain. He knew even if she did let him explain, she would still be defensive anyway, just like how she had been reacting to many other little things he did or said.

Maybe both of us can benefit from me going back to the office. Just for a couple of hours a day first…

He wanted to and felt responsible to be around Iris and Max. However, he did have a full-time job, which he could not work at home indefinitely, and he was most afraid that their constant tiffs were going to escalate into full-blown quarrels if he did not do something about it.

He picked up his phone and called Louis.

"Hello, little brother," Louis answered the call after a couple of rings.

Thomas smiled at Louis' giddy voice.

They were so different, him the obedient son and Louis the black sheep of the family. After Leila was gone and he joined fedpol, Louis completely turned around and became their father's right-hand man. He had transformed from a reckless rotter into a respectful businessman and from a philanderer into a devoted husband. Thomas believed Eva was the one taming the beast.

Thomas cleared his throat and said, "Iris and I talked, and I am going to be in the office tomorrow."

There was silence as if the call was disconnected.

"You there?" Thomas asked.

"I am here. Tomorrow? Just like that? Is everything all right?" Louis asked.

"Yes. Why?"

"Nothing." Louis paused for a few seconds and added, "You know that by law you have ten days of paid paternity leave, right?" Louis joked.

"Yes, I am aware of that." He laughed because he had been taking more than ten days off by now and he was sure his brother would not cut his pay. Then he let out a sigh and said, "I need..." he trailed off.

Louis could hear the hesitation in his brother's voice, he quickly changed the tone of his voice and said, "Welcome back, Mr. Torian!"

"Thanks. And thank you for covering the work."

In Thomas' absence, Louis had undertaken the responsibilities of both their jobs. Florent had offered to help, but Louis reassured their father, who was overwhelmed by Thomas' kidnapping, that he was able to handle everything.

"Don't mention it. It's my old job. Remember? Piece of cake." He brushed Thomas off. "By the way, Eva will not stop talking about Max." He raised his voice, apparently saying that to Eva.

"Hi Tommy. We want to babysit Bébé Max!" Eva's voice came through the phone.

"We?" Louis asked his wife.

"Yes, my love. We. You are the one who bought all those toys. Remember?"

Thomas chuckled at their banter.

Eva and Louis had been married almost ten years but never once talked about having a child of their own. Thomas knew Eva had dedicated herself to her job, but he was not sure if that was the reason they decided to wait.

A knock on the door…

"Come in." Thomas turned towards the door.

Iris walked in, holding a mug in one hand and the baby monitor in another. She set the mug down and mouthed to him, *Louis?*

"Yes. Eva as well. Come say hello." He wrapped one arm around her hips, pulling her down to sit on his lap, and then put Louis and Eva on speakerphone.

"Hi," she said to the phone.

"Hi Iris," Louis responded.

"Hi darling," Eva greeted cheerfully.

"They volunteer to babysit Max," Thomas said to Iris. "We can plan our holidays now."

"Yes, we do. Take good use of those ten days of paid paternity leave, Tommy." Louis laughed.

"That's very nice of you," Iris said softly.

"Anything for you, darling." Louis' voice became earnest.

They chatted on the phone a bit longer and then said goodnight.

Iris nestled in Thomas' embrace, resting her head on his shoulder. "Your tea is cold now. Do you want me to make you a fresh cup?"

"That's all right. I would rather sit here with you like this." He caressed her arm.

She was silent and then let out a sigh. "I am sorry…"

"Iris…" He kissed her hair. "Don't be."

"I…I just don't feel like myself."

"It will get better."

"You think?" She let out another sigh.

He did not answer her but held her tight.

"I love you…" she whispered. "So much… Please, don't give up on me."

Her voice was full of sorrow and fear, making his heart ache.

"Never…" he said and kissed her forehead. "Never, my love." He lifted her face up and placed his lips on hers gently and softly, not wanting to unnerve her.

She cupped his face and deepened their kiss.

CHAPTER 14

IRIS' picture appeared on James' phone screen, and almost immediately his phone started vibrating on the conference table.

"Excuse me." He hastily grabbed his phone and fumbled with it. "I have to get this," he said to his colleagues and walked out of the conference room.

"Hi sweetheart…" He answered the call.

"Hi James. Are you busy? Am I interrupting anything?" Iris asked.

"Nope. I am walking into my office now. How are you?" He quickly headed to his office and closed the door behind him. "I am so happy to hear your voice."

He had visited her several times at the hospital since she rushed back from the States. After her meltdown, her family declined all visitors, so he could only care about her and the baby from afar.

"I am fine. We are home now. I mean the one by the lake."

"Wonderful. How are Thomas and the baby?"

"They are fine, too," she replied, although her voice was missing her usual jaunty nature and James noticed that.

"That's fantastic…" He leaned back in his chair, debating if he should just ask her if everything was all right. Her voice was telling him she was *not* fine, and he loved her too much to beat around the bush with her.

"What's the matter?" he asked, his voice gentle.

Iris was silent at first and then let out a loud sigh. "Jame…"

"Sweetheart, I can tell by your voice that something is bothering you…"

"Would you…would you like to visit me?"

"Of course. Let me know when and—"

"Today..." Iris interrupted him.

James was surprised and not sure what to respond all of sudden. He was right, and her need for him to visit her *today* just confirmed it.

"If you are busy, it's all right..." Iris quickly said when James did not respond.

"I am leaving right now." He was already on his feet.

It was Iris' turn to be surprised and not sure what to say.

"Are you still there?" James asked.

"Yes... Really? You can leave now?"

"Anything for you... If you need me, I will be there." The hesitation and quivering in her voice worried him.

"Thank you. I...I just... I need someone to talk to..." she trailed off.

"Is Thomas there?" He wondered if she and Thomas were having problems.

"He is at work."

"I see... Sweetheart, I am leaving now and will be there in less than an hour." He grabbed his jacket from the back of the chair and picked up his messenger bag from the side table.

Iris opened the door, welcoming her guest.

James was thrilled to see Iris, but he did not expect to see her in a rainbow unicorn onesie. He blinked several times.

"Don't say a word." Iris gave him a warning look. "It's a gift from Antonio. Maxipoo has a matching one."

He chuckled, stepping closer to her to kiss her cheeks.

"Come on in." She stepped aside to let James walk in and closed the door. Then she gestured for him to follow her to the living room. "Would you like something to drink?"

"I am fine now. Maybe later." James sat down on the sofa, patting on the seat next to him. "Come sit." He gazed at her, feeling a little emotional. She did not look traumatized and frightened anymore but definitely thinner and fragile. He still remembered how shocked he was at her state of injury when he saw her at that hospital bed. She was covered with cuts and bruises and looked absolutely devastated.

Iris sat down next to James, her brow furrowed.

He gently held her hand. "How is Thomas doing?"

She turned to him, smiling. "He is doing great. Starting working out again, amazing with the baby…" Then the smile vanished. "He was the one who was kidnapped and badly hurt, but he seems to be recovering so fast and…and I…"

"Don't be too hard on yourself. He was a well-trained police officer. An undercover agent! That's pretty major."

"I know… I…I just don't feel like myself," she said, her voice little.

"What do you mean?" He gave her hand a gentle squeeze.

"It's just… I feel fine, but…" She felt defeated, not sure what to say.

James wrapped his arms around her shoulders. He was silent, trying to find some proper words to comfort her, but he did not know what to say until he knew more about her problems.

"May…maybe you can tell me if I am the same person." She leaned her head on his shoulder.

"Honey, I think you are too hard on yourself. You have been through so much. You are the bravest person I have known and—"

"See," She pulled herself away and looked at him. "I would have cried by now, but nothing had happened. Rien! Nichts! I feel *too* calm, and the days just go by like nothing." She let out a deep sigh. A sigh of relief, actually. It felt good to be able to voice this indescribable feeling that had been bothering her.

James looked at her, raising one eyebrow—quite comical, even for a handsome face like his.

She stared at him, waiting for his reply or comment, but he just looked at her, completely silent.

"Say something, James."

"How about this…" He smiled. "Let me meet the baby first. Maximilien… What an amazing name!" His smile broadened. "And then we will figure this out together. Okay?"

"I guess…" She was skeptical about what they could figure out together, although being able to talk about it was already better than she had expected.

"Where is the little prince?" James' eyes sparkled.

"He is napping now." She stood up, holding his hand, and headed towards the bedroom.

"I will be very quiet but cannot guarantee that when I see him." James followed her.

She stopped at the empty nursery and took a step inside. "This is his room." She shrugged. "I haven't finished it yet."

"Wow…" James walked into the room, scanning the murals on the walls and ceiling. "Did you paint those?"

"Yes. It took awhile."

"It is amazing. You are so talented."

"Thank you," she replied absentmindedly because all she saw was an empty room. "I need to order the furniture, window coverings, and more baby supplies. I hope I have the energy to finish this room before he can legally drink."

James chuckled. "I am sure you will."

She shrugged.

James glanced around the room and asked, "Do you need help?"

"Probably, I don't know… I have this image in my head of how this room is going to be, but I just don't have the drive to finish it. I had to force myself just to finish the painting."

"This doesn't sound like you," he said, gazing at her.

She headed out of the room, murmuring, "I know…"

James followed her out of the nursery and then into the master bedroom.

"There he is," she whispered, not wanting to waken the baby. She walked towards a white wooden crib at the far end of the room, James right behind her.

Yup, matching onesie. James held back his laughter. "Cutest unicorn I have ever seen!" He whispered to Iris, gazing at the adorable baby with a yellow horn hood over his tiny head. "You and Thomas really made a beautiful baby."

"We did, didn't we?" She felt satisfied and content every time she saw her little miracle. However, something was missing in her. Something that she saw in Thomas' eyes when he cradled Maxipoo in his arm.

"Now that I have seen the cutest baby, I am satisfied and have no regrets now."

"He is not only the cutest but also the easiest." She could not move her eyes away from her son, her voice proud.

"Really?" He gave her a skeptical look.

"He sleeps through the night most of the time and is always playful when he is awake."

"Really? No midnight feeding?"

"Nope. Then when I told my mom that he should be given a medal for being the easiest baby, guess what she said?"

"Congratulations?"

"She told me to tell her that again when he is teething." She smiled at her baby proudly and muttered, "Not sure what's her point."

James chuckled and added. "Yeah, tell me what you think when he is teething, too."

Iris glared at him.

James wrapped his hands around her shoulders and whispered, "Let's chat in the living room."

She nodded and both of them tiptoed out of the bedroom.

"I am going to have a cup of coffee. Can I get you something to drink?" she asked, heading to the kitchen.

"I will have coffee as well, please." He followed her into the kitchen and sat on a bar stool at the kitchen island.

"Americano?"

"You know me well, darling."

"Of course." Iris gave him a soft smile and turned on the espresso machine.

"So, what do you think is wrong?" James went right to the point while Iris reached for coffee cups and saucers in the cabinet.

"Nothing. And everything…" She sighed, preparing coffee in silence, her mind going through what had happened the last three months.

James gazed at her, patiently waiting for her to enlighten him. The last thing she needed was to be rushed. He remembered how she was when she first arrived at the embassy... It took days before she could look at him; weeks before she would talk to him; months before she opened up to him. Now she was not timid and traumatized like she was when he first met her, but nor was she lively and cheery like she was after she and Thomas reunited over a year ago. He thought she should have found contentment in Thomas' safe return and Max's survival. But... She was right. She was not herself.

The Iris he remembered wore her heart on her sleeve. She would have told him what was on her mind already when she called him. She would have jumped into his arms after she opened the door earlier. And she would have burst into tears and told him to *stop the Scheiße* the moment he gave her all the affectionate remarks.

This Iris in front of him was reticent and distant.

"There you go." She placed the coffee in front of James along with some biscuits.

"Thank you, sweetheart." James picked up the coffee and inhaled the almost nutty aroma before he took a sip.

She gave him a soft smile and picked up her own cup.

James watched her holding the cup beneath her nose and closing her eyes. She took a much needed breath, breathing in the warm air and the fragrance of the coffee as if she needed to calm herself, even though she looked as calm as she could be.

Then she opened her eyes, took a sip of her latte, her eyes staring into the distance.

Something is definitely not right... James frowned.

"I... I mean... Everything..." She finally spoke but struggled with words. Putting down her cup, she sighed and looked at James. "I feel numb."

He gazed on her expressionless face, reaching one hand to cover hers. "How long?"

She frowned, trying to remember. Her memory during her stay in the hospital was a blur. "After Maxipoo was born. Maybe..."

James knew he was not a specialist or anything close to that to help her with her mental health, but he could listen. "Let's sit on the sofa." He got off the stool and picked up his coffee and biscuits. "So we can cuddle, just like the old times."

She gave him a bright smile and picked up her cup.

"Everything is too calm, like nothing had happened in the past few months." Iris started to open up. "I almost lost both my husband and my son, for crying out loud."

"You and Thomas went through so much. Maybe—"

"Exactly!" she interrupted him. "Too much. I thought Thomas would never come back alive. And I thought I had lost the baby when I saw all the blood. Shouldn't I be all emotional?"

James reached for her hands, not sure what to say. He had witnessed how devastated she was after Thomas was kidnapped.

She was too emotional then. Why is being calm now a bad idea? He gave her hands a comforting squeeze.

"I just... I feel too peaceful." She let out a deep sigh. Again. "Peaceful isn't even the right word." She gave James an embarrassed look. "I... I don't even have a sex drive."

"Come again?"

She pouted, glancing at him. "I know, right? We are talking about Thomas. He is like sex on a stick."

"Not going to argue about that," James chuckled.

"It's like someone had pushed a pause button on my emotions and senses, and...everything." She let out another—James had lost count—deep sigh.

"Honey, you lost me..." James looked at her, furrowing.

"Huh?"

"I was told you were very unstable, I mean emotionally, after the surgery. That's one of the reasons they restricted the numbers of visitors."

She became quiet, remembering how shattered she felt after visiting her baby in NICU. "I was..." she murmured.

He held her tight, kissing her hair.

"Max... He was... He did not even look real..." Her voice was just above a whisper. "He was so small, covered with tubs and bandages. It's all my fault. I put him there."

"Ahh, sweetheart. It was never your fault."

"James..." She pulled away and turned to face him, her

expression regretful. "I…" She was not sure she had the courage to tell him what she did after she visited her baby.

"What is it? You are scaring me."

"I…I was put on heavy duty medications because…" Her voice was trembling.

"Honey?" He squeezed her hands, knowing he was not going to like what he was about to hear.

"I hurt myself…" She lowered her head, feeling ashamed.

He was speechless as she was one of the bravest persons he had ever met. Self-harm was never in her dictionary.

She looked down and added, "I…I didn't… Well, I remember I missed Thomas so much and then thought the baby might not make it… It… God… I don't think I can describe how I felt then. And the next second my mother and Janie were crying, and I saw blood all over my arms and thighs. I didn't even feel it. I mean the physical cuts or scratches I did to myself."

James pulled her in and embraced her, caressing her hair. "It is all over now…"

"Are you disappointed in me?" she whispered in his embrace.

Instead of answering her question, he asked, "Are your doctors still monitoring your condition?"

She nodded.

"Good. I am sure the medications work well. You are here now with your beautiful family."

"I guess… I wouldn't—" Suddenly, she pauses. "James…" She pulled back and looked at him, her eyes widened.

"What? What?" James mirrored her expression.

"That it is, James. You are such a genius."

"Okay…" He smirked. "I know I am a genius. Care to tell me what I did? Or said?"

"I am so lost, James, I have been lost… I am missing…" She was babbling.

"Hey… Hey…" He put his hands on her shoulders, calming her. "Take a deep breath…"

She looked at him, eyes blinking raptly.

"You are not making sense now. So just… Just take a deep

breath and clear you thoughts first."

She fixed her eyes on him, slowly breathing in and out.

He leaned in and kissed her forehead. "Take all the time you need. We will make sense of everything together."

She nodded.

"Remember what I said to you after the outing with Thomas?" Iris asked James after taking minutes to clear her thoughts.

"Yes. How could I forget? You were over the moon."

She blushed, remembering their first kiss.

"You told me you felt so protected," he continued. "Thomas was like your guardian angel. You would not shut up about him."

She grinned, fluttering her eyelashes at him.

"What?" James took a sip of his second cup of coffee, arching one eyebrow again.

After Thomas dropped her off at the embassy, Iris was so surprised to see James when she walked into the lobby. He was waiting for her return as he had told her. At that moment she thought to herself how lucky she was to have met a friend like James. He ended up spending the night at the embassy because she needed someone to talk to.

"I am so grateful that I had met you," Iris said to James, her voice soft and affectionate.

He beamed with a hint of shyness. "That's so sweet of you to say that. But we are talking about Thomas now, not me."

Iris' family was traveling all over Europe and visited all U.S. Embassies to spread the words. James was just obsessed with Iris' story when he first learned about her case. He knew she was taken in Paris but never had thought he would be the one in charge of her arrival in Bern and everything after that. The more he got to know her, the more he was drawn to her. They clicked, and the bond and friendship was unexpected.

"I know… But I want you to know that you are very special to me, too."

"Oh, I know. I am not threatened by your guardian angel." He tried to joke around to conceal his emotions. Although he was not joking last summer when he told her that he would fall madly in love with her if he were not in a relationship with Tim. Iris was one of few women who could arouse his interest. Their platonic relationship was something he held deeply in his heart.

Iris gave him a sweet smile and continued, "You saw what kind of progress I made with Eva."

He nodded, remembering how she was able to interact with people slowly but still struggling with her PTSD.

"After I went home, the therapy and medications helped but only to an extent." She sighed.

He knew that as well because he talked to her on a daily basis after she left Bern. Her condition had gradually improved, but she was healing in a cocoon.

"Everything changed when Thomas showed up at my door steps." She gave James a contented smile. "He is my guardian angel, my savior…" she trailed off, furrows appearing in her brow. She lowered her eyes, staring at her hands clenching on her lap.

James was not sure why mentioning Thomas made her mood change so swiftly. He reached for her hands and gave her a comforting squeeze.

"He…he is…" She suddenly felt emotional, a feeling that she had not experienced for a long time. "He is the best thing that has ever happened to me."

"I see that in your eyes every time you talk about him." He tugged a strand of hair behind her ear.

She turned her face up to him again and gave him a smile, but the smile faded almost immediately. "When he was abducted, I thought I had lost him…forever. I…I was in a very dark place. So dark, so…" She frowned, remembering how she had lived her days in despair during the time when Thomas was gone. "I…I…"

"Shh…" He wrapped his arms around her. "Take your time…"

"I thought…I thought being trafficked was…was the worst thing that could have happened to me. But it wasn't…" She leaned her head on his shoulder. "Losing Thomas was…"

James could not find any words to comfort her. He could only hold her tighter.

"I had tried my best to survive in captivity. But when they took him away from me, I didn't want to live a day without him. I..." She nervously twisted her fingers. "I was still pregnant then. If I hurt myself, I would have hurt my baby..." Her voice became small, barely above a whisper, feeling ashamed to admit that.

"Oh, honey..."

"I... I have been relying on him so heavily. I am burdening him."

"He loves you more than anything in this world. He would never think you are burdening him."

Won't he one day if I am still so messed up? She did not say this thought out loud because she knew James would rebuke her hastily. "James, I am not well." She slightly shook her head.

"What? Do you need to lie down?" He pulled away to look at her face, his voice worried.

"No. I am...I am physically fine." She smiled softly at him, squeezing his hand. "I mean my...my mind is not well."

"But you are better now..."

"Am I?" She murmured.

"Of course you are." He frowned. "I saw how you were before. And now you have a beautiful family."

"But Thomas has to take care of me like...like a caregiver. I want him as my husband, not a caregiver."

"Okay... Hmm... Let's take a moment here." James paused, trying to figure out what to say. "You take care of each other. I mean... Tim and I take care of each other, but I don't think I would consider him as a caregiver."

"It's different..." Iris frowned.

"Different how?"

"I need medications for anxiety and depression. I couldn't function properly without them. I know that because when I found out I was pregnant, I got off my meds thinking they might harm the baby. I...I should have talked to my doctor first. But—"

"Wait..." he interrupted her. "You just stopped taking your medications?"

"I know. I know. I've learned my lesson." She gave him a rueful side glance.

"Sorry... I didn't mean to interrupt you. Go on..." he said, his brows furrowing in concern. "But you had better learn your lesson." He added.

"I really did." She winced at his rebuking tone. "I became really agitated when Thomas was not around, like something horrible was going to happen to me. We thought it was because of the pregnancy hormones, so we just tried to deal with it. I was a mess. I didn't want to leave the house again, so Thomas worked from home, doing everything he could to take care of me. Anyway, it got better after I mentioned that to my doctor. She put me back on different medications."

"It sounds like the medications help. What are you worried about now?"

Iris frowned, remembering how much she had relied on those medications after Thomas was kidnapped and the baby was born. "I...I need those meds...."

James became speechless as she sounded like an addict. He was sure it was not that serious. "Honey, are you still taking them?"

She looked at him, nodding her head. "I am afraid to get off the meds. They...they keep me..." she trailed off, not sure how to describe what the drugs did. "I think... I really needed them when I was in the hospital. I couldn't remember much, but I remember I was calm, not so sad anymore. And I...I think that's the problem."

"Problem?" He was confused. "The medications?"

"I needed them when I didn't know if Thomas was alive and if Max could make it or not. I was... I was..." She nervously twisted her fingers. "I was going crazy, so they had to calm me down."

James furrowed his brow, staring at her. "So, you are saying that you are too calm now because of those meds?"

She took a moment to consider the word 'calm' and said, "I think so..."

"Enlighten me, please."

"I am calm, and that's good, especially now I need to take care of the baby and get back to our normal life again. But..." She paused to think about how she had been for the last several weeks. "That's how I feel all the time now. Calm. Nothing excites me, or saddens me." She looked at James. "I don't feel like myself. I...I miss laughing out loud."

James smiled at her words, remembering her carefree laughters.

"I miss how much I wanted Thomas all the time."

James grinned.

"I feel like I am losing myself..." She suddenly felt a burning sensation in her eyes, and she welcomed it. "I even miss being mad at him..." She was now remembering the time when they fought over him having a drink with his ex-girlfriend.

Tears merged and were rolling down her cheeks.

She blinked several times and burst out laughing. "I am crying!" she exclaimed, wiping the tears off her face.

James wrapped his arms around her. "Whatever he did to make you mad is all worthy now."

"I guess it is..." She laughed, remembering how heartbroken she was when he did not text or call and did not come home until very late that night.

"What do you plan to do now?"

Her emotions were quickly gone, and the calmness deserted her. "I have no idea..." She sighed.

"When is your next appointment with Dr. Fournier?"

"Tomorrow morning. I almost canceled it because I...I thought... I don't know what to think anymore...."

"Would you like me to go with you?"

She leaned her head against his chest. "That's very sweet of you, but thank you though. Thomas goes to all my appointments with me."

"Are you going to talk to him about it?"

She frowned. "I should..."

He dipped another kiss on her head. "Everything will be all right."

"Thank you for listening...."

THOMAS glanced at his watch—for the hundredth time since he sat at his desk. It was not even noon yet. He turned to another page of the document he was reading and tried to be as productive as possible.

Today was his second day back to the office. And since Iris texted him James was visiting her, he decided to work a bit longer than yesterday. However, he was eager to go home. The break he thought he needed did not really *de-stress* him.

He only stayed at work for two hours yesterday, but the drive to and from work took almost another two hours. Even though Iris told him she was fine, he still felt guilty for leaving her home alone with the baby for so many hours.

He picked up his desk phone and called his assistant.

"Travis speaking."

"I am heading home now. Please reschedule my one o'clock to tomorrow morning. Wait…" He paused, remembering Iris' doctor appointment was tomorrow morning. "I will not come in tomorrow. Just reschedule it."

"Of course, Thomas. Is everything all right?"

"Yes. I am going to stop by Gloria's shop before I go home," Thomas said.

"Would you like me to call Mrs. Gloria and have the arrangement ready for you?" Travis smiled, knowing immediately for whom the flowers were meant. He had ordered flowers from Gloria's Flower Shop for Thomas too many times.

"No, thank you. I am going to choose the flowers myself."

The temperatures plunged rapidly as the winter season began to set in. Thomas walked out of DeMont Hotel into the cold. He pulled up his coat collar as he strode across the street to the flower shop, where he regularly bought Iris roses.

The bell over the door dinged when he walked into the shop.

"I will be right with you," a young female voice responded to the sound of the bell.

He did not see anyone and was surprised by the young voice. Gloria was a lady in her late sixties. She owned the shop and was the only person he had ever seen working there.

"Damn it!" the young voice cursed. It was apparently coming from behind the counter.

He walked closer. "Excuse me," he said, poking his head over the counter, and saw a lady squatting by a pile of broken glasses. "Do you need help?"

The lady looked up, her face pale. She looked young, probably early twenty.

Thomas saw her hands holding together and blood dripping down from them.

He quickly walked around the counter and grabbed some paper towels from the dispenser on the wall. Carefully and gently, he pressed the paper towels over her hands.

"Do you have a first aid kit?" he asked.

"In the closet…" She tilted her head towards a door behind her and slowly stood up.

Thomas retrieved the first aid kit and came right back to her. "May I?" He looked between the young lady and her bloody hands.

"Ye…yes…" She put her hands on the counter, revealing the wounded hand. She winced at the pain and the view of the cut on her right palm.

"The cut is shallow. I don't think you need stitches," he said, examining her injury.

"Are you a doctor? Nurse? Paramedic?" She stared at him.

"No." He gave her a smile, his blue eyes soft, making her face turn pink. "Just well trained." He ignored her sudden shyness and turned to the first aid kit to find what he could use to patch the cut.

She could not move her eyes away from this handsome man, who just happened to walk in to save her…hand.

"This shouldn't sting." He read an antiseptic wipe packet first before tearing it open. And then he gently held her wounded hand and cleaned the cut. "You are not Gloria," he said, trying to distract her.

"Huh?" His comment brought her back from her musing. "Oh. Me. No… Gloria is my aunt."

"I don't see any glass fragments. Does it hurt when I put

pressure on it?" he asked, his eyes fixed on what he was doing.

"No...no..." She looked at her hand, grimacing.

He nodded and started to apply antibiotic ointment on the wound. "She has never mentioned she has any relatives in Bern," he said, his voice casual.

"What?" She blinked her eyes.

Thomas secured a dressing on the wound and gave her a polite smile. "There you go." He removed his hands from her bandaged one and walked back to the other side of the counter.

"Thank...thank you..." Her eyes moved from her hand to Thomas.

"You are welcome." He nodded.

And then the young lady just stared at Thomas.

"I want two dozen red roses," Thomas said since she was silent.

"Oh. Right..." She looked and sounded embarrassed. "I am so sorry. It... Everything... Never mind. Two dozen red roses," she murmured and walked towards the floral cooler.

Thomas kept quiet, watching her ungainly taking the flowers out of the cooler and bringing them to the counter to arrange them.

The first time Thomas stepped into the shop was after Iris came back to Bern with him. He wanted to surprise her with her favorite flowers, and Gloria came to his rescue. She asked him about Iris and made a beautiful rose bouquet for him. And ever since then, she had prepared many arrangements and presents for him to amaze Iris, who later asked Gloria to decorate the château for their wedding.

"So, who is the special lady?" the young lady asked while she was working on the arrangement. She added greenery to the roses and wrapped them with a black paper.

"My wife," Thomas answered, his left thumb inattentively rubbing with his wedding ring

She glanced up at him, disappointment in her eyes. Then she quickly looked back down and carefully tied a red ribbon to the bouquet.

"Is your aunt on holiday?" Thomas asked. He would like to know if Gloria would be back in the shop soon as he needed her expertise to raise Iris' spirits.

"Who?" The young lady frowned.

"Gloria." Thomas tilted his head, wondering if she was still in shock from the cut.

"Right. Gloria. Yes, she is." She forced a smile. "By the way, I am Emma." She extended her wounded hand for a handshake. "Oops." She quickly put the bouquet down and gave him her left hand.

"Thomas." He shook her hand.

"Nice to meet you, Thomas. And thank you again for…for saving my hand." She blushed again, staring at their joined hands.

Thomas pulled his hand back to avoid another awkward moment. "I have an account here."

"Right. Your last name, please." She turned to the computer on the desk behind her.

"Torian."

"Torian…" She moved and clicked the mouse. "Got it." She turned back to him and looked a bit embarrassed. "Can I verify some information with you since…since I don't know you?"

Thomas frowned and reached into his back packet for his wallet. He took out a credit card. "I will just pay it now."

"Oh…" She looked at the card in his hand for a few seconds before reaching for a card reader on the counter. "Sure. I am sorry for the inconvenience." She keyed in the amount before placing the reader on the counter top.

Finally, Thomas had the flowers in his hand. He said goodbye and pivoted on his heels.

"Wait!" Emma called, scurrying around the counter to catch him.

He stopped and turned around.

Then something unexpected happened as if it was a carefully choreographed dramatic effect for their already awkward encounter…

Emma tripped and was tumbling towards Thomas. He reacted immediately, taking one quick step towards her and catching her before she fell on the ground. She landed right onto the flowers he was holding, sending the rose petals flying.

Thomas quickly helped her stand on her feet, her hands grasping his forearms tight.

"I...I am so sorry. I swear I am not always this clumsy," she said, her voice nervous. "Oh my god!" She shrieked when she saw the destroyed bouquet, her grip tightened. "I...I will make you another one!"

Thomas pulled his arms free with a bit of effort and stepped back. He looked at the bouquet, speechless.

"I can't believe this..." Emma took the bouquet from him. "Give me—"

"Don't worry about it," he interrupted her, stepping further towards the door.

"Wait!" She walked closer. "Just give me ten minutes."

"Really, don't worry about it." He reached for the door handle.

"Let...let me give you a refund then." She stepped even closer.

"I really have to go now." He gave her a polite nod and walked out of the shop as fast as he could.

That's just... He frowned, having no word for what just happened. He quickly pushed the whole thing out of his mind and walked back to the hotel. *I am sure there's another flower shop around here.*

After he sat in his car, he started to search for floral shops on his phone. He called the closest one to make sure they had red roses and placed an order before he drove over there.

Iris' face lit up when Thomas walked into their apartment. It made all the effort worthwhile.

"I am so jealous," James said, looking at the lovebirds from where he sat.

Iris winked at James and walked into the kitchen to put the flowers in a crystal vase.

Thomas exchanged pleasantries with James before he went to the bedroom to check on his son and changed out of his suit.

"I am going to go now," James said when Iris walked back to the living room holding the blooms.

Disappointment appeared in her eyes.

He walked up to her, took the vase from her, and put it on the coffee table. He then wrapped her in his arms, kissing the top of her head. "I am only a phone call away."

She nodded.

"Let me tell Thomas you are leaving." She looked up.

He released her from his embrace.

Thomas walked out with the baby when Iris was heading to the bedroom.

"Look who is up?" She smiled at her son.

"He is even more adorable when he is awake." James walked up to the little family, gazing at the baby.

Iris placed a kiss on her son's forehead, feeling content. She turned to face James. "Wanna hold him?"

"Yes…" His smile brightened. "Should I sanitize myself first?" He looked at Iris.

"You've washed your hands a thousands times since you got here. You are fine." Iris chuckled.

Thomas walked closer to James and carefully handed his son to James.

James drew in a breath as if he was about to handle a delicate piece of china.

When he heard Iris had an emergency c-section and the baby was delivered at thirty weeks, he rushed to the hospital right away. He was told the newborn was critical and had to be kept in the NICU for as long as needed. No one had the heart to tell Iris her baby's condition. Fortunately, this little miracle came through within a week.

"You are too cute!" James cooed, mirroring Bébé Max's pouting lips. "I need to get myself one of these," he murmured.

"You would be a great daddy," Iris said, wrapping one arm around Thomas' waist.

James sighed, his eyes misty. "You think?"

"Just look at the way you hold Max. James, you are a natural," Thomas said.

"Aren't you the cutest…" James grinned at the baby.

Bébé Max made cooing noises, one chubby hand reaching for James.

"Oh my god, he loves me." James let the baby grab his nose.

After James left, Thomas and Iris bundled the baby up and took a walk along the lake. They then had an early dinner and enjoyed a quiet evening cuddling on the sofa and watching TV.

"Why didn't you buy the flowers from Gloria?" Iris asked when she was in bed waiting for Thomas.

He walked out of the bathroom and climbed underneath the warm duvet. He lay on his side, propped up on his elbow, one hand supporting his head. Then he told Iris the peculiar encounter.

"You think she didn't see your wedding ring?"

Thomas gazed at her, free hand intertwining her hand. "She was not flirting with me."

"Women always flirt with you," she said, staring at their interlocked hands.

He brought her hand to his lips and kissed it. "Don't care."

She grinned and turned to face him. "About my appointment tomorrow…" she said, changing the subject. "I want to talk to Dr. Fournier about my medications."

He frowned, his eyes concerned. "Why?"

She shrugged. "Just discuss the side effects and see if there's other options."

He was still giving her a worried look.

"Don't worry. I feel fine." She gave him a reassuring smile. "And…and I think it's time I go there by myself." She looked at him intensively, waiting for him to object or question her reason.

Is this a sign of her progress? He studied her face, seeing the seriousness in her eyes. "Okay. But I am taking you there regardless. I can pick you up later or wait there." He gazed at her, showing her his support. "And I will have Max with me," he added.

"Okay," she responded right away. "After the appointment, if you need to go back to the office, you can drop us off at the apartment. Maxipoo has never been there." Her eyes sparkled. "We should have a nursery there too!"

He smiled, happy that she was seemingly excited about doing different things.

Before he was kidnapped, she had improved so much that she was able to shop in markets and eat in restaurants. She had fewer nightmares and, if he remembered correctly, no panic attacks after their wedding day.

She was clingy after his safe return, but it was understandable. He refused to be away from her as well. Everything seemed fine until she screamed in her sleep one night…

She had dreamt about herself back in captivity. He suspected that knowing Vera was behind his kidnapping had triggered her nightmares, but Iris refused to talk about it.

Thomas gazed at his loving wife, his love for her stronger than ever. "*Je t'aime tellement,*" he whispered.

Iris reached one hand and cupped his handsome face. "*Je t'aime aussi.*" She looked into his deep blue eyes. "I don't know what I've done to deserve you…"

"I think that's my line," he said softly.

She leaned in and kissed him.

He sneaked one hand behind her head and deepened their kiss. Then he sensed her resistance. He broke the kiss first and pressed his forehead on hers.

She let out a deep sigh, pulling herself back, but he held her in place.

"I miss you," he whispered.

Her breathing became heavy, but not because of the arousal and excitement she used to have when Thomas touched her, but because of her nonsensical nervousness and disappointment—or sadness if she could find any of her emotions back.

"I…I am…"

"Shh… It is all right." He caressed her cheek.

"Something is not right… I am going to talk to Dr. Fournier about it tomorrow."

He leaned back so he could look at her.

"I…I want our life back…" She pressed one hand on his hard chest, her eyes fixed on his muscled chest. "Our…our sex life back."

"*Mon amour…*" He covered her hand with his.

"At first I just felt…felt…" She paused to find the right words, her eyes moving up to look at him. "Not in the mood."

He raised his eyebrow. "Not in the mood to play with me?" He teased her.

"I know, right? When did I ever?" She widened her eyes.

"Never." He chuckled, missing her adorableness.

Her face turned crimson. "I read some articles online about some types of antidepressants causing low sex drive. Well, loss of libido is my problem." She rolled her eyes.

"I don't mind being in the room with you to talk about it with Dr. Fournier."

"I just… Well, just in case I need to describe our sex life in detail."

"I see… You are ashamed of our sex life."

"Of course not!" She turned red again.

"I am teasing you." He laughed, pulling her in and tugging her next to him.

She snuggled closer to him, closing her eyes.

Everything will be all right…

CHAPTER 15

IRIS stared out the window, fidgeting with her fingers as she considered what Dr. Fournier had advised her after she told her she wanted to come off antidepressants and sleeping pills, whatever she was taking now. Iris completely understood the possible withdrawal symptoms.

But months? I don't want to wait that long… Iris felt discouraged.

"We can try to reduce the doses for a week first and see how you respond to the adjustment," Dr. Fournier said after Iris became quiet.

"I have to do it… For Thomas and Max. But months?" Iris murmured.

"Be patient, Iris." Dr. Fournier removed her reading glasses and looked at Iris.

After moments of silence, Iris turned to face her doctor and asked, "Do you think I am too attached to Thomas?" This was the real reason she did not want Thomas here today.

"Do you think you are?"

Iris nodded. "Maybe…maybe I need to heal on my own now."

"Would you tell me what makes you think that?" Dr. Fournier gave her a soft smile.

When she took Iris as a patient, she only knew about Thomas' kidnapping. Then she received Iris' medical record and learned about Iris' own abduction. She had reached out to Eva, Dr. Thompson, and Dr. Warren in the States to have a better understanding of Iris' condition. She was optimistic about Iris' chances of having a normal life in the future.

Iris let out a deep sigh and said, "I have been thinking a lot lately…"

Dr. Fournier put her reading glasses on, ready to take notes.

"I wonder how my life would have been if I had never been..." She stopped in mid-sentence, not able to say the words.

Why can't I say the words? Abducted. Trafficked... How hard can it be to say them out loud? Iris frowned.

"We cannot change what has happened," Dr. Fournier said.

"I know... It's just..." Her eyes moved to the windows again. "I was optimistic, independent, outgoing..."

"You are making wonderful progress, Iris."

"He is my savior. My protector," Iris switched her subject to Thomas, ignoring Dr. Fournier's last comment.

The change of subject did not surprise Dr. Fournier because she knew Iris' mind was still all over the place. Therefore, as long as Iris was willing to talk, she would listen. Although she did not think idolizing Thomas was healthy for Iris, she would leave that topic for a much later session.

"He has been the only person who can keep me calm, keep me... together." Iris continued.

Dr. Fournier gazed at Iris earnestly, giving her all the time she needed to open herself up.

"He...he..." Iris lost in her thoughts, remembering one night when she jerked awake from nightmares...

~ ~ ~

She gasped, reaching for Thomas who was sound asleep next to her.

"Mon amour..." He knew she had a nightmare. "Where were you?" he asked, holding her tight.

"In the recovering house..." Her voice was trembling.

"I was there, remember? I would never let anything bad happen to you."

~ ~ ~

She then remembered another time she was awakened by Thomas' calling...

~ ~ ~

"Iris..." Thomas seized her wrists gently, trying to awake her.

She opened her eyes, her heart pounding. She blinked her eyes many times and burst into tears when she recognized his face.

He pulled her in his arms, caressing her back.

"You... I can't..." she sobbed.

"Shh... Where were you?" he whispered.

"I...I ran into...into the woods. I couldn't...couldn't find you. They caught me."

"I was right there. I would always find you..." he consoled her.

~ ~ ~

"Iris," Dr. Fournier's voice brought Iris back to the present.

Iris looked at her doctor, her eyes blinking rapidly.

"We can talk about this during our next session if you prefer," Dr. Fournier said since Iris did not seem to be able to finish what she wanted to say.

"I grabbed on to him like a lifeline," Iris said, turning her head to face her doctor.

Dr. Fournier smiled, gently nodding her head, encouraging her to continue.

"I didn't want to talk about what had happened to me, except when the police interviewed me. When I finally was home, I tried very hard to forget about...everything. Including Thomas. It's easier that way. You know..."

Dr. Fournier gave her an understanding smile.

"I guess everything was sort of swept under the rug. I couldn't see them, but they were still there." Iris let out a sigh, turning her head towards the window again.

Dr. Fournier's private practice was near Aare in the heart of Bern. Iris stared out the window and into the distance. Behind the beautiful city landscape was snowcapped mountains.

"Sometimes... I still cannot believe I am here," she murmured.

"Here in my office?" Dr. Fournier asked, responding to Iris' changing of subject again.

"Switzerland." She turned back to look at her doctor. "I swore I would never come back here when I left." She chuckled.

Dr. Fournier completely understood Iris' reason for not wanting to return to where the trauma had occurred. She knew Iris faced her fear and came back here with Thomas. *Did she regret her decision?*

"Do you think it is a wrong decision to come back?" Dr. Fournier asked cautiously.

Iris quickly shook her head. "It's the best decision of my life." Dr. Fournier smiled.

"He..." Iris tilted her head, considering how to put her thoughts into words. "I was very confused and scared when he was back in my life."

"Why?"

"He...he is my hero, you know." She smiled radiantly, then her expression became solemn almost immediately. "He is also a reminder of what had happened to me."

Dr. Fournier was curious that Iris used *present tense*. "Tell me something, Iris. Why do you think Thomas *is* still a reminder of what had happened to you?"

Iris tilted her head, realizing she did use the word *is*. "It's not... It's not in a bad way, really. He became a part of my life the moment he broke the protocol and saved me. Sometimes when I look at him, I can't help but wonder what would have happened to me if he weren't there..." She paused and looked back out the window. "I know I would have still thought about the same thing if he weren't in my life now. And for all my life, I probably would have been wondering who this undercover officer was."

"So he is not a reminder of the horrifying experience."

"Oh no... He is a reminder of why I had survived. But..." Iris let out a sigh, her mouth curving into an ironic smile. "Still a reminder of what had happened to me. Kind of ironic... Does that make sense?" She looked at her doctor.

"Perfectly." Dr. Fournier smiled at her softly.

"To be with him, I had to face what I had been avoiding. All those memories that had triggered my anxiety attacks. I actually had more nightmares after we started living together." She shrugged. "But he was like a protective shield when I coped with the dreadful remembrance of my abduction and faced my fear and anxiety. Then I started to have less nightmares because I knew nothing would harm me as long as he was around. And I was able to learn to live my life again, knowing he would always protect me."

Iris extended both hands in front of her, palms facing up. She looked at her right hand and said, "Thomas, my hero, my guardian angel." Then she turned to stare at her left hand, her brow furrowed. She suddenly became silent, her breathing heavy.

"Take you time…" Dr. Fournier said.

"I haven't thought about it for a long time. I mean it's always there. It's a part of me…" she trailed off. "Anyway." She took a deep breath and said, "Memories of being drugged, trafficked, and forced…forced to…forced to…"

Dr. Fournier wanted to tell Iris that she did not need to say it, although in her professional opinion it would benefit Iris if she could face her fear.

"Let me try again." Iris glanced at her doctor with an embarrassed smile and then turned back to her left hand again. "A huge load of bollocks."

Dr. Fournier laughed, nodding in approval. She was glad Iris was able to talk about it regardless of her choice of words.

"It's a no brainer." Iris raised her right hand and lowered her left one. She then put both hands on her lap again.

"It sounds like you had a clear mind when you made the decision to be with him."

"I wouldn't say I had a clear mind then. More like…" She paused, considering how to explain her thoughts. "I… I didn't need to say anything, and he just knew exactly how I felt."

"Because he was there," Dr. Fournier said, referring to Thomas as the undercover police officer when Iris was abducted.

Iris nodded. "People only think I must be brave and blinded by love when I took a leap of faith with him. You know, love makes people do crazy things." She chuckled.

"You don't think you were brave then?"

"Honestly, I have no idea." She frowned, "Like I said. I grabbed on to him like a lifeline. I needed him to keep me sane…"

Everything she said so far sounded positive. What made her think she should heal on her own now? Dr. Fournier wondered.

"Dr. Fournier…" Iris looked at her doctor, a growing realization of her perplexity appearing in her eyes. "I think I am still clinging to

Thomas to stay afloat."

THOMAS went back to the hotel after dropping off Iris and Max at their apartment in Bern. He only planned to work for a couple of hours and then spend the rest of the day with his little family.

His desk phone rang.

"Torian," he answered.

"Thomas." Travis was on the line. "You have a visitor here in the lobby. I have tried to handle it, but she insists on seeing you. And… she would not give me her name."

Thomas frowned. "Can you put her on the phone?"

"Of course. One moment, please." Travis did not put the phone on hold, so Thomas was able to hear Travis' conversation with his unexpected visitor. "Excuse me, Ms. Mr. Torian would like to speak with you."

"But I need to see him," a young female voice replied.

"I understand and I have already told him that. He is on the phone now. Maybe—"

"Fine…" Her response sounded annoyed.

"Here she is," Travis said to Thomas before handing the receiver to the lady.

"Hi Thomas," she said to the phone. Her voice had become pleasant and soft. And she called Thomas by his first name as if they had known each other very well.

"Hi." Thomas did not recognize the voice, not sure how to address her properly "How can I help you? Ms…"

"It's Emma," the young lady said pleasantly.

What in the bloody hell? Thomas frowned. "Hi Emma. How can I help you?"

"I have something for you. I want to thank you for what you did for me yesterday. You were so amazing," she said, her voice carrying a hint of shyness and sexual allure, and she was loud as if she wanted anyone around her to think whatever happened between them was intimate.

"It is not necessary." He kept his voice solemn.

"It is!" Her voice became higher. "And you must accept the gifts I have for you."

Not wanting to stay on the phone with her, he said, "Okay. You can leave the gifts with Mr. Saunder."

"No." Her response was instant. "Sorry. I mean…" She paused, trying to come up with excuses. "My aunt won't be happy if I don't deliver the gifts to you. In person."

Thomas let out an irritated sigh. "I will be right there," he said and heard her telling Travis that he was going to see her in a disdainful tone. He hung up the phone, shaking his head. Grabbing his suit jacket from the wooden suit stand, he put it on and headed to the lobby.

When he appeared in the lobby, he immediately noticed that Emma was waiting for him anxiously.

"Thomas!" She called out in a cheerful voice, her eyes sparkling, smile radiant.

Travis gave his boss an apologetic look.

Thomas gave him an acknowledging nod, hiding his irritated expression. He approached his visitor, who was holding a huge bouquet of red roses and a small wrapped box.

"Hi," Emma walked up to him. She got on her tiptoes and seized his bicep with her free hand to kiss his cheek as if they were close friends.

Thomas was caught off guard. He did not want to embarrass her in public by pushing her away, so he stayed still and moved a step back when Emma stood on her feet again.

"Can we grab a drink?" she asked casually.

Thomas was, again, caught off guard by her bizarre behavior. "Emma, I appreciate your thoughtfulness. I am quite busy at the moment. I am afraid I have to decline your invitation."

"You are so businesslike." She giggled. "These are for you." She handed him the flowers and box. "I hope you like chocolate. Who doesn't, right?"

Awkwardly, Thomas looked at the gifts.

"Oh. The bouquet is for your wife." She burst out laughing. "It will be really awkward if I am giving you flowers, won't it?"

"Travis." Thomas turned to his assistant. "Can you... Please?"

Travis quickly stepped up, reaching for the gifts, but Emma glared at him.

"They are for you." She smiled broadly at Thomas. "How about lunch? You must take a lunch break."

What is wrong with this woman? Thomas had lost his patience. "Excuse me. I need to go back to work. You can speak with Mr. Saunder if you have more questions." He turned around and walked away.

"Wait!" Emma chased after him, but Travis stepped up and blocked her. "Hey!" Emma stopped abruptly, her eyes fixed on Thomas who soon disappeared from her view. "Damn it!"

Travis had witnessed women's heads turning when his boss walked into a room. However, this woman was too... Strange? Obsessed? Then he noticed this worried look on her face.

"Are you all right?" he asked her.

Emma ignored him. She turned around and left, bringing the bouquet and chocolate with her.

Travis shrugged and headed back to the office. He knocked on Thomas' door, eager to find out what was going on. He knew it was not his business, but if he was going to fight off admirers or stalkers for his boss in the future, it was his business.

"Come in," Thomas answered.

Travis opened the door and gave Thomas a lopsided smile.

"Is she gone?" Thomas asked.

Travis nodded and asked, "Who is she? I mean... Where did you meet her?"

"Yesterday at Gloria's." Thomas leaned back in his chair. "Gloria was not there, but that woman was. She said Gloria was her aunt."

"Wait. Gloria said she did not have relatives in Bern." Travis leaned against the door frame.

"Maybe Emma is here visiting. I don't know."

"Something is off." Travis stared at the carpet, thinking about the expression on Emma's face earlier.

Thomas shrugged and straightened in his chair. "I am going to finish viewing the budget now. Thanks Travis."

Travis gave Thomas a salute and left the room, closing the door behind him.

CHAPTER 16

IRIS' smile faded when she saw Thomas walking in looking anxious and troubled. He had called her earlier and told her that something came up and he would be home late. And that was all fine with Iris as things happened. Although, he had never brought any stress home from work.

"Thomas?"

He gave her a forced smile. "I need to show you something," he said. "But let me change and wash up first." He then walked into the bedroom.

Ever since they brought Max back from the hospital, washing hands and changing out work clothes before holding him was a must for everyone.

What's going on? Iris walked into the living room and sat on the sofa by her baby, a dark cloud over her head.

Little Maxipoo started to coo and gurgle, making his mother break into a smile.

"Aren't you the cutest..." Iris picked him up from the rocking cuddle and rubbed her son's belly, making him laugh broadly.

"You guys are having fun?" Thomas walked up to them. His upset expression was replaced by a radiant smile.

Iris looked up at him, noticing a big envelope in his hand. "What's that?" she asked.

He stared at the envelope, the troubled expression back again. "I received some photos today." He sat down next to her. Then a big smile appeared on his face right away when his son extended his hands towards him. He felt an instant contentment in his chest. He put the envelope on the coffee table and picked up his son from Iris' lap.

"Photos?" She reached for the envelope.

"Those are just photocopies. Julia took the original," Thomas said, standing up with his son in his arms.

Iris withdrew her hand as if the envelope just burned her. "Julia?"

"You will understand why I needed to reach out to her today when you see the photos." His eyes switched between Iris and the envelope.

She picked up the envelope and carefully took the contents out. Her eyes widened as she saw the very first photo.

"Your girlfriend?" she asked, tilting her head and staring at an image of a beautiful woman with long curly blonde hair holding a huge red rose bouquet kissing Thomas' cheek. If he did not tell her about that unexpected visit from Gloria's niece two days ago, Iris would have thought that woman was showing her appreciation after receiving the flowers from Thomas.

Thomas chuckled, walking into the kitchen. He knew Iris would never doubt his fidelity, but he did not want what was happening to trouble her since Dr. Fournier just modified her medications.

"Hum…" She looked at another photo. It was a close-up shot of Thomas and the same woman looking into each other's eyes as if they were deeply in love. "You didn't tell me this Emma person is so beautiful," she said, bringing the photo closer to examine the photoshopped image. It was taken in Gloria's shop, but Iris could spot so many flaws.

And the next photo raised her eyebrows. "Were those roses for me? They were so beautiful… What a waste." She sighed, looking at an image of that woman in Thomas' arms and rose petals flying.

If Thomas did not tell her his encounter in Gloria's shop, she would have wondered what was going on when she saw these photos. And people would easily believe that Thomas was having an affair.

There were more, but she had seen enough. She put the photos down and looked up at Thomas, who was walking back from the kitchen, baby in one arm and a mug in one hand. She did not know what to say, just staring at the man of her life carrying the most adorable baby.

He handed her the mug with hot tea.

"She isn't even your type," she said, receiving the mug.

"What's my type?" Thomas chuckled, sitting down and placed a kiss on her forehead.

"*Moi* is your type." She took a sip of the hot tea. "Blackmail?" she asked. "How much are they asking? What a cheesy idea!"

"Did you read the note?"

"What note?" She put the mug down and picked up the stack of papers again. She flipped through them until she saw a photocopy of an elegant stationary with a message typed in German. She read it a couple of times and believed it asked Thomas to go to Bellevue Palace alone at 9pm tonight if he did not want the photos to be sent to the press and his wife.

"Someone is blackmailing you to meet him or her in Bellevue Palace?" Iris turned to look at him, frowning.

Thomas just shrugged.

She stared at the copy of the note again. "Whoever planned this obviously doesn't know us well. I would just laugh at the photos, thinking it's a prank."

"But the press is going to be an issue."

"Who would want to do this to us?" She frowned. "And you just got kidnapped not long ago. Do they really think you would just show up alone?"

Bébé Max cooed and gurgled as if he had an answer for his mother.

Thomas leaned back, putting the baby on his lap to face him. "*Donc qu'en penses-tu, ma puce?*" he asked his little sweetie what he thought about it in French.

Little Bébé Max replied with burbling, bringing a big smile on his daddy's face.

Suddenly, Iris reached for her phone and tapped on her contacts. She found Gloria's number and tapped the call icon.

Thomas looked at her, frowning.

"I am calling Gloria,"

"I called her after receiving the photos, and she did not answer."

Furrows appeared in her forehead as the phone kept ringing.

"No answer?" he asked when he saw her disappointed expression.

She shook her head and ended the call. "I am worried about her now. I don't think she is involved."

"I don't think so, either. Julia is looking into that, too."

The name 'Julia' caught Iris' attention again. "Why did you call Julia?" She knew Julia was a human trafficking task force special agent. Calling her for blackmail was like using a sledgehammer to crack a nut.

Thomas' hesitant expression made Iris' heart pound.

"Just tell me. Please." So many possibilities and scenarios were going through her mind. "Does it have anything to do with your assignments before? Are we safe?" She was really concerned about her baby's safety.

"Yes, we are." Thomas wrapped an arm around her. "Julia has been keeping me updated about..." He paused, not sure how much information he should share with her.

"About what?" Iris pulled away, staring at him. "Vera?"

Thomas frowned.

"This... You think Vera is behind this?" Iris' voice was trembling as saying the word 'Vera' was like drinking acid. "She is... This is too immature for a person like her. She kidnapped you all the way from the States. Why would she...why would she plan this kind... this kind of..." She started to breathe heavily.

"Shh..." Thomas pulled her in and wrapped one arm around her while holding on to his son with the other.

Bébé Max giggled when Iris leaned into him.

"It makes no sense..." She murmured.

"Julia told me their intel has indicated that her organization has dropped her," Thomas said, his voice as soft as possible.

"Dropped her... What does that mean?"

"As in cutting her off. She used the organization's resources to kidnap me...for her own gain. They considered—"

Iris looked up at him, frowning at the words *for her own gain*. Her piercing look made him stop in mid-sentence.

"Nothing happened," he quickly clarified. "She wanted me to work with her. And when I refused, she asked for ransom instead."

The thought of Thomas being in the same room with Vera made her nauseated. "She was always all over you."

"I was doing my job." He sighed.

"I know…" She tried to push aside those unpleasant images of Thomas and Vera together. "So what happened?"

"Well. Apparently, my kidnapping is a failure because fedpol has tracked her and her accomplices down. The organization considers her a liability."

"So she wants to take her revenge out on you for her misfortune?" Iris was pissed. "Or she is obsessed with you."

"Well, if she is really the one behind this scheme, then she is making a huge mistake. She has gotten away with what she did and can hide in another country. She probably will never get caught. So we are not really hundred percent sure if she is behind this."

"I think her fixation with you must have clouded her judgment," she said with disgust.

"If that's the case, then it will be a great opportunity to catch her." Thomas was talking like a law enforcement officer.

"What if it's a trap? Other criminals you had dealt with before?"

"There is only one way to find out," he said casually.

"Wait…" Iris pulled away, staring at him. "You are going to Bellevue Palace tonight?"

Thomas gave her a silent answer.

"You are not an undercover agent anymore," she said, her eyes widened. "Let the police do their job."

"Mon amour…"

"Don't *mon amour* me. I almost lost you to that woman. Let the police do their job."

"Julia will have her team—"

"No!" she exclaimed, cutting him off.

Her suddenly loud voice startled her baby. His tiny lips twisted, bottom lip pouting, then came the wailing.

Iris turned away from them, tears flooding her eyes, regretting her outburst.

Thomas held the baby against his chest, gently bouncing and rubbing his back. He leaned towards Iris and placed a kiss on her hair. "Let's talk about this later," he whispered.

There is nothing to talk about. She wiped away her tears.

THOMAS walked into the Bellevue Palace and stopped in the lobby atrium under the impressive stained glass ceiling. He removed his black leather gloves, his eyes scanning the room. He did not know what to expect as *Come to Bellevue Palace at 9pm tonight. Alone* was all he had.

Julia had already gotten in touch with Bellevue Palace management and received their cooperation. Even though the hotel was not able to provide any information about their guests due to their privacy policy, they allowed several plainclothes police officers to patrol the hotel and some to lounge in the lobby pretending to be hotel guests.

Thomas kept his expression solemn when he recognized a couple of his former colleagues. During his decade-long career in law enforcement, he was on similar police operations numerous times. He could not deny the adrenaline rush he was getting and how eager he wanted to solve this case. However, he did not miss his old job at all now that Iris and Max were in his life.

The only reason he told Julia he must be here was that he would do everything to protect his family. He needed to find out who was behind this exaction and put an end to it.

Was it about DeMont Enterprise? They doubled that because his family ran honest businesses in the hospitality industry. He and Louis had gone through all the deals they had been working on this afternoon and did not find anything suspicious.

He honestly wished it was Vera and she had been careless and committed this immature crime. He vowed to put her behind bars so he and Iris would never have to constantly look over their shoulders.

But Iris could not understand his reason. She had a meltdown before he left home and locked herself in the bedroom. Thankfully,

Eva and Louis were there to be with her and the baby. He hated himself for having to leave her like that and hoped that she would forgive him after it was over.

"*Entschuldigen Sie bitte!*" When he was about to remove his black coat, a young lady approached him, seeking his attention in German. And before he could react, she handed him an envelope.

All undercover officers in the lobby were on high alert, fixing their eyes on the encounter.

Thomas received the envelope, his eyes on the young lady, who looked too young and innocent to be committing a crime, although he would not lower his guard.

"*Tschüss!*" she said goodbye, a big smile on her face, and headed towards the front entrance.

"*Bitte warten Sie!*" he asked her to wait but she had already walked through the revolving door. He knew the officers posting outside the hotel would catch her for questions, so he did not follow her. He opened the envelope and took out a folded paper.

It was a simple message telling him that a limousine was waiting for him outside.

Someone might be watching him, so he could not notify any officer in the lobby or Julia of the new message he just received. However, he was not worried as they had suspected that a meeting in a hotel was too easy and were ready for any unexpected situation. He looked up and stared at the front door for a few seconds before he marched out of the lobby.

A luxury black limousine was parked right outside the entrance, a chauffeur holding the backseat door open for him.

Thomas cautiously walked towards the car. In his peripheral vision, he saw several plainclothes officers getting into unmarked cars.

"Good evening, Sir," the chauffeur greeted Thomas in English when Thomas walked up to him. "This is for you." He handed him an envelope, just like the one he received earlier.

"Thank you." Thomas accepted it and stepped into the car. He hastily took his next instructions out, eager to know where he was going.

The note read: *"Turn off your phone and give it to the chauffeur."*

He frowned and then realized the door was still open. Apparently, the chauffeur had his own instructions to follow. Thomas took his phone out from the front pocket of his coat, turned it off, and handed it to the smiling chauffeur.

"Thank you, Sir." The friendly chauffeur accepted the phone, and closed the door. He walked to the driver seat in an unhurried manner and got into the seat.

"Please leave it down," Thomas said when the chauffeur pushed the up-button to close the partition. He needed to be able to see all surrounding areas.

"Of course, Sir," the chauffeur replied and pushed the down-button to lower the half-closed partition.

Thomas was not worried he would be kidnapped again or in any danger because he was well prepared this time and his former colleagues were right behind him.

It was dark outside, but he was able to see they were leaving Bern and heading east. Soon, the city night lights of Bern fell behind him, and they were heading to remote rural areas.

Roughly twenty minutes later, they drove up to a wrought iron gate, which Thomas found looked very familiar. The gate swung open upon arrival of the limousine.

At that moment, Thomas knew exactly whom he was going to meet. He turned around and looked through the back window. The gate closed immediately after them, keeping the police on the outside of the property.

He remembered this place, but it was not significant enough for him to remember when and why he was here.

Think! He fixed his eyes on the windshield in front of him, trying to see anything that might trigger his memory about this place.

Then a full picture of when and why he was here popped into his head when he saw a gently lit farmhouse standing straight ahead of them.

He escorted Vera here one time when one of her bodyguards was sick. She gave him no reason and purpose why she was here and was in that farmhouse for several hours. He and other guards were asked to wait outside the entire time. He had asked Julia to look into this place, and all she told him later was that this place was irrelevant.

Thomas stared at the double doors when the car stopped right in front of them. He was not sure if he should go inside... Not only was he not a police officer anymore, but he also had a wife and a son to think about now.

He looked around and saw many cars were in the parking lot and several uniformed drivers were casually standing by their cars, just like what he did the last time. They all looked harmless. Plus, the officers, who were following him earlier, would have notified Julia by now. She had checked into this place before, so she knew where he was and would have sent backup already.

The chauffeur opened the door for him and handed him a small black velvet box. "Sir, you need this to go inside."

Thomas hesitantly received the box and opened it.

A sparkling star shaped diamond ring sat elegantly in the center.

Thomas looked up at the chauffeur, who nodded gently at him with the same friendly smile, which he had been wearing since he picked up Thomas.

Thomas took the ring out of the box and put it on his right middle finger. He frowned as it felt odd and tight on his hand. He then removed it and put it on the right index finger instead.

"Very well, Sir," the chauffeur said as if he approved of it, holding the door wide open for Thomas patiently.

Thomas stepped out of the car. He scanned his surroundings first before walking up to the double doors, which swung inward before he reached them. He stepped inside with extreme caution and found himself alone in a foyer illuminated with only candles on the walls. He turned around when he heard the double doors slowly closing behind him. When the doors were completely shut, another set of double doors on the far end of the room opened up, mellow music muffled behind them.

A tall woman appeared in the doorway. She was wearing her red hair in a high ponytail, heavy makeup, black sky-high heels, black lace mini skirt, and...nothing else.

"*Bienvenue à l'étoile, Monsieur Torian,*" She spoke French, welcoming Thomas to L'étoile in an alluring voice.

L'étoile? He wondered if it was associated with Marcus' club Étoile and quickly made a mental note to reach out to Marcus after the whole thing was over.

Although he tried not to look at her almost perfect breasts, the star-shaped necklace pendant hung between them caught his attention. It was identical to the ring he was wearing.

"I am Tiffany. May I take your coat, Sir?" She kept a pleasant smile on her face.

Thomas removed his coat and handed it to her, keeping his eyes above her chest.

The hostess turned around and gave his coat to a young man standing to her left. Thomas tried to suppress his surprise when he noticed the young man was wearing nothing but French cuffs with cufflinks matching the pendant and the ring.

Sex club? Thomas wondered.

"Please follow me," Tiffany said and pivoted on her heels and opened the heavy red velvet curtains behind her.

Following Tiffany, he walked into a modern, luxurious, and full of half-naked people lounge.

Scratching that. He just spotted several completely-naked women and men lounging around.

Tiffany led him to a narrow hallway and opened a door. She stayed in the hallway, motioning Thomas to the room.

He took a deep breath and stepped inside, coming face to face with Vera.

CHAPTER 17

***IRIS** is going to go out of her mind,* Thomas thought when he saw Vera, who was smiling at him seductively.

She was sitting on a lush royal blue sofa, a leather braided whip in her hand. The outfit she was wearing screamed dominatrix: a lavish black lace-up short bustier corset barely covering her bust, black fishnet skirt revealing a rhinestone g-string, and a pair of black lace-up thigh boots. And a star shaped diamond ring was glittering on her right index finger.

"Hello, Thomas," she greeted him. Her eyes moved past him, and she winked at Tiffany.

Tiffany hastily closed the door and left Thomas alone in the room with Vera.

"Please have a seat." Vera's voice was deep and smooth.

He scanned the room and sat down on a single seater across from her. "I did not expect to see you so soon." He spoke first.

"Me, either," she said, her fingers playing with the whip.

"Just cut to the chase. What do you want?" He rested his elbows on the armrests, fingers steepled.

"A favor." She uncrossed and crossed her legs, the sparkling g-string fighting for attention.

"You really think you are in the right position to ask me for a favor after you ordered my kidnapping and put my wife and child in the hospital?" His piercing eyes were fixed on hers.

She shrugged. "How's my lovely Iris?" she asked.

He glared at her. "Do. Not. Say. Her. Name." Her mentioning Iris' name ignited fury in him. This woman had ruined many lives including his Iris, who was still struggling with anxiety, flashback, and mistrust.

"Touchy, Thomas. It doesn't sound like you." She smiled, not intimidated by his harsh tone.

"You can easily contact me and ask for this favor you want. Why go through the trouble?" Thomas kept his voice calm, refusing to play her game.

She shrugged again. "Just wanting to have some fun with you."

Seriously? Thomas raised one eyebrow.

"I had my girls all over the place waiting for you. All the bars, shops, restaurants around your hotel. I was surprised you didn't even notice those breathtaking women lounging around your hotel."

Thomas took a deep breath, trying to tame his anger.

"Do you think Iris will be upset when she sees those photos?" Vera asked as if it was a fun game, completely ignoring Thomas' warning about not saying Iris' name.

"You are going to send her the photos regardless, aren't you? His brows were knitted.

"Just want to spice up your marriage." She winked.

"Well, sorry to disappoint you. She has already seen them. And you have wasted your energy for nothing."

"Nothing? Not even a little…upset?" She blinked her eyes. "Ingrid, I mean, Emma is very young and beautiful. Too bad I had to fire her because she could not even get you to have a drink with her. Imagine if I had a picture of you two flirting in a bar… Or even better, making out—"

"Where is the flower shop owner?" he interrupted her, ignoring anything she was saying. Julia had not given him any update on Gloria, so asking the mastermind could save everybody's time.

"Oh, that woman…" Vera laughed. "She really thought she won a Bahama Vacation." And when she saw his sullen expression, she added, "She is having the time of her life in the Bahamas now. Give me some credit, please."

While he felt relieved to learn that Gloria was safe, he was troubled and puzzled by Vera's mindset. "What do you want from me?"

"I am intrigued by you, Thomas. I only wish you—"

"What do you want?" Thomas cut her off again. "And what

makes you think I will help you?"

She frowned at his grating voice, furrows appearing in her smooth brow as if her feelings were hurt.

Thomas did not have any sympathy for her. Ideas of how he could stall her until Julia and her team arrived started to go through his mind.

"Turn me in," she said, her voice determined with a hint of trembling.

Thomas was shocked, not sure if he had heard her correctly.

She stood up and walked towards him, making his body tense up. "Darling, I am harmless." She ran her slender fingers over his arm when she walked around him. She then walked towards the minibar. "Can I get you something to drink?" she asked while she was making herself a martini.

"No, thank you."

She walked back to her seat, a martini glass in her hand. "By the way, I will need that ring back." She glanced at Thomas' finger. "That's my very last favor here. It looks really good on you though."

Thomas wondered what other favors she had collected from l'étoile so far and again wondered if Étoile in Paris had anything to do with this place? He kept his eyes on Vera, removing the ring and placing it on the table between them.

She took a sip of her drink and said in a lazy voice. "The big guys are mad at me." She sighed. "And you know how much they loved me before." She raised her martini glass towards him. "So, can you imagine how pissed they are now?"

What she just said confirmed Julia's intel; the syndicate in Italy did drop her. He knew exactly how much they valued her before because of the revenue she generated and because she had many politicians and billionaires at her fingertips. Thomas could not believe they would just cut her off.

"I believe they got you out of jail the last time. Why go back to the jail voluntarily now?"

She tilted her head, gazing at him, her lips turning upward slightly. She averted her eyes and took another sip of her drink. "There is no *second-chance* in their world. Not even my father can save me this time."

Father? He knitted his brows, processing the newest information and making a mental note to pass on the information to Julia.

"Nobody knows." She perceived the bewilderment on his face. "I mean, except those big bosses since he is one of them."

"Why not run away. Disappear."

"From them?" She widened her inky eyes as if his comment was ridiculous. "I am safer in a Swiss prison."

So they did not just drop her. They are after her. But why am I here? He nodded, his brows still knitted. "You can just turn yourself in. You don't need me."

"Like I said. I just wanted to have some fun with you before I go away." She finished her drink in one gulp and stood up, heading to the bar to make herself another one.

He shook his head, wondering what kind of fun she was talking about since they were apparently in a BDSM club.

"Don't worry. I am not going to whip you." She chuckled, seemingly reading his mind.

He frowned at her comment, not finding it amusing.

She leisurely paced around the room, sipping her drink. "I want you, Thomas."

He shut his eyes, not wanting to have this conversation. Again.

"I know I cannot have you, but that doesn't mean I cannot fancy you. Right? We all have our fantasies. And here…" She raised her glass to the ceiling as she turned to face him. "L'étoile is my fantasy land." She sauntered back to the sofa and lounged on it. "I am a dominatrix. I am sure you have already figured that out. But you, somehow, make me want to be…submissive." She let out a deep breath. "You messed up my head, Thomas."

Do I really want to hear this? He was becoming impatient by the second, wondering how he could speed things up.

"So I thought I would mess up Iris' mind a little," she added. "Oops, sorry about saying her name again and again."

Thomas took a deep breath to calm his growing anger.

"I love how easy I can push your buttons simply by mentioning her name." She took a sip of her drink and set it down on the side table. "Just chill. So, tell me, Thomas. Were you an undercover officer when you worked for me?"

He raised his eyebrows and then smirked, trying to pretend he was actually flattered by her question. "I wish I were good enough to be one."

"Hmm... I have been racking my brain to figure you out." She stared at him, her long legs crossed, arms over her chest, and the index finger with the star ring resting on her cheek. "Since you had billions in your trust fund, I really don't think you would want to become a police officer."

Thomas felt sorry for her. A person like her would never understand why he had dedicated himself to crack down human trafficking organizations.

"But why a security company?" she asked.

If she wants a reason, then I will give her one, as long as I can put her behind bars, he thought. He leaned back on the sofa and said, "I was bored and wanted to have legit excuses to beat up people."

She raised her eyebrows. "So your rap sheet is real."

He shrugged.

"What...what made you change your mind? We worked so well together before."

Is that wishful thinking in her voice? Thomas could not believe she still thought she had a chance with him. Maybe she needed to hear the truth. "Iris," he said.

She frowned, not pleased to hear the name this time.

"She not only made me change my mind but also changed me. She makes me want to be a better man. She makes me happy," he continued to strike her with his real feelings for Iris. "She is the love of my life, and she is my fantasy coming true."

She chuckled, averting her eyes to hide her disappointment and humiliation.

"How do you want to do this?" he asked, done playing her game.

She shook her head, a slight smile on her pale face.

Did she change her mind? Thomas was suddenly worried. He had no problem restraining her and walking her out of this room. But was he able to walk out of this club? Even if he were a police officer, a club like this would protect their patrons first. And he had no way of knowing if Julia and her teams were nearby.

Letting out a deep sigh, Vera reached her hand to the side of the sofa and pressed a button.

Did she just press a silent button for security? Thomas clenched his fists. A knock on the door made his body tense up.

"Come in, Tiffany," Vera said softly.

Tiffany opened the door and walked in submissively, holding a phone, which Thomas recognized.

Vera extended one hand towards Tiffany. When Tiffany handed her the phone, Vera covered Tiffany's hand with her other hand.

"You are one of my favorites," Vera said, gazing at the young lady with affection.

"Thank you, Mistress Vera." Tiffany blushed at the unexpected compliment.

Instead of letting her go, Vera pulled her in and gave her a passionate kiss on her lips.

Thomas could not suppress his surprise and a reaction a normal man would have while witnessing such an arousing act.

"Thank you, my love," Vera said after pulling away and letting go of Tiffany's hand. "Leave us be."

"Yes, Mistress Vera." Tiffany scurried out of the room, closing the door behind her.

Vera handed Thomas his phone, her face inexpressive as if she had not just kissed a beautiful woman earlier.

Thomas cleared his throat—and his mind—before taking his phone back.

"Call your fedpol lady-friend now. I know you have been in contact with her after the kidnapping," she said. "Tell her not to come here but meet us at her office."

He looked at her skeptically.

"And tell her to get me a good deal if she wants to know what I know." She winked at him.

Thomas turned on his phone and made the call, his eyes fixed on Vera, who picked up her drink and took a sip.

Vera was in a plain black sweater and jeans when she walked out of the club with Thomas. They got into the same limousine that drove Thomas here and sat in silence all the way back to Bern.

Julia and many officers were waiting for them when the limousine pulled up to the federal office building entrance.

"I guess that's it." Vera turned to look at Thomas, who did not respond to her comment but opened the door and stepped out of the car.

One officer opened the door for Vera, who stared straight ahead accepting her destiny. Wrapping a red cashmere scarf around her neck and shoulders, she gave herself a smile before stepping out of the car gracefully. Her eyes became concerned when she scanned the surroundings.

Thomas walked around the car and stood by her side. "You are safe. Julia made sure all of the buildings around here were thoroughly checked out."

She gazed at him for a few seconds and then gave him an appreciating smile.

If she had not done so many unspeakable things to those women, not to mention his beloved Iris, he might feel sorry for her. Now he was only glad that one sinner was off the street.

Julia walked up to them and signaled two officers to escort Vera into the building. She then turned to face Thomas. "Good job, Torian."

Thomas nodded, suddenly feeling exhausted.

"Are you sure you don't want to come back?" She teased him, although her voice was serious.

Thomas gave her a gentle smile. In his peripheral vision, he caught Vera flinging her face to their direction. He turned to look at her, knowing she had heard Julia. He fixed his eyes on Vera's astounded expression and said to Julia, "No. Iris and Max are my priority now."

THOMAS was finally home. He quietly opened the door and saw his brother jumping up from the sofa in the living room. He also saw his son sleeping peacefully in his bouncer next to the sofa.

Louis walked up to him and pulled him in for a bear hug.

"It is over now," he said to Louis, who was having a hard time letting go of his baby brother.

Thomas was not worried when he left home earlier because he was confident that he would never be in any danger. The operation this evening was nothing compared to the nature of his missions before.

However, he had done a lot of thinking when he was driving home. He reminded himself that his family and Iris were not trained to deal with criminals. He needed to put himself in their shoes and understand what he did tonight had distressed them.

Louis was still speechless, not able to let go of his brother.

"How's Iris?" Thomas asked.

"She…" Louis finally let go of Thomas and took a deep breath. "Eva was finally able to calm her down. I think she is sleeping now. Eva is in there with her."

Thomas nodded, putting his coat on the back of a single seat sofa. "Thank you so much," he said, keeping his voice low.

"Don't mention it." Louis patted Thomas on the shoulder. "Eva and I can take Max so you and Iris can spend some time alone. We are going to stay at a nearby hotel."

"That would be great." Thomas turned to look at his son and then back to his brother. "I should…" He tilted his head towards the master bedroom.

Louis nodded and walked back to sit by the baby bouncer.

Thomas headed down the hall. He took a deep breath before he gently opened the door.

A smile spread across Eva's face when she saw Thomas appearing in the doorway. She slowly stood up from the chair by the bed, trying not to make any noise.

Thomas' eyes landed on Iris, who was lying on the bed facing the balcony, away from the door. He quietly walked in.

Eva stood on her tiptoes to give him a kiss on his cheek. "Be patient with her," she whispered in his ear.

He nodded, his eyes fixed on Iris.

Eva left the room and closed the door behind her.

Thomas crawled in bed slowly and scooped Iris from behind. Just as his hand touched her, she burst into tears.

She was not sleeping. How was she able to fall asleep when she thought Thomas might be in danger?

"I am so sorry…" he whispered.

Her body started to tremble violently.

"Shh…" He kissed her hair and said, "It is over now. Vera was taken into custody tonight."

"What…what…what?" she asked between sniveling and hiccuping.

"We never have to worry about seeing her or hearing from her anymore."

Iris turned around to face him, her eyes red, puffy, and full of tears.

He felt as if someone had tightly squeezed his chest. "I am so sorry," he said and placed a kiss on her forehead, feeling repentant.

He just handed Vera over to the authorities, so he was supposed to feel triumphant and thrilled now. However, he was feeling powerless now while holding his vulnerable wife in his arms.

He had assumed Iris would be supportive of his action, so he put his eagerness to take down Vera before Iris' mental welfare.

More snivels and hiccups… Iris buried her face in his chest and sobbed even harder as the past few hours had been sheer torture. She left as if the whole world had collapsed when he walked out of the door after she pleaded with, yelled at, and threatened him.

He doesn't care that I need him, we need him.

He is not going to make it because they are waiting for him to walk into the trap.

He is never coming back…

Those thoughts were all she believed regardless he had repeatedly explained to her why he must go. And no matter how hard Eva had tried to comfort her, no words were able to get into her head except her own pessimistic thinking.

She was going insane and felt like being tossed back to months ago when she was told Thomas was kidnapped. And this time... Not only was she mournful, but she also felt abandoned because he was not taken... He walked away from her.

CHAPTER 18

IRIS' beautiful face appeared on the screen of Thomas' silenced phone set on the table, bringing a content smile on his face.

"It is Iris," Thomas said to his brother and Eva, who were sitting on the other side of the booth. They were having lunch in a small diner near DeMont Bern.

Thomas had not left Iris' side since that dreadful event, and he finally agreed to go back to the office after Iris begged him to two weeks ago...

~ ~ ~

"I don't need a twenty-four-hour babysitter! Please go to work, and bring home the bacon," Iris grumbled.

Thomas chuckled. "I am sure we have plenty of bacon."

"You know what I mean." She rolled her eyes.

~ ~ ~

Thomas did not follow up on Vera's arrest, nor did Julia give him any updates. They seemingly had a mutual understanding that his family would be his only concern now.

It had been uneventful in the last two weeks. And even though Iris was irritable sometimes, Thomas had learned to give her the space she needed to avoid any argument.

Holidays were approaching, and they could not wait to celebrate Bébé Max's first Christmas.

"Hey..." Thomas answered the phone.

"Thomas..." Iris was choking with sobs. "Can...can...can you come...come home...now? Please..."

"Are you hurt?" He jumped up from his seat, grabbing his coat hung by the booth. "What happened? Is Max all right? I am...I am on my way." He headed towards the door.

Louis and Eva were on their feet as well. Louis put a couple of bills on the table to cover their lunch and followed Eva and Thomas out of the diner.

"Please…" That was the last word Iris said to Thomas before she hung up. He took off running towards the hotel, wishing they still lived in their Bern apartment instead of a forty-minute drive away.

"I will drive." Louis and Eva were right behind him.

Iris dropped her phone on the bed and picked up Bébé Max, who was cooing and gurgling, making the cutest noises. He scrunched his tiny nose and waved his two chubby arms in the air. "Daddy will be home soon…" Iris whispered to him, tears falling down her cheeks.

It was the hardest decision she had ever made, but she believed if she wanted to get better and keep her little family together, this was the only way.

After her last meltdown, Dr. Fournier increased the dosages of her medication for anxiety and depression again. She was able to take care of her baby and did not have to worry about mood swings. The medications did their jobs but also numbed her emotions. Again.

Thomas' spontaneous hugs and kisses had no longer aroused her. His tenderness had become unaffecting when it used to make her melt into a puddle of bliss.

She wanted to hold Maxipoo and feel that overpowering love she saw in Thomas' eyes when he had the baby in his arms. She wanted to look at her son and be able to feel the pain in her chest when she imagined how her life would be without him.

She still regretted that she was not able to be by his side when he was lying in the incubator, but she was too broken physically and emotionally then.

And she also regretted that she had promised her son the world but could not even give him a healthy mommy.

She was not there for him then, but she wanted to be here for him now. But how?

"My little-one, Mommy will get better for you and Daddy. I promise," she whispered to Bébé Max and kissed his forehead, inhaling his angelic scent.

She got out of the bed with him in her arms and walked to the window. Looking out to the lake, she felt so exhausted but yet also hopeful…because of all the emotions she was feeling now.

Hopeful was what the optimistic and cheerful Iris used to feel all the time, and she had missed that Iris so very much.

Can I find her again? She slowly sat down on the floor as the forceful feeling of despair was becoming too unbearable.

"Iris." Thomas' calling pulled Iris back to reality from her spaced-out status.

She opened her eyes, not sure how long she had been sitting on the floor with Maxipoo sleeping in her arms.

"Iris." Thomas' calling became louder.

She stared at the doorway, and soon he appeared into view. Then she saw Eva and Louis right behind him.

"I…I am here…" Thomas whispered when he knelt down in front of her. "Did you fall? Are you hurt?"

His attentiveness was breaking her heart…

She handed him the baby and said, "I am fine. Just very tired…"

He received his son with care and tenderness. The affection in his eyes was so powerful that it brought tears to her eyes.

She gazed at them, wanting this image of Thomas holding Bébé Max to be deeply imprinted on her mind.

And unexpectedly, Thomas turned around and gave their son to Eva, who carefully received the sleeping baby. He turned back to Iris and said, "Louis and Eva will look after Max for a while."

She smiled at Eva and Louis with gratitude.

"Call us later," Louis said, wrapping one arm around Eva's shoulders.

"Take as long as you need," Eva said, smiling at Iris.

Iris watched them turning around and leaving the room. Her eyes stayed at the empty doorway, tears gushing down.

"Mon amour…" Thomas gently touched her cheek to bring her attention back to him.

He had sensed Iris had been more emotional lately, but he thought it might be because he went back to work and she was adapting to the changes. But this… He frowned, letting out a deep sigh. This was unexpected.

Iris could see the sadness and perplexity in his eyes and so much more emotions that she could not understand.

Suddenly, he got up and walked into the en suite, and then he marched out holding her medications. He just stared at her, his blue gaze perplexed.

Iris was not sure what was happening. She had never seen Thomas looking so lost.

"When did you stop taking them?" he asked, his voice low, hurt, and accusing.

Her eyes moved to the bottles in his hands. They were almost full. Then she looked at his glowering expression again, more fat tears rolling down her cheeks.

Thomas drew in a deep breath to calm himself down before he walked towards her and knelt back down in front of her again. "Did you talk to Dr. Fournier about this?" he asked, trying to keep his voice calm.

She averted her eyes and said, "Her plan takes too long…"

"Iris!" He raised his voice, "Do you know how dangerous it—" He hastily stopped and took a deep breath to control his growing anger when he saw her flinching at his harsh tone.

He dropped the bottles and reached for her. "I am sorry…" He held her hands, relieved that she did not withdraw them from him. "You know how dangerous it is to stop taking your medications without talking to Dr. Fournier, don't you?"

She nodded, staring at their joining hands.

"How long?" he asked, his voice tender.

She shrugged and said in a small voice, "Three…three weeks…"

He let out a frustrated sigh. "Why?"

And, that single word brought more tears to her eyes. She turned her head away from him.

"Talk to me, please," he pleaded softly.

She drew in a deep breath and said, "I want to go home."

"You are home. I don't understand…" he said, but somehow in his heart he knew exactly what she meant.

"I need the sun, the beach, the salty air, and...and things that remind me of my childhood..."

"Okay," he replied right away.

She turned to look at him, not expecting him to agree with her without a fight, an argument of some kind.

"I will get the passport for Max as soon as possible, and we will go home to the States," he said in enthusiasm.

She looked into his blue eyes, her soul torn into pieces. She pulled her hands out of his and cupped his face in them. She shook her head, not able to make a sound, tears gushing out.

"What is it? Tell me..."

"I...I want to go home by myself."

His face turned pale, frowning. "Why?" he said, holding her hands and grasping them tightly.

"Thomas," her voice was weak and sorrowful. "I need to get better...on my own."

"I don't understand..." His expression became painful. "Am I... Did I...did I do something wrong?"

"Oh no, *mon amour*..." She got on her knees and leaned forward, her face inches away from his. "You are perfect."

"Then why?" His voice was becoming impatient, thin moisture coating his cobalt blue eyes.

Iris shut her eyes as the desperation and sadness in his eyes were too unbearable. She slowly took several deep breaths while Thomas fixed his eyes on her with apprehension.

She then opened her eyes again and smiled at her beautiful man. "Do you know how much I miss kissing you passionately?"

His tips started to tremble.

"I...I cannot feel that passion and lust when I am taking the medications." She caressed his cheek. "I want to get better."

"We can get you better together." Tears were rolling down his cheeks.

She leaned in and kissed his tears away. And he immediately embraced her in his arms.

"I realized one thing when I was talking to Dr. Fournier last month..." she whispered. "I...I..." She paused, choked with emotion.

He held her tight, waiting patiently for her to continue.

"I...I am still clinging to you like...like a lifeline."

He blinked, trying to understand what she meant, and slowly loosening his hold.

She leaned back to look at him. "I knew...I knew what Vera's plan for me that night," she said, remembering that dreadful night. "Mia had painted a very clear picture for me. I..." She swallowed hard as if it just happened yesterday. "I had prepared to end my life if...if she...if she—"

"Shh..." He gently put his fingers over her mouth to stop her. "I would never let that happen to you."

"But I didn't know." She pulled his hand down. "When you asked me to trust you, you became my only hope... Only option... My lifeline..."

"And I thank you for trusting me." He brought her hands to his lips and kissed them.

"You are thanking me?" She chuckled.

"We saved each other, Iris. Getting you out of there made me... made me feel hopeful again."

She tilted her head, feeling baffled. Thomas had never talked about his own experience as an undercover agent then.

"Witnessing what all those women, you, had gone through..." He ran the back of his fingers along her soft cheek. "That undercover task had badly weakened my mental strength."

"Mon amour..." She remembered she often found him looking dejected. But back then, she detested him too much to care about him. Only if she had known what he was going through...

"When I saw you walking towards Julia, one step closer to your freedom, I got my strength back. I knew I could continue to do my job."

She threw herself onto him and wrapped her arms around his neck, bursting into tears. "I..." She sniffled. "I've never known..."

"Vera is behind bars now. That should put our minds at ease."

"Thanks to you," she whispered.

Thomas smiled, feeling relieved and believing he had changed her mind.

"That's why I think I can do this," she said, her voice barely more than a whisper.

He pulled away from her, his eyes confused and troubled.

"You don't need to be saved anymore, but I do," she said, her voice calm.

"I don't understand...."

She reached her hand up to brush a strand of hair off his forehead. Her heart started to beat a little faster when his blue eyes gazed at her with so much affection. She smiled, one hand pressing on her heart, which was now pounding heavily for him because... because she could feel her love and passion for him again. She closed her eyes and inhaled deeply, welcoming the sensation.

She opened her eyes and met his doting gaze again. "Mon amour..." She cupped his face. "You've done your job. Let me do mine."

"I should...I need to be around to help you," he pleaded.

She bit her bottom lip, her heart aching. "I have to do this on my own."

"This—"

"Thomas..." she interrupted him. "I am not...not leaving you. I..." She paused to take a deep breath and continued. "I love you more than...more than words can describe. I have to do this on my own. Please understand..."

"I don't, so make me understand." He squeezed her hands, his voice anxious and frustrated.

She frowned, averting her eyes, not sure what she could say to make him comprehend her reasons.

"Try me. Talk to me. I promise I will listen." His voice was trembling.

She interlocked their hands and got on her feet, pulling him up with her. "Come," she said, walking out of the room and heading to the living room.

"Can you bring me a glass of water, please?" she asked after sitting down on the sofa.

"Sure..." He took another glance at her pale face before walking to the kitchen.

Iris wiped the foggy window glass and looked out into the distance. The ground was covered with fresh snow, which was sparkling in the sunlight. She had not felt so alive for a long time. Full of love, joy, devastation, and even sadness. She wiped away the new tears rolling down her cheeks, smiling as she knew this was the right thing, the only way to have herself back.

"Here…" Thomas handed her a glass and sat down next to her.

"Thank you." She took a sip first and then proceeded to down half of it. She held the glass in her hands and whispered, "I can feel you are suffocated."

"No, I am—"

"Thomas," she interrupted him. "You have to be honest with your feelings. Otherwise…otherwise one day, probably soon, everything between us will be gone."

He shook his head in despair, one hand running through his dark hair.

"Because of me, you are disappearing," she continued.

"I—"

"Shh… You've promised me you would listen." She put the glass down and held his hand. "I want you to be you."

"I am fine." His eyes were tearing up again. Sparkling drops made his blue eyes even brighter.

"When was the last time you hung out with your friends?" she asked softly.

"I have you and Max…"

"I know you enjoy dining out, live music, and theater." She ignored what he said. "But you haven't done that since we met again." She sighed and continued. "You fit in with my…my crippled needs when I cannot join you to enjoy what you like to do."

"There is nothing crippled about your needs." He held her hands close to his chest, feeling disheartened.

"Afraid of strangers? Refusing to go out? Nightmares?" She looked into his eyes.

"You have been out," he rebuked.

"But only when you are with me."

He wanted to argue, but he could not deny the fact that she was only able to do those things if he was right by her side.

"You are the one who was kidnapped and brutally beaten, but I am the one who completely fell apart," she said. "I had..." She breathed out to calm her emotions. "At...at one point, I had...I had given up hope when I thought you were never coming back. I—"

"Stop..." He could not bear to hear what she had gone through.

"You promised, Thomas. So let me finish." She stared at him. "I didn't think about the baby, my family, or your family. I...I just wanted to end everything if I couldn't have you in my life because... because you were my antidepressants, my anxiolytic, my hypnotic, my..." Tears streamed down her face. She could not continue as she was choked with emotion.

He shut his eyes so he could not see her devastated expression.

"I...I didn't realize that I had stopped trying to get better since you were back in my life."

He flung his eyes open, baffled by what she had said.

"Because I had you. I took you for granted. I clung to you and believed you would heal me." She pulled her hands from his and cupped his handsome face and added, "And I truly thought I was healed and normal again, but I am not."

"We took the vows..." Small teardrops were running down his cheeks. "For better, for worse."

"I have to do this, so we can have a better life, my love. Maxipoo needs a healthier mother." She wiped the tears off his face.

"No..." he leaned in and held her in his arms, whispering in her ear. "No... No..." His pleading was shaking her will, but it also made her want to be better.

"I have to heal, Thomas. For you and Max. I know I can do it," she whispered back. "You have to help me...by letting me do it on my own."

"*Je t'aime...*" His body was trembling as he knew he could not win this fight. He leaned back and pressed his lips on her, kissing her as if it was their last kiss.

She wrapped her arms around his neck, deepening their kiss.

When their lips parted, he pressed his forehead on hers, both breathing heavily. He did not say a word, just holding her still. It had been a long time since the last time she had returned his affection with fervor. He needed to calm himself down or he would lose control.

"Okay… But you have to call Dr. Fournier right away." Finally, he voiced his thoughts.

She nodded, too overwhelmed to speak. She was glad that Thomas had agreed, but at the same time she started to feel regretful and uncertain.

"And Max has to be with you."

She pulled away, her eyes on his. "I…I cannot take him away from you."

"One of us has to be with you." He sounded determined. "This is nonnegotiable. And we will make plans after you speak with Dr. Fournier."

She gazed at him, feeling so much love from him. "*Je t'aime plus que la vie,*" she whispered to him that she loved him more than life itself.

He leaned in and sealed her lips with his again.

A moan escaped her. She wrapped her arms around his neck and sat astride his lap. She was drunk in his tender touch and alluring kisses. The burning sensation in her body and the craving for more of him were so strange and so familiar.

His hands grasped at the skirt of her dress and pushed it up. She raised herself up so he could get the skirt over her hips, and she raised both arms above her head when he pulled the dress up and over her head.

"I have missed you…" he whispered, his breathing picking up as he unclasped her bra and gently slid the straps off her shoulders.

"Not as much as I have…" She leaned in and kissed him, her hands unbuckling his belt, unzipping his dress pants, and slipping inside.

He groaned, lifting her up and off him. She was surprised by his action but smiled broadly when she saw him swiftly shoving his pants and boxer briefs to the floor and kicking them away.

He sat back down and pulled her back to sit astride his lap again.

"This will have to go soon." He ran his fingers over her thong.

She was busy pulling his tie loose and started to unbutton his dress shirt.

Thomas gripped the shirt hem and pulled with a jerk, buttons flying all over the place.

A heartfelt laughter burst out of Iris. She cupped his face, her lips crashing down on his.

THOMAS gazed at Iris, who was sleeping soundly next to him. She once joked that he was her best sleeping aid as the more orgasms she had, the deeper her sleep was. He smiled, gently brushing a strand of hair off her cheek.

How could I be so wrong? So naïve? He truly believed that he could heal her as long as he was by her side.

Am I too overprotective? He still remembered the fear in her eyes when he first saw her in the recovering house and knew all too well about the agony she had gone through. He could not erase those horrific events from her memories, but at least he could give her all the comfort and security she needed to have a normal life. He had vowed to himself to shield her from any mental or physical harm.

But she was not a damsel in distress and did not need a knight in shining armor to rescue her from her PTSD. She needed professional help and her own strength to heal.

Can we really do this? Can I do this? Maybe I need her more than she needs me... He chuckled at his last thought as he knew how desperate he was two years ago...

~ ~ ~

Iris had already gone back to the States when he came back from his assignment. She had left him several text messages and a couple of voice messages, which he had listened to over and over again...

"Hi, this is Iris. Hmm... I... My parents and brother are here. They are looking forward to meeting you." She let out a small laugh and continued, "My mom is super excited. So don't freak out if she gives you a big hug. Ahem... Call me back. Or text me."

"Hi, it's me... I am going home today..." Then there was a long silence before she spoke again, "Well... Thank you so much, Thomas. Have...have..." She paused and let out an audible sign before she said goodbye.

He called her back, but her number was no longer in service. He wanted to reach out and explain to her that he was undercover and could not contact her and that he did not mean to ghost her.

"She was doing fine." Eva would only tell him that much as she was bound by professional confidentiality rules.

Afterward, he dived into the family business with the regret of not being able to keep in touch with Iris.

She is safe with her family now. He had to remind himself that when he thought about her—on a daily basis.

Time did help. He had met some nice ladies and gone out on some dates, but there was never a second date because by the end of those dates he was thinking about how nice it would be if Iris were with him at that restaurant, the bar, or the club. Believing it was unfair to those ladies, he decided to take a break from dating and just hang out with his friends.

He did enjoy Anna's company, and she was, after all, his ex-girlfriend, so he gave it a shot.

"This is an amazing place, Torian," one of his friends commented when a group of them came to his apartment for an after-new-year-party party.

Anna started helping him entertain the guests like a hostess. He really appreciated her as he had never hosted any gathering at his place, not even a family dinner. The night went on, and they cuddled on the sofa chatting with their friends like an old couple. When people started leaving, she kissed them goodbye and intended to stay.

Suddenly, Thomas had an image of Iris standing by the door saying goodbye to his friends with her charming and slightly shy smile. His heart started palpitating, wishing Iris were there with him.

"I...I have an early morning meeting. I should get some rest," he said to Anna and reached for her coat and scarf in the coat closet. The disappointment in her eyes made him avert his eyes, but he could not be with her if all he thought about was another woman.

"Call me," she said and gave him a lingering kiss on his lips.

After that, he limited his social life to just a small circle of friends and family.

One morning when he opened his traveling schedule during a board meeting, his eyes glued to one particular destination—DeMont Beverly Hills.

"Thomas?" Louis' voice pulled his mind back to the meeting.

He turned to look at his brother. "Yes?"

"Dad is asking you about the annual gala." Louis found Thomas' distracted expression unusual because Thomas was always focused, probably due to his police training, and he had been devoting almost all his time and energy to learning the business.

"I have to see her," he said to Louis, his voice determined.

Louis frowned, not sure what Thomas was talking about. Then his eyes landed on the schedule in front of him. His lips turned up slightly, and he said, "Then you should go."

Thomas broke into a broad smile.

After the meeting, Thomas went back to his office and continued to stare at his schedule. He started to pace around, thinking about how to get her contact information without asking Eva, plotting a visit that she could not decline, and imagining all possible scenarios when he saw her.

~ ~ ~

Thomas placed a soft kiss on Iris' cheek and then rolled off the bed. He picked up the discarded clothing on the floor and put them in the hamper before putting on sweatpants and a t-shirt.

Quietly, he walked out of the bedroom and tried to locate his phone, which was in his coat pocket. He walked into his study as there were a couple of calls he had to make.

The first call he made was to Dr. Fournier's office. Regardless of what they decided to do, Iris needed to discuss her medications with Dr. Fournier as soon as possible.

The doctor's assistant was able to schedule an emergency appointment for Iris the next morning. That was a relief.

He then called his brother. Louis and Eva had already checked into a hotel nearby, just wanting to stay close in case they were needed.

Thomas knew that both Louis and Eva adored Iris and Max and that they would do whatever they could to help them. But they were not babysitting Max now because he wanted to take his wife out for a date night. They were here because Iris had an emotional breakdown.

This was not what he had imagined when they were pregnant, preparing their wedding, and eager to build a life together. And he was very certain this was not what Iris had wanted either, and he understood why she wanted to be off her medications and to heal.

"Stay for dinner. I will cook," Thomas said after Louis told him they would bring Max home soon.

"Sounds great!" Louis replied immediately as Thomas was well trained by Mrs. Carson.

Thomas chuckled at Louis' enthusiastic response. "I…I also want to talk to you about something."

"Tommy, anything you need."

CHAPTER 19

IRIS double-checked the address on her phone and looked up at the beautiful beach house in front of her. "This is it," she said to Jane, who was sitting behind the wheel.

"A very fancy office…" Jane widened her eyes.

They both got out of Jane's Tahoe, two pairs of eyes fixed on this modern structure in Malibu.

"I don't see any…" Jane stopped in mid-sentence when she saw a small metal plate underneath the house number. "There!" She pointed out the sign to Iris: Nicholas Sachtleben, M.D. Clinical Psychiatrist.

Dr. Warren had retired, and she referred Iris to her protégé Dr. Sachtleben, whom, according to Dr. Warren, was her best student and the only psychiatrist she would recommend to Iris.

When Iris called after she was back in the States, the first available opening was in three months. However, Dr. Warren was able to make Dr. Sachtleben see Iris in two weeks. And Iris believed this new doctor must have read her medical records because he called her back himself instead of any of his staff and suggested his private office for their first session.

"Ready?" Jane gave Iris' hand a little squeeze.

"Yup." Iris sucked in a deep breath and walked up to the black front door. She rang the bell and stepped back to stand next to Jane.

The door opened soon after. They were greeted by a mixed-race, beautiful lady in a grey knit dress and black knee-high boots. She reminded Iris of the British actress Gemma Chan, although not quite so Asian.

"Hi, I…I…" Iris cleared her throat and continued, "I have…I have an appointment with Dr. Sachtleben at ten," Iris said nervously.

She had told her friends and family that from now on she wanted to interact with people herself instead of relying on everyone around her. And this lady in front of her was her very first in-person-interaction-with-a-stranger.

"Mrs. Torian." The lady gave Iris a warm smile. "Yes, we are expecting you. Please come in." She stepped aside, holding the door for them.

They walked into an elegantly decorated waiting room. Iris' interior design sense was stirred up. The contemporary exterior might have given a hard and bold impression, but the interior was comfy and relaxed. It was very welcoming.

"I am Summer. Would you like a cup of tea or water?" the beautiful lady asked, looking at Iris and then turning to Jane. Her smile was contagious.

Summer? Iris mirrored her smile. *It suits her so well. Beautiful Summer...* "Water, please." Iris replied.

"No, thank you," Jane said, removing her Jacket.

"I can take that," Summer said to Jane. She then turned to Iris, indicating she could take Iris' cardigan as well.

"I am fine." Iris shrugged, closing the open front of her cardigan, hugging herself.

"Please take a seat. I will be right back," Summer said in a gentle voice and left the room.

Iris looked around, feeling anxious. She had googled Dr. Sachtleben after Dr. Warren told her about him. She did not find much about him online. It could be a good thing, meaning he was a private person. She saw several pictures of him and found him looking very young for being early fifty, but she thought those might be old photos. He looked handsome and a little mysterious, sort of reminding her of Thomas. When he called her, she found his baritone surprisedly warm and comforting. Perfect for a therapist.

"Sweetie, don't worry. I will be with you the entire time." Jane wrapped one arm around Iris and steered her to a loveseat.

Iris rested her head on Jane's shoulder after they sat down. "What if I don't like him?" she whispered.

"What if you like him?" Jane whispered back.

"You are right…" Iris smiled.

Summer walked back into the room with a bottle of water in her hand. "Dr. Sachtleben will be with you shortly." She handed Iris the bottle and walked to a stained gray wood writing desk by the door.

As Iris and Jane were whispering back and forth, a tall man walked into the room. He was in a white dress shirt, dark suit pants, and a silver tie.

"Mrs. Torian." He smiled at Iris, walking up to them. "I am Dr. Sachtleben."

She froze, blinking her eyes rapidly.

He then moved his eyes to Jane, "You must be Mrs. De Waal, I presume."

"Yes, call me Jane, please." Jane responded, standing up. She extended her hand for a handshake and Dr. Sachtleben took it.

Following Jane, Iris also stood up. "Iris. Please call me Iris." She averted her eyes, feeling uneasy.

"Iris, Jane." He gave them both a warm smile. "This way, please." He pivoted on his heel and led the way down a hallway.

Taking in a deep breath, Iris grabbed onto Jane's hand and followed Dr. Sachtleben.

They walked through a set of double doors and into a fully furnished large room with floor to ceiling windows facing the Pacific.

Iris walked towards the windows, smiling at the ocean view.

"Please, have a seat," Dr. Sachtleben said and sat down on a beige armchair.

Jane sat down on the three seater sofa against a wall and looked at Iris, who was still gazing out the window.

"It feels like my living room," Iris said.

Dr. Sachtleben did not respond but simply observed Iris.

She then turned around and walked towards where Jane was. She sat down right next to her, giving her new doctor a quick glance. She wondered how familiar he was with her condition.

"You have a place by the ocean?" he asked.

She nodded.

"Then I hope this environment makes you feel comfortable."

"It does." Iris finally looked at Dr. Sachtleben, who had salt and pepper hair, tan skin, and a pair of light brown eyes. He was a well-muscled man and very handsome, and he did look very young for being in his early fifties.

"Fantastic." His smile became broader. He crossed his long legs and rested his elbows on the arms of the chair. "Iris, how about we start with how you are feeling now?"

Iris frowned, her eyes scanning the room but avoiding Dr. Sachtleben's gaze. "Nervous... Because...because I don't know you."

"That's reasonable. How about we get to know each other first?"

Iris finally looked into his sincere eyes, which were almost golden in this sunlit room.

Maybe it is a good idea to have a new doctor... she thought. *Someone, who will guide me and help me to face my future with a different perspective.*

THOMAS kept checking the time, wishing he could be there with Iris during her first session with her new psychiatrist. He was in DeMont New York now, four-thousand kilometers away and feeling restless. He could not focus on work, so he canceled his afternoon meetings and just sat in the living room of the family suite. He missed her so much.

They flew back to California after the holidays, and Thomas stayed for a week before he came to New York. The separation was hard for both of them.

He remembered she cried like there was no tomorrow before his departure...

~ ~ ~

"I am only a phone call away," he said to her, suppressing his emotions and trying to be strong for her.

"I know..." she said between hiccups and sniffles.

"We will talk everyday." He kissed her hair.

"I know..." She burst into a sob of despair.

~ ~ ~

He was still not convinced that being apart was the right thing to do, but if it would help her, whatever he thought or believed did not matter.

Letting out a deep sigh, he looked out onto the Manhattan skyline. He missed having Iris here. And even though Max was still too young to appreciate the city, he would love to show him how big and fascinating New York was.

It had been four days since he was here. Business dinner invitations were flying in, and he should be socializing with restaurateurs and hoteliers. But he could not put his mind to it, not when he left his heart in California with his wife and son.

His phone rang and a picture of Iris snuggling with Max appeared on the screen.

"Hey…" He answered the call right away.

"That's quick." Iris' laugh brought a smile to his face.

"I was staring at my phone," he said, standing up and walking to the window. "How's the session? How's Dr. Sachtleben?"

"It was nice. We just left. He is different…"

"Good different or bad different?" Thomas was concerned because it was essential for her to have a psychiatrist who could work well with her.

"Good. I think I will continue to see him."

"Fantastic." He wished he was there with her, but he did not say, not wanting to have that I-should-be-there-for-you conversation with her again.

"How's your day?" she asked.

"Same." He went on and told her how excited Travis was since this was his first time in New York.

"You should go," she said after he told her Travis had planned to go out every night. "You didn't get to go out when we were there the last two times."

"Maybe…" Thomas brushed her off.

Iris knew him too well to understand the tone of his voice, so she changed the subject. "By the way, Janie is bringing her yoga instructor to the house to give me lessons."

"I did not know yoga instructors make house-calls."

Iris chucked, "I am special."

"Yes, you are." He smiled. "I am sure—" Suddenly, his phone beeped, interrupting him. "Love, give me a second." He looked at the screen and saw Louis' name. He put the phone back to his ear and said, "Louis is calling me. I probably should get it." He let out a sigh.

"Of course. I will FaceTime you later with Maxipoo. *Je t'aime.*"

"*Je t'aime,*" he said, and Iris hung up the call. He then answered Louis' call. "Shouldn't you be in bed now?"

"Three in the afternoon?" Louis laughed.

"That's my time." Thomas walked towards the kitchen, going to make himself a late lunch.

"It is mine, too. I just landed."

"You what?"

"Care for some company?" Louis asked.

Thomas could hear some noises in the background. Actually, it was Emma's voice. "Seriously?" He laughed heartily. "Did you sense my distress signals?"

"Too strong to ignore. I will be there in a couple of hours."

"See you later."

Both brothers hung up the call.

I cannot believe it. Thomas shook his head. The last time they were in New York at the same time was when he was in high school. A family trip. With their mother and Laila.

Thomas and Louis had dinner at the Dine, and Louis suggested having a drink at The Carlyle Hotel's Bemelmans Bar instead of their own distinguished bar Ta DeMont.

Thomas would say he would much prefer Ta DeMont's atmosphere to Bemelmans Bar, but he would love to have a night out with his brother, no matter where he wanted to go.

How pathetic, he thought because he had not stepped a foot out of the hotel since he arrived.

Is Iris right about me losing myself? He felt perfectly content when he was with her. Although they had never gone to any bars or clubs together, he was fine with that and had never felt that he had missed out on anything.

What could I be missing out on if she is all I want and need? he thought. *I need her as much as she does me...*

They decided to walk because The Carlyle was only a few blocks away. It had not snowed for a couple of days, so the walk was not bad. And as far as the cold weather was concerned, it was nothing compared to what they had back home.

During dinner, they talked about business, about how they planned to make their hospitality brand more contemporary while still keeping the DeMont legacy. However, sitting at the bar near the piano and nursing his second cognac now, Thomas suddenly felt sentimental.

"Thanks for coming," he said to Louis, eyes staring at the amber colored liquor in the glass.

Louis blinked at his little brother's unexpected uttering. Although he was five years Thomas' senior, he always thought his younger brother was so much more mature than he was, and Laila reminded him that all the time while they were growing up.

"Who would forgo New York?" Louis gave Thomas a grin.

"It...it is so fucking hard," Thomas said, ignoring Louis' joking tone. He picked up the glass and swigged the rest of the drink in one gulp, wincing at the burn going down his throat.

Louis suddenly became speechless. He cared for Thomas and Iris so much, but he was not sensitive like his wife was. Eva was the one who encouraged him to come here.

"Tommy needs you," Eva emphasized when she basically forced him to get on the jet.

When Thomas first mentioned Iris to him, he was skeptical. He thought his brother must have some kind of hero syndrome, which made him think that he must save someone or save the world. He first thought saving Iris was just Thomas' way of grieving for Laila, and then when he knew Thomas had fallen for Iris, he was not sure if it was right, or even healthy. Although, he had never said anything to Thomas. Who was he to judge when he was the rebellious and impulsive one of the family?

Then he saw the change in Thomas who was happy, driven, and alive when he was with Iris. She had brought positivity to his life again. Actually, to all of their lives. And Bébé Max... He must be born with wizardry of some kind. That little man made him think babies were adorable and made Eva think about having a child of their own.

Eva's line of work had made her hesitate to have a child. She told him she could not imagine how she would react if their child was abducted, even though she specialized in counseling trafficked victims and their families. And since he had never been a fan of babies, he was perfectly fine with that. However, things had changed after Bébé Max was born. She saw hope instead of uncertainty, and he just thought they would make an even cuter baby—a baby girl with that wild brown curling hair like her mommy's.

Louis raised his hand to get the bartender's attention as his little brother could use another drink.

Seemingly, the bartender had already had two drinks for them. He approached them and sent two snifters in front of them. "From the ladies by the piano," the bartender said, tilting his head towards the piano.

Louis turned his head to thank whomever buying them the drinks while Thomas frowned and told the bartender to send the drinks back.

"Thank you. We will keep the drinks," Louis quickly said to the bartender, who gave him a nod and walked away. He then picked up one snifter and turned back to the ladies, who were smiling at him broadly. Both were brunette, young, and attractive. He gave them an appreciative nod and took a sip.

"What the fuck are you doing?" Thomas asked.

"Enjoying a free drink."

"Like you cannot pay for your own drink. Shit! They are coming over." Thomas growled. From his peripheral vision, he saw the two ladies standing up from their seats. He was in no mood to socialize.

"Just chill," Louis whispered to him and smiled at the two ladies, who did not hide their interest in them at all.

"Thank you for the drink." Politely, Louis said to them in English when both ladies reached their seats, holding their wine glasses.

"Our pleasure. I am Tabitha. This is Beatrice." The one with a high ponytail spoke in perfect French, her eyes screaming flirtation. "We heard you speaking French. Are you visiting?"

"Yes," Louis replied while Thomas indifferently said the word *no*.

Both women laughed as if the two handsome men were making a joke.

"Where are you from? France?" Beatrice asked, speaking in French as well.

"Yes," Louis replied while Thomas said, "No." Again.

What the bloody fuck? Thomas shot his brother a glare.

Both ladies seemed to enjoy the duet. They laughed and stepped closer. Tabitha fixed her eyes on Thomas while she walked to the empty seat to his left and set her wine glass down. "Are you brothers?" she asked.

"Yes," Louis replied.

Thomas was eager to say *no*, wishing Louis were not his brother at this moment. He knew Louis would never cheat on Eva and was just enjoying a night out. Shaking his head, Thomas held his empty glass up to get the bartender's attention for a refill. It was not that he was too arrogant to accept the drink from these ladies. He just…did not want to drink it.

"I thought I asked the bartender to bring you the same thing you were having," Tabitha said to Thomas, placing her hand on his forearm.

Thomas did not want to be rude, but her touching was not welcome. He withdrew his arm and showed her his wedding band. "I am married."

She chucked, trying to hide her embarrassment. "I…I didn't notice that."

"Yes, you did," Thomas said and turned to Louis. "And he is, too." He shot a warning glance at his brother. *Who is the asshole now?*

"Happily married!" Louis showed the two women his wedding band as well, not bothered by the awkwardness.

"Drink to happy marriage!" Beatrice seemingly took the rejection very well. She clinked her wine glass against Louis' sniffer.

"Thank you, ladies. Let me buy you the next round. Same thing or?" Louis smiled at both of them, especially Tabitha, who had already walked around Thomas and was now standing next to her friend.

"I would like a pink lady, please. Thank you." Tabitha said, smiling at Louis, but she took a quick glance at Thomas, who sat lazily on the bar stool, ignoring his brother.

"I'll have the same," Beatrice said.

"Fantastic." Louis turned to the bartender, who just brought Thomas his refill, and placed the order.

"So, what's your name, Mr. happily married?" Tabitha asked.

"Lancaster," he replied and pointed at Thomas, "This is Timothy. I call him Timmy."

Thomas just shook his head, staring at his drink.

"Timmy. That's cute." Tabitha said, turning her smile towards Thomas, who seemed to block all three of them out.

"No, no, no." Louis suddenly looked serious. "Never use 'cute' on a man."

"Oops." Tabitha covered her mouth with her hand.

"So, Lancaster. You are from France and your brother is not?" Beatrice asked, emptying her wine glass.

"Yes and no." Louis seemed to enjoy this meaningless chit chat. "I was adopted when I was a baby and grew up in Paris. He…" He turned to Thomas and met a cold blue glare. He suppressed an urge to laugh and continued, "He grew up in Monaco."

"*Bist du betrunken, oder was?*" Thomas said to Louis 'Are you drunk, or what' in German on purpose since his brother was bullshitting those ladies in French.

Just then, the bartender delivered the drinks.

"Two pink ladies for two beautiful ladies," Louis said, picking up the reddish drinks and handing them to Beatrice and Tabitha. "It is a pleasure to meet you, ladies. And please excuse us. We have some serious business to discuss here. I hope you enjoy your evening." Louis politely excused them.

Thomas let out a sigh of relief when he heard that. He took a swig of his drink.

After both ladies walked away, Louis put his hand on Thomas' shoulder and laughed, "Come on, it is not that bad. Cute Timmy."

"Shut up!" Thomas smiled, shaking his head.

CHAPTER 20

IRIS felt quite uneasy all day because tomorrow Janie was coming over with her yoga instructor Alice to give her a private class.

Alice was not a stranger. Iris had taken her classes for years before the trip to Paris. That meant she had not seen Alice for more than three years and she was not sure how much Alice knew about her condition.

"I can do this, right?" she asked her baby, who was lying right next to her on the sofa, sucking on his clenched fist.

She felt better about herself more and more each day. Dr. Sachtleben felt like a good fit, and if she worked harder on her end, her little family would be together soon.

She still remembered that day when Thomas left after spending a week with them…

~ ~ ~

She stood by the front gate and saw him driving away. It seemed so easy for him, but she knew he was hurting, too. After closing the gate and dragging herself back to the house, she collapsed on the floor and cried some more. She could not get herself together until Bébé Max started to wail.

Holding her baby in her arms, she called Janie.

"Is everything okay?" Jane asked because Iris did not say a word and all Jane heard was a duet-crying. She immediately knew Thomas must have just left.

Jane and David offered to be there with Iris, but Iris insisted that the three of them needed to say goodbye in private and that she would be all right. Apparently, she was not…

"I will be right there," Jane said to Iris.

Since then, Iris and Bébé Max had been staying at David's

ranch. Thomas actually felt relieved when Iris told him about the arrangement and especially pleased that her parents also decided to stay.

Her mother was a baby miracle worker. Bébé Max seemed to bond with her the moment she held him. He often stared at her with his big brown eyes, cooing and gurgling as if he was trying to tell her all about his adventures. Nobody could be a better person to help Iris with Bébé Max.

After staying at David's for more than a week, Iris decided to move back to their beachfront house.

"I have to, Mommy," Iris said to her mother when her mother suggested she should stay at the ranch because she needed all the help she could get. "I am doing so much better. Really. Thanks to all of you. But I can't rely on you."

"But that's what family is for..." Her mother said with sadness in her voice.

"I know, Mommy. But I came home to..." She paused, trying to find a better way to express herself and not sound ungrateful. It was definitely easier just to accept all the help from her family and friends—even Antonio checked on her everyday. But she wanted to get better soon and be with Thomas. "I didn't leave Thomas and come back here to rely on you guys. I...I want to be better."

Her mother wrapped Iris in her arms and said, "I know... But..." Her mother did not just give up. She continued to suggest if she could move in with Iris and the baby, just to stay closer.

Iris knew all too well that her mother was a tough negotiator, so she countered that her mother could continue to stay at David's and visit her and Maxipoo everyday.

"That's fine... As long as I get to see my grandson." Her mother pouted, finally giving in. "He is my favorite now anyway."

Her family drove Iris and the baby back home, and when she walked towards the front door with the baby in her arms, a sudden sadness emerged.

I want my Thomas....

"Iris..." David called from behind.

She turned around and saw her brother handing her his phone.

"Someone likes to walk into the house with you," he said.

Iris frowned. She switched her son to her left arm and received the phone.

"*Mon amour...*" Thomas' face was on the screen, smiling warmly at her.

Iris blinked, her mouth slightly open. She could not believe her brilliant brother had FaceTimed Thomas so they could walk into the house together. Iris looked up at her brother, tears in her eyes.

David leaned in to kiss her forehead and said, "I can't take credit for this. It's all Thomas."

Iris looked at the screen again, speechless, and Bébé Max reached for the phone and sucked on one corner. She laughed and held the phone up so both of them could look at Thomas.

"Look, who is here? *C'est papa!*" she said to her son.

"*Oui, ma puce, c'est papa.*" Thomas' smile could not be brighter.

They walked into the house *together* and stayed on FaceTime until Thomas was called into a meeting.

"*Je t'aime,*" they said to each other before ending the call.

~ ~ ~

Since this separation began, they found that neither of them wanted to end the calls first. Thomas even told Iris that he would stay on the phone until she fell asleep for the first couple of nights. Then they decided that they would say *I love you* and end the call together.

They texted each other practically every second, called several times a day, and definitely FaceTimed at least once a day to see each other. She knew he missed Bébé Max as much as he did her, so being able to see his son everyday—even by means of FaceTime— was very important.

Sometimes Iris wondered if Thomas was as lonely as she was. But she was afraid to ask him because if he was, then she was the one to be blamed.

It was a peaceful night tonight. She was lounging on the sofa, listening to the soothing sound of the ocean *and* her son's gurgling noise.

It was a night like this when Thomas sat on this very spot,

holding her in his arms, and told her he had left fedpol and did not have a wife or a girlfriend.

Iris smiled at the memory. She chucked when she remembered they were making out on the sofa and had to stop because they did not have condoms.

She loved every second of her life with Thomas and never thought she would be back here to heal…without him. It felt like her life had taken a detour so she could meet the love of her life and they could make a new life together.

He is worthy, and Maxipoo is worthy…

She found that her love for both of them was so much more than life itself. The thought of losing either one of them scared her all the time because…because she was once too close to lose them both. Just the memory itself made her forget to breathe.

She grabbed her phone and texted Thomas…

Iris: *Je pense à toi.*

She texted him that she was thinking of him.

Thomas: *Je pense à toi à chaque instant.*

He replied almost instantly that he was thinking of her every moment.

She smiled, able to breathe again.

Jane arrived early in the morning with Alice the next day.

"Auntie Janie is here," she said to Bébé Max, who was on his bouncing bed in the living room sucking his toes, and scurried to the door. She buzzed the front gate open, feeling anxious and excited, and hurried back to her baby.

"Hello!" Jane opened the door and walked in, followed by a petite young lady with strawberry blonde hair.

"Come on in." Iris waved at them.

"Your house is so beautiful," Alice said in astonishment, following Jane into the living room.

"Thank you." Iris gave Alice, whom she had not seen for more than three years, a nervous smile.

"Hello precious…" Jane walked up to Bébé Max.

"Nice to see you again, Iris." Alice leaned in and gave Iris a hug, which caught Iris by surprise.

Iris forced herself to hug her back and successfully managed her rising anxiety.

"Oh my god! He is too adorable!" Alice's eyes flung to Max. She put her bag and yoga mats down on the floor and stood closer. "I want one, too."

"Everybody wants one after they meet him." Jane laughed.

"Thank…thank you for coming," Iris said to Alice.

"Don't mention it." Alice gave Iris a bright smile. "This…" She gestured to the living room, floor-to-ceiling glass sliding doors, and ocean-view. "This is the best yoga classroom."

"Agreed." Iris' smile broadened.

"Do you like to have our session in here or another room?" Alice asked.

Not sure what to say, she looked at Alice and then Jane, shrugging her shoulders.

"I think right here is great, don't you think?" Jane asked, gazing at Iris.

"Okay…" Iris nodded.

"Great! Let me wash my hands first." Jane walked into the open kitchen adjoining the living room. After she was done, she walked back to Bébé Max and picked him up. "I will take this little guy…" She whispered to the baby, "Hello, Little Prince. We will have our party downstairs."

"Thank you, Janie." Iris kissed her son's forehead.

"No problem," she said to Iris and then switched her voice to a singsong tone and said to the baby, "We are going to have so much fun, aren't we?" She turned around and headed towards the stairs.

Iris stood awkwardly, waiting for Alice's instructions.

"Shall we?" Alice picked up the mats she brought with her. "I brought two mats with me. Or do you like to use your own?"

"I…I'll use mine," Iris said and walked briskly to the den. When she came back to the living room, Alice had already laid her mat down on the open space between the living room and the kitchen. Iris put her mat down, about six feet away from Alice.

"Please sit down and face me," Alice said to her, sitting on her own mat and facing Iris.

What Iris liked the most about Alice's classes was that she focused on calming the mind and balancing the body. And she was desperate to have a peaceful mind.

Iris nodded and followed Alice's instructions.

"We are going to practice our breathing first and also calm our mind," Alice said to her in a very soothing voice. "Close your eyes and listen to my voice."

Iris took a deep breath and closed her eyes.

"Relax your shoulders…"

Iris did as she was told.

"Very well…" Alice's voice became even softer. "Now… Breathing in… Very well. Now… Breathing out…"

Okay… This is not hard. Iris thought, breathing in and breathing out, just like doing her breathing exercise.

"Keep your eyes closed. And in the next fifteen minutes, you are going to focus on yourself, think about only yourself, and love yourself," Alice continued, her voice soothing like meditation music.

Okay… This is not hard, either. Iris smiled. *Wait… Actually, hmm…* Her smile vanished as images of Thomas and Maxipoo were pouring into her mind. They were all she could think about.

"What is your favorite color?" Alice's voice interrupted her thoughts of *the most handsome man in the world* and *the cutest baby in the universe.*

"Red," Iris replied.

"Why?"

"It's…sexy."

"Nice… Now, who is your favorite singer?" Alice's voice continued to guide her thought.

"Hmm… Lara Fabian. I think…" She had been listening to Lara Fabian to learn French and grew to like her a lot.

"What do you miss the most…about yourself?"

Her mind suddenly went blank, and an overwhelming emotion was surfacing.

I miss… I miss… I miss everything. Carefree, optimistic, adventurous, undaunted, enthusiastic… Hot tears flooded her eyes and streamed down her cheeks.

Alice gazed at Iris, her heart aching for her. Jane had been keeping her updated about Iris, from when she went missing till Thomas was kidnapped and released. She was glad that she had this chance to help Iris, and she would offer her all the support she could give.

"Focus on one thing. One thing that you miss the most about yourself," Alice said softly, trying to keep her voice calm as she could feel tears in her own eyes as well.

"I…" Iris breathed out a word.

Alice was quiet, waiting patiently for Iris to look inside herself for her answer…

Carefree… A deluge of tears gushed out and rushed down Iris' cheeks. She could not withhold any emotion any longer. She could feel *that* Iris, who vanished three years ago, was trying to fight her way out but she was pushed back by a forceful feeling of dread, which was so dark and cold and ugly.

She wanted to hold *that* Iris in her arms and shelter her….

She wanted to encourage *that* Iris to be brave and embrace everything that had happened to her, to let the bygones be bygones, and to look forward to her future because nothing would and nothing could hurt her anymore…

She wanted *that* Iris to know that her life was so wonderful now because Thomas and their baby were with her…

———

THOMAS marched into Louis' office and threw a newspaper on his desk.

"Good morning to you, too." Louis did not even look at what was thrown on his desk, his eyes fixed on the computer screen.

Beside supporting his brother, another goal he had planned to achieve in New York was to finalize the acquisitions of several boutique hotels. Since he was not sure his brother really needed him here, he vowed to at least accomplish his other mission.

"Page Six!" Thomas growled.

Louis gave him a side glance. "When did you start reading American gossip columns?"

"Since we are in it!" Thomas rarely raised his voice, but he really could not suppress his anger now. "Travis brought it to my attention earlier. I had never been in a gossip column before. Why am I even in an American tabloid?" Thomas slumped onto one of the guest chairs in front of Louis.

Since Thomas sounded so desperate, Louis glanced at the paper and burst out laughing. He picked up the paper and started to read it. Then he picked up his phone and took a picture of the page.

"What the bloody hell are you doing?" Thomas asked.

"Send it to Eva." He tapped on his phone several times, texting the picture he just took to his wife.

"I am sure it is on their website, too." Thomas snarled.

"True. But this feels more original. Classic." Louis chuckled.

"You think this is funny? It's all your doing!" Thomas folded his arms on his chest.

"It is hilarious. You should send it to Iris, too." Louis put his phone away, his eyes back on the document he was reading earlier.

"She will be furious!" Thomas growled, his eyes landing on the pictures of him and Louis *and* two young women—Beatrice and Tabitha.

Apparently, someone at Bemelmans Bar took some pictures of them, and now they were the gossip of the day. The pictures looked like they were having a great time, and one of the shots was when Tabitha's hand was on his forearm. Thomas knew he was grumpy the whole time, but that picture somehow captured a shot that made him look like he was flirting with her. And the headline was such a nightmare: Wealthy socialites Beatrice and Tabitha are looking for richer husbands. Are the Torian brothers in the market for new brides?

"I doubt that," Louis said, his tone indifferent. "There will be more new gossip tomorrow, and then we will be forgotten."

"We shouldn't be in it in the first place." Thomas could not understand why his brother was not bothered by this. How was Louis okay with being painted as a rich philanderer?

Thomas' personality and previous employment—especially being undercover—valued privacy to the extreme. This whole thing was unacceptable.

"Well, think of it this way. Tabloid press only reports famous people. We must be famous in the States for them to talk shit about us," Louis said, trying his best to suppress another laughter since his little brother did not think it was all that funny.

"I have to call Iris before she hears or reads about it," Thomas murmured, ignoring his brother. He stood up and headed back to his office.

Louis picked up the paper and dropped it in the waste bin. His attention was back on the document again.

Thomas closed his office door and called Iris.

"*Salut papa,*" she answered the call with a baby voice.

"*Salut maman,*" Thomas smiled and replied with the same endearment as well. "How's your day?"

"Very good," she said, letting out a relaxing sigh. "I had a yoga class this morning."

"I am glad." Thomas sat down on the sofa. "How's Max?"

"I am worried about him…" Her voice suddenly became serious.

"What happened?" He stood back up, his heart pounding.

"He might be developing a fetish for his toes…" Iris said and laughed out loud before finishing her sentence.

"You almost gave me a heart attack!" He sat back down, her laugh easy on the ear.

She is in such a good mood. Do I want to mention Page Six? He thought, one hand loosening his tie.

"He is perfectly fine…" She laughed more. "Napping now. I will FaceTime you when he is awake."

Her voice sounds so cheerful. He hoped it was a sign that they could be together soon. "I…I am going to be in a meeting from three to five."

"Okay. Actually…" She paused.

"Yes?"

"I was going to call you before you did because…" She paused again.

"Yes?"

"Are you looking for a new bride?" she asked and let out a stifled laugh.

"*Putain!* You saw it." Thomas swore, although he was relieved that she sounded amused by the news.

"I have a Google alert on your name. You know…after what happened."

"I promise I was having a shitty time then. Those pictures—"

"You looked very handsome," Iris interrupted him. "Even when you were having a shitty time."

He let out a sigh and said, "You are amazing…"

He appreciated that Iris had always trusted him. She once told him that she would never stay in the relationship if she could not fully trust the person she was with. He could not believe he was worried that she might be upset over the gossip column.

"I am glad you went out with Louis. But why did you have a shitty time?" she asked, her voice tender and soothing.

"I…" He wanted to tell her how much he missed her and Max, but he had promised her to be supportive, so he would have to keep his feelings to himself.

They both became silent…

The silence often happened when they both hesitated to express their longing for each other.

Respectfully giving Iris the space she asked for, Thomas had forced himself not to express his feelings. And Iris had definitely noticed that because he was never shy about conveying his affection for her.

"Do you…do you want to spend your birthday with us?" Iris spoke first, in hesitation.

Thomas was turning thirty-six next week. However, according to their plan, he would fly back to Switzerland on his birthday and come back to see Iris and Max next month. Iris would hate herself if he could not celebrate his birthday with them, especially since it would be his very first birthday as a father.

"Of course, *mon amour.* But, I mean… Can I?"

Iris' heart ached when she heard him saying that. "Of...of course, you can." Her voice became emotional.

"I miss you..."

"I miss you, too. So much..." Her voice was trembling.

"If I leave now, I can be there in six hours." His voice was now full of enthusiasm.

"But...but... Didn't you say you have a meeting later? What about work?"

"Louis is here." Thomas was on his feet already, ready to head upstairs to pack.

"Thomas..." She was choked with emotion.

"*Je t'aime,*" he said. "Don't cry. I am on my way now."

"Are you...are you..." She started to sob, not able to get her words out.

"Am I in love with you?" He finished her sentence, jokingly assuming that's her question. "Yes, I am. I am madly in love with you."

She laughed, appreciating him for lightening up her mood. She was going to ask if he was disappointed in her because she was the reason they were apart now.

CHAPTER 21

IRIS slowly took in a deep breath and held it… Then when she could not hold it anymore, she breathed out, letting it spew out through her mouth, her shoulders relaxing, her muscles slackening, and her mind unloading. She was up before dawn and had been meditating since then.

"Come back to bed," Thomas drawled. He pushed his upper body up on his elbows and scanned the room, and then he spotted her sitting on a blanket on the floor by the balcony sliding glass door.

A big smile spread across her face. Iris opened her eyes and saw the brightening sky. She turned her head and met his lazy blue gaze. Her eyes took in his messy black hair, remembering how she had run her fingers through it last night and gripped it when he gave her that never-ending orgasm.

She got up from where she sat and scurried towards him. She jumped on the bed, pushed him back down on his back, and sat astride on his thighs.

He put his hands on her hips and pulled her closer to sit on his erection. "That's better," he said with a hoarse morning voice.

Iris squealed when her soft and still tender lady's part slid over the cotton duvet cover.

"No, it doesn't work…" he grumbled. "Get in here." He lifted the duvet.

Iris moved underneath the warm bedding and resumed her position.

Thomas groaned, closing his eyes.

She fixed her gaze on his handsome face which was so beautiful that it still took her breath away. She moved one hand between where their skins touched and repositioned herself. Closing her eyes, she slowly guided him into her. She moaned, taking in his thickness.

He opened his eyes, gazing at her aroused expression. His hands roamed along her thighs, moving up. He cupped her buttocks and gave them a gentle squeeze when she started rotating her hips, grinding her needy lovebud against him. He knew this was her favorite position as she could take control and stimulate herself with the precise pressure at her own pace.

One nightgown strap fell over her right shoulder, revealing her round fleshy breast undulating gently. Thomas cupped it with his big hand, and his hips started to move to her rhythm.

"Thomas…" She started to move faster and frantically, her breathing picking up.

He lifted his hips, driving into her deeper and harder.

"Oh god…" she rasped. Her body leaned forward, almost collapsing on top of him. She gripped the headboard, her body trembling. Her moans of ecstasy nearly made him lose right there.

He wrapped his arms around her waist, chasing after her climax.

She wanted to go back to sleep, especially after that incredible orgasm. Every time she thought she just had the best orgasm ever, then the next one would always surpass it.

She remembered once she and Jojo were comparing notes on their sex life…

~ ~ ~

"Sky is my orgasm limit," she said to Jojo and made her rolling on the floor laughing.

"I am serious." She looked at Jojo with a I-shit-you-not expression. "I urge you to have a talk with Mr. Viking."

And that only made Jojo laugh even harder.

~ ~ ~

Iris let out a loud sigh and rolled off the bed.

"Where do you think you are going?" Thomas tried to grab her but missed.

"Stay. I will be right back." She turned her head around and gave him a big smile.

Thomas assumed she was going to check on the baby. They had

converted a guest room to a nursery, but when Thomas was not around, Iris would put the crib in the master bedroom so the baby could keep her company—not the other way around. So Thomas believed Iris was still not used to having the baby in the other room.

"I did not hear anything," he said, glancing at the baby monitor.

Their son was a long and deep sleeper, but when he awoke, he would make sure to announce it until someone physically picked him up.

She grinned at Thomas and left the room. She took a peek into the quiet nursery before walking upstairs and into the kitchen to make a cup of coffee, the way Thomas took it, and walked back down to their bedroom.

Thomas smelled the coffee before Iris walked into the room. He opened his eyes, frowning. "It is too early for coffee."

"I need to talk to you about something." She handed him the mug and climbed back in bed to sit by him.

Thomas sat up and took a sip, feeling content. "Can I stay here? Forever?" He pressed his forehead on her shoulder.

Surely it sounded like he was asking to stay in bed forever, but what he truly wanted to ask was to end this separation. And Iris knew him too well to hear the hidden meaning.

"Only if you are in charge of changing Maxipoo's diapers," she joked, then her voice turned stern. "Seriously, are you fully awake yet?

"Almost…" He took another sip of the hot creamy drink.

Iris rolled her eyes.

"I saw that." He gave her a side glance when he took another sip. "Okay now. Talk to me."

She gave him a big grin and said, "I want to start working again."

Thomas nodded, processing the information.

He had always encouraged her to do anything she wanted to do, so if she wanted to work again, he would definitely support her decision. However, living in Switzerland and being a mother might have limited her opportunity to continue her profession.

How? He wondered if she was thinking about resuming the

arrangements she used to have with Antonio and Jasmine. *Remotely?*

Where? He was worried that she was thinking about staying here…indefinitely. He suddenly broke out in a cold sweat.

"Are you all right?" She tilted her head to look at him. "Did you hear what I just said?"

He raised the coffee mug and took a big gulp to hide his uneasiness.

No need to make the unnecessary assumption, he reminded himself. He nodded his head, answering her question.

"I've already spoken with Antonio and Jojo. I will start with just working on design concepts, and other designers and assistants will team up with me. Remotely, of course. That way, when we are traveling, I can still take on some cases…" Iris went on and told him about Antonio dating their new designer Skye, who was a single mother of an adorable little girl, and how serious he was about her.

Everything she said after *'when we are traveling'* became inaudible to his ears.

Is it what I think it means? He gazed at her, smiling.

"What is it?" She mirrored his smile. "What's that smile for?"

"For you." He leaned in and kissed her.

"Thank…thank you…" She blushed.

"You seem happier." He brushed a lock of hair off her forehead. "I…I am sorry that I was skeptical about your decision to come back here without me."

Iris gave him an appreciative smile. She knew she still had a long way to go, but she was heading in the right direction.

Thomas flew back from New York two nights ago as he had promised her, and they had enjoyed every blissful moment they had together. Much as she would want him to stay after his birthday, she knew she had to do this for everyone who cared about her.

"When is your next appointment with Dr. Sachtleben?" he asked and took another sip of the coffee.

"Next Friday."

"Oh…" He frowned.

"What is it?" She did not like the frown appearing on his face.

"Well… I'd like to go with you if…if my schedule allows it," he said with hesitation, and he knew it sounded lame as he could decide his own schedule. His birthday was next Monday, and he was supposed to fly back to Switzerland with Louis soon after. The only way for him to accompany her to the appointment was to extend his stay, and he would do it in a heartbeat. But... Would Iris allow him to stay that long?

"I would love that!" she said almost immediately.

Thomas blinked his eyes several times, confused by Iris' response and also thrilled that he was able to stay longer with her and the baby.

Without perceiving Thomas' surprised expression, Iris started sharing with him what she and Dr. Sachtleben had been talking about.

"During my last session, he asked me a specific question," she said to Thomas. "My first reaction was: *Did you seriously just ask me that question?*"

"You really said that to him?" Thomas chucked.

"No..." She smiled. "Just in my head." She then let out a sigh and continued, "He asked me... 'Why are you trying so hard to forget what happened?' His exact words..."

Thomas frowned, not sure what to say. He probably would ask the doctor the same thing.

"He then did this little exercise with me." She widened her eyes. "He asked me not to think about coffee, and then asked me again what I was thinking."

"What were you thinking? Coffee?"

"Exactly!" She reached for the coffee mug and took a sip. "I was going crazy about how much I loved coffee. Caramel brulée latte was my favorite. Peppermint mocha creamer was the best..."

Like a light bulb just went on in his head, Thomas suddenly understood the reason and purpose of Dr. Sachtleben's question, and it also reminded him of his own sessions with his therapist after all his undercover assignments. He was eager to share those with her, but he said nothing, wanting her to express her thoughts first.

"Then again, he asked me not to think about dogs," she continued. "Then I started thinking maybe I should bring my baby

Liam back because he could be Maxipoo's buddy. Isn't it crazy?"

Thomas smiled at her dramatic expression.

"That's my assignment this week," she added.

"What do you mean? You have homework to do?"

She nodded. "Think about the answer to his question, and we will talk about it next Friday."

"It does sound like he has a different approach than Dr. Fournier, doesn't it?"

She nodded, her mind turning. "Well… Eva, Dr. Warren, and Dr. Fournier are kind of like ER doctors. They had to give me emergency care and treatments to stabilize my condition first before it became irreversible. And Dr. Sachtleben is working on my chronic issues now. Does it make sense?" She frowned, biting her bottom lips.

"It makes perfect sense," Thomas said, the invisible pressure on his chest suddenly feeling lighter. It had been a long time since he felt this relieved and optimistic about her, about them, and about their future.

"Anyway…" She let out a deep breath. "At least I only need to think about it and don't have to turn in an essay." She chuckled.

"That's the spirit," he tapped the tip of her nose with his index finger.

"Oh, about your birthday tomorrow—" She changed the subject but was interrupted by a high-pitched bawl.

"I will go." Thomas handed her the coffee mug. "That boy surely has a pair of strong lungs."

THOMAS and Iris were in the kitchen preparing dinner in the evening when the doorbell rang. They looked at each other, bemused.

Thomas' birthday party was tomorrow evening at the ranch. All the guests were expected to be there tomorrow; even Louis was at DeMont Beverly Hills now.

"Are we expecting any delivery?" Thomas asked, walking to the security panel and turned on the camera's live view screen.

Iris shook her head.

He stared at the screen, his brow furrowed.

"Who is it?" Iris walked out of the kitchen and halted when she saw his expression.

He turned his face to her, furrows in his brow deepening.

"You are scaring me, Thomas." Iris moved a couple of steps closer to him.

He raised his hand, asking her to stop. "Stay here and don't come out." He then opened the door and headed out.

"Thomas!" Iris was freaking out.

Thomas strode across the front yard. He took a deep breath before he opened the gate and came face to face with Mia. He had never forgotten a face, and he remembered all Vera's victims.

"It's...it's...it's really...really you..." Mia was stuttering.

He stepped out and pulled the gate close behind him. "Mia."

"You...you...you..." She took a deep breath and said, "You remember me."

"How did—" His sixth sense kicked in. He hastily looked around, checking for any suspicious people or cars.

Mia mirrored his behavior, looking around as well, but not sure what she was supposed to check.

"How did you find this place?" Thomas asked, frowning. "What are you doing here?" Because of what happened to Iris and him last year, he was on high alert.

"I...I...I saw your picture—" Mia started to explain and paused when the gate was opened again.

"Mia..." Iris appeared in the doorway, her face pale and her body trembling.

Mia's appearance was so different now. Her long bleach blonde hair was now shoulder-length light brown, and her petite body was wrapped in a huge black sweater instead of the fitted dresses she always wore. However, that pair of saucer green eyes were the same.

Thomas immediately stepped closer to his wife.

"Oh my god!" Mia covered her mouth with both her hands, her knees giving up.

Thomas took a step forward and caught Mia before she fell onto the ground.

"Thomas, let's bring her inside." Iris stepped inside the gate and held the gate open.

Thomas seized Mia's elbow and steered her into the front yard.

Mia stared at Iris, her mouth open, while she slowly walked through the gate.

"This way…" Iris headed back to the house.

Mia followed Iris and froze when she stepped into the foyer. "Wow…"

"Come on in." Iris gestured to the living room, her eyes fixed on Mia.

She had not seen Mia since the night she left the mansion. She knew Julia's team took all the women out of there and sent them home. And it had been almost three years.

Thomas walked past Mia and into the kitchen, his eyes fixed on Mia as well.

What has happened to her after she was rescued? Iris wondered. "Please, have a seat," she said to Mia, who was scanning the impressively beautiful place.

"Thank…thanks." Mia adjusted the backpack on her shoulder and walked into the living room. She hesitated, not sure where to sit. Then she walked to the single seater closest to her and sat on the edge, hugging her backpack in front of her

"Water?" Thomas put a glass of water on the coffee table next to Mia and sat down on the three-seater sofa.

"Thank you," she said, her voice timid.

"What are you doing here? How did you find this place?" Thomas repeated his questions.

Iris sat down next to Thomas, wanting to know the answers as well.

"I saw your pictures in the newspaper…" Mia said, still holding her backpack tight in front of her like a shield.

"Bloody tabloid," Thomas muttered, making Mia wince at his irritation tone.

"Go on, Mia." Iris gave her a small smile.

"Yeah, That. Page Six. I was so surprised. I mean I wasn't sure that was you at first." She looked at Thomas. "So I googled you. It was really confusing because your name and the stories I had read were all...not you. You know." She nervously picked up the glass and took a sip. "So I kept digging. I called your hotel in New York since those photos were taken in New York, and they transferred my call to your assistant. I believe his name is Travis."

Thomas frowned, ready to fire his assistant if he indeed gave her his private information.

"He was tough. Jesus. He gave me a lecture, telling me you were a happily married man and I should've never bothered you."

Iris bit her bottom lip to suppress a grin.

"Then I tried again and pretended I was a reporter from The Travel Magazine and would like to interview you. Then I was told you left New York already and I should try DeMonet Beverly Hills."

Iris and Thomas looked at each other, impressed.

"Then it's a dead end. They only connected me with your PR people and refused to tell me anything about you."

"Yeah?" Thomas raised his eyebrow, feeling proud.

"Then," she stared at Thomas and continued, "I came across a news article online, about your kidnapping. You know, once posted online, it stays online." Her eyes became sad when she continued, "I am so sorry for what happened to you." She turned to Iris as well, giving her a sympathetic frown. "I didn't know it was you. I just thought it was a coincidence that his wife's name was Iris. All of the articles were about his background, family fortune, how much he was—"

"Mia, how did you find us?" Thomas broke in.

"Oh, right. That. Some articles mentioned you were on your way to your in-law's in Laguna Beach. That totally narrowed down my search area."

Both Thomas and Iris frowned, wondering if Mia really searched for them all over Laguna Beach.

"Public records are available," she said and looked at Thomas. "You are not an American, but I found your residence history here in the States."

Mia was excited to share her *investigative skills* while Thomas was truly troubled by how easily she could locate him—old habits died hard for a formal undercover agent.

"Mia, why are you here?" Thomas asked, his tone harsh.

Her eyes suddenly brimmed with tears. She lowered her head and shrugged. "I don't know…" she whispered. She really did not know why she tracked him down. "I just… I just wanted to know if the man in the newspaper was you." Then she flung her head up and looked at Iris. "I…" Tears rolled down her cheeks. She quickly wiped them away. "I…" She took a deep breath and said, "You don't… you don't know how…how happy I…I am to see you."

Iris smiled slightly, not sure how to respond. She had such mixed feelings towards her.

"I thought Max, I mean Thomas, took you away. And…and…" She suddenly was choked with emotion.

Iris reached her hand and patted Mia's, "I am fine. That's all that matters now."

Mia nodded, staring down at the floor. After a couple of minutes of silence, she cleared her throat and stood up. "I should go now," she said, clutching her backpack on the chest.

"Wait…" Iris stood up hastily. "We…we are making dinner. Stay for dinner."

Mia glanced at Thomas, not sure if it was a good idea. As for her, he was still *the* Max.

"Please, stay for dinner," he said politely, his voice much gentle now.

Mia looked between them and finally nodded.

"Why don't I get the dinner ready while you two talk?" Thomas stood up and headed towards the kitchen.

"Thank you." Iris smiled at her thoughtful husband. When she turned back to Mia, she found her staring at her with watery eyes. "Mia…" She reached for her and held her in her arms. Her embrace made Mia burst into tears.

Iris took her backpack and set it on the coffee table, and she pulled Mia down to sit next to her on the sofa. Mia was only twenty when they met…still a baby when she was abducted.

"Where do you live now?" Iris asked when Mia was finally calm down.

"Vegas," Mia said, wiping her tears with the tissue Iris gave her.

"You came all the way here? You were really determined to find him."

Mia shrugged. "I just... I was shocked when I saw his picture. I just had to know, you know. And when I found out he might be in California, I thought that's not too far. So I just got on the bus—"

"You...you took a bus here?"

"Yeah, Greyhound took about seven hours. Not bad," Mia said.

Iris suddenly fell silent. She was curious what Mia's life was like after she came back to the States.

"The beach is so pretty. I actually sat at the beach for hours before I got the courage to walk here." Her tears were dry. Her beautiful face was smiley again.

"Do you have a place to stay tonight?"

"Yes, I am staying at a motel. It's only a thirty minutes walk to get here."

Iris nodded. She had so many questions to ask her but was not sure where to start.

"Can I ask you a question?" Mia whispered, apparently she did not want Thomas to hear what she was about to ask.

"Of course," Iris whispered back.

"You and Max? I mean, Thomas?" Mia peeked at the man in the kitchen busy preparing dinner.

"I know, right?" Iris winked, remembering how often Mia and other women at the mansion talked about *the* sexy Max.

"The articles said you were pregnant..." Mia trailed off. She did not find any article about what had happened to Thomas' wife after the accident. What if... "I am sorry..." She regretted asking such a sensitive question.

"Why? The baby is sleeping. Would you like to see him?"

Him? Mia's eyes widened. "A boy?"

"Come," Iris grabbed her hand and stood up. "We are going to check on Maxipoo," she said to Thomas.

"Dinner will be ready soon." Thomas smiled at her and gave Mia a polite nod.

"Maxipoo?" Mia frowned. "You and Ma…, shit, I mean, Thomas wouldn't be that cruel to your son, right? Seriously? Maxipoo?"

Iris chuckled and said, 'His name is Max, Maximilien."

"Wow. Really?" Mia almost lost her footing. She looked at Iris in astonishment, her eyes red and misty again.

Iris looked into her eyes, knowing Mia got it. "Max is very special to me, to us."

"Oh god, I got goosebumps just now." Mia rubbed her arms.

"Wait until you see him. He is a mini Thomas."

CHAPTER 22

IRIS tossed and turned, her mind going a million miles an hour. Finally, she slipped out of bed, grabbed her phone from the nightstand, and padded upstairs. She grabbed a bottle of water and sat on the sofa facing the ocean.

It was too cold to open the window to listen to the sounds of the ocean waves, and it was also too dark to see anything outside.

She had never thought she would see Mia again. Another reminder of that dreadful period of her life. After learning what Mia was going through after she came back, Iris could not be more grateful for what she had. If she were really an *iris* plant, she was definitely one that was pampered and protected in a greenhouse with perfect temperature, sunlight, and moisture. And compared to her, Mia was like a wildflower, which was uncultivated, tough, and growing freely.

Conversations with Mia were playing over and over again in her head...

~ ~ ~

"Does your family live in Vegas?" Iris asked while they were enjoying Thomas' delicious garlic butter chicken.

"No." Mia gave a quick and short answer and turned to Thomas and said, "Dude, this chicken is the best I've ever had."

Dude? Thomas winced at the word. "Thank you."

Iris waited for Mia to say more about her family, but she seemingly avoided the subject.

"Then why Vegas?" Iris changed the subject. She knew all too well about pushing someone to talk about something they tried to avoid.

"I'd always wanted to see Las Vegas!" Mia turned to her, excited about the new topic. "I grew up in a tiny, tiny town named Fairmont in Oklahoma. I mean, you can walk around the entire town in thirty minutes." She chuckled.

Iris smiled at her, feeling good about how Mia was willing to share things with her and Thomas. Even though she was curious about Mia's family, she decided to know more about her current life first.

"How long have you been living in Vegas?" Iris asked. Then she picked up her wine glass, which was only half full, and took a small sip.

"You still can't drink much, do you?" Instead of answering Iris, Mia said with a teasing smile.

Iris froze, her lips on the rim of the wine glass.

Mia turned to Thomas and said, "Do you know she could get drunk with like half of the glass? She stole bottles of wine from the kitchen and got drunk before going to those parties." She talked about things happening in the mansion like they were just causal incidents.

Thomas gazed at Iris, worried about her reaction, and to his surprise, Iris just glared at Mia and said, "You, Snitch."

Mia turned back to Iris and laughed, putting another big bite of chicken in her mouth.

What did I miss? Thomas raised one eyebrow.

Iris put down her wine glass, the end of her lips tilting slightly upward. She had never shared with anyone, not even her therapists, many things that had happened in the mansion. Thomas, then Max, had no way of knowing what they did or talked about behind their bedroom door.

"Do you enjoy Vegas?" Iris asked Mia another question since she did not answer her last one.

"Oh, right." Mia took a sip of her water, remembering what Iris just asked her earlier. "I've been there for almost two years. I…" She paused, seeming to decide what, or how much, to say. "They couldn't… I mean the police or whoever got me out of Switzerland. They couldn't find my mom. Who knows where she is now." She rolled her eyes and continued, "So I told them I liked to go to Las

Vegas. That's the first place that popped into my head. Those people were very nice. They put me in a home there. They took good care of me."

Iris suddenly felt a burning sensation in her eyes. She picked up her water glass with her slightly shaking hand and took a big gulp of water to hide her stirred emotion.

Thomas caught Iris' reaction. Sitting across from Iris, he fixed his concerned eyes on Iris, wanting to reach over and hold her in his arms.

I am fine, Iris mouthed the words to him, giving him a reassuring smile. Then she turned her face back to Mia and asked, "Do you still stay at the same place?"

"Oh god, no." Mia widened her eyes. "It's...it's not like it's a bad place. It's just a halfway home, you know." She shrugged. "The people there helped me get jobs so I could afford my own place."

Just then Iris noticed Mia averting her eyes, just like the way she did in the mansion when she had something to hide. "What is it?" Iris narrowed her eyes at Mia.

Mia grimaced and leaned towards Iris, putting a hand over her mouth.

Iris leaned closer, giving Mia one ear so she could tell her the secret.

"I still had those fancy gifts with me when I left. I sold some of them so I could get a nice place to live," Mia whispered.

Iris smiled, a warmness filling her heart. Who would have known that those gifts, which she once thought Mia had traded her dignity for, had helped her when she had no family or friends after she came back to the States.

"Your secret is safe with me," she whispered back to her.

Thomas frowned, curious about what they were talking about. He did feel at ease when Iris was so collected and not perturbed by Mia. Therefore, as long as Iris was doing fine, they could keep all their secrets from him.

Mia sat up straight again, stealing a peek at Thomas, who was simply enjoying the food in front of him.

"So what do you do now?" Iris asked.

"I work at Caesars Palace. Nothing fancy. Just a housekeeping job. And I—" She suddenly shut her mouth, doing the eyes thing again.

Iris leaned in, waiting for another secret.

"I did some stripping in the evening…" she whispered.

Stripping? Iris felt a sudden tightness in her chest.

"But I am taking some evening classes in the city college now," she added. "I don't have time for that anymore."

"That's amazing, Mia. What classes are you taking?" Iris asked. She then looked at Thomas and explained, "She is taking classes at the city college now."

"That's fantastic!" Thomas gave Mia a broad smile, wondering why it was a secret.

"I really like journalism and public relations, but I am working on GE credits now."

"Journalism? You really have that in your blood. Look where you are now," Thomas commented.

Mia smiled sheepishly.

"Oh, Mia…" Iris tilted her head, gazing at Mia. "You amaze me."

"I do?"

Iris nodded vigorously, blinking back her tears. "And I admire you very much."

They invited Mia to Thomas' birthday party, but she declined the invitation because she had to catch a bus in the morning. She did not want to miss her classes in the evening since school just started.

Iris offered to buy Mia a plane ticket back to Vegas, but she claimed that she loved the bus ride. She finally gave in to the offer of flying when Iris pleaded if she could come back to their house for breakfast in the morning so they could chat more. However, Mia insisted on paying for her own ticket.

Refusing to let her walk back to the motel so late at night, Thomas gave her a ride after she put up a big fight about not wanting to trouble them.

~ ~ ~

Iris let out a deep sigh, wondering if Mia was sleeping well in her motel room now.

She did not see a hint of the Mia she knew before. Or did she really know Mia at all?

The Mia in the mansion did not have any problem flaunting her fancy wardrobe and splendid rewards, which were given to her by the patrons for her *special* services, and she seemingly enjoyed the luxurious lifestyle in the mansion. But this Mia, who just had a pleasant dinner with them, was wearing a plain old sweater and leggings and carrying an old canvas backpack. She refused to accept an eighty-dollar airline ticket from her...

Iris wanted to help Mia. Her maternal instinct was kicking in again, just like when she first met her.

But how?

Iris looked at the time on her phone. It was nine in the morning in Switzerland.

I hope Eva is not busy. She tapped her phone and called Eva.

"Hello darling." Eva's voice was cheerful. "Cannot sleep?"

"What's new, right?" Iris chuckled.

"I am sorry that I will miss Tommy's birthday party. I will make sure to buy him a drink when he comes home," Eva said. There was shuffling noise in the background.

"He would love that. Hey Eva, I..." Iris suddenly did not know what to say. Those ideas in her mind were still so raw and unorganized.

"Yes, darling?" The shuffling noise stopped as if Eva had stopped whatever she was doing and was giving Iris all her attention.

"Are you busy? Can we talk?"

"Of course! I am all ears."

Iris started with the unexpected guest they had, then she went on to tell Eva how much she wanted to help Mia, even though Mia did not seem like she needed her help.

"There is so much I can do for her." Iris sounded frustrated. "She just... She just sounds so alone in this world." She was choked with emotion. "When I was talking to her, I felt that she was so strong and tough because...because she had to. Life has never given her a break…" Tears were rolling down her cheeks. "And I am here whining about nightmares and anxiety when I have all you guys around me."

"Iris, darling. There is no comparison. Let's take a step back first." Eva's voice was comforting.

"Okay…" Iris sniffled.

"Let's focus on what you can do for Mia. What's on your mind? Anything…"

"I am thinking, maybe I can persuade her to move here. I will find her a place to live around here so she can be close to me. After I go back to Switzerland, she still has my family and friends."

"That's very thoughtful of you," Eva said. However, she could not agree with Iris just yet because she did not know Mia at all to know if that was a good option for her.

"I can help her get a job at my company or the hotel. I don't know. I have to talk to my friends and Thomas about it. She is so smart, I am sure she can learn whatever is needed for the job she takes. If she accepts the offer, of course."

"Okay… How about school?" Eva asked.

"She can continue to go to school here. I want to pay for her college."

"You sound like you know what you want to do for her already."

"I do… I just don't know how. She seems too proud to accept my help."

"How about starting with something small? And there is the Elizabeth and Laila Foundation at your disposal."

"What?" Iris' voice came out hoarse. She took a sip of her water and asked, "What do you mean?"

"As a member of the Torian family, you automatically have a seat on the board of directors. And we could not ask for a more suitable director like you." Eva started to explain what Iris could do as a member of the executive committee. "Iris, there is so much you can do for Mia and many more like her."

Iris started to snivel when she heard what Eva said last.

"I have been waiting for the right time to talk to you about this. Iris, I think you are ready."

"But...but..." She sniffled loudly. "I am such a mess."

"Not when you are thinking about helping other victims, thinking about making this world a better place for them."

Eva's encouragement only made her cry harder. "You really think I can do this?" Iris asked with a nasal voice.

"Absolutely." Eva's voice was resolute.

A shadow caught Iris' attention, then Thomas walked into the living room. He put the baby monitor on the coffee table and sat down next to her. He pulled her into his arms and placed a kiss on the top of her head.

"Eva is telling me about the foundation," Iris said to him.

He gave her an understanding smile and rested his head on hers.

"Here is Thomas," Iris said, tapping on the speaker icon on the phone screen.

"*Bon anniversaire, Tommy!*" Eva's birthday greeting came out of the phone.

"Merci beaucoup," he expressed his thanks.

They then chatted for a few more minutes before saying goodbye.

"Can we sit here for a little bit?" Iris asked, snuggling closer to Thomas.

"Of course." He grabbed the throng on the back of the sofa and laid it over their laps.

THOMAS was feeding the baby in the kitchen when Iris and Mia were chatting over coffee and breakfast crepes. He heard Iris sharing her thoughts with Mia and was surprised when he heard Mia politely refusing Iris' offer.

"It's too much, Iris." Mia sounded touched by Iris' suggestions, but, as Iris had been worried about, she was too proud to accept her kindness.

He walked towards them, debating if he should say something. If helping Mia was Iris' first step of being involved with the foundation, he should help. He had to help her.

"Elizabeth is my mother, and Laila is my sister," Thomas said to Mia.

Iris had avoided making the connection because she did not know how much information she could reveal. She gazed at Thomas, reading his expression.

"What?" Mia frowned.

Iris reached her arms out for the baby and the bottle, giving the stage to Thomas.

Thomas put the bottle on the table and gently placed Max in her arms.

"You guys are so cute together." Mia grinned.

Thomas sat down across from Mia and continued, "My family owns the foundation—"

"Hold on…" Mia raised her hand up, right in front of Thomas, to stop him from talking. "Iris just told me that Laila was abducted and trafficked…"

Thomas nodded.

"And one of the missions of the foundation is to help human-trafficking victims…"

He nodded again.

"Then why the hell did you work for Vera when your own sister was trafficked and your family owns a foundation like that?" She glared at him, her voice full of accusation.

Thomas exchanged looks with Iris and said, "I was an undercover agent."

Mia fell silent, her eyes fixed on him. Her mind probably just went blank because she simply could not process what he just told her.

"I know it is a lot to take in, Mia." Thomas' voice was soft and tender. "The operation was going on for more than two years before you were brought there—"

"But…but… You were there when…" she interrupted him. "How could you let them take those women away?" Mia's voice came out as a mumble first, and then she shot him a fierce glare and exclaimed, "April and Linnéa were both gone. They were my friends!"

Bébé Max was startled by Mia' sudden outburst, his little bottom lip trembling.

Hastily, Iris stood up and walked away with the baby.

"I'm sorry. I'm sorry." Mia turned to Iris, tears in her eyes.

"Mia…" Iris stopped and smiled at her. "I am sure your friends are fine. Give him a chance to explain. Please…" She then walked into the den.

"What did she mean that my friends are fine?" Mia turned back to Thomas.

"April and Linnéa were transported to our headquarter in Bern —"

"No, no, no…" Mia cut him off. She stood up and started to pace in a circle. "They told me they were sold to some shitty pimps who were going to turn them into sex slaves."

"Mia…" Thomas stood up as well.

"I…I…" She halted, jerking her head to look at Thomas. "I was so afraid to be sold." Her voice was trembling, tears gushing down. "I…I did whatever that bitch told me to do. I let those men rape me!" She fell to the floor, burying her face in her hands.

Thomas knelt down next to her, his hands right above her shoulders.

"Why…why didn't you save me?" She sobbed into her hands.

Why didn't I? He had asked himself that question countless times. Watching any of the women suffering was a torment for him because they made him think of what Laila might have been through. While he wished he could save every single one of them, he had to remind himself again and again that taking down the syndicate in Italy was their ultimate mission.

He felt a gentle touch on his shoulder, and then Iris knelt down next to them.

"I got this," Iris whispered to Thomas, tilting her head towards the den.

Thomas sighed, switching his role with Iris.

"Mia…" Iris embraced her, gently rocking her like a baby. "You are safe now. That's all it matters."

Mia wrapped her arms around Iris' waist, clinging to her like a lifeline. She had not cried for a long, long time. She did not even remember when was the last time she shed tears before yesterday. She had never had the luxury to cry or to feel sorry for herself. Her chest hurt so much, and she felt like she could not catch her breath.

"I...I think I am gonna die..." she said to Iris in fear.

"No, you are not. I know exactly how you feel. I've been there so many times," she comforted her, stroking her hair.

"Why does my chest hurt so much? I am...I am afraid that this... this pain..." She sobbed, clutching at her chest. "It'll never go away..."

"It will. I promise you it will..." Iris leaned back so she could look at Mia. "I am going to find you a good therapist."

"I don't think my insurance— "

"Don't worry about it," Iris interrupted her. "I'll... I mean the foundation will cover all your costs. You will get better." Iris smiled at Mia.

You will get better. Iris repeated the same words to herself, and this time she actually believed them.

CHAPTER 23

IRIS stared at Dr. Sachtleben, waiting for him to say something after she poured her gut out.

She had to cancel her last session because she was so occupied with relocating and settling Mia. She had not been so busy and felt so fulfilled for a long time that she completely forgot about the homework Dr. Sachtleben gave her.

Well, she did not completely forget about her doctor's question. It was always in the back of her mind. She still remembered how she frowned at Dr. Sachtleben in displeasure when he gazed at her earnestly with his stunning amber eyes and asked, "Why are you trying so hard to forget what happened?"

For the past few days, she finally found some alone time to think hard about the question and what she had been feeling since Mia showed up at their door…

~ ~ ~

After Mia's meltdown that morning, there was no way Iris was going to let her go home by herself in that condition. Iris insisted Mia stayed at their house and went to Thomas' birthday party with them that evening.

Iris called ahead and told her mother about the unexpected guest they were bringing. Koto made sure everyone at the party would treat Mia normally, and she embraced Mia like her own daughter.

"Your mother is so funny and graceful and beautiful," Mia whispered to Iris, who was cutting the cake for everybody. "I wish mine was like that."

"You should tell her that. Seriously. I am sure she will adopt you right on the spot." Iris laughed, handing Mia a big slice of cake.

On that same day, Thomas advised Iris to reach out to the foundation's office in New York and find out all the resources she could use, and she did exactly that the next day.

The first thing she did for Mia was giving her a safe and comfortable place to live in LA. DeMont Enterprise provided employee housing, so all Iris had to do was snap her fingers and a one-bedroom apartment was ready for Mia. It was that easy.

Since the semester just started, Iris persuaded Mia to transfer right away. It might result in a loss of credit and tuition fees, but all could be managed.

Since Iris was busy with Mia, Thomas left for New York with Louis two days after the party. Iris found that she was not as sad, lonely, and scared like she was the last time Thomas left. She knew she did not love him any less or was used to or enjoying the separation, and she still cried her eyes out when he drove away. However, she felt settled and gratified, and she was excited about being able to help Mia overcome her stress and anxiety that had been buried deep inside her.

Iris and her mother helped Mia move into her apartment in Santa Monica. It was small, but it was home. A real home for Mia.

"I...I want to give you this," Mia said to Iris, handing her a small black velvet pouch.

"What is it?" Iris received the pouch, feeling the weight landing on her palms. *Jewelry?*

"I don't need them anymore..." Mia then added, "I don't want them, either. Can I donate them to the foundation?"

Curiously, Iris opened the pouch and emptied the content in her hand. "Mia..." She was astonished by the sparkling bracelets, earrings, and necklaces.

"I can't believe those perverts gave me real stuff. I thought they were just crystals or something," Mia said. "I..." She suddenly lowered her voice as if someone would hear their conversation. "I hid them in my bra when the police came to the mansion that day. I am glad I did."

Koto wrapped her arms around Mia's shoulders and leaned her head against hers. Iris saw the tears in her mother's eyes, knowing Mia would be in good hands after she went back to Switzerland.

~ ~ ~

"So?" Iris pressed on since Dr. Sachtleben did not say a word.

"Are you fishing for commendation?" He looked amused.

"At least give me a grade. A plus? A plus plus?" She gave him a big wishful smile.

"Hmm..." Dr. Sachtleben tilted his head, really giving it a thought, and said, "B minus."

"What?" Her eyebrows arched.

"If it is A plus...and plus, like you just asked," he said, crossing his long legs. "Then there's no room for improvement, don't you think?"

She lowered her eyes and stared at the throw pillow she had been hugging on her lap. "True..."

But improve what?

I guess no-medication-at-all is the final goal. She only took her medications when she needed them, and she had not been needing them lately.

I guess I should be able to talk about what happened more freely. She was able to talk more about her captivity, thanks to Mia, when she used to refuse to even think about it.

I guess I need to step out of my comfort zone more often. She had tried to take short walks around the house. By herself! And just like right now, being in the room with Dr. Sachtleben without Jane was a big step, too. Although Jane was just a few feet away in the waiting room because Iris still could not come to the appointments by herself.

"I guess you are right," Iris mumbled.

"You guess?" Dr. Sachtleben believed Iris had more to say.

Iris gave her doctor a shrug.

"All you have shared with me was amazing, Iris. Mia has inspired you."

She nodded.

"And you think the reason you are trying so hard to forget what happened is if you could forget, then the whole nightmare might not be real. Correct?"

She nodded again.

"To which stage of grief do you think it belongs?"

Iris had learned that denial, anger, bargaining, depression, and acceptance were the five stages of grief which was a response to losing either someone or something that was important. And she had been grieving for the most important thing she had lost: herself.

So, her answer was actually just the *denial*...

And when something reminded her of her misfortune, she became agitated, so that was the *anger*...

Then she would have so many regrets and start asking herself what ifs, so that was the *bargaining*...

And when she could not answer all her what-if questions, she started feeling hopeless, so that was the *depression*...

Then she would wish she could forget everything...

And the cycle repeated.

I am just bouncing between the first four stages... She just had a realization that she had never come to terms with the tragedies, including Thomas' kidnapping and the emergency c-section. Just the thought of the possibility of not having Maxipoo in her life made her chest hurt.

"I've never...never accepted it," she said, her voice small.

Dr. Sachtleben smiled as that conclusion was what he was waiting for from her. "I think I might change the grade to a B."

"Not B plus?" Iris looked up and gave him a witty smile.

"We are going to leave enough room for future improvement," Dr. Sachtleben said, feeling great about Iris' progress.

"Okay..." She let out a sigh of relief. "Can I ask you a personal question?"

He removed his reading glass and tapped it on the notebook in his hand, considering her request. After a few seconds, he said, "Yes. Although I cannot guarantee that I will answer it."

"Fair enough," she said, lightly nodding her head. "Is Summer your wife?"

Dr. Sachtleben was surprised by Iris' question. He read her

expression and found only curiosity. "What made you think that?"

She shrugged and said, "Just the way you look at her. It...it's just like the way Thomas looks at me. And you are wearing matching wedding bands."

"Very observant."

"It's my forte." She smiled brightly. "I always have this great difficulty of remembering people's names. So I used to pay detailed attention to people and nickname them."

"Used to?" he asked.

"Yeah..." She stared back at the pillow. "I just don't care who they are anymore. Why bother nicknaming them?"

"What will you nickname me?"

Iris flung her eyes up and smiled broadly. "You've already had one."

"So, you do care." He gave her a warm smile.

Iris blinked her eyes rapidly, wondering if her doctor was right. Did she really start to care whom she met now? She did name Mia's apartment manager Mr. Adonis after she met him.

"So, what do you call me behind my back?" Dr. Sachtleben joked since Iris became quiet.

Iris focused on her doctor again and grinned. "You have to admit that Nicholas Sachtleben is not an easy name."

"Let's hear it." He gave her a serious look. "I might oppose it."

A laughter burst out of Iris, and it made Dr. Sachtleben smile.

"Dr. Warlock." She gave him a sheepish smile.

"May I ask why?" he asked, suppressing his own laughter.

"Well... Your eyes. They are amber, almost golden. They make you look like you have some kind of magical powers. And your voice. It's very deep and..." She paused to find the right words. "It echos. No. It sounds like it is vibrating in your voice box. Very hypnotizing. And you have this vibe of domination."

Dr. Sachtleben was extremely interested in her last observation: domination.

"Seriously, I bet you can easily make people submit to you. Like having magical powers. Hence, Dr. Warlock."

"I am very impressed, Iris."

"Thank you," she said, feeling conceited. "So, is she?" she asked.

Dr. Sachtleben nodded, giving her a warm and content smile.

THOMAS did not fly back to Switzerland with Louis as planned. He took a commercial flight back to California and stayed in DeMont Beverly Hills before he figured out what to do next. He hated to lie to Iris, but she insisted that she needed more time and he wanted to give her the space she needed—just from a closer distance.

For him, Beverly Hills was still too far. Therefore, a couple of days ago he moved into a small condo which was only a fifteen-minute walk to their beach house. And David was his accomplice who found this place for him.

When he called David several days ago and told him about his plan, David was on board and offered any help he needed.

"Just don't tell anyone," he told David.

Then soon after that, Jane knew. He could not really blame David for telling his wife because he would have done the same thing.

And then he got a phone call from Koto telling him how happy Lucas and she were. He was not surprised that his in-laws knew about it as the De Waal family was as close as the Torian family.

The plan was: Iris' family would call Thomas when Iris needed someone to babysit Max, usually just doctor's appointments or visiting Mia. Thomas would show up after Iris left and watch their son. He loved spending time with Max, even just for a few hours.

When they FaceTimed each other, Thomas made sure to sit in front of a plain wall so Iris would not notice anything out of the ordinary. Thankfully, Iris was never a suspicious person, and she only focused on him.

He had the urge to be close to Iris and Max all the time, and sometimes he found himself walking towards their house like a stalker, just wanting to steal a peek of them. Like right now…

He knew Iris was home not long ago from her appointment with

Dr. Sachtleben because he had been playing with Max and left about twenty minutes before Iris got home. Instead of going back to the condo, he grabbed some lunch at a small diner first and had been wandering aimlessly until he ended up back at their street.

He halted and ducked behind a car when he saw the front gate open. He peeked behind the car and saw Iris standing in the doorway for a long time. Then she finally turned around and pushed the stroller out. She pushed Max for about half a block and then turned around, scampering back home.

Bravo, ma chéri. Thomas had his eyes on them the whole time, wishing that he could be there with them and that they could take a stroll down the beach together.

CHAPTER 24

"IRIS!" Jane exclaimed when Iris walked into their ranch house. She scurried towards her, her head turning left and right as if looking for something. "You...you are back early!" Her voice sounded way too loud.

Iris looked at her, bewildered.

Just then David appeared from nowhere. His breathing was a little heavy as if he had rushed to the foyer like Jane did.

"Iris is back!" Jane said loudly, exchanging looks with David.

"I thought... You told us you were going to Mia's after your appointment," David said, his voice a bit shaking. The always calm and cool Dr. David De Waal sounded nervous.

"I forgot Antonio and Skye were taking her to a meeting today." Iris walked into the house. "She really enjoys working with them."

Mia had started working in their interior design firm as Antonio's part-time assistant while attending Santa Monica College at the same time. She insisted on making her own living and not receiving monetary help from the foundation. Iris could not be more proud of her.

"You are back early..." Jane repeated, her eyes widened like saucers.

"What's wrong with you two?" She looked around and asked, "Where is Maxipoo?"

Iris had gone to her appointments by herself for several weeks now. And since she planned to visit Mia after her appointment and might be gone for a long time, she dropped off Max at the ranch instead of having someone come to her house to babysit him.

"Dad has him!" David said.

"Mom has him!" Jane replied at the same time.

Iris pivoted and looked at them. "Okay... Mom and Dad have him. Where are they?"

"They went to the beach," Jane answered straight away.

"Yeah, they are at the beach now." David stood behind Jane as if taking shelter from Iris.

"Seriously... What's up with you two?" Iris asked again.

They looked at each other again.

"Did he get sick?" Iris suddenly had a bad feeling.

"No, no, no." Jane waved her hands and shook her head. "Don't you worry. He is perfectly fine."

"You two..." Iris stared at them. "You two are very bad liars."

"We are absolutely truthful," David said. "They are at the beach now."

"Where? Main beach park? Or Wood Cove?" Iris asked.

Her parents took the baby to the beach quite often, especially when they babysat him at the beachfront house. She was not sure why David and Jane were acting the way they were now.

Jane frowned, averting her eyes.

"By the house?" Iris asked again.

Jane looked up at David and then turned back to gaze at Iris. She nodded.

"That's not too hard, is it?" Iris started to walk out.

"Where are you going?" Jane asked.

"Going home."

"They will be back soon. You might miss them if you go looking for them now," Jane said, her voice a little too keen.

Iris raised her phone that she was holding in her hand. "Don't tell me they forgot their phones."

Jane winced at her sarcastic tone.

David sighed and kissed the top of Jane's head. "Let's take her there."

"Where?" Iris asked, not enjoying this secrecy, especially when her son was involved.

"Your house." David walked around Jane and wrapped one arm around Iris' shoulders. "Let's go."

Leaving her car at the ranch, Iris rode with David and Jane back home. She was sure Maxipoo was fine since he was with her parents. They not only took good care of him but also spoiled him rotten. If they were not at the beach or the house, they were probably pushing him along Broadway Street or PCH, showing him off in those art galleries and boutiques their friends owned.

Why are DD and Janie insisting on taking me home? Iris stared at her brother and met his eyes in the rear view mirror. He gave her a nervous smile.

Something is going on and they just don't want to tell me. She returned his smile with a frown.

Twenty minutes later they arrived at her house. Iris jumped out of the car before David even made a complete stop. Key in her hand, she rushed to the front gate, ignoring Janie' calling.

She stormed into the house and found both her mother and father drinking coffee in the living room and looking like deers caught in the headlights when they saw her. Just like Jane and David's reaction when she walked into their house.

"Is Maxipoo napping?" Iris asked. Now they were really making her feel anxious.

Neither of her parents answered her question. They looked over her shoulder and exchanged looks with Jane, who was walking in right behind her.

"What's going on?" Iris sounded worried.

Koto sighed and walked towards her daughter. "Come with me, Sweetheart." She smiled warmly and held her hand. She turned around and nodded at her husband.

Iris did not ask anymore questions. If they wanted to tell her what was going on, they would have told her already. Taking in a deep breath, she let her mother lead the way downstairs.

Iris had been doing so well the last few weeks, thanks to Thomas, her family, Dr. Warlock, Mia, and…everybody in her life. She was able to go to the stores alone, take Alice's yoga classes at her studio, and drive to her appointments by herself.

Just a couple of days ago, she took Bébé Max to the beach by herself for the very first time. She was so overwhelmed by happiness and excitement and not by anxiety and panic she used to have. It was a feeling of satisfaction and contentment. How much she wished Thomas was there with them, and she knew he would be so proud of her.

"Who is watching Max?" Iris asked when they reached the fun room.

Koto only gave her a small smile and led her towards the beach. She then turned around and stood behind her daughter, steering her towards the lifeguard tower direction.

Iris immediately spotted her son, who was sitting on a beach towel, reaching his little arms towards...towards his daddy...

Iris forgot to breathe suddenly.

Thomas knelt down in front of Max. He gently picked him up, saying something to him in the process. He held him in his arms and kissed his little cheek. Then he pointed at the ocean and whispered in the baby's ear.

When did he come back? Why didn't he tell me? She thought, mesmerized by that beautiful father and son picture.

She turned around and found her mother had already walked back to the house. She was standing by her father, and David and Jane were right behind them. They were all watching her, smiles on their faces.

She took a deep breath, blinking away her tears. Then she turned back around and slowly walked towards her little family.

Either Thomas could sense her presence or he happened to turn his head towards the house. He spotted her, and a bright smile spread across his face.

Holding their son in one arm, Thomas extended his free one to her.

Iris walked into his embrace, keeping her eyes on his striking blue gaze.

"Hi..." he whispered and dipped a kiss on her lips.

Bébé Max noticed his mommy. He babbled and reached his arms towards her.

"I think he wants his mommy." Thomas handed their son to Iris gently and wrapped them both in his arms.

Iris had not felt so content and peaceful for a long, long time. She looked up at her loving husband and said, "I am ready to go home."

THE END

NOTE FROM THE AUTHOR

HAVE you ever had a dream which was so vivid that your heart was still pounding after you awoke? I had one three years ago...

It was just a fragment of the dream that made me feel upset and anxious, and I remembered clearly the surroundings, persons, and the fear I had in that particular fragment: I was forced to ascend stairs while followed by a woman. It was a poorly lit, narrow staircase. I was scared, fearing for my life. Then a man blocked the stairway, and his presence petrified me. I had to squeeze past him to reach the landing, and as I was walking by him, he suddenly stepped closer. I froze, believing that he was going to harm me in a horrific way. Then, I awoke abruptly and my heart was beating as hard as it was in the dream.

I was so preoccupied by the fear I had in the dream and the two persons who frightened me that I wrote it all down so I would not forget. I also talked to my husband and two children, who were eighteen then, about why *I*—the person in the dream—was so scared, about who would those two persons be, and about what would have happened to *me* if the dream had continued... My conclusion was *I* must be living in captivity, presumably trafficked, and the two persons were my captors.

Weeks later, I told my daughter that I was going to write a fiction inspired by my dream. And that became the prologue of *The Very Thought Of You Duet*.

Some narrative threads of the story are my personal and close friends' experiences, such as psychotherapy, the side effects of antidepressants, and medical procedures. They have a great impact on how I value my life.

Lastly, I would like to note that human trafficking take many forms, and it occurs across the world in countries rich and poor. If you see suspicious activity, please report it to your local law enforcement. You can protect your family, neighbors, and community and can you save someone whose life may be in jeopardy.

RESOURCES

IF you or someone you know is in immediate danger, please call 911 (Americas), 112 (Europe and parts of Asia), or local emergency telephone numbers.

If you or someone you know is a victim of human trafficking, GET HELP NOW:
- US National Human Trafficking Hotline 1-888-373-7888
- UK The Modern Slavery helpline 0800 0121 700
- 27 European Countries European Commission National Hotlines
- Organizations fighting human trafficking and supporting survivors

Understanding Human Trafficking :
- Polaris
- DeliverFund
- The National Center for Missing & Exploited Children (NCMEC)
- A21

ACKNOWLEDGMENTS

THANK you for reading The Very Thought Of You Duet, the journey of Iris and Thomas.

Special thanks to my wonderful husband Jeffrey, our twins Randall and Winona, and my dear friend Brooke Hanson. Thank you for believing in me.

ABOUT THE AUTHOR

MY college degree was in German Literature, but my profession was interior design. As project manager for a commercial design firm I often put in twelve-hour days sprinting around construction sites. I am now retired and, along with my husband, an empty-nester. And I now have time to devote to my writing, and my obsession with the tales of the characters in my books. My writing tends toward contemporary and historical romance novels that are intricate, humorous, and a bit erotic, which hopefully brings my readers both laughter and tears. I love to incorporate my personal experiences, and those of my close friends, into narrative threads that are especially close to my heart. When I am not lost in reveries wherein my heroines and heroes stumble over obstacles before they live happily ever after, I enjoy reading, photographing, painting, indulging in TV or movie marathons, and traveling.

Visit me at
www.SufenAdams.com

TITLES BY SUFEN ADAMS

ÉTOILE SERIES

The Very Thought Of You Duet

This duology must be read in order. *The Very Thought Of You* includes the prequel and contains a cliffhanger. *The Very Thought Of Us* concludes the story.

16 Reasons

(Book form expected Spring 2023)

This book can be read as a standalone and does not contain a cliffhanger. It is highly recommended that you read it after *The Very Thought Of You Due*t.

I'm Hanging Up My Heart For You

(Expected 2023)

This book can be read as a standalone and does not contain a cliffhanger. It is highly recommended that you read it after *The Very Thought Of You Duet*.

STANDALONE

Bound

It is a historical romance novel.